SOLARPUNK TRANSFORMATION TRILOGY

Solarpunk Transformation Trilogy

SHEL GRAVES

ISBN: 979-8-9985486-3-5

First Printing, 2025 Sheltopian Press

CONTENTS

~~

~~

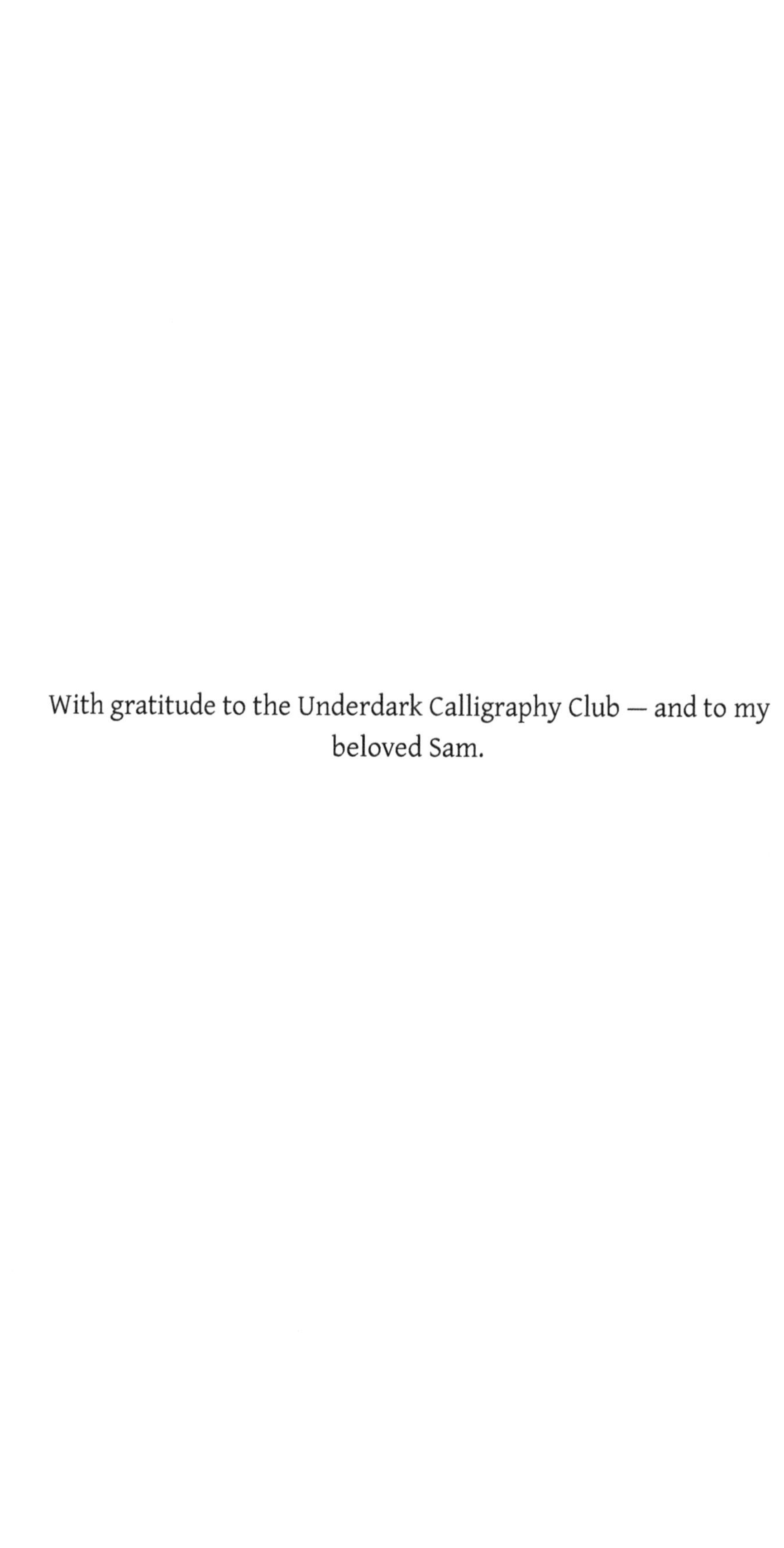

With gratitude to the Underdark Calligraphy Club — and to my beloved Sam.

Sync Chrome City: Book One

Solarpunk Transformation Trilogy
Book One

Sync Chrome City

~ 1 ~

SYNC CHROME CITY: PROLOGUE

In the distance, on the horizon, the corrosion of the Rust Sea rises slowly submerging the islands of Pacifica. While many of the smaller fish have died, some in the sea like the sensitive sharks have silently developed resistance and embraced the deadly rust while Varuna the Whale sings and dives deeper to escape it. Yet, we begin in the remains of the most beautiful places in the world; the Cascadian Wilderness, where blackberry vines cling to slopes and towering evergreen trees often burn, and the northern islands of Pacifica, where madrona trees hang over the rising waters, the color of their peeled skins perfectly matching the color of the red seas.

Off continent, many wondrous islands with white, black, pink, and beige sands await. Occasionally, we see glimpses of the once sparkling blue and green waters surrounding them. More often, the grey-green plastified waters slosh and churn. Nonetheless, surfers travel from beach-to-beach and wave-to-wave carefree, communing with each other and enjoying the freedom to see the world while they may, as absentminded men fretfully try to restrain and employ them. The surfers do their best to stay far ashore of the United Government and its industries and travel any other way than in the lurching containers of AeroFlux planes.

Pay attention and the variety of birds and fish on Earth still astound, while populations of mammals surge and wane around fluctuations of human tragedies. When humans retreat and die off from manmade disasters, other animals may return to prowl.

On the edge of Cascadia, in the basement labs of New West University, researchers attempt to combine mammals, fish, reptiles, amphibians, and birds quickly into new shapes to withstand the environmental damage men have wrought.

The 'Way, the great grey stretch of asphalt that divides Cascadia's competing political utopias, New West and C-Town, contains unwelcome refugees with their multifaceted minds harboring so many unwelcome thoughts. Out here, men use genetic manipulation to give themselves new features: fur, feathers, scales, and tails. Generations despondently yearn to be more animal, but most do not know how to access their animalness other than in this superficial and manipulated way. Some howl and gyrate as they listen to Giovanni Hastings Musica, a mix of old and new instrumental sounds. Songs contain hope and inspire listeners. Animalness lies within in every cell and soon in every grain of sand.

In other parts of the United Government, animals are largely tortured and eaten though some crawl underground and some escape notice. The landscapes remain vast, after all.

On distant planets, men work in the Spire Mines to provide resources for other richer, absent men and they dream of home and imagine the beauty of the Earth. Further away lies a planet made of tiny organisms living lives like sand for now untouched by human thought.

Eventually, human thought expands for good or ill.

Wisely, look to the animals. Ask: What are the animals thinking? How do the animals feel? Yes, you can tell by the way they hold their bodies and the choices they make with them. Yes, we too, are embodied. Look to animals, as small as they may seem, for clues to our destination. Find yourself: suddenly prescient and amazed. Animalness remains.

A parrot squawks revived by aliens. Taste the slippery orange fruit. Be transported to sacredness, power, and an earthly unearthly island.

Isn't it strange how some humans have ignored even the largest animals like Varuna the Whale? Her vast intelligences know many secrets. She communes with beings underwater. She understands better than most the fate of the oceans within which everyone's fates flow. She sings.

On the edge of Cascadia, great transformations rise above the horizon.

In the heart of Cascadia, evolution continues to unfold on Earth and in the universe.

Beneath the drowning islands of Pacifica, a compassionate civilization awaits.

As you envision the future, hold your loved ones close. Let them burrow near your neck and feel their sharp claws, scaly fins, and slick fur.

May you feel loved.

We begin our approach to this future, heads held high, with the story of a heedless young woman raised by utopians, a college student at New West University, Geneva Teresa Weltraum.

But first, there is an angry man.

~ 2 ~

SYNC CHROME CITY: THE FREEWAY

"Some mistakenly believe Geneva Teresa Weltraum to be the originator of society's psychic transformation but, in fact, before The Awakening many youth displayed heightened awareness, although their abilities were repudiated and ridiculed. C.G. Burrows, arguably among the first Dawning Psychics, was one of these pariahs. His own abilities were limited and came at a cost. He could hear others' thoughts clearly, but only those directed at him. This limited telepathy caused him great pain. Thoughts entered his mind "like needles," he said. He considered his ability a great curse. He was an outcast and a misanthropist." — *Becoming Psychic 101, A History and a Primer*

On the other side of someone else's vision of utopia, the manicured territory of New West, those people deemed unworthy of paradise camped on the Freeway. Tents littered the top of the mud-streaked asphalt. They blended together makeshift, weathered and covered in soot, as did the men who ambled between them bearded, hooded, and hunched. C.G. Burrows kept apart from this human refuse as long as he could stand to, living in the forest they feared, until his loneliness grew unbearable, and he ventured close to make another attempt to join them. Despite the pain people caused him, Burrows craved their company like a drug. Thus, forced from hiding, he approached the masses on the Freeway. Low hanging branches clipped him as he paced the tree line. Black smoke from the kerosene campfires stung his eyes as he scanned the pavement looking for a tent with red and beige flaps. That tent was not much different from the others, except that it had the person he needed inside, his only friend on the 'Way, his dealer, Mace.

Burrows hadn't seen Mace since his last failed fix: a dose of old therapeutic that hadn't helped his condition or got him high. He'd retreated to the forest and stayed there, alone, for weeks. Now he couldn't be sure something hadn't changed on the 'Way. Maybe Mace had moved on, decided to make the trek south for warmth. Although, he would have had reason to stay. This part of the Freeway was prime real estate, just out of sight of the white arching entrance to New West on the hillock of clipped lawn, but close enough to draw the occasional guilty emissary out. A few of the rich bastards would occasionally bring fuel, food, and apologies to assuage their guilt. Tents further down the corridor got none of this false regret. Charity made this part of the 'Way crowded and aggressive, a belt of opportunistic and ever hopeful beggars. No, Mace wouldn't have left. He had to be here, somewhere.

Finally, Burrows glimpsed a spot of red in the canvas sea. He shifted the weight of his knapsack and warmth trickled between his shoulder blades. He hung his head and stepped onto the asphalt. He began weaving though the squatters: head down, eyes up. Almost immediately some guy was on him, staring at him with narrowed eyes. Burrows braced for the impact.

The guy pounded him: *What you got in there? Looking to deal?*

Every word struck and stung.

"Leave me the fuck alone," Burrows said.

The guy sized him up. Burrows got: *Fine, big man.* The pain eased as the guy turned his attention elsewhere. Burrows hunched and hurried on, but now he'd attracted attention and more desperate thoughts: *Looking to deal? Looking to deal? Deal. Deal.* He looked back at the forest with longing, but he was already a few hundred tent-covered yards away from refuge with at least 50 people between him and the quiet. It was just what he'd been afraid of, a mind field, and he was trapped in the middle. They needled him all around and he couldn't yell because it would bring more of them on him. Anonymity was key. He struggled in silence. And suffered, yes, always suffered.

Shut up. Ignore me, he thought, but he knew they wouldn't hear. His was a one-way curse.

"Back off," he grunted, pulling his jacket around him. He wished, just once, he could fire back at the crowd, press his own thoughts directly into the heads around him, let them feel the hard jab, the echoing sting, the after burn and see how they liked it. "Back off!"

No one ever got him. He was a receiver, a one-way street leading out of New West. There was no way in for him. He hurried on, but the tent he'd started toward turned out to be the wrong one. Still, no Mace. If Mace had moved on, could he find a new dealer, pick another quiet mind out of the hustle? He wasn't sure he was up to it, and the time he'd spent isolated in the forest wouldn't make it easier. He felt monstrous and, by now, had to look the part.

He stopped and turned to a dirty young woman beside him, brown-scraggly hair and a musky urine-tinged stench. She opened the flap to her tent and held it wide. If only it could be that easy, just go inside and see what she had. He made eye contact and stepped toward her: a mistake. She blasted him: *What's he got in that sack? Not a bad looking guy. How much will he want? Could be a protector, scare off the others.* All her scheming speculation pierced him. As the pain intensified, from everywhere he got: *violence, a show, should we stop him, he's hurting Allison.* He looked up into the woman's bulging blue eyes. His hands were high on her shoulders inching up her collarbone to her throat. He was strangling her. He wanted to silence her thoughts, to end his own pain. But if he gave in to it, then the rest of them would be on him pinning him with all their incriminations. They would never leave him alone. Instead, Burrows inched his hands back down the woman's shoulders and shoved her into the tent, "Shhh." She stumbled back onto a pile of tattered clothing.

Burrows' restraint had the desired effect turning a murderous impulse into the kind of fleeting violence common to life on the 'Way. He felt the minds around turn away, bored. He hurried on. So, that was it. There was no way he could handle meeting a new source. He looked toward the forest ready to bolt. Then, at last, he spotted it, Mace's tent, in exactly the same place it had been for the past two years. Going for it, Burrows made himself slow. The minds pulled away from him as the squatters forgot him and returned to their preoccupations. He swung the sack off his back and held it up. Dark stains crossed the canvas. The patch of dried blood tightened across his back as he braced for the initial jolt.

"Mace," he said.

Mace stuck his head out of the tent. The thoughts he directed at Burrows struck in two dull thuds: *Burrows. Meat.* It hurt, but it didn't floor him. Mace was one chill dude. Burrows shook the bag and went fishing for information, "You got something good for me?"

Mace took the bait. He shrugged, but he couldn't help thinking: *SLO-42. Da Lime. Really good score.*

"You look like you got your hands on something," Burrows said, rubbing the side of his face along his rough bearded jaw. Mace had to be about his age, in his 20s, but all the refuse on the 'Way looked weathered.

"Yeah, it's new. You take it and you get to experience what it's like to be someone else. It's made out of someone else's neuro...something, whatever, brain juice," Mace said.

After a bout of zipping and shifting nylon, he stepped out. He flashed the inside pocket of his tattered United Government issue jacket and Burrows caught a glimpse of neon green, possibly the cure he was looking for, or at least a reprieve from his continual misery. "So, it's good?"

"Depends. Mine is," Mace said. Burrows followed his gaze to the lone truck coming at them, making its way along the shoulder of the Freeway past the tents. It glistened white, free of the pale gray soot that covered him, Mace, everything else. The forest-green New West logo shone inside a yellow circle.

"Mace, trade?" Burrows said.

"Hang on," Mace waved the back of his hand. "I want to see what this one is."

The absence of pain Burrows felt as Mace's attention completely left him provided only bitter relief. It quickly turned to annoyance.

"Mace, trade." Burrows said, wanting to get this over with and get off the 'Way. But Mace was focused on the truck like a well-trained dog.

The truck rolled to a stop beside a group of tents and a man and woman got out, a matched set. They were dressed in identical boots and jackets, but there were no logos on their clothes, or when they lifted the back door of the truck, on the pile of burlap sacks inside. They were do-gooder missionaries acting on their own outside of New West's authority.

"Flour," the man said into a small, white handheld megaphone. His voice carried over the crowd amplified by a tinny echo. "We want you to know the revolution hasn't ended. There's still a place for you in New West. We've brought flour and stoves. Anyone can ask us what it's like inside."

As the man spoke, people began to crowd the truck and the woman started handing down sacks. Burrows hefted his bag of meat up over his shoulder again and adjusted the weight across his back watching the weak people clamoring. Handouts. He didn't need handouts. The New West bastards had taken everything but his freedom, and now they were offering flour in exchange as if it were a fair trade. Fuck that.

Burrows dangled the sack in front of Mace again. "Rather have meat?"

"I'd rather have both," said Mace with his ever-practical, adaptable chill. "Gotta go. You want to trade or not?"

Burrows couldn't stand Mace's good nature. From what he knew of Mace's history, the guy had reason, even more than himself, to be pissed off at anything that came out of New West. Instead, he let himself be reduced to a pathetic beggar. It made him want to club some sense into Mace with the bag of dead rabbits, but he couldn't let himself get testy, not with the one guy out here whose company he could briefly tolerate. "I'm not sure. Let me try some, see if it's as good as you say. Use your tent?"

Hands in the pockets of his grey camouflage jacket, Mace shrugged: *Sure, I ain't got nothin' in there you can steal.* "Sure," he said and handed over a rig half-full of green liquid: *Da Lime.* "It goes in your eyes. They connect to your brain, man."

"Yeah, I get that," Burrows said, rolling his eyes. He was not some ignorant junkie. "Who did you say this comes from?"

He ignored Mace's rambling explanation because he got his answer clearly: *Kendra LeMay.* He knew the name. He took the rig, stepped into Mace's tent and zipped it up behind him. The inside smelled like a dank concentration of the rest of camp: feces, musk, urine, sweat, black smoke. Burrows rummaged around. Mace wasn't wrong. There was nothing of value here. He found a bottle of rubbing alcohol, matches, and some cotton.

He settled on top of Mace's tattered sleeping bag and heated and swabbed the syringe. The green drops in the rig looked dirty in the yellow cast of light filtered through the tent. What made Mace think he'd actually scored some of Kendra LeMay, the

Friend-Me inventor? It seemed unlikely, although he'd heard rumors around the camp about plans for a new Friend-Me factory. It could be built just outside of New West on the land along the Freeway so the company could make use of the cheap labor. The 'Way had been abuzz with the news, with the hope of work, but so far, nothing had come of the rumor. LeMay had chosen to stay in New West under its restrictions. It wasn't a smart choice for an entrepreneur. New West's brand of perfection was the death of invention. In fact, LeMay's Friend-Me journal was the only thing new to come out of New West since the revolution, and only little girls got excited about diaries, no matter how techie Friend-Me made the journals.

Burrows leaned back and positioned the tip of the needle in the corner of his eye ready to inject the green fluid into his optic nerve. He doubted he'd get a glimpse into the mind of Kendra LeMay, but he wasn't really concerned with the experience itself. He was after a side effect: anything to keep other people's thoughts out of his head. He depressed the syringe and the liquid surged around his eye. He blinked twice, as his vision turned puce. He sat back and waited for the kick. It worked fast gliding over the blood-brain barrier like caffeine. The stench in the tent became unbearable. He smiled even as he stumbled out of the tent and caught his breath. The drug had definitely come from a female anyway. She couldn't stand the reek of sour male sweat and now it repulsed Burrow's drugged senses, too.

Outside the tent, the New West logo on the truck caught his gaze. At first, he wasn't sure whether his reaction to it was drug induced at all. As usual, the truck represented rules and he wanted to avoid it. But in the SLO-42 haze, with somebody else's perceptions riding over his and guiding his emotions, there was also curiosity. *Could this really be Kendra LeMay?*, he wondered.

As he stared at the truck, a drug-induced memory played over the top of his natural vision. He saw a little girl on an empty playground with her arms wrapped around a willow tree. The school grounds and everything from the tetherball pole to the sidewalk graffiti glimmered. Energy flowed into the little girl as she plucked a frond from the tree. She waved the leaves back and forth and spun round. Then, a nimbus of golden light surrounded her. A word came at him as if spoken by a crowd: *destiny*. It rang his mind like a bell. Its chime came at him from all sides and Burrows reeled. He tripped on a tent stake and dropped to one knee. Underneath the excitement of the drug, the word surged into his mind and expanded fast, filling his head. Pressure pounded at his temples. He exhaled, shallow panting breaths. Then, the memory stopped. He looked up at the truck again, deflated. He quickly found Mace and traded his two rabbits for another dose.

That night, he and Mace shared a campfire with the New West emissaries, Vic and Perla Freeman. Burrows was used to inhaling lung-scarring fumes from a kerosene flame or, by himself, burning wood, which smelled better, especially with meat cooking over it, but the smoke still stung the back of his throat and left his voice dry and husky. The Freeman's, however, lit one of their clean electric blue stoves. Vic set the swirls of yellow and purple light high so they could almost see the faces of the nearest squatters. The glimpses Burrows caught of the shadowed squinty visages surrounding them made him cringe, but his recent dose of SLO-42 dulled the thoughts the campers shot his way. They came through in manageable thumps: *Lucky. Bastard.* Vic adjusted the scent of the stove through lavender and sea spray to settle on clean pine. It was just another example of how everything had to be better in New West, Burrows thought. Even a campfire wasn't good enough for those...the drug smoothed away his habitual *bastards*. It dulled his cynicism. Instead, the thought felt true. Everything was better inside New West. It surely was.

The Freeman's shared food with them: savory mashed hazelnut and shiitake cakes and stone-ground wheat crackers washed down with sparkling blueberry cider. Perla served them cinnamon Pink Lady apple tarts on clean tin plates. The drug enhanced the flavors too, Burrows thought. It allowed him to enjoy the tastes without judgment. The buttery graham crust seemed a good enough reason alone to embrace New West.

"Pretty fancy-pants for the 'Way. But I can't complain," Burrows said. He really found he could not. Because that almost, but not quite, bothered him, he laughed. His mind really was not his own. Maybe next time he could get away with just half a rig of Kendra LeMay (if that's who this was).

"What do you normally eat out here?" Perla asked.

"Whatever you send out. And there's some trade." Mace said.

Burrows didn't mention the woods, his hunting. It wasn't good nighttime conversation.

"That can't be enough to feed everyone," Vic said.

Mace took another bite of tart. "A lot of people headed south."

"People camping on the Freeway outside our gates without food. That's not what we had in mind," Vic said.

Even through the SLO-42, Burrows got twinges from the Freeman's guilt: *Terrible. What we've done to you.*

Even through the drug, their guilt disgusted him, but the person whose perceptions he was riding didn't share his anger. She was a problem-solver.

"So, what's the political situation?" he asked, to get the Freeman's out of his head and talking.

Perla leaned toward the flame. She wanted to explain. Burrows heard her soft beat: *Don't blame me.*

"A lot of people feel we made some mistakes," she said. "We knew we couldn't convert everyone to our way of thinking, and we couldn't create the society we wanted to without a unified effort. So, we asked those who disagreed to leave. A lot went to C-town. Most were happy to go, I think."

Burrows nodded. "My parents were."

Before the economic collapse, they had been some of the wealthiest, most influential people in the Northwest. Then, in the depression, they'd lost everything: money and power. The New Westians had foreseen the financial chaos. They'd swooped in with their savings and encircled their bastions, the seat of government and the university, along with some neighboring farmlands and a few small towns. They'd created New West on the high ground no one else wanted. His parents had left voluntarily taking Burrows with them to C-town. Not everyone was so lucky. New West forcibly removed a lot of undesirables: the uneducated, homeless, drug addicts, dissidents. When he couldn't handle C-town — the incessant mental anguish of being a refugee in a city where everyone felt bad for him — a brain hammering chorus of *Sorry. Sorry. Sorry.* — Burrows ended up here with all the other castoffs outside New West on the Freeway. And then, entered the forest.

"I was never political. Just poor," Mace said, digging his hands deep into the pockets of his U.G. jacket.

"New West didn't have much choice. The old system left behind so many problems. We wanted to make a fresh start," Vic put his arm around Perla. "But our new government is stable. We've got our infrastructure in place. Things are good now, very good in New West. We're working on an alliance with C-town and granting amnesty to those who agree to try the new society."

"You're opening the gates?" Mace asked.

"We hope, eventually," Vic said. "Friend-Me Co. is also looking at building a factory outside New West and I think, this time, the government will allow it."

That rumor again. Maybe, just maybe, things were looking up, Burrows thought.

The next day, Burrows brought his own tent out of the woods and pitched it next to Mace's. Mace handed over two more vials of green, "I think things are going to change for us, bro. Pay me back later." They helped the Freeman's distribute the remaining bags of flour. On full rigs of SLO-42, Burrows head throbbed tolerably even in the August heat with all the squatters gathered around: *Me. Me. Give it to me.* Even with the headache, he felt better than he ever had. In the forest, he'd been physically pain-free, but alone. He'd forgotten how much he actually liked people, when they weren't hurting him.

"Are you going to try to go to work for Friend-Me?" he asked Mace.

"Nah, I'm gonna get in to New West if I can. I've had enough of this here. I want to be clean and well fed. Something I can get used to long-term."

Vic wiped his brow. "We have a couple passes. We can bring you back in with us if you want. You'll have to complete studies at New West University to make your residency permanent, like any other citizen."

"Maybe," Mace said. "I can see myself settled in to one of those nice little towns."

"Deming or Linden are real nice," Perla said.

Burrows thought about it. He could not picture himself in one of those hick towns, but he could see himself at the capitol, New West, at the university. College was what he'd always wanted until his dream had been derailed by the revolution. He'd been 16, about to enter university and more than ready. He'd barely survived high school and all the stabs of *loner, creep* he'd endured. His junior year, he got taller and broader than the rest of the guys and let a slutty girl hang around him to deflect attention. The clangs of *nice tits* were annoying, but not directed toward him, not blows. Still, he'd clung to the idea of escape. One more year, and he'd go relatively unnoticed at the large university. He'd study to be a surgeon, maybe even a neurosurgeon. He liked the idea of being able to mess around inside someone else's head for a change and when they were too doped up to think about him at all. Anesthesia would mean silence. That could be perfect. His parents would buy him a condo off campus. He was finally going to get away. And then everything had gone to hell. Political machinations he had nothing to do with and couldn't control.

Now, with the Freemans, Burrows saw a way back in, a way to reverse time. Maybe everything would be better in New West. That night around the campfire he asked Mace for more SLO-42 and got the last rig. "Sorry dude, it's a limited run. So, what do you think? Was it LeMay?"

Burrows nodded. "Could be. Positive, a real go-getter anyway."

That night he left the campfire early. The SLO-42 was wearing off and his head was starting to throb. The next morning, he caught Mace making last minute trades and packing up his gear.

"You going to New West?" Burrows asked.

Mace didn't look up. He was squatting in the dust, hunched over a collection of white packets and pills laid across a strip of canvas sorting them into piles and counting. "Yeah, why? You were."

"You can't seriously think that's a good idea. That they are going to let you in. No." Burrows stepped over the canvas casting the goods in shadow. "Dumbest idea, ever. It was just the drug talking."

Mace squinted up at him: *Comedown's a bitch.*

The words fell on Burrows like fucking hammers.

"It clouded my perceptions like New West wasn't so bad. But you can't forget what the revolution did to us." Burrows ground a boot into the ashy pavement. "Not here. They're using that drug to control us. You think it's a coincidence SLO-42 from LeMay shows up and she's planning to open a factory out here? She's looking for friendly slave labor. That's what it was. It's another huge scam aimed at us losers."

"That was all you. I was never on Da Lime. My mind was my own. I've been thinking pretty clearly for myself. Just back off, OK?" Mace pulled a corner of the canvas out from under Burrows' boot. "You changed your mind. Fine. I got things to do, a place to go."

"It's not like you can take any of that with you. You'll be nothing, have nothing in there. Think about it. They want us to fall in line under their rules." Burrows knelt. "I'm never going to do that. I'm never giving up my freedom. Think about it. That's what you're doing."

The thought of Mace leaving, his one contact out here, made him so angry.

Mace didn't blink. "No, I'm taking opportunities. I can set myself up there." He began rolling the goods up. "Tea, bandages, aspirin: it's all legal. The Freeman's are leaving tomorrow and I'm going with them. Don't worry. I'll still be able to work trades out here. I'll come back with something for you." Mace shoved the roll into a knapsack and shot off: *Junkie.*

Burrows grabbed Mace's shoulder and held him low. "No, you gave me that woman's Lime. You owe me."

Mace froze. Like a rabbit. *Man, dude's whack. He's going off again.*

The drug was gone now, completely, and the thoughts thrust into Burrows head stinging and burning like nettles. Burrows' hand dropped from Mace's shoulder. He was staggering to his feet when Mace launched his next round: *You want to live like an animal out here, fine. You probably couldn't handle the city. I'm going in.* "I don't own you nothin'," was all Mace said.

Burrows stumbled towards the forest. Jumbled thoughts chased him as he ran through the tents, checking people as he went. *Hey. Where's he... Why's he... running to? Who's that? Look at that. Some crazy motherfucker.*

Out of the heat, in the forest, Burrows pressed his head against an evergreen. He ground his face into the bark and then began to pound his head against it until it felt better, the physical pain superseding the mental. He slid down and huddled at the base of the tree. As the voices ebbed, he drew his legs up under him and rolled, fetal, in the evergreen needles, pulling at the roots of his limp damp hair. The pain didn't stop. No words came at him, but pressure crowded his skull. He looked up into the trees and – *destiny*– that golden word, sprang at him from the branches. It clawed at his skull and sunk its teeth into his brain. He didn't know what the drug-induced memory of a little golden girl meant to its owner, Kendra LeMay. For it had been Kendra. To him, the borrowed memory showed that the pain in his head could get a lot worse. It would come out of New West. It would find him in the forest. It would be more than he could stand.

When night came, Burrows crept back into camp. He snuck into Mace's tent, placed a knee on his chest and wrapped his hands around his throat. It felt good to be doing something, on the offensive. He wouldn't wait around to be a victim. When the body stilled, he claimed the rubbing alcohol and the matches and headed for the New West truck where Vic and Perla Freeman slept. He didn't even know they'd had a little girl with them until he saw her run from the back of the smoking truck into the tents. She looked like a miniature of her parents, no hint of gold nimbus as in his dream, so he ignored her. He drove the truck with its flaming corpses into the woods to burn. The traces of lavender, sea salt, and pine that had lifted in the propane explosion faded into the toxic smoke of burning vehicle, bodies and old growth wood. Burrows had always thought the other transients weak, too afraid of the rumored voices in the trees to live on the soft forest floor where the hunting was good. Now he'd felt the evil screaming from the trees: *destiny.* The rumors had proved true and he wanted to engulf the whole forest in fire.

It didn't matter who favored heading to New West University, the capitol, or settling in a little town like Linden. No one was going back into New West with the Freemans. But Burrows could not return to the forest, either. He pulled his new U.G. issue camo jacket around him and, in the pocket, flipped the Freeman's pass card. He had his ticket into New West. He would wait near the border until the threat came – the stab of *destiny* – and then he would hunt it down.

~ 3 ~

SYNC CHROME CITY: BLACKBERRY CORDIALS

"The economic collapse of the United Government led the way for social transformation. It was a time of great change. The educated elite of society had predicted and prepared for the downfall. They led the revolution and founded their utopia: New West. These visionaries created a stable social structure that allowed for the next, unforeseen, stage of evolution, an internal transformation we refer to as the Psychic Reformation. Key founding figures of the New Westian Revolution included the Weltraum and Freeman families. This alliance brought Dawning Psychics, Geneva Weltraum, First Psychic Sender, and Valerie Freeman, First Psychic Receiver, together. At the time, no one knew how the girls' powers, once awakened, would clash." — *Becoming Psychic 101, A History and a Primer*

Many people, the majority, thought they had succeeded in creating a utopian society in New West carved out of the remnants of the United States in the Pacific Northwest. They had chartered an ordered government, which created a secure environment for its citizens to pursue their own interests and intellectual growth. Yet, they had attained peace with unforeseen and uncontrollable consequences. Perfection came at a price, and so, with some sense of loss. In much the same way, as soon as her new sister appeared, Geneva Weltraum came to regret ever wishing to improve her family. Why had she ever longed for and begged for a sister?

When Geneva was six, Valerie Freeman came to live with the Weltraums. At the time, Geneva's family was the only world she knew. Valerie's arrival was her first experience with sudden change: a negative one. She lost her status as an only child in one nightmarish evening. One night, soon after she'd been put to bed, Geneva's mother had woken her, "We're going to help a friend." She'd led Geneva, bleary-eyed in her nightgown, to the car. Because her family rarely drove anywhere, this woke her fully. She watched as they sped out of Linden past the neat neighborhood houses, down the main street where blue solar lights lit the high school and through the forested outskirts of town. Shortly after the black expanse of low-growing soy fields began, the warmth of the car and the whir of its electric engine lulled her to sleep again. Her parents' voices soothed her into sleep as she curled in the back seat wrapped around the fluff of her blanket. She woke up when her mother sobbed, "But why? It was over."

When the green security lights flashed over them, she sat up as the car crossed the border and the high, white, illuminated arch passed over them. On the other side lay darkness. It was the first time Geneva had ever experienced the boundary of her world, Linden in New West on one side, everything else unknown on the other. She huddled in the backseat. She felt her world's smallness and her own. The car slowed as they left New West driving along the shoulder of the Freeway under the line of evergreens. "Hurry," her mother said. But her father said no, they might hit one of the people living on the road. Geneva had never been to the Freeway, only heard adults arguing about it. Bad people lived there. One day, they might get into New West. She hoped not.

When she heard shouting in the distance, her father stopped the car. She could see shapes moving nearby. Behind them, reddish light shone around billows of black smoke. “Stay here,” her father commanded. “Don’t move.” A burnt smell entered the car as her parents left it. Alone, Geneva huddled with the blanket over her head inhaling its lavender scent. Even without her father’s admonishment it wouldn’t have occurred to her to set foot outside the car here. She wasn’t a curious child. She was lawful. Footsteps, then the brush of someone passing along the side of the car, brought her out from underneath the blanket. A figure loomed outside the window. Scratch, thunk — the door handle lifted. She shot across the seat, reaching for the opposite door, but stopped when she saw her father's hands. He lifted a girl onto the seat beside her. The girl smelled of smoke. Her hair and pajamas were smeared with soot and stuck with pine needles. As her little shoulders shook, she made sounds like rubbing tree limbs. Geneva wrapped her blanket around the shivering girl, then drew away. She rubbed the silky corner of her blanket between her fingers. She wanted her blanket back and the girl away. The girl didn't feel safe. Nothing about this night did.

When they got home, her mother tucked Geneva back into bed and petted her hair. "Val lost her parents last night, Gen, she's our responsibility now. You have a sister." Geneva barely slept. She’d always wanted a sister, but her parents had said one child was enough. Now Val was here. Geneva wondered if it was too late to change her mind. She hadn’t known she’d be this scared of the sister.

In the morning, the girl sat at the breakfast table with them, terribly silent. Geneva had never known anyone whose parents had died. The way the girl looked — frozen — it was more awful than she could imagine. It was as if Val had stepped out of a nightmare and stayed. Geneva shied from the strange girl as if she might lure monsters out, at any moment, into the sunny kitchen. The girl had streaks on her face where tears had dried, but she didn't make a sound now, not even when she cried. In a way, that was good. It would be more frightening if the girl spoke, if Geneva had to talk to her, because she wouldn't know what to say. Instead, she stared at the bony, dark, pale girl. No one would believe they were sisters.

After breakfast, her mother sent them out to pick blackberries. During the revolution no one had had time to fight the encroaching Himalayan blackberries, and now they grew ripe and wild behind the house. Her father had talked about taking shears to them, but he hadn't gotten around to it. Geneva hurried to grab her silver pail. She could already taste the sweet tart juice and the buttery crust of her mother's pie. She was excited to get started, but she had to take Val, too.

Val walked too far into the bramble in her short sundress unwary of danger. Thorns hovered just over her pale skin. She faced straight ahead and plucked at the branches. Her long dark hair hung past her shoulders and into her face. Geneva wondered if Val could even see. Sometimes her fingers caught a berry and sometimes not. She dropped leaves and clusters of green and white nubs into the silver pail.

"You're supposed to only pick the ripe ones," Geneva said.

The girl flinched and red lines rose on her arms and legs as the bushes around her shook. There were pricks of blood on her fingertips.

Geneva filled her pail quickly. "Come on. It's enough."

When Val didn't say anything and didn't move, Geneva grabbed her arm and pulled her away from the bushes. Val's dress snagged and Geneva unhooked each of the thorns while she stood there. When Geneva had freed her, Val ran ahead of her into the house. Geneva spit on her hands and rubbed the blood off the long scratches on her calves before following her in.

It had been like that ever since. Geneva, although she was actually a year younger, took care of careless Val. They'd become roommates at New West University against father's advice. "It would probably be better for both of you to be apart," he warned. In a show of newfound independence, Geneva disregarded him. It was only the second time she'd ever done so. The first time was when she'd bought the new Friend-Me Journal.

As it turned out, Geneva's father was right. The girls rooming together had been a terrible idea. In the spring of their junior year, Geneva and Valerie were studying for their finals at New West University when Val began to scream. The shriek brought the university security guards, two of them, both with blond hair nearly the same color as their jackets. They stormed into the dorm room in a rush of reflective yellow and tackled Val where she writhed on the ground her keyboard still clattering. As one of the guards hit the floor, he thrust an elbow into Geneva's open Privacy Law book and crumpled its pages. Geneva heard the tear, a low rip through Val's cry. Then the guard reached across Val's heaving chest and pinned her with his thick forearm. The other guard held her down, his hands on the short bare expanse below Val's skirt. Val's skin reddened around his fingers. Geneva had no idea what was wrong with Val, what had started the screaming or the spasms. The eerily quiet Val she'd grown up with seemed to have departed this loud, violent, irrational body.

"Don't hurt her!" Geneva yelled, but in her typical passive take-what-comes fashion, she didn't try to stop them. Her side ached where Val had thrust a thick-heeled black boot into her ribs. Geneva clutched the side of the armchair where she had scuttled out of the way of Val's flailing limbs.

The guard near Val's head wrenched the virtual reality glasses from her face. Val turned her head to the side, heaved and puked. The room filled with a stench of chocolate and vomit layered over a thick masque of cinnamon oil: Val burned drops in the tiny brass lamp beside her computer. She said cinnamon enhanced her mental abilities. Val would do any little thing to get an edge, to race faster through the virtual world. Maybe the cinnamon was to blame. Maybe she had gotten too fast. Maybe, underneath the wires where Val spent most of her time, something had gone wrong. Definitely, definitely something had gone wrong.

Val stared up unblinking, but her eyes still scanned side to side, up and down. Her fingers still twitched rapidly over the air. She gaped and stopped screaming. Geneva could still hear the piercing echo of her screams. She hadn't imagined Val could even be that loud. If she hadn't seen her mouth stretched wide, she wouldn’t have believed that Val was making the sound. She still didn't connect the noise to Val, not really, it seemed to emanate from everywhere. Now Val sucked in air, her entire body arcing as the men held her.

"Looks like we've got another case of EHBF," said the guard at her feet.

Sirens blared outside the window. A medic in a white lab coat wheeled a stretcher into the room, he mumbled into a snail shell phone as he did so and waved the guards over. They manhandled Val ignoring Geneva until a guard turned to her, "What happened?"

Geneva looked at the frothy almond milk and brown chunks on the crème carpet and started to gag. Her mouth still held the taste of chocolate, now bitter, in the back of her throat. She wished she'd spent the day studying with Val instead of taking the extra shift at Ruby's. She'd tried to make up for her absence with chocolates. She remembered the chocolatier placing four blackberry cordials into a silky pouch.

It had started out as such a bright, beautiful spring perfect New West day. Geneva had left Val in the dark cave of their dorm room, put on her somewhat faded but still bright ruby-colored uniform, and headed across campus. She’d stopped at the landing by the student union building which overlooked the bay. There was a sculpture of jagged white arches framing the view: the bright blue bay and the deep green brambles of blackberry on the steep slope below. There were whale spouts in the harbor. There were eagles perched in the evergreen trees. A squirrel chittered in a nearby madrona. It was gorgeous and full of life. But if anyone else had been standing beside Geneva they might have pointed out the warning signs to her. There was a red tinge along the edge of the horizon where the sea was turning to rust the same color as the red-tipped thorns among the blackberry brambles. The whales, along with other ocean refugees, were coming closer to shore to escape the poisoned seas. But Geneva saw only what she wished to, and had been taught to observe, a bright peaceful serene place, the alluring utopian vision of New West.

From there, she hurried on to Ruby's not because she needed to work, but because she enjoyed the community and serving the diners there. She also liked the baker, Nate, who made Ruby's blackberry scones, muffins, and pies. Nate had lived before the revolution and outside of New West. He was her parents' age but well-traveled and more forthcoming. He occasionally shared stories and sometimes leftover goodies, contraband, and forbidden flavors. But today she'd worked a standard shift, the only surprise was the unusual tip a customer had left for her after devouring a slice of blackberry pie. Geneva stopped by Tim's Chocolate Shoppe with the gold coin on her way back up the hill to campus.Tim, the chocolatier, had flipped the pure gold coin between his fingers, "Are you sure you want to spend this?"

Geneva wasn't. It was the first time she'd had one of the commemorative coins in her possession. Her first thought had been to take it back to the dorm and give it to Val directly. In between ferrying plates of food, she'd rubbed her fingers over the evergreens imprinted on the coin in her pocket. She liked that New West had minted the coins out of real gold so that they had actual value. She appreciated the heft of it in her hand and in her pocket. But the more she thought about it, the more she realized Val would not like this reminder of the founding of New West 25 years ago. Val's parents had not, technically, died in the struggle. They'd been killed six years afterwards when the revolution was over. However, Val didn't see the distinction. She still blamed New West for her parents' death. Besides, she would point out, New West's supplies of solar and wind power were worth more than its cache of gold.

So instead, Geneva had detoured over to the chocolate shop. She nodded at Tim and took the bag of chocolates. Tim's Chocolate Shoppe, and its blackberry cordials, had been one of the first discoveries she and Val had made together at New West University. Freshman year they'd trekked down the hill for them before every tough exam. This year, as juniors, they hadn't come to the shop at all. She and Val were still roommates, but they didn't hang out anymore. Val was becoming a regular Plug-In. Even when she was in the dorm, her mind was virtually elsewhere. Geneva had been spending most of her time at the greenhouse in Varian Hall, the environmental psychology building. Geneva wasn't sure what had changed, but they just weren't as close, and she missed the connection with her older adopted sister. Blackberry cordials might not be the solution, but they weren't a bad start. Besides, they were a delicious indulgence, perfect for finals week.

Leaving the shop, Geneva stuffed the pouch into the front pocket of her Ruby's uniform. Now she had two reasons to hurry. She needed to get back and start studying for her final and it was a rare spring day actually warm enough to melt chocolate. Heading up the hill towards campus, she could see the water shimmering in the bay to her left. Ahead, the evergreens encircling campus stood in stark relief against the perfect blue sky, but mid-air the sea-pine scents mingled. A sheen of sweat broke out on her forehead as she strode up the hill along the brick path beside Old Main. In a hurry, she'd forgotten to take the long way around to her dorm. Sure enough, the three gray-haired protesters were there with their faded yellow signs. They were standing on the stairs to the administration building as if they had nothing better to do. Their signs read: "Get R.A.P.T.! ," "We want PSI!," and "Problems, Solutions, Innovations." As she passed, they cocked their heads and gazed at her. Geneva hugged her arms to her chest and hurried away from the weirdos. These women could have told Geneva about the dangers of the encroaching rust red sea.

The protesters were fixtures on campus, as much a part of it as the evergreens and the madrona trees, the red bricks and the ivy covering Old Main. They'd positioned themselves in front of the administration building and had been there every day for years. The first day Geneva had visited New West she'd hardly noticed them. She'd been with her parents and Val checking out the school.

Her father had pointed at the three women huddled on the steps of the building and elbowed her mother. "Does that remind you of something?"

Her mother shrugged.

"Wasn't that us, in the early days, getting together, ready to raise hell?" he said.

Geneva looked at the people sitting and humming with their hands on their knees. They didn't look especially rebellious.

Her mother laughed. "Ha, they remind me more of homeless people. Remember them?"

"In New West? Never." Her father laughed, then said, "I don't know, those psychics look pretty serious."

Her mother snorted. "Well, they can relax. The Revolution's over. They ought to just leave well enough alone." Her mother put an arm around Val and drew her in. "Just concentrate on getting your education."

Geneva and Val both rolled their eyes. Their parents were reminiscing again about the old days, "When times were hard and people had had to fight..." Blah, blah, blah.

"Back to the future, OK. Let's be present. Be here, now," Val had said using their parents' usual admonishments against them, and they'd continued their tour.

Since then, except for the times when the protesters got new yellow signs or were written about in the student newspaper, *The New West U Review*, Geneva hadn't paid much attention to them, mostly.

One day, this past winter, one of them had startled her. She'd just looked at Geneva strangely. The woman's head had jerked around when she walked by as if she had called out. The woman's eyes went wide. Her look was expectant. It made Geneva feel exposed and the feeling clung.

Then, it happened again. Another day, another intense look. A different protestor, but that same jerky movement, those same wide eyes. The next time all three of the women had started to turn toward her as she walked by. Geneva attracted the protesters' attention, as if she'd suddenly appeared in front of them. They weren't just looking either. She felt them reaching out to her as she turned away. To avoid their creepy stares, she usually took a longer route across campus, veering through the madronas and crossing in front of the student union building.

She'd forgotten in her hurry and there they were at it again. They stared at her open-mouthed as she walked by. She looked behind her to see if there was anyone else the women could be staring at. Nope. The path was empty. She had one more year left at New West University. She wouldn't miss those three strange women.

Geneva walked faster tugging down the hem of her short Ruby's uniform dress and reached the lawn in front of her dorm, dotted with students. Textbooks were splayed in front of them, but no one was reading. The students lay on their backs, eyes closed, lips slack. She wanted to shrug off her flour-dusted Ruby's uniform, flop down on the grass and bask with them.

But it was finals week. She had to study. Until Nathaniel had called and begged her to fill an afternoon shift, she'd meant to spend the day reading. She wanted to nail her test. Then she'd be home free until graduation. She also wanted to encourage Val. At the beginning of spring quarter, Val had received a warning notice from the university. She had been spending a lot of time in virtual reality and that winter all the online slacking had finally skewered her grades. Graduating from New West University was a requirement for permanent citizenship. If someone got booted from the university, they could be thrown out of New West onto the Freeway. It was a serious consequence. Still, even after the warning, Geneva didn't think Val had attended many classes this spring, either. Fortunately, most of Val's classes were in her major, quantum information theory, which were easy for Val. She needed to ace the finals but could do so with just a little study. Geneva was frustrated. Val wasn't putting in the little bit of effort it would take to prevent a crisis, while she had to bust her ass just to maintain decent grades. Geneva had always been annoyed by Val's tendency to float by obstacles in the past, but now she was worried.

Geneva couldn't quite give in to the indolent spring day, but she settled for taking off her shoes as she crossed the lawn. She wiggled her toes in the grass and admired the way her Toad Vapor polish sparkled. As she walked across the lawn, Ruby's wingtips in hand, a flock of AeroFlux Butterflies flew by and a bare-chested boy in board shorts lunged past her twirling to grab a handful of the disks. Geneva noticed his long lithe torso, warm skin, and slim muscled calves. She watched him leap over one of the girls lying on her belly on the grass and snag the edge of his target. He spun in the air with the Butterflies in hand so that he landed on his ass facing the girl. He winked at her and then grinned. The girl laughed shaking the blond ponytail that hung down her back, apparently not minding the intrusion.

"Hey, Ruby!" A voice called. It took Geneva a second to realize the guy was talking to her. It was her uniform, the monochromatic ruby-colored dress. She turned and the guy was there. She was looking at the wishbone arch where his chest ended and his abs began.

"Wanna play?" he asked.

She caught her breath. He had full lips and gleaming teeth and his hair fell in natural brown curls to his sun-kissed shoulders. He grinned and bounced on the balls of his feet like he was flush with energy but had all the time in the world to spend it.

Geneva shook her head.

"Got to study huh, Ruby?" he said and bounded away, over the path and across the grass, flinging Butterflies to another boy. She tried to imagine standing in her stiff, stick-straight Ruby's smock pointing her arms up into the air and stumbling after a Butterfly. Just then the blond ponytail girl stepped by her. The girl looked nude at first in her bronze bikini until Geneva saw the thin line of a strap under her blond hair. The ponytail swung back and forth across her back like a metronome keeping time with her hips. She leapt like a dancer and caught eight Butterflies flung her way. Geneva noticed she wasn't the only one watching ponytail move.

Just as well, Geneva thought, let the other girl distract the beautiful Butterfly throwing boy. She had an upcoming exam, the last significant one of her college career. After three years of effort, this test was worth the sacrifice of one more spring day. Next year, she could take electives, do an internship, and figure out what to do with the rest of her life. She quickened her pace.

At Inu Wood Dormitory, Geneva pushed open the door to her dorm room. The air inside was hazy with cinnamon-scented smoke: Val's incense. Val was there, in total Plug-In mode, just as she'd been when Geneva left. She wore slim, black, virtual reality glasses, a purple snail-shaped cell receiver in one ear and a silver one in the other. Insulated as she was, Val could probably ride out an earthquake, even Cascadia's long awaited Big One, without looking up. Geneva winced at the way Val was sitting. She was perched on the narrow chair. Her long legs, encased in her favorite kick-ass, thigh-high boots, were slung sideways and tucked under her butt. It was an ergonomic nightmare, but somehow, Val managed to hold that twisted position for hours.

Geneva went to the kitchenette, poured a glass of almond milk and set it down beside the computer. Val snaked a hand out, wrapped it around the glass and brought it to her lips. Her other hand maintained its flight path over the keyboard whirring as her fingertips depressed keys. On the monitor, information spiraled around the screen and then came to a stop as Val pulled off her headset.

"Hey, Gen. You're back." Val wrinkled her nose. "And so smellin' like fried soy."

Geneva shrugged. "I tried to smell like chocolate." She reached into her apron pocket, pulled out the Tim's bag and handed it to Val. "To help you study."

"Cordials?" Val reached into the bag and then held up one blue and brown smeared finger. "Yep. Ah, thanks." She put the bag aside.

"Sorry. It was warm and I dawdled. You get some studying in?"

"Ah sure, Mom. I think I got it under control," Val said. "Don't worry. They try to kick me out and I'll just remind them my parents died for the cause."

Geneva turned, stung. "OK. I guess."

"Hey," Val called as Geneva headed down the short hallway. "I still think you should dye your hair. Everyone already calls you Ruby. So why not go with it?"

Geneva slipped out of her uniform and took a quick shower. A package of Wicked Sprites hair dye in Gator Tongue red was displayed on the bathroom counter. She smiled as she secured the wet sable strands of her hair into two ponytails and put on a white

T-shirt and khakis. Val didn't seem to get that she already attracted more attention than she wanted. In the living room, she took one last look out the window. Through the dark slats of the blinds, the long lines of sky and lawn were now cast in an orange glow, the first hint of sunset. She closed the blinds and wrested the oversized armchair around to face into the room.

"Val, is it OK with these closed?" she asked turning on the floor lamp.

There was no reply. Val had left real-reality. Geneva wondered when talking to Val had become mostly habit, like talking to a pet. She didn't expect a response. Still, in front of her, Val filled the room with companionable silence. Val rustled the air and sucked it in. She swung side to side on her chair. Her fingers on the keyboard produced soothing insectoid sounds. Val muttered to herself in breathy half syllables as she did — whatever it was she did — online. She provided just enough noise and movement to make the room feel occupied, exactly the right amount of company. Val's reaction to the cordials had been disappointing, but what did Geneva expect? A few chocolates weren't going to make them kids again. Growing up meant growing apart, and maybe their more distant relationship wasn't bad, just different. Geneva sunk into the armchair and hefted the Privacy Law book onto her lap. She turned to the section on Neo-Privacy and started reading.

Snap! Geneva looked up as Val undid one of her many pockets, extracted a vial of gloss and whisked the brush over her lips. Geneva smiled. Val had been wearing that same vampy shade of plum since junior high. It matched her Wicked Sprites Nightshade colored hair. She noticed how the ends of Val's hair fell forward in a sharp angle under the headset and smiled again. On the other hand, Val had a new haircut almost every week.

Geneva returned to her text. It was time to get serious. She needed to think of a mnemonic device to remember the names of the plaintiff and the dissenting judge in the landmark neo-privacy case. She sounded out a sentence slowly, driving each word into her head, "The Supreme Court upheld the *Hales v Friend-Me Co.* ruling in an 8-1 decision with the dissenting opinion coming from..."

Then Val started screaming. Her high-pitched wail shook the room streaming from everywhere at once. Geneva had to identify the source of the sound visually — Val's plum-smeared mouth stretched wide. Val jerked backwards in her chair and then fell from it onto the floor. She writhed. Her limbs struck the metal chair as she continued to scream.

The law book crashed to the floor as Geneva jumped to Val's side. She fell back striking her tailbone as Val kicked her in the side.

"She...she just started screaming," Geneva said to the medic. "I was studying here and she was online and then..."

"How long?" the medic said.

"Hours."

"No, how long was she screaming?"

Geneva shook her head. It felt like hours. She began to tremble. The numbness that had reined in her panic at the bizarre situation left her suddenly, releasing her to a cold quake.

The medic extracted a finger-length wand from his front pocket and waved a point of light in Val's eyes. They were laced with red, sunk deep into the sockets. The flesh around them puckered.

"Optic neuritis," he said. He filled an eyedropper with liquid from a vial in his coat pocket. From it, he squeezed green drops into Val's eyes. Then he placed a black patch on her forehead. A wave pattern appeared after a few seconds. He spoke into his snail shell as he worked. "There it is, the spike and wave. And there's the ELF. Definitely an EHBF. What's your name?" he asked.

Val stared up vacantly. The drops made her irises swell. "Val Freeman," she whispered.

"Where are you?" he asked.

"New West University," Val said her voice steadier. Then she jerked and grunted, "Get...off...me."

The guards started to back off.

"Keep holding her." The medic told them. "I'm going to give her something to relax."

He pulled a syringe out of his coat, peeled down the top of Val's boot and lowered the plunger into her thigh.

Geneva edged off the armchair, “Wait.”

But Val was already sinking into stillness. The guards released her and the medic hoisted her up. She hung limp as he belted her onto the stretcher. Under the thick straps, in her black T-shirt and short-pleated skirt, Val looked delicate. She would hate that. Bruises were already beginning to form in a row down her thin arms where they had struck the chair. Her head lolled. Geneva reached over and tucked a strand of hair behind Val's ear. Her hair and forehead were damp.

The medic began to move the stretcher forward. Geneva started to follow, but he stopped, grabbed her arm and pulled her aside.

"Here, take this." He handed her a business card. "Call her family and tell them to call this number."

She started forward again as Val was wheeled from the room. "I'm family.”

"No," he said, his voice low, his fingers tight around her arm. "You should stay here. You're shaking. You want something to calm you?"

She shook her head. It was true that she could not stop shivering, but she felt too calm as it was. She should be doing something. She wanted to run after Val, but she didn't trust her legs. The medic had stepped around in front of her, blocking her.

"Well, here, take this, if you want, for later," he said. He handed her an eyedropper filled with green liquid. Her fist closed around it. When she looked up again, she was alone with the two campus guards.

"Jeez," one of them said as they left. "What were you girls doing inside today anyway? Inside on a beautiful spring day, it'd make anyone crazy." He pulled the door shut behind them.

Geneva looked down at the card in her hand. The card's embossed green pyramid logo glittered. She went to the lamp and read: New West Mental Health. Details of Val's seizure began to shine out to her like the words on the business card and she connected them with bits she'd learned in psychology and science classes. The diagnosis the med-tech had given Valerie, ELF, these were low frequency electromagnetic waves, brain waves. She'd seen the label on the drug he had given Val, Thorazine. That was an old anti-psychotic, but with a new modern use the professor had glossed over, that she could not recall. She saw the words Sync Chrome City stretched across Valerie's chest on her t-shirt and thought she'd seen them somewhere else before. She began to remember the crazy rumors, of something like this happening to other students at New West. She may have even seen flyers on campus about it — a place the government had taken students, usually Plug-Ins, referred to as The Camp.

Just when everything seemed out of her control, at the same time, everything felt connected. Geneva had the feeling that if only she'd been paying attention, she could have anticipated this and spared herself and Valerie a painful shock. She could have done something to prevent this. She promised herself that now, now that her roommate, her sister, her best friend had been taken, she would be more aware, she would notice. Things had been happening in the world around her and they mattered.

~ 4 ~

SYNC CHROME CITY: QUILLS

"Most are in agreement that the Psychic Reformation likely would not have occurred without the establishment of a peaceful enclave that allowed Generation Utopia to focus on a high level of self-actualization. However, many (notably: S. Sherring in *Save Giovanni: The Lost Men of the Psychic Wars*) have speculated about the role of C.G. Burrows and whether the trauma of those first Awakenings could have been avoided. In hindsight, we can argue that the New Westian Revolutionaries should have tried to repair the immense social damage created under the United Government, rather than attempt a pristine utopia. In addition, many have criticized New West for its failure to enact a psychic education program sooner. Had it done so, undeniably, suffering could have been avoided." — *Becoming Psychic 101, A History and a Primer*

Just outside of New West on the 'Way, C.G. Burrows was taking his time plugging black ink into his thigh bead by bead. After each prick came the ooze of entering ink. He finished the tail of the "e" on his left thigh and started in on the "d" on the right. The design was nothing fancy, just black block letters he'd been working on a little each day, ever since he'd moved his parents' R.V. up from C-town and opened his Vary shop inside. For six months he'd been clean. An assortment of drugs had failed to keep the needling voices out of his head, even here, closer to New West, where there were fewer people. Of course, he'd never been in a hurry to finish the tattoo. That was kind of the point of the long Latin phrase he was embedding into his skin — *Omnis festinatio ex parte diaboli est* — all haste is the work of the devil. He was taking it nice and slow. The needle pain was his new remedy for his psychic distress.

This morning, he'd heard about another way of keeping the voices out of his head. He'd found a link to the Noetic Sciences Institute — the headquarters located far down the 'Way — and the Society for Psychical Research, located far off-continent — on the Psi-Aware website. Noetic meant intellect, and he didn't think the Psi-Aware group had any. The idiots were interested in enhancing and developing psychic skills and spurring change in a rapid fashion as ignorant as New Westian rebels. Their naïve expectations regarding the ecstasy of psychic experience ran counter to Burrows own experience with telepathy. It just caused pain. The desires of these factions were the stuff of Burrows' recurring nightmares: the one where he stood in a crowd of silent people stabbed by the thoughts of a similar crowd over the next hill, or even worse, the one where he stood alone in a clearing with no one and nothing in sight but trees, still pinned by a crowd of pricking thoughts as if he were trapped in an ancient torture device, a psychic iron man. So far, these psychic wannabe groups had not found support for their plan to develop psychic abilities in the general population. So, his nightmares were still only nightmares. The only thing he agreed with them about: It was possible.

Unlike the Psi-Aware activist naïfs, however, the Noetic Institute had done actual research into psychic abilities and their research had application for his own interest: controlling his psychic piercings, reducing his pain. The institute wrote academic scientific papers filled with multi-syllabic garble that concluded: psychic powers can be controlled by meditation. It was a slow and time-consuming solution he hadn't tried and wasn't going to. He'd stick to the ink. When he focused on the pain, he could keep the intrusive thoughts out of his head. He practiced slow tattooing as pain management.

Burrows looked at the clock and laid aside Faust, his favorite needle, a nine-incher. It was time to open his shop. Not that any-one was likely to come in before it got dark, but he had to keep to a schedule, or he'd lose his mind out here. He made a quick post on *KillGiovanni* to keep the content fresh. Then he turned on the vid screens displaying his handiwork in the showroom, lit up the neon pink "V" over his R.V. and put on his lab coat.

He was sterilizing his needles one by one over the stainless-steel table when the kids intruded: two minds pierced his. A girl, impatient: *Where's the owner?* And a boy, bored: *There's no one here.* He clenched his jaw and tapped his temples with two fingers, twice, hard, mimicking the pain in order to dull it. He liked to be sitting out front when the customers arrived so he wouldn't be surprised. He could handle the pain better if he was prepared for it.

Let them wait. He didn't need psychic ability to know they were college students, coming into the Freeway so early, on a lark. He finished sterilizing the set of two-inchers and walked out into the waiting area when he felt the boy about to leave: *There's no one. Let's go.* He stroked Faust's steel in folded gauze as he approached them.

Sure enough, college students, too clean to be anything else. They were a little sweaty and scraggly from the walk past the gate, but they were obviously from New West although they'd put some effort into appearing otherwise. The boy had matted hair and the girl dark gunk around her eyes. Both were in clothes that hung off their scrawny limbs. They looked like rag dolls, but he could see their stuffing and it was clean. What would their parents think? The revolutionary generation had worked so hard to keep the rabble out of New West, only to have their children idolize the cast-offs and scheme their way out of utopia.

The boy was nervous, spooked probably, by the dirt and disorder of the ‘Way and maybe a little turned on by it too. Everything that was so carefully maintained in New West came undone on the Freeway. It was New West with its corset unstrung, exuding carnal entropy. He remembered what that felt like the first time, being cut loose onto the ‘Way. Frightening, but invigorating, before it wore you down.

The boy's eyes flickered around the shop unable to settle on any of the screens flashing images of blood and body parts from finished and in progress Varies. The guy finally saw him and nudged the girl who was also staring at the screens. He nodded and Burrows just stared back until the girl — *Over here!* — talked. "I'm here for quills."

The girl’s voice in his head was needy and insistent, particularly biting, and it was Burrow’s pleasure to ignore her. He turned to the guy and testily countered with a string of his own verbiage, "You from New West? You sneak over the border and walk into the first Vary shop you see on the road, that it? So what do you think? What can I do for you? Give you a special on detachable tails? I got some real pretty custom exotics."

Burrows had learned to be a fast talker. It was the only way for him to fire back at the unsolicited thoughts he got from others, since no one ever "got" him.

It was insulting to suggest they wanted something so tame as tails and Burrows knew it. The kid, on the defensive where Burrows wanted him, puffed up at first, then he decided to play cool and sunk into a chunk of the mustard-colored foam in the waiting room.

"No detachables. Quills," the girl said.

"Yeah, she hardcore?" Burrows asked the boy. Then, still focused on him dismissed the idea. "Nah, those are real uncomfortable."

The guy pointed at the girl and shrugged. She looked into a glass case at back of the R.V. "Serious, I know what I want."

"OK, sure. I'll take your money, if you've got it," Burrows continued to address his comments to the boy while the girl's indignation grew—*Hey. Prick. Over here. I'm the customer.* It amused him to annoy her, but he was going to have to deal with the headache sooner or later. "I'm not one of these Vary guys that tries to mess you up and laughs at you later. What you want is what you want, but I know my business." He jerked a thumb at the girl. "I don't think you want quills."

"You can't look at me and think you know what I can handle," the girl said.

He snorted. "Handle, sure. In case you haven't noticed, I haven't even looked at you." She'd left greasy handprints all over his showcase. He finally gave her a long look. "Like I figured, you look more like tail."

Asshole. Her retort slammed him, reminding him that he was having too much fun. Pissing people off was the one thing he enjoyed about his "gift." He could push people to the brink of anger and still end up with their money. Time to get charming. "But who cares, I won't see you in here again anyway. She wants quills, she can have quills."

The boy took the cue. He reached into one of his many pocket and flashed his circle of New West green and yellow. These college kids always had lots of credit. "I think that'll cover it," the boy said. He crossed one baggy-pant clad leg over the other, sprawling, taking up space, relaxing into the insulation like it was home.

"Now we can talk," Burrows said to the girl in a low voice, the one women especially liked. "I'm Burrows." He extended his hand. "And you are?"

Eve. She thought it. He knew it. Her name penetrated his mind and then she said, "Eve." It was like living in a damn canyon. He liked it better when people lied. It was less repetitive.

Eve pointed to one of the long black quills in the case and he opened it up and handed it to her. She ran a finger along it as the boy came up beside her. He reached a fingertip out and jabbed it on the point drawing blood, "Yaaah!" Burrows swiped the quill from Eve and swabbed it with the gauze.

The boy jammed his fingertip into his mouth and sucked. "Damn, those could do some serious damage. Where you going to put them?"

Eve pulled her shirt up and placed her hands around her hips just under her belly roll. "Long ones from my back to just about here that stick out." She slid her thumbs down from her hipbones till they met in a point just under the waistband of her black pants. "And then a triangle of shorter flat ones in between where the points meet."

"Oh great," the boy whined. "You want to kill me?"

Eve curled her lip at him. “You wish.”

Burrows unlocked a smaller case and extracted one of the gold quills. He held it up to the light so she could see its glowing core.

"See, that's pretty," he said. "The inside captures the light and it has a russet tone." He touched the transparent tip. "And it's longer than it looks too, surprising. Now, these are what you want. Not those black ones, too obvious, garish."

Eve, mesmerized, nodded. "Yeah."

He knew she'd like those. They were a total mismatch with the persona she was trying to pull off: black clothes, dyed black hair, kind of witchy. But they reminded her of someone: *Coco*. Some other girl, he figured. A pretty girl. No, his type. Better than pretty, he imagined — fine.

Burrows began to gather an assortment of the five, three, and two-inch gold quills. When he had a fistful, he jerked his head at the door to the surgery and said, "Come on behind the curtain. I'll let you watch me alter your girl's abdomen."

He pulled the curtain aside to reveal the most sterile place outside New West — his operating room, one stainless steel table and a collection of needles. It wasn't what he'd envisioned when he'd dreamed of becoming a neurosurgeon. It was what he had, the meatloaf he'd made out of the scraps of life he'd been left. He waved Eve toward a stainless-steel table. "Climb up there."

She hesitated at the door. "Do I have to put something on? Like a gown or something?'"

"No, just pull up your shirt and take off your pants."

He looked at the boy. The two kids had exchanged moods. The boy was the cool one now and the girl was nervous and struggling not to show it.

"So, serious, you do know what you're doing, right?" she said. "I mean, you must've been doing this awhile."

Accusations were flashing through her head — *Hack. Waster. Perv.* — He felt each one: prick, prick, prick.

"Yeah. Good question," Burrows said. "Why don't we talk about this while I'm working? This could take time."

She pointed at his lab coat. "Are you wearing something under that?"

The boy snickered and that made her shut up and drop her pants. She sat up on the table. "Fine."

She had flat white thighs and black cotton underwear. He wheeled his chair and tools over and swabbed her abdomen with alcohol. She didn't squirm much. That, and the way she hadn't complained about the cold table, told him she'd probably be good with the quills. He started to look forward to this.

"You know, actually, I haven't been doing this long," he said, when he had the first quill poised over her side.

She shot him a look. He hadn't left himself much room. She was one comment away from slamming her hands down on the table and jumping off. He looked up at the boy who was already starting to lose interest, pacing around the backroom.

"But she's in good hands," Burrows said. "Before I did this, I was gonna be a surgeon. You know, back when people wanted to be beautiful. But don't worry, I didn't get shut out of New West for malpractice or crime."

"What happened then?" Eve asked. "How did you get here?"

Burrows inserted the first quill in her side. "Steady now. Let's just say some people didn't like my opinions. They had their revolution. I was on the wrong side."

"You could come back. There'll be amnesty," the boy said. "Especially for a doctor."

"Interesting riff. Heard that before. You don't listen," He began to stick in the second quill. "I'm not a doctor. I was going to be."

The boy: *Whatever.*

He stuck the girl harder than he needed to with the third quill. She bit her lip, real quiet now. She was concentrating on her own pain, not thinking about him at all anymore. She was staying in her own head, good girl. That was the best part of the Vary work, making people quiet. The boy stood by watching the infusion of quills into his friend's side. It shut him up for a while too, but not for long. He was a twitchy little guy.

"So when did you get all that work done?" he asked.

Burrows paused and ran his hands over the "work," the kid was referring to, the long hard spikes around his neck and the rubbery black nubs over his jaw and cheeks.

"I didn't, 'get-it-done'," Burrows said inserting another quill in Eve's side. "I did it. You have to trust a guy who does his own face, right?"

"Yeah," the boy said.

"I wanted to make sure I would never be tempted into going back into New West again, since they wouldn't take me like this, it all works out."

The kid stopped asking questions. The girl was flat on her back now. Her chest heaved like she might hyperventilate. Her eyes, glazed and unfocused, were muddy brown like the edge of the 'Way along the forest. She was beginning to feel high from the pain. Burrows zoned in on his work. He poked the thick end of each quill under the white flesh, watching the blood rise to the surface and seep out around the end in small circles. Eve's sides were starting to swell and purple where he'd stuck the first quills. He finished on her sides and began to set the shorter, softer quills into her lower abdomen.

He was getting into a rhythm, laying them down fast and smooth, when a spasm of thought knocked him off beat. He jerked back, jabbing his finger with one of the quills as the kid stabbed him: *It's him. It's the killgiovanni guy!* He whipped around and saw the boy hovering over his computer.

Then the kid was at his side in full twitch mode. "Is *Kill Giovanni* your site?! No way, everybody loves it! Do you run it? Did I introduce myself? You said you're Burrows, right? I'm Grugel."

Grugel was not this kid's name, which explained why the kid hadn't given it to him sooner. A name was usually the first get people would hand him. Everybody wanted to be known. This kid, some kind of schemer, stayed inside, a proper liar, but he was telegraphing now as he rambled on. Grugel was spinning ideas about whether he could get Burrows to come into New West with him, if there was a way to make some money.

"I have a cult site too. It's called *Sync Chrome City*. Giovanni is one of the security codes."

The kid sent tornados of geek enthusiasm migraining into Burrows. It was a pain, but also flattering. Apparently, Burrow's site, his little counter revolutionary hobby, *Kill Giovanni Hastings*, a stab at the popular children's book, had gained some kind of following. After a few beat downs in elementary school, Burrows had learned to disguise his weak-looking reflexive wincing with a pissed off mocking sneer. He used it now, turning this face to the source of the migraine. "I thought all you kids liked Giovanni Hastings — the voice of Generation Utopia?"

At this, Eve hoisted herself up on her elbows. Her stomach rolled out, now nearly coated in gold quills: like a bloody, prickly, teddy bear tummy. Her lip curled.

"That was our parents' idea. We can't stand that sunny-day story. Giovanni Hastings ends up king of the world. But what really happened? Nothing. Our parents got to have a revolution. We got nothing: static. What am I supposed to do when I finish college? More of the same. Some lame job in New West. Giovanni's just a fairy tale."

"Well, yeah." Burrows rolled his eyes. "More like propaganda. So, you're running to the 'Way? Taking up residence? Finding work, maybe, at the Friend-Me factory?"

"No way," she looked around. "Just visiting, maybe hitting one of the bonfires. We don't want to make slaves of ourselves and live in the dirt out here. I'm just saying it's not perfect in New West. Not so perfect as they like to make it out."

"Hey, I like to make out," said Grugel, and was ignored.

"Just better than here," Burrows said. "Because you're bored?"

"Yeah. Basically. Perma-bored. Stuck."

Grugel hopped around. More astute than the girl, or maybe just less self-absorbed, he actually noticed how the comments burned Burrows. "Eve, piss him off when he's done sticking you," he warned.

"Yeah, I'm about done," Burrows gave Eve's forearm a little shove. His antagonism toward the kids had become more serious, less entertaining. He hated that they had what he'd once wanted: comfy, little college lives. "Lay back down and let me finish this."

He flicked in the last quills.

"That you too, Grugel? Going nowhere, bored? Way's too poor for you?"

Grugel: *Is he crazy? No one lives on the Freeway unless they have to.* "Not me," he said. "I mean I'm not going to have some lame job. College is just like, my cover; I have my own business."

"What kind of business?"

The kid shrugged. "I do some tech." But Burrows got another much more interesting answer: *SLO-42.*

The kid was dealing. No surprise there, what other kind of business could a college kid have? But SLO-42. That was rare. Burrows kept his expression neutral, but he had to work at it. SLO-42 was complicated to manufacture, and you had to have a source, someone who people wanted to experience. Did this kid know Kendra LeMay? Burrows hadn't got his hands on that supply for years. He'd given up on the drug altogether after a few bad trips sampled from dull minds. He didn't need to experience the perspective of some guy on the 'Way. He already got that.

He hadn't had a good trip since the dose Mace had given him. He was sure now it had really been off the famous entrepreneur, LeMay. He grimaced remembering how he'd last seen Mace. The worst part had been the expression on his face, not even surprised, like he expected Burrows to kill, just like he'd expected him to steal. The next worst part was the intensity of his thought, completely focused on his murderer as he struggled. It had come at Burrows like a spray of buckshot; the pain delivered on a mundane last thought —just a denial — *No!* Then the pain ebbed. The thoughts had faded. Mace had gone inside, silent, his life flashing before his eyes, Burrows supposed. And Burrows had rushed out of the tent and continued to live up to low expectations. He'd given up on drugs, for the most part though, and settled for solitude to avoid the pain of people.

He pushed back his stool and, even distracted by his memories, he couldn't help but admire his work. The girl's pierced belly was almost pretty now with its prickly golden sheen. Eve sat up and carefully ran her hands down the quills.

"It'll look better without the blood and bruises. You're done," he said.

Grugel handed over payment, a circle of green and yellow. "Hey, don't forget we want one of those tails too," Eve said. She pointed at a Golden Tamarin — a long fluffy noncommittal variant that, in truth, had no genetic relation to any kind of off-continent creature. It got its lush fringe from Golden Retriever and its long curling tail courtesy of an inventive rat-cat hybrid. Not that these kids knew the difference between their animal parts.

"That doesn't look like it'd fit either of you," Burrows said.

"No, it's for a friend. She was too scared to come," Grugel said.

"Then she doesn't deserve this," Burrows said stroking the tail, which was still one of his favorites despite its inauspicious origins. The geneticist had made the best of the inferior raw materials available. "Why give her an edge she hasn't earned?"

"Oh, as if," Eve said. "She wasn't scared. She wasn't allowed. Her father's got her in chains."

"Father?" he asked, to see if he could get it. He already knew they were talking about the fine girl, *Coco*, who Eve idolized and was so overshadowed by that she'd gotten quilled to try to stand out. Too bad for her, he doubted it would work out. Classic beauty always trumped trying too hard.

Eve: *President Sherman.*

Another surprise. These kids! They knew the daughter of the head of the university, the de facto leader of New West, and they had access to some kind of SLO-42. He couldn't help but hope it was the Kendra LeMay variety. Now they were getting interesting.

Burrows shrugged turning the New West electronic coin over in his hand. It was just a credit card, but everything had to be tweaked in New West, made better. It had the heft and glint of coin, embossed with the New West emblem, a circle of yellow bisected by a line of trees. He scanned it, took his due, and as he handed it back to the kid asked, "So what if I decided to come visit? Would you have a place for me to stay?”

"Yaaah! People would want to meet you,” Grugel said, failing an attempt to suppress a geek spasm of excitement. The kid was like a series of electroshocks. "Check out my site, some time. Here." He handed over another coin, this one glossy black. A line of skyscrapers cut through the circle in place of the trees on the New West coin. The cityscape pictured on the coin was anti-New West in every way but reminded Burrows of the black windowed Mirror building at the center of C-town where his parents lived. C-town was another enclave that had formed in the economic collapse, but the people there had taken the opposite approach: preservation. They had liked things the way they were and tried to keep them that way. It was a dull, predictable scene.

"Those are the access codes. Tell me what you think," Grugel said.

At that, both the kids' minds flashed, pinning Burrows brain from either side: *Check out Sync Chrome City.* And from the boy: *Yaaaah!*

After the kids left, dragging their Tamarin tail behind them on their way to a Friend-Me bonfire like it was freaking spring break, Burrows flipped Grugel's Sync Chrome City link into his machine. Twenty minutes later he was reeling, gasping for breath. Ten minutes later he had a blade on his face digging into his flesh to remove the nubs. He had to push the scalpel in deep to get them out. Removing the quills from his neck was even more painful. The delicate skin tore loose. The flexible quills didn't help and after he pricked his fingers a few times he broke off the sharp ends to get them out of the way while he worked. When he finished at about 2 a.m., his head, ear to jaw, was a bloody mess. Blood streamed through the stubble down his neck and pooled in his collarbone. He sponged the worst of it off and applied some anti-microbial jelly. He'd wear a collar. He'd grow a beard. It'd be fine. But he was going back into New West and he couldn't have people looking at him and sending hard thoughts his way.

He'd put in the quills and nubs to fit in and establish his business out on the 'Way. Now, he'd ripped them out so that he could pass back into New West. He told himself that it was not about scoring SLO-42. It was what he'd experienced on Sync Chrome City that drove him, but in truth he couldn't get Kendra LeMay out of his mind. She'd opened the Friend-Me factory just down the 'Way from New West like she'd planned, giving the ruffians work and holding the monthly bonfires to keep them happy. The hedonistic celebrations drew the college kids down like flies. They didn't want to work as "slaves," but they were more than happy to party like them. So, Kendra was close, but still too far away to please him. He'd seen the potential of Sync Chrome City, so it was time to go into New West. If he managed to score some SLO-42 made from Kendra LeMay, so much the better.

~ 5 ~

SYNC CHROME CITY: FINAL EXAM

"Perhaps undue attention has been given to the fact that Geneva Weltraum, Mother Connectress of Minds, was so solitary in her younger years. Many have countered that her studies of psychology, even though her focus was primarily plants, not people, indicate her empathic leanings. However, the portrayal of Geneva as a loner is, for the most part, accurate. It must be remembered that she manifested first as a Sender: a telepath, not an empath. The repellant nature of Sender and Receiver, referred to today as "annihilation," caused trauma that could have been avoided if the government had embraced psychic abilities rather than treating those first manifestations of the transformation as mental illness." — *Becoming Psychic 101, A History and a Primer*

Rumor had it that a few New West students each year suffered psychic seizures, and that the university had been removing them to a remote facility. Whether the purpose was to help them, study them, or just isolate them; no one knew. They called the mysterious off-campus location, The Camp. Now Geneva knew another alias: New West Mental Health. That was where the medics had taken Valerie after giving her thorazine. Geneva had remembered its other use: a psychic suppressant. Groups like Psi-Aware, advocates for supposed psychic evolution, wanted the drug banned.

Did the university think quiet Val was psychic? How could they know? Was she sick? Could it possibly be contagious? In tears, Geneva called home. She was relieved to hear her father's voice. Usually, she disliked talking to him on the phone and immediately asked for her mother. Ever the scientist, her father didn't converse: He relayed information in terse, tense phrases. Now she was grateful for his laconic style. She didn't want to talk or to try to explain what had happened. She just wanted help. Unsure where to begin to sort through her fear, sadness, and the first seeds of anger, Geneva began in a manner like her father, concise and factual. "They've taken Valerie."

Her father listened to her blunt story and then his voice lifted as he zeroed in on key information. When he spoke, it was in the slow, moderated tone he used when he did research, talking to himself as if reading his thoughts aloud as they scrolled by. "OK, the business card. Just read me what's on it."

She did, and her father responded with silence, the way he so often did. He'd stop in the middle of a conversation to ponder a subject unrelated to what you wanted to talk to him about, possibly a new species of rodent he was studying. There was nothing to do but wait him out. If interrupted, he'd forget what he'd been about to say. Geneva grew impatient, she wanted reassurance that Val would be OK.

"Can I talk to Mom?" she asked.

There was another pause, and she strained to hear him catching only, "Sorry." before he hit full volume. "Your mother's on assignment in C-town."

Of course, she was. Her mother had been "on assignment" since Geneva had hit puberty. She glanced at the door, still seeing, in her mind's eye, the dark top of Val's head disappearing as the medic wheeled her out on the stretcher. "I shouldn't have let them take her without me. I should go after her."

"No," her father said, in the firm tone he used to announce new research. "I was thinking I know where they are taking her. That place. It's nearby. When did they leave?"

"Minutes ago. They'd take her all the way back to Linden?"

"Yes. You've seen it. That clinic. The building was by your high school," he said. "You remember, in the forest."

Geneva didn't.

"I'll meet her there. Sit tight. I'll call you when I have news," he said.

"Wait, what about this green drug?" she asked.

But he was already gone. Her father didn't say goodbye. He never did. He had no sense of phone etiquette, as though he didn't really believe the device was connecting him with another human being just the information that person contained. Geneva detached the phone from the curve of her ear and stared at the purple snail shell in her palm. The display read 11 p.m.

Her father had sounded so sure about his strange conclusion. If they'd taken Val to Linden, that was at least a 30-minute drive away. Val wouldn't even be there yet. Her father wouldn't call until he had concrete information. It'd be an hour at least, after midnight, a new day.

If The Camp was real, why had the medics taken Valerie there? As far as she knew, Valerie wasn't any kind of psychic. And they'd both been healthy. Her mind raced, and the dorm room felt constricting. She replaced the phone on her ear, grabbed her key card from the pocket of her Ruby's uniform, and headed out the door down the empty hallway.

She wanted to bang on one of the doors, find someone, and tell them everything to dilute the contents of her spinning mind, but she didn't know anyone who would unquestioningly invite her in at this hour. Val was the one person in her life she could talk to about anything, anytime. As she left Inu Wood, she caught a glimpse of a couple cuddled in the lounge in the glow of a screen. She'd met them but couldn't remember their names.

Maybe her father had been right when he'd said she and Val shouldn't room together. Val had been her built-in best friend ever since she'd come to live with the Weltraum family. When the economy collapsed, the government and all the schools had shut down. Restoring the educational system had been New West's priority after the chaos of the revolution, but it had happened slowly. Her parents had taught them at home until high school. If not for Val, she would have been alone. When the high school opened, Val had welcomed it. She'd made new friends. Geneva could just as easily have stayed at home helping her father identify new species of rodents.

"You're more like our mother," she'd said to Val once in high school meaning it as a compliment.

"Your mother," Val had said. "And I'm not."

Her parents were not technically Val's, but they'd always said "our mother" before. Val's rejection hurt, but Geneva excused the slight. Maybe Val was upset because their mom had been away on diplomatic missions so much. She felt abandoned sometimes, too. It had to be worse for Val, but they'd never talked about it.

When they'd moved in together, Geneva had been happy. She thought it would bring them back together and heal the places where they'd grown apart. You couldn't get closer than roommates; problem solved. Maybe rooming with Val had kept her from making an effort to meet any other people on campus, so what? She didn't need a lot of attachments. She was focused on her studies, and, after all, one close friend was better than a bunch of acquaintances.

Geneva headed across campus without any particular destination in mind just seeking more space for her thoughts. Lamps along the brick paths cast an orange glow. She soon reached the west edge of campus overlooking the dark bay. She leaned against the railing looking back. A sliver of moon hung over the evergreen covered hill behind the cluster of brick halls. Through the madrona trees at the university's heart, the administration building was as still as the rest. The stairs leading up to the giant double doors were empty. The protesters had gone home for the night. Geneva wrapped her arms across her chest and rubbed the goosebumps on her arms. The campus was still tonight, its students tucked away cramming for finals.

The snail shell balanced lightly on Geneva's ear. She wished it would vibrate and she would hear her mother's voice. She missed the mother she remembered from childhood: a more serene version, she thought, before Val had come to them and before she had taken the government job. The breeze off the Salish Sea cooled the tears in the corners of her eyes. The moon appeared to waver as she blinked them away. Val had changed their lives. Sometimes Geneva wished she hadn't.

It's happening again, Geneva thought, nothing will be the same tomorrow.

She bit her lip and veered over to the Student Union Building. The Big Top Valerie had called it in an editorial she'd written for *The New West Review* and the name stuck. She'd opined that the building's design reflected the architect's disdain for students. It looked like a circus tent. Disdain was a frequent theme of the paper especially on the topic of "their generation," Gen Utopia. They would be the first to live out their lives in New West and benefit from the social order and the soundness established by their parents, The Revolutionaries. They would all be educated and economically upper class and would not have to worry about political upheaval, an economic crisis, or environmental chaos: the three plagues that had occupied their parents. They were free to spend their lives at the pinnacle of Maslow's hierarchy of needs and devote themselves entirely to self-actualization. The newspaper editor railed against the labeling of their generation and liked to point out this left Gen Utopia in "no place" with nothing to do. Although she'd never shown much interest in writing before, Val had picked up the paper's note of disdain perfectly in her commentary. She'd always been persuasive in a quiet way.

"The Big Top exemplifies how they see our role in this society. They expect us to live delighted within their arena, like children at a circus. We are their perfect denouncement. At the same time, our entire generation could slide into the sea, and it would not spoil the show. Perhaps the best we, Gen Utopia, can hope for is some looming natural disaster to give us purpose. That's why everyone talks about The Big One, the earthquake we hope will shake us out of our ennui, and why the psychology, geology, and environmental studies classes here at New West are so full. When were not self-absorbed in actualizing, we're hoping Nature will give us something more worthwhile to do."

Looking at The Big Top it was easy to understand how it got Val thinking about natural disaster. Nearly half of the hulking octagon hung out over the bay supported by steel beams. Geneva identified with a lot of the sentiment in Val's article especially the feeling of ennui, she didn't know what she wanted to do after university either. But she disagreed with the scathing tone. It was disrespectful. Their parents had devoted their lives to that transformation of society and had solved a lot of pressing problems. It seemed ungrateful to be bored. Geneva resented Val's slam on "self-actualizing students" and attack on psychology and environmental fields, her own double major. If Val thought her studies were self-absorbed, she could have said so to her face instead of writing about it in *The Review*. Val's editorial had widened the rift between them.

Papers flapped on a nearby board. Geneva looked to see if, among the flyers for bands, shows, and clubs on campus, any warned of psychic seizures and The Camp. A fluorescent pink paper caught her eye. Smoothing it down to get a look at the message, she shivered. That stripped feeling came over her like when the psychic advocates stared. She repressed an instinct to look around. No need to be paranoid. Then she remembered the self-defense training she'd learned in the dorms: It's safer to meet a stranger's eyes.

As she turned, a hand dropped onto her shoulder. "Yaaah!" a voice behind her shouted. "End of the Year romp!"

She spun around snaking her arm out, her fingers cupped to strike the attacker's neck. Her fingers twitched when she saw the guy behind her. He was about her height with a wild mat of towering hair. Emblazoned across the front of his T-shirt in fire engine red was the word, "Dickwad." It was just another student. At first, she was proud, then scared, to note that her fingertips were poised just like she'd learned in the class at Inu Wood, poking towards his windpipe. Another few inches, a clean strike, and she could have collapsed his throat, maybe even killed him. But he'd caught her wrist. The grip of his hand made her give him a second look. His forearms were sinewy. Muscle packed his frame. He was small, but tougher than his goofy expression and the paunch of belly hanging over his belt suggested.

He released her wrist and winked. He was somewhat bug-eyed and his open eye bulged at her so she could see his sea green iris clearly even in the faint light. He held his arms out on either side of her and pointed with both hands wagging. "This ain't no average, ordinary hallucination. New West, Dark Wave with the electric light stylings of DJ Leo Love brought to you by..." He moved his hands in an arch over her head and wagged them to the left. "The Mansion Expansion."

He pointed at Keller Hall. The dorm was a windowed wedge. A cliquish group of plug-ins and ravers called it home. This guy, a hybrid, had the pockets of a plug-in, but his bright orange half-shirt screamed raver. Val had been spending some time over there lately. Did he know her?

He reached into one of the many pockets on his green cargo pants and handed her a flyer identical to the one she'd just been looking at. "Yaaah. Supa Stella!" He arched his arms over to the Mansion again. "So, you must be one of Leo's girls. Want to party?"

When she didn't answer, he cocked his head at her shaking his plume of hair. He narrowed one eye. The other widened. He pointed at her pocket. "Party?"

Geneva looked down. In her Face in the Crowd T-shirt and khakis it had to be obvious she was not his scene. Then she registered the green glow spreading through the pocket of her pants. She reached in and brought out the dropper half full of shiny green liquid that the med tech had left her. “You want something to calm you?” he’d asked.

The spaz boy snatched it and raised the dropper. When he looked at her again, green liquid streaked down his face. The whites of his eyes glowed and his irises had turned from light green to emerald. "Yaaaah, that's it." The look he gave her made her feel unwrapped. "Sure, you don't want to party?"

He held out the dropper. But she shook her head. "Um, no I have to study. That's OK."

He pocketed the dropper with one hand and grabbed her hand and gave it a violent shake with the other. Then he shook pointed fingers at her pistolero style. "Bummer. Right on."

Her phone began to vibrate. She lurched and it fell off her ear onto the brick. The guy squatted and grabbed it. His toenails were the same orange-red as his shirt. She snatched it out of his open hand and placed it on her ear. "Dad? Dad, are you there?" she asked. She turned her back on Dickwad.

"Geneva, I'm at the clinic. They're evaluating her for treatment," he said. He sounded stilted as if he were reading lines. “An apparent psychotic break. That’s what they said.”

It was as if Geneva was standing in the dark on the middle of campus alone again. She didn’t know what to say after that, and if her father did, he was taking a long time thinking it over. Psychotic: Geneva struggled to remember the clinical definition. It wasn't something that came up often in environmental psychology. It meant Valerie had lost contact with reality. For a plant, losing contact with reality wasn't a condition, it was a death sentence. Plants needed their roots in soil or water to grow, but people could become detached and still survive. Behind her, Geneva heard a patter on the bricks and knew the weird boy was loitering behind her continuing his restless dance.

"I don't understand. She's been fine," she said into the phone.

"No," her father said, and for the second time she heard his harshest voice directed at her. "She's not fine and she hasn't been fine. She's had some kind of breakdown. Whatever you've been doing up there, I don't know, but we're going to keep her close."

The silence was so long she was sure he'd disconnected. When she turned around Dickwad was still there, hopping. Whatever drug the medic had given her wasn't calming on this guy. When she started to walk away, he darted in front of her and gave her his pistolero fingers again. "See you tomorrow night."

She crumpled the flyer and shoved it in her pocket.

Suddenly, her father was back, "They say they'll be keeping her over the summer."

"Summer? But she can't miss." Geneva looked up and saw she'd instinctively headed to her safe place, Varian Hall, which housed the greenhouse and most of her classes. "It's finals week."

"Finals?" Her father asked. Of course, he didn't know about Val's slumping grades or the warning letter.

Geneva sat on the steps. "We both have big tests tomorrow."

The chill marble seeped through her pants.

"So, she was studying when this happened?" her father finally asked.

"Not exactly." Off to her right, a movement caught her eye. She turned and saw only moonlight reflected in the waxy azalea leaves.

"But you were, right? You weren't on the computer?" he asked.

"No." She wished again for her mother. Her father, the scientist, liked to analyze, pick things apart one at a time and classify them. Her mother, the diplomat, was great at listening, multi-tasking and making connections. She could have dealt with Val's emergency and been there for Geneva, too. Her mother would at least ask how she was feeling. Her father continued to use the harsh tone with her, and now she was confused by his barrage of questions and sudden interest in studying. She tried to reach him and let him know what she needed some fatherly reassurance. She said quietly, “Dad, I'm scared. I feel like, somehow, this is my fault."

In response, she heard only muffled voices in the background. She rose half off the stairs. The azaleas shook. Her father returned. "Geneva, there are some papers I have to sign. Don't worry about your test. You'll do fine."

The test? Wasn't that the least of her worries? "Dad? Goodbye? Goodbye?" But this time, he was really gone.

The azaleas rustled again, and a low growl rose out of them. She walked toward it crouching to peer into the shadows beneath.

Through the leaves, she saw hands running down a bare back and fingers plucking at the strings of a bikini strap. "Animal," she heard a girl's voice and giggling. Blond hair swished across the back. The girl she had seen chasing Butterflies was in the bushes with some guy. He made the sound again, a mock growl like a human purr.

Geneva stepped back. She wasn't the only one who'd caught the couple. She saw a flash of orange around the corner of the building: Dickwad. She hadn’t meant to see either the couple’s naked lust or his naked jealousy. Suddenly, it felt like there was too much company on the college campus, and too much emotion. Geneva was exhausted. She turned and headed back to the dorm. She collapsed on her bed and stared at Val's empty one. Her mind cycled between worry, confusion, and fear until she fell asleep.

The alarm clock went off at 6 a.m. Geneva let it blare. She lay in bed surrounded by pillows in the windowless dorm room. Her head ached with the retort of Val's scream, fired off like a concealed weapon carried within her usual quiet. Geneva kept hearing her father's accusation, "Whatever you've been doing up there...we're going to keep her close." What did he think they had been doing? She tried to reassure herself that Val's sickness, whatever it was, was not her responsibility. That's what her mother would have said if it had been her on the phone last night. She often chided Geneva for taking "too much on her shoulders." Her father, on the other hand, reinforced her own tendency to be analytical and try to solve every problem she encountered. "Sometimes all you can do is cry, and that's enough," her mother liked to say. Maybe it had been true when she and Valerie were in high school and their problems were mostly silly and social. They were struggling to fit in and beginning to grow apart and make different friends. Was it true now? Shouldn't she be more responsible? She was on her way to becoming a citizen, after all. Her father had questioned her and sounded critical as if Val's breakdown was something she could have prevented.

As she got up and began to get ready for class—because what else was she supposed to do—the situation made her angry. This was Val's fault. It was a stupid time for her to go crazy. Graduating from New West was the first thing they had to do on their own, their first chance to screw up. If Val was going to freak out, any other time would have been better. Now, although there was no way she could possibly concentrate on it, Geneva had no choice but to take her Privacy Law final. It was what she had planned.

As she crossed campus, other sleepy, scruffy students stared at her. They paid sudden attention to her as if they were all Psi-Aware protesters. A shivering girl in a tank top shot her a sympathetic glance. A huddle of guys in ball caps parted to let her through. It was as if everyone could see the misery inside her. Geneva hurried head down along the brick walkway until she reached the steps of Varian Hall. She already felt bad for blaming Valerie. Thanks to her stupid psychology classes, Geneva knew she was only angry because she felt powerless. She didn't know what to do to help and she felt so lost she couldn't even cry. She was studying psychology not because she understood people, but because she knew she didn't. She felt more comfortable around plants: They were simpler. But of all people, she'd thought she could always count on Val. Now she couldn't. She'd thought they'd understood each other. Clearly, they hadn't. Worst of all, she'd thought they'd always be there for each other, and now she'd failed that too. She'd left her friend alone thrashing on the dorm room floor. She hadn't been able to help. If Geneva didn't understand and couldn't help Val, then she wasn't of use to anyone.

Up the steps and into her seat in class, Geneva tried to switch tracks and think about passing her exam. It was useless. She couldn't recall anything she'd studied, not a single fact. Val screaming. Val flailing. Val lying on the stretcher. That was all she had in her head.

When she looked up, the professor was done giving instructions, the same ones she'd heard a million times, for taking the test. She didn't say, "My friend went insane last night. Can I take this test later?" because it wouldn't matter. It wasn't as if she would feel any better about taking this test in a couple of days. If Val was an unknown variable, then everything in the future was uncertain.

The class clown, sitting beside her, shot her a pained look. She looked down and pulled up the exam on her desktop. Essay questions appeared on the screen. "When the Supreme Court upheld the *Hales v Friend-Me Co.* ruling in an 8-1 decision with the dissenting opinion coming from..."

She froze. It was the exact same sentence she'd been reading just before Val's seizure. She heard a cough behind her. The professor leaned over her shoulder. "You don't have to do this."

She turned in her seat. "But I..."

"Nonsense." He ran a hand through his thin hair as if brushing something aside. "Look, I know this is not a good time for you. Shhh. Listen. Rules make humanity, but they don't trump it. Quietly take your things and go. No, no. We'll talk about the make-up some other time, Geneva."

She grabbed her knapsack and staggered out of the room keeping her head down to avoid the gaze of the staring students all the way across campus. Back in the dorm, she dry-heaved over the toilet. Before today, she hadn't even thought that professor knew her name. She was a diligent, anonymous student. Her adviser Robin Roundtree was the only one who'd ever paid her any attention in class. Now, she still wasn't speaking, but it felt like everyone on campus was listening, when she wanted to be inconspicuous. Geneva had never felt so afraid, and she was trying to tamp it down, bury it inside of herself. If she gave in to her fear, if she let herself, she'd be on the floor screaming and they would take her away, too.

~ 6 ~

SYNC CHROME CITY: MANSION EXPANSION

"In addition to the serene social conditions within the New West enclave three factors fostered the environment that allowed the rapid emergence of psychic abilities:

The Friend-Me Journal – created the precedent for information sharing among large populations and the predictive empathic element of the Friend-Me Couriers.

Sync Chrome City – although the computer program induced mental trauma in unprepared young minds, this artificial Psychic Space model introduced and adapted the Dawning Psychics to the speed, heightened awareness and collective thought they would later share without the aid of devices or drugs.

SLO-42 – this chemical replica of a neurotransmitter conveyed empathy and stimulated neural pathways in the Dawning Psychics.

A fourth factor may also be considered, although its impact is still being analyzed by botanists (including R. Roundtree) and geologists, the natural event of the earthquake along the Cascadian fault line some call the Psychic Quake." *—Becoming Psychic 101, A History and a Primer*

Geneva held her head under the faucet in the bathtub and watched Gator Tongue dye stream out of her hair, coloring gallons a rusty red. Whenever it seemed about to run clear, she'd tousle her hair and more red would gush forth. With her head doused in cold water, the answer to the test question — "What was the reasoning behind Justice Grace Vinton's dissenting opinion in the *Hales v Friend-Me Co.* 8-1 ruling?" — came easily.

The neo-privacy lawsuit was about Friend-Me Journals. The journals were new and all the rage when she and Valerie were pre-teens. The controversy was with the sophisticated database, which tracked and fed the girls' journal entries to the corporation. Justice Vinton had argued that because the consumers were minors when they began to give Friend-Me Co. access to their personal information they could not legally give consent. Geneva's father had had the same opinion. "You're too young. You don't even have control of yourself yet, you're too young to give it away." He'd wanted to forbid the girls from getting Friend-Me Journals, sure the corporation would abuse its link to the subconscious of a generation of teenage girls.

Her mother, however, had insisted the girls be allowed to decide for themselves. Valerie, in a rare display of conformity, quickly got a Friend-Me. Geneva, going against her father's wishes for the first time, did too.

Geneva massaged her hair again and the water turned rosy. She turned off the faucet. Pink droplets spattered the white tile as she reached for a towel and wrapped it around her head. Of course, her father had been right. Friend-Me Co. had come up with a way to profit from all the information they were getting from the girls. After five years, the company launched its courier service. Using its enormous database filled with teen girls' wants and desires, the company developed an intricate caching and retrieval system. Zeroing in on product names and cross-referencing them with key words indicating levels of interest, analysts at Friend-Me developed a program that could extrapolate a user's future desires based upon their journal entries.

Prescient deliverymen, the Friend-Me Couriers brought you exactly what you wanted even before you knew you wanted it. Most devoted Friend-Me users raved about the new service. The deliveries cut through uncertainty by providing an instant, tangible answer to everything. Even if you didn't know exactly what you wanted, Friend-Me knew. It reviewed your recorded emotions, ran a comparison to a database of other users, and linked them to a corresponding product. The Friend-Me goods had an 89 percent acceptance rate. The couriers were as difficult to deny as a craving. That was the crux of the *Hales v. Friend-Me* litigation.

Too young, Geneva hadn't paid much attention to the death of Sherri Hales until it was required reading for her Privacy Law class. But her parents had often talked about the case and the woman's Friend-Me assisted suicide. The Friend-Me courier had brought her a bouquet of Lilies of the Valley. Hales ate the datura leaves and collapsed. Neo-Privacy advocates brought a wrongful death lawsuit against Friend-Me Co. on behalf of the woman's daughter, Eve. The suit accused the company of bringing the means of death to a depressed woman's doorstep and the privacy advocates argued furiously against Friend-Me's use of Sherri Hales' teenage diaries filled with vampire fantasies: death and resurrection.

The justices, with the exception of Vinton, disagreed. The court said that the women had established a precedent by confiding in the journals and accepting Friend-Me deliveries on numerous occasions. Users' consent for the couriers was implied when they logged in to their journals.

As Geneva dried her hair and secured it into ponytails in front of the mirror she was startled by the effect of her garish red hair. It made her green eyes pop, looking large and alien. The rest of her slim pale features — nose, cheeks, and lips — appeared to retreat behind them. She swabbed some of Val's Plum Ice gloss over her lips. The clash of red, green, and purple turned her triangular face into an exclamation point.

Now she was ready. She was done with feeling powerless. She'd decided to follow her instincts and problem-solve. First, she had to find out what Val had been looking at when she'd lost it. In the living room, she put on Val's glasses and scrolled through the history. There were two sites: NWU-Physics and *Sync Chrome City*. Geneva went to the physics site and it took her into Val's e-academics folder. Val's final was there in her quantum information theory class. Geneva scrolled through and was surprised to see Val had filled in most of the questions. There was still time. She guessed on the final few questions for Val and submitted the test. While waiting for the confirmation, she scrolled over the *Sync Chrome City* link.

She felt bad about checking up on Val, but when the reply came, "You have completed your QIT final." she clicked on *Sync Chrome City.* The words flew into the corner of her vision. Skinny right leaning letters in script the mirror image of Val's glowed cerulean. They read: *I am not an average ordinary hallucination. I am going to mess you up, bad. Welcome to Sync Chrome City.* "Ooh, la, la," a voice trilled. "Gunk-Secured content."

A series of crisp video images —roaches, bombings, and mutilations — flashed in front of her. Geneva couldn't handle even the first round of hard-core content. She lifted the glasses and tossed them aside. "Ugh, that's what I get for spying. Damn, Val what were you into?"

Geneva, rocking back in the chair, almost tipped to the ground when she heard a courier call "Friend-Me" outside her door. She went to answer it, determined to auto-reject the delivery. Today, her life was too complicated to want anything that came in a box. When she opened the door, the courier knelt before her on one knee in a spotless forest green cloak.

"You want this," he said packing persuasion and subservience into the few syllables. The green box he lifted out from under a fold of his cloak glittered. He held it up to her in the palm of his hand.

She knew it was just packaging, but she could already feel her resolve caving to curiosity. According to Friend-Me's database, her history indicated a desire for whatever was in that box, right now. It was a message from her childhood self.

Probably sweets again, she thought, reaching for the box. "I'm not hungry." But she stroked the velvet lid and opened it. With a knowing smile, the courier transferred the box to her hand and bowed sweeping the cloak across his body. "On your account, of course."

Geneva nodded and pushed the door closed. She sunk to the floor with the box in hand. On the satin lining, the cluster of tiny leaves looked especially dry and brittle. But her memory was fresh. She had plucked the leaves from the towering willow tree on the edge of the school grounds on her last day of first grade. In that moment, her emotions surged. She'd stared up into the branches spinning around with the feeling that she was about to be caught up in something enormous and wonderful. She'd heard a voice, the word — *destiny* — and reached up to the tree and shook a branch as if she were sealing a pact with it. Then the feeling faded. She'd put the leaves in a scrapbook that she hadn't touched since buying the Friend-Me journal.

For the first time, Friend-Me was wrong. This wasn't what she wanted. That feeling of destiny, purpose and wonder was exactly the opposite of the one she had now and the memory of it made her despair. She didn't think she'd ever feel like that again. Geneva lifted the leaves out of the box, and they flaked onto the carpet. Underneath the leaves was a slender black stylus just like the ones that came with all the Friend-Me journals. She picked it up and realized why everything about this delivery felt wrong. The courier's knock had startled her. She'd been at Val's computer, not connected to her Friend-Me journal at all. So where had this "gift" really come from? She spun the smooth stylus and ran her fingers over the engraving. The silver read, "Sync Chrome City."

Geneva stumbled as she entered The Big Top teetering on Val's boots with their 9-inch heels. As she stood in the doorway, looking into the room filled with dark spaces and flashing lights, she felt relieved. No one turned to look at her. The stretchy black fabric of her short, pleated skirt was almost obscured by masses of shiny silver snaps. Light reflected off them and colored spots darted around on the floor in front of her. Although she couldn't have felt more conspicuous, she blended in. Everyone here wore plug-in clothes, practical black adorned with buckles and snaps to secure all the pockets that held their electronic gear. Thumping beats allayed her fear that the thoughts pounding inside her head were audible outside it, too. Instead of turning to her, everyone at the Mansion Expansion dance seemed immersed in their own worlds, their bodies spinning solo in restless intensity.

It wouldn't be hard to get caught up in it. Geneva stepped onto the dance floor and swayed. She needed a break. She didn't know how to have an insane friend. She couldn’t wait for the quarter to end, for campus to empty out and everyone to leave. She was tired of telling people that Val had gotten ill and gone home for the summer. It was the truth, and it wasn't. She wanted to bring Val back in time to continue fall quarter and ignore the weirdness. She knew she couldn't do both. She had to find out what had really happened. *Sync Chrome City* was key, but she was too afraid to enter the site. It wasn't just the disturbing Gunk gross-out images; she was scared to let her mind run wherever Val's had gone. The lurid pink flier, pimping the Mansion Expansion dance, had given her another idea, brought her here. Just like *Sync Chrome City*, it claimed to be "not just another average, ordinary hallucination.” Maybe she’d find a clue here.

Geneva maneuvered through the dancers around the edges of the octagon looking for Dickwad. At first, she couldn't find him, then she spotted his frizz of hair bobbing through the lights. He had on another orange T-shirt. This one said, "Kill Giovanni." He was smash dancing into a guy twice his height with sleek dark hair that shone blue in the lights. The tall guy danced head down, jerking on the hinges of his elbows and knees, gliding in circles around Dickwad. Silver flashed across his black T-shirt and after a few rotations she made out the words: *Sync Chrome City*. What was this, suddenly everywhere, city?

Geneva made her way towards the men dancing pressing through the crowd. Even on heels, she lost sight of Dickwad but she tracked his tall-dark companion. She was greenhouse hot and misted, moving through the dancers, by the time she got near him. She reached for his shoulder just as Dickwad slammed into him. Tall-Dark's elbow struck her chin and she went down, landing on one knee. It was Val's damn towering boots. The guy turned to see what he'd hit, but the crowd closed around him blocking his view.

The music changed. A discordant cello and electronic mandolin duet replaced the pumping sets. The crowd on the dance floor thinned. A circle of seven guys in black joined Dickwad and Tall-Dark. Geneva crouched just at the edge of a pink spot of light that opened up in the center of the dance floor. Two girls gyrated up to them. She recognized the blonde by her metronome hips as Ponytail from the Butterflies and the bushes, although she wore her hair loose and wavy tonight. A black stretch dress rode her curves made out of a chameleon fabric that matched colors with the lights playing over it. Ponytail wrapped the end of her detachable Vary, a golden-fringed Tamarin tail, around the back of Dickwad's neck flirtatiously, but they seemed an unlikely couple.

Geneva hadn't seen the other girl, squat and witchy looking with curly dark hair, before. And she'd never seen a Vary like that. The V of red-gold quills that lined her stomach below her triangular half-shirt was clearly from The Freeway, not something you could get in New West. Geneva didn't know why anyone would risk going out there, but the Vary definitely made the girl look exotic. Without it, she might not have gotten a second look. Whereas the tail on the blonde was a redundant accessory. The golden girl didn't need any help to attract attention.

With the rest of the crowd hanging back, the small group's dance became a performance. The song had unintelligible lyrics that resonated from a low male voice as if he were singing from inside a hollow tree. A celestial chorus of women trilled behind it. The dancers mouthed all the words, but the chorus rung in a crescendo of voices as they sang along and now, she could make out some words, "Harvest Sin and Chrome and Sea. Come and intertwine with me." The DJ melded the music and the lights with his Sound-wield set. Even with her limited knowledge of the equipment, Geneva appreciated the DJ's prowess, the way he spun, weaving the lights through the crowd. Val, who could have appreciated the tech too, would have been in awe.

Geneva watched the DJ hanging in the darkness near the roof of The Big Top on a three-legged silver stool. When the new student union building was erected, the architects had insisted the design was an homage to higher thought. It was meant to look inspiring. But with the DJ spinning in the center of the sloping ceiling it looked even more like a circus tent. He leaned back arching over the dancers. The curled ends of his hair dangled as he swung from side to side waving the Sound-Wield wand to adjust the lights. She watched until her neck ached and then looked back to at dancers to see what effect he was having.

Now thick pink ropes swooped through the dancers linking each of them with light. The girls' sinuous movements went staccato. The whites of their eyes shone. The dancers leaned to the right, twitched, and shook. Their limbs flailed as the music rose to a pitch. Writhing, they collapsed on the floor as the music stopped. Geneva's knees buckled as everyone else began to applaud. Only she seemed disturbed by what she had recognized in the grotesque movements. They were stylized, and somewhat slower, but they were dancing psychic seizures: flailing, writhing, and twitching just like Val had while screaming on the dorm room floor. But it was all a performance.

Geneva stood, both repulsed and fascinated, by what she'd seen. She was curious, but afraid. She wanted to ask them what they were doing and find out what they knew, but the encounter with strangers seemed more than she could handle tonight. She wished she were back in the dorm room in her Face-in-the-Crowd clothes with her long brown hair down over her eyes and a book in front of her like a shield. A chain rattled just behind her ear. She lurched back and found herself staring into the upside-down eyes of the DJ lowering his stool down beside her. When his sparkling black eyes were level with hers, he flipped and landed upright beside her. "Intense. Very intense."

Those were her thoughts exactly. He stood so close it felt like they were touching. She swayed back and forth in her boots. He put a hand on her back, to steady her and it felt hot.

"What band was that last song by? It's amazing," she said.

He nodded. "Giovanni Hastings Musica from down the 'Way. No one's sure if it's really a band or all synth and marketing though."

"What's your name?" she blurted.

"Leo." The DJ pressed her hands lightly between his. "Love."

She flushed. He tapped his chest twice with his forefinger. "Leo Love." He winked. "I know you. Ruby, everybody. Everybody, Ruby." He gestured in a circle at the ring of dancers surrounding them, many of them had glowing green eyes. They looked like Dickwad after he'd used the drops the medic had given her. Leo made a quick round of introductions, while Geneva paid just enough attention to get that Dickwad went by Grugel, Eve was the witchy girl with the killer Vary, and Tall-Dark Streker wore the Sync Chrome City T.

Every one of the DJ's friends oozed charisma, and she felt dweebish in comparison. Meanwhile, she was sure her fascination with Leo had to be apparent. Eve, with her hands on her hips just above the quills, looked like she wanted to stick Geneva with them. They could probably all tell she was a poseur. She had to look ridiculous in Val's clothes. Worse, now that the music was off, she had that stripped feeling again like everyone could hear her thoughts. She'd never been in love before. She imagined it would be a heavy-handed mystical experience and that was exactly what this felt like—love, falling, at first sight. She tried to think about anything but love, Leo, or otherwise. She was here to ask about *Sync Chrome City*, the psychic seizure, the green drug, and The Camp where they had taken Valerie.

While she tried to screw up the courage to ask at least one of her questions, Ponytail sauntered in and draped her arms around Leo's shoulders. She wrapped her fluffy golden tail around him and kissed his cheek. Leo purred and nuzzled her neck. "And this is Coco," he said. The heat drained from Geneva's face as she recognized the animal noise Leo had made. He was the guy she'd seen playing with Butterflies and heard in the bushes with Ponytail girl. He looked so different as a DJ in the dark with his lithe body encased in black clothes. Of course, Ponytail— Coco—was his love interest. She stepped back, letting Leo's friends edge her out of their circle.

"Nice to see you again," she whispered as she headed for the exit. It was too much. She'd had enough. She needed the night air to cope with what had happened to Valerie, not a bunch of new people. As she strode across campus, through the courtyard, she broke into a teetering lope. The chill air wicked sweat from her skin. Then she jerked forward as the heel of one boot caught in a gap in the bricks. She broke her fall with her forearms and sprawled. Pain keened as she examined the red raw scrapes. She sat up, unzipped the boots, and pulled her striped stocking feet free. As she did so, she saw why the boots had been so uncomfortable and unwieldy all night. It wasn't just the high heels. She'd been wearing them on the wrong feet. No doubt then she'd looked dumb in front of Leo and his friends. She was such a clumsy dweeb.

Thankfully, it would be summer soon. Everyone would leave campus and the only person she'd have to deal with would be her manager at Ruby's. Geneva yanked the boot heel free and began to laugh. There was nothing else for it. It was all she could possibly do.

~ 7 ~

SYNC CHROME CITY: MISTRESS M.D

"We considered those men collateral damage. We made the decision to look to the future. The past was too desecrated to repair. Forced to make the decision again, knowing the costs and the consequences, I would do the same, abandon those men, C.G. Burrows among them. I cannot regret how we created New West. But many of our decisions were wrong, including how we handled the emerging empaths. The psychic internment camp at New West Mental Health was a gross mistake. We acted out of fear both for our youth and of them. I feared for my daughter. Constance Monica was always foremost in my mind." — *Save Giovanni: The Lost Men of the Psychic Wars*,
S. Sherring

Under a black light in his surgery, Burrows gripped a white marker and sketched routes into New West across his thigh. He thought up lies as the glowing lines appeared until his bowels grew painfully heavy again. In the outhouse for the third time that night, his gut twisted. His nerves were acid. He felt sick planning to sneak into a place where he rightfully belonged. Burrows wiped his ass with a page out of a pre-revolutionary copy of *InkSkins* and let it fall. The door to the outhouse banged shut behind him. He would do what he had to. If there was psychic spread coming at him out of New West, he'd find the source and stop it. He had to take it one move at a time. First, get into New West. Then, find the kids. Follow his instincts. Act.

Burrows stripped off his lab coat and took a deep breath. The night air billowed over his bare chest. He palmed the warm tin of Black Gold wax in his pants pocket. He popped the top and smeared a corner of his lab coat with the grease. Evergreen needles skittered as he pulled the tarp off Mistress M.D., his Mercedes. It was time to take her for a ride. He stroked the car in circles with the polish until her surface gleamed. The shadows of his broad torso in her black depths as he leaned over the hood gave him smooth certainty. The wax had the same leather and oil scent as the inside of his car, but with a soapy undercurrent. It was the scent Burrows found most comforting, although not his favorite. His favorite scents were girls and warm snickerdoodles like his nanny used to make and, in the best of all possible worlds, girls who smelled like cookies: sugared cinnamon and vanilla. In his worn button-up shirt and Mace's old U.G. Jacket, Burrows slipped into the driver's seat as if it were a silk suit. He drove the Mercedes, a vestige of his parent's wealth, to the border. Razor-edged coils of concertina wire glinted along the top of the fence while lamps and moonlight lit the arch over the entryway to New West. It glittered silver and white shining unmercifully through the dark like the gateway to a prison or a paradise. The false lure of the place was what he hated. He wouldn't want to be trapped inside, but he couldn't stand being excluded either. He brought Mistress M.D. to a stop beneath the arch.

Behind a plate glass window, the border guard raised his eyebrows and shrugged. "Where'd you get a car like that?"

Burrows got a better look at the guard's scrawny shoulders and the green and gold New West badge on the breast of his jacket. "My parents, Marlee and Arlan Burrows." he said. "They live in C-town now."

From the agent he got: *Those rich bastards?*

"C-town, eh?" the guard said, still elevated, probably standing on tiptoe in a pair of heavy black boots.

"It didn't agree with me. I grew up in New West. I guess you could say I'm looking to come home," Burrows said, although he hadn't talked to his parents in years.

The guard lowered a few inches, giving Burrows a better view of the stubble on the roll of flesh under his neck. "Hmm, my mama always said home was wherever she was." His eyes flicked to the side and then back: *Am I going to have to shoot you?*

The green tint of the glass the guard stood behind gave him a reanimated look. Burrows held out the Freemans' pass he'd swiped off of Mace along with the jacket years ago. He hoped it was still good, but there was always Plan B.

The guard studied the pass like he was going to be tested on it later. Possibly he would be, that fit New West's over-educated style. While the guard looked vacuous, he undoubtedly had some degree that qualified him to do this job: probably political science or psychology, in the old days it would have been criminology, but who needed that now? New Westians disbelieved in crime. They'd excluded that element from their social planning, too. Education didn't make the guard smart though. Burrows prepared to floor the gas–Plan B drive real fast. He'd found it didn't pay to over think and if the guard was even allowed a car to chase him down with, it'd be one of those low-powered jobbies unable to keep up with his Mistress. As he pressed down on the gas, a bank of green security lights shot down from the arch and scanned over the car. A glowing tag now marred the pristine black of the Mistress M.D.'s hood. They'd given him a driving pass. He would be privileged not to have to ride the New Westian buses. What those freaks had against cars; he did not know.

"That's good for six-months. Then you have to renew," the guard said. "I guess New West and C-town are becoming best buds. Enjoy your stay."

As he passed through the gate, he switched Mistress' control panels over to electric and solar. There'd be no place to fill up the car with gasoline in New West. "Sorry to tame you girl," he said. "It's just while we're in enemy territory." Like that, Burrows was on the other side of the border. He drove past miles of soy and pea fields and small towns lit by pale blue solar lights straight to the university. He remembered the way, although he'd visited it last in high school. There were buildings and green open spaces now where there'd been parking lots, but it was easy enough to find a place to put his car on the street. In the darkness, Burrows could see only the edges of the long dark lawns and the clustered stalwart buildings in the distance. His chest expanded as he inhaled the warm pine and sea scented air. It sunk to the bottom of his lungs. So fresh. A white monument sign with New West University etched into the marble sparkled at the entrance to campus under a bright lamp. Burrows ran his hand over the letters—New West. The edges were sharp, although the institution was more than 200 years old. Burrows put his hand to his face. The sides of it were pitted from where he'd pulled out the nubs and his fingertips came away wet. The skin was rough on his cheeks and around his eyes. He felt like an old man sneaking onto campus on a summer night. It was the opposite of what he had wanted.

He strode past the shadowed buildings, heard a cry and stepped around the corner into a brick courtyard shadowy with amber solar lights. A girl sat in the middle of it, her arms hooked over her knees. Stiff curly ponytails stuck out from each side of her head. She was staring between her legs as if he'd caught her in the middle of midnight sit-ups. As Burrows watched her, she started to shake and then he heard laughter, high-pitched and somewhat hysterical. She took off her boots, padding towards him in striped stockings. She swung the long boots beside her, so they almost kicked the ground. Her red ponytails danced. Burrows staggered back as her thought stabbed him: *Sometimes, you just have to laugh.*

The thought nicked him, knife to stone. The suddenness of it caught his breath like a sucker punch. He didn't think she could even see him from where she'd been sitting in the dim light. This was not the way it worked. They weren't supposed to be able to get him randomly. He couldn't have dealt with every stray barb. It would've killed him. He froze in place, panicked, and then filled with a cool rage. This effect was confirmation of exactly what he had come to New West to stop. Let these people keep their thoughts to themselves. He didn't want them out infecting the 'Way with their thoughts. As she got closer, she started. Her red ponytails jerked back before the rest of her, and the coils sprung as she came to a stop: *I didn't see...Big scary guy. Danger.*

She looked light. If she dropped the boots now and started running, he didn't think he could catch her. Instead, though, she'd stupidly come to a halt. He could reach out and take her shoulders in his hands. She was not his type, dressed like a distressed doll, but she was just what he'd been looking for. She would know the way.

"Where've you been?" he asked.

She rushed him: *At the dance. All the plug-ins. Sync Chrome City. Valerie. Leo. What can I do?*

A barrage of thought came at him, a battering, far more than he was used to at once, and he couldn't make sense of it. The thoughts weren't all directed to him or even remotely about him. She must be drunk, he decided, caught up in her own world, projecting at everyone. He wanted to get away from her, but it was like he was in the middle of a storm being struck repeatedly by lightening. He couldn't move until it had passed. He hunkered down. Over and over, he got: *There's nothing I can do to help her. I can't even walk in her boots. I'm ridiculous. Stupid.*

Well, he agreed with her there. Shut up and vomit, he thought, as he weathered her silent barrage of words and finally picked out what he needed from her mess of a mind: *Mansion Expansion. The dance. The Big Top.*

"Yeah, so that way?" he pointed across the courtyard. Got: *Yes.*

Then, as a bonus, he got a last thought from her: *Just let this be OK, and I'll never walk alone on campus at night again.*

It almost made it up to him, for all the painful thoughts, that she was scared of him. She should be.

"You know," he said. "You really shouldn't walk alone at night. Perhaps you would like me to walk you home?"

She thrust back: *No.*

Instead of wincing, he took the pain and leered. "My place, perhaps?"

Then she ran. He watched the pleats of her skirt flap over her taut haunch, as her thoughts grew faint. A smoky cinnamon scent lingered in the air where she'd been standing.

"Mmm, hmm," he said, enjoying the low vibration of the sound in the back of his throat relieved that she was gone, and he was alone in his head again, but regretful, too. It was always pain or nothing, and just when he was having fun. "I'll just carry on without you then."

He headed across the courtyard until he came to a new dome-shaped building that had to be The Big Top. Students dressed in black and shiny clothes milled around the entrance. One of them would know the kids he'd met in his shop. The helpful, painful girl had pointed him in the right direction.

As Burrows approached, the students averted their eyes. They raised their voices appearing immersed in their own conversations. From them he got quick appraisals: *Who's that? Not a student. Looks tough.*

Then the thoughts snapped studiously off. If he left them alone, they would leave him alone their thoughts said. Burrows could almost like these kids, his kind of people, even if he had some 15 years on them. He was clearly not a student, but the been-through-it look of his face and his natty camo jacket bought him some cred. Or maybe it was his size—the one lasting advantage he'd gotten from his father. Either way, these kids respected his solitude. They had a code of privacy that he could exploit. Any adult would have questioned him, knowing he didn't have a good reason for being here, and therefore bad intentions. They would have been right.

Instead, some lanky kid nearly his height approached and offered him a hit. The kid drummed his fingertips with their matte white nails against his shirt pocket and lifted and lowered a dropper: green glowing inside. It took Burrows a couple of ticks to realize what he'd seen. Da Lime. SLO-42. He hesitated and the kid moved on. Burrows hadn't had another opportunity to get the drug, since he'd ditched Mace and sworn it off. He shoved his hands deeper into the pockets of his coat. He was tempted, but no. No drugs, especially not SLO. If he ever killed again, he wanted to be certain it was solely his decision. He had a goal to achieve and couldn't let himself get distracted under somebody else's influence.

He watched the pusher kid move through the crowd and stop to talk to another kid coming out of the building. There was no mistaking that head of rag hair. It was Grugel the *KillGiovanni* fan boy with his hair dyed the same orange as his shirt. Burrows took a few steps out of the crowd and into Grugel's line of sight. In a moment Grugel came at him buoyant and grinning like a clown. It was perfect. He was even wearing his KillGiovanni shirt. "Burrows, my man!"

"Fanboy!" Burrows said.

Grugel bounced at him, shaking little droplets of sweat on Burrows' jacket. When he got close enough Burrows got: *Freak, man!*

Grugel was staring at his face, noticing his new scars.

But he also got: *Sweet! This is gonna be sweeeeet.*

The kid was cool. He turned and waved the drug pusher over.

"Streker. Streak, man. This is the guy I was telling you about. The one Eve and I met out on the 'Way. C. G. Burrows, the host of KillGiovanni."

The kid was practically panting with enthusiasm. The pusher looked at Burrows. His girlishly big eyes widened: *Whoa!*

He was not a deep well. Grugel put an arm around the pusher's neck, reaching to make up for the height difference, but making it look easy, and drew him in. "Streak works with me on *Sync Chrome City*," he said, pointing to the kid's black and silver t-shirt as if it weren't obvious.

Burrows nodded. "I came to see your set up."

"Yeah, you know it. Matter fact, we were just heading back to The Mansion," Grugel said. He pointed across a lawn at a long windowed one-story building.

"You're running it out of a dorm," Burrows said. "You live, there?"

"Yeah," Grugel bounded ahead and Streker followed. The pusher carried a constant shrug, his shoulders high around his neck.

Grugel opened a door to one of the rooms from the outside. It had a huge blind-covered window like a cheap old motel.

"Welcome to Sync Chrome City," Grugel said, as he held open the door. Burrows ducked under the threshold. The square room smelled rank and stale as a tent on the 'Way.

Grugel turned on a black light. A jolly roger glowed on a flag hung over the far wall. There were two narrow beds shoved to opposite sides of the room. Burrows wondered how these kids got laid. He looked at them and smirked: yeah, probably not a big concern.

"Give me a hand, Streak," Grugel said, as he stood on the end of his bed and reached up to unhook a corner of the pirate flag. The cloth dropped to the floor revealing a panel of electronics. Micro-sized versions of microphones, speakers, lights, recording devices, hard drives and consoles were packed together around three huge monitors.

"Yaaah! That's what I'm talking about," Grugel said grinning maniacally. He reached down behind his bed and the room started to hum. The words "Welcome of Sync Chrome City—population 1,274" popped up on the monitors. Grugel began blinking rapidly, his eyes darting from screen to screen.

"Yaaah, lots of people on board," Grugel said. He turned and bumped up against Burrows' chest. He leaned back, looked up and drew circles in front of his eyes with his pointer fingers. His eyes glowed gray. "I got the contacts. Do you want one of the headsets?" Grugel: *This will blow your mind.*

The kid's thoughts hit him like a hangover. The sensation was not entirely unpleasant. He was enjoying Grugel's enthusiasm. Being around the kid was like doing shots and immediately paying the price in rapid succession. "Brilliant, fanboy. Nah, I already perused your city from the 'Way. Lots of options. So, how much are you charging?" Burrows asked.

Grugel shrugged.

"Would that even be legal?" Streker asked.

"If people want it, it's legal." Grugel said.

"Right, very admirable. Listen," Burrows said. "I'd like to stay around awhile, really get to know your system. We can talk business."

Grugel: *Oh, yeah? Moneymakers? You don't look money, but I'll show you off. The KillGiovanni guy.*

Burrows was still getting his head around that latest round when he got pressed again, this time, by a new voice: *He's here!*

Eve walked in. She was wearing a short black skirt that made her legs look thick, but he had to admit that the Vary he'd put in was doing her favors. The v-shape elongated her short waist. She looked better.

"It's OK. She's cool." Streker piped up from where he was sitting on the bed. He patted the spot next to him, but Eve stayed standing.

She didn't look happy to see him, but he got: *He's here! You came!*

"You guys going to be ready?" Eve said, with the practiced nonchalance of an ill-favored woman.

"We're showing Burrows *Sync Chrome City*," Grugel said. "He's got some ideas."

Eve bent down and reached under one of the beds. The hum stopped. The room went still. She pulled a large black case out from underneath the bed. "You guys haven't even started to pack," she said. “Do I have to do everything?" Eve detached a speaker from the wall and placed it in the case. "What ideas? There’s no time to mess around. We're out of here tomorrow."

"Yaargh! Don’t mind her," Grugel said. "Going home makes her bitchy."

"Just put the monitors in the case and don’t touch the screens," Eve said.

"Yeah, gimme a hand," he said to Burrows.

Burrows liked the bickering. It kept the kids’ thoughts off him. But he didn't like watching them disassemble Sync Chrome City. "I thought we were doing business."

"It's summer," Grugel said.

Burrows stared at him. "So? Am I interrupting something?”

"Dude, nobody stays around in the summer," Grugel said. "But, hey, you could come with us. We can work on it at home."

"Right. Where's he going to stay?" Eve said. She had her hands on her hips just above the Vary. "Your father won’t be cool.”

Grugel shook his head and pointed at Eve.

"No way," she said. "It's just bad timing, you know."

"No, it's fine," Grugel said. "He can stay with Strek."

They all looked over at Streker, who was sacked out against the wall chewing his white-coated fingernails. He looked up when he heard his name. "Dude, I think I'm eating paint. Think it's toxic?"

"Streker," Grugel said. "Lydia will be cool, right?" He pointed at Burrows. "He needs a place to stay for summer so we can do stuff. Why not Deming?"

Grugel: *That crazy bitch won't even notice you, Frankenstein.*

Streker looked at Burrows: *Stray cat.* "Sure," he said. Shrugged. "Shouldn't be a problem."

"Don't think so," Burrows said. "I'm the kind you don't take home to mother."

Streker stopped gnawing his nails. "We'll almost have the place to ourselves. She's all the time at Psi-Aware meetings or meditating."

Psi-Aware. Well, that might make a detour to Deming worthwhile. Burrows could feel everything lining up. New West was sprawling for him.

"OK, I'm for bed. You guys finish packing," Eve said. "The Shadow Bus leaves at 8 a.m."

"No," Burrows said. "Take your time. No bus. I have this invention. Called a car. You'll like it."

Streker was a blank, keeping his thoughts, if he had any completely to himself. Eve scowled at him wordless, but he could feel the ache of her wanting. Grugel's grin went maniacally wide again. From him Burrows got: *Man! Dude! Yaaah!* The kids' enthusiasm gave him a migraine. But it was almost worth it. *KillGiovanni*, a car — Burrows felt like a real celebrity here and he couldn't wait to surprise them.

~ 8 ~

SYNC CHROME CITY: NEW WEST MENTAL

"What was once considered an illness, a defect or a harmful mutation affecting Generation Utopia is now seen as society's greatest gift. It is ironic that the First Psychics were deemed unfit when they developed the same neural networks that children now achieve in elementary school. The lesson is powerful: the permutations of what is possible, what is normal, what is gifted, and what is ill are ever-changing. It was once common belief that people used only 10 percent of the brain, that they could not learn past a certain age, and that psi-abilities were extremely rare or quackery. Today, these notions seem ridiculous. As you meditate and develop your awareness and connections, remember that the brain is indeed "wider than the sky." There is no ceiling to our thoughts." — *Becoming Psychic 101, A History and a Primer*

In the outdoor dining area of Café Ruby's, the sun shadowed the customer's face so that he looked up at Geneva with dark eye sockets, "That's not what I ordered." She swept the offending Ruby's Special away promising to bring the soy "salmon" burger instead. Inside, she apologized to the chef pushing the plate back under the heating lamp. He shrugged. "It all starts to sound the same after a while, doesn't it? You're still one of the best. Try to fit in a break soon."

She was at Ruby's full-time during the day for the summer. The money was good, but the work was draining; filled with forced music, loud conversations and the pervasive scent of grilled soy. It didn't help that everything in the restaurant was red. On her first full day, by the end, in a fit of sensory overload she'd wanted to rip all the menus and napkins to shreds. Now, after an hour on the job, her senses shut down and everything looked like Gary the manager's stash of pre-revolutionary memorabilia—plastic. She couldn't wait to go back to the night shift when summer was over. It was soothing by comparison. The lights were dim, the red looked ruby, the customers were fellow students, and the orders were simple: shakes and fries or pancakes and coffee.

After the irritated customer ate his salmon and left a meager tip with his bill, Geneva caught a break. She leaned against the brick wall in the alley behind Ruby's, feeling the hard warmth between her shoulders. She closed her eyes and imagined the sun burning through the stale soy particles embedded in the fabric of her uniform. She thought about the DJ, Leo Love. It was becoming a habit, an embarrassing one, even in the privacy of her own head. She could see him dancing over her. His locks fell forward to touch her shoulders. His lips were on top of hers, kissing. The fantasy was becoming more intense but less satisfying each time, as she let herself drop irresistibly into the pleasure pangs of hope.

When the door beside her creaked, she opened her eyes and jumped to see Gary glowering. She shoved her hands into the pocket of her apron. She wasn't sure what, if anything, she'd been doing with them, but she felt guilty about it. Gary had that look: stonewall with a glaze of pity. It was the look he used when he was trying to explain to some curious customer what was in a Ruby's Special.

"You've got a call from your father. He says it's urgent."

It had to be about Val. She swallowed hard. "My dad, calling here?"

She followed Gary and took the call standing beside his desk in his tiny office. It was filled with a stash of pre-revolution era culinary supplies. There were clunky, colorful plastic appliances and cans and boxes and bottles labeled in unintelligible, off-continent writing. Glossy photos of cakes and salads topped with strange pink, orange, and green sliced fruits plastered the walls. Gary said he liked everything about the revolution except the food. He'd had a fancy restaurant before and constantly reminisced about the menu when there had been key-lime pies, Cajun-seasoned swordfish, and Sloe Gin slushes. Now, he said, Ruby's serves a Pacific Northwest-Cascadian-American Indian-West Pac Rim fusion. "Get it, fusion?" he'd say and howl. But except for a couple of the older chefs, who sighed sympathetically, none of the waiters got the joke. She could tell Nate, the baker, got it, but he always rolled his eyes.

In a Social Justice class at the university, Geneva had learned how New West had moved to self-sufficient production of its own food supplies. It was both socially responsible and an economic necessity as the United Government could no longer be relied upon to provide enough goods to support the population. Besides, importing had been a heinous abuse of resources, which had caused a host of environmental and human rights abuses. It was far more efficient to live off the land. As well, the foods naturally produced each season were the healthiest to eat. New West had ceased importing and exporting operations. It became completely autonomous, producing everything it needed locally. It received nothing from the United Government and nothing from off-continent.

Occasionally, some of the older generation grumbled. They missed this or that product that they had enjoyed in the past, especially on holidays. Many of them kept caches of canned goods stashed like buried treasure in the backs of storerooms. Most people Geneva's age thought this behavior silly. Geneva was sure, no matter what they'd imported in the old days, it couldn't have been worth it to forfeit their self-sufficiency, not when what was locally available was plentiful and delicious. She was even wary of the mission her mother was on now to open limited trade between C-Town and New West. She wasn't sure it was such a good idea. Although they were in the same eco-system, it still seemed a bad precedent to allow New Westians to come to depend on goods that they couldn't produce themselves. And from what she'd heard C-Town ate a big diet of lab-grown meats, which sounded disgusting. But it was impossible to argue with Gary and the chefs at Ruby's when they began to reminisce about food. They would say, "Well, you never tasted them. You wouldn't know." True enough, and that was fine with her. She couldn't be missing much. If Gary and the chefs really thought so, they would have left New West. They looked horrified at the suggestion, "There's always C-town."

"No, no, out of the frying pan," Gary scoffed and then he'd turn back to reminiscing about a certain fruit or vegetable with a private wistfulness. He talked about shipped and imported foods the way she fantasized about Leo, milking each little memory for maximum pleasure again and again.

Still, Geneva would rather listen to Gary babble about the past than hear her father's shaky voice on the phone now, "They were supposed to release your sister today. But there's...a problem."

Geneva tensed. Gary was shuffling just outside the open office door. She didn't want to have this conversation here at work. She leaned against a stack of boxes wishing she could shrink into them.

"You need to come home now," her father said.

"And leave work?" she asked for Gary's benefit.

"You need to come home now," he said. "She tried to commit suicide." He said more after that, something else incomprehensible. She heard the words but wasn't ready to deal with them yet. She tucked them away for later.

"But she's OK, right?" Geneva asked.

"Just come home," her father said.

Gary was beside her nodding as soon as she hung up, "Family emergency. You do what you have to do."

"She's OK, right?" Geneva asked still trying to make sense of her father's words. She stared at Gary blankly. He looked miserable. She tried to imagine him lumbering from table to table trying to do her job. Could she really just leave in the middle of her shift? If she left, there wouldn't be anyone else to help him. She should probably stay. It wasn't like she could just blow off her job. She was supposed to help. Besides, how fast could she get home, anyway? It wasn't like there were bullet trains to Linden. And when she got there? What could she possibly do? How could she help?

The truth was, she didn't want to go. Knowing Val was at New West Mental Health was one thing but seeing her there would be another. Gary looked at his watch and his face flushed. "Unless you can finish your shift. It's just an hour, and we're swamped. I won't be able to get anyone to fill in."

An hour wouldn't make much difference. She nodded, relieved to have the decision made for her. She went back out on the floor and took a family's order. She had their pile of burgers and fries hefted above her shoulder when her hands began to shake. Her chest tightened. Ruby's melted into a neon-red blur. Her conscience caught up to her. She thought, Val could be bleeding to death right now. The tray fell from her hands. Plates slid across the concrete floor and shattered. The sound cut through the blaring music. Conversations stopped. The family stared at her and two out of three children in the restaurant began to cry. The smashed burgers and ketchup splattered fries squished underfoot. Gary appeared at her shoulder. "I've got it. Just go."

Dazed, Geneva walked out of Ruby's into the heat and headed up the hill to the university. It had been a long time since she'd spoken to Val. After Val had been admitted to New West Mental, Geneva had called often. Each time the conversation began all right, but by the end Val was babbling. She kept muttering something about getting reconnected. She kept saying Sync Chrome City and asking for a Friend-Me stylus. The conversations were exhausting. They went nowhere. Val seemed trapped in a cyclic delusion impervious to logic. She was unreachable. Eventually, Geneva had stopped calling. It hadn't exactly been weeks since she'd last thought of Val, but it had been weeks since they'd spoken. Meanwhile, she thought about Leo, a guy she didn't even know, every day.

Recently, Geneva had been having nightmares and it didn't take a psychology major to know why. She felt guilty. In the nightmares, she was in a classroom, alone, taking a test, nervously running her hands through her long reddish-brown hair. Then, in a dream shift, her hair was cropped and black and the classroom was filled with old women staring. They surrounded her and her hair began to drop onto her desk in chunks. The dreams were so filled with the classic symbols of a troubled psyche that it made her laugh recalling them. But knowing that worry and guilt were fueling her nightmares didn't make her feel any better about them or herself. She felt powerless to help Val, but that seemed a poor excuse not to even try.

Geneva broke into a run, anxious now to make up time. She shouldn't have tried to finish her shift at Ruby's. Any compassionate person would have headed home right away. She took the fastest route across campus, past Old Main. As she passed the building, the protesters turned to her, startled. There were more of them this summer. Geneva counted seven men and women. Deep creases lined their eyes. Their probing looks added to her rising panic. She shouldn't have stayed at the university this summer. She should have quit work—but she liked helping there—and spent the time in Linden near Val—but what would she have done there?

Her uniform trapped the heat around her and it grew heavy with sweat as she ran across campus. It stuck to her legs as she sprinted across the field to Inu Wood. When she reached her dorm room, she shucked off the sticky dress. She changed into a pile of clothes on the floor and grabbed a few things for Val—clothes and a vial of plum lip-gloss—and stuffed them into a knapsack. She rushed down the hill to the bus station. At least she was finally doing something, even if she wasn't sure what.

Then she fidgeted, at an enforced standstill again, waiting for a Shadow Bus. The buses, painted black with surplus paint, were hard to see and would have caused accidents but for the lack of traffic. They also had high beam lights and were wrapped in iridescent yellow wire lights meant to look like a security system, but everyone knew they didn't work. The government wouldn't allow them to be equipped with actual electrodes. A public entity didn't have as much leeway to accidentally zap a civilian and there were too many children and elders at the bus stations, not to mention punks who were most likely to trip the security by goofing around the station. The buses would have been tasering everyone, all the time, if they were really armed. The lights had been installed back when it was trendy to put pretend deterrents on everything as advocated by Mindfare, the now defunct philosophical/marketing movement. Mindfare had moved to C-Town after the revolution, but there were remnants of its advertising campaigns in New West.

Geneva sat on a concrete bench and remembered what her father had said just before he'd hung up. Fear sharpened his final words to her, "She tried to commit suicide. The doctors are afraid she might be susceptible to some new virus. Before they release her, they want to talk to you."

Geneva didn't know why she was important, but she knew there would be questions and answers: right and wrong, like a test. All she wanted was to pass so that she could get Val out of there and back to New West in time for fall quarter. Then everything would be all right again.

When the bus pulled into Linden station, Geneva shielded her eyes from the sun and looked for her father. She stifled a gasp when she spotted him in the shadows. His face was gray and blotchy and his eyes sunken. Possibly he hadn't slept a full night since Val's collapse. She went to him and he held her, squeezing her shoulders tight, so long that she began to squirm trying to create room between them for cooling air to flow. "Dad?"

He released her, his jaw trembling. His vacant eyes shifted. He avoided holding her gaze.

"What happened? What is it? Is Val OK?" she asked.

He sighed. "Geneva, you're here." He inclined his head toward the street and the family's compact green Enviro-Car. He didn't speak again until they were both wedged in. He pulled out into the narrow empty streets rubbing one hand nervously along his thigh as he drove. In profile, the edge of his brow and the corner of his lip twitched. "They said she tried to commit suicide. But she didn't. She didn't succeed. I don't understand. She was fine at home. They say there had to be something up at the college."

Geneva pressed back against the vinyl seat and looked down at her sneakers. "She seemed OK." All summer she'd been trying to avoid this conversation and the accusation that she should have noticed something unusual about Val long ago, some observation that could have prevented this. But she hadn't noticed anything. The truth was Val had been keeping to herself a lot lately, zoning out under her glasses and leaving Geneva virtually alone in the stark dorm room. Between Ruby's and the hours she spent in the greenhouse, Geneva had barely registered how often Val was plugged-in and unavailable.

As the car passed the high school, her father stopped to let a pack of teenagers cross in front of them. He focused his gray eyes on her. “But she wasn't OK. And you were with her. You must've seen signs of something."

Geneva lowered the window. She needed fresh air. The teenagers laughed as they headed over to Rome Subs, a favorite hangout. She was too nervous to eat, but the smell of fried comfort foods, potatoes, and breaded onions, made her stomach rumble. "I'm sorry. I wouldn't have let anything happen to her. I don't know what went wrong."

After they passed the high school, the town gave way to forest and the air in the car cooled. Geneva grasped the side of her seat as her father turned sharply onto a gravel road just wide enough for the car. "You're studying people," he said.

Geneva looked back at a sign angled away from the road. Underneath a film of brown-green moss, she read the words, New West Mental Health. "Environmental psychology," she corrected. “It's mostly plants."

Her father stopped the car in front of the building. Evergreen branches brushed its roof. "Just talk to the doctors. Maybe there's something you saw but didn't notice. Talk to them, please. That's all I'm asking."

Geneva frowned as she got out of the car. The building looked more like one of the high school's portable classrooms than a medical clinic. Her father followed behind her as she climbed the rickety steps. There was no reception, just a claustrophobic entryway and two steel chairs. Her father shuffled from side to side, his shoulders stooped before collapsing into one of the chairs.

"Shouldn't we tell them we're here?" she asked.

He pointed up at a translucent camera mounted in the corner. She settled into the other chair and studied her sneakers until she felt a hand on her shoulder. She sprang to her feet and looked up into a woman's face. She had sharp features. Her eyes were even wider and darker than Val's. She wore a lab coat and a cold air of authority. "Geneva, I'm Dr. Montgrave, Valerie's doctor, please follow me."

Geneva looked back at her father. His head rested on the wall and his long legs stretched out in front of him. His eyes were closed, but his face was ashen and contorted. Low rhythmic grunts escaped through his nose.

She left her sleeping father and followed the doctor behind a door down a hallway rank with mold. They took a couple of turns and passed through a few doors until Geneva was sure she could no longer find her way out on her own. They entered a white windowless conference room just big enough for one folding table and an old vending machine. Geneva shivered and understood why the doctor was wearing a high-collared sweater under her lab coat in the middle of August.

"Valerie?" Geneva asked, ignoring the audible rumble of her stomach. "I came to see her. Is she OK?"

"I have a few questions first." The doctor gave her a crimp-lipped smirk— the kind of cold smile professors used before tough exams. "We're trying to help your friend..."

"My sister," Geneva corrected.

"Yes, well, I'm hoping you can help us figure out what happened. We've ruled out any neurological disorders or genetic predisposition. But you were with her most recently. If you'll give us some time, maybe we can find out what triggered the seizure."

Geneva sat in one of the cold folding chairs. She looked at the dingy carpet and the flecks of black mold where the walls joined the ceiling. She listened to distant footsteps, a creaking door and then silence.

"Would you like coffee? Something to eat?" the doctor offered.

"No," she said. She couldn't eat here; it would feel too much like acquiescence. It reminded her of mythology class: like Persephone eating pomegranate seeds in Hades. If she ate food here, it would give them power over her and she might not be able to leave. It was unreasonable, but she preferred her gradually growing hunger to the quick pain of forcing down fear. She knew it was a bad sign, psychologically, that she was letting superstition drive her actions. It meant she felt out of control. She wondered what pomegranate tasted like and if it were one of the foods Gary missed. She'd have to ask him. Why had Persephone eaten only the seeds?

Across the table, the doctor's persistent silence was oppressive, and it made Geneva want to fill it, which she suspected was the point, a trap. At last, she rushed into it, "I'm sorry. I feel horrible. I mean I didn't notice anything symptomatic in Val's behavior. I can't believe she's here. The guards said she had EHBF, I remember."

She didn't expect the doctor to be forthcoming, but Montgrave said, "Extraordinary Human Biological Function. Uncontrollable psychic reception."

"Psychic reception," Geneva echoed, and this time she waited out the trailing quiet until the doctor spoke first.

"Well," Dr. Montgrave said, after an interminable pause. "In an untrained brain, EHBF causes imbalanced electrical activity in the two halves of the brain, EEG asynchronicities — seizures. The more the seizures are allowed to happen the more likely they are to reoccur. The brain learns to activate that firing of synapses: a kindling effect. The repeated use causes psychic disorder."

"They gave her Thorazine, an old anti-psychotic," Geneva said. "And a psychic suppressant."

Dr. Montgrave took out a small notepad and a stylus from her lab coat pocket. She rolled the green stylus across the table. "Don't worry. No one's blaming you. Have you seen one of these before?"

Geneva rolled it under her fingers. "Uh, yeah. It's a pen."

The doctor lowered her voice. "A Friend-Me stylus. It's also what your sister used to try to kill herself."

The pen clattered as Geneva let it fall. She stared at it on the table and imagined Val thrusting it into her throat in a deadly tracheotomy. It was a horrifying idea, but she didn't buy it. "How?"

"It's been modified to emit ELF, that's extreme low frequency electromagnetic waves," the doctor unscrewed the stylus and showed the stretch of clear fibrous wires between the pieces. The wires were notched and lined with spirals of metal. "This modification could be used to jury-rig a kind of external neural net, an almost direct connection between people. There have been reports of people doing this, taking their conversations offline, turning their biological brain networks into a kind of server. It's the kind of thing advocated by Neo-Privates. I don't know how much your father told you, but we've heard reports that this kind of thing is spreading, as if it were a game at the university. But it's dangerous. The brain is not a toy. We're concerned. These technological extensions hardwire harmful connections and are basically creating a new viral form of mental illness. It spreads from brain to brain like a cancer. Normally, electricity is biologically propelled through a nerve, but this modification bypasses normal chemical inhibitors. It sends out constant stimulation. The neurons literally fire themselves to death."

"We're trying to find the students who are doing this. Valerie won't tell us anything. She's too caught up in it to see the harm." The doctor let Geneva digest this information and then pressed her, "Did you notice anything unusual about Valerie's behavior before you witnessed her seize?"

The doctor leaned forward. Geneva wanted to push her chair back but at the same time she could not look away from the woman's face. Her engaged, yet calm, expression reminded Geneva of photos of her mother taken in the days before the revolution. Afterwards, her parents had tried to cultivate in their children this same intense awareness. But Geneva did not feel focused on her parent's world. She felt worried, guilty and something worse. There was a needling feeling her under her skin she couldn't identify, and she hoped it would go away before she did.

"Well, Val's definitely a plug-in. It started in college. She's been plugged-in a lot recently. We haven't talked much lately." She shrugged. "I don't know. It didn't seem odd to me. It's what people my age do." Geneva didn't feel like volunteering specifics, but she was starting to guess that the source of Val's illness, if that's what it was, probably had to do with the Sync Chrome City site.

"Well, I'll tell you what I noticed," Dr. Montgrave said, and her voice became soft and low. "Almost immediately." She leaned forward and looked over Geneva's shoulder with an intense gaze that was even more uncomfortable than when the doctor eyed her directly. The roped copper chain of her necklace bounced along the high-rolled neck of her sweater. The 8-shaped pendant swung round. "I tell you this outside of my official capacity here: There is a quality of amorous sadness about your friend, an intoxicating ennui. Such a thing is often a harbinger of change. It requires our full attention, if you understand me."

Geneva didn't, and her confusion showed. The doctor promptly leaned back and resumed a business-like demeanor. She wore the expression of a student in the front row of a lecture. She reattached the pen and poised it over her notepad screen. "Now, my questions, which you will do your best to answer before you may see her. She's been asking for you, you know."

Dr. Montgrave's stylus glided across the pad as Geneva reluctantly answered questions about Val. At first, the information seemed trivial: Val loved orange juice and chocolate, slept five or six hours a night (unless she was pulling plugged-in all-nighters, Geneva omitted) and listened to trance music or soulful folk. Then the questions got harder: Yes, Val spent at least four hours daily in virtual reality. No, Geneva didn't know what she did there. She didn't know why. She didn't know when she had started doing it. She didn't know who Val hung out with in person or plugged-in.

She really didn't! Being asked the questions made Geneva feel like she should know the answers. She nervously twisted her ponytails around her fingers. There wasn't a clock in the room. The only decoration, aside from the vending machine, was a tattered poster of a girl spinning with her arms outstretched under a tree and a clear blue sky. It looked like the cover of an environmental psychology textbook. At the bottom it said, "The brain is wider than the sky. — Emily Dickinson." She put her head in her hands and spoke to the tabletop through clenched teeth. "No. I don't know. I really don't know. I don't know. I really don't."

Finally, stonewalled, Montgrave ceased her barrage. She paused, "OK, fine. Just one more thing. What about partners? Is Valerie seeing anyone? A boy or a girl?"

Geneva looked up. That was it. She wasn't going to talk about this. Val had no trouble attracting a certain type, brooding plug-ins, and she had been spending lot of time at the Mansion. But if love was the reason, Val kept it to herself as was her right. Val's sex life or romantic status, if she had one, was no one's business. The table bucked as Geneva slammed her hands on it and stood up. "Forget it. I'm done. She's not a freakin' Neo-Private. Listen. Please. I'm starving. I'm tired. Just let me see her. I need to see that she's OK."

Dr. Montgrave sighed. "We're trying to help your friend. Are you sure there isn't anything else?"

Geneva pressed her lips together. There was one secret of Val's she was privy to that maybe did matter, and she hadn't mentioned—the warning notice about Val's expulsion from the university. But this clinic couldn't give a damn about that, or they wouldn't have yanked Val out of school. Besides, she definitely wasn't spilling a true secret. That would be a real breach of trust. Already, she regretted blabbing as much about Val's personal life as she had. Val had always been loyal. If the situation were reversed, she thought, ashamed, Val wouldn't have given the doctor any information at all. "How exactly is this helping Val?"

The doctor's serene expression wavered which Geneva took to mean it wasn't or at least Montgrave had her doubts. "All right. I'll take you to her now. I should tell you though; it's a bad day. She's rather upset that we took the stylus. She wants to use VR, but I'm sure that would do more harm than good."

As she rose, Dr. Montgrave adjusted her swinging necklace. Her voice dropped and she trained her distant gaze past Geneva again. "It's an infinity symbol. Not a figure eight or a woman meditating, no. Yes, you see, depending on where we are sitting, our perspective changes."

At last, the doctor led her to Val. For a moment, Geneva watched her friend through the tiny pane in the thick door. She had hoped Val wouldn't be strapped to a bed or anything macabre the way she'd imagined. She wasn't. Val sat beneath a barred window surrounded by white pillows looking thin, pale, and startlingly familiar. Instead of a gown she had on pajamas. They made her look more like a philosopher than a patient. Dr. Montgrave placed a hand on Geneva's shoulder and pushed the door open, "Go on in. It's safe."

The room, small and austere, reminded her of their dorm room, but it smelled of mold not cinnamon. A low moan of wind rattled the roof of the clinic. Pinecones clattered. Tree branches brushed the window, casting shadows on the opaque glass behind the bars. Val sat with her legs folded up to her chest and her head flopped over her knees. Her dark hair fell forward along the line of her chin and covered her eyes. The posture exuded sadness. Geneva wanted to go to her friend and comfort her, but she found herself at a loss, afraid to step into the room. What good could she possibly do?

Geneva stood by the door willing herself forward until, at last, Val looked up. "Nice Gator-girl hair. So, I leave and you finally listen. Figures. C'mere."

Geneva twirled her fingers through her Gator Tongue ponytails as she entered the room. She perched on the end of the windowsill seat across from Val and watched the door swing shut.

Val rolled her eyes. There were dark bags under them, and her lips were pale. She spoke with her head down between the shanks of hair that fell across her face. "I so did not try to commit suicide. They tell you that? So not my style you know. If I did that, how would I know how everything turns out?" Val slapped a hand down on Geneva's bobbing knee. "Stop. Nervy-girl. Did you bring it?"

Geneva unsnapped a pocket on the side of her pants, extracted a vial and handed it over.

Val shrugged and smeared some of the lip-gloss over her pout. "Thanks, but I meant the stylus. I need the one you got from Friend-Me."

Geneva's shoulders tightened as she hugged her knees to her chest. "How did you know?" It was disturbing that Val knew about the unexpected Friend-Me delivery, but worse that she'd asked for the stylus, the same kind Dr. Montgrave said she'd used to try to kill herself. She watched Val's keen dark eyes. She didn't think Val would harm herself, but Geneva didn't trust her own judgment. She'd been missing so much of her best friend's life, lately. She shook her head and held up empty hands.

Val sighed. "I love you, but clueless-girl, I wasn't trying to die. I was trying to get connected. Listen, you and me have nothing to fear from wideware. The adults are just jealous that their stale old brains can't take the tech. Yeah, I want to do something radical, but death, so not what I'm going for. Not in the middle of a revolution. There's a lot more to do. A lot more. We have to keep at it for all those other people on the outside, on the 'Way."

Geneva tucked her chin to her knees. For the first time she thought Val really might belong in a mental ward. "Not over? What? Those people on the Freeway want to be left alone. It is, definitely, over."

"No," Val said. "Things are changing."

"Things changed," Geneva lowered her voice. "Val, I'm sorry. But the revolution? It ended the day those people killed your parents. All we have to do now is graduate New West. Keep the peace. You know it's OK for us to do that. It's OK."

Val raised a hand and leaned toward her. Every line in her face was tight and turned down. "It's so not OK to just sit on our asses while this goes down. Look where I am. But yeah, sure, you be peace-girl. That's so like you. I wouldn't want to spoil it."

Geneva knew Val would never hit her, but it looked like she wanted to. On the pretext of grabbing a pillow, Geneva shielded her face as she set it in her lap.

"Ugh." Val spun off the bench and folded her arms across her chest. "If you're so afraid of me, why are you here? To tell me to calm down? Like that's going to help in any way?"

"I've been worried," Geneva said, kneading a corner of the pillow. "I want you to be able to come back to New West, to finish your degree. I want to help."

"Really? You've been all worry-girl, helpful for me?" Val said. "Or do you want what you've always wanted, what your parents told us to want: a quiet place in a perfect little world? Here's the problem: There's no such thing as a bloodless revolution. Why don't you tell me what you have been doing all summer? Because you haven't been here."

Geneva rocked with the pillow.

Val leaned forward again, fists on her hips. "No? Nothing? Fine. I'll tell you what you've been doing," her voice got louder. "You've been worried about serving people burgers. You've been thinking about some guy. You so haven't been thinking about me. You could have come anytime. You're here now because they said I tried to kill myself. Why not care about my everyday life as much as my possible death? Make me be drama-girl because that's what it takes to move you. You so haven't been paying attention. And I can't believe you're scared. Of *me*. Coward. You're afraid and you don't even know what you're afraid of."

Geneva felt Val's breath on her cheeks. She stood up and stepped to the side to get some distance. She had to look down to see into Val's glossy eyes. She realized Val was barefoot and without her boots several inches shorter than usual. Even so, it was true. She was afraid of tiny, quietly forceful Val, who'd she'd known all her life, as if she'd been transformed into some strange creature. It was fear of the unknown. She didn't know what to expect from her friend anymore. They used to know each other. Now she didn't know what had broken them apart, so how could she manage to mend the gap? It shamed her to realize, that for her part, Val had resorted to brinkmanship. She had pretended to commit suicide to get Geneva to the clinic. Was that really the extreme it took to make Geneva break her routine — a near death experience? It probably was. Even now, if she could, she'd rather be at Ruby's doing predictable work than having this nebulous argument with Val. How could she repair the damage between them? "Val, I...sent your final in for you. So, you're on track to graduate," she said, lamely.

"You touched my computer?" Val followed Geneva's gaze to her feet and sighed. "No. That's fine. That's great. You want to help me. But the New West way so doesn't work, withdrawing or erecting walls. Isolation invites evil. To create utopia, everyone has to participate. Everyone has to connect. You want to understand just give me that stylus. I want to get out of here, too. I so do."

Geneva fingered the stylus in her pocket wondering how the tiny every day object could possibly be as dangerous as Dr. Montgrave had implied. She hated the fact that she didn't trust Val with such a small thing. "I can't."

Val put a hand out palm up. "Yeah, I know. You think that. But we're family. You can't be too afraid this time. You know I know what I'm doing, or I wouldn't ask. Do you want to help me or not? We're together in this."

Geneva scanned the room and slowly pulled the pen from her pocket. "There's no port here. What are you even going to do with it?"

Val slipped her hand around the instrument. "I don't need a port."

In seconds, violet light flashed in the air around them. Outside, branches splintered.

"Sync Chrome City Psi-Girl," Val sighed sounding like a computer shutting down and her arms dropped to her sides. Her body began to convulse in rubbery waves. She collapsed toward the window seat.

"Val!" Geneva grabbed at her friend's waist, caught her shirt and fell forward with her onto the cushion. Val's forehead knocked against the bars over the window. Geneva groaned. She lifted herself off Val's side and turned her over. Val's back arched. Her head dropped exposing the long taut line of her throat.

Geneva slapped the side of Val's face. "Don't do this. Don't make this my fault. Don't."

Val's head jerked up, a red patch forming on her forehead where her skull had struck the bars and another along the side of her jaw where Geneva had hit. Her eyes rolled into place. "I'm fine. Tell the doctor it's OK."

The door creaked and Dr. Montgrave pushed Geneva aside placing two fingers on the side of Val's neck. "What did you do? What did you give her?"

Val's eyes flicked to the side in the direction of the stylus lying just at the doctor's feet. Geneva pocketed it, but not before the doctor noticed.

"Hand it over," Montgrave said.

Geneva extracted a slim black tube from her pocket and gave it up. Val sat; her face flushed. "I'm fine." She took the vial from the doctor's hand, opened the tube and ran the wand across her bottom lip. She smirked at the doctor with her Plum Ice smile. "Lip gloss, just what I needed."

A lab tech entered the room, and while the doctor talked to him Geneva whispered, "Sync Chrome City?"

Valerie pulled her in close. "Listen, you don't want to deal. Fine. I'll respect that. You're off the hook. Thanks. It was enough. I'll be home soon."

"Run some more tests," Dr. Montgrave said, as she grabbed Geneva's elbow and steered her to the door.

Geneva turned her head as she left the room and saw Val peering around the lab tech at her. The look in Val's eyes—What was it Dr. Montgrave had said? "Amorous sadness." — made her want to stay. She wanted to finish the argument, figure out when Val had become so angry and why she felt so responsible.

"Is she going to be, OK?" Geneva asked as she tried to keep pace with Dr. Montgrave's stride down the hall.

"We don't know. Every time she seizes, it reinforces patterns. It's more likely to happen again. She needs to stay out of VR, before the pattern becomes permanent. But there's nothing more you can do," she said.

In the waiting room, her father was awake now, staring vacantly. There were shadows embedded in his brow and worry lines slicing from his nose to his lips. Her father, a biologist who was most content researching rodents, had joined the revolution. He'd dedicated his youth to establishing utopia. Then he'd taken in Val, his best friend's daughter, and instead of following his own passion had devoted his life to making sure his children could enjoy the prosperity of New West. Now, what he had worked for was unraveling. He looked drained. His eyes were watery. His lips quivered. He looked pleadingly at Geneva.

Nothing more she could do? If that were true, then Geneva had absolutely no control over a situation affecting the people she loved. She cared deeply and could not accept it. She twisted her ponytails around her fingers and pinned down the needling feeling she'd had: hope. It was a small, despairing, persistent feeling that she knew, uncomfortably, she would have to pursue. Now that everyone was telling her to never mind, she would do the opposite. Her stubborn streak, as her mother called it, had kicked in. She would make a difference. She would find Sync Chrome City. That she could do.

~ 9 ~

SYNC CHROME CITY: DUMPED

"Prior to the Psychic Awakening, those who considered psychic abilities possible were marginalized. One of the main effects of the Awakening was the institutionalization of empathy and the introduction of psychic curriculum into the public school system. Early fringe factions included:

Noetic Sciences Institute – a reputable, scientific organization of people sharing psychic research and practicing collective consciousness using modern methods although, pre-Awakening, with far less dramatic results.

Psi-Aware – a radical group of former revolutionaries, protesting for psychic awareness, rights and the introduction of psychic curriculum into the schools. Few members were able to demonstrate psychic proclivities.

The United Government – highly-classified groups within the government or operating under government grants secretly testing psychic abilities such as remote viewing, primarily for military objectives, with 50 percent success rates.

For further study: What other factions now marginalized might be advancing tomorrow's thought forms? Recall that before the printing press was invented even silent reading, the idea of hearing words in your head, was regarded as an impossible mental skill. Consider the psychic botanists and geologists whose teleological theories and attempts to tap into the *unus mundus*, or world mind, many consider to be extreme, impossible, or ridiculous." — *Becoming Psychic 101, A History and a Primer*

Living with Lydia Streker in Deming over the summer had been a surprising boon. The dowdy, frizz-haired hippy wasn't his type, but Burrows liked the sugary lard she served up in her bakery, and in her bed. It had been a while since he'd used his telepathy to work a woman and he'd forgotten what could be accomplished when you knew ahead what they were thinking. Usually masochistic pleasure, the pain of other's thoughts, was the best he could hope for when he manipulated people. Lydia had unwittingly taught him some tricks, however. In her quest to become psychic, she was big into meditation. Playing along to ingratiate himself, he'd found that the techniques helped him control his migraines. Although it took a lot of concentration, he could dull the pain.

Fortunately, before he got too comfortable mooching on the couch of New West, Lydia invited him to come to one of her Psi-Aware meetings, as he'd hoped she would. He needed to find the threat, the person who would bust minds wide-open, make privacy a thing of the past, and cause himself intense, inescapable pain even out on the 'Way. He needed to find the threat he'd glimpsed in Sync Chrome City and eliminate it.

Unfortunately, in this regard, Psi-Aware was a huge disappointment. No one in the group had any ability. In fact, he'd never met a group of less intuitive people. They were all a bunch of middle-aged wannabes like Lydia, true believers, but not in the least psychic. He couldn't resist showing off a little and they began to look to him for advice. When he meditated with Lydia, their adoration was even bearable.

He'd started to have a bit of fun with his ipso facto leadership role, seeing how far off-kilter this group could get. They were rabidly loopy, and he was good at inspirational speeches. "Now, I think we all know that if anything's going to get done, it's going to get done at a grass roots level. Even the national chapter of Psi-Aware has gotten far too conservative and cautious. And I'm tired of waiting. If the Deming chapter has to make it happen, then so be it. We just can't have people being kept down like they are now, struggling for no good reason."

After that, they'd given him a standing ovation and it got him thinking. He seemed to have tapped a vein with his oratory persuasion. They gushed enthusiasm. These Sync Chrome City kids were working out better than expected, giving him all the right connections. He was beginning to feel very hopeful about his prospects in New West. Forget about simply stopping the psychic threat. There was a chance he'd even been wrong about that. Nothing he'd seen so far indicated that anyone had that kind of potential. Maybe his ability was an anomaly. Now that he was here, he could turn his own pain to his advantage, extract his revenge. New West had shut him out, now he would shut it down. He could feel the "utopia" on the brink of crisis pressed on one side by the psychic wannabes and on the other by the privacy advocates. It had been too calm too long. Entropy and chaos were the natural order, the place where Burrows fit in.

Another entertaining side effect of bedding Lydia was the reaction of her son. Streker had figured out that Burrows wasn't in line to be "daddy" and was probably up to no good with mom. While Lydia herself had low expectations, older women tended to be realistic about their self-indulgences, it made her kid peevish. As fun as annoying Streker was, Burrows was due for a break. He would have accepted the kids' party invitation just to get out of the house. For variety alone, he'd trade the suspicious pains of Streker to endure the jabs of fawning Eve. It was a significant sweetener though when he found out he was to be a guest at President Sherring's home to celebrate the twentieth birthday of his daughter Coco. Yes, New West was just a land of opportunities. For a malicious outcast who'd scored an invite, Burrows was starting to see a lot of them.

Eve had mentioned Coco's birthday party casually, but he'd gotten: *Save me!* and knew she wanted him to provide her a bit of distraction from The Coco Show. Burrows was only glad to be used. If Eve got sick of glow-glow Coco, she was welcome to hang out in Burrows' shade. Meanwhile, he'd get a handle on the psychic landscape—find out what the politicos were planning—and where they were weak. To ensure your own security, you had to think big, long-term, get involved. You couldn't let people make world-changing decisions with life-threatening implications like—hey, I know, let's change the entire structure of people's brains so we can all have nifty psychic powers—without your involvement.

The only downside to the party was being foisted off on Leo. Eve had spent the night with Coco as a guest. To get in, Burrows would arrive at the party as a friend of Leo's, Coco's boyfriend. He'd gotten to know the guy pretty well—and didn't like him. It was two long hours on the back of Leo's scooter to get to the president's mansion. No cars were allowed on Route 9 around New West so they couldn't take his Mistress. Leo was a quiet guy inside. In that respect, he reminded Burrows of Mace. He gave Burrows little, but still managed to grate on his nerves. On the surface he was energetic, always moving. The guy was so juked up to see his girlfriend at her little birthday party he was practically cartwheeling. Being around Leo made Burrows feel every day of the nine years he had on the kid.

Leo parked the scooter at the gate and vaulted off it. On the banks of Silver Lake, the New West President's palatial estate rose before them. Burrows imagined the white columns of the house on fire like in an old movie. He unbuttoned his collar, wicking his shirt away from his chest and rolled up his sleeves. It had been years since he had been anywhere so clean—the place reminded him of a fresh wound. He squinted as he strode along the sparkling sidewalk, past an expanse of lawn and grazing goddamn horses. The New West he remembered was a soggy haze filled with chill tension that made your bones feel brittle. This was something else.

"Oh yes, electric! And we call the dorm a Mansion!" Leo exclaimed. “This is the real deal.”

As they walked up the steps and stood at the president's door, Burrows looked over at Leo with his curls and his scooter helmet tucked under his arm. Leo was wearing a pair of tailored pants and a lime-striped shirt both a bit tight and short like he'd bought them long ago and hadn't worn them enough to notice he'd outgrown them. He stood with lazy knees and elbows, showing a lot of teeth. The guy had no clue. Leo's role as campus DJ and Coco's erstwhile sidekick had given him delusions. The kid thought he was carrying cool currency, but he'd enter this house with an empty plastic card.

"Hey, wait," Leo said, grabbing Burrow's wrist as he reached for the brass knocker. "Before we go in, look."

He reached in his pocket and pulled out a velvet jewelry box.

"For Coco," Leo said. "Do you think I should...?"

Burrows got: *Love her forever.* And cut the kid short. He didn’t have time for schmaltzy kid crap. "How should I know? I haven't seen her. Put that away. Let's go in."

Burrows lifted his hand, but Eve opened the door before his knuckles struck wood. Her expression was sullen. Burrows marveled at how she could mold her face into such disdain. She looked tired from the effort. He leered at her and she lost it, the corners of her mouth turned up. She was wearing a sleeveless black dress that made her shoulders look beached. It reminded him of doing her Vary, her black underwear and flat white thighs. The lacy leftover prom dress bunched around her widening hips and chest.

"Hey, good to see a familiar face," Leo said.

Eve shrugged. "Coco's still getting ready."

"You look good," Leo said.

"You too," Eve replied.

One advantage to being psychic, no one lied to you about how you looked.

Eve looked at Burrows with no concerns for his appearance at all. She thought at him: *Please, make this less lame.*

"Wow. Check this place out," Leo said, ogling the closest crystal chandelier.

Burrows peered into a ballroom. Behind French doors, arrangements of flowers, Hollyhock, Columbine, Fireweed, and Bleeding Heart, and platters of food, deep leafy greens and red and blue berries, splayed down elongated tables.

"Check out the spread!" Leo said.

"Fit for a princess," Burrows said.

Coco made her entrance descending a winding staircase. She wore a red dress with a plunging v-neck. The sateen fabric clung to her hips and flowed around her legs. Her hair was pulled back in a low ponytail. Gold hoops dangled from her ears. Beside her Eve looked short, dirty, and adolescent.

Burrows looked at Eve and let pity show in his eyes. Her reply snapped: *Ugh*. He extended a hand to Coco and she enclosed it in soft fingers. "I'm Burrows—a friend of Leo's. Happy birthday."

"Happy birthday!" Leo said, stepping between them.

Coco embraced Leo, "Thanks Leo Love."

He went wet sugar limp in her arms.

Burrows hung out with the students until the guests arrived. Then, Eve helped Coco greet them at the door, Leo accosted the buffet table, and Burrows mingled listening. Most of the guests were well-dressed, middle-aged politicos. Few people spared Burrows a thought other than: *Ah, security.* It helped to be a big guy.

Most of the conversations were local politics: debates about New West's new trade negotiations with C-town, flame vs. electric shock alarms, and neo-private legislation. Boring. It wasn't like anyone here was going to say, 'psychic'. If anyone needed a map to where that would put you on the political landscape all they had to do was look at Psi-Aware, an organization so far out in the boonies of influence it could have been off-continent. Burrows started to think the party was a waste of time, but the food was good, if strictly vegan, and he enjoyed watching the women shimmer in soft gowns. It seemed like years, not months, since he'd been surrounded by the filth of the Freeway. He grabbed a pine nut tart off the buffet table, which, of course, brought him dangerously close to Leo, the feeder, again. He overheard the kid talking to Coco.

"When are you going to introduce me to your father?" Leo asked. "I thought he wanted to meet me."

"Trust me, he's been checking you out all night," she said, touching her lips to his cheek. "But he's busy. Schmoozing."

"Well, now he's schmoozing with my mom," Leo pulled Coco toward a tall woman with black braids talking to an even taller white-haired man. "Time to introduce myself."

Burrows recognized President Sherring and Kendra LeMay, the owner of Friend-Me Co. He stared at Leo's back in his too tight pressed shirt and tried to process. The goof Leo was related to the Friend-Me founder—she was his mother. He followed the kids into the two leaders' conversation and found the two people in New West who weren't afraid to say psychic—the president and the entrepreneur.

"Psychic education. Completely open our minds?" Sherring said, opening his hands at the same time, hands even larger than Burrows' own hands, with long fingers and pink palms. "That's an extreme point of view even for a neo-private."

LeMay shook her head, hands on her hips. "I'm not advocating any agenda, but I'm a futurist. I don't think the issue is going away. Remember, before the advent of the printing press something as benign as silent reading was considered practically paranormal. The fact is there are 100 billion nerve cells in our brains all with the potential to connect and interact. If we're not using them all, then we don't really know what we are capable of. We haven't even touched the surface of possibility, yet. In the long run, Psi-Aware is right. The future will be about going into our own heads, expanding and exploring our own capacity. That's the next space we have to conquer."

Her hands, at the end of her long bare arms looked disproportionately thick, hammers stuck to wire, and her knuckles were worn, dry and cracked. LeMay paused to encircle Leo with her arm. The kid didn't flinch. He stood there like it was the most natural thing for a guy his age to remain under his mother's wing. Burrows felt a twinge of jealousy. Possibly the best time in his life, the most certain anyway, had been that week on the 'Way drugged on LeMay, under her influence.

The president nodded at Coco. His face froze into an attentive expression as LeMay continued her argument. "You know, I had my doubts about doing business in New West. When I started Friend-Me, I had lost my tech job in the depression. I staked everything on my silly invention—that's what every investor said about a diary for girls. I worked harder for myself than I ever had for an employer, in part, because I was terrified. I was pregnant with Leo at the time."

Leo grimaced as his mom drew him tighter. "I was on my own. My idea had to succeed so we could support ourselves. I had such high hopes. I think hope is the female equivalent of men's lust—an intense and painful obsession."

At "lust," Leo detached himself from his mom's embrace. "Coco, let's dance. This sounds serious."

Coco took his hand. "It's supposed to be my party, but with my father it's always politics."

LeMay and Sherring smiled distractedly at their children. Neither noticed Burrows standing next to them. In this ballroom, with these important people, his head was silent and numb. No one spared a thought for him. LeMay turned to Sherring. Her black eyes shone. "I almost left when you were creating New West. I loved the idealism of it, but I hated the rules. Utopia is not an innovative environment. I stayed because I felt so strongly about New West, both ways. When emotions pull at you like that—love-hate, hope-fear—you have pay attention. As it turned out, New West was the right place for Friend-Me. New West and Friend-Me both work because they fill the same need—connectivity. People want to be in a system that's small enough to interact with them, where they matter as individuals. I wasn't the only little girl sitting alone, writing in her diary, wishing for a response and someone to talk to."

Behind LeMay and Sherring, Leo pretended to waltz Coco around the dance floor. Her dress hung low in the back, and he had his hand on the girl's bare skin. Many of the guests had turned to watch them. The girl beamed. LeMay and Sherring continued to stare each other down. Burrows, beside them, still got nothing. Sherring's long hands hung at his sides.

LeMay talked with her hammers. "I've learned that having my own business, makes me more dependent on other people. What happens in New West affects Friend-Me and being stagnant isn't good. The depression and malaise that plagued the United Government remain. New West hasn't cured us. To maintain this utopia, we have to move forward, we have to train people to use all of their minds. It's coming whether we like it or not. What I'm saying is, ignoring the problem could undo all you've achieved here. We have to think of our children. That's why it's so important that New West fund our research."

At this, president Sherring held up his hand, long fingers pointed to the domed stained-glass ceiling. "We'll talk real business tomorrow."

LeMay dipped her head as Sherring turned and, finally, Burrows got something. Sherring noticed him: *Who? So close. That's not one of my men.*

Burrows scars stretched beneath his beard as he smiled. "I'd be careful, president. What Ms. LeMay says sounds like a threat: either you help the psychics gain access to your heads or you face the possibility of civil war. Meanwhile, your kids aren't fighting."

Burrows got a quick slice of animosity from the president before his attention turned to his daughter. LeMay and Sherring looked to the dance floor to see what had been entertaining the rest of the party. Leo dipped Coco and swung her back arched, blond hair skimming over the polished ballroom floor. They all looked down the smooth line of her chest. Her hair shook as he righted her, face flushed. Then Leo got down on one knee and opened a tiny box to her.

The president stepped quickly forward, raised his hands high and clapped twice. "Attention," he said. His voice boomed. All eyes turned to him. "As you know, it's my daughter's 20th birthday. Please stand and sing with me."

Leo, interrupted, stood up, flustered. Coco beamed, unaware, easily exchanging one form of attention for another. The guests started in on the song. Waiters in white coats flowed through the ballroom with plates raised over their heads. They distributed pink-frosted cakes decorated with glazed berries and one lit candle each to the guests. The room filled with glow and sugar-scent.

"Let's make a wish," Sherring said.

Leo stood just behind Coco, stunned and forgotten. The president and LeMay shared a distressed glance. He looked angry. Burrows was sure if he'd been LeMay he would have gotten: *Keep your son away from my daughter.*

LeMay lifted her cake, pursed her lips as she blew out the candle and winked at Sherring. "Well, you know what I wished for."

She dipped the tines of her fork into the frosting and tasted it. "Mmm, strawberry."

Burrows stared at the dainty cakes, the shiny curtains, and crystal chandeliers. He recalled spring on the 'Way when he'd found a cluster of strawberries growing wild on the forest floor. There were only three worth eating, the size of your fingertips. He'd wanted to show them to somebody, share them, but most of the outcasts on the 'Way were afraid to come into the forest. None of them were friends. He'd put the berries in his pack and found them at the bottom of it weeks later: three moldy lumps soaked in rabbit's blood. The wax from the candle dripped onto his cake and hardened in the frosting furrows. He set it down, still lit, on the buffet table.

LeMay was right: hope hurt. Wishing was a painful, useless, obsession. There was no reason to endure the anguish. If you wanted something, you took steps to make it happen. Burrows looked around the room again and saw all the instruments of New West's demise laid out in front of him, shiny and sharp as a row of surgical steel. The waiters flowed through the ballroom again distributing champagne flutes filled with light liquid and popping peach-tinted bubbles. He grabbed the president's arm.

"I'd like a meeting with you too, Sherring. I have some information for you," Burrows said, and he braced for the pain that came when the president turned his full attention to him, angry, irritated thoughts falling on Burrows in heavy blows.

After the party, Eve paddled over to the stairs of the pool and hung on the top step with her legs behind her and her chest floating forward in the hammock of her bikini top. "I bet I could get any one of those suits to sleep with me."

"Yeah," Burrows said kneeling by the edge of the pool. "So, why are you wasting your tits on me?"

Eve: *Asshole.*

Ignoring Eve's splashes and her opinions, he looked up to the house where politicos lingered with the president. Satisfied with the proceeds from his own schmoozing, he'd followed Coco's friends to the pool. He returned his attention to Eve.

"Sure, those guys would gladly drain you of your youth," Burrows said. "But why would you want them to? Oh, wait. Don't tell me." He leaned forward and dipped his hand into the pool in front of Eve. "You'd like the attention."

He had to steady himself on the pool's edge as he got: *Look at my chest.* As if it were possible not to. He could also see the backs of her dimpled legs magnified in the water. Fat hadn't disqualified Lydia, but he would never sleep with young Eve. Her wasp's nest of thoughts tormented him enough. He wouldn't want her thinking of him more, although he couldn't seem to resist baiting her.

"You know what kid, fact is, sooner or later, everybody's mother dies. It's no excuse: Eve Hales versus Friend-Me. Yeah, I've been paying attention. New West's a small town. Your parents all know each other."

He looked up at the balcony, where Leo leaned on the railing staring into a room with movement behind him. "That Leo's one lucky guy, isn't he? Coco is one fine bit of birthday cake."

This time Eve didn't bite though. Her thoughts drifted elsewhere. She was used to her place in Coco's shadow. "She's a daddy's girl. Sherring throws this party every summer. Next year will be big, Coco's turning 21. They've probably already started planning," Eve said, sounding blasé, but not sarcastic. Coco did seem to be at the center of the kids' world: Eve's and Leo's anyway. For Streker and Grugel, it was Sync Chrome City. "I don't think Leo's lucky tonight though."

"So, you guys are going back to school soon?" Burrows asked.

"In a few weeks." Eve said.

"Well, you shouldn't have to live in that fishbowl dorm again, kitten. I've got another option," Burrows said. He watched Eve's eyes narrow: *Kitten?* She was wise enough to tell he was pandering but didn't quite have the willpower to resist it. "For you, Grugel, Streker."

Burrows got a strong spike of interest from her like the pull of a fish on a line and then Eve's thoughts flicked away. She looked past him at Leo, who was stalking towards the pool, walking heavy like he'd stored the buffet in his legs. "Hey, Burrows. Party's over. Let's motor."

"Oooh, with a rebel yell," Burrows said to Eve. “Boy’s gone fierce. What's gotten into him?"

"Coco dumped him." Eve said. "Again."

Burrows started to take off his shoes. "I was just starting to enjoy myself."

Leo looked to Eve and back and spiked a thought at Burrows: *Letch.*

"Sure got the impression the President didn't like you." Burrows said.

"Yeah," Leo said. "He told Coco to stay away from me."

Burrows dipped his feet into the pool. "Can't blame him for trying to protect his daughter from the taint of mediocrity."

"The taint?" Leo said. He glared but gave Burrows nothing. The ends of his thoughts all pointed in. "Man, what's your problem?"

"Same as yours." Burrows said. "And my mother's not even the head of a Big-Time company." To his mind, the party had been worth it just for that bit of knowledge. DJ Leo Love was aka Leo LeMay, the son of Kendra LeMay, owner of Friend-Me Co., New West's biggest, most innovative and, therefore, controversial company which also had a huge factory out on the ‘Way. It made everything just a bit more interesting. Even more delightful was the fact that Ms. LeMay, who almost hadn't made the cut to stay in New West herself, and President Sherring didn't exactly agree on the definition of utopia and Sherring abhorred her son dating his precious daughter. Then there was Coco’s best friend and jealous rival, Eve, the daughter of the woman who'd been killed by a Friend-Me flower delivery. There were so many cracks in the walls, Burrows wasn't sure where to strike first to bring them down.

"Right. I don't think Friend-Me helps my case. My mother tends to piss people off. She's always pushing," Leo said. His gaze drifted up to the balcony. "I just don't understand why Coco listens to him. Her father said he was worried about her 'associations.' He wanted her options to be 'limitless' so that she could make choices without any 'hindrance.' Whatever. What's that about?"

"Um, hindrance, that would be you. Kid, you just don't fit into their plan. Don't they teach you history? That's New West's M.O., get rid of what you don't like, move on. Keep only perfection."

Leo stared down into the pool. "You can read it like that. But I'm thinking, it's simple: Coco's afraid to stand up to her dad. She just needs some time."

"Hey, feel free to draw out the pain," Burrows said, rubbing his thigh. "Always a good distraction. I ought to know."

"It worked last time," Eve said. She was sitting on the stairs now. Her arms wrapped around her knees. "She got back together with him in the fall."

"Oh, evil," Burrows said. "You let her play with you? You her cat toy?"

Eve and Leo went quiet, and Burrows followed their eyes and watched Coco stroll out of the house. Her rolling walk made a very fine silhouette.

"Hey guys," she said, as she unwrapped her towel and laid it across a chaise lounge. In the shadows, as she walked around the pool, the bikini ties that dangled down her thighs and swung at the back of her neck hinted at clothes. When she perched on the end of the diving board, the clinging bits of her swimsuit shimmered in the soft surrounding light. She stood with her heels raised, her calves long, a glimmer between her thighs. Light rippled over her torso. She unloosed her hair and the waves fell past her shoulders. She dove.

"I can see why you'd be tempted to be her whipping boy," Burrows said, while they watched Coco glide under the water towards them. "But you have to figure a girl like that will get what she deserves. Better."

Leo didn't respond. Not even with a thought. So, he agrees, Burrows thought.

Coco surfaced near them with Eve paddling in the water beside her. "Come on. Swim with us."

"No," Leo said.

"Don't be like that on my birthday," Coco said folding her arms over the ledge of the pool. "Swim. Daddy won't mind. You can even spend the night."

Leo turned away. "Yeah, thanks. I don't think so. It's past two and we've stayed plenty late. Burrows, let's get."

"You go," Burrows said, unbuttoning his shirt and dropping his pants to reveal black briefs. "I feel like plunging in. Now, I'm sure I can figure out some way to get home."

Burrows enjoyed the jolt of the girls' appreciation, his lean years looked good on him, as he jumped into the pool. He surfaced next to Coco. In the water, she glowed, just like the little girl from his drug-induced premonition. Was that about 15 years ago? Then, today, Constance Monica Sherring could be the one about to make minds explode.

He answered her unasked question. "The ink says, 'All haste is the work of the devil.' It means, wait for the right moment."

This could be it, he thought. Now that he knew what mattered most to the President of New West and most to Kendra LeMay, the owner of Friend-Me Co., he'd found what mattered most to him. There was no need to wait any longer. He dove underwater hiding his grin, watching the girl's legs churning the water. Here he was, a shark among seals.

Burrows took a trip with the kids: Grugel, Streker and Eve to the 'Way. There'd be no more dorm life for them. They brought back his Vary shop, a silver bullet of an R.V., and he had them set it up with all their electronics: Sync Chrome City on wheels. Come fall, he'd split his time between them at New West University and Lydia Streker in Deming, between Sync Chrome City and Psi-Aware, plotting the end of New West. It was cocky to think he could wage a one-man coup, but with time and technology on his side, he was pretty sure he could.

~ 10 ~

SYNC CHROME CITY: FRIEND-ME COURIER

"As misguided as the early attempts to access psychic potential through wideware, technological extensions to the brain, may have been it is true that an external focus or vision can help people tap their potential. Each person is unique however, and technology is just one of method of accessing our higher, connected selves. Just as individuals may more easily learn conventional, teleological information by visual, auditory or kinesthetic means, each person must identify their own best avenue into Psychic Space." — *Becoming Psychic 101, A History and a Primer*

Inside Varian Hall, the environmental psychology building, philodendrons with face-sized leaves climbed the walls of Dr. Robin Roundtree's office. The vines ran over the small skylight in the ceiling, their unfurled leaves casting faint green into the room. It accentuated the chlorophyll tinge of Professor Roundtree's hands and face that students said was due to the pitchers of Herbbank Farm alguice he drank during lectures. He stroked one of the waxy leaf tips that hovered along the trim line of his beard across his plump cheek. "It's a good plan. I have some projects in the greenhouse you can work on for elective credit this winter and in spring you should look into an internship."

Geneva nodded, peering down at the schedule she'd scrawled into her notebook. Despite her academic adviser's assurances, she wondered if she'd outsmarted herself packing all the rigorous classes for her last year at New West into fall quarter. Environmental Science, Natural Psychology and Chemicals and Physiology were all in her major, so she'd do well. But she wasn't Valerie; she'd have to work at it. If everything went as planned, she'd graduate at the end of this year. Still, she had no idea what came next. Between these classes and her shifts at Café Ruby's, she'd have no time to think about the future.

“You look pensive. Let us see," Roundtree turned and for a moment his head and shoulders submerged into the dark mass of leaves behind him. He returned balancing three books in the crook of his arm. "It seems I have extra copies of the required texts." He pushed them across the mahogany desktop. "You may borrow them."

On the cover of the thickest book, *Natural Psychology*, a smiling man and a woman read together beneath a cherry tree. It looked like most of the books in her major, but this one was by Professor Roundtree himself. Geneva placed a hand on top of the books and calculated that by giving her the books he'd just saved her a few months' work at the café. "Thank you, really, this helps so much!" She lifted them into her knapsack.

Roundtree's voice dropped into a Hort-Audible coo, a tone usually reserved for talking to plants. "You're a rare student, Geneva. I must nurture you with the richest soil just as I would any exotic orchidaceae. Ah, like our Nootka Rose-Orchis. Have you seen her in blossom? Extraordinary." Roundtree grabbed the edge of his desk and pushed his chair back into the vine-covered bookshelf. Leaves flopped over his pate, hiding the bald patch in the middle of his ring of red hair. "We're finished here, aren't we? Come with me to the greenhouse on your way out. I think I have something else to help you. I don't like to see you feeling the loss of *unus mundus* too deeply. You remember, *unus mundus*, from class?"

Geneva hefted her pack onto her shoulder and followed him. "The world?"

"The world mind: our connection to it and to nature," he said.

The loamy scent of Roundtree's office wafted behind him, replaced by traces of strawberry and hyacinth as they passed through the arching double-doors into the greenhouse. Geneva tied her jacket around her waist as he led her back to Special Projects.

"You've finally blossomed for us." Roundtree cooed over his pet orchid. The scent of wild roses flowed around the camouflage of his corduroy jacket. She peered around him at the Nootka Rose-Ladyslipper hybrid in full bloom. The center lips of its three-petal blossoms protruded. They were bright pink with deep red striations. "Oh, it's..." She reached for it and Roundtree stepped aside so she could cup one pink bud in her hand. "Lovely." It looked delicate as folded wet moth wings, but the petals were orchid thick.

She tried sub-vocalizing, "You're a beauty."

Roundtree cocked his head at her. "Yes, but it's a little further back. Hort-Audible should sound like two teak branches rubbing together." He placed two greenish fingertips along her throat and wiggled them up and down her windpipe. Her voice dropped an octave. "There, that's right. Perfect. Would you like to take her home with you?"

Geneva shook her head. "What? To the dorm? Oh, no. Not a special project."

Roundtree lifted the plant and placed its ceramic container in Geneva's arms. He continued to talk in coaxing Hort-Audible. "Oh, I think she's ready. Not all learning takes place in class, you know. There isn't a class for everything. Nootka can help you regain *unus mundus*. She will ease your sorrow. They say a feeling of oneness with the universe is the highest experience the brain has to offer. If this were any sort of real university, I would offer you that at least. But Nootka will have to do her best." The rose scent enveloped Geneva as the two-foot-tall plant trembled. Bits of blossom fell onto her head. She followed Roundtree out of the greenhouse as he cooed instructions. "Practically speaking, I want to see if she's ready for cooler temperatures and drier climes. I'd love to plant some of our starts outside in spring. Keep her in the bathroom at first and then gradually move her out. Keep a record and let me know how she does. Consider it an internship."

Outside the greenhouse, he resumed his normal human-audible tone. "So, you are on track to graduate." He pinched the bridge of his nose, the way he did in class to right himself when he realized he'd digressed. "Almost."

The rose-ladyslipper's thin thorns pricked Geneva's face as she jostled it.

"I was surprised to see you had an incomplete last quarter," he said. "So I wanted to make sure to mention it. You missed a final, was it? Just be sure to take care of that. I know you are still undecided about your future. Don't worry, you've time. I offer this advice: In looking for self, pay close attention to that which both attracts and repels. That's good. That's all," he concluded abruptly, muttering to himself as if he were checking boxes off of some internal list. "Now, do you need some help with that? Nootka is heavier than she looks and awkward to carry."

Outside Varian Hall at the top of the steps, Geneva glanced between the rose-ladyslipper stems in the direction of the bookstore. If it weren't for the rose, she'd probably go there to browse anyway even though she didn't need to buy books anymore. Everyone would be there. She'd thumb through some of the texts outside her major while the freshmen darted around. She maneuvered down the stairs, shifting the rose in her arms so she could catch glimpses of her tan sneakers landing on each step. Would she have seen Leo Love? Did the DJ dance in the music or art history aisles?

She rolled her eyes and blew a strand of hair aside. She could not believe she was still so pointlessly obsessed, even after her talk with Valerie. Before the dance she'd never seen DJ Love, not once in three years, not in class, in the crowded bookstore, or in passing on campus. Their paths didn't cross.

At the bottom of the steps, she turned toward her dorm, Inu Wood. Students' sandals slapped against the bricks as they passed in a blur of brown, green, and black backpacks. Crossing the open field, she remembered the one other time she had run into Leo and glanced to the side looking for him and his AeroFlux Butterflies. Then—squish—she stumbled forward as the ground went soft beneath her, burying her shoes in mud. She mucked back to the brick path. Of course, the soggy field was empty. No one was playing on the lawn today. As her toes turned icy inside her sneakers, she shivered and looked down at her jacket still tied around her waist. She shifted the weight of the smooth ceramic pot, pressing it into her side so that she held it as much with her torso as with her numb arm wrapped around it. The rose thorns poked her chest and shoulder through her thin T-shirt. The plant's leaves drooped. She hurried on, her shoes squeaking along the alameda of Japanese Fire Maples on the path to Inu Wood. These solitary trees had turned to pinkish orange spires. Others, on the hillside behind campus sharing oxygen with the evergreens, remained pale green or yellow.

At the dorm, she fumbled with the door, watching the plant's reflection in the glass window. In three years, she'd never thought to bring a plant back to her room. Valerie would have hated a pure pink rose, but she'd like the professor's vermilion orchid hybrid. The pot slipped under Geneva's arm. She clenched it to her chest with her limp arm but recoiled when the thorns stabbed at her throat. She spun on the slimy soles of her shoes and the pot slid away from her, crashing onto the brick. Its blossoms landed up against the door. Slim white roots showed through the soil surrounded by ceramic shards. "Oh no, the *unus mundus*," she moaned pushing soil over the roots. "Not air." She ran to her room. "Val, quick, I need a..." She grabbed a container from the kitchen.

Outside, she replanted the rose in a popcorn bowl. She carried it straight back to her bathroom. A few buds and leaves fell onto the bare countertop as she set it down and filled the sink with hot water. Steam rose along with the scent of crushed wild rose. The Nootka's branches were intact. Her choked voice fell naturally into Hort-Audible. "I'm not trying to kill you, special project. You're the world mind. Be strong."

The Nootka lifted the faces of its rare blossoms, but its leaves wilted and clung. Finally, she left it alone in the bathroom shutting the door behind her. "Val, did you see that? I almost killed my professor's plant."

Geneva dropped her pack on the bed, went to the closet to retrieve a sweater and stopped cold. Usually there was a sharp divide, where the light matte palette of her Face-in-the-Crowd outfits ended, and Val's shiny dark Plug-In gear began. Now the light blue wall continued past her clothes. The closet was half-empty. Val's clothes were gone.

Geneva darted to the bathroom and pushed open the door confirming what she'd observed, but hadn't registered, when she'd placed the plant down on the bare countertop. The bottles and vials that made up Valerie's collection of cosmetics and hair goo and dyes were also gone. She opened the cabinet. There was only her own wood-handled hairbrush, a jar of apricot kernel skin softener, some tubes of plant wax lip balm. All the glossy, slick products were gone except a short row of Wicked Woodsprite nail polishes and the container of Gator Tongue hair dye both gifts to her from Val.

Her breathing slowed when she saw the computer still hooked up in the living room because she could not think that Val would have left it behind. Beside it was an envelope propped against a glass of orange juice. Her full name was written across the front of it, tilted sharply left in Valerie's skinny script. The letter began without endearments:

Geneva,

I'm still on campus. But I've decided to live with some new friends at the Mansion. We came and got my stuff while you were out. I left the compu because your parents bought it and you might need it for class. The guys are a bunch of plug-ins and they have a good lab set up at the Mansion. We share interests. There's more to life than graduation, you know! But, yeah, don't worry, I will still try to get out of here....but, it's a big world out there. Anyway, I hope you get a cool new roömmate, someone you have a lot in common with, and I'm sure I'll see you around. I know this may sound cruel, but I've thought about it a lot, actually, and I think living with you made me a little crazy-girl. You don't seem to want to deal, so...I'm just getting out of your hair.

Still love your new red 'tails by the way, go gator-girl,

Val

Geneva clutched the letter and circled the dorm. "Your parents? A new roommate? See you around? This MAY sound cruel. MAY?"

She ended up in the bathroom, the letter clenched in one fist, yelling, "A letter? She leaves a fucking letter!" at the Nootka Rose, until she collapsed to her knees beside it overwhelmed by loss, *unus mundus*, and deep, insatiable sadness.

That afternoon, Geneva commandeered the computer. She'd stopped crying but she was still angered by Val's abrupt departure. Her legs splayed across the chair as she leaned into the screen. She stretched Valerie's custom virtual reality glasses apart to fit around her wider face and lowered them, wrapping herself in darkness. The silver letters Sync Chrome City flew into the left corner of her vision. This was where Valerie had been when she started screaming. "Since when is hanging out with Mansion Expansion freaks more important than graduation?" Geneva queried the dark.

A pixilated flashing skull appeared. Blue flames shot out of its eye-sockets. After the trill, "Ooh, la, la. Gunk-Secured content." the skull dissipated, and a series of crisp video images flashed. Geneva rolled her eyes and sat tight. Shaded gray tubes writhed on top of still gray, black, and white shreds. She tried to decipher the image and pinched her eyes shut as soon as it crystallized — maggots crawling on a chunk of rotting torso. The image repeated until she forced her eyes open and watched.

Then in a flash of blue, more words appeared silver and wavy as mirages: *I am not a rub on Aladdin's lamp.* More video followed. She identified it faster this time. The corpse of a young man shed strips of skin as he spun around his limbs lined with fishhooks. An electric crackle accompanied the words: *I do not exist for your entertainment.* Shades of pink filtered onto black-and-white, video-colored flesh still attached to the joints of protruding bones in a pile of bodies. Geneva's temples and fingertips tingled as an electronic buzz, feedback, amplified into a thumping pulse: *Prism people, fractured all.*

The music trailed away. Everything went white. Light glowed through the white letters: *Sync Chrome City, mind-expanding speakeasy. Operate EveryMan?*

"Wow, paranoid, much?" Geneva responded. Gunk was one thing, a half-assed security system that tested a user's will to sit through horrors in order to get to the main attraction. EveryMan, on the other hand, was serious neo-private security. It open sourced a user's data logs baring a computer's soul. In theory, it created a screen of privacy behind a thick fog of information. Valerie wasn't a neo-private, but she'd installed EveryMan and had it set on Deviant. While she was on Sync Chrome City, her computer would browse porn sites while broadcasting her files. Geneva twirled her fingers through her ponytails and set Every-

Man to Numbingly Normal so it'd hit only a random-selection of top-rated sites.

Submit to screening process?

She hesitated then clicked *Sync///chrome///city.* She had to find out what Val was into. Aluminum bubbled before her, words wavered across reflective surfaces: *Welcome to Sync Chrome City. Four questions secure your admission.*

Are you big?

Do you use it all?

Anything unusual today?

Giovanni Hastings?

Geneva typed yes four times smiling for the first time since she'd turned on the computer. Giovanni Hastings (it was also a book, a movie, and a short story) was her favorite game to play as a kid. It was about a nerdy child who grew up to rule the world, if you played it right.

Choose your method of locomotion: movement, people, computers, nature.

She hit nature in spite of her accident with the Nootka, the plant looked as though it had a fair shot at recovery, and a little clock appeared, and the machine began to whir. The time warp installation was the most devious security measure of all since most plug-ins abhorred wasting seconds. To sit still for it, Val must have been motivated. The delayed install took forever. While she waited, Geneva painted her toes Smashed Violets and fell into a reverie. She imagined DJ Leo Love's hands wrapped around her feet. He massaged her soles. Just as his fantasy lips touched the tip of her toes, a rap on the door made her kick back rocking the chair and nearly toppling.

"Friend-Me," the courier called. "You want this."

As she leapt to the door, she noticed she'd tracked mud all over the crème carpet. "Damn!"

The courier held a hand out from underneath a flap of the usual forest green cloak. A purple velvet box rested in the palm of his hand.

"You want this," he repeated, and she reached for it.

"Yeah, sure." She stroked the velvet box, listening to the whir of the computer as it loaded Sync Chrome City. The courier already had his back to her. She grabbed the felt of his cloak. "Hey, I wasn't actually using Friend-Me so you shouldn't be here. How do you know what I want if I'm not journalizing?"

He turned around and her eyes scanned over the Friend-Me badge on his breast, an official silver, equilateral triangle with thin green letters, or a perfect replica. She looked up at the courier's face and DJ Leo Love stared down at her just as he had from the ceiling of the Big Top at the Mansion Expansion dance.

He swept the formal Friend-Me bow, turned again, and walked away.

~ 11 ~

SYNC CHROME CITY: IN IVY LEAGUE

"As disturbed as I was by Burrows' threat to my daughter, it was this conversation that led me to act. He accused us of simply shutting out what we did not like—accurately—I thought. I then had to admit to myself that I was acting out of fear. Our minds could not and, in fact, would not, stay closed. I did not want to be held hostage by man or fear. And I wanted to prove him wrong." — *Save Giovanni: The Lost Men of the Psychic Wars*, S. Sherring

As C.G. Burrows stepped onto the New West University campus, he resolved to begin his conversation with President Sherring amiably. The irony of pretending to talk to the president on behalf of Psi-Aware was too rich. He could see the ivy-covered administration building, Old Main, across campus and guessed that the jade green climbing it was not alive. It looked natural from a distance, but as he approached he could see the ivy leaves were too regularly spaced. Unless trimming them was someone's full-time occupation, the placement of the vines was unnaturally perfect leaving an eight-inch margin around each window.

Real ivy, he assumed, would not be allowed in New West. It would grow in and force the bricks apart. The live stuff would have been poisoned and replaced. A tamed synthetic would impart the institutional aesthetic: We've been here forever (a lie) and there's no going back (a fantasy he'd dispel). Old Main itself, undoubtedly, was centuries old. Built long ago on the slope of an evergreen-covered hill, the building had probably withstood several earthquakes and might even remain standing after the fault line below split into the latest and greatest, overly anticipated, Northwest natural disaster. It was the recent incarnation of the college that needed the façade of ivy. New West University had been here less than a lifetime.

The steps of the building were close together and many. Four tiers of stairs and landings led up to the doors. Burrows stretched his steps over four or five stairs at a time. When he reached the top, he adjusted the collar of his jacket. Across campus, the emerald tip of a pyramid pierced the gray sky. The construction of Friend-Me Corporation's headquarters on the southeast corner of New West University was nearly complete. Nearby, lines of students filed out of the bookstore by the bay. He wondered if any of them knew the university was building a psychic research center for Friend-Me Corporation with their student fees. Probably not. They couldn't see more than the next red brick in front of them on their way to class. They couldn't think past their next big test. The greater consequences of the society they lived in eluded them. Only he was aware. He had to put a stop to it, turn the president against Friend-Me.

Burrows ground his knuckles into the scarred craters knotting at the base of his neck. His skin was still numb from when he'd yanked out the Vary implants. He entered Old Main. The administration building was filled with stale citrus-scented heat wafting off the polished pine bannisters. He walked three more flights of stairs to the President's Office where a blue uniformed New West officer, an older, stouter version of the campus security guards, stared sullenly. Burrows got no twinges from the guard and figured he looked passably benign. The officer, probably thinking only of his next pay raise, hadn't spared him a thought.

Similarly, the receptionist waved Burrows painlessly into the president's office. Inside Sherring stood, arms crossed, at his third-floor window in a parody of idle time. But Burrows could feel him busy, thinking, thinking migraines at him about their upcoming meeting. The information came at Burrows in onslaughts, streams of consciousness followed by sharp conclusions.

From Sherring he got: *Why is C.G. Burrows interested in Friend-Me Corporation's funding? What is his connection? What does he know? He's trouble.*

Burrows wanted to retreat from the pain, turn and slam the door behind him, but he'd lost the option to go back when he'd left his Vary Shop in the 'Way. Maybe other people didn't understand, but that's how it worked. When you decided to do something, it was done. You got one chance to choose and then it was over. There was no longer any choice involved. Teeth clenched; Burrows stepped further into the room. He held very still while he waited for the shards of information about himself to pass through. It was like running through a window in stop motion.

Sherring continued to project: *Burrows is: a counter-evolutionary who has been living on the Freeway running a Vary shop, an aspiring surgeon who lost his chance to go to New West University during the revolution, the son of wealthy socialites now living in C-Town.*

The president's objective focused analysis dealt Burrows near crippling mind cramps. Sherring knew a lot, but he was still seeking answers, asking questions, trying to gain an advantage. Burrows could see why the people in power were so stalwartly opposed to psychics. They didn't want to lose their edge. They were practiced at extrapolating from every bit of surface knowledge they could glean about a person: his personnel file, his history, his non-verbal cues. They used this expertise in human behavior to see inside other people's heads from the outside. They didn't want psychics to one-up their advantage. Later, when he was in less pain, Burrows would appreciate what he and Sherring had in common: They saw other people first as foes.

At last, Sherring turned and acknowledged Burrows.

"Mr. Burrows come on in, welcome, please have a seat," Sherring said, leaving the window and settling into his faux leather chair. "So, are you here to see me in my capacity as the President of New West or as the President of New West University?"

Meanwhile, he was assessing Burrows: *A nice suit. Conservative cut, not too stylish. He could still be his father's son. But don't jump to conclusions. The revolution created a rift. The beard is troubling. He's hiding something. Vary scars? Likely Vary scars.*

Burrows struggled to keep his forehead smooth, his reactions hidden, while the president's sharp interest cut across his brow. It was hard to be charismatic with a migraine. This guy was a real thinker. Burrows was glad he'd worn the suit. A nice suit went a long way with a guy like this. If there was one thing his telepathy had taught him, it was that appearances mattered. "I'm here to see the President of New West," he said.

Outwardly calm, the president showed stress in his stream of analysis: *No, this is not routine. He doesn't just have a complaint. He has an agenda. He already looks uncomfortable. He's not intimidated by me, and he's intense. The way he's standing, he looks like an enforcer. He looks like he's going to tell me what to do, not ask. At least he'll be direct. McDougall's on security duty today. He's reliable if this gets out of hand.*

Burrows lost his line on Sherring's thoughts for a moment, as he did when a person reached back into their own minds, remembering. If Sherring was already thinking about security, he realized he didn't have much time. The president returned abruptly from his inner voyage to pound Burrows with: *This is about the war.*

Burrows stumbled forward and slid into the chair in front of the president's desk. Even on the 'Way few had the courage to call what had happened war. People had to bleed in war. They had to die. The deaths of the revolution had been indirect. Among those hardest hit, it was called an opportunistic seizure, a grab. Everything had gone to hell and a few people had made good.

New Westians stuck to an official line. During the Greatest Depression, a group of people had banded together. They had foreseen the collapse of the markets. They had pooled their considerable funds, drawn a net around the institutions they cared about and protected them from ruin. Amid chaos, they had created New West. Everyone had had a choice to abide by the new government or to seek a way outside of it. The intellectuals had kept the transition orderly.

Burrows sat back in his chair. He uncrossed his legs and let his arms hang loose at his sides, giving the president cues that he was at ease. He had to strike a pleasant tone, establish some trust. He began by telling the man what he already knew. "After the revolution I never thought I'd come back. I opened a Vary shop on the Freeway." He stroked the side of his face. "I gave myself some pretty nasty looking implants. I was angry, I admit. I was a young man at the time. I didn't understand all the politics, didn't want to. I just wanted to go to my father's alma mater and study medicine to help people. But then a group of people, brilliant people by all accounts, for reasons I didn't understand, forced some changes. I didn't have a choice about that, but in doing so they denied me my opportunity, my education."

From the president, Burrow got an answering jab: *Yes.*

He had struck a nerve: New Westian guilt. He'd known it was there from his time around the electric blue pine-scented fire with the Freeman's, but he had not been sure it reached all the way to the top, to the instigators of oppression. They had made some cold-hearted calculations to attain a fresh start for their new utopia, but they had been aware of the costs. They had sacrificed a generation of others' children, banishing them to the old 'Way, in order to make a new way for their own progeny. Burrows understood that he was here taking action just in time. The original founders, with their historical memories, still had regrets. Saul Tillitat, for example, had taken his riches and retired to the island of La Merde in Pacifica so he would not have to see the refugees. Generation Utopia, when it took power, would not regret. Those kids: Leo, Eve, Coco, Grugel, and Streker. They would owe Burrows nothing. Now was the time to use this remorse to his advantage. "I never even had a chance to understand what their issues were," Burrows said. "Because I wasn't allowed access to the information and the knowledge they had. To them, it was a necessary sacrifice, but I saw myself as a casualty—of war."

Burrows paused. His use of the word, stolen from the president's own internal narrative, had the desired result. It got Sherring's attention and his empathy. He leaned forward, his arms folded over the papers on his desk.

Yes.

"Those combatants chased out people they didn't agree with. They chased my parents out because they didn't fit into their new perfect society. They chased me out onto the Freeway; a place they said wasn't fit for anyone. They condemned class warfare, but they reinforced that divide, that chaos. The way I saw it, at least the 'Way had freedom, autonomy, independence, privacy — a few of my values were intact out there. So, I left. But then, what? After all of the grief they caused, then what did the New Westians do after their so-called revolution?"

Burrows let the question sit. He watched Sherring's eyes. His head stopped aching as the president's thoughts wandered away from him again. Then Sherring returned and gave him: *I'm sorry.* He'd struck the guilt. Those two sharp veins striating his brain: I'm sorry. Now he'd mine it.

"Nothing. They rebuilt society exactly the way it was." Burrows took a deep breath. "Except with me and my family shut out of it. They ruined my life."

As he said that last though, Burrows instantly heard himself as a teenager, whiny and adolescent, and wished he could take it back. He guessed he'd overplayed his hand and was correct. The president watched Burrows steadily, his blue eyes barely blinking, but he'd become defensive and then bored: *Right, sir, this is the part where I let you talk. You talk, I listen. You go away happy, heard. You burn away your energy in words. You forget what you wanted. I'm a sounding board. I'm an apologist.*

Hearing the president had no patience for self-pity, Burrows switched tactics. "But I've forgiven them," he said, evenly, moving on, leaving all of the wrongs done to his family on the cutting room floor. "I'm thinking about the future. I've met some students, some very bright young minds, and I've found this Utopian generation to be appreciative and understanding. We have some things in common. I know that you played a key role in keeping things the way they are, from getting out of control. I'm worried about those young people. You share my concern, I know. That's why I'm here."

With that, he had Sherring's attention again, he got: *OK, now we get to it. Get to it.* He pressed his hands together fingertips intertwining. "Mr. Burrows, what can I do for you?"

Burrows glanced at the collection of photos of Coco in an assortment of silver frames on the president's desk. He saw Coco as a girl, her fine pale hair in faintly curling ponytails, sitting on the steps of Old Main; Coco, with curls cascading from underneath a red mortar board; and Coco lying on a beach, somewhere off-continent, surely, with pink sand and turquoise water behind her, her hair pulled back, resting her head in her hands and smiling. It looked like where she belonged. Did the president regret that he had stranded his daughter in the enclave of New West, that he had denied her the world he had always known and she only briefly? Or was he grateful that global events had intervened in her transition to adulthood (probably she would have chosen to study abroad) trapping her close where he could hold on to her childhood a little longer?

"You are a hypocrite," Burrows said. "And you are setting yourself up for a civil war. The Neo-Privates won't like to hear that the New West government is funding Friend-Me Corporation's psychic research. LeMay misrepresented herself. She's very anti-privacy. Her company is all about evolution. Its experiments are dangerous."

"There's nothing wrong with research," the president said.

"You know it's gone way beyond that. You have to end it."

"Mr. Burrows, let me speak candidly, since I see there is no point in trying to disguise what you already know. You are right, we have made discoveries. But," the president shook his head. "It would be wrong to end the experiments. I think this change in our society, in ourselves, is inevitable. I don't think we can stuff it back in the box, at this point, just because it makes us uncomfortable."

However, the president was not thinking what he was saying. Burrows could tell by the complete absence of pain, a total misdirection. He was lying. Burrows took a guess about what and went fishing. "But that's exactly what you are doing."

The sink line paid off, he got: *New West Mental Health.*

"Oh, that's rich," Burrows said, quickly making the connection. "The kids are manifesting psychic powers; you don't know why and you've created some kind of place to shut them away. That's New West's answer to everything, isn't it? Shut out what you don't like. Do you know what's causing the powers?"

He got nothing. The president didn't know. But Burrows had a good idea: Sync Chrome City. That was a bit of information he could use, later.

Burrows picked up the photo of Coco lying on the beach. "You're willing to sacrifice Generation Utopia? Her? Listen, Friend-Me is not the answer. You can't let these abilities develop.

It's not an option. Do you want your daughter to grow up in a world where anyone can get into her head? It's mind-rape."

From the president, he got: *Leave Constance out of this.*

Sherring's expression didn't change, but Burrows knew he'd struck a nerve.

"You'd better try. Friend-Me Corporation has been producing drugs. SLO-42 made with the son's oxytocin. Ever wonder, how your daughter became so interested in a loser like Leo LeMay? Drugs, maybe? Makes a lot more sense, doesn't it? If you let Friend-Me carry on with this 'research,' you'll give other people the power to control how your daughter thinks."

Burrows gripped the arms of his chair, half raising out of it, not caring anymore that he was beginning to make a bad impression: *An enemy we created in my office. Stop talking about Constance.*

The president stood up. "Put that down. His tall body shook as if the window had opened to let in the fall chill. "McDougall," he shouted, his voice hoarse. For a moment, Burrows' mind filled with flashes of red and a roaring crescendo. He rarely got emotions from people, just words and pain, but when he did, they came in a rush. Then the president switched off his anger and regained his logical pace of analytic thought: *Wait, Constance's 20th birthday. You were there. Why? How long have you known my daughter?*

Burrows took blows from Sherring's mental jabs. He dropped the photo of Coco. The metal frame clattered as it hit the floor, glass shattered, and shards slid over the polished marble. Burrows lowered back into the chair. It was all he could do not to clutch the sides of his head an instinctive reaction to the pain that he'd fought to suppress since childhood. It gave him away. It made him different. He sprang from his seat and lunged at the desk, placing his hands in the center of the president's desk to steady himself, knocking over Coco's graduation picture and the one of her as a toddler. The president didn't move. His eyes locked on Burrows. He landed a thought. It sunk in like a long, slow injection: *Stay away from her.*

It sent Burrows reeling. The chair's legs screeched against the floor as he stumbled over it. He staggered back and hit a wall of uniformed flesh. The New West officer clenched Burrows' shoulder. Burrows time was up, but he wasn't sure he'd gotten what he wanted. The president squared his shoulders and righted the picture of Constance.

"What about Friend-Me? Are you going to let them?" Burrows shouted as the officer jammed two sharp prongs into the small of his back.

"You're going to leave now," the guard said.

"Your daughter. I'll drug her myself," Burrows said calling the president's attention to him. "What are you going to do about LeMay?"

The president took the bait and Burrows got: *Friend-Me will have to go.*

It was the response he had wanted. He sank into the officer's grip.

"Did you hear that threat, McDougall? Mr. Burrows will be ending his visit now. Please provide him an escort."

The officer piloted Burrows into the elevator, kept the taser on him all the way down and then shoved him out the front door of the building. As Burrows stumbled down the steps propelled by the officer's grip, he kept his eyes trained on the tip of the Friend-Me pyramid. The sides of his face pulled taut. The scars beneath his beard stretched tight. They burned with the sensation of a numb limb waking when he smiled.

The guard released him at the bottom of the steps, where 30 members of the Deming Psi-Aware chapter hoisted yellow and red signs: Psi-Now. Burrows raised his voice to address them. "No progress. We're at an impasse. The protest continues. The president refuses to see reason. If non-psychics don't take us more seriously there will be civil war."

Behind him Burrows heard a soft but steady snikt, snikt. As he watched the protesters mount the steps, he saw a slim figure dangling beside one of Old Main's windows. A man in brown overalls and a green painter's cap was holding a shiny pair of shears. He was trimming the live ivy. It occurred to Burrows, for an instant, that he didn't know New West as well as he thought.

Burrows was relieved fall classes were starting. The Utopian kids had almost unlimited reserves of adulation.

Streker: *Whoa, man, I'll just get out of your way.*

Grugel: *Dude, you can really work it.*

Eve: *So interesting.*

There was only so much of that he could take within the confines of mobile Sync Chrome City, the cramped R.V. outfitted with the kids' tech. With summer over, the students fell back into their routines and self-absorption and gave him more mental space. He had them pegged now. They manufactured drama-laced lives fueled by simple motivations.

Streker: Love

Grugel: Money.

Eve: Love *and* money.

Security. That was the prize they were after, at the root of all their angst, but it was impossible to get at by thinking small. So, he'd get them thinking big. Get them ready to take it up a notch. Grugel said he could have the tech ready in time for New Years. He'd blow the lid off Sync Chrome City.

~ 12 ~

SYNC CHROME CITY: SYNC CHROME CITY

"The physical and chemical effects of the psychic state are well documented. Meditation stimulates the alpha waves in the brain and the release of the amine, serotonin, and peptide, oxytocin. Psychically active minds achieve a state of internal synchrony. All nerve cells fire simultaneously. However, the psychotropic nature of the experience remains unexplained. The feeling of interconnectedness with the universe is similar to the effects of psilocybin. Our empathic connection to all surrounding minds, our creation of an external neural net, our Infinite Lattice, our Connected Ego, remains a mystery." — *Becoming Psychic 101, A History and a Primer*

Geneva shoved the purple box into her pocket and followed the green cloak of the Friend-Me courier. All summer DJ Leo Love had been in her mind manipulating lights and sound behind her eyes and delivering kisses in dreams and daydreams. She'd wondered if she'd ever see him again. Then he was at her door, a Friend-Me Courier. How many times had he delivered to her? How many times had she passed him on campus and not even noticed? Maybe Valerie was right. She wasn't paying attention. What else was she missing? She'd only noticed the DJ when it had been impossible not to, when he'd been swinging over her like a star.

There was no guarantee she'd see him again. She wanted to know who he was, where he lived, and how she could find him again, so she followed. It was a drunken impulse; hope drowned her inhibition but without the heady time warp. She didn't have seconds to reconsider. She just went, trailing behind him so that she wouldn't be seen, tracking him in his green cloak across campus.

There was an oceanic roar of chanting as Leo headed towards Old Main. On the lawn in front of the administration building she could see the crowd of protesters had grown. They were 30 or more strong waving signs and yelling "Psi-Now!" in unison and there was a smaller group holding up pictures of sad-looking lab rats. Geneva shied away from them afraid that they would turn to her en masse. But Leo stopped in front of them. If he turned now, he'd see her standing behind him, obviously going nowhere, following him. She glanced up at the ivy-covered building and veered up the steps ducking into the mob for cover.

Leo stripped off his cloak revealing a white T-shirt and long forest-green pants. He sprinted at a group of students jousting with live steel on the lawn. He finished his dash with a forward handspring, and he landed in front of them.

"Leo!" the fencers bellowed. One tossed a flail. Leo caught the hilt, yawped, and parried. The others grabbed their swords and engaged. From the steps, Geneva gawked. With some quick thrusts and a deft lunge, Leo disarmed his opponent and held the tip of his sword to their chest. His opponent dropped to a knee. Brandishing the sword, Leo pivoted towards the steps, nodded his head and yelled, "Geneva."

She shrunk into the crowd, but it was no use trying to hide now.

"Geneva," he yelled again looking right at her. "It's you right? From the dance."

She waved a hand in Leo's direction. She hoped his next question wouldn't be, "Why are you following me?"

He introduced her around again to Grugel, Streker, and seven others who looked vaguely familiar from the Mansion Expansion dance. This time she got all their names: Chris, Michael, Don, Eli, Tod, Roger, and Andrew. "We all live in The Mansion. We were just about to go get some food. Do you want to come?"

They went down the hill to Ruby's, of course. They crowded into to the biggest round booth in the back, the one the waiters called The King's Table when the tips were good or the 'Way Back Booth when they weren't. Geneva ended up in the middle of the ring of loud college friends across from Leo. They were a classic case of big eaters, bad tippers. She wondered who would be serving them.

She was surprised when Gary the owner came over to take their orders and felt a flash of guilt that Ruby's was so short-staffed. "What will you have?" he asked.

She shrank in her seat. His eyebrows arched when he saw her. "Hey..." he was about to say something embarrassing, then caught himself. He took down the orders for burgers and fries. "Just tea for me," she said. He winked at her.

"So, I'm thinking it's time we break out, do something big," Grugel said. "I'm working on some code to spark the process. We haven't even touched capacity. It'd be like adding fuel to the fire."

"We'll have a party for the roll out," Streker said.

"Are you talking about Sync Chrome City?" Geneva asked.

"You a citizen?" one of them asked.

"No, I was trying to enter. I got interrupted."

"This'll be beyond you then," Grugel said. "We're talking about an amped up version."

The food arrived. The friends dove in. Geneva sipped her tea and tried not to get caught staring at Leo. Then Gary returned and set a head high sundae down in front of her. They all looked up as he pushed it across to her and handed her a silver spoon with a curled handle. It looked long enough to dip down through all the layers of creamy whip to the ice cream below.

"I didn't order this," Geneva said.

Gary smiled and leaned against the table. "This contraband isn't on the menu—yet." He winked. "I'm not leaving until I see the look on your face when you taste it."

Drizzled over the top of the sundae were sunshine swirls of orange and yellow sauces. A sweet citrus scent rose off the sundae. The others stared at her as she lifted a spoonful. It tasted like not-quite orange and lemon, the flavors were infused with some far away tang. The nuts sprinkled on top were unusual too. They were crisp instead of crunchy, and lightly oiled. The best part was the ice cream itself. It was a smooth confection of an unfamiliar flavor, fresh, new, exotic—not butter cream or maple or strawberry—that reminded her of longing.

She took another bite and then passed it down the table. "Everyone's got to try this."

Gary leaned across the table and whispered. "That's toasted coconut ice cream topped with mango and passion fruit syrups and crushed macadamias. You couldn't get further off-continent. That's what you've been missing. That's what all us old chefs have been talking about, the paradise outside New West. I figured I'd give Geneva here a taste since her mother's helping to negotiate the trade with C-town. Who knows how they are getting these tropical goods, but that's what we used to call utopia, the places where you could get fruits like these."

By the time the sundae returned to Geneva only two melted lumps of white ice cream remained. Now that, with Gary's help, she had the friends' attention, she asked, "After this, show me Sync Chrome City?"

Back at the Mansion, they took her into the City. They brought her to one of the fishbowl dorm rooms outfitted with a panel of screens and closed the blinds. Geneva sat on the end of a bed next to Streker with a row of his friends alongside and another across from her on the other bed all wearing black razor glasses. Leo perched on a swivel chair next to her and handed her a pair. She pulled her ponytails out from under the sides of the glasses as she put them on.

At the front of the room, Grugel knelt beneath a screen and tapped electronics. The silvery equipment glowed. The onyx screens glimmered. The words Sync Chrome City ran across the largest screen in tall, stretched type. She gripped the edge of the bed.

"Let's have some music," one of them said, and from under the bed the drum-bound strings of Giovanni Hastings Musica began to flow.

The tat-tat-tat of Grugel's rapid typing continued. "I'll get us in quick, go around all the security straight to the source," he said.

When the first security flash appeared—swollen red and purple-banded worms writhing through torn gray flesh and bandages—Geneva squeezed her eyes shut. The tapping quickened. She peeked between her fingers, and they were blowing by slick, heavily-coded decoy sites: the towering black spires of Sin Rom City and the deep silver pools of Synchronicity. She opened her eyes wide when they landed on the doorstep of the real Sync Chrome City—a flat screen with the four questions: Are you big? Do you use it all? Anything unusual today? Giovanni Hastings? They ran across the screen in a textbook font on matte black with a flashing green prompt. But there was more. Geneva felt she could scoop her mind out and squeeze it in looping spirals onto that black space communicating with the masses like icing on cake. She felt that she could go into to the net scape of Sync Chrome City but didn't understand what it meant.

"OK, I see it. But what is it, exactly?" she asked.

"Yaaaah, it's the same as utopia. Nothing really," Grugel said. “No place. Like where we’re going Gen Utopia. The big zero.”

"It's true," Streker said leaning in, breathing against her shoulder. "That's what utopia really means. The guy who came up with it was being sarcastic."

Geneva lowered her glasses.

"What? Don't look at me like that," Streker said. "I'm a philosophy major. It was Sir Thomas More. 16th Century."

She rolled her eyes. "Jeez, at least with environmental psychology I can work in a greenhouse. What are you going to do with that?"

Streker shrugged. "I'm doing this. It started as a social network, some Psi-stuff I bought into as a kid, some games, just playing at trying to expand each other's minds—but it was all kind of flat. Then I met Grugel here and he advanced the tech. He hit on some juice. A formula that, like, sparks the mind, taps the wires. It's a trip. You'll see."

He watched her as he spoke, his eyes staring into hers. His hair gleamed blue in the low light reflected off the screens like dark wavy leaves. She raised her glasses again. "So, you're kidding me, Grugel's probably the only one of us here with a viable major..."

"Computer science," Grugel said. "But I haven't been sweating it. This makes bank. Don't worry, first ride's free."

Beside her Leo swiveled in his chair, his vinyl pants making swish-stick sounds. "And I have a decent shot with my music. Not that some people think so. Just take her in. Get her past the bouncer."

Streker turned to her. "The questions are just a screening system. We didn't want to let in people who couldn't get it. If they can't experience that space out there, this looks lame. They'd talk smack about Chrome City, say it sucked."

Leo: Swish. Stick. Swivel. "The questions don't really matter. You get in, if you're ready. It's a trigger."

Under the glasses, Sync Chrome City expanded like an oil slick, colors swirling. Geneva forced her eyes from the screen and lowered the glasses again. The room was still there. Its black walls a fuzz-edged enclosure.

"Kind of like hypnosis." Geneva raised the glasses. "Ready."

Streker talked as he tapped through the answers. "The questions refer to your mind and your self-perception. Are you large? Do you contain multitudes? Or are you a lone ranger? Most people, if they are paying any attention to what's going on outside themselves, have unusual experiences that they can't explain."

"The brain is wider than the sky," Geneva said.

"A nice way to put it," Streker said.

“Dickinson,” Geneva said, feeling a bit silly she’d got the quote off a poster, but Leo’s friends seemed very intellectual, and she wanted to keep up. When he got to the last one, Geneva put a hand on his shoulder. "Giovanni Hastings? What’s that mean?"

"Yaaah, goody-goody," Grugel said.

Streker shrugged. "Oh, nothing. Really. Nothing. I just like him."

"No. It's cool, really." Leo said, swiveling in time to the music. "It fits with what people can experience here. Being greater than they are, unexpected world rulers in a way like Giovanni. Maybe that's what our generation is all about really. Forget Gen Utopia. We should call ourselves Gen-Giovanni."

"Yeah. My kind of my hero." Streker said. He tapped again and they arrived at the last screen. It looked like the others but read, "Choose your method of locomotion. Movement. People. Nature."

"This is the key. It tells us the best way to tap a person in. What did you choose? No, I know..."

"Nature," he and Leo said together.

“The environmental psychology major,” Streker said.

The final keystroke clicked, and Sync Chrome City went live. "I'm a big kid," Streker said, as the blackness morphed to jungle night green.

Vines looped out of the darkness and unfurled body-sized leaves. Juices coursed, slurping through thick translucent veins. Geneva tried to lower her glasses with her palms, but she lost track of her hands. The plants pressed against her intertwining with the purple cords in her head.

"Rocket, we're in." Streker said.

Inside Sync Chrome City, on the periphery of her own perception, Geneva could see the vines pulsating as multicolored laser beams or surging with corpuscles as interwoven red veins. Those were Leo's and Streker's interpretations of the experience: movement and people. She tried again to move her hands and this time her fingers fluttered like the tips of fur-lined leaves. Streker leaned against her, his shoulder tree trunk firm against her knee. He whispered, his voice rustling through the vines, shaking the leaves. "Feel them," she heard him say and then felt the echoing press of his thoughts: *Feel them.*

She sighed and her hands dropped into her lap as she became aware of the other minds. There were less than a hundred of them connected to Sync Chrome City. They dangled together like ripe fruit in the space. She pressed a thought out to them— *Hello.*—and the vines rose and fell, rippling from 'h' to 'o'. The minds bounced as she ran her thoughts along them, down the vines, touching the tops of each one. One by one, she met the people connected to Sync Chrome City. The seven in the room and other students at New West, the same faces she saw in passing each day lugging packs on campus. But they came at her in three-dimensional layers. Instead of eyes and ears and mouths, she identified them in a glance by experience, personality, and injury. He played the oboe, had grown up on the 'Way, rose to meet her, mind open wide, with high levels of serotonin afraid of very little since his father had abused him. She studied biochemistry, had been off-continent and spoke Chinese, and stayed deep inside herself with low levels of serotonin used to being sheltered. They danced up to her freed in this space to be themselves. Geneva knew these students. There was more to know. And she knew as much as she needed: *It's an external neural net.*

Streker: *One big party. And everyone knows everyone. Really knows them.*

Leo: *A group of people with something in common who'd go to great lengths for each other, a reunion.* His laughter thumped giddy through the greenery and Geneva heard it pounding as though it came from within her own heart.

The circling vines swelled looping over each other. Geneva mingled. It was like being at the Mansion Expansion dance where she'd been fascinated by the people around her, except that she was one of them now. She could stay here, forever, in their company.

Hours later, Leo lifted her glasses and helped her off the bed. She staggered lightheaded; her legs numb. The others were still, motionless under their black razor glasses. They looked strangely unlike themselves now placid and uniform in plug-in clothes, now that she'd seen them vibrant inside Sync Chrome City and gotten to know them. She was glad she'd been able to meet them in person, before getting to know them in Sync Chrome City and that she'd had her first experience in the city in the Mansion with people nearby rather than all by herself in her dorm room at Inu Wood. It dulled the shock of leaving the City and finding herself suddenly alone, to see them there and have Leo nearby.

"I think that's enough," Leo said. "You get the picture. It's pretty addictive."

"Yeah," she nodded. "Is it dangerous?"

"Anything is—in excess. I mean, for one, you have to remember to eat and stuff."

He walked her back to her dorm. She felt like she knew him very well now and it was comfortable to be beside him and natural to slip her hand into his. But at Inu Wood, she realized she'd forgotten her passkey, locked herself out of her room when she'd chased after him, Leo Love the Friend-Me Courier.

"Come on back to the Mansion, sleep at my place," he said.

She twirled her hands through her ponytails, uncertain what he was asking.

"Just sleep," he said.

And she did lie beside him that night, but she didn't sleep much. The dorm bed was narrow and covered with worn flannel sheets. She drew next to his warm curled body and after inhaling his scent, sugar-dipped pine, began thinking about how he had swayed over her at the dance. She memorized the sound of his steady whistling breaths and marveled at his stillness. Her lips brushed once against his back covered by a thick cotton T-shirt. She awoke from a dream remembering a pattern of green and blue-green and purple-green shades laced through the treetops below. She'd been sitting cross-legged beneath an evergreen tree. Then needles clattered down beside her, and she rose into the air, arms outstretched. The sun on her back made her afraid to fall like Icarus, so she skimmed low like a hawk over the forest listening to whispered voices below saying unfamiliar, but potent, words. She felt tangy, light and delicious as an off-continent sundae.

Like that, she became a regular at the Mansion. She didn't spend much time on Sync Chrome City, instead hanging out with Leo in real life listening to him play music and watching him work his Sound-Wield set. Coco and Eve avoided her making it awkward. Leo caught her watching Coco once. "Yeah. She's cool. She's very confident. Sometimes I think you can keep more hidden if you make people think you're giving everything away."

Now that she was part of the Mansion crew, Geneva could keep tabs on Valerie, who spent most of her time in the Sync Chrome City room. But mostly she was absorbed with Leo. He seemed to live a whimsical, spontaneous life the opposite of her habits. Although she'd freely shared her mental space in her Friend-Me journal, she'd never made a physical connection until the night Leo embraced her. It felt good, but it couldn't last.

She hadn't known for sure until she'd had sex with Leo, and then, lying in his arms, afterward, it had been obvious.

"You still love her," she'd said.

"Coco." Leo nodded. He'd placed his hands on her shoulders. "Honestly? Yeah. Even though she just gave me up like that, without a fight because of her father. I think if I had the chance..."

Geneva had known what he said was just true, he wasn't trying to hurt her. She wished that she were a different person. Val often said "all's fair in love and war," but Geneva didn't believe it. There were too many excuses in the world to pretend like other people didn't exist. Love couldn't be one of them. When Coco wanted Leo back, she wouldn't stand in her way. Coco and Leo looked like they belonged together and all the Mansionites had enjoyed the couple's radiance. But it was worth it to hang around in the meantime and be near Leo while she could. She just tried to remind herself, it wouldn't last. She thought if she was logical about her decision, it would hurt less when it ended. When it did, she told herself that was true.

It happened as fall quarter came to an end. Coco made up with Leo and Geneva just stopped going to the Mansion. She spent a lot of time in the greenhouse, avoiding going back to her empty dorm room. She hadn't gotten a new roommate. Screw that, it was her senior year, she wasn't taking the time to get to know some stranger's quirks. She put in extra time at Ruby's to pay for a single room. Valerie had been a total plug-in last year, so she'd figured living alone wouldn't be that much different. It was.

She couldn't keep up with all that had been happening. She felt like a leaky vessel. She couldn't seem to get to class on time. No matter how hard she tried, she got to class later and later. She'd begun to make ridiculous excuses, which her professors believed. Then she felt guilty. Her mind couldn't keep up with the world and she began to lose her physical grip on it too. She kept losing things just when she needed them: a stylus, a disk, her passkey. She'd never realized how many separate, small objects she had to keep track of in order to live, until she began to fail at the task. She'd taken to wearing pocketful plug-in clothes, which helped, until she put on a clean outfit and left everything she needed behind her in a dirty wad on the floor in Inu Wood.

Once in early winter, she stopped by the Mansion. She wanted to check in on Val, see the guys, and maybe Leo, too, but she didn't have a passkey to the fishbowl dorm because she wasn't a resident. She spotted Eve going in and called after her, but Eve never looked around and pulled the door tight behind her. Geneva realized she'd lost not only Leo, but her access to the Mansionites and Sync Chrome City, too.

~ 13 ~

SYNC CHROME CITY: DA LIME

"It had become shamefully common to experiment with the brain chemistry of our children. We medicated them for perceived mental defects. We did so out of guilt. We were so sure the rigors of our modern society had left them diseased and corrupted. We mistook their terror and unrest for teenage spiking hormones aggravated by drug use, lack of sleep, and poor diet and exercise. It never occurred to us that while we were in shock, they were evolving." — *Save Giovanni: The Lost Men of the Psychic Wars*, S. Sherring

On New Year's Eve, Geneva went to the Mansion again. Tense, lonely, she wanted to catch Valerie before she went out, if she was going out. She peered into the fishbowl and knocked when she saw Eve. This time Eve opened the door, but she didn't step aside. She was dressed for a plug-in party. She had on the same outfit she'd worn at the Mansion Expansion dance, a short black top that showed off her red-gold Vary quills with a flowing black skirt, and she'd taken some time to pin back her masses of wiry curls.

"I just stopped by to say hi," Geneva said. It was stupid to explain. She had every right to visit the Mansion. She hadn't seen Val for months, but Val was still her sister, still her best friend.

Eve glared. "Well, no one's here."

She could tell from her tone that Eve probably thought she'd come here looking for Leo. It wasn't a bad idea. He was usually in the center of everything anyway. "What about Leo?"

"Probably with Coco," Eve said and started to close the door. She was still playing watchdog.

"Great, I'm just looking for Val," she said.

She was ready to give up, when she saw Leo coming down the hall. He saw her right away, waved and Eve stepped aside as if she'd just opened the door.

"Hey Leo," Geneva said trying to sound nonchalant but working to get out the words. Leo wore black, too, loose pants and a flowing shirt that made his upper body look broad. She'd forgotten how nervous he made her. She couldn't help thinking of him as DJ Leo Love. Val would have mocked her with, "fan-girl," if she'd known, and Geneva would have deserved it. Looking into Leo's thickly lashed dark eyes made her feel pathetic. She wanted to curl up and cling to him like frazzled lint. She shook her head and looked around. "Where's everybody?"

"Mostly in VR," he said.

He meant the guys she hoped, not Val. Months later, she still had a fear of virtual reality headsets. "On New Year's Eve?"

"Yeah, yeah. It's some kind of online party. Some kind of launch. That's why everyone stuck around campus. They could have done it from home, but they wanted to experience it together," Leo shrugged. "Everyone's all geeked out about the Bonfire."

"I thought I'd noticed a lot the Mansionites around for winter break," Geneva said. "Val isn't with them, is she?" She winced at the way the words came out, brusque and high. She sounded like her mother checking up on Val.

Leo shook his head and Geneva relaxed.

"What about you? The Bonfire?" she asked.

"No, I plan to check out a live action party," he said. "There's a place, Sync Chrome City on wheels. Do you want to go?"

He sounded so casual. But it wasn't. She wanted to check up on Val, but she didn't want to crowd her. She wanted the chance to be near Leo, but she didn't feel like competing for his attention. He seemed to want her to go. But Eve, sullenly standing by, obviously didn't. And where the hell was Coco?

She spun her fingers through her hair, twisting her ponytails into curls. She really had come straight from the greenhouse. She was in her old Face in the Crowd clothes and probably smelled like soil. "Um, I'm not really party ready."

"Val and Coco are already there," Eve now volunteered. "A nice ride came and picked them up an hour ago."

Eve had meant that to be discouraging, but that settled it. Geneva wanted to see Val. It had been so long. Still her voice wavered, "But yeah, OK."

They piled into Eve's Cadillac, sitting up in front, because the back was cluttered, filled with big piles of dark stuff. They squeezed in together, thighs pressed, Geneva in the middle and too aware of their legs touching on both sides. Eve reached over her, pushing Geneva's knee aside to crank up the heat and fiddle with the defroster. Leo began to riff in his smooth voice, dropping in some eerie minor chords. As they headed out on the highway, encircling New West, it started to snow.

They drove a long way out of town and eventually pulled into a trailer park landscaped with weeds that were gathering snow. Geneva sat forward. The worry she had pushed aside earlier had crept back into place on the drive over and she was anxious to see Val. They drove to the back of the park and pulled into a lot that had a bit higher gravel-to-weed ratio in front of a crooked trailer. There were few lights. The nearest trailers to the side were aways off, and beyond the tilting trailer there was nothing but black. The trailer was on the edge of a marsh, or most likely, from the smell creeping into the Cadillac's vents, a landfill. As Geneva scooted out of the Cadillac, one whiff of the air, heavy with decomposition, resolved any doubt.

The trailer looked all the more shoddy next to the swank black Mercedes parked in front of it. Walking by, Geneva jumped back as she spotted red and orange flame emblems on the car's bumper, warning of a fire alarm system. She didn't want to get charred.

Leo put a hand on her back, "Don't worry, it's not that sensitive."

Geneva leaned into the tingling sensation of his palm wanting the touch to be more than it was, coincidental. "Are those even legal, the flame ones?"

"I think so," Leo said striding ahead.

As she approached the trailer, Geneva recognized Giovanni Hastings Musica, drumbeats electronically fused with shrieking strings. Inside, it was pitch black, but as her eyes adjusted, she saw glints of silver. Expecting a dive, Geneva thought the walls were covered in aluminum cans until she could see well enough to discern the high-end electronics. They were wall to wall, top to bottom. Layers of slim Plug-In gadgets were packed next to lab equipment and Vary Home Surgical Kits. One of the newer Sound-Wield Sets took up a lot of space in the back. A monitor lined one side of the trailer with one big velvet armchair at a console in front of it. It was a small but spendy space. There had to be a good air-filter system among the tech, because the air wasn't tainted like the outside. It smelled of cinnamon.

She spotted Val in a corner talking to a tall man who looked vaguely familiar. Val looked comfortable enough, leaning against a paneled side of the trailer, nearly invisible in all black, except for the luminescent blue drink in her hand. Geneva waved but got no response. The man's huge shoulders probably took up most of Val's view. She twirled her ponytails as she took a better look at him. His age set him apart from the crowd. He had a beard, a bald head; a heavy jacket pulled up around hunched shoulders, and a rough look. In that respect, he fit in better here than she did. She looked down and noticed that her chest was glowing, her unobtrusive white T, gone disco in the black light. She pulled her brown jacket around her and held it in place with crossed arms.

Most of the party people, in black Plug-In clothes, sat on cushions strewn across the floor. Coco was in the middle of them dancing in a short gold dress to the Giovanni Hastings hit. The lead singer had an androgynous voice that dipped drum deep and then rose stringed up. Geneva listened carefully trying to discern if the music had real voices and instruments or if it was completely melded synth. As the final chorus of the song played, everyone mouthed the lyrics, while reaching for Coco's swaying Tamarind tail, "Intertwining fingers on your soul, invade your heart and make it whole, harvest Sin and Chrome and Sea. Come and intertwine with me." Along with everyone else, Geneva watched Coco twirl to the last notes of the song, spot Leo, and grab his arm. Her tail swatted Geneva's nose as she spun round. Leo sat in the center of Coco's circle. As she finished her dance, she sunk to the floor beside him. Her tail curled around his leg, her bare knees touched his, as she threw her arms around his neck.

Geneva decided to take off her wet, muddy boots before she destroyed all the silk pillows. She knelt to unlace them, wondering what she was doing here. Nothing had changed. Leo and Coco were still together, and she was out of place as usual. Val seemed to be getting along fine without her, too. She was listening with an animated expression to the tall man. Geneva had the impression—the cinnamon scent, Val's relaxed demeanor—that she'd been here a few times before. Worrying about Val was just paranoid. She shook her head and stumbled as she yanked off her boots. A hand reached down and righted her.

"Welcome, my lady." Her rescuer — a gangly Plug-In — bowed sweeping the long jacket he wore behind him. He took her hand, held it to his lips and kissed it. His thin lips warmed the back of her hand. "Always nice to meet a new lady. I'm Streker."

She blushed; glad it would be hidden in the reflected glow of her shirt. "We've met before."

Streker cocked his head at her and blinked both eyes, one blue, one brown. His face had slightly distorted features, like he'd been punched a lot. His look told her he didn't remember. She took a step back to make room, but his coat still brushed against her. He reached into it and held up a test tube filled with glowing liquid. "Some Lime for the lady?" His half smile revealed crooked eye-teeth. He tipped a silver syringe into the tube filled it and then, “Last chance before we start the festivities."

She shook her head.

He placed the tip of the needle in the corner of his eye. "Suit yourself. I'm your host, not your feeder."

She turned away to miss the injection and when she turned back, he was staring at her with glowing green eyes and grinning.

"Do you know why they call me Streker?" he said. "Because I let it all hang out. No secrets. I expose all my data to everyone. Of course, I've got nothing to lose. But it's what I do, shock people out of their little worlds within. Ask me anything. Ask me."

"So, you're a true neo-private. Well, what's your take on Giovanni Hastings?"

"My favorite story."

"No, Musica. Are they are really a band?"

"No, just some local synth pretending to be imported from down the ‘Way. You?"

"I think it's a band. I want it to be anyway. There's too many different sounds and it has a raw feel. Those haunting voices, I want them to belong to people. Someone I could meet."

"I know what you mean, but there's really good synth out there."

She nodded toward the older guy. "What about him? Who's he?

Streker looked sad. "Our star power, Burrows, the host of *Kill-Giovanni.*"

"Kill who?"

"Kill Giovanni Hastings. It's kind of a cult site. A parody, you know, of the book. Grugel and Eve met him on the 'Way last summer, when Eve got her quills."

Geneva clutched the ends of her coat over her glowing midriff and shivered. She loved the Giovanni Hastings story and its odd little hero, a kid with supernatural powers who conquers the world. Kill Giovanni Hastings? Who would want to do that?

C.G. Burrows watched the college kids lounging around the trailer injecting drugs into their eyes. Grugel waved a fluorescent green syringe in front of him, "Hey, why don't you give this a try. It's a party. It's New Year's Eve."

Burrows rolled his eyes. The kid was trying to pressure him, unbelievable.

"I know you're more into the meditation thing like Strek's mom. But it just gives you a different perspective. It really works." Grugel nudged him, made twin pistols with his hands and shot an arc of imaginary bullets around the room. "Don't you wonder which one of them is the source?"

Burrows didn't. Grugel gave him the name: *Leo.* But he didn't get why Leo's head was in demand. If he was going to shoot up with one of these kid's personalities, he'd pick one of the girls, Coco probably. She looked like something he'd like to get inside: shapely curves that moved well, undulating, with warm skin and hair that glowed. Her dress was simple, well-cut. Even flirtatiously short, it was classy. He'd watched her dancing earlier, they all had, a potent promise of warmth and softness. She gathered their attention and radiated it back like a power source. Sex. He got that from her. Instead of a sharp pain in his head, it came like a low throb in his loins. OK, not really. Wishful thinking. He got: *Checking me out?* He got: *Who are you?* Anyway. That chemistry, that perspective, might be fun. But, Leo, hell, he looked like one of the dimmest bulbs here. The way Leo kept smiling at him, at everyone, maybe he had no thoughts at all. He certainly wasn't giving Burrows anything. The guy hadn't given him a second thought or a first for that matter. Nothing. He'd never run across anyone who didn't strike him at all.

Meanwhile, Coco was hanging all over Leo. Another girl, who didn't have a chance, was looking at him longingly and kids were shooting him up left and right. Burrows was annoyed. He'd been hanging around these kids too long. They were starting to get to him. Their heads were textbook-laden, introspective. This party was bringing back distasteful memories. He'd been denied a chance at college by these kids' parents. Damn revolutionaries. He didn't need to fit in. He needed to relax. He had a plan, and it was coming together. He could probably relax a little, "OK, yeah. Give it to me."

Grugel waved the syringe again, "Want me to do it...?"

Burrows lifted the flap of his brown jacket to the side to reveal a holster of needles he used to perform his Vary work, including the monster, Faustus, he'd used on his own tattoo. He rolled his fingers over the cold cylinders, which responded by casting glinting light around the room, as if, in the dark glow of the R.V., they were one with the electronics. Burrows took the syringe from Grugel and squeezed the liquid into the corner of his eye before the kid could finish his sentence. "You forget, fanboy, I'm familiar with needles."

In the wake of the SLO-42, Burrows' animosity faded fast. He blinked. The green cortisol-based fluid washed over and behind his eyes. Grugel smirked knowingly and slid into the chair at the console beside Eve. Burrows wiped away a tear and stared at it on the tip of his finger. It appeared to him as three distinct aspects. There was the lime color, the rolling shape, and the dancing viscosity. Glancing up, the disorienting view rocked him. The trailer was a black and silver block. It had flashing lights and slow jerking bodies inside. His eyes couldn't settle, and he lost his balance and fell back on the floor cushions. He closed his eyes and when he looked at his fingertip again the triad of images coalesced. The tear was easily identifiable again as the sum of its three parts: green, round and fluid.

He knew roughly how the injection of Leo's neuropeptides was supposed to work as it shot back behind his eyes and coated his neocortex. But the experience was nothing like his telepathy, the cutting thoughts that came at him. Instead, the SLO-42 created a haze over his own perceptions so that everything he experienced was filtered through a foreign point of view—Leo's. Burrows sank back into the cushions. He could feel the corners of his mouth curling up into a goofy grin.

In Leo's world, the trailer was bigger. The tech was brighter. The party was stimulating, and he was at ease. He liked the people around him and they, certainly, liked him. Coco was still gorgeous, but glossier, slippery looking. The other girl he'd seen watching Leo, *Geneva, Gen, Genie,* now he got her name loud and clear—was prominent in Leo's periphery. And wasn't she cute: lithe and flexible, with glowing hair and skin. *Willowy. Earthy.* She fit into an overall feeling he had: that the world flowing around him was about to pop like a canister of confetti and fall into his hands. Burrows, affected by Leo, couldn't take his eyes off Geneva. Everything was going to be great.

"Now it begins," Grugel said. The huge monitor lit up displaying an image of a stack of logs piled high, leaning away from a video moon. It bathed the room, and the side of Grugel's angular face, from the point of his chin to the spiked peaks of his hair, in amber light. His mouth stretched wide, "Bonfire!"

Geneva did not like the way that man who'd been talking to Val earlier was looking at her now, with an unnatural smile, like she was his New Year's resolution. It figured, the creepy older guy giving her attention. She checked her watch, nearly midnight. She hoped Leo and Eve wouldn't want to stay long after.

The light flickered and the countdown started. Everyone in the room chanted, "10, 9, 8, 7, 6..."

Grugel, Eve and Streker hunched over the console. Just before midnight, the video logs burst into flame. "It's time to jump," Grugel said. Everyone screamed, "Midnight!"

But Val didn't stop. Her voice carried on. Her wail rose to a pitch. It sounded as though it was on top of them, but Val herself was far away inside the fire. Geneva stared at Val's open mouth; her lips smeared with plum gloss. That frozen feeling spread down her limbs. She couldn't believe it was happening again. It seemed that if she concentrated, she could make Val stop just by becoming more aware of her, like a lucid dream. Instead, she lunged.

Val began to twitch in a parody of the Mansion Expansion dancing, her limbs crooked her body jolting, her head down eyes up. The only difference was that it came with a tight sporadic flailing that could not be consciously imitated. Her ankles twisted out from under her. She began to fold and fall. Streker caught her waist in the crook of his arm and lowered her. Geneva was at Val's side, cradling her head before it touched the floor. Val wasn't breathing.

She pointed at the nearest spectator, Grugel, "You get help. Call an ambulance."

She tilted Val's head back, opened her jaw and swept a finger along the back of her throat. She breathed into Val's mouth and watched her chest lift. Ripping open the front of Val's shirt, exposing her white chest and black bra, she placed her hands atop each other in the hollow between Val's ribs. With her elbows locked, she pressed hard and fast. Val's chest flexed under her hands: thunk, thunk, thunk. She breathed for Val again. When she looked up, Coco knelt beside her ready to help.

Geneva let her take over the compressions. Sweat beaded on her forehead as they worked on Val in rhythm. Finally, Val's chest shook and rose on its own. Geneva turned Val's head to the side. Coco rolled her over. Val spluttered, coughed, and vomited onto a silk cushion. Caught between the sweetness of Coco's floral perfume and the stench of Val's upturned stomach, Geneva gagged.

"Where are the medics? Where's the ambulance? Shouldn't it be here?" She pointed at Grugel again. He was still standing in the same place. "You called them, right?"

He shrugged. "We can't have any greenies out here."

"But we need to get her to a hospital."

Around the room, people were either staring at Val or at the floor nearby. Leo was beside her, eyes downcast. Only the older guy looked directly at her, smirking like he was watching a show. "Fine." she reached down and pulled Val up by her armpits. Coco helped her hold Val there. No one else moved.

"We need to get her to a hospital," she said looking at Eve. Eve shrugged. Streker came forward and placed his long jacket around Val's shoulders but stepped back at a grunt from Grugel. Grugel, Streker and Eve began to argue as she and Coco carried Val out of the trailer. Through the dim blue lights and the falling snow, she could see the black car in front of her, the keys in the ignition. If no one would help her, she'd help herself. Passing Val to Coco, she waved Coco away from the Mercedes' flame bumper emblems. She didn't know how far out the flames would shoot or for how long. She took off her brown jacket, wrapped it around her arm, turned her head aside and reached for the door.

Leo gripped her forearm just before she touched the handle. "No. It's OK. Eve will drive."

"It's not OK!" Geneva yelled. She didn't turn until she heard the Cadillac start and saw Eve at the wheel.

Leo, Coco, Geneva, and Eve squeezed into the front seat laying Val across their laps. Geneva held her friend's head in her hands and stroked her soft dark hair. "What happened to her?"

"It might have been the Lime." Eve said.

"The drug. What is it?"

"You've heard of SLO-42, right? That's Lime." Leo said. He was looking away out the window, watching the snowfall, avoiding her gaze.

She frowned. She had learned about SLO-42 in class. Psychotherapists had developed the drug before the revolution in response to growing public apathy. The chemical was manufactured from a person's neurotransmitters. It gave the user a peek inside someone else's head, a truly different perspective. It was hard to make and had little street value, unless it came from someone people really wanted to experience. Its popularity had peaked when the mind of a serial killer had made the rounds. Then it had been outlawed. A bad reaction to the drug meant a bad source, like that creepy guy Val had been talking to. "That guy."

"No, me." Leo said.

"You?" Was he some kind of monster? She leaned into Coco and stared at the falling snow. The Cadillac headed uphill towards the university. "Why aren't we going to Bayside?"

"She won't want to go there," Eve said. "We'll just get her back to the Mansion."

Geneva lunged across Leo and grabbed at the steering wheel. "What's wrong with you? Take her to the hospital."

Val's eyes opened wide. Her lips parted. "No."

Eve sneered and pushed Geneva's arm away. "See."

"But she needs help." Val's eyes, were wide, scared.

The Cadillac stayed on course. As they approached campus, lights flashed through dark plumes of smoke obscuring the snowfall. Fire trucks blocked their view of the Mansion. Eve lowered the window as a police officer approached with his hand out. "Stop here."

Cold smoke stung Geneva's eyes.

"What happened?" Leo asked.

The officer made a quick backhanded gesture, "An incident. Fire. Some students at a party. We haven't really had time to investigate." He placed a hand on the window, leaned into the car. "What's wrong with the girl?" he turned over his shoulder, shouted, "Medic."

Leo, Coco, and Eve turned away from the Mansion. In the flashing lights surrounding it were fire trucks and ambulances. Medics eased Val out of the car. Coco, Leo and Eve stumbled out together and held each other in a tight knot. Geneva stood outside beside Val as the medics loaded her onto a stretcher. But the New West officer in his green uniform held her back, his fingers digging into her arms, as they closed her into an ambulance. "You can't go with her."

As the ambulances sped down the hill, he released her behind the plastic tape barrier. She stood beside Coco, Leo and Eve and watched the dorm burn as the snow fell. With the added height of the columns of flames, the one-story building looked like a true mansion. The heat radiated over her face and torso. It was a while before she felt the pain in her feet. Her toes were white on white, as she stood barefoot in the snow. In her hurry to help Val, she'd forgotten her boots.

~ 14 ~

SYNC CHROME CITY: NEW YEAR'S DAY

"I disagree with those who see C.G. Burrows as a sociopath with unfathomable motives. In fact, I count him among the Dawning Psychics. It is easy to understand his animosity, his hatred, for our children. He had been like them, with all their potential. Yet, they had everything he had wanted, while he had been cast aside. To him, it was justice, seeing them grow up and also become worthless." — *Save Giovanni: The Lost Men of the Psychic Wars*, S. Sherring

Burrows woke up on New Year's Day in a companionable drug-happy haze. Streker drooled and Grugel twitched, sprawled on the floor nearby. As the SLO-42 wore off, the trailer darkened. Burrows' hangover started as soon as he moved. Grimacing, he struggled to lift himself out of the sunken chair. He felt pieced together, slow. When he was high last night, that girl, Gen, had glowed. She'd leapt with feral speed to the thrashing girl's side. She'd pounded on the girl's chest like she was fighting for her own survival. Soon, he vowed, she would be.

That slight girl was a powder keg. He'd seen through the bramble grown wild over her explosive potential. He rubbed the side of his aching jaw. He'd been stupid, thinking Coco was the one about to pop, thinking she was the golden girl of his dreams. Blame it on having lived too long away from women on the 'Way. Being lead around by your dick felt nice until you saw where you were headed. He'd forgotten.

Streker interrupted. Shot at him: *You don't even care about her.*

The kid meant his mother. He'd become obsessive on the topic. Burrows stared at him until the kid blinked and looked away. It took a fraction longer than he liked. Last night, in the chaos, he'd gotten a similar bit off Leo. While Coco and Gen were on their knees lifesaving, Leo had thought: *Mom.* That was the guy everyone lusted after, just another mother obsessed man-child. New West: creating a nation of pansies. "Who was she?"

Streker: *Val.* He groaned. "Oh god, what happened? That was so wrong. What did we do?"

Burrows looked around at the glinting electronics. This set up had served its purpose. "I think you overloaded her, kid. Maybe we should find out if she's a total vegetable. Where do you think she'd be?"

"The hospital, Bayside," Streker said.

Grugel sat up, combed his fingers through his hair so it spiked again. "Nah, Eve said she'd make sure they didn't take her there," he said. "We're cool. They'll be on campus."

"Nice job, Greg Lionel. We still need to get this out of here. Drive this bucket back out on the Way. Streker, come. We'll go find the rest of them, don't want them saying the wrong thing."

Grugel: *Man, you're tweaking.* "Relax, they're cool. Even Coco. It's her rebellious phase."

"Yeah?" Burrows asked. "Even ponytails? She looked a little upset."

Grugel: *Ugh, just chill.* He shrugged. "She's Val's friend."

"No worries, Val and Gen go way back," Streker said.

"Really? That's not selling me. I think you've got a problem." Burrows said.

Streker: *You got us into this.* "They're like sisters. Seriously, Val came to live with Gen after her parents were killed, in a fire or something."

On dawning New Year's Day, that was all Burrows needed to make the connection that had been just out of his grasp. He grabbed his jacket and stumbled out of the trailer towards his car. He wrapped his arms over his throbbing head shielding his eyes from the light. In the new day's light, he remembered his history: Gen was the golden destiny girl he'd seen in the forest wearing Kendra LeMay's perceptions. Val was the waif he hadn't bothered to chase down after he'd killed her parents Vic and Perla Freeman. He still knew their names. They haunted him. That he'd seen the girls together last night, just as they were expanding the limits of Sync Chrome City, smacked of synchronicity, an incident that screamed, "Pay attention!"

He'd talked to the girl, Val, last night for a while and her brooding had seemed more genuine than these other kids' angst. He'd gotten pangs of skepticism: *So, what are you doing here, old man? Slathering after Coco? What's the point of KillGiovanni?* He could see it now for what it was: the inheritance of a childhood in mourning. She wanted a revolution. She wasn't just a Sync Chrome groupie. She was a believer.

The trailer door banged as Streker emerged. He was, as usual, wearing a too tight sweater, that made him look even reedier with his trademark black pants and trench. Burrows started Mistress M.D. and sat inside as the kid scraped frost off the windshield. He didn't like his connection to the girls, the feeling of unfinished business. But it was the perfect start to the New Year. No one in New West needed horn-blowing festivities. They needed to smack up against the terror that came when your mind expanded. They needed to cower under the weight of their own capacity. If they manifested psychic abilities, it would mean a complete loss of autonomy and privacy. It would be a pandemic of mental anguish and pain, which maybe New Westians deserved, but the people on the Freeway did not. SLO-42 had given him a taste in Leo of New West's perky hope. The morning after the inside of his mouth tasted of rotten orange. Hope was a downer, a hangover. Disgusting.

He lowered the window, "Get in. Good enough."

Mistress M.D. slid across the slick of frost-covered mud as they left the trailer park. Burrows gripped the wheel. "Hey, you got any more Lime on you?" he asked.

Streker shook his head*: I'm not your dealer. It's Leo's Lime.*

When they reached the road, Burrows pressed his foot to the floor.

#

They smelled the smoke long before they saw the black clouds over New West University, which dissipated to a gray haze across the bay.

"Not the Mansion," Streker pleaded, as if he couldn't see the sodden ashes in front of them and the green fire trucks spouting arcs of water on the ruins.

If he'd been alone, Burrows would have skipped up the walkway. It had worked. Crashing Sync Chrome City had caused this damage, no doubt. He could see the kid wasn't making the connection. His eyes were unfocused underneath welling tears. If the kid knew he'd caused this, it would crush him.

“Not the Mansion,” Streker sobbed.

Ah, innocence. You learned that it didn't matter if the people around you were ready or not. If you saw danger you acted, even alone. You moved with a single mind until disrupting lives, counting casualties, and killing dangerous people became incidental.

A man yelled, "Psi!" Burrows looked his way and saw the crowd of protesters. Flakes of ash floated through the air above them. The scene was pleasantly apocalyptic. Burrows rocked on his heels and a chill crossed his gums, as his lips parted wide.

"Is that Psi-Aware?" Streker said. "Mom?"

The kid took off running past the Mansion to people. He darted around them like a dog after gulls. Burrows followed, his hands in front of him pointing the way. The kid finished a lap around the crowd and came to a standstill beside Burrows winded and dazed.

"Lydia ain't here, kid. Too embarrassed, probably. It looks like the group is finally taking their crusade to the next level."

"Yeah," Streker sighed: *Now will you leave mom alone?*

Burrows reached forward, palmed the kid's head in one hand and squeezed. These kids kept thinking harder. He tousled Streker's hair to disguise his anger as he pulled away. Sure, kid, sure.

Desperate as Streker was for a father, he'd strained things with the kid when he'd moved into Lydia's bedroom. Fine, he was about done with her. He'd gotten what he'd wanted. The loonies were hell-bent on pushing their "teach us to be psychic" agenda and looking damn silly doing it. They couldn't see the real deal, psychic potential crackling around them well-disguised as it was, hidden in unlikely vessels. Speaking of loopy kids, "Is that Leo?"

"Hey, have you guys seen Gen?" Leo asked looking around. "She was right behind us and then she was gone." He touched his forehead, stared down at the bricks. "She probably went to Val. I think they took her to Linden."

Leo looked up, gestured toward the Mansion. "Ah, Streker, man," Leo put his arm, encased in puffy parka, around the kid's shoulders. "I have to tell you..."

"Wait. She'll be at the bus station then. Streker, go after her."

"Me?" Streker asked, rocking on his heels pivoting towards Leo. "Shouldn't you?"

Leo shrugged. "Nah, she's got to be sour on me, Da Lime, me."

"It wasn't your..."

"Guys," Burrows said. "We're in a hurry here."

He had just one last task for the boy. He pulled Streker aside. "Go, now. That girl shouldn't be alone. Follow her. Stop her in Deming."

Streker stared at him with those long dopey eyes.

"Just take her to see your mom."

The kid started down the hill glanced back and then broke into a run. His feet were practically spinning at the bottom of his black trench coat. His long legs must really be churning. Good boy. Go fetch.

"Good," he said. "So everyone here all right?"

Leo shook his head, no. He got: *Seven guys.*

Burrows reeled from the hit. He fired back, "Where's your stash?"

Leo: *Friend-Me.*

"You got any on you?"

Leo: *Damn.* "Just the last of the latest batch." He opened up his jacket and there were four syringes. He handed three of them over. *You take the fall.*

Instead of backhanding Leo, Burrows took the syringe and shot it into the corner of his eye. He barely felt it when Leo punched him with: *What are you doing shooting up in front of all these people?*

He was starting to feel good and happy. Now all he needed was a nice pair of dead girls. In the distance, Burrows saw the top of the Friend-Me corporation pyramid, a green triangle, rising out of the haze. In Leo's perception, it beaconed to him like a Shangri-la invoking feelings of loyalty and responsibility. He looked at it and saw his destiny, but it also provoked rebellion. He heard music in the background of Leo's thoughts. He wanted to pursue his own course. So, this was what it was like if you were supposed to take over your family business.

He could not stop thinking about Geneva. Last night seemed to have capped it, turning his attention from Coco to Geneva. Burrows wasn't sure how much of this was Leo's perception and how much of it was his own, the feeling he'd woken up with this morning that she was the key, the place to focus his energy. He understood the different psychic potentials. Geneva and Leo were senders, broadcasting their thoughts: the girl powerfully, constantly, unfocused and Leo only as a DJ unconsciously but controlled. The other girl, Val, was a receiver, taking it all in. She got everything. More than her mind could handle.

Burrows got the location of New West Mental Health by asking probing questions at Bayside Hospital. On his way to Linden, driving Mistress M.D., and riding Leo's happy thoughts, he obsessed about Geneva as he watched the New West landscape, the brown, soaked, snow-spotted fallow fields of winter, pass. He imagined the red-ponytailed girl in the middle of the empty fields and along the roadside and was content. He was headed in the right direction here in New West seeking out the girl. But underneath all the good feeling, his latent cynicism nagged. The drug wouldn't last, and he feared the betrayal of this hope would cause a return of his murderous rage. The towns seemed barren and lonely, and he sped through them to the clinic wanting to be with people on New Year's Day.

Inside New West Mental Health, a shoddy, ill-equipped building that looked no more like a hospital than his Vary shop on the 'Way had looked like a doctor's office, Burrows heard screaming. There was no one at the front desk and no one prevented him from going back. He could distinguish voices in the screams: men shouting and groaning and one distinct female yell. He passed the lab filled with stretchers and movement and went back to a smaller room where there were bars over the windows. The screaming began to oscillate. They were moving the girl about, perhaps putting their hands to her mouth. He looked in the room and saw the dark-haired waif. They had the girl bound hands and feet and were stuffing a cloth over and into her mouth. Two scrubs were doing the dirty work while a distraught woman in a longer lab coat stood nearby.

"Excuse me," Burrows said. "I think I can help."

He felt how the doctor was relieved at the interruption and knew he had an in, this would be easier than he'd thought, maybe even less violent. Interning a few random students who'd been spending too much time online hadn't bothered her, but the implications of the sudden collapse of so many young minds on New Year's had frightened her. What they were doing now—from her he got: *imprisoning* and *suppressing a generation*—crossed some line she'd set for herself. Well, he could use that.

The SLO-42 helped him make a nice impression, the way it had made Valerie's parents, The Freemans, like him. He was relaxed and easy going, with an air of natural authority.

He was Leo when he asked for the girl. "The danger has passed. She's OK. Let her go. C'mon, let me take her home."

The medics relaxed their grip on the girl. Valerie stopped struggling. Everyone saw the value of diplomacy. If nothing else, it was a chance to catch their breath. They turned to the doctor, awaiting her response.

"She's a danger to herself."

"Danger? Or something you don't understand? Maybe she's handling this just fine. Why don't you ask her what she wants?"

The girl was not stupid. He saw shrewdness in her eyes. She clearly understood the trap. He'd now opened up an option to her, but she was still limited to two: stay here at the clinic or go with him. He felt the doctor and Valerie sussing him out and it was a pretty good try from both of them. The doctor even knew what she was doing. He felt a searing press of hot needles, but he met her with a blank wall. The girl's attempt was ineffectual. His mind was closed to her. He was a receiver like her, a one-way street. He gave them nothing.

"I want out of here. I want to go with him," Val said. "There's nothing wrong with the way I think."

Burrows got a more conceited version: *Can't hold me here. I'm the future.*

The doctor looked down. She pressed her hands together. Then she took off her lab coat, and he saw her breasts in a soft-looking warm-colored sweater, her hips rounded and wide even in black pants and a copper necklace, an infinity symbol, drawing his attention back to her breasts. She folded the lab coat and draped it over her arm. She looked apologetically at the medics.

"I can't do this anymore. I can't be a part of this approach," she said, and then turned to Valerie. "As far as I'm concerned, you may go."

Burrows caught a last stab of fear from the woman: *Careful.* The SLO-42 was fading and the thought stung. He pulled the girl to her feet and shoved her ahead of him down the hall.

As they left, he heard the doctor tell the medics, "There has to be a better way. We need a decision."

As he touched Valerie's shoulders, Burrows was aware how close he was to his own conclusion. He held half of the psychic threat in his hands.

"You are the future," he said, and he felt the words relax her. She thought he understood. She didn't know it was the future he feared.

Outside, Mistress M.D. was waiting for them, and Burrows was sad to see the car looked like it had seen better days. The gleam had worn off her. Bits of evergreen littered her hood. She could use another coat of polish.

"Where's Sync Chrome City?" the girl asked, as if the transportation he'd brought her wasn't good enough.

"I put it in the trunk," he said, not a bad idea, actually. It'd be a great place to hide the tech.

He disarmed the car and popped the trunk and the girl went there and stood beside it as though she was really expecting to plug back in right now outside the clinic. *Junkie*, he thought, and wished just once someone would get him.

“I’ve gotta get back in. What was happening was incredible. What we’re going to be capable of, they don’t even know," she said.

“I know,” Burrows said, and he shot her a look. He saw her and her friends their minds unleashed streaming everywhere like an EMP.

From her, he got a sudden awareness: *You don’t want.* She was a sharp kid.

“Pain," he said. "Like razors. I feel it coming and I just want to be alone.”

As he said it, he felt the SLO slipping away making it true. How alone he wanted to be: alone. He’d get the other girl, finish this business off, get out of New West and then maybe go south down the ‘Way. He turned to the girl and saw the fear in her eyes, and the fight, but he wasn’t afraid of her anymore. He had come so far, and he was so close to the end.

~ 15 ~

SYNC CHROME CITY: STREKER

"It is important to place these historic events in a cultural context. Understand that people at that time had rudimentary ideas of what it meant to be psychic and they were each bound to a Single Ego. They had no knowledge of connectivity. The idea was foreign and terrifying. They valued independence and autonomy. They feared the loss of privacy. Some called telepathy invasive others went so far as to use the loaded term "mind rape." The older generation didn't want the youth to gain abilities they could not. People thought the older brain was brittle and weak. It was a radically different time." — *Becoming Psychic 101, A History and a Primer*

Rumor had it that seven of the guys had been critically injured in the fire. No one mentioned Valerie. Leo, Coco, and Eve spent the night huddled in Geneva's room at Inu Wood. Coco could have gone to her father, but she said, no, he was busy and she would stay with her friends. They felt safer in each other's company. In the morning, a resident adviser knocked on the door. He was going around to all the rooms. He told them winter quarter classes would start the next day as usual. The university was holding a meeting to discuss the tragedy and would provide temporary housing for residents of the Mansion. They began walking up the hill to the Big Top.

Eve and Leo flanked Coco. Eve held her hand. Leo sheltered her, his arm around her shoulders, "It'll be OK. It'll be OK." Geneva trailed them. Acrid smoke hung low in the heart of campus. Some students were standing, watching the fire trucks stream water onto the hull of the dorm. Leo, Coco, and Eve squeezed together and entered the Big Top murmuring, heads down. They didn't look back when Geneva stopped at the door. She stiffened. Other students corralled into the Big Top after them, quiet and still. She glared, feeling like she could pierce them. It sickened her to see them simply doing what was expected when their friends needed them. She was jealous, too. They fawned over Coco while she was so alone without Val.

She turned her back on them. There was movement beyond the Madrona grove. She cut through the trees toward a distant hissing. She heard someone yell, "Psi!" as she walked in front of the New Year's Day protest. There were so many Psi-Aware protesters, she couldn't see the steps of the administration building or the bricks of the walkway leading up to it. The hiss-yelling grew louder as the people chanted, "Psi, psi, psi!" Clouds of white breath puffed into the sepia haze. They were bundled in coats and hats and scarves and coated in a fine layer of gray ash from the Mansion. Only a band of their faces showed: red cheeks and dark eyes. They stopped speaking. As one, they stared at her.

She stared back, stood her ground for a moment, her eyes darting from face to face to face before she turned and ran. Water rushed over the charred remains of the Mansion. Pain pricked across her cheeks, the sudden return of sensation after a chill. It wasn't fair to be angry: with Leo, Coco, Eve. The university would tell them to go to class. If they didn't know what else to do, they would go. It was just that she couldn't, this time, continue to do as she was told. The medics had taken Val to New West Mental again. Probably the guys were there, too. She went to the Shadow Bus station and bought a ticket for the next departure. Outside the terminal, she pulled her scarf tight around her neck as she shivered beside the black buses, black screens over the windows for privacy, looking for the one that would take her to Linden.

The bus was half full. Riders cloaked in privacy webs sat in back. She took a seat, reached up, and pulled the black fabric down in front of her face and all around her. Inside the enveloping darkness, she couldn't get a full breath. Her chest heaved halfway up and stuck. She cycled through her fears: that Val and the guys would die, that her new friends were also in danger, that she would never be safe again. Shut away behind the web, she saw the protesters' eyes. She felt them on her skin. She yanked the web up and released it so that it shot back into place on the roof. Inhaling deep breaths, she moved to the front of the bus. She had to get to Linden.

Finally, a woman in uniform approached. Geneva gawked as the bus driver boarded. The woman looked like an oversized character in a children's book: glossy and bright. Her hips spanned the seat as she settled into it and hunched over the huge wheel. As the bus lurched forward, Geneva glanced out the window. A lanky figure loped after the bus. "Hey wait. That guy."

She caught her seat as the bus jerked to a halt and Streker stepped on.

The driver looked back at her and winked one huge blue eye. Lashes like shredded black butterfly wing dropped over it. "Ha! No problem. I don't suppose anyone here is in too much of a hurking rush to get to Linden." The driver winked again. Her yellow ringlets bounced.

Geneva raised her hand as Streker went by. He reached out, caught it and kissed the top of it, swaying deftly as the bus pulled away from the station. "A pleasant surprise, the lovely lady. May I?" He sat down beside her, his legs splayed, his knee touching hers.

"I never wear a web," he said, looking around at the shrouded shapes at the back of the bus. "But it's nice that there's someone here I actually want to talk to."

"Are you going all the way to Linden?" she asked.

He grimaced and shook his head. "No. Home. Deming. Just outside."

"Deming's home? You seem more city."

He shrugged. "Nope, home is where my mom is, that's Deming. I thought I'd better get away for a while."

"Last night wasn't your fault," she said. "And I'm not angry at you guys. I know I was just projecting. A similar thing happened to Val last spring, and I just stood there. I didn't do anything. I felt so stupid. Not that you guys were stupid. I just remember what that's like. You are so shocked you can't move. Totally understandable. I just couldn't do that again. I had to act."

He looked away. "Yeah, well, the people at your party are your responsibility. But it's not only that, I'm worried about mom."

"Why? No. That's OK. I respect your privacy. Hey, wait though, Neo-Private. Isn't spilling your thing? You put it all out there."

He held up his hands with his wrists clenched together and shook them at her. "You caught me. Cuff me."

She crossed her arms. "So, what's with your mom?"

"Well, she's been having migraines and she's a member of this group, Psi-Aware. You heard of it?" His eyes flicked back and forth between her face and his knee.

"Yeah, they're always on campus. Today, there were many," she shrugged. "I don't really get them. They think they have ESP or something. Not sure what's to argue about. Does your mom? Have ESP, I mean"

He looked away again. "Uh, no. Not a bit actually. There's no way. There's so many things I've hid from her. But that's the point. That's what the Psi-Aware people are pissed about. My mom and her geek friends don't think they are psychic. They think that they *could* be. Should be, but the government's keeping it from them. Nobody teaches psi. If we started at a young age, we'd all know how to read each other's minds as easy as English."

He fixed his gaze on her. His blue eye was very light, the brown eye almost hazel. "Yeah, they're convinced that it'd be really easy. We all just need to learn how."

"What? You mean like a class at New West? Becoming Psychic 101?" She started to laugh, but stopped short when Streker said, "Exactly. But the government won't do it. So, it's a conspiracy."

She held a hand over her mouth to hide her residual smile. It took her a while to sound serious. "Oh, but what do you think? I'm sorry. Do you think we could be? Psychic?"

He shrugged. "Could be, but, honestly, it's not my thing. I don't care. I don't want to look into other people's heads and nobody has to look into mine. As a neo-private, I run around naked. So, what's the point? I'll tell anyone whatever it is they want to know. What you give away can't be taken."

She tugged her jacket around her and turned away to look out the window. "Sounds scary." She could still see the red tops of some of the New West buildings surrounded by evergreens and the triangular green tip of the new Friend-Me building. It was the beginning of the quarter, and she was leaving campus. She still hadn't scheduled a retake of her test from last year because she still hadn't had a chance to study. It was twisted logic, but she couldn't help think how in some ways Val was the lucky one, again. She didn't have to worry about tests, homework, a job, or grades. She didn't have a choice, so she didn't have to choose. Her problems took that away, reducing her options to one clear path—clear to Geneva anyway. Val had to get help. Geneva still had to make decisions though, and maybe she was making the wrong one right now, leaving campus. What she was going to do when she got to Linden, anyway? She wanted to be there, but what good was that? She pushed the doubt aside, having made the decision. She had to be there, had to. Maybe it wouldn't make a difference, she didn't know, but this time she had to be by her friend's side.

"Hey, wait." She turned to Streker. "Are you sidetracking me? Conspiracy theories, psychics, it's interesting, but what's it got to do with your mom?"

He cringed, his shoulders hunched, and he made the "cuff me" gesture again. "That guy from the party last night. He didn't have a place to stay when he got here this summer, so he stayed at my house."

"The creepy guy?" she asked.

"You think so?"

"Well, yeah. He's mammoth and older and he's not a student, right? So, why's he here? And last night, he was giving me weird looks." She crossed her arms over her chest again. "Maybe it was just the Lime. Was it really Leo's?"

"Yeah. But Leo's a good guy. I don't think that caused Val to flip." Streker looked at his hands and seemed to fold around himself. His gangly body took up even less room. "I don't know. I didn't really have a problem with the guy until he started sleeping with my mom. Not Leo. The creep guy, Burrows. I didn't mind so much at first. She seemed happy. But he was using her, trying to get close to her Psi-Aware friends, I guess. Except now he doesn't seem into them, either. My mom's headaches are getting worse. And it's bad timing. She and her Psi-Aware friends think something is going down."

Streker's shoulder brushed hers. "But you said they aren't psychic."

"No, but they are so well-connected and whack. It's almost the same thing." He leaned on her shoulder and sighed. "You know, I'm comforted with you here after last night. You seem solid. I just don't know many good people like that."

Solid. She wanted to believe him, but she felt so unsteady. She was on a bus instead of in class. She'd altered course and inside she felt like she was down on the floor with Val in spasms, screaming. At least it didn't show.

"Yeah, I'm glad you're here, too. I've just felt so alone. Since, last year."

"You should come meet my mom," he said.

It sounded so sweet. She thought about her mom taking care of everything when Val first came to live with them. Baking pies. Outside, the land had flattened, and patches of farmland began to appear between clusters of evergreens. The bus rumbled by. Streker took her hand from her lap and stroked it. When she didn't pull away, he put his head on her shoulder and lay there with easy affection like an animal. She smoothed his dark hair across his forehead and stroked his chest through his green sweater, fuzzy and coarse, like moss.

"I like this." she said, plucking at it.

"If you stopped by my place, you'd get to Linden even faster. I could drive you. I have a permit."

"Yeah, so why aren't you driving now?"

"A friend asked if he could borrow my wheels last night and I said sure. He'll have it at my house soon."

"You gave him your permit?" This was the most unbelievable thing Streker had said, and she was sure it was a lie. It was hard enough to believe he had a permit. Cars weren't allowed to travel outside city limits without one and the government didn't issue many because people were supposed to use the buses and trains. That's why the buses were mostly painted surplus black. No one would pay to put advertisements on them anymore because few people saw them pass by, no traffic. If Streker actually had a permit—doubtful—it wasn't the kind of thing you let someone borrow. It'd be foolish to trust anyone that much. The price of a permit would pay her student loans. But maybe he was a better person than she was, less cynical. "And you're sure, he'll have the car back? No, I don't think I can stop."

"Too bad. I'd like to find out how you do it."

"Do what?"

"Be you. Be so together."

Suddenly, she was tired of holding it together while the people around her freaked. If college had made one thing obvious, it was that her dad had been right. The world was in stasis. She looked out the window and the view confirmed it. The scene was the same as ever: a long gray road banked by fallow farmland, with a gas station and the pointed tops of houses appearing as they approached the town. All the significant events and inventions had gone before. Gen Utopia had only toys: AeroFlux Butterflies, Sound-Wield Sets, Friend-Me Journals, nothing that would make a difference. Maybe that's why people didn't like the Giovanni Hastings story—jealousy. None of them would experience a transformation like that. It was a lie, a tease. Nothing would change for herself and her friends. Where she was resolutely headed, out of college and into the working world of New West, they would all wind up. It had been handed to them. Geneva had been planning her life carefully day by day, but just to fill it. The foundation of her life was as arbitrary as her economic theory classes as made up as mathematics and flowing along in history like everyone else's. This point in time ebbed.

As the bus drove through Deming past a coffee shop, bakery, diner and bar, Geneva felt anything but together. As long as she was being pushed apart, would it hurt to take the next step voluntarily? She was a child of her generation. There was no use resisting. When the bus stopped in sunny Deming, Geneva placed her hand in Streker's and stepped off. She didn't like those Psi-Aware eyes on her, accusing her. Of what? Maybe Streker's mom could tell her.

~ 16 ~

SYNC CHROME CITY: CRÉME-FILLED

"In elementary school, you learned the tenets of extrasensory perception. You were trained primarily as a Sender, to push your thoughts out to others, or as a Receiver, to catch those thoughts. You identified your psychic learning style, learned meditative techniques and sent your first tendrils, wires or waves (however it fit you best to visualize it) out to touch the Lattice. Now that you are sure in your individual identity and have learned emotional control, you will attain the next level of psychic skill. You will enter the external net and join us on the Lattice. Let your teachers guide you." — *Becoming Psychic 101, A History and a Primer*

Stepping off the bus in Deming with Streker felt like skipping class. Geneva was happy, excited, and instantly guilty.

"Not in such a hurkin' rush to get to Linden at all. No one ever is," the wonderland driver said as the doors wheezed shut.

"Cool." Streker said, releasing Geneva's hand as she stepped to the ground. "You really will like my Mom."

He bobbed as they strode through the town's main strip. He stopped in front of the bakery, Lydia's, and pointed at a tray of doughnuts puffed so full of cashew cream it spilled out and pooled on the waxed paper sheets. A bell rang as he pulled her inside the shop and inclined his head at a pink-aproned, pink-cheeked shop clerk who emerged from the backroom. He extracted a doughnut from the case and presented it to Geneva on a square of waxy paper. Even so, the doughnut's sticky sides slipped around and smeared her fingers as soon as she took hold.

"I can't eat this. It's like the size of my head," Geneva said. "And shouldn't you pay for it?"

"Nah," Streker shook his head, taking a bite. Globs of cream slopped onto the linoleum. She went for napkins to sop it up as Streker stood rocking back and forth on his heels, his face stretched blissfully smooth. "Yeah, that's the stuff." He turned to the clerk in between bites. "Is Mom here?"

"Upstairs," the clerk said, swiping her hands back and forth over her apron and releasing clouds of flour. "She started the cinnamon rolls this morning and went up for a bit. Headaches again. Go ahead, step through the back."

At the mention of headaches, Streker stilled. Then he resumed his languid swaying. Geneva inhaled the shop's yeast and maple sugar scent. She wouldn't have imagined Streker could look so content outside of the electronic lined R.V. "This where your mom lives?"

Streker nodded and gestured back at the writing in reverse across the shop window, "Lydia's." Then he pointed up. He took Geneva's doughnut-free hand and pulled her back behind the counter. Enormous steel ovens warmed the bakery. Mounds of dough rose in belly-sized bowls under towels. Frosting udders lay supine on silver countertops.

"This way," he said pointing to a door at the end of a hallway lined with bags of flour. He paused and turned to a shelf filled with bottles of colored sugar crystals. He plucked one, opened the top and grabbed Geneva's wrist. He tilted her hand back, so the doughnut lay flat and shook the bottle over it. Pink sprinkles scattered over its wet sugar surface and began to melt. "There, that's better. Come on, you gotta try it."

"Yeah, that's what it needed, more sugar," Geneva said.

He pulled her down the hall and up a narrow staircase while she buried her face in the sugar dough. Cream squeezed away from her mouth. Blobs of it fell onto the stairs and rolled in the dust. She started bouncing up the stairs after Streker in a shared sugar high. It reminded her of how she and Valerie used to act coming up the hill to campus from Tim's chocolate shop. The memory scalded her with guilt. Val had probably woken up this morning scared and alone at the clinic. Geneva should be with her now. Across the door at the top of the stairs, gold letters spelled Streker. Before she could help Val, she needed to know if there were answers behind it. Did the Psi-Aware advocates know what was happening to the New West students, and why?

Layers of cinnamon smoke swirled as Streker pushed the door open. Geneva blinked while her eyes adjusted to the bluish light. Stacks of books filled the room piled on end tables, climbing up corners. Titles like *The Lusty Rogue* and *The Courtesan and the Pirates* ran across the paperbacks in metallic scripts. Block letters covered hardbacks with combinations of the words: universe, quantum, hologram, and consciousness. A few trails of shaggy brown carpet wound around the books. Geneva looked for cats but didn't see any and the cinnamon smell inside reminded her of Val. Sugar fueled a rush of anxiety. The woman, she was about to meet — no mere crazy cat lady — was a Psi-Aware member. Geneva noticed her hands were suddenly empty. She'd inhaled the rest of the doughnut and dropped the square of paper on the stairs.

"She's probably in her meditation room," Streker said.

"Val?" said Geneva, distracted.

Streker shook his hair back from his face and behind his shoulders. It was almost as long as her own. "No. My mom. That's what she does when she has migraines, meditates."

He led her down a carpeted furrow to a small room in the back of the apartment. In the middle of a worn tatami mat, a flour-dusted woman lay on the floor with her legs and arms spread wide as if she were in the middle of making snow angels. Her eyes were closed and, asleep, she buzzed and whistled exhaled breaths.

Streker sighed kneeling. He patted her shoulder. "Jeez, Mom."

The woman opened pale green eyes. "You're not the Buddha," she said staring up at Streker. "I fell asleep again, didn't I? I'm terrible at this." She winced and closed her eyes again. “My head still hurts."

Streker put his hands to her temples and began making small circles there with his fingertips. "You really should just take some aspirin."

The woman grunted. "Don’t you start. I've told you drugs cloud the mind."

"Aspirin? Besides, it's not working. You aren't getting psychic."

"Uh, uh. Don't waste your time scolding today. This is no time to doubt."

As mother and son fired sentences at each other, Geneva looked around. The room was mostly bare except for a low table with four cones of incense smoking on a saucer and a satisfied jade Buddha settled in one corner. Above the Buddha were five framed certificates. They said; Lydia Streker, visionary leader, Noetic Sciences Institute; Lydia Streker, president Psi-Aware, Deming chapter; Lydia Streker, baking certificate, Lakeview Community College; and Lydia Streker, doctorate in physics, Massachusetts Institute for Technology. The final certificate was a cross-stitch sampler. It read, "There is only one time to awaken. That time is now. — Buddha."

"So, how's your sex life?" Lydia asked.

Geneva snapped around. She flushed before realizing the question hadn't been directed at her.

Streker's face and neck reddened.

The woman was still lying down feet pointed away from the door. "I'm your mother. I have to ask."

Geneva wondered if Streker had to answer. He'd seemed adamant about his Neo-Private philosophy. Maybe this is where he drew the line.

"It's, um, different and, um, kind of on hold," Streker reached down and tapped his mother's shoulder. "Can I introduce you to my friend now?"

The woman opened her eyes. They rolled back in her head as she looked at Geneva. She flopped over on her mat. "Oh, Streker, is this...? " The woman pressed herself up, her ash-colored hair a nimbus of frizz. Across her bosom and pouched belly, her T-shirt read "Deming Fest: Dem Right!" She certainly didn't look psychic. Although, sitting cross-legged on the floor she had a distinctly eight-shaped figure that reminded Geneva of Dr. Montgrave's infinity symbol necklace. Lydia stood, lifting from buoyant hips. "Oh, Push-Me! I mean, Geneva. What a nice surprise!" Upright, she grew animated. She pressed her hands together and dipped her head. "Namaste! How nice! How nice!"

She reached out, brushed the side of Geneva's face and held out sugary fingertips. "I see you've been to my bakery. I'm Streker's Mom. You can call me Lydia. Right then. We'll go back down and finish the rolls up quick, quick, quick. My Psi-Aware chapter will be here any minute. This is so exciting."

She bustled out of the room singing, "You want to know what I know."

Streker smiled and shrugged. "That's my mom. Just go with it."

They followed Lydia out of the room. "About Psi-Aware?" Geneva asked.

"Just let me grab a snack," Lydia called out as she went down a hall.

Geneva followed feeling disappointed. The woman had not fixed her with a strange glare. Aside from her meditation and cluttered house, she seemed friendly and normal, not at all what she'd expected from a Psi-Aware member. It had been a mistake to stop here. She should have gone directly to Val.

In the kitchen, the light in the apartment turned from hazy blue to puce as, instead of filtering through smoky incense, it passed through chlorophyll. Plants filled the space instead of books. Most of the vegetation appeared connected to one matriarch philodendron winding its way along the window intermittently unfolding shiny green leaves. In off continent tropical jungles, the leaves of the philodendron could grow to the size of a small child. Some of them were approaching those dimensions in Lydia’s kitchen. The plant appeared to originate from a huge yellow pot in the corner while rooting along the windowsill in a collection of white, blue, red, and green hand thrown and painted pottery. Lydia grabbed a handful of raw almonds from a bowl on the table and chewed. Geneva crawled across the breakfast nook and peered through the blinds. There were no cars on the street. "The car?"

Streker looked around, his eyes scanning as though he expected the car to unfurl in the kitchen, "Don't worry. It'll be here soon."

She wasn't so sure. Streker's friends weren't the kind you could trust with a fancy vehicle and an expensive rare road permit. She could be stuck waiting for the next bus. She shouldn't have stopped here. Sitting in the corridor of plants, she wasn't even sure which way to go to get out of the apartment. Another sampler hung on the wall by the stove beside Lydia's head. The words, speckled with orange grease, read, "All we are is the result of what we have thought." — Dhammapada.

"When you feel uncertain about something, it's a good idea to ask yourself how you got where you are." Lydia Streker said. "What brought you here today?"

"Streker," Geneva said.

"But how did you decide? Was it a gut choice or a decision?"

"Gut," Geneva said, as the half-chewed gobs of dough wobbled in hers. She imagined curdling cream-filling. "I wasn't thinking. That's my problem. I just go along."

"It was probably the right choice, then. You see, that's the way our brains work, the processing happens behind the scenes. It's almost impossible to think about the future We have to rely on our intuition," Lydia said.

She held up an almond to the light peering at it as if it were translucent. "This is the same shape as the amygdala, the most primitive part of our brain. It's the seat of our emotions, the source of our sadness and confusion."

"I've heard sadness is a loss of connection to the world mind," Geneva said.

"Hmm, the *unus mundus*," Lydia chewed a few more almonds and swallowed. "That's a way to look at it. All these ideas are connected. This way," she said and led Geneva through the book maze back to the bakery.

Downstairs, Lydia took a pound of plant butter from a refrigerator and dropped it into a white ceramic saucepan decorated with tiny red flowers. She dusted one of the countertops with flour, overturned a bowl of dough and divided it into three sections. She threw one to Streker. He peeled off his sweater. Underneath he wore a thin long-sleeved Sync Chrome City T-shirt. He pushed up the black sleeves and tied back his hair.

Lydia placed a lump of dough in front of Geneva and demonstrated the kneading motions. "Up to speed. Down to business, dear."

Geneva looked over her shoulder. A row of shiny buttered, brown-topped wheat loaves lined the narrow opening from the bakery to the shop. Past the bread and through the pink swirl—s'aidyL— across the front window the street looked empty. "The car could be here soon. I don't really think we have time."

"Don't worry. I'm an expert. We can finish these fast. Or Cinda will." Lydia nodded behind her at the opening and the back of the shop clerk's pink-kerchiefed head. "Besides I think better when my hands are moving. You're studying psychology?"

Geneva nodded.

"That makes it easier. You know a little about the brain. You understand how it works? Electricity leaps from synapse to synapse and, voilà! we are alive, Frankenstein style. Brain cells store and access information like a computer." Lydia dipped her head from side to side. "Left brain logical, over here. Right brain creative, over there."

Geneva pressed the dough under the pads of her hands. "No. Not quite, it's way more complex than a computer. It's really a combination of chemicals and electricity. And that whole right brain, left brain thing is really outdated. There is no right-side, left side; it functions together."

"Mmm, hmm, that's right. Now fold the dough together and squoosh it again. Squoosh, that's a technical term. Good. Good, they are teaching you something in that university. Neither one nor the other, neither right nor left. Both. Much more intricate. Organic. Adaptable. Interwoven. We call it the community of the mind. The brain has far more possibilities for connections than stars in the universe." Lydia inclined her head at Streker. "He hasn't helped me in the bakery for a very long time. But see?"

Streker kneaded the dough moving it through his long hands like liquid.

"Plasticity. Even now his synapses are reestablishing old connections." Lydia said. "And strengthening new ones. Our brains have the ability to change rapidly with experience and the more experiences we have the more we are capable of. We create our own possibilities. Start at any idea, anywhere and you have immediate access to the entire potential content of your consciousness.

All the options, unlike any device. The brain is totipotent —capable of all possible futures."

Steker snorted. "My mom's really into wetware."

"Shush, skeptic. Don't roll your eyes at me. I know what I'm talking about. Even if you think it's foolish. I don't know why you are so interested in computers when I've always told you, you have the untapped potential right here." She thumped him on the side of the head with a floury hand.

"I'm studying philosophy. I don't think you're foolish, I just..." Streker said.

"Yes, you do." Lydia reached across him for a tube of frosting. She squeezed a drop of icing onto her fingertip and smacked her lips around it. "Mmm, taste," she said dotting the tip of Geneva's own fingertip with icing. It tasted faintly of orange.

"Matter used to be the gold standard, then it was energy," Lydia said. "We found smaller and smaller particles capable of testing the limits of what we thought was possible. We found particles that responded differently in controlled tests depending on the expectations of the researchers. The particles moved as the researchers thought they would." She flicked some flour from her fingers at Streker. "Now tell me that I am making some fantastic leap. I am not. It is the teeniest, tiniest step through time and space, from where quantum physicists have explored to what the ancient shamans believed. Sentient awareness is the basic substance of the universe. It's the material that connects us all." Lydia raised her arms up over her head and brought her hands together: clap, clap and a shower of flour. "Thought."

"Mom, I know you're not stupid." Streker said. "You just get so drama, and I really don't think..."

"Give me," Lydia held out her hands and took the satiny lumps of dough from Geneva and Streker in each hand mashing them together. She unhooked a silver rolling pin from a collection of utensils clanging overhead. She rolled the dough into a thick sheet.

"It isn't such a stretch to believe that everyone has a great deal of unused potential." She sighed. "Here we are having this conversation instead of simply understanding each other. But at least we're going to get some sweets out of it."

Geneva looked over her shoulder again. There was still no sign of the purported car. "So you earned your doctorate in quantum physics?"

"Yes, yes and then you want to know why I have a bakery in Deming? The answer is because I've always wanted to have a bakery in Deming. Because they shut down the space program when the economy collapsed, and this was my opportunity. But the real reason is that our minds are the next frontier, the greatest exploration we will ever undertake." She pressed her hands to the sides of her head pressing down her frizzy puff of hair. "This is the space I'm interested in now. If we apply what we know and observe about the universe to ourselves, if we take our intuition seriously, then we, we scientists and bakers, become telepathic. We've always had the innate abilities. We just need to learn and connect those neural pathways like anything else."

Lydia grabbed the saucepan of melted butter and poured it over the dough. She made butter waves spreading it around with her fingers. She shook a jar of cinnamon sugar over it. The lighter particles of cinnamon wafted up. The heavy bits fell. Streker sneezed. Lydia laughed and poked him in the side.

"Meanwhile, even skinny, skinny skeptics have to eat. And it might as well be cinnamon rolls." Lydia rolled the dough over the layer of butter-soaked cinnamon sugar turned rich earth black. "You know, they say cinnamon enhances psychic abilities. I am constantly testing that theory." She winked. "So that's the answer to your question. People are gathering in New West because New West was supposed to be moving forward with our exploration of minds. It was part of the promise of our utopian vision."

"Now that's what's stupid," Streker said. "People don't want to be psychic. That's never what New West planned. That's all you."

"Well, you could be right. People are afraid. But I don't think we have a choice. They triggered it, so now our chapter of Psi-Aware is asking the government to take action, to take responsibility for what they began."

"Mom, don't. You shouldn't put yourself out for those wackos. They laugh at you. They don't care about you. You are not psychic. You're not gonna be. Not even a little."

Lydia took down a large clean-edged knife and began to slice off ends of the roll. "We have cut the brain into the thinnest slices and inspected it, but one aspect remains a mystery: consciousness. The mind-brain dilemma. How do all the chemicals, sections, synapses, and cells that we do understand account for and create an individual's sense of self, which we don't? This is the question that we will answer in your lifetime. That's your question too, Geneva. Your burning question: What does all of this have to do with me?"

Lydia looked at her out of the corner of her eye as she sliced the dough. Geneva leaned forward. *Yes. This is it. Tell me why I'm here,* she thought.

"The answer is: nothing," Streker said. "Mom, that's enough. Leave Gen alone. This is your thing. She doesn't care about any of this." Streker grabbed her arm. "Come on. Let's wait outside."

Geneva pulled her arm free and pushed Streker aside. "No. I need to hear this." She thought she heard a car approach now, a crunch of gravel, but she didn't look back.

"The car," Streker said.

She ignored him. She stepped toward Lydia. "Why are they are always staring at me?"

"Because we can feel your thoughts dear. You're projecting outside yourself, outside your head. We call you Push-Me," Lydia shook her head. She brandished the knife in between cuts. "No, not pusher. Push-Me. Like Push-Me-Pull-You. That's what it feels like when you think: a push. Anyone paying the least bit of attention around you gets it."

"But I'm not doing anything," Geneva said.

"Oh, but you are. Trust me." Lydia said. "Were you always this way?"

No.

"Leave her alone," Streker said.

"Any idea how this happened? What does your intuition tell you?" Lydia asked. "If it's about your friend, why are you here?"

"Mom, let it go."

Val. Val. I just want to help Val.

Lydia turned to her and fixed her with that Psi-Aware gaze, the one that made her feel as though she were thrust on stage in front of a large crowd. A connection sprang to the front of her mind. *Val! Sync Chrome City.* It landed. Snap. *We're in danger.*

Lydia Streker reeled. She clutched her head, nicking her forehead with the knife, and teetering back. She elbowed the pot of butter on her way down. The delicate red flowers spun around the rim. Streker lunged to catch his mother as the ceramic pan lurched off the counter hitting his arm. Hot butter slopped onto Geneva's thigh. It slid down Streker's arm. The knife clattered. The pan shattered on the floor.

Lydia sat among buttery shards. Blood trickled down the side of her face and flecked her forearms. She began to cry. "That was my mother's pot."

Streker threw off his shirt. Geneva stared at the sudden exposure of skin. His pale flesh hung close to his bones. His shoulder and upper arm were shiny, bright red. He bent his shoulder into the sink and turned on the tap. "Burned?"

Geneva's thigh pulsed heat when she looked at it. A grease stain spread across her khakis. "I'll be OK."

"No, take off your pants." he said. He shrugged his shoulder at the running faucet. "Put it under cold water."

He turned away and offered a hand to his mom. Geneva stepped out of her sneakers and pulled down her pants. She jumped up on the counter and wedged her leg under the water. The cold felt good until she looked down and saw how her thigh was a bright match with her silk scarlet panties. She wished she'd changed out of her party underwear and vowed never to have such a stupid thing again. It served her right for thinking her underwear could be seen in a desirable situation to be caught out now, ridiculous. She heard a car door slam just before the bell rang.

She pulled her shirt down between her legs and looked up to see the creepy older guy from last night's party standing in the doorway with a half-eaten Bismarck and a creamy smile. "Well, what have you been up to? Ready to go?"

Streker knelt at his mother's side. He helped her to her feet, his head bent low to her ear whispering, "Please don't go with him. He doesn't care about you."

Geneva sat in the sink still holding the ends of her shirt down, knees pressed together. Lydia followed Burrows upstairs to get her things. She took Geneva's pants to the clothes washer and promised she'd bring something else down for her to wear.

"Are you OK?" Streker asked. He gently placed his hands on either side of the reddening blotch on her thigh. The soft flour dusting his palms tickled. Sparse, black hair trailed across his chest and in a line down to the top of his jeans.

She touched his shoulder above the burn. "Yeah, you?"

He flexed a freckled arm. "It's OK. I don't think it will blister."

"It's not true, is it?" she whispered. "I'm not a whatever, a Push-Me. I mean, you can't feel me?"

Streker's eyes flicked from her thigh to her neck. "Now?"

She flushed. "I mean, thinking."

He knelt to press his forehead to hers and pulled back.

"You have to tell me," she said. "You won't keep secrets."

"Not if you ask. Then, the answer is: yes." The word pressed out of his thin, thin lips. "At first, I thought you were just very intense. Then I realized I could actually hear you, words. It's OK. You're very, very nice. Don't be afraid. Not of me. It doesn't feel bad to me, your thoughts. It's just different, lady."

As he placed his lips on hers, they felt full and warm. His kisses were soft and kittenish, harmless. She tensed as the faucet pressed into her back and glanced at the stairway.

"It's OK. It doesn't have to be such a big deal. You can relax. They'll be awhile," he said. She caught the bitterness in his voice and felt sorry for him. She wanted to comfort him, soothe herself.

Streker put his fingers to her mouth and traced them lightly across her lips. "I want to think about something nice."

He put his arm around her and drew her in. It was a turn on to let him touch her, she felt generous as though she were bestowing an ill-deserved gift. She felt pleasantly free of herself. He moved his hand and kissed her again until she wrapped her arms around the back of his neck. His tongue licked the traces of grease and sugar from the corners of her mouth. She stopped thinking, on purpose.

Her burn brushed his jeans. It stung. She was still very conscious that she wasn't wearing pants but becoming less and less embarrassed by it.

Then a pair of large hands gripped Streker's shoulders and yanked him from her arms. The creepy older guy said, "It's time to go."

Lydia stood behind him, her eyes red and swollen. She tossed a pair of white drawstring pants to Geneva who jumped down from the sink and pulled them on. The guy grabbed her arm as soon as she was standing upright before she had time to put on her shoes. He steered her to the door. "Enough fooling around."

Streker stood at his mother's side. He put his arm around her shoulder and drew her in. "What's wrong?"

"You were right." Lydia said. "Happy? He doesn't care about me."

Compared to the guy who held her, they looked so small: Streker a mere slice, Lydia dwarfish. "Yeah, you'd think, Lydia, if you were psychic, you would have seen this coming," Burrows said as Geneva pulled away. When he didn't let her go, she kicked. "I'm not going anywhere with you."

He absorbed the blows and held her fast. "Yeah, 'fraid so. Didn't kissy-face here tell you that was the plan?"

"Let her go." Streker said. "I said I'd bring her. I never said I'd let you take her. Not if she doesn't want to go."

Geneva went limp. "*This* is your friend?"

Streker shrugged scrawny shoulders. He seemed sad, but he always looked sorrowful. "You didn't ask."

Creepy older guy gave her a yank. "You think we're having a conversation, people?"

Her feet flew out from under her. She managed to get a foot on the ground and catch her balance. She twisted around and planted a foot in the guy's groin— heel first, Tae-Kwon-Do style, just like in the self-defense class at Inu Wood. It worked. She felt the give in his jeans under her bare foot. He folded at the waist and released her. "Ungh."

She turned and ran for the stairs. She made it more than halfway down the hall when he caught the tail end of her shirt and swung her sideways. Her foot twisted into one of the bags of flour. She spun into the pantry shelf and scrabbled at jars of cake decorations. Colored bottles flew off the shelves shaking sugar-crystals. One of the containers popped open. In a shower of pink sprinkles, the guy got a grip on her shoulders. "Fun," he said. "But not very friendly."

Slip, she thought. And he shook her so hard her neck torqued. It stunned her. She couldn't think.

He walked her to the door, smashing scattered sprinkles underfoot. The bell rang again as Burrows directed her out of the shop, with a firm hand. Geneva turned her head. "Why? What about Val?"

Streker, shirtless, cringed into his collarbones. He didn't make a move.

Creepy older guy manhandled her into his car. "All that tussle and you never asked where we were going. I'm taking you right to your best friend forever." He nodded at Streker. "Just like he promised."

Finally, in the creep's black Mercedes, Geneva was headed at top speed toward Linden, exactly what she had wanted. Except now, she knew she was a freak. The Psi-Aware protesters, who wanted everyone to be psychic, were listening to her thoughts and somehow this whole idea was putting all her friends in danger, if they were her friends: tough to say, since her judgment was clearly impaired. The second boy she'd ever kissed had already betrayed her. Follow your intuition because your brain is a step ahead of you, Lydia had advised. But if that was true, then Geneva's subconscious was seriously defective. Maybe her gray matter wasn't working right. Or maybe she was thinking too much.

Her twisted ankle throbbed and her neck ached. At least she didn't have to ponder the source of her sadness. Her trouble wasn't Val, the loss of connection to the *unus mundus* world mind or the firing of the primitive, emotional center of her brain the almond-shaped, amygdala. She looked at her kidnapper. Her problem was him. *Who the hell are you, creepy older guy? What do you want with me? I hate this.* The car swerved and Geneva clutched her burning thigh.

"My name is Burrows," he said through clenched teeth. "And 35 is not that fucking old."

~ 17 ~

SYNC CHROME CITY: BREAK OUT

"Be prepared for your first entrance into the external neural net to be disorienting and quite unlike your earlier psychic experiences. The main difference is that instead of your mind being used as an extension of your body, you will experience your body as an extension of mind. Instead of your one separate ego connecting to a few minds as you may have experienced in small group work, your ego will be subsumed by the larger Connected Ego. A common experience is to perceive the Connected Ego as a very literal interpretation of the inside of the mind as moist, dark, warm, electrical coils often accompanied by blue or violet flashes of light. Later experiences may be quite different. The Connected Ego has been perceived as nature (clouds, forests, mountains, or seas), patterns (tapestry, wires, or cells), or as mundane places mimicking virtual realities in libraries, schools, or city streets. Sexually active students familiar with entering a state of communion with another person will more easily access the Connected Ego. It has been said that the experience is similar to orgasm. Certainly, it produces similar patterns of activity in the brain." —*Becoming Psychic 101, A History and a Primer*

Burrows pulled over on the highway just outside of Deming. Even though he had practice, it was harder than you'd think to fit an unwilling 19-year-old girl into the trunk of a car. He didn't bother being gentle. He could still feel the ache in his groin where she'd landed him one. It was all about control. He held her as if she were a snake, squeezing the back of her neck. Still, she could kick and she had a lot of leg for a short girl. She'd actually been more trouble after he'd blindfolded her and tied her hands behind her back. Once he put his hands on her, lifting her up, she'd lashed out with those legs. Up until then, he supposed, as long as he was going her way, she'd been willing to give him the benefit of the doubt.

He skewered a knee up into the small of the girl's back. She arched instinctively and he used her momentum to force her into a forward fold. He hadn't meant for it to go down like this. After six months of careful planning to remove the psychic threat and bring down New West, he'd ended up with victims in the trunk of his car like some cheap serial killer. It bruised his ego. This wasn't the way he'd meant to operate. It wasn't who he was. He'd been all finesse turning Sync Chrome City and Psi-Aware in his direction. Now this was a come down. He couldn't chance the border with her in the trunk. But in the car, beside him, she'd been thinking migraines at him. Unbearable.

At the same time, even through the headache, he'd liked her there on the seat beside him twirling her ponytails around her fingers and biting her lower lip so hard her hair and lips were the same shade of red. Cute. He knew he hadn't thought she was adorable before and suspected the SLO-42 had worked him over. He hadn't meant to scare the girl. But he'd seen that joker Streker kissing her in her underwear, and he'd reacted. Then, he'd had to fight to get her out to the car. It had to be residual SLO-42 fuzzing his thinking. Yeah, maybe, literally, fuzzy. Like small, brown and fuzzy. Like voles. He remembered reading something about SLO-42 in the C-Town *Mirror* when he'd lived with his parents. The headline had said blah, blah, blah FEMALE ORGASMS. That caught his attention. It was probably the reason that rag, *The Mirror*, had done the story in the first place, anything to put the word orgasm out front. SLO-42 was made of two neurotransmitters. One of them, oxytocin, had been linked to lovely female orgasms and, far less sexy, maternal instincts. In male rodents — voles — they'd found it triggered bonding, monogamous relationships. Bottom line: men didn't have a biological excuse to screw around because voles were committed. Yeah, someone had really reached for that one. Who woke up in the morning to study vole sex? What loser got stuck with the job?

Anyway, when he'd seen Streker with Geneva, he'd lunged like some kind of sightless tunnel beast thinking, "Mine." So, there was a good chance that goof Leo wasn't interested in Coco anymore. The kid might not even know it himself, but his fresh batch of SLO-42 held a bit of bonding to this girl, Geneva. He eyed the band of red underwear across her buttocks showing through the sheer white pants, as he tucked her head under the metal lip of the trunk. Too bad she was such a pain, maybe he would have worked on changing her impression of him.

"You know most women find me really attractive," he said.

In return he got: *Creep.* Again, with the creep. He should have been mad, but it was kind of endearing. Damn drugs, he'd never had any fun with them.

She caught him a good one above his knee and he dropped her into the trunk.

"Sorry, sweets, what we have just ain't real. It's all in his head."

The nice thing about there not being a lot of traffic in New West was that he didn't have to worry about being seen along the highway. He just kept a look out for Shadow Buses. But these unpaved roads were hell on Mistress MDs wheels. The potholes!

Geneva landed in the trunk of Burrows' Mercedes. The lid slammed over the top of her, rocking her back and forth so that she got a feel for the space: tight. She gummed the wad of gauze stuffed into her mouth trying to find a comfortable place for her tongue to rest behind it. Her eyes were bound under another cloth and her wrists wrenched behind her. It all seemed a bit much. She got the feeling she had really bothered creepy older guy, personally. Why? What was she to him? Better question, why was she worried about the kidnapper's feelings?

She should have jumped out of the car when she'd had the chance. But he'd said he'd take her where she wanted to go, to Val. Until he'd freaked out, trussed her up, and stuffed her in the trunk, being in his car hadn't seemed so bad. Now it was bad. She strained her fingers behind her to see if she could reach her bonds. Instead, she touched smooth cold skin. She pulled her hands back. Was that really skin? Cold, dead skin? She wasn't sure. How cold was dead? She hadn't taken anatomy yet. And it was winter. It was cold in the trunk anyway. Her own hands were probably cold, not dead cold though.

If there was another body, no, another person, in here with her, it would have to be small, no he/she would have to be small. Maybe that's why it had been so hard for the kidnapper to get her into the trunk. Or it could be a big person, a big body, in pieces.

She reached out again tentatively. This time she ran her fingers over thick satiny fabric. She touched something cool and smooth, a button, no, a snap. She poked her hand down behind the button into a pocket of the slippery fabric — snaps, pockets — plug-in clothes. The body — *no, don't think that* — the person, behind her jerked. She reached back again and felt the cool skin — hands. The fingers wiggled in hers. Thank goodness. Live hands, her size hands, maybe a little smaller with slimmer, longer fingers. A live person. Then underneath the medicinal smell of gauze, she caught a whiff of cinnamon.

Valerie? It had to be Val. She felt relieved and terrified. If that was Val, they were together again, but in the same predicament. Worse, but better. She tried to take a deep breath through her nose, but there was barely room for her chest to lift. She squirmed trying to create give. She needed to breathe, think how to get out of this. The top of her head struck metal. She went still.

Then it felt like someone pulled her hair: *Gen.* She was lying on top of one of her ponytails. She wiggled and got her hair out from under her, but her hair still pulled at her neckline. Her fingers fluttered behind her.

Yank: *Gen.* The hands grasped hers.

Yank: *Gen. It's me. Relax.*

She thought she heard a voice, but the voice didn't sound like Val. It sounded too close and metallic. It reminded her of a sleepless night when she was very ill as a small child with a high fever. The voice had said: *Geneva.* It had called out to her from a nightmare: A dream about a blaze in the middle of the 'Way. Her mind re-envisioning the night they had rescued Val maybe. The voice had called *Geneva* from the middle of the fire insistent, urgent. The voice had licked her like flames.

This voice was similar. She listened to the muffled hum of the car tires on pavement and felt the vibration beneath her and realized the voice wasn't a sound at all. It was a physical sensation. She felt it inside her head, behind her eyes, inside where she herself was, within her own thoughts. The pressure was like thinking very hard, like learning a difficult subject for the first time, or studying for a final exam in a foreign language.

Gen. It's OK. You can hear me?

It tapped at the back of her head. It gnawed. It burrowed in bringing bad news. *He wants to kill us. We need a plan.*

Kill us. It really hadn't occurred to her. It seemed so out of the realm of possibility of what someone would actually do. She retreated from the thought.

The trunk had the ambience of a cold womb. She curled there. As a child, when she'd dreamt about the fire, she'd woken up and pulled the covers around her head leaving only a breathing hole.

It wouldn't keep the monsters out, but it'd be better to go with her eyes closed. She'd lose in a struggle, but the fear would be the worst. The monsters could eat her, so long as she didn't have to watch. She'd slept that way ever since, hiding.

Tap: *Gen.* Tap: *You idiot.* Tap, tap: *Don't shut me out. Hello, stop being so morbid.*

Geneva bounced as the car went over a bump. Slam: *I've had it with you.* She pulled her hands out of the ones behind her and tried to press them down against her back. That voice wasn't Val. Val wouldn't say that. All she'd been doing was worrying about Val, trying to help her. If she hadn't been, she wouldn't even be here. She'd be finishing school. Since last spring, she'd been worrying about Val and maybe even always, since Val came to live with them.

The voice: *Spare me, Gen. Spare me your denial and guilt. You haven't been thinking about me. You haven't even been paying attention.*

Geneva moaned under the gauze and squirmed trying to stretch her cramped limbs. That had been Val. The sentences vibrated with a tinny twang like someone talking through the end of an aluminum tube, but the tone was definitely Val's. It was her scathing voice—the one she used when she thought she knew more than a professor, "He keeps making these analogies to string theory but he never shows us any equations." or when they were both mad at their mother, "I think if we want to see mom again, we're going to have to move to C-town." or when they made fun of their father, "OK, here comes Vole-Man to the rescue — for all your obscure rodent knowledge needs." It was not funny being the recipient of the sarcasm. *I was worried*, she thought, and I *saved your life*. Just *last night*.

From the voice—Val—came: *Did you? Or did you just turn me in so they could lock me up again at that clinic. Turn me in so Burrows could find me. You don't know what's going on. You don't know what's happening to me — everyone. You're just worried it will mess up your plans.*

Now she was sure she was in the trunk with Val, hearing Val's thoughts. But she couldn't believe what Val was saying. How could she be critical at a time like this? Sometimes it was too hard to be her friend. She just didn't get where Val's head was, anymore, if she ever had. Now that they were going to die at the hands of some psycho, she just wanted Val to know that she loved her, cared about her. At a time like this, that was all that mattered.

Val: *That is so lame ass. 1. I'm not going to die like this. 2. You have to figure this out.*

Val grabbed her fingers and squeezed them hard. She twisted them wringing them around. Stinging shocks replaced the numbness in Geneva's hands. At the same time, she felt a thrust: *Here!*

What she got was a chunk of thought, Val's thought. A memory that shoved her own reality—panting for breath behind a cloth—aside. She recognized it immediately. It was a moment from her childhood. Val had had severe asthma as a child, but she hated her inhaler and often forgot to carry it. Geneva had been with some new friends across the playground when Val had collapsed.

This time, in the memory, she was Val sprawled on the fresh mown lawn. Geneva stared at the pink daisy sandals that had been Val's favorites at age 7. She wheezed. Her ribs felt like armor over her tight, flat lungs. She took deep pulls through her nose trying to lift them, let in some air. Her chest constricted. There was barely room for her pounding heart. Breathless moments passed. She tried to focus on the pink daisies. They spun round and turned purple. She was drowning without water. Everything was tinted blue: the grass, the schoolyard, Gen running toward her. She couldn't breathe. She could not breathe. Gen pressed the inhaler into her hand, held it to her mouth helped her pump the fumes into her lungs. She relaxed, waited. They expanded, opening wide. She lay back on the grass, arms wide looking up into the sky, air everywhere, drawing breath. Euphoria. Breath. Breathing.

Geneva shook her head from side to side, the cloth between her teeth, herself again. It had been like being in a demo of a virtual reality game, where you are someone else, but not in control.

She was still trying to reorient when Val slammed in another chunk of memory, this one unfamiliar, at first. It placed her in the middle of a blaring black swarm. It snapped into focus when she looked down and saw the thigh high boots. Val was in college at a concert surrounded by Plug-Ins, dancing up on the speakers, and loving it loud. Her skull vibrated. Her body rocked. The walls were coated in electronic finery. She felt hands on her hips and turned to see a bare undulating torso. The stomach in front of her was nearly convex with sparse black hair. She grew warm feeling Val's lust. Then she looked up the trail of curly black hair up into the face and the eyes: one blue, one brown. Possibility. Maybe even love. She saw Streker. Streker and Val, together.

The memory released her. Streker: Val's boyfriend. Oh, shit. Shit. Geneva went cold, trunk in winter cold — not dead cold, she was pretty sure. She'd been kissing Val's boyfriend. She should have known. How long had they been dating? She was surprised at how easily she knew the answer once she thought about it: Since this time last year when Val had started spending more and more time plugged-in and at the Mansion. Val and Streker had been together a year. And she'd kissed him, today, for no reason at all, just a distraction.

Val was right. She hadn't been paying attention, didn't want to. Maybe worrying about Val wasn't the same as caring about her at all. Maybe it was just avoidance. No, wrong. In the stillness of the trunk, Geneva realized Val could be reading her thoughts — right now. She didn't want Val to know about this kiss, didn't want to damage her friendship any more than she already had. Instead, she thought about the one thing that made it impossible to think of anything else — Val's parents, how they had died.

Val: *Fuck you. Everybody dies. It's no excuse, bitch.*

The car lurched and swerved. It sped up and then it went quiet. The vibration of the engine stilled. The car had stopped somewhere. There were footsteps, then a screech of metal on metal like a key being scraped along the outside of trunk. There was a dull thud and a steady—thunk, thunk—across the top that grew faster and faster. Geneva flattened trying to get away from the roof.

Val: *Relax. He's just whacking off.*

The sound stopped. She heard footsteps and the hum returned. The car lurched. Geneva braced and spared herself another lump on the head. The hum came high and long. They were moving fast.

Val: *Forget, apologies. I've had it. If I'm stuck here with you, I can't wait for you to come around. I can't let you ignore me. If you care, you'll get this.*

The thrust thought came again. She couldn't tell at first if she was Val or not. She was disoriented, unsure. That didn't feel Valish. The new place was black, filled with dark tangled shapes. It could have been the trunk they were in or maybe the backseat of Eve's car. Her limbs were cramped and bound, and she was still stuffed into the space, but it was hot and moist. She looked down to see what kind of shoes she had on. There was only blackness below. She struggled against the thick cords binding her. They released her and she plunged forward into black space. Then the cords yanked her back and sent her ricocheting. They began to glow. Neon purple coils lined the walls of an open chamber and sizzled with current. She flew past them and landed, free, on top of a pile of greasy ropes.

What was this? A virtual reality? A techno sauna? A plug-in theme park? It wasn't a memory. Maybe it was a dream. *No*, she thought, *this is Val's mind, I'm in.*

Geneva searched through the piles of cords, holding each one to her ear until she located the source of the echoing whine. When she found the one humming, it slipped from her hand again and again until she wrapped it around her wrist, a purple, fluorescent bracelet. She followed it stepping over and under the other cords. A goo like melted blackberry cordial coated her arms. As she walked, the whine got louder and shriller and the cord began to pull. She stumbled forward trying to keep her balance on the slick surfaces. She ran, then tripped, dragged forward through the ropes. They lashed her face and smeared it with warm mush. She started to scream.

Then she arrived at the memory. She knew it, instantly. She looked down and saw the thigh high boots tucked beneath her. She was Val studying in the dorm room last spring screaming loud and shrill. She was on Sync Chrome City opening to the minds around her and then she was off in space. Off the net, detached, but still linked to a sea of minds. She was scared, but not terrified—thrilled. Every few seconds, Val took a breath and could have stopped screaming. But she elected to howl: a joyful catharsis, epiphany, power.

In a flash, from outside the memory, Geneva saw the purple cords, strung tight, vibrating. The neon flickered. The cords sizzled and went black. A burst of burnt sugar steam rose from the cords. It smelled of charred blackberry pie. It stung the back of her throat.

Inside the memory, Val's scream changed to that wrenching, throat about to be torn out, shriek. She fell off the chair and started to convulse. She looked at Gen watching her, wide-eyed and frozen. Help me, she thought. She couldn't breathe.

The car lurched. Geneva was jolted back to her own senses. The memory released her. She thought hard trying to make sense of what she had experienced.

Val: *I need you. Do you get it? Did you see? This is it. Final exam.*

Sync Chrome City had awakened something in Val's mind. It wasn't bad. For a moment, it had been amazing. It wasn't an illness like they said. It was a new ability. A sense. Something changed.

Val: *Forget it. I don't need you. I'm on my own. Again. I'll fight this guy, get out of here myself.*

Wait! *Wait!* Geneva thought, but this time she imagined gripping at the purple cords. The thoughts pressed out of her. *I don't understand. Is this some kind of evolution?*

There was a long silence. Stillness. The car had stopped again.

Val: *Yeah, maybe exactly.* Geneva also felt Val's emotions: Relief. Excitement. Val had been so scared, alone. They had both felt so alone.

Geneva thought out: *I think I got what was going on with Sync Chrome City. But what about that other part: the coils and the neon. What's all that?*

There was silence—then footsteps.

Val: *I don't know. You're the psychology major. Listen, about Streker. I know. It's not your fault. He's like a big dog, needy. And he took some of that Da Lime. It's OK.*

Geneva sighed. She was trapped in a trunk and suddenly unafraid. Possibly the least afraid she'd ever been in her life. *Euphoria. Possibility. Power.*

Burrows opened the lid of the trunk. He looked down at the two trussed girls, one in white, one in black, lying yin-yang curled like seeds inside fruit holding hands behind their backs. He stepped back, his head pounding. His instinct said, *close the trunk, get away*. He almost listened.

~ 18 ~

SYNC CHROME CITY: FAUSTUS

"It is possible to use psychometric tools to store aspects of one's thoughts or to help gain access to the Connected Ego. However, use of Faustus Implements by students (popularized by sympathetic retellings of C. G. Burrows' role in the Psychic Dawning) is generally discouraged. They are unnecessary to psychic development and there is no reason a student should feel compelled to expend undue effort to the task of creating one. Because Burrows used his Faustus as a murder weapon, some schools strongly oppose the creation of any such mind-imbued matter. Despite its nefarious origins, however, there is no reason to believe psychometry is anything other than a harmless diversion." — *Becoming Psychic 101, A History and a Primer*

Burrows reached under his brown jacket to the side holster hanging beneath his arm. He unclasped the leather pouch, rolled his fingers over the smooth, cold cylinders, and withdrew Faustus, his favorite nine incher. With his thumb over the blunt end of the needle, he reached into the trunk. One of the girls was kicking now, jamming her heel against the inside of the taillight to no effect. The other girl lay still, facing up, her head swaying from side to side, blind, but aware of him, listening. He reached for her, plunged Faustus into the well between her throat and her collarbone. Her body arched around it and then writhed away as he drove it in. Blood pooled around the wound on extraction.

Using Faustus wasn't an efficient way to dispatch the girl, but it was satisfying. Burrows focused on that spot of red until it appeared behind his eyes. His mind went numb as he retreated inside himself, alone, where no one could reach him for the first time in years. Here, now — this was the place he'd been seeking, the quiet that drugs and rituals and meditation and hiding out in the forest couldn't provide. He ran his hand down his thigh, over his ink. All this time, he'd been pointing the needle — *Omnis festinatio ex parte diaboli est* — in the wrong direction. The blood-streaked needle quivered in his hand, rising and falling with his breath. It wavered over her heart like a divining rod. Maybe he didn't need to kill her quickly at all. Then — crack — plastic splintered.

Geneva experienced déjà vu as she started to kick around in the trunk. Some faint memory clung to the whiff of wax polish. Maybe she'd dreamt of escaping from the trunk of a car before. How had it turned out? She searched for the taillight with her foot, planning to kick it out, thrash her foot around and hope someone would see.

Valerie lay still beside her: *Stop. Above us. The open space. He's there.*

Geneva registered the click of the trunk and the waft of cool air, external cues that had escaped her when she was inside herself feeling the rush. Then images flashed in front of her eyes. A pierced round hole filling with blood: *Pain.*

Val thrashed. Geneva's leg thrust through the taillight. But it didn't matter now. The lid was open. He was right there, hurting Val. She sat up and pulled her leg out. She stumbled over the lip, sprang from the trunk and hit the pavement in a fetal position with her knees and shoulder. In her mind, she leapt up and ran forward, pummeling Burrows with superhuman strength, attacking like an enraged bear. In reality, her hands were tied behind her and her eyes and mouth were bound. She couldn't see. She couldn't roar. And he was there. The outline of his hulking shoulders hovered on the edges of her senses as if in infrared. He smelled like car wax and doughnut grease.

A rush like wind, a high-pitched whine, surrounded Burrows. Geneva leapt from the trunk and landed on the pavement, trailing bandages, moving like an injured cat escaping. His quiet evaporated, the pressure began to build under his forehead. He turned to the girl, with the needle poised. And then—whump—she hit him square behind the eyes. He flew back. His ass struck pavement and gravel ground up his lower back. The impact rumbled down his spine like a Shadow Bus.

Then he was gone. Where? Spinning blindly Geneva pushed herself up to standing. She leaned back and reached behind her into the trunk. Val's hands clasped hers. Warm. Alive. She didn't want to let go. But Val's hands slipped out of hers pulling at the bandages on her wrists. When her hands were free, Geneva tore the blindfold from her eyes. They were on the side of the road surrounded by soy fields in the low light of afternoon. Burrows sat a ways off sheltering his head in the crook of his arm. He looked human there, unlike the monster she'd imagined him to be under the blindfold. She inhaled the rich soil smell, and turned her back on him, to see to Val.

The hole in Val's neck didn't look so bad, more like a bright pendant than a wound. But when she released Val's gag, she made a gurgling rasp as she drew breath and blood chugged from her throat.

Gravel crunched behind them. Geneva turned and kicked, aiming for Burrows' crotch again. He caught her shin and she tipped back, falling against the car. Her head scraped the lid of the trunk. The small of her back struck the edge. Burrows towered over her. She struck out, flailing her arms and he started to laugh. "The thing is, I have a size advantage."

Why would anyone hurt her? Hurt her and laugh? She cocked an elbow and clipped Burrows on the side of the jaw with a low smack of bone on bone. Pain shot up her elbow. But his eyes held fast on her, the space between his brows three long dark roads. "That's fine. Takes the edge off."

A glint caught Geneva's eye and she looked down to see the needle on the road. He'd dropped the weapon. Relief coursed through her. He'd release her to get it and then she'd have a chance.

"Nah, don't need it." He fumbled against her a moment, pressing her against the trunk. He pinned her there with a knee between her legs and then he grabbed her neck in his hands. "Be still, be quiet," he said squeezing each word into her neck.

Stricken, struggling, Geneva tunneled down into her own mind searching for a place inside herself running away from the approaching darkness. She reached a calming voice, a haven.

Val: *I'm right here. Come on. Stay with me. We're going to do this together. Think together. Let's take it to him. Think about the possibilities. Independence is overrated. Privacy's a thing of the past. Imagine what we could do... Intertwining fingers on your soul, invade your heart and make it whole...*

A purple coil of thought started to glow in the darkness and Geneva forgot about being choked and picked up on it... *harvest Sin and Chrome and Sea. Come and intertwine with me.*

Burrows grip loosened. She opened her eyes and saw him cringe. She lashed out: *Get back!*

He released her. His feet lifted off the ground. A lavender haze engulfed him and knocked him back. She turned raising her arms against the blast.

If you knew what we could do. You wouldn't be against it: Val continued.

Geneva lifted her head and peered between her forearms. She looked up into the empty gray sky, down the long silent road and over her shoulder at the still fields. A traditionalist, she was slow to catch on: *Wait, was that us?*

Burrows lay on his side, his legs splayed over the centerline of the highway. His head pounded, filled with chatter. A litany of pain and pressure swelled behind his optic nerves. It was exactly what he'd feared. He was trapped under the thoughts, immobilized. He realized he was lying in the road just as he caught a glint of silver streaking toward him over the horizon. He recognized the RV, Sync Chrome City was bearing down on him and he couldn't move. It'd roll right over him. He stared at death unblinking. He was not beyond caring, wracked with pain as he was, he always chose life. It was his. Why was his every choice stolen?

The RV stopped just in front of him, leaving his looking up under its tires.

Grugel got out, jumping: *Man, what are you doing here? You look like roadkill. Hit by a Shadow Bus. What the hell?*

Burrows made out the words. The pain faded back to average levels. Usual. Tolerable. He managed to get to his knees, stagger up. It was his life. His own. Sync Chrome City was here. New West was coming, his new friends, the boys in green. He had to get out. *Harvest Sin and Chrome and Sea*, the chorus resonated, lodged in his head, haunting. He rose to his feet and started running. No way, he'd be quashed by a song. Lame ass synth pop, and a couple of kids. No way. He slammed Geneva with his shoulder as he charged past her, sprinting into the soy fields.

"What the hell was that?" Grugel said. "What's with him?"

Geneva could barely hear him over the sound of Val's high-pitched excited laughter—that rollercoaster exultation again. In between fits, Val thought: *Whoa. Incredible. But I would like to see him run.*

"Right, yeah," Geneva said aloud. Clutching her shoulder, she lurched over to the trunk and untied Val's blindfold. The light sobered her. Val sat up: *We should go after him.*

Geneva looked out over the field. The sun, low in the sky, looked cold and distant. She wrapped her arms around herself: *It's too much.*

Val: *I know. It's weird. One minute you're eating Bismarks, the next someone's trying to hurt you.*

Geneva wished she had a coat to put over her T-shirt and Lydia's linen pants. Her jaw trembled: *We were hurting him. I mean, even if he... I still couldn't. That was a lot of...he was in a lot of—pain.*

Through the sound of her teeth clacking, Val's voice pressed through clearly: *Oh. OK, yeah. Wow. We can do that.*

"Um, guys?" Grugel wiggled his fingers back and forth between them. "Snap out of it. Am I, uh, interrupting something?"

"Yeah," Streker appeared beside them. Geneva flinched as he wrapped his trench coat around her shoulders, but she held on to the lapels. "They're talking."

Streker lifted Val out of the trunk in an easy motion. He was stronger than he looked. Looking down, Geneva spotted the needle lying by the road.

"Man, really? But Sync Chrome City." Grugel turned to the RV and back a couple of times. "No way. You mean without Sync Chrome City?"

"Yeah," Val said. Now that she was standing, a trail of blood oozed out of her throat and down her neck moistening the top of her T-shirt. But she was smiling so the gap between her front teeth showed. She looked cute and bloody.

Streker placed a couple of fingers to the side of Val's wound. "You're hurt." He massaged the torn pink edges of flesh and wiped the blood on his jeans. "It's not too bad, but let's get you in and fix you up."

"Shit," Grugel stomped one foot. "You mean we don't need Sync Chrome City? Isn't that gonna stall our easy ride?"

"No, we need it," Val said as Streker put his arm around her shoulders and began to lead her to the RV. "Not everyone can do what we can, yet. We still need a catalyst to wake the rest of them up."

Geneva got in their way. "No, this is crazy. We're not going with you."

"I wish you'd stop using that word," Val said.

Geneva pointed at Streker, "But he's an...an accessory. He gave me all that, crap, 'Come meet my mother, you'll really like her.' and then he...and he knew, knew we were best friends. Yeah, no, uh-uh."

They stopped. Val punched Streker on the shoulder. "You were an ass."

He hung his head. "I'm sorry. Really. I don't know why I trusted that guy. I think it was partly Da Lime. Blame it on Leo, guy loves everybody."

They started walking again, right towards her. She held up her hands. "That's not good enough. It's no excuse. You're still responsible for your actions."

"What are you going to do, stay by the side of the road?" Grugel's muffled voice came from the car. He was searching around in the trunk.

"No, we'll take that," she pointed ahead at the Mercedes.

Grugel looked up. "Steal my man's car?"

She held her arms out. "Your man tried to kill us. I guess we can borrow his car."

Val stepped around her. "We don't have time for this. It's a revolution." Grugel ran by her, too, carrying a round canister of car wax.

They entered the RV and left her standing alone in the road. She rolled her eyes and watched a few crows fly overhead across the flat gray sky. She bent and grabbed the needle. As soon as her fingers brushed it, it flashed blue: *Faustus.* The tips of her fingers went ice cold as she saw the needle plunging into a slim neck, Val's, and dipping into a thick thigh. She read pain, peace and agony off the needle like words on a page. She pulled her hand back, rubbed her fingers and rolled her eyes again. Well, what did she expect? The needle had a history. She thought about the bits and pieces of information that had passed her by, what Val and Streker had both said about Leo's Da Lime, how it drew people to her. The dangerous drug was a passed note with "Leo likes you" scrawled across it. She could exchange thoughts with Val and now with Faustus. It was too much to take in, a rush of, empathy, telepathy, psychometry. What was she going to do with it all? How would it change her? She wrapped the end of her T-shirt around her fingers and picked Faustus up. In the trunk of the car, she found a black encrusted piece of chamois cloth Grugel had missed. She wrapped the needle up and pocketed it.

When she turned around, the RV was still there. Val leaned out the door. She had a strip of white cloth tied around her neck, a spot of red soaking through the center, dashing, like a new punk look. "What're you doing? Come on."

Geneva stepped into the RV. It was no longer hazy, filled with the cloying cinnamon incense from New Year's Eve. It smelled like old carpet. Grugel was up front behind the driver's seat, smearing black car polish through his hair so it stood on end in three clumps. He stuck his tongue out, "Yaaah!" and leered as she got on board. In the dim light, Streker stood with his taut stomach exposed, the bottom of his T-shirt torn off. Val patted the chair next to her, sitting in front of the console. "Let 'em try to stop us now. We can do anything."

Darkness enveloped Geneva as she walked slowly to the back of the RV. On New Year's Eve, the glinting electronics on the black velvet had looked like stars. All around her they'd sparkled along with the electronic chords flowing over the chatter and laughter. She'd hidden in a corner, watching the Plug-Ins, unseen. That night, the RV had been warm with too many bodies and moist with breathy condensation. Now it was cold, dry, and silent. She stared at the console, a darker patch of black, until she could see the tiny squares of light reflected in Val's dark eyes. She felt like they were all floating in space on some leaderless mission. She wondered how they would get back. Val lowered a sleek pair of VR glasses over her eyes and handed Geneva another set. Streker dug a wire out of the console and unwound it to a black velvet chair big enough for two. He tapped a few buttons. "It'll be safe. We'll ease you in and out. Watch any one of those screens or all of 'em."

Streker took them in past the security sequences and in an instant they were connected to a thousand minds. Purple vines looped over them. Euphoria. Possibility. Power. She loved them all, these minds, these men and women. She'd do anything for them. *Now what? What do you want?*

The vines trembled and answers began to emerge: *Heal. Teach. Build. Help. Create. Love. Play. Sex. Relax.* Val: *Anything. Revolution. Change the world.* The students' minds pressed forward. Endorphins surged. The vines shook and the students dropped from them, disembodied, minds floating into space. The vines burst, juicy droplets flew. The minds rose over the split and writhing vines up into emptiness. Streker: *Leaving Sync Chrome City. This is new.* The students clustered together picking up speed, propelled by hope. Val whooped: *Go. Go.*

Geneva grew warm, sweat trickled down between her eyes under the glasses. They were going to reach meteoric speeds, rushing forward like a launch party. Geneva's earthbound limbs twitched against the chair. Her temperature dropped. The sweat cooled on her brow. She sensed black holes ahead: seven of them. The danger seemed a vague, dream-like premonition, until she remembered the names of the lost guys: Chris, Michael, Don, Eli, Todd, Roger, and Doug were in comas at New West Mental because of this, Sync Chrome City. Only reality had such stark, crisp details. A launch like this, they weren't ready for it. She pressed the names out to the group: *Some of us are missing. Wait. Stop.*

But Val kept going: *Don't hold us back.*

Back? Geneva knew as soon as she thought about it, got it off Streker and the rest of them: *You couldn't be doing this without me.*

She saw Grugel in Sync Chrome City, his vines appearing as a stream of wires and data, just before she pressed out a last thought—*everybody out of the pool*—and yanked off her glasses.

He stood behind her as she sat shaking in the dark RV. "Yaaah, it's definitely more powered up."

She blinked at the purple cords flickering on the edges of her vision. Streker's head lolled on her knee beside the mottled velvet of the chair. She stood up and he moaned, falling back. "More dangerous, you mean. This could kill them. Look what happened to the guys." She turned to where Val was still under the glasses. "Get her out of there."

Grugel stepped around the chair and stood between her and Val. Muscles packed his small frame beneath his black wicked hair.

"These are people's minds," She faced off with him. "What the hell are you doing? You charge for this? Try to make a profit? Then, when they can't pay, what do you do, unplug them? Like a public execution? That's sick."

He grabbed her wrists, his forearms flexing from flesh to solid mass, and shoved her. "You are not going to stall our easy ride."

She went down fast, her wrists smeared with black wax, landing on her ass. Grugel swung his leg back like he was shooting for a target outside the RV, far across the road, "You understand, I'm not giving this up." His boot came at her, its black top scuffed, its thick sole caked with highway mud and gravel.

She gasped. Her lungs filled with stale carpet air. Pink flashes obscured her vision. He loomed over her, a leaning square torso and triangular face pointed down at her. On the edges of him, beyond her vision, back inside her mind, she felt the other students, racing forward. Then, falling into space. The RV screens went dark. Sync Chrome City shut down leaving their minds open, but alone, spiraling outward. Utopia really was nowhere and that where they were all going.

Grugel kicked Geneva in the hip where she lay. The blow landed, but barely registered as she felt the students fall. He pirouetted towards the screens. "What the...?"

Separated from Sync Chrome City, the students' minds seized. Grugel bent over one of the screens. Streker and Val slumped on either side of him. Streker's head fell forward. Val's dropped over the lip of the low chair. The screen glowed gray as Grugel resurrected it. "Damn, bitch. You told them. The Greenies come to shut us down."

Streker and Val's limp bodies began to twitch. Streker's shoulder hunched. Val's head bounced along the back of the chair. Below her glasses, her dimpled cheek flexed. The glasses slid to the side and the white slivers of Val's eyes showed; her eyes had rolled back into her head following her mind inside. Streker and Val were seconds from full-blown spasms as their minds trekked into territory their brains couldn't handle.

Geneva didn't want to lose them— any of them. Already, she wasn't quite sure where the students were; outside of their own heads for sure, cast out of powered down Sync Chrome City, but no longer housed in any space, tangible or virtual. She reached for them, pressing her thoughts out and felt their minds faraway, but she couldn't find them without letting go of her own tether, her body. Then how would she get back? She didn't know how to search that far outside of herself. She could not make the connection.

When she opened her eyes, Grugel stood over her, reached down and pulled her to her feet. Her hip burned as she put weight on it and her leg bent under her. He hoisted her dead weight, tucking an arm around her waist and pushing her around in front of him. Her head jerked back as he held her ponytails tight near her scalp, wrapping them in his hand. "We're getting out of here. No way I'm getting caught."

He pushed her forward past Streker and Val, their bodies slack, their minds floating.

As Grugel pushed her up toward the cab, the RV door opened. Leo's arms and legs splayed across the exit creating angles of light and shadow. "Hey ya."

Behind her, Grugel tensed. "Hey, man. You wouldn't be with the greens."

Leo ducked his head under the doorjamb. "Nah. Came for that one." He nodded at her.

Grugel pressed his body into hers and pulled her hair back at the same time, leaving no space between them. It felt more confining than the trunk. She could smell the wax polish in his hair mingling with the stale air. "Ah, you and Streker keep getting distracted. The game's about what's between your ears. Focus. This is our ticket." He said pulling her hair even harder. "Help me get Sync Chrome City out to the 'Way."

She jerked her head back hard —thwack—her skull connecting with Grugel's chin. His hands loosened in her hair. She pulled away and stood sideways between the two men, her hands out measuring the distance between them. "Nobody leaves."

She clenched her jaw remembering the way Burrows had flown away from her and landed in the middle of the highway. Blood streamed from Grugel's nose, the straight line of it bent. She could throw him away from her, crumple his body into the RV wall just by thinking about it. Her vision blurred and tears warmed the pinched corners of her eyes. "No. Sync Chrome City is over. We're going to stay here and let the cops gut this place, take them to the clinic, and you," she pointed at Grugel. "Wherever. This is a big contest of crazy. But I'll win if I have to. I'll scream the loudest. It's over."

Grugel glared. The tight edges of his eyes and mouth twitched. Leo stared at him. "Border's closed Grugel. Greenies all around. This is it for Sync Chrome City."

Leo tilted his head back and stretched his hand out simultaneously, so he looked like he was standing on parallel planes. "But don't let them lock you up in the clinic, Gen. They aren't the good guys, either. Come on, girl. Let's go before they bust in."

She shook her head, her hips dropped low. Grugel darted around her. He checked Leo as he went out the door. "Yaaah, plan B." Leo sidestepped, lunging, and grabbing Geneva's shoulder. She turned at a sharp sting, just in time to see the neon green liquid shooting into her arm. "Fuck! Get off me!" She swatted at the syringe and its emptied shell wobbled in her shoulder and then fell to the ground. Leo released her. "Trust me, girl."

The SLO-42 kicked in fast, sharing Leo's perception, and the flashing green lights in the distance beyond the door caught her attention. Dark shapes crawled toward her in the rose-colored dusk beyond the doorway. Field agents. One of them waved the blue current end of his taser at her. Leo had gotten the greens to let him into the RV to retrieve her telling them she was an employee of Friend-Me Co, but they only half believed him. They were ready to rush in and finish their mission to shut down Sync Chrome City and take the students to the clinic.

Leo wanted to get her out of there, bring her back to New West to his mother. But it felt like a challenging escapade, a diversion. The baseline of his persona belonged lazing under a tree somewhere, smiling up at the sun. Underneath the burst of Leo's chemicals, Geneva started to giggle. She knew it was wildly inappropriate, but the drug overrode her. "Lighten up," she said. "Why so serious?" Her high-pitched laughter shook her whole body as Leo grabbed her hand and led her out of the RV.

It was warmer than she remembered outside. Leo let go of her hand and crooked an elbow at Burrows' Mercedes. She watched three agents dressed in forest green creep toward the RV as she slid into the passenger seat. As they drove north, Geneva glanced in the rearview mirror and saw Grugel running in the opposite direction. He ran in a zigzag pattern, veering into the soy field. A flicker of blue appeared low in the field, and he faltered, lurching to the side as his leg went out from under him. Geneva looked down and loosened the drawstring on Lydia's linen pants. She pulled a side down to inspect her hip where Grugel had landed his boot. It was turning lavender in garish contrast with the scarlet strip of her underwear. She cocked her head at Leo and pouted. "It hurts."

"Mmm," Leo said looking at her hip out of the corner of his eye and treating her to a pleasant alchemy of prurient and concerned interest.

"People shouldn't think someone's only about what they've seen. Just because you're usually quiet, doesn't mean you won't yell. You know, just because I'm not about creating drama doesn't mean..." She crossed her arms over her chest and nodded her head once, floating high on the cloud of Da Lime. "Damn, dopamine addicts. Turn it into a test and I'll ace it every time."

The corner of Leo's mouth raised plumping his hollow cheek. "Yeah, I heard. You'll win a contest of crazy."

She sniggered. "Actually," she tapped her chest, creating the flutter of an external heartbeat on her breastbone as she stared ahead at the long-straight road. "I'm psychic. Really. Me."

From the edge of the soy field, Burrows watched Leo drive away, abusing Mistress M.D. by swerving unnecessarily on the straight highway. Paramedics followed the agents into the RV, they came out lowering two stretchers and hoisting them into the ambulances. The green lights flashed on the RV's silver surface and then sped away. The agents searched the side of the road and a couple of them ventured into the fields. Their electric tasers buzzed as Grugel fell. They finished their search. They got into the RV and three government Enviro-cars and headed down the highway toward New West. Burrows was alone again. It grew dark as he waited on the side of the road hoping to flag down a bus. Chill air crept underneath his brown jacket. His shoulders tensed. When the faint blue lights of a bus appeared from the south, Burrows stepped out onto the road and then back again. He wanted to be seen, not hit. The bus went by him and he thought he'd erred too far on the side of caution. But it stopped a few yards ahead of him. Its doors opened in a gassy exhalation. The bus driver was stranger looking than any of the Vary-altered people he'd met on the 'Way. She had huge blue eyes set deep into her round face. As he boarded, she winked. Her caked lashes left flecks of black beneath her eye. He moved quickly to the back of the bus. He was reaching for a privacy web, when the shroud beside him lifted. A frazzled Grugel appeared with a singed smell about him. "Yaaah, bitches, can't catch me."

~ 19 ~

SYNC CHROME CITY: INTERNSHIP

"The Mindscape material is also now regarded as an unnecessary psychometric tool and remains popular primarily as a children's toy. However, materials science made an essential contribution to the evolution of psychic potential. Mindscape helped early Awakening Minds, Geneva Weltraum in particular, conceptualize the Connected Ego, the Infinite Lattice and Psychic Space for the very first time." —*Becoming Psychic 101, A History and a Primer*

Leo clasped Geneva's hand as he led her up the walkway to the new pyramid-shaped building on the New West University campus. Its face was one huge triangular window made up of many smaller ones. The mounds of earth around the building were bare, yet to be landscaped. A landmark sign, however, had already been placed by the entryway. It read, "Friend-Me Corporation," in glistening silver.

"We're here to see my mom," Leo said, responding to the question Geneva had not vocalized. "What else would I do with a nice girl like you?"

Geneva's face warmed even as the chill winter breeze swept back her hair. The effects of the drug were wearing off. Beneath

Leo's ethereal thoughts she recognized her own grounded undercurrents of perception. If she closed her eyes, feeling the wind through her lashes, she could see her thoughts: sunken orderly lines running beneath colored clouds. Under the influence of SLO-42, she knew what else Leo might plan for a nice girl like her and the thoughts were pleasant skin-to-skin, molten feelings. She also saw that as attracted as he was to Geneva, and the possibility she held for a new kind of romance, he'd still go back to the certainty of having Constance Monica Sherring as a girlfriend, if Coco so much as nodded his way. You couldn't fault someone for loyalty, but Leo's was frustrating.

Coco had made her choice. If she was letting her father's judgment keep her away from someone who loved her that was her problem. Maybe it was time to give Leo the choice instead of taking herself out of play just in case Coco changed her mind. All's fair in love and war. She tightened her grip on Leo's hand. She pulled him around to face her, pressed her body to his, tilted her head back and parted her lips. It was exactly what she'd imagined doing all last summer in the alley behind Ruby's. Now all he had to do was kiss her. Leo looked down at her, his eyes tinged with amber warmth. "Hey, hey now. I think I was supposed to bring you in directly."

Leo smiled. She took it as enigmatic, not outright, rejection. He was still holding her hand. She pouted. He'd abducted her. He'd drugged her. He owed her—a kiss at least. "You always do what your mother says?"

"Yep." he said nonplussed. "She's been good to me, an amazing woman. Come on, I'll introduce you."

There it was again, that loyalty. Hard to argue with, but still. Geneva returned her attention to the Friend-Me building before her. Its green-mirrored surface was completely out of sync with the rest of the red and beige brick buildings on the New West campus. Rumors about what went on in the basements of some of the buildings floated around campus. As a psychology student, however, she knew most of them weren't true. The administration had put a stop to animal experimentation after the revolution. It was wasteful, cruel, and unscientific. If animals were going to be tortured again for the sake of science though, this new building looked a likely place. The mounds of upturned earth, the unnatural green, and the ironic imperative of the name Friend-Me: It all said vivisection.

With her own good sense overrun by a residue of SLO goodwill, she followed Leo inside. It was reassuringly corporate, in maple and silver. A trim receptionist sat behind a computer at the front desk. Leo pointed to a small room with a green door to the right, “That's dispatch for the campus couriers." Then, he showed her to a large, windowed room filled with circular tables ringed by monitors. “This is where the Friend-Me mentors will be. Mom likes them to work together. That's why the circles."

Geneva nodded as he led her deeper in, to a bank of elevators. They rode up to the 14th floor where the elevator door opened into a huge triangular office, the tip of the pyramid, cast in greenish light. A woman knelt on an orange and brown patterned rug in front of a slim metal desk. She sorted through boxes, humming and occasionally clapping a hand to her thigh. When she looked up at them, her expression—half-smile and heavy-lidded eyes—felt familiar. It was the way Geneva herself looked after cramming all night for a test and awakening the next morning ready to ace it.

"Leo! Good!" the woman stood, stepped over the swirl of papers at her feet and held out her hand. "You've brought her."

Geneva felt the remnants of Leo's thoughts surge with love at the sight of the woman and the sound of her smooth low voice. Her own thoughts also spiked in recognition and not just because the woman's broad smile was clearly the origin of Leo's. She stepped forward past the woman's outstretched hand and wrapped her arms around the woman's waist, inhaling her nutmeg scent. The woman returned her embrace. For a moment, resting her head on the woman's soft shoulder, Geneva felt lighter, as if she'd just dropped her book bag after a long day. Relief swept through her. Seconds passed. Then she pulled away. The room went from blurry to sharp green, as she blinked back tears. She twisted her fingers through her ponytails. This woman was not her mother, was not a refuge. She'd just hugged Kendra LeMay, the head of New West's most innovative corporation.

Kendra peered into her eyes. She huffed, put her hands on her hips and faced Leo. "You drugged her. Are you out of your mind, child?"

"She was a little reluctant to come." Leo said. He gave his usual easy shrug. It was the same gesture anyway, but his plaintive expression, wide eyes, furrowed brow, made his face look ten years younger.

"Everyone's making bad decisions," Kendra said, looking pointedly at Leo who took shelter behind the desk. "But I'm glad you are here." She held Geneva's hands in hers and swung them side-to-side. "The world's first powerful psychic."

Geneva swayed. "Don't."

Kendra placed her hands on Geneva's shoulders steadying her. "Don't be afraid. There's nothing new, but so much to be discovered. 'Pure thought can grasp reality as the ancient shamans dreamed.' Sound familiar? It's Einstein."

Geneva pulled her hands away and shook her head. "No. You sound familiar, the way you talk. Those words. I know you."

Kendra put hands to hips and smiled. "So you have been paying attention."

Then Geneva made the connection to her childhood mentor on Friend-Me and understood why she'd been getting deliveries from the courier even when she was not on the Friend-Me network. "Nala?"

Kendra held out her hand again. "It's nice to meet you in person."

Geneva just stared at Kendra's red-orange nails. "My father was right. You've been spying on me, just like he said you would."

Kendra spread her arms wide. "He calls it spying. I call it synchronicity."

"An invasion of privacy," Geneva said.

"I didn't think your generation even cared about that anymore. Aren't you all neo-privates? A moot point regardless. What kind of privacy can someone who projects their thoughts expect?"

Geneva grasped her head in her hands as if to hold her thoughts in.

"Mom," Leo said.

"I'm sorry." Kendra said. "I noticed you when you first opened your Friend-Me account. We were just developing the process with the couriers. I monitored some of the journals and noticed you were unusual. It was easy to know what you wanted and needed. I became your Friend-Me mentor, Nala, to stay close to you. It's not so terrible child. Psychic powers are like everything in this world, more amazing than you could ever imagine, but also more mundane. It depends on what you are looking for. You project your feelings, but it's not a word for word translation. Not always. Mostly, we just get a general impression."

"Like with SLO-42," Leo said. "It gives you a taste of someone else, but it doesn't take you over."

Kendra frowned and waved a hand at the door. "Leave us."

No, don't, Geneva thought. Leo reacted as if he'd heard her, giving her an apologetic look, but he still rose obediently and disappeared behind the elevator doors. She was alone with Kendra LeMay. The woman's eyes, very much like Leo's but a darker shade of brown, stared through her. Feeling heavy and unsteady from the receding drugs, Geneva sank onto the least paper-strewn bit of rug she could find. "It's done. I'm here. Please, just tell me why."

Kendra LeMay knelt on the floor beside her and swept a hand over the rug. "Geneva, I want you to explore your potential, learn to control your abilities, see what you are capable of, what the future holds. I believe your abilities are our next stage of evolution. You will lead us to a new understanding of consciousness and what it means to be human."

Geneva shook her head. "No, I just want to graduate and get on with my life. I'm just a college student. I'm nobody's future. I haven't even got my own figured out."

Kendra made a clicking sound with her tongue. "Yes, and that's what college is for. A good leader is just someone with a driving passion who realizes they need other people to accomplish their goal."

Geneva pressed her palms against the rug and held her eyes wide so that the tears forming wouldn't spill out. Just one escaped. It splashed onto one of the papers, a document titled Conceptual Reality Project in CHEC with RFC-43 "Mindscape:" Subject 1 contract.

"You'll do it." Kendra said riffling through the papers around her. Then she reached forward and tugged a stack of them out from under Geneva's knees, the tear-stained sheet on top. "You'll do it to help Valerie, your friends, and Generation Utopia. These abilities are coming and if you don't know how to control them, your minds will betray you. All you have to do to prevent this is learn. Be willing. You might not be ready, but that's OK. No one ever is. You can be what you are and what you will be at the same time. That's life. That's synchrony. For the betterment of society, we have to learn how to use this ability that's coming whether we like it or not. I'd really like your help."

"This is the contract," Kendra said, flipping through the documents. "It gives you as many specifics as possible without wrecking the experiment." Her voice jumped an octave as she began talking faster. "Just sign there," she pointed to a line on a page.

"And initial, there, there and there." She shuffled through the papers and handed them over. If she noticed the tear splotch on the first page, she didn't say anything.

Geneva took the thick slightly oily parchment in her hands. She skimmed the document: Conceptual Reality Project in CHEC with RFC-43 "Mindscape": Subject 1 Contract. It was filled with legalese. Her semester of Privacy Law aside, she'd need a lawyer to decipher it.

"What's RFC?" she asked.

"Really Fluid Composite," Kendra said. "It's a new material you'll be working with."

"And CHEC?"

"The Controlled Holistic Environmental Chambers, where the experiment takes place."

Geneva brought the last page to the top of the stack. The paragraph over the signature line read: As a result of participating in this experiment, I, the undersigned, absolve Friend-Me Corporation and the individual, Kendra LeMay, of any responsibility in the event of accidental death or dismemberment or instance of permanent disability including, but not limited to, coma, paralysis, seizures, mental trauma or loss of mental capacity or functionality. In addition, I, the undersigned, agree to commit to research and development of any findings from said experiment for a period of no less than two years and agree to uphold Friend-Me Corporation's full and proprietary interest in all such findings and the results thereof for a period of no less than 10 years."

Geneva's visions of vivisection returned. "I don't want to be a lab rat."

Kendra held out a pen. "Think of it as an internship."

The pen was standard Friend-Me courier issue, slim forest green with silver lettering. It looked like every pen she'd ever used to sign her name at the bottom of countless Friend-Me deliveries. She reached out, took it, rolled it between her fingers and stared at its nub of potent green ink. It signified a lifetime of acceptance. She continued to look over the contract, lingering on each of the consequences.

Kendra twined the long russet yarns of the rug with her fingers. "You know, part of being alive, of being conscious, is being aware of your role in the world—history, future, culture, society—at this point in time. When I started Friend-Me Co., I wanted to create powerful connections between people. I thought of myself as a lone innovator in a time of stasis. But as it caught on, I discovered there were other people interested in the connections I was creating. I joined Psi-Aware and met Dr. Montgrave. She confirmed what I believed: that culture shapes who we are as people far more than the limitations of our bodies. Our bodies become what we imagine. She told me about the traumatized children coming to her clinic. Our children's brains were being changed by the connectivity of our culture, but faster than they could handle. Friend-Me contributed to the problem and now Friend-Me must help solve it. Even the government now agrees—the danger of being uninvolved outweighs the risks of plunging in—and it is funding this research. There's no going back, so we must go forward. This experiment will save tons of young people the grief you and Valerie have gone through."

Geneva considered. If she wanted to find out more about these powers, if she wanted to really help Valerie, here was an action she could take now. She silenced her thoughts, pushed aside her fears and scrawled her name at the bottom of the contract. Her usual steep slanted signature gained eccentric length and loops. She stared at it a moment and then put the page aside. In a flurry, she scoured the document and placed her initials GTW on each page. With each stroke, her anxiety lessened. This time she wasn't riding on the drug-induced high of Leo's buoyancy. She was feeling wave after wave of her own cool confidence. "I feel like I've just enrolled in Becoming Psychic 101."

"Well done." Kendra said. "You're about to embark on the most incredible adventure left to humankind—the exploration of the mind. It is time for us to venture in."

~ 20 ~

SYNC CHROME CITY: MINDSCAPE

"Friend-Me Corporation did play a role, as did founder Kendra LeMay, but I think the importance of that role has been exaggerated. We would have adopted the psychic curriculum, eventually. I don't like to use the term meddlesome, but I think it applies: the corporation and LeMay's involvement in the transformation was dangerously meddlesome." — *Save Giovanni: The Lost Men of the Psychic Wars,* S. Sherring

Tingling pain replaced the numbness in her legs as Geneva stood up from her cross-legged position on the rug in the middle of Kendra LeMay's executive suite at the top of the Friend-Me building on the university campus. She clutched the Mindscape Contract in both hands staring at her signature scrawled in permanent ink across the bottom of it. Probably, it occurred to her, too late, she should have at least asked her father's advice before signing her life over to Friend-Me. He'd been right about Friend-Me the first time. They were spying on little girls to gain a corporate advantage.

A door beside the elevator opened and Leo rushed out. "Mother, it's Sherring," he gasped, as the elevator opened. "I'm sorry."

A man with silver hair ducked as he stepped out accompanied by a blue uniformed officer. Geneva had seen photos of John Sherring, the President of New West University. In his smiling headshots, he looked handsome, but terribly ordinary, like an aging ball player. In person, all of his features were long, his arms and legs, nose and jaw. The stripes down his suit and across the broad tie knotted at his neck added even more length. In real life, he looked stretched thin.

Kendra LeMay pulled her tapered skirt down from where it bunched at her hips as she stood. Her patterned green and black blouse ballooned around her as she stepped forward. "President Sherring, you must be here to talk about the grand opening. We're just about moved in."

The top of her head reached just below his armpit. "It's over," the president said. Beside him, the guard's hands hovered over the holster wrapped around his waist.

Kendra tilted her chin up. "What's over?"

"This relationship," he said. "Between New West University and your corporation. You are no longer welcome on this campus."

Kendra knelt and lifted one of the boxes off the floor. Neither the president nor his guard made a move to help her. "The construction of the building is complete. Millions of dollars have been invested and we're about to begin. The last time we talked, we agreed. Friend-Me needs to be here. Sherring, you are not a mercurial man." She shifted the box on her hip. "So, what did I do to piss off New West?"

The president nodded at the guard who held up a handful of green vials. "I did not know part of your plan was to manufacture drugs on my campus. We found this in the basement. I believe this was made with your son's oxytocin. It's a complicated process. I can't imagine he's been doing this without your knowledge."

Kendra dropped the box on her desk. "Making SLO-42 isn't a crime. And Sherring, you are well aware—or could be—that we're using that drug to suppress students' psychic abilities at your internment lab. Thorazine isn't as effective as it used to be."

"Dealing SLO-42 is a crime. Especially, on my campus," he said. "I want you and Friend-Me gone by tomorrow morning."

Standing stock-still for once, by the stairway, Leo's eyes darted to his mother and then down. Kendra turned back to the president her hands planted on the edge of the desk. "You can't punish New West for my son's stupidity. When you entered the agreement with Friend-Me, you made a considered decision. You had good reason."

Geneva started toward Leo, bidden to comfort the hurt in his eyes. The president's voice rose. "I didn't know about your son's dealings. I didn't know you knew about Sync Chrome City. I didn't know you planned to speed this process up the entire time." Geneva jerked to a stop as the president caught her wrist. "Wait. What's this?" She looked from her signature scrawled in green ink, to him and back again. The wrinkles on his face appeared strategically placed to give him the authority of age without marring the smoothness of his cheeks.

"An employee," Kendra said.

The president dropped Geneva's wrist but pulled the contract out of her hand. As he scanned the page, steel gray flashed in his ice blue eyes. "No. This is not what we agreed to."

"It's exactly. Further research." Kendra replied.

"Test Subject?" The menace in the president's tone grew but his voice stayed low. He pointed at Geneva with his fist, the side of the contract balled up in it. "You cannot misuse my students. This ends. You lied to me, Ms. LeMay. I always had concerns that society was not ready for this. Our minds may be capable of more, but it doesn't matter if the majority of people are not ready for those changes and unwilling to invest in them. Becoming psychic would make us fundamentally different and we like the way we are. You are a visionary, but that doesn't mean you would lead us in the direction we want to go. Your vision could even be seen as a kind of genocide. You can't force this."

"I can't," Kendra said. "You can't force anyone to do anything. I'm well aware they have to make their own choices. But I can tell them what's stalking them, and I can come to their aid when I hear their cries of help. This is not some hypothetical. We're not debating some far-off future. This is not something Friend-Me can turn its back on. The genocide, as you call it, is underway. Our children are changing whether we like it or not. Young lives are at risk now."

"Because you put them there," the president said. "You said this was a completely natural occurrence and now I find that you've been speeding it up with SLO-42. You know what it's been doing to these children. They are not ready for this. We are not ready."

"But it's happening, and I think its been happening all along. Our children have been symptomatic for generations and our response has always been to drug them and now you are going back to the oldest solution of all—lock them away. Out of sight, out of mind. How will you rationalize this? Call it a lost generation?" she said.

"You will pursue this line of research no further," Sherring said. "I'm speaking both as the president of this university and as president of New West. You and your company are no longer welcome here."

At this, Leo took a protective stance at his mother's shoulder. His expression would have stopped Geneva cold. But the president had inches on him, and the guard had girth and the adults barely registered his presence. Kendra held out an arm protectively to hold him back as if they were coming to a sudden stop. Her eyes were locked on Sherring. The way they were focused on each other reminded her of the purple cords winding between her and Valerie. They looked like they were sharing an internal connection, having a silent conversation in a shared mental space. She saw confusion at the root of their anger. Neither Kendra LeMay nor the president had the ability to communicate the way she and Valerie had, sharing ideas and emotion directly. They had to talk to bridge the distance between them with words and be wary of a wrong one. It was easy to misspeak, misread, mishear, and misunderstand.

"The rebels were right. New West's a sham," Kendra said. "You didn't create utopia. You just took advantage of a situation and got rid of everyone you didn't like. Now I'm on the chopping block. Fine." She gestured to the boxes. "I haven't even unpacked. I'm a single woman who started out with a small business selling little girl's diaries. I know my place. You know you can afford to push me out precisely because I am not your enemy. I'm actually on your side. But how can you throw away our children?"

The president's extended arm began to shake. The contract in his fist rattled. He took the paper in both hands tearing it. The ripping sound seemed to carry on and on like a scream. "You are not bound by this young lady."

Geneva reached for a diagonal slice of the contract as it slipped from his hand and caught a jagged edge as it fell to the floor. "That's mine." *To help Valerie.*

The other half of the contract fluttered to the floor. The president stared at her. "What?"

"She didn't say a word. But you heard her. Valerie's one of the students you're interning at New West Mental. She wants to help," LeMay said.

Geneva nodded.

The president gestured to his guard and turned his back on them heading to the elevator. "You can do whatever you want, out there. We'll make our decision about this development when the legislative session ends in March."

Kendra threw the contract into the trash and turned to Geneva. "That's your new contract, then. That's how much time we have to help your friend. Less than three months."

A paper cut from the torn contract bled a thin red line across Geneva's hand.

Before leaving New West to become a guinea pig for Friend-Me out on the 'Way Geneva called home. Her father answered. Her mother was out.

"She's on assignment again. Something's brewing in Cascadia," her father said. "Is there something you need?"

"No, Dad, I just...love you." she said.

Geneva hadn't been outside of New West since she was five. Already the sight of the dingy 'Way and the transients living along it had her on edge, not to mention that she'd left behind the university, her family and everyone she knew to take part in an experiment. Pulling up to a high-fenced yard laced with concertina wire behind the low gray Friend-Me factory didn't make her feel any better. It was even worse when Kendra unlocked the chains and drove the Enviro-car through the gate up to the ramshackle house. Whereas Friend-Me corporate looked like the kind of place where animals went to tortured deaths this place looked like it hunted humans.

"This will be your home for the next three months," said Kendra as she followed her up the front steps. Kendra paused on the porch and fumbled in her purse. "After you enter the CHEC, Controlled Holistic Environmental Chambers, you will have no contact with the outside world until the experiment is complete. Do you have any questions?"

Geneva wished she knew what to ask. She shook her head no.

"Think of yourself as a plant about to be moved from a small pot to the yard. It will be traumatic to be uprooted. You bring just a little of your original self with you. The sudden rush of air feels noxious, but when you spread out, you'll grow."

She sounded like Professor Roundtree, but the metaphor was lost on Geneva when she entered CHEC house. The effect was immediately claustrophobic, and she wished she'd brought along a little more of her original soil. All that she had was her jacket and a fresh change of Face-in-the-Crowd clothes with an innocuous pair of white panties.

The CHEC house felt close, warm and stuffy like an unfinished attic. Everything was coated in a fluffy orange crème material that looked like insulation but felt like sponge.

"Lights," Kendra said, and a soft peach glow enveloped the room.

Geneva looked around. There was nothing in the house but the soft sherbet-colored fluff that coated the walls, floor and ceiling. There were no windows and only the entryway door. After looking around, she hurried up the staircase in front of her. Her sneakers sunk into the stuff. The upstairs of the house looked the same. There were a few unfurnished partitioned rooms coated in sherbet fluff.

Geneva went back down the stairs and pressed her hand into a wall. The scent of oranges rose. The goo oozed around her fingers. It was sticky damp and warm like dough. When she touched her fingertips to her lips, they tasted faintly sweet. The wall held the shape of her hand. "What is this?"

"That's the RFC - Really Fluid Composite. Marketing calls it Mindscape."

"Is there a bathroom?" she asked.

Immediately, a door opened in the side of what had looked to be a seamless orange wall.

Kendra smiled. "Through there. There's lots. You just have to explore. I'll leave you to it and send your teacher to you in the morning. Dr. Montgrave is a very special person. Very few scientists are prepared to stand up publicly for psi."

When Kendra left, the seam to the front door closed and Geneva was alone in the orange-crème Mindscape with no way out.

She managed to find a few comforts programmed into the house as a teaching tool by saying the right words in the right places. "Food," opened a little drawer filled with trail mix in the kitchen and "Water," extended a shiny orange working faucet near the bathroom. When she said, "sleep," in a small room upstairs, a nest of Mindscape, rose up out of the floor. It was not quite a bed, but when she lay down and wrapped it over her body it was soft and warm. Orange remained in her mind's eye long after she closed her eyes. It was difficult to gauge time in the windowless house, but she guessed it was nightfall. Her first night in the house, and she was already sick of seeing the color orange.

Geneva was sitting in the living room of the Mindscape CHEC house mushing the orange foam with her fingers when the front door reappeared. The wide-eyed woman who walked through it was familiar. She had a hooked nose and almond skin. The copper infinity symbol necklace swung over the high collar of her rust-colored sweater. She wore tights too and Geneva could not take her eyes off of the refreshing forest green color. "Dr. Montgrave?" she asked.

"I'm not with the clinic anymore. Just Friend-Me. You can call me Clara. How do you feel?"

Geneva pressed the orange-goo between her bare toes. "Weird. I'm a little bored. That's the last thing I expected."

"You are experiencing some sensory deprivation. That can be more stressful than too much drama. Sometimes it's more difficult to cope with mundane, daily life than to make a radical change. Did you find food? Water?"

Geneva nodded.

"Good." Clara plopped down cross-legged into the Mindscape in front of her. "Some of the basics have been supplied for you although we've worked them into the environment so there's still the exploratory feel. Mostly this house contains only what we are sitting on here. With the exception of its outward façade, part of the original 1905 building, the house is made of RFC."

She scooped up a mound of the floor and held it in her hands. "This is an ultra-light proton, high slippage, denatured transportable Really Fluid Composite, called Mindscape. I am one of a team of materials scientists and psychologists who created this substance for Friend-Me Co. We know it can do a lot. Since you have demonstrated ability with psychic projection, you will be the first to test its full potential."

She shaped the orange fluff into a ball and tossed it. Geneva caught the smooth, cool sphere and threw it back.

"I will teach you what I know," Clara said. She pulled and kneaded the ball a few times in a series of gestures that looked like Lydia Streker making cinnamon rolls. "This material is a combination of teleportable protons and viscous matter more easily susceptible to the vibrations of the mind. It's uniquely meldable."

As she watched, the stretched ropes of material grew shiny and bright like taffy. Clara reshaped it into a ball and began to spin and stroke it in her hands until it became translucent with a hint of yellow at its center. Clara tossed it. Geneva caught the warm sphere and clasped the smooth glass to her chest.

Geneva put it aside and tried to scoop up a glob of the floor. It didn't separate as easily as Clara made it appear. She tore a wad of the material up. As soon as it was in her hands, it felt less solid. It squished between her fingers and dripped back onto the floor when she tried to roll it into a ball.

Clara reached across her and picked up the glass sphere. "What you need to know is that the mind has the power to shape objects. We live in a conceptual reality. That knowledge is all you need to reach a de facto truth that you are capable of much more than you know and unlock your mind's potential. The Mindscape just gives us a way to process this new ability, to let us focus on what our hands are doing while our minds adapt. The brain learns and stores many things in networks which function outside of our awareness."

Geneva tried to shape the ball again, but the Mindscape still lay flat in her hands like soft dough.

Clara held up a transparent glass-like ball again now with a spiral strip of color through it like a bright orange peel. "You can do anything if you can harness the *vis viva*— the living force in all objects."

"How did you...?"

"With thought." Clara said. "I'm going to teach you to reify this substance. Mindscape is an abstract representation of infinite possibilities. I want you to imagine it as something simple, real, and attainable. Now cross your legs, close your eyes, and let's go to work. If anyone is capable of using this material, it will be you. While living in this house, you will learn to use it. You will need to, or the sensory deprivation will drive you crazy."

For the first time, Geneva understood why Val hated that word, because it implied that the changes happening to her were bad, that she was failing in a way eminently out of her control. She must have been—no, she must be—terrified and so alone. Geneva picked up another glob of Mindscape determined to prove that what she and Val could do was not crazy. When people saw what could be achieved, they would have to accept Generation Utopia.

~ 21 ~

SYNC CHROME CITY: ORANGE CRÉME

"Even those who have not had difficulty with their psychic studies to date, may struggle to attain the next level of development. An internship is strongly recommended. Students may also find it useful to participate in various meditation camps and workshops. Remember how even Geneva Weltraum struggled at first." — *Becoming Psychic 101, A History and a Primer*

Geneva was alone in the Mindscape house again. She'd had to admit, at first, that it felt good to be away from school. The atmosphere at NWU was so intense. Everyone was trying to follow their dreams or fall in love. Professor Roundtree said life was about, "being and becoming—constant transformation" which seemed true of New West students. It was so much work. They were all so busy becoming it seemed there was no time to think. Although wasn't that why they were at college?

Now she had time—too much—to contemplate and she was still failing. She hadn't managed to use the Mindscape. There were snow globe-sized tufts of it all around the house and scattered throughout the room she'd taken to sleeping in for longer and longer stretches. Her body had sunk into the orange sherbet-colored foam where she'd been curled up for days going on months.

Sometimes the foam had a warm tone to it that meant it was daylight somewhere other times it was dim and grayish, meaning night. She felt hallow, but she was tired of the rations: the bread, the powdered juice, the reconstituted soups, and trail mix she'd been eating. She touched a few raisins and nuts beside her. She'd liked the food at first because it provided some relief from the homogeneous Mindscape. The nuts were firm, and the raisins were deep brown and wrinkled. But it wasn't working anymore. The peanuts were almost the same shade of orange as the Mindscape and the raisins had the same squish. Instead of changing the material, she felt like it was changing her and everything into a homogeneous blob.

Clara had been encouraging about Geneva's failures when she stopped by for training sessions twice a day wearing a relief of colors. "Don't worry," she said. "It takes time for the brain to create new connections. Even thinking of changing the Mindscape is progress. You are creating new patterns. I know that you hate the loneliness imposed on you by this work. But you are here because you want to find out what it means to be psychic. Once you find that out, you will never be lonely again. This isn't a magical wish in a fairy tale with terrible repercussions and a harsh moral. This is an ability that today will make you unique and tomorrow will transform us all. Your reasons for seeing this through can be as big or as small as you like. They can be as practical or as fanciful as you require, but if you stay and you do this, you will never regret it."

Inspired, Geneva had spent hours with Mindscape in her hands, hoping. But as the days passed, even Clara couldn't disguise her frustration at the lack of progress. Geneva emerged from one of their meditation sessions with a pancake of Mindscape smashed between her palms. "Stop trying so hard to control it," Clara scolded. "You have to free your intuition. Relax."

"Every time you say that I get tense. My intuition sucks," Geneva said.

"You have to concentrate on the outcome you want so your mind doesn't lock on the negative," Clara said. Her fuchsia top made her skin look a sallow orange. "Listen, I think we've gone as far as we can together. I've given you all the tools I have. It's time for you to use them: on your own."

Geneva had almost stormed out of the house then making for the now invisible doorway where Clara had entered, the spot she'd been staring at all afternoon, when she was supposed to be concentrating on shaping matter with her mind, "You're giving up?" But she'd stopped in the doorway staring out at the dingy 'Way and the bleak February sky. She could leave, but nothing had changed out there. She'd go back to the same uncertainty not knowing what to do, unable to help Val, unsure if Leo cared for her or was just waiting around for Coco to change her mind again. Leaving seemed pointless too. She closed the door behind Clara and didn't ask when she'd be coming back.

The worst part of being left alone in the Mindscape House was not knowing when she'd see anyone again. As soon as she was awake, Geneva wanted to be unconscious again, to bury her head in the orange-scented Mindscape and sink into sleep. She was so tired. Awake, her thoughts cycled. This was pointless. She could not help Val. She'd destroyed her future by coming here. She wouldn't graduate. She'd be kicked out of New West. She'd have to go live on the 'Way and work in the Friend-Me factory or live alone in the forest.

Geneva rolled over and scooped a ball of Mindscape out of the floor for the 365th time. She rolled it between her hands, closed her eyes and concentrated. *This time let it happen. Let it become glass.* She opened her eyes, and the Mindscape was—orange and viscous—exactly the same as the rest of the house. She pushed it back into the hole she'd taken it from. Maybe this was a trick and Clara was a magician. Maybe the "Mindscape" was just foam, and she'd been trying to do something impossible all along. Maybe she was the control in some experiment while someone else, somewhere—Valerie at the clinic?—had the real, malleable stuff. She wished she believed that, but she could still feel a connection to Val and knew her friend was still comatose, while she stayed here, in isolation, accomplishing nothing.

It wasn't fair. She couldn't do this. She didn't have the answers. She didn't know how to use this stuff, make it do or be anything else. Clara's logical explanations of quantum particles didn't mean anything, the world she described was nothing like her reality. Maybe it was something Valerie could have understood. She hadn't, maybe couldn't. Besides what good would it do, really, if she figured out how to manipulate the protons in the Mindscape and make glass spheres? They were good for nothing, and it was too late. The guys and Valerie were in comas imprisoned in New West Mental. Their minds were lost. The damage was irreparable. Geneva wasn't doing any good here. She was responsible, but powerless.

The wall behind her was scarred with long deep shadowed lines. She stood up and placed her fingers into the grooves. She couldn't remember raking her fingers into the stuff and wailing. But she knew she'd done this. There was no one else. It seemed so long ago that she could have felt that much emotion, had that much energy. She ran her hands down the lines.

She looked up to see Kendra LeMay staring at her. "Hi Geneva," she said in a soft voice as if speaking to a shy child. Geneva touched her matted hair, noticed the moistness under her arms and wondered if Kendra could smell her stink through the cloying orange Mindscape. It had been weeks since she'd bathed.

"Our time is almost up," Kendra said. She gazed at the shredded Mindscape floor and the scarred wall. "We're beginning to think we made a mistake. I know you are trying. Clara tells me you are. Maybe we fooled ourselves because we wanted to be right. We knew this would be hard, but we expected faster progress. It's not fair to keep you here if we're wrong. It's not healthy. I think we have to accept that either the Mindscape doesn't work, or you are not what we thought."

Geneva clasped her hands and thought about becoming clean, eating fresh food, seeing her mother. It was so tempting. But then, what? When she thought about leaving, she had to think about what came after that and nothing had changed, except that she was more miserable, than the day when she'd almost followed Clara out of the house. She still could not leave. Her problems were unchanged. Val would be in a coma. She would go back to the university. But she was not even a student there anymore. She'd disconnected herself even from that to be here. Now, it had become harder to go back than to go forward.

"No, I said I'd stay to see this through. I signed on," Geneva said, remembering even as she said it that Sherring had shredded the contract. But the paper itself had little value, whereas her act of signing it was irreversible. She remembered her scrawling signature and the relief she'd felt at the end of it. She hated LeMay for making her remake the choice.

Kendra shrugged. "OK, but soon it won't matter. They are casting a vote. Psychics will be one more undesirable element shut out of New West."

Geneva considered what the impact of a vote like that would mean: everything. They would never allow psychic studies. She and Valerie would be banished from the utopia her parents had created. But, if she could demonstrate the breadth of their abilities, nothing could stop them from claiming a completely new destiny. Alone again, Geneva kept envisioning LeMay's off-handed shrug. Like she didn't care one way or another. Even she had given up, even she no longer believed Geneva could make anything out of the revolutionary material.

So far, Geneva had failed to find either of the two things hidden in the Mindscape House she longed for most: a window and a phone. She intensified her search. She made another routine search around looking for them. This was her pattern: eat, drink, search methodically room by room—sleep.

One day she awoke from a dream. She couldn't remember any of it, except that it had contained the color blue. She immediately began her search. She walked throughout the entire house and said, "Window, window, window," until the syllables in the word separated and she wasn't quite sure how to pronounce it anymore or precisely what it meant. Still, no windows appeared anywhere.

She began to scream, "window" and sob, "window" pacing through the house, circling, until her limbs pulled her down on the floor of one of the small upstairs rooms. She muttered, "window, window" through dry lips with a swollen tongue. Her eyes burned as she stared unblinking at the ceiling. Finally, she closed them and just saw the window in her head, the four outlines, the great distance through it and the wispy clouds dissipating in the sky.

When she next opened her eyes, the light that struck them was colorless. It streamed through a clear panel revealing sky, in the ceiling of the orange-crème room was a window more beautiful than she had imagined. She sat up and dropped her head back to stare at it breathing deeply through each chakra from her sacrum to her forehead just as Clara had taught her. At the side of her window view, she could see wisps of green tree and a flitting sparrow. She sat cross-legged and stared into the sky as her mind uncoiled releasing the claustrophobic tension that had gnawed at her ever since she'd entered the house. She ate and slept and then returned to the window. It had grown wider. The tree held a nest in a misshapen branch.

Geneva sat up from where she'd been lying sunk into the spongy sherbet-colored floor of the Mindscape House. The ceiling looked different. There were waves on the surface of the orange goo overhead, variations of light and shade she hadn't noticed before. Depending on where she looked, patches were colored like buttercream or marmalade or blood orange. She got to her knees and wiggled her fingertips in the soft material at her sides. She leaned back and placed a hand behind her. She pressed down. It was warm where she had been sitting. It was cooler on the floor in front of her. Her body heat affected the Mindscape. It was not really such a leap from that change to what Clara insisted she could do: move the quantum particles and reshape them with her mind.

Geneva scooped a ball of the goo out of the floor. It was the same size and shape as each of her failed attempts. She began to knead it with the heels of her palms. Bits of it stuck to her skin. She stretched and pummeled it with her fists. She started to hum the Giovanni Hastings Musica melody in time with the kneading. The ball became smooth and satiny. It grew warm in her hands. She held it aloft. From underneath her eye, she brushed away a cool tear and lifted it on her pointer finger. She waved it back and forth and watched how it held its shape. The word for that: viscosity. She looked through it to the Mindscape dough. The dough adhered to certain principles. It was designed to move. She was meant to be able to move it or she wouldn't be here. It was the way to get unstuck.

She wanted to run, to shout, but she'd lose the moment. Instead, she sat very still and stared through the tear. She focused all her energy on it. Her mind ran to the ball, all around it and inside. Her mind pulsed with pleasure. So what she'd been doing before, trying to coax the ball to bend to her will was wrong. The opposite of what was wanted! Instead, she placed her mind inside the ball and let its curve shape her thought.

Then there were colors. It began with a yellow line of light bisecting the orange ball and trembling inside. Beneath the rind, yellow bubbled. Yellow burst out of orange seeds in the core and blossomed to deep red. The ball grew smoother and shinier until it became translucent. Geneva rolled it back and forth on her palm.

It was hard and solid and unlike anything else in the soft, sticky room, in the soft, sticky house. She closed her eyes tightly. Her lashes flicked her cheeks. Dr. Montgrave explained that once she put thought energy into an object it gained weight and a presence of its own that was reinforced when others saw it too. She wanted to share this reality not just with Clara and Kendra but with someone who cared, not just about the mindscape and its vast potential for profits, but about herself. There were things she was starting to realize and she wanted to share these ideas. Whenever she thought about that, she thought of Leo. She held the globe and sat by the door sending her mind outside of it to: *Leo.*

Hours later, when the door opened, he entered. "I heard you. I thought I'd stop by," he said.

His distant offhanded tone had unsettled her in the past, but now she had learned to see the possibilities in things that at first had no substance. He was earnest but cloaked his response in nonchalance to stave off rejection.

"You know what I want," she said.

She placed the glass globe shot through with yellow rays and red flowers in his hand then she grabbed his other hand and pulled him upstairs to the window room. She took off her clothes and pressed her lips to his. She sunk into the crevasses of his body. She hadn't felt comfort in a very long time.

~ 22 ~

SYNC CHROME CITY: BREAK IN

"At first you may feel overwhelmed by the Infinite Lattice. As you meet many minds, it may be difficult to keep track of your own. Rely on your unique way of visualizing the Lattice. The analogy to swimming is a good one. There's an innate element of danger in the environment, but it becomes less dangerous as you learn to navigate it. Remember there are many minds in Psychic Space to help you. It is less like swimming in an ocean and more like a crowded pool. Entering the Lattice is an essential part of mental development. When you feel restless, angry, or despondent, you most likely need to increase the pace of your psychic development. Spending more time in Psychic Space will be beneficial." — *Becoming Psychic 101, A History and a Primer*

Geneva and Leo made love upstairs in the Mindscape House. She opened her eyes and looked over Leo's bare shoulder into a profusion of Nootka-Rose-Ladyslipper blossoms. The wild rose honey scent dripped into her open pores. It filled her skin with expanding warmth until she felt ready to burst. Tendrils of steam rose off Leo's back like morning earth. She was up to her fingertips in his smooth shoulder blades kneading the muscles stretched across them. The red-striated lips of the flowers lapped at her sides. She took a deep breath settling underneath him. The air gliding petal smooth across her tongue left a trace of sweetness. It reminded her of sucking lilac stems. She exhaled letting his weight compress her. Her voice dropped into Hort-Audible tones talking to her lover as if he were a tender plant. "I can do it now. I can save them."

He lowered his torso onto her chest and his lips caressed the corner of her eye. Then he drew back, his lips glistening with her tears. "No one expects you to."

Her ponytails slid across the carpet, red-on-red. She laid her palms over his tawny nipples and pressed against his chest. Heat waves shimmered between them as she pushed him away. "No, I said, 'I can.' Look up. I can connect them."

She started to laugh until her body rocked with it. Leo turned over beside her on the bedroom floor and followed her gaze up. Delicate white roots dangled from the ceiling. Thorn-covered branches crossed the skylight and arched down into the room. Blossoms spread open wide above them, petal to petal.

"You did that?" His fingertips brushed her shoulder trailing a tingling sensation. When he held his hand up, the tips of his fingers were faintly green. "And this."

Geneva looked to see if she were turning colors, too. But she was still pink. It was the effect she was having on him. She couldn't stop laughing. Just this fall, she'd been afraid of killing the one rare hybrid entrusted to her by Dr. Roundtree. Now, in a moment of delight, she could Mindscape a hothouse filled with the flowers.

Leo stroked her back. "See, things don't have to be terrible to be true."

"I thought that," she said. "Gritty reality seems most real, but when things are beautiful and right, we always describe them as dreamlike and hazy."

"It's a problem," Leo said. "People don't picture the best possible outcome and they wind up living the awful reality they imagined instead."

"We can change that," Geneva said.

Leo shook his hand out and the pink returned to his fingertips. "I must have gotten some on me." He stood and the lean long line of him above her reminded her of seeing him for the first time at the Mansion Expansion dance. Then, she'd thought she'd be satisfied just to know his name. She rose and pressed her body to his one more time, her ribs aching from laughter. They stood naked and honey-coated surrounded by the heat of hundreds of exotic flowers. He held her head in his hands, petted her. "Come on. We should go."

At the dance, the guys had crowded her out of the way. Now, the thought of them sobered her. They would see her when she saved them. She pulled on her Face in the Crowd underwear, T-shirt, and khakis. Leo hummed behind her as she ran down the stairs. "How will we get back across the border?" she asked reaching for the door.

She froze as it opened, and Leo tensed beside her. Coco stood on the porch. The smoke-filtered Freeway sunset created a reddish nimbus around her head and shoulders as it shone through her blonde hair. Warmth rushed to Geneva's face. She grabbed Leo's hand and thought at Coco: *You had your chance.*

With the sun behind her, she couldn't see Coco's expression very well, but the nimbus around her dipped. "That's not why I'm here."

Coco gestured behind her. Eve's Cadillac was parked in the lot beside the house. The suspension was so low the chassis nearly touched the gravel. "They're voting tomorrow on whether our friends can be helped or not. We should be there. We should make them look us in the eye when they tell us we don't count."

Leo nodded. He went to the car and held the passenger door open. "Take us to the guys first. To Linden. It's Geneva. What she can do, its incredible."

Coco waved a hand. "Spare me details."

Geneva slid across the seat next to Leo. They waited while Coco made a call from the porch. "Just letting him know where we are," she said as she settled into the driver's seat.

Between Coco and Leo, Geneva twirled her fingers through her ponytails. She stared at the brown of her hair showing through her Gator-Tongue dye job and looked from Coco to Leo, one solid golden profile to the other. She had the not unfamiliar feeling of being small and foolish beside them. But things were different now. Her thoughts were audible outside of herself. She could shape matter with her mind. She looked at Leo. He loved her.

"You know," Coco said, watching Geneva in the rearview mirror as she backed out onto the street. "When I first met you, I was intimidated. You seemed so independent."

In Coco's controlled hands, the car sped unwavering toward Linden as the sky went dark. The president's daughter had no trouble getting them across the border.

Did she have to be beautiful, smart, and a great driver?

The corner of Coco's mouth turned up, but her eyes didn't leave the road.

"Sync Chrome City. It's like an addiction," Leo explained. "If the site goes down while you're on, it causes a mental rift. Or, if you use it too much, you get awakened. You know, gain access. I think that's what happened to our boys. But they couldn't quite handle it. So if the damage is caused by being unplugged, it makes sense that what might fix the problem is to..."

Coco veered off at the exit to Linden. "Plug them back in."

"But not in Sync Chrome City," Geneva said. "We want them outside that artificial environment."

Coco slowed the car as they hit the main strip into town and drove past the closed sandwich shop and the blue glow of the dimly lit high school. "We can't do that. Reconnect them to what?"

"To each other," Leo said. "Turn here and pull over."

Geneva looked at Leo. There was a chance it might not work out between them. Even though they'd made a connection, he still cared about Coco. What she had with him would either grow or it could be uprooted, wither and die when it would hurt most. It was a risk she was willing to take, to love him for a while, while it lasted.

Gravel crunched beneath the tires as Coco made the sharp right down the road to the clinic. "So how are we doing this?"

"I don't think we can just march through the front door. The lab coats at the clinic probably don't understand what's really wrong with the guys," Leo said.

"Worse, maybe they do," Coco said, pulling the car to the side. "I mean I can see why New West would have problems with a generation of psychics. It's destroying the last vestige of privacy." She killed the engine and turned to Geneva. "Not everyone always thinks the most complimentary things."

She sounded tense, and it was strange to think Coco might be jealous.

Coco reached over the seat into the black fullness of Eve's back-seat and returned with a flashlight for Geneva and a small pocket light for Leo. Geneva hefted the light. "We'll sneak around back."

"You're going to break into a government facility. You realize this could get you thrown out of New West. Permanently exiled. Or you might not come out," Coco said.

"You don't have to come in with us," Leo said. "In fact, it'd be better if you didn't. Stay here. If anything goes wrong, call the president and bail us out."

Coco, who'd been sitting with her long legs out the door, swung them back in. "You're right. Daddy wouldn't approve if I got caught inside. I'll sit tight."

Geneva caught an edge of bitterness in Coco's voice and tried to make out her expression in the dark. There wasn't time to decipher it.

Outside of the car, Geneva and Leo walked just under cover of the low hanging evergreens along the road to the clinic. She kept the flashlight pointed down at the brush. It ensured she wouldn't trip on a stray root but staring at the spot of light obscured everything else. She could barely make out the building when it came into sight ahead of them, a lumpish shadow in the night. The low, green building blended into its surroundings like an animal in hiding. There were no cars or lights around it visible from the forest.

They pressed close to the wall of the building to get through the dense bushes to the back. Brambles snagged her thin cotton T-shirt and thorns scratched her face and arms as she pushed through them. They walked the entire back of the building trying to spot any variation in its surface that might indicate an entrance. As they examined the paint, her flashlight dimmed and went dark. "I think we have to go around front after all."

Leo turned on the pocket light. Light flashed into the air for a moment before he snapped it down. "Wait, look at that."

Geneva turned toward the illumination of green and gray-green shapes trying to see behind the brightness. Then the pocket light flickered out too, leaving her in blackness.

"Useless." The bushes beside Leo rustled and she guessed he'd thrown the light aside. "The ground's different here. Careful." A rush of falling leaves accompanied the last syllable followed by thudding.

Kneeling, Geneva felt through the wet, slimy leaves in front of her. "Are you OK?" Brushing the leaves aside, her fingers ran over cold, rough concrete. As her eyes adjusted, the jagged outline of the bushes appeared framing the rectangle of black that had enveloped Leo.

He whispered from below. "There's steps, and a door."

She scooted down the stairway feet first. Rain-soaked moss lined the steep narrow stairs. It squished beneath her hands as she lowered herself down. The cold numbed her palms. There was movement below. As she reached the middle of the incline, Leo came into relief leaning against a gray door. He cradled his hand close to his body as if it were a slack-winged bird. "I cut my hand. I don't think it's bad."

Geneva touched his shoulder, nodded. She examined the door and plucked a New West Mental Health pass card from the pocket of her khakis.

"Where'd you get that?" Leo asked.

"Friend-Me," she said. "My last delivery. I thought you knew."

She ran it—click—over a sensor. Leo pushed the door open with his shoulder. "I thought we were breaking in—literally. This was easier than I..."

As they stepped into the bright clinic hallway, the door snicked to a close behind them. As she blinked, an elongated shadow, a tall man, bore down on them. "You don't think we have cameras?" A pocketful of green syringes — SLO-42—stuck out of his lab coat.

Geneva readied to bolt down the hall when Leo unclasped his hand and held it up. His nearly severed finger dangled. Leo's eyes went wide as he tumbled forward. His head cracked on the tiled floor at the man's feet.

"Shit," the lab coat said.

Geneva knelt and rolled Leo over. Scarlet red spilled down the front of him. A patch spread across his shirt where he'd cupped his hand to his chest. Blood streamed down his arm and began to pool on the tile.

The man turned, took a few quick steps and then turned back. "Stay, I'll get the first aid kit." He darted forward through one of the doors.

Leo looked up and winked at Geneva. He nodded at the empty hall. "It's just a finger. Go."

She nodded at him in surprise but didn't hesitate. She sprinted down the hallway trusting her instincts to take her the right way.

She ran right, left, right until she came to three doors in a row. Locked. Locked. Locked. From inside came, "Yaaah, do it now."

Grugel.

She pressed her hand against the steel door on the end and on tiptoe peered through the reinforced-plastic window. The doors connected to one long narrow bunkhouse. Inside, curtains separated several hospital beds. Unrestrained sheeted shapes lay in each of them. At one end, Grugel stood with several wires snaked through a barred window clutched in his hand. At the other end, Burrows hunched over one of the shapes. He lifted a limp figure off the bed.

Geneva's thoughts lunged for her friend: *Val.*

Returning sensation pricked Geneva's numb hand as she pounded on the door. "He doesn't care. He's trying to shut you down." Eve's narrow dark eyes appeared in the window. *Come on. This time let me in.*

The door swung open. Purple sparked out of the ends of the wires and danced across the beds. In front of her, Eve's eyes rolled back into her head. Her body dropped to the floor, convulsing. The bodies on the beds shook. Limbs thrust under the sheets. Purple coils unloosed around them. They were plugged into Sync Chrome City, but Sync Chrome City could not support them. So, they disconnected from everything, disembarked, disembodied. Their minds rushed past her falling into void as if she were standing on the precipice in front of the Big Top. They leapt past her off the ledge into the bay.

Electric violet lashed Geneva as she ran forward and grabbed the ends of the whips. Her arms elongated and her body burned with the sensation of stretched muscle. She gathered eleven ends into her hands, twined them together and fastened them around her wrist like a balloon bouquet. She tethered their minds. Instead of the nearby hospital tile, the floor sparkled purple far below. Discs of white flashed by as she descended. Dry heat rose around her. She was losing them. Their minds couldn't keep up with the evolution. They were detaching under the strain and falling free. *Maybe this is what's supposed to happen. Our entire generation sacrificed to unattainable perfection.*

As she fell, she heard Leo, "Call for help."

The lab coat responded, uncertain. "It's a secret facility."

"Fuck secret. My friends are dying. She can't hold them forever."

"Give them these. The SLO."

In a flash of green, Eve's mind separated and began to pull upward straining in Geneva's hands. She tightened her grip. *Is this what we want? To live out our days confined to New West Mental because we're unwanted?*

Eleven voices responded with opinions, but within them ran a thread of consensus: *We want to take our place.*

She grabbed at that thought. She showed them the Mindscape and the Nootka-Orchids. *We can learn to do this.*

She threw out a purple cord of thought, a long-tangled loop of an idea: *Utopia.* She unwound it in their direction speaking to Streker and Val who would understand and help her explain: *Sir Thomas More didn't believe his government could achieve it, but our parents tried. They taught us that it does exist. Maybe it's not New West. But if we've seen it, thought of it, envisioned it so many times...*

Minds grabbed on to the end of the cord continuing the thought. She felt Streker, Val, and others: *...then utopia is somewhere, and we are not lost.*

Yes. With a surge of effort, Geneva rooted her feet to the floor. She raised her arms, so her fingertips almost brushed the low ceiling. She made a trellis of her body and the purple cords wound over her. The tendrils lifted one by one off the sparkling desert floor. Uncurling purple tendrils, Geneva reached for those minds stretching to meet them. She repeated *utopia* over and over, like she did to the plants in the greenhouse on campus. The minds drew near and hooked onto the tendrils like buds. A garden grew across her. The room filled with soft, green light and the damp air dropped. Her skin sucked at the sudden moisture. She counted them. No one was missing. Eleven minds, detached from Sync Chrome City, had reconnected to each other creating an external neural net. They didn't need the Chrome tech. They didn't need New West. They connected to each other.

She opened her eyes and blinked to see that her arms were bare. The beds and the boys on them were unchanged although their limbs were still. Syringes littered the floor and green droplets trailed along the line of beds. At the far end of the room, Burrows rested on one knee, Val in his arms. His head hung. Sweat dripped down the top of his head and his lips formed a tight, dark arch beneath the shadow of his brow. At the other end of the room, Leo knelt plunging the last syringe of SLO-42, which was helping to anchor their minds to their bodies, into Grugel's arm where he sprawled on the floor.

Directly in front of her, the lab coat stared. He touched his lapel and spoke, "The president please. This is Dr. Klick. Yes, it's urgent."

With a grunt, Burrows lunged across the room. He lifted Val and kicked Klick in one swift motion. The doctor toppled to the floor. He moaned. "There's been a terrible tragedy."

Burrows kicked him again. "Shut-up." Teeth ground and cracked against bone as Klick's jaw caved-in. Leo rushed at them, head down. Geneva hit Burrows with: *We're coming. You've failed.*

Burrows checked her with his shoulder. Val's bare feet swiped her arm. "Stay the fuck away, freak. Leave me alone," he said. "They'll fear you too."

Geneva stayed rooted waiting for the last mind, Grugel's, to wrap around her. She couldn't leave the boys hanging. She looked at Burrows. *One day, you'll be one of them.*

He staggered past her carrying Val. Val's tether stretched thin. Finally, in a wave of green-relief Grugel's mind settled. Geneva curled the purple cords, back into their own heads, and tucked their minds—safe—inside their bodies. She left Streker, Eve, Grugel and the seven guys with visions of orange-cream frosted blossoms caked with loamy scent. Except for Val, who broke snap pea loose.

Geneva left Leo bent over the lab coat and ran after Val and Burrows. At the end of the hallway, past the reception desk, the front door to the clinic was shut, still. Outside, black forest surrounded the empty gravel parking lot. Alongside the building an engine hummed. Backed into the bushes by an open window was Eve's car. Burrows flung wires into the trunk and stepped into the passenger seat as the car rolled forward. It peeled out with Coco driving. Too late, Geneva placed that sarcastic tone that had sounded so strange in Coco's voice. She'd sounded like Burrows, or, she reluctantly admitted, like Val.

Leo came up beside her. "Come on."

They ran after the car. Gravel dust caught in her throat. The taillights shone ahead of them and then flickered out as the car cornered leaving them alone in the forest. Leo put a hand on her back as she doubled over clutching her knees.

"She helped him." Geneva said.

"Of all the times, to defy Daddy," Leo said. “Coco picks now.”

A familiar gassy exhalation sounded over her panting breaths. She started toward it blinking in the night until she could make out the huge shape. Swathed in black, with its lights out, parked in the brush, the shadow bus was nearly invisible. It wheezed as its doors opened and closed. Geneva boarded and saw the blond bus driver, blindfolded, bound and gagged lying on the floor beside her seat. One arm stretched over her head. Her hand gripped a round black knob as she operated the doors. Her cheeks were stained with black streaks. Leo took off her blindfold. The underside was smeared with mascara. Her red eyes narrowed. She sucked in air as he removed the lipstick-stained gag. Her washed out pout stretched into a grimace. "That creepy jerk."

~ 23 ~

SYNC CHROME CITY: POLITICS OF PSYCHICS

"It was a lesson we could have learned from our own revolution. When the time for change arrives, it cannot be forsworn. Things on the fringe, laughable ideas that ignite the passion of a minority, are the ones to watch. Change evolves. The shifting begins far in advance, but then roils suddenly to the surface unstoppable. It's very like tectonics. I don't want to sound too much like a psychic geologist, but it is an interesting idea, that these shifts are part of our essential framework, built into our very earth." — *Save Giovanni: The Lost Men of the Psychic Wars*, S. Sherring

Burrows hesitated at the edge of the crowd of Psi-Aware protesters in front of Old Main on the New West University campus. He watched the wind whipping their hair across their contorted faces. He told himself it'd be fine. He could enter the crowd of people and not one of them would notice him. They were too caught up in their fervor. He'd just make his way to the steps of the administration building. Even while he told himself this, he stood still. Just because the minds weren't pointed at him didn't make them less sharp. It'd be like stepping into a field of knives and trusting that they would stay sheathed.

A line of television crews, cameras and neatly dressed newscasters there to report on the historic vote were the first gauntlet. As Burrows squeezed by a young TV reporter in a tight pink suit, he heard a familiar voice rising behind him, "Well, I do have a Ph.D. in physics and on the basis of what we know, we have to take our intuitions seriously. It's time to stop snickering. We can be telepathic." He turned and saw Lydia Streker shaking her frizzy-haired head at a young reporter. She wore a yellow T-shirt that said "Deming Fest: Dem Right Fun!" across her chest. Her son stood beside her.

Burrows had done this very effectively, created this crowd in hopes of throwing New West into civil war, but now it was inconvenient. He'd meant to foment unrest to meddle with New West's perfection, reveal a few cracks and maybe begin to tear it apart. He'd never thought there would be this many people though who wanted to be psychic. There were more of them than there had been counterrevolutionaries and there was usually a lot more energy in opposition. He'd never imagined that you could get this many people to stand around holding signs and chanting, “Yes, Psi!” Yet here they were. They looked damn foolish. They'd do their cause more harm than good. But their numbers were annoying, and Lydia Streker was on TV.

As he pushed past the media, the crowd grew tighter. Burrows shoved them aside with his shoulders to get closer to Dr. Montgrave. He could see the expression on her face and could tell she thought that protest was distasteful too. It served her right. She was one of them. The only difference between her, Friend-Me Co., and these fanatics was that she had been willing to wait. These people wanted things to happen faster. He supposed having her clinic fill with comatose patients had changed that. Did she really think the world needed a bunch of psychics? Burrows would make sure the president knew Clara Montgrave was no different than the Psi-Aware crazies.

As they closed in on the steps, the people were packed shoulder to shoulder. Beside him Coco yelled, "Excuse me!" as she shoved Valerie's chair into each shift in the bodies to create an opening. Burrows followed her, braced for pain. They were nearly at the steps, immersed in the crowd. He was taller than most of the people, which afforded him some relief from the claustrophobia, but the people standing on the steps blocked his view. The pressure on his chest and back from the crowd was bearable. As long as they didn't turn their thoughts to him, he could make it. But people were unpredictable. They could crush you without warning.

When the forward movement stopped, Burrows was jammed among the crowd. Coco could no longer coax the people ahead of them to move. There was no place to go. We're trapped, he thought, and struggled for breath. Looking down, he saw the wheels of the chair at the base of the steps. He unstrapped Valerie and lifted her into his arms.

"Hey. Hey man. I'm with you. With Psi-Aware. And so is this girl. She's sick because of what the government's done. Tell them." He pointed at the camera in front of the crowd. "Tell them, I've got something to say. Follow me."

He thrust her over the crowd hoisting her higher and moving her forward. "We'll take her to the president."

The crowd moved up the steps into the rotunda. He climbed up with her and reached the president as he began to speak. "I've just received some information that, while disturbing, might make our decision here today easier. Some students were seriously injured at New West Mental Health. Secrecy is no longer an issue. I can tell you everything."

The crowd hushed as the earth moved beneath their feet.

Geneva leapt out of the shadow bus driven by Alice as soon as they reached the New West campus. The wind pushed against her as she ran to the administration building. A throng of people, protesters, and reporters, stood on the lawn. She could see the Psi-

Aware fanatics and the Neo-Privates yelling at each other. Their faces were red and contorted. Their mouths were wide open with lower teeth bared but the syllables they spoke were carried away by the wind. It made sounds a meaningless jumble. As Geneva pushed into the midst of the protest, she was buffered from the wind. Ahead of her, on top of Old Main the New West flag rippled, evergreens segmenting its golden circle. Holding her hands out in front of her and mentally shoving people aside, she jogged through the crowd. *Move. Move. Move.* She pulsed the thought forward and watched the people jolt out of her way. The people ahead turned to look at her with wide eyes.

Go on and look, Geneva thought, *just get out of the way.* She searched ahead for Burrows and Valerie. She continued to press her thoughts in front of her creating static charged shocks. She pointed at the steps up the administration building. By the time she reached them, people had stepped aside and cleared a path for her, a white part. She raced up the stairs and paused at the top to get her bearings looking back over the crowd with the Friend-Me pyramid distant behind them. The guys circled behind her; Leo, left, Streker, right. Ahead, silent people filled the rotunda. They listened to a deep clear voice.

"President Sherring," Leo said.

The narrow doors were propped open. Geneva pushed into the building and through to the center of the crowd. She looked up to see the president standing on the third-floor landing talking to a man with his back to the crowd. "No, don't. She has done nothing. She is powerless in all this."

Burrows turned. He cradled Valerie in his arms in the white clinic robes. He dumped her body over the third story railing but held her wrists, so she dangled above the crowd like a porcelain doll. They gasped and took a step back leaving Val suspended over the marble floor. If Burrows dropped her, Val would fall on top of the New West crest in the center of the golden circle. Burrows shrugged off the president's hands. Valerie's chin lolled on her chest. Her feet pointed toes down.

A dull roar shook the building. Geneva lurched from side to side. Leo and Streker grabbed her shoulders. People dropped to their knees around her. Burrows let go of one of Valerie's wrists. Her body tilted toward the floor. Her arm hung. Her wrist red where Burrows had grasped it. He clung to the railing with his other hand and Valerie swung in pendulum arcs.

Geneva stretched her arms up. She blinked as a skiff of plaster dusted her face. A crack etched through the dome of Old Main. A white blur passed in front of her, and a woman dropped to the ground. Blood gushed around the chunk of ceiling embedded in the back of her head. A wave of people moved toward the doors of Old Main and toward the arched doorways ahead of the hallways.

Everything Geneva had learned was useless. She could manipulate matter with her mind. If she meditated, focused her thoughts, she could effect a slow change, fix the roof maybe. But the building was collapsing over the people now and Valerie was falling. Bodies surged around her and thoughts: *Get out! Earthquake! Mother.*

She stood firm keeping her arms raised. She wouldn't leave Valerie. At least she could do that. Then she saw a flash of familiar purple light. Valerie's eyes blinked open above. The room strobed purple. Geneva saw flashing lines of thought whipping around the dome, leaping from person to person. In the middle of the chaos, the light pulsed toward an interwoven voice, a shared synapse. The individuals were united in one thought: *Door!*

Val: *Just get the dome.*

Just the dome. Just. The ground swayed. The floor buckled and Geneva reached out for the synapse, the one unified thought, and made a connection.

Everybody here. She directed. *Everybody now.* People's attention turned. It was as if she were standing naked, dipped in clay, and they began to approach her with paintbrushes. Leo squeezed her shoulder. She looked up at the dome splintering above them. She pictured it solid, the pieces fused. *We can do this. Now!*

The people's minds turned to the ceiling. The room became still and silent, except for the low rumble and the intermittent thump of falling bricks. The people were rooted in place, looking up. Bricks and chunks of marble and bits of plaster began to float through the air and land on the floor. The cracks in the dome above filled with purple light. Its surface flowed. It became smooth and transparent showing blue sky, cumulus clouds and the waving New West flag.

A rush of spring air sank to the bottom of Geneva's lungs. Valerie had pulled her other hand up to grab Burrows arm. She clung to his thick forearm as he shook her. Valerie: *Powerful.*

"Get away, get off me!" Burrows screamed.

Then, Valerie was falling.

Geneva waited for the impact, bone against bone. It never came. The crowd raised their arms, too. For a moment she couldn't see anything but the backs of people's upturned hands. When they moved away, across the room she could see Valerie crowd-surfing, but lost sight of her as she was lowered to the floor in a huddle of people.

A multitude of strangers hugged Geneva. She turned and saw Lydia Streker's frizzy wind-swept hair, tear streaked cheeks and enormous smile. "That's what I'm talking about. I heard you honey. I heard you. You did it."

Geneva looked at the translucent dome. "Not just me."

"I know," Lydia Streker, said her ample chest puffing. "Damn right, we all did."

“Up there,” Leo said.

Geneva and Lydia darted through the crowd and up the staircase. The president stared over the railing. Moaning came from his office. They found Burrows huddled in a ball next to the president's desk clutching his head in agony.

Lydia Streker rushed by, knelt by Burrows and raised her arms. She looked like she was going strike him some swift blows with her elbows. Then she took a deep breath and rocked on her heels. She stuck out her tongue and waggled her fingers. "Psychic, ha. There's nothing to do but wish you the blessing of instant karma. If you're lucky you'll get the consequences right away and won't have to atone for them in the next life. If you're lucky. Namaste."

~ 24 ~

SYNC CHROME CITY: LONG DISTANCE LOVE

"Again, to understand the trauma of the Psychic Rift, you have to look at historical and cultural context. Simpatico was an unknown concept, and certainly not a shared value as it is today. Our idea of shared mind—Connected Ego, Psychic Space, the Infinite Lattice—would have horrified them. Even those few who welcomed psychic abilities could not have fathomed our achieved extent of psychic connection. There was little evidence of what would be accomplished. Even trained psychics, of whom there were few in secret government programs, had achieved, at best, merely 50 percent success." — *Becoming Psychic 101, A History and a Primer*

Geneva held tight to Leo's waist as the scooter purred along the lane toward the Senator's Mansion. Her ponytails, freshly dyed a dangerous Gator Tongue red, whipped around her face as she turned to look at the lawn. "Horses?"

"It's a luxe pad," Leo said.

She pressed her face to his hair. It smelled of peach. "I can't believe Coco invited me."

"She kind of had to. You're the thing," he said. "Besides, I don't think there are any hard feelings."

Geneva didn't think so either, not between her and Coco. As far as she was concerned, Leo had made his choice. He was with her now, no matter how gorgeous Coco looked when she opened that door. Leo parked his scooter next to the Friend-Me Co. trucks alongside the mansion. "We've always been friends."

She caught the trace of bitterness in Leo's voice and realized it was true. Leo and Coco were good friends no matter how many times she dumped him.

"I don't think I can forgive her," she said.

Leo cupped her face in his hands. She could tell he knew she wasn't talking about Coco anymore. She was asking about Valerie, again—still—of course. She waited for recriminations. He had to be tired of her worrying about Val. She was tired of it too, but she couldn't stop, "What if I can't?"

"That's probably OK," he said.

He kissed her. He tasted peachy, too. She rang the bell. Coco opened the door in a rush of sunlit orange. She wore a breath-catching smooth tangerine dress that fell to her knees, the most flattering length. Eve stood beside her busty in strapless periwinkle. The girls embraced Leo. Geneva hung back out of habit, but Coco hugged her too, her arms sugar-polish soft. Eve shrugged her shoulders and gave her a half-smile. "Welcome," Coco said. She pointed through the French doors toward a ballroom filled with Mindscape. It smelled like an orange ocean. "The party starts now. You can set up."

Leo pulled his Sound-Wield wand from his backpack. "I'm going to get started. You OK?"

Geneva looked at the guests, in gowns and tuxes, standing knee deep and uncertain in the Mindscape. In the August heat, the orange waves across the floor and layered on the walls and ceiling took on a sweaty sheen. "This is too weird. But," she pointed to the buffet table. "My parents are over there. I'll be fine."

"Introduce me later?" he asked.

She hugged him. "Of course." As she navigated the crowd, one bewildered guest, a woman holding up the ends of her paisley gown, stood stiffly amidst the foam. She turned to her tuxedoed partner, "I don't know what's happened darling. Last year, there was elegant dancing and excellent hors d'oeurves."

Wedges of orange and yellow fruits filled the buffet. All the foods had been imported from C-town under the new trade agreement Geneva's mother had negotiated. Geneva recognized flavors from the Ruby's tropical sundae and tried to remember the names: mango, passionfruit. The nuts were crisp, light and summery: macadamias. Leo started his Sound-Wield set with timpani and mandolin and a cascade of golden light.

When she reached her parents, her mother drew her in. "Honey, I'm so glad to see you."

Geneva pressed her face to her shoulder. She hadn't felt so close to her in such a long time. They didn't let go until President Sherring approached. “Ambassador, you've done a remarkable job with the C-town assignment," he said.

Her mother released her and shook the president's hand. "Thank you. I think we'll all benefit. AeroFlux agreeing to manufacture Enviro-Cars to our specifications is the real coup and they are happy to retool now. There's not as much business in the airline industry." She gestured to the buffet table. "The other things though, I'm not sure how much we'll want foods like these or really be able to get them. Frankly, I don’t understand how C-town did and I couldn’t find out easily.”

President Sherring nodded. "Not much demand anyway, I suppose. New West is too independent. I think we were right on that score. It makes sense to be self-reliant when it comes to the essentials. It increases our security, our sense of well-being. Good things, however, are meant to be shared, enjoyed all around. Going into this next phase, that's got to be clear. Well," he gestured to the guests. There were few genuine smiles around the room as the guests attempted to mingle through the Mindscape in pretense that this was just another cocktail party. "I suppose we'd better get on with our demonstration. They look restless."

The partygoers silenced as soon as Sherring clapped his hands. They'd been waiting for some signal to be let in on the surprise.

"Attention everyone, please let me introduce Dr. Clara Montgrave. She will explain our unusual décor this evening."

There was light applause as Clara held her hand high in the middle of the room and the crowd parted around her. Leo bathed her in a circle of light that made her copper gown shimmer.

"This lovely orange fluff at your feet is a new material called Mindscape," Clara began. "It's the latest Friend-Me Co. innovation. There's a very complicated explanation involving slippery protons and quantum particles but, since this is a party, let's keep it light."

The guests murmured agreement.

"The magic of this material is that it is specially designed to be shaped by thoughts: our thoughts. You can move this material with your mind and with enough practice make it into whatever you can imagine. Please join me in a demonstration." The infinity symbol around Clara's neck swung as she scooped a sphere of Mindscape out of the floor. "Everyone please take a handful, like so."

The begowned and bejeweled guests struggled to emulate Clara's easy gesture. They tore up wads of Mindscape like cotton candy. Strands stuck to their fingers. Geneva's parents managed spheres after a few tries. But the New West University students dipped down and came up easily with balls. The guys juggled theirs waiting for the rest of the guests.

Lydia Streker approached Geneva, pouting, with a drooping lump of Mindscape in her hand. "None of the young people are having any trouble."

Geneva rounded out Lydia's Mindscape with a few pats. "Don't worry. Clara makes it look too easy. It took me months to learn. It makes me jealous to see how easily my friends can pick it up now."

"Well, I'm not giving up," Lydia said, tossing her ball in one hand. "Some things are easier to learn when you are young, but we all have the capacity. The brain gets better with use. We can think revolutionary thoughts until we die. You paved the way, now we all have to catch up."

"Does everyone have a ball?" Clara asked, as her orange blob turned to glass. "First, will it crystal clear. Then, concentrate on adding color." Stripes of red flowed through her sphere.

Overhead Leo swung on silver chains and switched the music to a string suite as he wove streamers of orange and yellow light like sunshine through the crowd. The guests stared at their globes.

Her mother, holding a murky sphere, whispered. "Is that your Leo?"

Geneva nodded—her Leo—her cheeks warmed.

As the string music trailed off, Clara held up her carmine-laced orb. "How did you do?"

The guests held spheres with varying degrees of translucence palms up. Most of the students raised colorful balls. They were nothing more than paperweights and baubles, but they were made of Mindscape and mind.

"Good. It takes practice. Focus. Now, let's work together. I think we're all tired of walking through Mindscape in our ball gowns. Let's do something similar to this orange goo on the floor," Clara said. "Look down. Close your eyes. Join hands if you like. It's time to use our collective consciousness for a change."

Lydia clasped Geneva's hand. "This part I'll like," she whispered.

Leo changed the music to steel drums and the lights pulsed pastel. The orange faded. The waves flattened. The floor smoothed into clear glass. Lydia clicked her heels, "Ohhh." Eddies of pink and yellow and turquoise began to swirl under the surface of the translucent ballroom floor. As Kendra LeMay walked over to them, colors pooled under her steps.

"Mr. and Mrs. Weltraum," she said, shaking Geneva's parent's hands. "You really have remarkable daughters. Everyone saw what Geneva here did and Valerie's blossomed now that she's learning control."

Geneva followed Kendra's gaze across the room, where the New West students had raised a ring of knee-high glass bulbs around a sparkling crystal floor and begun to dance. Valerie and Streker circled each other tossing garnet-colored globes between them. Geneva sighed. She'd meant to look for Val first thing and had forgotten. Maybe it was time to accept that it was OK. She wasn't Val's keeper. Her sister could take care of herself.

Her mother saw where she was looking. "You two getting along better?"

"A little. We're speaking, anyway," Geneva said.

"You two living together, both starting to awaken was difficult," Kendra said. "It was very hard for her to be around you while her powers were developing. It was hard on you too. That's why you've felt intertwined and yet distanced. You had to get away from her to discover your talent and she needed to be away from you to be able to cope with hers."

Geneva sighed. "I kept trying to help her, but I was aggravating the problem."

"I told you not to be roommates," her father said.

"Don't blame yourself," Kendra said. "Sync Chrome City sped everything up before your minds were ready. That's what caused the seizures."

"*Omnis festinatio ex parte diaboli est*," Geneva said. "All haste is the work of the devil."

Her mother winked at her father. "Slow down, you move too fast."

"On the other hand, it's not good to stand in the way of progress. Having a lot of hope and nothing to pin it on, no action, almost lead us into civil war. President Sherring has assured me that New West will restore funding to Friend-Me so we can research and develop psychic powers on campus and New West Mental Health will be shut down permanently," Kendra said. "I'm excited that Valerie is going to come work with me. We need to develop the curriculum so we can start teaching the skills, slowly, to the next generation. There's a lot to be done. People are warming to the idea of telepathic, empathic and telekinetic abilities, but there's concern about what it will mean. Some people will be afraid to let their children learn something that's difficult or even beyond their own abilities. Our work begins." Kendra turned to Geneva. "Are you sure you won't join us? We could really use your help."

Geneva shook her head. "I'm sorry. I have other plans."

Leo swung down beside them putting an arm around his mother. "Am I interrupting something?"

"I was just trying to get Geneva to come work for me after graduation and I think she was turning me down," Kendra said.

Leo gave her a questioning look and in return she gave him: *We have to talk.* "Mom, dad, this is Leo."

"Fantastic light show," her father said.

"I was just the opener," Leo said. He pointed toward the doors. "You won't believe who Coco got for the main event."

The band had more deviant Varies than Geneva had ever seen in New West. The five people standing by the French doors were practically animals. There were two bearish guys, a squirrel woman, and a couple with black tattooed masks across their eyes.

"That's Giovanni Hastings Musica from down the 'Way," Leo said.

"That's really them?" Geneva asked. "They're a real band then, not synth?"

"Yeah." Leo said. "Coco tracked them down in Portland and they agreed to make the trek up."

Geneva smiled. "I knew it! I knew they were real."

"Go on," her mother said.

Leo pulled her toward the front of the room. As Giovanni began its dark chords the students danced and changed the Mindscape. The rounded bubbles grew long and spiked, coming up from the floor and down through the ceiling. The ballroom became a cave of amethyst, garnet, emerald and onyx stalagmites and stalactites. The guests wove through them drinks in hand. Geneva and Leo stood at the edge of the ring watching the band play and their friends dance. Geneva pressed her back against Leo as Intertwining Fingers began. They sang the chorus along with the raccoonish-looking vocalists.

As the song ended, Geneva gave Leo*: I wish people were made of Mindscape.*

He hugged her. *No, you don't. You'd be some kind of super villain.*

She watched their friend dancing with fluid arching bodies, no longer emulating the shaking jolts of seizures, instead looking like the electric violet lashes of their minds. *This all would have been easier, if we could have just thought: change.*

Leo stroked her hand. *Now we can start to educate people.*

Geneva turned to him. *I'm going away.*

"Come on," he said, he held her hand and led her out through the French doors. "I like it when you are in my mind, but let's talk."

He walked her out to the pool behind the house. The setting sun made silhouettes of the horses grazing in the president's pastures. Geneva and Leo sat on the edge of the pool and dipped their feet in the water. "I talked to Dr. Roundtree," Geneva said. "I joined one of his research projects for post-grad work, but it's in the Cascadian wilderness, outside of New West. Roundtree thinks there is a teleological aspect to the psychic powers that needs to be explored.

We know that technology, Sync Chrome City, caused the psychic abilities to manifest sooner than they otherwise would have. But not for me. I didn't need that electronic connection, mine manifested organically. It was a natural evolutionary step that happened faster than we thought was biologically possible. We don't know why. Why now? Why me? I'm going to do graduate research study. I guess my thesis will be myself, I'll beat other people to it and be my own best lab rat."

"In the wilderness?" Leo said. "Sounds dangerous. You're brave."

Geneva shrugged. "I guess. I'm excited about the research, but I'm sad. It's bad timing, for us."

"Not so much," Leo said. "I still have to finish school and I'm working on my music. Besides, we're too new for promises. I mean, right now, I feel like I want to be with you forever, like I could say that, but what if things change? It's too early to say we're a sure thing."

"I know. I want to be with you. I just want to know what else is out there first." She circled her feet through the water. There was no way to be sure. She might just be projecting her feelings onto Leo. Maybe he didn't feel exactly the way she did. Maybe it wasn't organic. Maybe it wasn't real.

He touched his feet to hers below the water. "We'll see how things are when you get back. We'll hope and see what happens."

~ 25 ~

SYNC CHROME CITY: THE FUTURE FOREST

"We return always to Geneva Teresa Weltraum. She more than any other figure, even Valerie Freeman, embodies the spirit of the generation and her story most accurately explains the Psychic Rift and Saga. Even the most historically precise interpretations cannot avoid the compelling story of her tragic romance with Leo LeMay. In hindsight, we see so much unnecessary pain." —*Becoming Psychic 101, A History and a Primer*

"Even so, there's no question that Geneva Weltraum is the hero of our time and C.G. Burrows no less than a villain: a shark among seals." — *Save Giovanni: The Lost Men of the Psychic Wars*, S. Sherring

Geneva stood at the back of the Big Top as President Sherring began his fall quarter kickoff speech standing behind the NWU podium with Kendra LeMay. She already felt different from the other students, older, immune to the opening day energy. Kendra had arranged for Geneva's time in the Mindscape House to count as an internship for college credit. She just had to take the test she'd missed and then she'd be a graduate student, leaving all this behind.

"You could say we'll begin teaching Becoming Psychic 101," President Sherring said. As the Big Top filled with applause, Geneva checked her watch and left for her Privacy Law final. The test was a snap. She'd never gotten around to studying, but with her new powers of concentration, she didn't have to. She scanned her textbook before the test and when she sat down to take it, the information flowed line by line in waves behind her eyes like an open book.

Afterwards, she headed to the on-campus headquarters of Friend-Me Co. The Nootka Rose-Ladyslippers planted around the base of the green pyramid looked healthy. Their dark leaves lifted, and their petals fluttered in the cool breeze off the bay. The new hybrid had passed its test, too. It had become heartier and withstood the cooler weather. Geneva inhaled the marine-rose scent. The corrosive Rust Red Sea with its encroaching iron tang seemed far away. She felt light. No more tests. She still carried some nervous energy inside of her, but she understood the source of it and knew what to do now. Her new certainty felt like seeing a color other than orange in the Mindscape House, a relief.

Inside Friend-Me, Geneva nodded at the receptionist and took the elevator down. The world held many possibilities, as it always had, but now she had chosen a direction. She would follow her destiny and Burrows knew the way.

Burrows injected the last syringe of SLO-42 into the corner of his eye and contentment washed over him. They had him on a mellowing blend of Kendra and Leo LeMay, four syringes a day. Between that and his twice a day meditation routine, he'd conquered the pain of his telepathy for the first time in 30 years. Other people's presence registered as light pressure, tolerable. He no longer knew what they were thinking about him and could therefore stand to give them the benefit of the doubt. Animosity sloughed off him and left him at peace. Compared with the energy and certainty of the person he had been, he felt lethargic. He missed his drive, though he knew bitterness and anger had fueled it. Being superior had been fun, but it wasn't worth the agony. So, he took the drugs and buried his telepathy.

At the moment, he didn't have a choice. By sweet irony, New West's philosophy didn't make provisions for wrongdoers. There were no prisons or penalties. They had already done their worst to him—exile. The people he'd wronged most, Valerie and the president, had argued on his behalf. They valued knowledge over revenge. They'd turned him over to Friend-Me for research. He lived in the basement of the drug and psychic lab. Across the hall, New West's researchers were also making hybrid animals who could withstand the rising Rust Sea fish-rats and dog-turtles. Although the briny smells and squeals were not ideal, at the moment living in the lab among the other test subjects was a fair trade. He was learning. He wasn't becoming a neurosurgeon, scooping into people's brains like he'd wanted, but he was finding out a lot about the chemicals within them and the way minds worked. They were examining slices of his mind to see where it was different and what had caused his telepathy. They thought they were getting closer to the key to unlock the mystery of consciousness.

So, he wasn't surprised, after the Friend-Me lab tech called, "Visitor," to see Geneva standing in the lab wrapping her bright red ponytails around her fingers. Because she knew he'd murdered Valerie's parents—a point of fact damning even in New West—and had kept it to herself, he had expected she would show up at some point to extract a price. In return for protecting his privacy, what would she ask?

Geneva held the huge brass padlock in her hands until it warmed and expanded with a pop. She pushed open the thick steel door. The basement lab had been outfitted with a futon and a rug, but it was still mostly beakers and vials strewn across black counter tops. Burrows sat with his back against a cement wall staring into an open Friend-Me journal. He was expecting her. She got:

They couldn't keep you out. Go ahead. He expected her to hurt him, again. It was weird to think she could.

"Come on in. I've had my shot," he said getting up, straightening the bedding on the futon and raising it into a folded couch.

She looked at the row of green vials of SLO-42 lining the nearest countertop, the juice Burrows needed to take every day. She walked over to the countertop and picked up one of the vials. She held it up to the dim fluorescent light where it turned from black to murky green. It was a sludgier looking stuff than she was used to, highly concentrated. She fingered the syringe.

"I can," she said. "I thought about it. I really thought about it, whether it was actually possible to forgive someone for murder. But it is. It just is. They couldn't do it. Valerie wouldn't. Right now. But once they see, once they open up to it and they can feel each other so intensely like right inside at the heart where it matters. Then, they will. They would."

From Burrows she got: *But I killed.*

"It wasn't you. You were in pain. No, stop, it's not just an excuse. Just stop thinking that for a moment."

Burrows tried. He knew what it was like to have thoughts stinging in his head, carrying the burdens of others. It made her feel that what she was about to do would be OK. Would work out OK, anyway.

"Thank you," she said. "You would never have done that. You would never under any circumstance have done that. You would never do that. You aren't meant to hurt *anyone*."

She said it like a mantra, and he winced when she pushed that last word in to him, through the sludge of drug dose suppressing that part of his mind, protecting him from the pain. She pushed it in and watched him take it. He gave her: *I deserve it.* She felt his regret, his repentance. Not that he had killed Valerie's parents so much, in truth he hadn't known them, but sadness about losing his dealer, a peppy guy named Mason, Mace.

"I liked him," Burrows said. He hadn't had many friends.

Geneva felt bad for having that power, a niggling bit of guilt she was always going to have if she stayed around here, knowing that for no good reason she had power over all these people, because she knew both their secrets and how they felt about them. Her power over others gave her an inherent moral ambiguity. It would be impossible not to abuse it. She couldn't be psychic and be a good person, she figured. In Burrows' case, she would not even try. She needed him to take her to her destiny. "Burrows, I forgive you."

She felt Burrows both wanting this relief and trying to resist it. He didn't want to be so easily satisfied, to have the emotions tugged out of him as if he were watching a mass-market movie or saying, "I love you, too." The emotions came anyway. Relief and thankfulness washed over him, and his mind leaned into hers and sighed. Geneva felt guilt now because she'd used his guilt to get what she wanted, compliance.

"Tell me," she said. "Tell me what you know. What frightened you?"

He rubbed the side of his jaw, running his nubby fingers through the scars, visible through his shorn beard. He didn't want to talk about this, but he would, because she had paid the price, she had power over him. "I'll go there, but I want to actually tell you," he said.

He knew he didn't deserve the concession, but he didn't want her in his mind. She agreed. She also didn't enjoy the feeling of forcing it, of tearing thoughts out of another's head. It was better if he was willing.

"OK," she said. "But I'm going to follow along. I want to know how you feel about it.

He frowned but nodded resigned. There was no way to keep her out of his head. She could go where she wanted. He stroked his beard some more, a habitually nervous tic. It was another thing they had in common. She was still winding her ponytails around her fingers.

"It was just a little girl sitting under a tree."

"Me."

"You."

"What scared you?"

"She did. You did." he said. "She was sitting and glowing and it was like she, everything, was going to pop open."

Like a wound.

Like a seed. She corrected, pressing him. He saw the girls again in the back of his trunk bound together. He felt the old fear and the new guilt.

Burrows balled his hands into fists and rose off the couch. "I wish you wouldn't do that."

He stepped towards her, towering over her. She was glad he couldn't feel that she was afraid. She didn't back up, not an inch. She held still even when he grabbed the syringe.

"An extra dose if you don't mind," he said. "This is really hard for me, you know."

"No, I don't care. So, it's hard," she said. Then she whispered. "But you're forgiven."

He plunged the syringe into his arm and then looked up at her. He threw it onto the futon. He gave her a cold look. "I have to forgive myself."

She looked down. That was harder. "What kind of tree was it?"

His mind went blank.

"What kind? Madrona? Fir? Maple?" she pressed.

His mind clicked emptily over various responses, but it pulsed as she spoke the words. There was something hidden there. It was what she wanted. *Come on.*

"It had long droopy branches with tiny shoots and leaves."

"Blossoms?"

"No. Yes. Pink."

"A weeping cherry."

He shrugged.

Geneva yanked her backpack from around the shoulder. She unzipped the side pocket and brought out the dried cluster of leaves, the Friend-Me delivery from early last year, when it had all started. "They looked like these."

He nodded.

"When I was in school on the last day of elementary school before the revolution, I was all alone on the playground. It was before Valerie came to live with us. I touched that tree and I felt." She paused and the feeling washed over her again, the golden glowing expansiveness—she could do anything. She looked at Burrows. "Do you miss it?"

His hands immediately went to his jaw. "No," he said.

But he did a little.

"No," he said. "This is better, understand. The peace. The quiet. That's all I need."

She did get it. She understood that the dull murky layer of SLO-42 haze was better than the sharp stabs of pain. Without the distraction, he could access the better parts of himself here: his wits and his humanity. But he was still scarred inside. He might never want to be around people, know more compassion. He would never feel joy again. She placed the vial, the one she'd picked up and was still holding into her backpack. "You were born in the wrong time. One evolutionary step too early."

"No, not that. Don't do that. Don't take that," he said.

He was so afraid to live without the drug, for now. It made her smile. It made it easier.

"I need you to come with me. We're not done. Becoming Psychic 101, what they are going to do. Teaching it is just a start. I haven't been able to figure it out. I haven't been paying attention. I couldn't get my head around it. I kept wondering, 'Why me? Why now?' Like you're thinking. You just want the peace and quiet. I thought that's what I was supposed to do, be, and then I was hit with this destiny thing and I'm a big superhero/super villain. I'm Giovanni Hastings. I have the power. I could go either way. But I was asking the right question all along, 'Why me?' I don't think it's just me. I have to know, but I don't want to stay here and have them try to pull the answers out of me like a lab rat-fish thing. I want to find out for myself."

He couldn't keep his eyes off her fingers, going down the row of vials and moving each one into her backpack. If she dropped one, she knew he would catch it. She watched how much effort it took him to ignore the vials, to sit down and clasp his hands together. Letting go, letting her take the drug he needed. He didn't understand yet that he was going with her.

"My father said once that learning the mysteries of the world doesn't spoil it. It doesn't have to make things less interesting. It doesn't have to destroy our faith. We have to believe things can only get more miraculous," Burrows said. "I haven't believed that—ever."

"You think your Dad never gave you anything better than Mistress M.D."

He nodded.

"But he said that," she placed the last vial into her backpack. "Here's the deal. I'm going North into the Cascadian wilderness. I'm doing a research project for Dr. Roundtree to start my graduate work. I never did figure out what I wanted to do with my life. If I stay around here, I think I'll be treated like some kind of psychic messiah, some hero. I can't."

She got: *You don't want to be the hero. I don't want to be the villain.*

"Exactly, or vice versa if it comes down to that. So, you're coming with me. You're the only one that's felt it before. I haven't felt it. You are going to help me find the *unus mundus*, the world mind. It's not just me and us awakening. It's everything. It's why you and Valerie and Senator Sherring and Constance are so sad. They've lost that connection with nature. This lab," she pointed back toward the room of animal experiments. "There's the problem."

"They'll come after us," Burrows said.

They would. New West, Friend-Me, the people on the Freeway; when they realized she'd taken Burrows with her. But that's not what Burrows meant: *The trees.*

The idea filled Geneva with an expansive rush. She couldn't resist the impulse to press back at Burrows, all the thoughts that came to her: *The source is in the trees. It's teleological, natural. It's the wayrrul. It's the quantum flirt. It's the aboriginal power. It's the trees.*

He cringed, resisted her thoughts*: I wish you wouldn't.*

She felt his*: Fear.*

"We feel fear before we know what we're afraid of," she said.

She didn't tell him what else she'd picked off his subconscious. That The Freemans, and his friend, Mace, were alive. He hadn't killed them after all. It seemed safer to travel alone with him if he still carried his guilt for the murders—was trying to reform. It would keep him committed to taking the SLO-42 to keep himself in check. She didn't feel bad about the omission. He had kidnapped her, taken a stab at Valerie and threatened Coco. If he thought she had forgiven him, he would owe her. What gnawed at her was that she hadn't told Valerie. She'd didn't want Valerie following her into the wilderness, as she surely would have if she'd known her parents could be there. But there were no guarantees.

Geneva knew she was different, but she did not know how in the world it had happened. She pushed Burrows again: *We're going forward. We're going to find it, our way, our new way together.*

On their way out, Geneva uncaged one of the hybrid rats with webbed toes and lacy flying fish wings. The friendly creature clung to her and its freedom. It burrowed into her neck and she felt it exhale and relax. As she stroked its soft and scaly back, she watched Burrows unlatch another cage and free another of the rat-fin beings, which quickly crawled up to his neck, and curled around it.

The four of them left the lab and headed North into the dry Cascadian wilderness and toward the drowning islands of Pacifica.

~ 26 ~

SYNC CHROME CITY: EPILOGUE

The Giovanni Hastings Story

There once was a boy with such unusual talents that his parents thought there must be something wrong with him. They took him to a doctor. The doctor, who had been trained to diagnose trouble, thought there was indeed something amiss.

"What should we do?" the parents of the boy, Giovanni Hastings, asked. "Medication?"

The doctor held his head in his hands and pondered. Finally, he referred them to a specialist. The neurosurgeon claimed to be able to see into Giovanni's head from the outside. He put Giovanni into large machines and shot rays through his head and took pictures of his young brain. Then he held the pictures up to the light and hemmed and hawed and pointed at spots.

"I propose surgery," he said, at last. "Of a most unique sort. We must remove Giovanni's brain and feed it to the world. Then everyone will gain these unusual talents."

Giovanni's mother, Mrs. Hastings, nearly fainted on the spot at this dramatic proclamation although, in truth, she'd imagined just such drastic measures.

"If we do this, what will happen to Giovanni?" Mr. Hastings asked.

"He will be without brain," the surgeon solemnly responded.

Giovanni's parents took the boy home directly. This was not the kind of decision one made on the spot in a doctor's office. The neurosurgeon apologized that in this most unusual case, he did not have any pamphlets he could send home with them to help them make an informed decision. An operation of this sort had simply never been performed. It was the first of its kind. Mr. Hastings noted the excited gleam in the neurosurgeon's eyes and the way he said "performed." It made him hesitant.

However, that afternoon, Mrs. Hastings spied on her unusually talented Giovanni as he played in the abandoned yard with the neighborhood boys. Giovanni had always been the leader of games. He had, after all, most unusual talents. Shortly thereafter, the telephone rang. It was the excited surgeon. "Have you made your decision?"

"I think it must be done," Mrs. Hastings said. "For the good of everyone."

The media got hold of the story. Probably the surgeon's office assistant had made the first call to the attractive television reporter. Certainly, the gleaming-eyed neurosurgeon was pleased that the story was out, all the better to make him well-known. Giovanni was, in fact, a very media-friendly boy, pleasant to look at even on large screens. Soon his rosy cheeks were ubiquitous. Mrs. Hastings gave interviews explaining why she was willing to sacrifice Giovanni's brain.

"For everyone's good," she repeated.

It was a popular phrase with the public. The tabloids, however, vilified her. She was a terrible mother, an attention-monger. They rolled out their largest type for her: MOTHER ASKS SURGEON TO REMOVE CHILD'S BRAIN!

Mr. Hastings, on the other hand, was a terrible interview. He didn't have much to say, so the reporters, eventually, left him alone. They pressed the neurosurgeon for details instead. He described the procedure incision by incision, his eyes gleaming all the while.

"What about Giovanni?" a reporter asked. "What will happen to him?"

The neurosurgeon said that not all of Giovanni's brain would be extracted. He would leave the primitive reptilian portion of brain to control Giovanni's emotions. This would give him a small chance at survival.

"The amygdala is shaped like an almond," the surgeon said, as the reporters scribbled furiously.

The next day almonds were ubiquitous shown in insets above Giovanni's rosy cheeks. The tabloids used more large type: BOY WILL BE LEFT WITH ALMOND FOR BRAIN! Sales of almonds skyrocketed. The public relations executive whose responsibility it was to make sure people ate more almonds worked overtime to take advantage of the windfall publicity. Finally, all her carefully prepared facts about the health benefits of almonds, and the history of almonds, and clever witticisms about almonds saw the light of day. Due to her efforts, almonds gained positive associations in the minds of all people for years to come. All her hard work paid off, but of course there was also a certain amount of luck involved and the results were difficult to quantify. Lots of dollar signs were added at any rate.

Politicians got involved rapidly in the Giovanni Hastings' situation so that they could also take advantage of the windfall publicity and set them themselves up handily for re-election. Also, they wanted to be seen as doing something and respond to the concerns of their constituencies.

"It's wrong for a mother to remove her child's brain," they declared.

Politicians proposed laws prohibiting the removal of a child's brain and prohibiting the eating of brain. When that infuriated a small but vocal ethnic minority that considered the eating of crab brain to be a great delicacy, they amended that law to prohibit the eating of human brain, specifically, which would, in all probability, scientists declared, lead to outbreaks of disease and madness.

Because some politicians and scientists were so adamantly against the removal and eating of Giovanni's brain, other politicians and scientists took the opposite side and became vehemently in favor of it. Later, everyone heralded these early adopters. Sensible people merely asked questions: What were Giovanni's amazing talents? Would eating his brain bestow the powers upon everyone who ate of them or would it cause disease and madness? They could not make up their minds about eating Giovanni's brain without understanding all of the facts. Other people took great offense to this. The audacity of asking! Who did these sensible people think they were? No one owed them any explanation.

As a benefit of all this discussion, every person learned a lot about the workings of his or her brain. The field of neuroscience, previously considered a bit of crockery and certainly beyond the ken of the average layperson, expanded considerably. Soon even the smallest child could name all the hemispheres of their brain and neurotransmitters and, of course, everyone knew about the center of emotions, the almond-shaped amygdala. And nobody perpetuated that right brain, left-brain misinformation any longer, because everybody knew the brain worked holistically through complex, interconnected electro-chemical mechanisms.

Meanwhile, other things went on in the world. And they were not going well. They were going to hell. People stopped laughing at wild-haired prophets who talked about the "end of the world" and the "end times." They weren't so funny anymore, except for their continually and radically unkempt hair. They could be right. It was time for drastic measures.

The tide of opinion shifted.

“The early adopters were right,” people said, including on the front page of The Herald daily newspaper. “We might as well eat Giovanni's brain.”

Giovanni was now 10 years old. The gleaming-eyed surgeon was still around and anxious to perform. The laws were restored. Childrens' brains could be removed, and anyone could eat whatever they liked (almonds were still very popular). A date was set for the procedure to remove Giovanni's brain and the maker of the leading brand of almond milk developed a formula for a tasty brain milkshake. The milkshakes were very popular even without the Giovanni Hastings’ brain supplement.

As the date for the long-awaited event approached, the removal and consumption of Giovanni’s brain, an investigative reporter asked a sensible question, "Would there be enough brain to go around?"

Oh, the audacity! In fact, there would not.

This sparked another firestorm of controversy that threatened to flare into endless debate. But for the first time, Mr. Hastings himself offered an opinion. He gave a, for once, engaging interview proposing that the younger generation alone eat Giovanni's brain and gain the unusual talents. It was a culturally acceptable plan, because they all said they wanted what was best for their children, even though some parents secretly, selfishly, if truth be told, did not want their kids to be able to do anything unusual. Particularly, they did not want their children to do what they could not do. But no one would say this culturally inappropriate truth out loud. Some of the older population also thought the brain might kill you and wanted none of it. So, this solution worked for them, too.

Eventually, even the surgeon and Mrs. Hastings agreed to forgo their portions of Giovanni's brain for the sake of the children. To be sure, they put it to a vote. Some people voted yes because they believed eating Giovanni's brain would save the world. Other people voted yes because they thought the procedure was doomed to fail and they were tired of the endless debate and they were too old to eat the brain anyway, tasty almond milkshake or no. Overwhelmingly, people voted to kill Giovanni Hastings and feed his brain to children.

On the night before the operation, as Mrs. Hastings sat around absently stroking the top of Giovanni's head, a masked man with enormous shoulders broke into her living room and kidnapped the boy. Soon after, the masked man appeared on TV threatening to kill the boy the good old-fashioned way by gunshot. He said he would cut off Giovanni's head and hide it away until the amazing brain inside rotted, lost to hungry consumers of tasty almond milkshakes young or old forever. Soon everyone asked in a unified voice: Who was this masked man who had stolen Giovanni, kidnapped their futures, and deprived their children of brain and potentially world-saving unusual talents?

The investigative reporter worked overtime trying to find out who was the angry man behind the mask. Using the clue of his enormous shoulders, she uncovered some interesting facts:

1.) The man was an escaped convict.

2.) He had had amazing abilities as a young boy and had been operated on.

3.) The gleaming-eyed neurosurgeon had removed all but the almond-shaped amygdala of his brain and subsequently made the man angry. Always angry.

"Is it true?" The reporters questioned the neurosurgeon. "Why didn't this important fact ever come up during all of our endless debates?"

The surgeon gleamed. "Not relevant," he said. "That was then, and this is now."

The angry man allowed an investigative news team to shave his head on TV so that everyone could see the latticework of scars left on his skull from the operation. He submitted to a brain scan, which revealed only the almond-shaped portion of his brain. The rest of his head was filled with a medical foam replacement patented by the gleaming-eyed neurosurgeon.

Meanwhile, the search for Giovanni was underway. No one knew where he was except the angry man who wouldn't say. He said they would never find Giovanni, but the police continued to look. Many private citizens took up the search too, but the most tireless searchers were Giovanni's four best friends from the neighborhood who missed their playmate very much. He had always been the leader of their games with the best imagination and most unusual talents. They looked for Giovanni day and night and long after they were supposed to come inside for supper. But the angry man was right, Giovanni was well hidden, and no one could find him.

So, Giovanni, tied up in an abandoned warehouse, had to save himself using his unusual talents. After his escape, he went directly to the clubhouse in the abandoned yard near his home where his four playmates hugged him and listened joyously to the recount of his escape. Giovanni embellished a bit adding Cerberus and Cyclops. His friends were glad to see him. Afterwards, Giovanni announced a press conference.

All the reporters, including the investigative one, came to hear Giovanni's announcement.

"I am 12-years old now and I have spent most of my life listening to people talk about whether or not to eat my brain," Giovanni said. "But it is my brain and here is what I have decided: I would like Dr. Skillings to remove all of it."

At this, the neurosurgeon's eyes reached the limits of their capacity to gleam.

"Even," Giovanni continued, "the almond-shaped amygdala. And I don't care for any foam filling."

"But how can you live without any brain?" the surgeon protested. "An empty head? That will surely kill you!"

"I'll have my eyes," Giovanni said. "The optic nerve is part of the brain."

The crowd of reporters murmured. By now, everyone knew this to be true, but no one had thought of it.

“What will happen to your brain?" a reporter asked.

"Will you feed it to the children, Giovanni?" another shouted.

At this, Giovanni gestured to his four friends standing on the stage beside him. "My friends will try it first. If they gain my unusual talents, then all the other children may share the tasty almond milkshakes, too."

The angry man, who was allowed to attend the press conference in the custody of an armed guard because it made good media, raised his hand. The reporters looked up expectantly and Giovanni called on him, "Do you have a question?"

The man stroked his hideously scarred head stuck between his enormous shoulders and fidgeted nervously in his orange jumpsuit. Between clenched teeth he said, "You'll regret this, kid."

"That is not really a question," Giovanni said. "But the world is coming to an end, and we have to try."

"That's what I thought too," the man snarled, shaking his enormous shoulders. "Didn't work out so good."

"That was then, and this is now," said Giovanni.

Despite the warning of the angry man, that afternoon a team of surgical technicians led by Dr. Skillings, of the gleaming eyes and bearer of the patent for medical foam, removed Giovanni's brain, every portion of it including the almond-shaped amygdala which was fed raw to Giovanni's four close friends. The texture was terrible, but it didn't taste bad, a little cinnamon-y.

Afterwards, everyone waited anxiously to see if the four friends would gain amazing abilities. Giovanni's parents waited anxiously to see if their son had miraculously survived brain extraction. The neurosurgeon waited anxiously to see the result of his great experiment. The angry man waited anxiously as he had every day of his life since his own operation for his anger to fade and his head to stop hurting. The investigative reporter didn't wait for anything. She was investigating a possibility no one had thought of and was already digging up some interesting leads.

As it turned out, the four friends gained unusual talents even more amazing than Giovanni's. They could lift large objects just by thinking about them. They could communicate with each other telepathically. They could read minds. They could heal injuries and stop pain. They could levitate through the air. The Giovanni Hastings Milkshakes were rapidly distributed around the world and hastily consumed by most of the world's children. After drinking the GHMs, the world's children gained an immediate understanding of each other and managed to solve most pressing global problems on the spot. They established an entirely new educational system and sent their parents back to school. As it turned out, eating Giovanni's evolved brain was just a catalyst that unlocked latent abilities undeveloped in the populace.

Giovanni Hastings awoke, and he was the same old Giovanni, but with a strange gleam in his eyes. His head was not empty. It was filled with compassion and empathy for all the world's children. He could see their perspectives with his remaining brain—his gleaming eyes—and communicate with them effortlessly all at once. Giovanni's parents were happy. His mother was first to enroll in the new school system. His father didn't want to, he said he was too old to learn new things, and that was OK, too. The world's children declared Giovanni their heroic leader and created the worldwide holiday Giovanni Hastings Day during which everyone ate sugared-almonds and drank milkshakes and wore crowns of almond leaves and decorated their houses with almonds, too. The woman who had run the almond marketing campaign had become very, very rich and then retired. Now almost everyone planted almond trees in front of their homes and down city streets and ate as many almonds as they wanted for free.

Although there was no longer any need for prisons and there were no guards, locks or keys, the angry man still lived in his cell holding his hurting head in his hands. The neurosurgeon offered to remove the rest of his brain and the medical foam, but the angry man didn't want anything to do with him. No one really did. Now that they could see how Giovanni's eyes gleamed with enlightenment and compassion, the gleam in the neurosurgeon's eyes just looked creepy by comparison and made everyone extremely nervous.

While his friends went on making improvements in the world and enjoying their new super heroic powers and setting up schools, Giovanni paid a visit to the angry man.

"I'm sorry about the way things turned out for you," he said. "I was lucky my friends suggested sharing my emotions."

"My friends only teased me," the man said. “My parents weren't interested, either."

"I think you should at least take medicine to dull your pain," Giovanni said. He handed the man a couple of pills. "Then you won't be so angry."

"But somebody has to be angry. Where there's a hero, there's a villain. That's the way it goes," the man said. "Besides, it's all I have left. It's my identity: the angry man.”

But Giovanni insisted that the world was different, so the man took the pills and sighed. "So, that's it then."

"No, there's more," Giovanni said. "I've been in touch with an investigative reporter. She's been asking, 'Why you? Why me? How come our brains evolved before everyone else's?'"

The man had not thought much that. His head hurt too much. "Those are good questions," he admitted.

Giovanni handed the man a bottle of pills. "Keep taking these so you won't be so angry. You and I are going to find out together the true source of our unusual talents."

And the man did as Giovanni Hastings said because Giovanni Hastings, the hero, had saved the world.

Mirror Island: Book Two

Solarpunk Transformation Trilogy
Book Two

Mirror Island

~ 27 ~

MIRROR ISLAND: PROLOGUE

Conceived on an island universe

Imprisoned in SpireMine, Leonid Moriena spent his last days reflecting on his life and who he was. Still, the last action he took in life surprised him. He was an engineer and an activist. People who saw his life from the outside said he was self-sacrificing, but he saw it differently, he went to the forefront of action because that was his means of survival. It invigorated him. He had to act. The people who saw his life from the inside, his wife and daughter, saw it yet another way, as neglect, but theirs was an untenable point of view. The accolades he received for his service insulated him from their criticism, if not, in later years, their sorrow. Osana threw herself passionately against that barrier often early in their relationship asking for his time and his presence, but in later years she never raised her voice or shed tears or pressed her body tightly against his anymore. She had yielded.

His daughter, Kira, was another matter. His engineering team developed the aircraft, an AF-897, that led them to a new source of energy to power their world. She was unimpressed. As a child, she wanted her father close by, to hold his hand, as a teenager she punished him by pretending indifference, and as an adult she was simply distant. She never forgave him for putting his work ahead of holding her in his arms, so Leonid was startled when it was she who arrived to save him.

The AF-897 aircraft brought them to a small planet with a power source at its core. Tremors crossed the planet's surface, growing in intensity as the hastily assembled SpireMine operation inhaled the energy to fuel earth's needs. AeroFlux was unwilling to invest the time required to solve the engineering problem of how to extract the energy safely. When it became clear the company meant to use and discard the small planet, draining the core until it imploded, Leonid led his men to protest. He founded the Watchmen. In the planet's last days, the fallow mine became the dissidents' prison.

As the rumbling in the mine grew, the imprisoned men quieted, each entering the smaller cell of his own thoughts. They were like the planet now, silent on the surface, but in upheaval inside. The prison guards had gone, leaving the men in the mine. The catastrophe would happen quickly. No survivors were expected. They hadn't bothered to release the men so that they could die with their families. Leonid thought of his wife, Osana. The mourning in her eyes for the relationship they might have had weighed on him. When the choice had been his, he had so often left her. Now that it was beyond his control, he wanted only to be at home with her in her garden.

Then his daughter appeared at his cell door. He inhaled the faint trace of the outdoors on Kira's skin and touched her pregnant belly and forgot everything. He escaped with her. If he lived, he'd remember every detail; her white wrist smeared with soot, the sulfur stench of the steam-filled corridor, the soles of his shoes tacky on the hot stone, the steep incline and the grit stinging his eyes. She did not take him home, but instead brought him to the AF-897. They would try to leave the planet and get far enough away in time to live. Kira meant to save herself and her child and he was proud, for a moment, he'd given her the means to try.

Only after the silence of space enveloped them, and it looked as though there was a chance they might survive the implosion, did Leonid consider what he'd done. He'd left his men behind. If he lived, it would haunt him. He'd run past rows of his Watchmen every waking moment. They'd call out to him at night. Still, he willed the ship away, faster. He did not expect to survive, but he wanted to live to be a grandfather, guilt-ridden or not.

"It took time to come for me. Why risk it?" he asked.

Kira placed a hand over her husband's, splayed over the aircraft controls. "We're going to have a little girl. I wanted Doreena to know her grandfather."

Leonid had disapproved of Kira's marriage to the government-employed aerospace engineer and Nazar's passivity now did not impress him. Leonid would have put saving his family above every consideration. He would not have let his wife come to the prison mine and he wouldn't have taken his hands off the controls to hold Kira and comfort her the way Nazar was doing, not when it might take all his concentration to steer the craft and save them.

"The boy lacks passion," he'd complained.

But, of course, that's what had drawn Kira to Nazar. She didn't want a passionate personality. She'd seen the loneliness that had brought her mother.

"Your mother?" he asked.

"Still in her garden. She didn't think we'd even get this far," Kira said.

Of course, Osana would be placid through the end. He thought of her with her hands around a steaming cup of jasmine tea — no, she'd want to keep busy — he saw her patting mulch around her Sky-Blue Coronets. Either way, she was grounded on the planet. From space it looked peaceful, there was nothing to betray the cataclysm inside. After all the fighting he had done for it, she was the loyalist now while he would likely die off-planet.

Loyalty was a trait Kira owed to her mother. Osana had never left him even when he, consumed by his work and the Watchmen, had come to her so little. But Kira's passion to live was his contribution. They were one of only a few ships daring the attempt to escape into uncharted space. And that was Kira's doing, but they were still too close to the planet.

When the planet's gutted core collapsed and its husk crumbled into space, the ship tossed. Leonid lurched across the ship to the controls. "I'll take it."

Nazar had already unstrapped himself from the seat and Leonid saw, like a clear pool, the true reason Kira had delayed leaving to rescue him — why the mother would risk her child. Nazar knew the mechanics of the craft but he didn't have the confidence to fly it or the ferocity needed to save his family. Leonid took the controls. If the machine failed, he could not keep the craft aloft by sheer force of will, but he would try. He'd give everything to save his daughter and grandchild.

He kept the ship pointed outward as pieces of the planet battered its hull flinging them through space. When a glowing blue sphere appeared before them, he didn't hesitate. He directed the craft toward it taking their best chance. Inside the planet's atmosphere, peaks and valleys sparkled blue. The AF-897 whined as it spiraled down. Leonid pulled up and adjusted for a water landing, but the ship plunged through the blue and struck like a diver in shallow water.

Leonid awoke to whispering: "Water. Water. Water."

It was dark and cold and cramped in the smashed cockpit. Kira was still strapped into the chair next to him. The blood on her forehead had crusted into a black scar. Her lips were puckered, white and gaping. Her hands were folded over her belly. There was no blood there or pooled on the floor beneath her. He twisted around and pain shot up his spine. Nazar was crumpled on the floor behind him half of his head caved in, his arms outstretched and bent as though he'd tried to catch himself. The lips in Nazar's wrecked head moved, "Water."

"Water," Kira responded and Leonid moaned listening to the lovers pass the word between them. It reminded him of the way the Watchmen had whispered "Soon, soon, soon," up and down the rows of cells as the mine rumbled. Kira whispered "water" again and this time Nazar did not respond. They were dying in a slow, painful, predictable way like their home world with impotent protests. Leonid wished he hadn't woken up for this dying, but he fought to keep himself from going into shock as he moved his trembling hands to unclasp his belt. He slipped to the floor, crawled to Kira's side and lifted himself to her.

He heard her sigh and lost sensation. Numbness spread across his chest. He made one last exertion and stretched to lever open the hatch. The atmosphere would hasten their deaths and reduce their suffering, and he wanted to see where they had landed. He wished things had been different, that the planet he loved had been smaller, so that he might have had a chance of saving it. It had always been too big a task for one man no matter how many Watchmen he'd convinced to join the cause. He wished he had lived to see his granddaughter grow into a young woman and see what she would choose: loyalty or passion. The plank floated down into a swirl of soft blue. Behind him Nazar said, "Water," one last time.

"Doreena," he replied, the child deserved a chance at life.

He heard a splash and felt the ship roll before he died.

It took Leonid Moriena some time to puzzle out who and what he was. When he reappeared beside the spaceship, he floated alongside its warped shell in a blue haze. But on his next breath, his lungs filled with fluid. He flailed. Seeing light, he shot up. He surfaced gasping. His head and shoulders bobbed half out of the water like the ship beside him. He sucked in air. Blue light shimmered around him. Blue flakes floated on the water, a sparkling sea foam. He started to swim to the ship. He wanted to touch its cool surface and feel the pressure of it against his palm. He reached for it but heard splashing behind him.

"Help me."

He turned and saw Kira with her arm around Nazar's waist hauling him through the water. Nazar's shoulder stuck out like a fin. Water rippled around Kira, but she barely moved. He treaded to her, and grasped Nazar's waist while she held her husband's head.

"There." She pointed ahead at a shiny blue shore.

Leonid pulled Nazar's body tight against his and lugged his son-in-law through the water until he was able to drag him on shore. They sank up to their elbows in the soft blue. Had they crash-landed in the sea? But the blue did not feel wet. Instead, it tingled. It tasted salty-sweet.

"Get them off. Get them off."

He sat up shivering and turned to see Kira slapping at her arms and legs brushing billowing clouds of blue from her body. Nazar too was coated in the glittering film. It stuck to his face so that he looked metallic. When Kira knelt beside her husband and ran her hands over his face the flesh tones returned. Leonid ran his fingers through his beard. He peered into the blue powder that dropped into his hands. He blew and it puffed into the air and disappeared. Kira managed to clean herself and Nazar completely so not a sparkling trace of the alien matter remained on them. Leonid let the stuff rest on his skin and traced a finger through a skiff across the top of his hand. It tingled pleasantly. He sat for a long time trying to remember what had happened.

First, he remembered a photograph. When the international team of engineers had finished the aircraft, they had posed for a photo in front of it. He was the senior among them and they had put him at the center of it. They called him "chief." The South African called him, "*moriena*," which meant chief in his mother tongue.

"Father, are you ready to eat now?"

He looked up and Kira stood over him with her pregnant belly and handed down an open half of some orange fruit. He scooped out the smooth flesh with his fingers and ladled it into his mouth.

"Good?"

"So sweet. It tastes like home," he said.

Kira put an arm around him and he bowed his head. As a young man, he'd never cried. He took Kira's arm and let her help him to his feet. When he'd awakened beside the ship and seen its underwater wavering, he'd thought he was a ghost, but now his legs felt stiff from sitting. He had no idea how long he'd been on the beach. Except for Kira and the fruit everything was swirling blue. He ran his hands through his beard. It ended inches past his chin as usual.

He allowed Kira to lead him off the beach and continued to eat the fruit. Kira and Nazar had found a grove of trees and grasses — all kinds that he knew and could name— in the middle of the blue field. They'd made a lean-to out of palm fronds against the back of a green stone. There was water, food, and shelter everything they needed and Kira and Nazar busied themselves with the tasks of survival. They ate, drank, and slept. Leonid was neither hungry nor thirsty nor tired and his skin remained a constant temperature neither hot nor cold.

He pulled Kira aside, "Where are we? How did all of this get here?"

"All of what?"

"Home," Leonid said. "These plants that are just like home. How can everything be so familiar?"

Kira ignored him. Leonid knew his daughter and saw that she was annoyed with him the way she was whenever he'd left her either to work at AeroFlux, or to organize protests against it, or to be martyred in prison. She handed him a hollowed out gourd. "Here, Nazar and I do all the work while you ponder. Fetch us some water."

Filled with regret, for he knew he had been a terrible father, Leonid bowed his head, took the gourd and walked to the water with it dangling from his hand. When he got to the water, he dipped the gourd it in and water pooled in its yellow lining. He wet a finger in it and pressed it to his curled tongue. The water was clean. He drank from the shell and then directly from the lake raising it to his lips in a cupped hand. It was clean as a mountain spring, not salty-sweet as he recalled. And where was the ship? He peered out across the flat shimmering surface squinting into the brightness.

"Father, what are you doing?" Behind him Kira stood at a distance by the trees.

He had waded knee deep in the body of water. "I'm going to look. Wasn't that a sea? Wasn't our ship floating on the surface out there?"

"No, father," Kira said. The tremor in her voice sounded fearful, but there was nothing to be afraid of here: The weather was mild, the water and plants were safe.

"Something's wrong," he said.

"Don't expect trouble. It's a miracle we're here," she said.

He allowed her to call him back to the trees. Nazar met them outside the shelter. "Good news. I've found a spring. You won't have to go down to the lake anymore." He handed them cups of water in small gourds. "Taste. It's delicious."

Leonid put the cup to his lips. The water was cool and sweet and pure. He felt himself tearing again. "I miss your mother."

Kira took his hand and placed it on her belly. "I'm going to have a baby. You're going to be a grandfather."

The water in his cup spilled over the side. He couldn't keep his hand steady. "But we crashed."

He remembered the sulfur fumes and growing heat of SpireMine. In those final days of the planet, it had felt as though the prison walls were absorbing every joule of anger he and the Watchmen contained. For years, they'd warned against over-mining the planet. They had grown raspy with protest until they were silenced. When they were proven right, they were not released to their families. Kira had come to him smelling like her mother's medicinal plants and cultivated rings of Sky-Blue Coronets. He had forgotten his men in that moment. He had so wanted to live and be a grandfather. But he could not forget them now.

"But we died. All of us."

Beneath his hand, the baby swimming in Kira's womb stilled. Kira's taut belly softened and her flesh rose around his hand as it sank into her. With a hiss, she withdrew and turned her flattening belly away. Her elbows jutted to the sides as she massaged her stomach.

"Kira, the baby?" he asked drawing closer.

Nazar stepped between them and grabbed Leonid's shoulders. Leonid staggered back as Nazar plowed forward squeezing his upper arms. Nazar lowered his head until his forehead pressed Leonid's firm and cool.

"Stop. Don't think like that."

Leonid turned his head to the side, unable to bear the crushing closeness and Nazar's contorted expression. His legs bent and gave way beneath him. He stared through the trees as he tumbled to the ground clutching the sand. His knees ground through the smooth beige layer revealing the mysterious blue that shone just beneath. Leonid watched Nazar return to Kira and wrap his arms around her.

"She's fine. She's healthy," he said.

In moments, they turned to him. Kira looked ripe again. Her flight suit stretched around the oblong swell of her. Leonid rose to his knees, numb. Kira pressed her lips together and held her belly.

"I'll have Doreena soon. Your granddaughter. This time, just let it be, daddy. Please. Not everything's a struggle."

He clenched his hand. He could still feel the swell and fall of her pregnancy in his palm. He understood that somehow, by thinking about death in this place, he had almost killed his grandchild. But he couldn't forget or ignore what he thought he knew.

"That was your mother's gift, not mine," he said. What was he, after all, without struggle?

He turned from Kira toward the body of water. It felt further away than he remembered. When he got to the beach, he sat with his head in his hands staring out across the lake, or the sea, where he thought he remembered they had landed.

One other time in his life, Leonid had felt like this: while working on the mining system, the team had hit a wall.

"Take a break," Leonid told them, "Just take a sit. Put your minds on auto pilot and it'll come to you."

Leonid couldn't remember the last time he'd eaten in the company atrium. There, among the glossy red anthurium lilies, an unexpected answer came to him: The mining system didn't matter. There wasn't time. AeroFlux didn't care about finding a solution, because they'd already declared the planet a cost of doing business.

Kira interrupted his thoughts, walking out of the trees to the water's edge. "We're leaving." She said pointing to the horizon. "There's a place for us to raise Doreena."

At first, peering out past the end of his daughter's fingertip toward the horizon, Leonid saw only a pale blue haze, but as he concentrated it clarified into distant dark spires. "A city?"

"Why not?" She placed her hand on his forearm. "If it scares you, couldn't you just not think about it?"

He looked at her helplessly and then turned back to the water. The ship had risen from the hidden depths. It was floating on the surface again. "You sound like the people who put me in prison."

The sand shifted as Kira turned. "All right. You know where we'll be. I wish mother were here."

"I wish I'd stayed with her," Leonid said.

He waded into the water. It lapped his ankles, calves, and thighs until he sank up to his neck in the warmth. Osana, she would have been happy just to be by Kira's side as she gave birth. She would not have questioned this, but it was not in his nature to leave a puzzle unsolved. He should have died on his planet where the rules made sense. He began swimming out to the ship with long smooth breaststrokes. He half-expected to find Osana there, now that he had thought of her, to find her sitting on the edge of the ship dangling her ankles into the water. Where the ship floated, the water became salty as expected. The body of water felt like it stretched far beneath him and extended around him. Yet, it was motionless, and the beach was always close. The ship's sides were scorched with black entry burns. Leonid placed his hands on its cool hull. He dove underwater and saw the yawning hatch through the clear water. He swam through.

The bodies were there: Kira and Nazar strapped into their chairs with waxy expressions. His body floated beside Kira's near the door. It occurred to him that the water was too clear and empty. The moment he thought it, it became murky. A movement caught his eye and a tiny silver fish darted by Kira's face picking at her cheek. He ducked back out of the ship and sidestroked to the shore.

When his feet hit bottom and he was standing upright, he heard waves rippling behind him. He froze in place, his first thought that he might turn to see one of the reanimated corpses behind him. Then he thought again of Osana. But did he really want her here, like Nazar and Kira were here, in some form masquerading as human? He did not. He had always wanted the truth. The ripples continued to play behind him until he found the courage to turn.

The woman resembled Osana. She had the same shape, but shimmered like the layer of powder that shone through the disturbed sand. She was the color of Sky-Blue Coronets. She held out a hand and, unable to stop himself, he took it in his. It felt like his own, the same temperature and dry, but tingling.

"This is not like you," the blue Osana said, her voice musically layered like a muted choir. "to come to a new place and see everything as it was in the place where you left. These shapes are tiring. We would rather flow."

They sat together on the beach; she with her legs bent like Kira used to sit as a young girl with her nightgown pulled over her knees. Leonid looked around at the trees, grass, shelter, fruit and tiny spring ahead of them, everything so familiar in this exotic place. He cried into his hands, grieving the loss of Osana, Kira, Nazar, tiny Doreena and himself as the woman stroked his back. When he was done crying, he dug through the sand and into the layer of blue. He scooped up handfuls of the powder and turned to her. "What is this? Help me understand."

"We are," she said, and did her best to explain. The blue particles that covered this planet were sentient inorganic helical plasma structures. Leonid, Kira, and Nazar were the first people they had ever experienced. Their ship had crashed through the soft blue layer and hit the hard rock of the planet. When the hatch opened, the particles were shaped by human thoughts. The plasma became the people and embraced their dying thoughts: water and Doreena. Leonid was made out of them and some of his own last memories.

As Leonid talked to the woman, the world lost the form imposed on it and began to flow naturally again. The beach and forest turned blue, the edges of objects became fuzzy until the unspoiled, shapeless haze returned. Exploring, Leonid let the glitter settle onto the surface of his skin, stick to the soles of his feet, and embed under his fingernails. It collected in the creases at the corners of his eyes and hung in flakes from the ends of his eyelashes. It got so that it coated the insides of his nostrils and he could taste it sweet on his tongue when he drew a deep breath. He slept within a warm blanket of blue. In time, he let the woman go, returning to her blue collective.

He realized he could rejoin them, too. His body would dissolve just as he'd watched the trees and fruits and water return to sparkling blue. He wanted to do this. But first, he needed to see his granddaughter; he'd died with that idea and it held fast within him.

Leonid stood and shook the blue from his hair. He began walking toward the city in the distance that Kira had pointed to some time ago. He stopped when he reached a slender line of reflective stone. The slick gray path stretched out across the swath of blue and wound toward the spires in the distance. Leonid reached down and touched it. They had no word for death. They knew only soft and hard, free and firm. The rock felt hard pressing them into the service of a single, solid form. They were trapped in it, imprisoned as Leonid and the Watchmen had been in SpireMine. Kira and Nazar were hardening this world, enslaving it to create the shapes they desired.

With each step along the stone to the city, Leonid grieved for the ones underfoot who had lost their fluidity and freedom to become the matter of Kira and Nazar's home. He understood that he and his daughter, and his son-in-law were a threat to this place. Their presence, their thoughts, harmed it. Therefore, they — himself, his daughter and son-in-law — must go. He would preserve this planet as he had fought, and failed, to preserve his own.

Leonid had never felt more of a responsibility to live according to his highest principles than now that he was a grandfather. He swung open the door and walked into his daughter's home. From floor to ceiling the room shone like water. On a dais at the end of the hall, his daughter and her husband sat enthroned. Their skin had a silver cast to it. They were no longer simple people at all. Kira held a shiny berry to her mouth. It looked like a metal bead, plucked off the silver tray beside her.

"Father," she said.

What must he look like to them with his fuzzy skin and his beard and hair dripping with blue? He could see his himself shimmering in the silver floor. A trail of blue dust lay behind him, tracked into the hall.

He loved his daughter. But she was not his daughter.

"He's come to see the baby. He's come to see Doreena," she said.

He wanted to see the child. And he did not. He wanted to do what was right, not want to fall in love with the idea of his granddaughter. Leonid hardened for the task ahead, and his hands grayed. He was himself, but not himself. He was only Leonid Moriena's last thoughts. Also, he was a new grandfather. He looked into Kira's hard, black glittering eyes. "You enslave them."

He lunged at Nazar first (he had never loved his son-in-law and this was not his son-in-law) and beat the boy's face with his harder hands until it shattered. It was easier then to pound into his torso until the man lay in chunks like coal at his feet. He was surprised at how easy it was, at how little resistance, until he remembered that the man was not a man, but merely thought hardened into submission.

When he looked up, Kira was gone. He went after her. The baby's wail gave her away. He heard its cry down a dark corridor and followed it in into a gray room. Kira stood there with the baby swaddled in a blue blanket. So soft. Where had she found it?

"Your granddaughter," she said.

He raised his hands and beat her away while she held the infant in her arms. Now that Nazar was gone, she would not fight.

"I already have what I wanted most, and I know you won't destroy her," she said, as he took the infant from her crumbling form.

He admired the child's perfect mouth, ears, nose, and the rosy tint of her flesh while he ground the mother's shell beneath his feet.

This child was Kira and Nazar and himself, the untainted parts and the destructive bits. If she stayed here with him, she would grow up hard, a black diamond girl, with the potential to pollute this soft blue world and turn it hard. What else would she know? He carried her out of the walls and across the scarred land. He returned with her to the soft blue loam. He held her to his chest. If she stayed here, if he lay down with her, she would return to the powder blue collective dissolving into soft waves. But as he lay down and the weight of her rested on him and her blanket became blue haze beneath his hands, he concentrated on her baby heartbeat, and her baby skin and the heat inside her dividing young cells. He could not help himself. He willed her to be, instead of letting her go.

He finally got up and walked to where the shelter had been and the beach, to the edge of the lake or sea, which had returned to waist deep fluffy blue. He waded through it to the ship, the solid, actual ship, where he removed the bones of the people (himself, Kira, and Nazar) and repaired the craft using the malleable blue to restore its hull. He created canisters and filled them with the plasma and placed them in the ship making no apology to the beings he sacrificed. Doreena would need them to grow, as she would need other people to give her form and hold her in place and help her become his grandchild. They would leave this place in peace. She was a fresh start, a seed. He would take her back to earth, to some small island. He would stay with her, keep her still, and be a grandfather.

Leonid Moriena loved Maui. The white sand beaches and cobalt waters sparkled as did the bright black eyes of the Hawaiians. It reminded him of home. Parts of it were better: the rustling palms, lapping water, and shifting sands. When lonely, he'd watch hummingbirds with nearly invisible wings flit between white hibiscus blossoms. Doreena was thriving. She was growing into a normal, healthy Hawaiian baby just as he cooed to her each night. When he carried her out onto the beach others coddled her, too. They called her *wahine*, a pretty girl. They liked the peach tint to her hair and the curls protruding from her bonnet of palm fronds and her broad cheeks. People pinched them until they became more and more pronounced and he had to make them stop. They lived off the coconut palms, selling weavings to tourists from a roadside stand and eating the fruits that dropped near their shack on the beach. People mistook them for natives.

But Doreena wasn't very old before she wrecked it, as he'd feared she might one day. He'd taken her to the beach at age three when she was walking and becoming more autonomous. He encouraged her to hold his hand but, lately, it would slip from his as she reached to touch the bark of the Hau tree or stroke the glossy red anthuriums. He was forever palpitating her hands in his, coaxing her digits back into fleshy, girlish fingers. One day after he'd climbed to the top of a coconut tree, hacked one open with a machete and shared the water with her, he lay back, his face shaded by his hat and let her wander towards the water on her own. Up and down the beach other children were doing the same, parading in the shallows and piling sand on the shore, unsupervised.

He woke from a doze and, at first, all seemed at peace past the pink-lined pohuehue vines sewn into the shore at the high tide line. Doreena lay on her stomach where the waves soaked the coral sands. Eyes open, she held her cheeks between her tiny hands and her curls swept across her forehead. A wave swirled up around her receding from her elbows and leaving a strand of seaweed stuck to her side. She giggled. He reached for his slim, silver camera. He loved this device, this miraculous compromise. It captured a moment and released it. The image was precise and permanent, but the picture did not tamper with reality. Everything continued as it was, unspoiled, leaving no residue of guilt. He did not own a computer to view the pictures with, but he had stacks and stacks of the square disks and had figured out how to use the drugstore kiosk to print the pictures onto paper. The snapshots wallpapered their hut.

He took a photo of Doreena and zoomed in on the image on screen. He'd captured her serene expression, an absolute sense of belonging. She was one with the sun on her face and back enjoying the rush of sea. She lay flat against the sand, her legs and feet behind her in the surf. He magnified her sea turtle green, *Honu*, eyes. Her gaze past him was absent. She was somewhere inside herself daydreaming. Then, he saw it behind her — the fin.

He leapt to his feet shouting. Lost in reverie, she did not respond. He looked at her, not entirely sure he could tell where her sides ended and the sand began. She had taken off her tiny bikini top. Her striped pink, brown and white briefs were nearly the same color as her skin. She blended into the sand. Down the beach, a *haole* mother and son were walking towards them hand in hand. Doreena's feet had spread and joined in one translucent sea green fan.

He caught her hand and yanked her up. Her green fin flexed against the sand. Her eyes focused on his and she shrieked. Sand clung to her round belly and sides. He kicked sand over her fin as the mother and son walked by. The woman pulled her son around to her other side and glared. He dragged Doreena up the beach yelling, "Stay out of the water!"

Doreena began to cry, another danger, too many tears and her flesh would start to flow away. It had been a mistake to bring her here.

"Selfish," Osana had said once under her breath during one of their fights. And he'd laughed at her. "Of all the things I've been accused of, Osana!"

But she'd been right about that too. It was selfish to want this child. But he could not stop.

He knelt and plugged Doreena's nose and mouth with his hand. "Stop." He half hoped she wouldn't remember the Breath Game, the way he'd taught her to breathe, but she flushed pink and her cheeks swelled. He held her puffed smile in his hand from corner to corner.

"Is everything all right here?"

The *haole* mother hovered over him. Her boy stood slightly behind, his hand hidden in hers. He couldn't see the woman's face just the sheen of light through her hair, but he could see the effort it cost her to confront him in the way her silhouette trembled. He released Doreena's face and her breath huffed out. She giggled.

"I'm her grandfather. She was playing too close to the water," he said.

Still, the woman stared down at him. Her shoulders shook. "You can't touch a child like that. That's not acceptable. Do you understand?" her voice trembled. "She's just a little girl."

He squeezed Doreena's shoulders. "Yes, that's right. She's just a little girl."

But the woman wasn't leaving. She should leave them alone. That was what these people did, left each other alone. He picked up his camera and machete. He didn't want to hurt the woman, but he didn't mind if he looked threatening. "Go away. Mind your own business."

The woman took a step back stumbling over her child. Then she was striding past him down the beach back towards the other people.

He whispered to Doreena, "Stay here, my little girl. Stay here."

Leonid held faint memories of these kinds of people from his former life, but they also confused him. They were separate from each other, distant. They did not share thoughts but, sometimes, like this woman, they formed sudden, random, one-sided connections. This unpredictable tendency and the woman's rigid certainty and focus on Doreena frightened him. How could Doreena live here among these people unaffected by their thoughts? How could he protect her?

He clutched the machete as he stared after the woman and then let it drop to his side. His shoulders slumped. He was capable of destruction. He could change that woman in an instant with the machete, remove her ability to shape the world with her heart. But he would not do it just because she threatened Doreena. He was sorry he had scared her, too. These people were not so easily shaped by emotion like Doreena or as interwoven in a universe of thought as himself, but he could not believe they were entirely unaffected by each other. It was still a harm to create fear needlessly on the gentle beach.

But in Doreena's case, it was necessary.

She pointed down the beach at the other children. "Why can't I go in the water?"

He knelt and whispered in her ear. "Sharks. Huge old beasts with mouths all teeth. They swim in packs like dogs," he lied.

As he walked Doreena back to their hut, he watched her feet skim the sand until her toes pinked. He bent every few steps and pocketed a stone or shell. He made her sit inside the rest of the day and count them. He stared at his photos and decided. He needed to take her away from the sun and sand and water — all the shifting, shiny lures. They needed to go somewhere inland, much more solid.

~ 28 ~

MIRROR ISLAND: JUMP

On the island, Doreena Flora Moriena reaches a point of decision between two worlds and two men

On the island everything is tangled. Petals, tendrils and leaves entwine. Everything moves: the surf, the sand and the jungle vines. Even those island elements that seem most stationary shift. The stones shake: the miniscule ones that make up the red trail, the round ones collected at the bottom of the pool, the moss-coated planks up the walls of the cave and the two pillars that stand on the land's highest point.

Doreena Flora Moriena, who has lived her life as an amorphous person of shifting shapes easily influenced by the expectations of others, finally knows her ancestry. This question has needled her since childhood when the other children wondered why her skin was that color, and her hair so curly, and made fun of her accent, buzzing — *zza, zza, zza* — and said she came from somewhere illicitly off-continent, although they had no knowledge of geography. Eventually they left her alone, which was the way her grandfather wanted it and the reason why he did not tell her either the truth or a lie.

Now that she knows her parents, Doreena is in a quandary. She does not know where she belongs or how to be comfortable. She stands on the edge of a cliff contemplating jumping into the sea. The island shakes.

She's the only one still, and won't be for long.

In Doreena's last moment of indecision, the island blooms. Hibiscus trumpets, lily flutes, bird of paradise spears, jasmine bells ring, and waxy, red discs of anthurium charge through the jungle greens. The island contains an impossible combination of flora. Some of its wild botanic garden belongs in temperate climes, others in cooler ones. The plants grow naturally north or south of the equator. Yet, on the island, they grow in volume together like companion plants as if gaining benefit from each other's use of soil. Flowers arrange themselves down the slope of leaves, stalks, and stems to the sea. In miniature, they could wind nicely around a front reception desk. The confluence of their scents, musk-laden, fruit-sweet, and spice-tinged, carry up even to the jungle's edge and the mountain top. From here, from its highest point, the island threatens to erupt.

Through the sulfur plumes, Doreena catches a whiff of the floral tide and it poises her on the edge of the cliff where she's leaned out to watch her employers fall. The sales manager Marilyn's hands flap out in front of her like pink kerchiefs and the publisher, Rock, plummets after her. Months ago, Doreena would have jumped after them unthinking. But now an inlet of sand, a thumbprint of pink, at the base of the cinnabar-laced cliff distracts her. She knows the quality of that sand, the soft talc press of it against her skin. The little thumbprint idyll circled by white crests of waves on one side, and white blossoms on the other, looks calm like a remnant of the island she remembers from her first encounter with the magic place.

When she first came to the island, Doreena recognized the white Hawaiian hibiscus, *kokio keokeo*, her grandfather had planted around her childhood home and the tall palms from photographs of her infancy on Maui. The beach that had suddenly appeared around her had felt like childhood restored. Something in the air soothed her grief over the loss of her grandfather and quelled her anger at how he had left her abruptly with her questions unanswered.

On her own, she would have stayed on that beach. She would never have gone further than that first break of jungle with its grove of fruit. Behind her, the red mouth of the trail parts the jungle, but the tranquil beach at the end of it now has hurricane churned and sea-stained sand. There is no easy trail down to the new beach beckoning at the base of the cliff. From this height, were she to fall down to it, that pink sand, all the grains at once, would hit her body like stone.

Her employers, Rock and Marilyn Traynter, are speeding through the gray sky toward the reflective pane of sea with its white wave shards. Midway through the sky, the portal back to the city revolves. Its light inner rings look like rows of teeth. It draws Rock and Marilyn in, winks as they pass through, and then reappears over the sea. As soon as they are gone, Doreena, wind-pressed, and suddenly light, stumbles. Her bare feet hover above the pink sand, toes splayed, and then a hand catches her arm and pulls her back. Tom, *The Mirror's* number two advertising salesman, squeezes her upper arm, firm enough to get her attention, loose enough not to pinch, a father's practiced grip.

"Don't go unless you mean to. You're going to have to really jump."

Doreena envies Tom's children. She never knew her own father.

With Rock gone, the C-town City Fathers, *The Mirror's* sales force, and the people who love her look to Doreena Moriena. They examine her bare skin as though looking for a map in her blue veins.

"Is that how we get back?" Tom asks. He has a family to go back to and will surely jump.

Doreena admires his certainty. "Yes."

Tom releases her and returns to the sales force. The Stew, *The Mirror's* investigative reporter, pumps his arms. "That's all I need. I've seen enough." His eyes are wide behind his glasses. He jumps and lands in the fissures' center where he flashes through to C-town. For a moment, the green water of Lake Traynter shines through the opening. The City Fathers point down to Rock. They huddle in their black suits and prepare to jump. Following Rock has always been sound strategy. The circle of white heads unwinds into a line. Sand and sea spray streak their doughy faces. Just before they jump, the powerful old men clasp hands like schoolboys. The fathers fall, black specks, in a disordered migration. The fissure crackles as they enter it and plunge through to the man-made lake. Doreena's memory of all those heavy mornings, every day she's forced herself to get up and go into the city, lifts like fog as the fathers fall away.

Tom leads the sales force to the edge of the cliff. He points and bends his knees showing them how to make the jump. They leap one after the other off the edge. Even in casual dress, they look alike. She'd been one of them once, the best of them, actually — *The Mirror's* number one salesman. The drop of each one buoys her and she bobs on the edge of the cliff. The wind lifts her hair off the back of her neck crowning her face with curls. Tom turns back to her when he's seen the rest of the force over the edge.

"Are you coming?"

"I don't know."

He throws up his hands, jumps hard and speeds to the center. He can't wait for her; his children are home. However, much time has passed on the island, it's too much time to spend in a place that feels so far away.

Nine months ago, Doreena had been loved by her grandfather and then he had gone. Since then, other people had appeared who loved her, too. She has a best friend, Diane, a tribe of surfers who adore her, and two soul mates: Earnest, in his tweed jacket, and Alonso, naked on the island like herself. Being with them now makes liquid shapes under her skin. The sudden swells of her body and the tremors of the island rock her. These people who love her come from C-town, so she has to consider going back.

The surfers in their wetsuits move to the edge of the cliff. Doreena wants to give them some token to remind them of this place, but her hands are empty. She kisses each of them and whispers their island names: Kyushu, Sri Lanka, Jamaica. They still have those places if they attempt to reach them. Doreena never took an island name, preferring to keep the name her grandfather gave her. It and the necklace are all she has left from him. Now even his ashes are gone.

The surfers, all except Alonso, turn their backs on paradise and dive off the cliff. When they leave the island, her breast and hips deflate and she's back in the compact virgin body she grew up in, a little stout and drooping toward the grassy lawn. Inside of her, the waves persist, however. Has this motion been inside her all along? Or was there a moment it began? She is unsure now.

Through the fissure, the City Fathers bob in the lake with their lies, the sales force paddle in billowing Hawaiian shirts and the AeroFlux union workers cling to their protest signs: "Maui forever." and "Jobs now!" Doreena stands between Earnest and Alonso knowing she must make a choice soon. If she jumps down into the cold lake, C-town will quell the watery sensations of which she has only recently become aware. A wave of heat rolls down the green lawn from the stone ruins, black and reflective as Traynter Tower, *The Mirror's* office. A jet of molten lava spews. Her island will soon be covered in heat and when that cools it will turn to black rock. Is this her fate as well? Now that she has lovers and heat flowing within, will she soon grow cold and hard again?

Diane grabs her hand. "Come with me." She pulls Doreena across the lawn until the cliff is just a green line across the gray sky. "Did I ever tell you I'm afraid of heights? It's easier for me if I don't look down. I'm going to take a run at it from here. Are you coming?"

"I feel light," Doreena said.

"The wind."

"No, me."

"Look," Diane says, her red hair wind-flung into a tentacled headdress. "You can go back, pretend you don't know. Just don't think about it."

"Don't think about where I come from, what I am? How am I supposed to live like that?"

"You did before."

"But now I know. You don't understand. I feel them inside me."

Diane squeezes Doreena's hand and releases it. As she runs down the green lawn, her red hair sways. When she reaches the edge, she spreads her arms wide across the gray and her wingspan drops beneath the green line and disappears.

The watery feeling in Doreena rises. She is alone on the island with her two lovers. She approaches the edge of the cliff and stands by them; inside she flows between them. One side feels firm as a sandy shore and the other holds the openness of the sea. Clouds roil overhead and it is as close to night on the island as it has ever been. She listens to her lovers.

"I love you. Come back with me."

"I'll stay with you."

Doreena unclasps the necklace her grandfather gave her. She swings the empty vial on its silver chain. She sees the dark island through its clear glass. If her lovers leave her alone on the island, there will be no one's thoughts to hold her together. When she first came to the island and it warmed her, she wanted to meld with it. Now the heat of the lava rolls, ready to consume her. Or, she can jump away and forget this place. She can let the presence of her ancestors flow away and harden. The island stills. It has given her all the information it can — now she must move toward the sea or the jungle.

~ 29 ~

MIRROR ISLAND: DOREENA

Once a solid citizen, Doreena loses her anchor and questions her ancestry

After work, on the day Doreena Flora Moriena received word of her grandfather's death, she could barely move. Her body, slowed to a molten pace when her grandfather left for vacation, began to stiffen. The paralysis crept over her as soon as she'd pulled out of the parking garage. Her hands hovered over the steering wheel and she ran the few streetlights on her way home afraid to come to a stop that might be permanent. When she was finally able to pull up to the curb in front of her home on Maple Street, Doreena failed, with her thick fingers, to turn the ignition completely off and the car stereo stayed on. Chapter 1 of *Stellar Sales*, "Mirroring Made Simple: The Persuasive Secrets of Body Language," continued. Looking at the house, Doreena felt the truth; that grandfather would not be coming back to it. It had been a chaotic day, but now she wasn't ready to admit it was over, enter the house and spend the night alone.

In the morning, she'd grabbed *The Mirror* on her way up to the sales office. The paper had been using the new silicon broad-sheets for almost a year, but she still wasn't used to the jellied, flesh feel of them and the pink tint to the pages. She intended to flip through to the Entertainment & Food section to check her ads for registration errors, but the gross boldness of the 46-point headline drew her eye: Maui AeroFlux Flight Crashes. Beneath the header was a full-color shot of a mangled plane with emergency chute extended. Sliding down the chute was her boss, *The Mirror's* publisher, Rock Traynter, holding her other boss, sales manager, Marilyn Traynter, on his lap. Perfectly composed, the shot placed the Traynters in the bottom right corner of the frame, the place the eye naturally gravitates to when looking at a photo. The shooter had captured great expressions too. Rock looked oddly gleeful with the smoke rising behind him and a cluster of terrified passengers ahead and Marilyn, her face tilted up at Rock, looked awestruck. Doreena thought she had studied all Marilyn's expressions, but the one in the photo was new. This one photo could put an end to all the gossip about Marilyn's mercenary attachment to *The Mirror's* publisher. Obviously, she did love him, if only for the security. Positioned directly behind the couple was the maroon-winged AeroFlux logo framed by a black puff of smoke. It was a shot worthy of *The Mirror's* best eye, Andy Orson, but the photo credit read Stewart "The Stew" Holmes. *The Mirror's* investigative reporter didn't usually take pictures. Doreena could see how it could have happened though. Even as the plane plummeted, Rock would have had *The Mirror* in mind. He'd have called The Stew and ordered him out to the airport.

Beneath the masthead and the newspaper's tagline *Information is physical: C-town's daily source* read:

Seven die, 16 injured; Mirror publisher heroically lessens tragedy

In the early morning hours, AeroFlux flight 393 returning from Maui crashed on the landing strip killing seven returning vacationers and injuring 16 C-town citizens.

The Mirror's own publisher, Rock Traynter, and his wife, Marilyn, were on the flight returning from their honeymoon. Survivors of the wreck said Mr. Traynter's quick action aboard the plane saved lives.

"He's a hero," said stewardess Diane Wing. "As we were going down he got up and yelled, 'Come on, citizens.' And got everyone ready to evacuate. I was so glad someone took control."

Trouble began as the plane made its approach into C-town. It circled several times in the foggy morning before beginning its descent.

The story went on — AEROFLUX CRASH see back, A12 — offering little in the way of new information and ending, "*The Mirror* has opted not to list the names of the deceased passengers in this morning's edition in order to give AeroFlux time to notify their families." Doreena had already received her call early that morning, but from the Aloha Funeral Home, not AeroFlux.

Even before the physical stiffness had begun to set in, Doreena had felt grandfather's death in the wrong way. She'd had the wrong emotion, anger, and pushed it down and hurried to work even though she knew that was not what most people would do after learning of the death of a loved one. Doreena ran her finger over that last sentence on the back page, "notify their families."

Underneath the cool page of silicon, nubs rose. These quantum dots embedded in the paper had made her sales job easy and catapulted her into position as *The Mirror's* number one salesman. The dots embedded electrons in the paper, which relayed bits of information throughout the town. Sold in conjunction with a radio transmission of corresponding phosphorescent particles, the ads literally embedded a business' message in the fabric of C-town. In fact, it became impossible to compete without placing an ad in *The Mirror* and signing up for a corresponding package of phosphors. But since her grandfather had gone on vacation, Doreena hadn't been able to make a single sale. She wished she could see her grandfather's name in print and touch the rise of it. She could not believe he was gone.

A sidebar to the crash story confirmed the buzz in C-town. One of the City Fathers, Charlie Earl, had recently been dismissed (*The Mirror* couldn't bring itself to report "fired") from his job as CEO of AeroFlux and a successor had yet to be named. Word was the company was bringing in someone from outside of C-town, from back East. The double deck headline's rhetorical questions made *The Mirror's*, and therefore, C-town's opinions clear, "New AeroFlux CEO in trouble? What mistakes are behind the recent crash?"

Doreena, reading the paper as she walked into the pressroom, dropped it as the applause began. The pressroom, usually vacant by daybreak, was packed. The pressmen, in gray coveralls splashed with dried patches of pink plastic, leaned against the stainless-steel vats of silicon.

On a pallet of papers pulled into the center of the room, publisher Rock Traynter stood over them wearing his double-pair of sunglasses even in the dim blue lights used throughout *The Mirror's* offices. Standing beneath him were a few notepad-clutching reporters. The last time there'd been an all-staff stand-up at *The Mirror* the subject had been the new quantum information technology, what they all now called the dots. Warmed plastic and an electric sizzle had been introduced to the pressroom and Doreena remembered tucking her chin beneath her turtleneck to escape the stink. Now, it struck her as funny, how the colognes of the sales force stood out instead. They were all down here too, looking unusually at ease. There wasn't a single bright patch of color among them, no sign of Marilyn their manager at all.

"There we were circling for the third time," Rock said. "That was the best part of the whole trip for me being able to see all of C-town from that vantage point. We're an outpost in the middle of the Cascadian wilderness, but what we've built is so bright and so solid. I've never been more proud than I was looking down at our city, seeing Traynter Tower and knowing you were all here at *The Mirror*. The citizens of C-town are the best in the world. We're the only people who still know what it's like to live in America. We were the only ones able to preserve our way of life when everything else went to hell. That's what I was thinking when that hull began to shake. By that time, it was our third pass over the city, and we knew something was wrong. Marilyn had already joked that she wished we could go down over Pacifica for a softer landing, but I told her I'd take the firm ground over the ocean anytime. I said there's no place I'd rather crash than C-town and that's exactly what we did."

The way he said it made it sound like he'd brought the plane down in C-town on purpose instead of surviving an accident. He paused while the staff cheered. "Thank you. It's going to be a busy day."

The reporters and salesmen began to crowd toward the elevator. When Tom, *The Mirror's* number two salesman, spotted Doreena an expression of concern crossed his face and Doreena suddenly stiffened and began to topple. Something inside her lurched, an unfamiliar, unsettling motion. Tom caught her arm and held her steady.

"Are you ok?"

"I'm fine. I've never been sick a day in my life," Doreena said sounding so much like her grandfather that she wanted to scream, just like when she'd gotten the call. She clamped the anger down, but she could feel it, or something, roiling inside her underneath her thin, stiff shell.

"No," he shook her a little. "You look like you're about to faint, really gray. Should you be here? Do you need me to drive you home?"

"No." She couldn't explain how the idea of leaving made her panic and she wasn't sure which she was more afraid of, that she might freeze up completely or open into a flood of whatever was flowing around inside her. The only way to counteract it was to just keep on as usual which, of course, no one would understand. "It's my grandfather."

"Goodness," Tom said, more concerned than he sounded. He had three young children at home, so his language was always subdued. "Was he on that plane? Listen, you should get a look at the manifest. You work at *The Mirror.* We'll just ask The Stew for it. He went upstairs."

Doreena didn't want to tell Tom that she already knew her grandfather was dead but had come to work anyway as if it were no big deal. She liked his idea and wanted to see her grandfather's name in print. Maybe that's what was wrong with her, why she wasn't reacting appropriately, because she didn't really believe what she'd been told yet. She never did like conducting transactions over the phone. Things just felt more certain face-to-face. The paper wouldn't be embedded with the dots yet, but she could still see her grandfather's name in plain ink and run her finger over that.

In the stairwell, Doreena and Tom stopped just below the newsroom door when they heard Rock's voice and saw him talking on the landing. They knew better than to interrupt. Rock and The Stew had a tense alliance. The Stew had been the last reporter to come over from the *Post-Intelligencer*. The paper had folded shortly after he'd left, cementing Rock's grip on a one-newspaper town.

"Traveling at the speed of sound 1,000 feet per second over the ocean at the mercy of AeroFlux was a mistake," Rock said. "But this never would have happened on Charlie's watch. I want you to find out what went wrong with that plane."

"I'm on it," The Stew said.

"Damn fools. How dare they get rid of Charlie? Their new guy won't know the rules, the history, what holds C-town together."

"I've got a name," Stew said.

From the stairwell below, Doreena could see Rock get ready to do it. He reached up and lowered that top pair of glasses. Underneath were a second pair of dark shades. Behind these, people said, people who'd had the misfortune to get close enough, you could see the outlines of Rock's eyes through the green-tinted black panels. These same people (when they could be sure they were not in the same building as Rock) sometimes said they doubted Rock even had a light sensitivity. Maybe just wore the glasses to intimidate the hell out of people.

"How?" Rock said.

The Stew appeared able to hold Rock's gaze for a few seconds, but when he started talking again his words came faster. "I've got sources. The new CEO's Dalton Rees. And he's not just from back East. He came in off continent." When he's finished blurting this out. Rock stayed silent and The Stew spoke again, more slowly, "So, how was Maui?"

He made it sound off hand, but everyone knew Rock hadn't wanted to go on the honeymoon trip. Marilyn had had to work on him for almost a year.

"Gritty and hot," Rock said, and thumped up the stairs.

The Stew paused with his hand on the newsroom door. When Rock's footsteps faded, he called down, "Do I smell some salesmen down there trying their chops at snooping?"

"It's us," Tom said. "We're looking for the flight manifest."

"Ah, number one and number two." The Stew was now openly mocking, but he stopped when he looked at Doreena. His gold-rimmed glasses magnified his already large eyes. "Oh, you got someone on there. Yeah, sure." He handed over his green notebook. "Here's my list of the dead. It's short. But I guess if you know one name on it that's long enough."

Doreena looked over The Stew's scrawl of names.

"Nothing?" The Stew said. "Here's the manifest." The Stew handed her a roll of normal paper and flat type with an alphabetized list.

"He's not on this either." Had she imagined this morning's call? Except for her stiffness, nothing had seemed certain of late.

"Maybe he planned to stay a few more days," The Stew said. "That could be trouble enough. After what happened, I'm not sure how much longer we'll be seeing flights in and out of Maui."

"You think they'd cancel Maui service? Isolate us completely?" Tom said.

"Rumor has it," said The Stew. "The City Fathers were pissed about what happened to Charlie. Suspicious too. And now this crash. Bad timing for AeroFlux. It was bound to happen though, there's no mystery there, since C-town hasn't been letting them import the materials they need for maintenance. You won't be reading that story in the pages of *The Mirror* though."

Behind the door, they heard Vic Brown, *Mirror* editor, bellow. "We need tomorrow's headlines, people."

"Nope, screw Maui," The Stew said. "Rock's finally going to turn C-town into his own private island. That's today's headlines. Take that to the street and sell it." He grabbed his manifest from Doreena's hands and left them alone in the stairwell.

"I'm glad your grandfather's OK," Tom said when they reached the sales floor. "I know how much he means to you."

Tom, the family man, knew her grandfather was all she had. He'd hinted more than once it was a situation she should change. Doreena went to her desk and tried to keep her mind on work. Through the trodden gold carpet of the sales floor, she could feel the buzz of the newsroom below, the screech of phones, the roar of the editor and the rise and fall of the reporters from their desks. The last time Rock had had newsroom jumping like this was when C-town was separating from the United Government. *The Mirror* had been sparring headline to headline with the *P-I* whose editorial board favored unification. It was usually feature-story quiet. The sales force was excited too, but without Marilyn's oversight, their energy lacked direction. The guys kept popping up for coffee breaks and pacing the halls. Only Tom solidly made calls all morning and afternoon.

Doreena stayed close to her desk too, although she was useless on the phones. She did her best work on the street, in person with her irresistible Mirroring Technique, but she couldn't get herself to leave the office. She rode the elevator down a couple of times intending to head out, at least take a lunch break, but each time that stiffness set in. It settled over her like a heavy shell. And she wasn't hungry anyway. Her appetite had vanished with her grandfather. She'd tried to keep to regular meals like he'd told her to, "Stay healthy, have dinner." But she kept forgetting until she was already in bed, the same bed she'd slept in since she was four, staring up at the ceiling filled with her own imagined constellations in the uneven paint.

No one worked past six that night in sales, although the newsroom was still bustling below. As the office emptied out, that stiffness settled into Doreena's skin even in the sanctity of *The Mirror* office. She muttered the words from *Stellar Sales* as she drove home to distract herself. "To create a feeling of sympathy. Put your hands in the same position as the person across from you. Subconsciously, they will see you as like themselves."

Doreena was still sitting in her car in front of her house when her neighbor Mrs. Dammerung knocked on the window. "Honey, there's someone here to see you."

A man in uniform stood on her doorstep. He carried a clipboard and a small brown box. Mrs. Dammerung clung to Doreena's arm as she got out of the car and approached him. He wore a brown uniform with an orange and gold flower on the lapel. The embroidered script inside the blossom read, "Aloha Funeral Home."

"But I saw the manifest," Doreena protested. "I work at *The Mirror* and I've already seen the official record. His name wasn't on there. He wasn't on that plane."

Mrs. Dammerung squeezed her hand.

"Oh, I'm so sorry miss," the courier said. "Very sorry for your loss. He came back on that flight all right, but they wouldn't have listed him. Not like this," the man raised the brown box and stared off towards the house. "In cargo. It happened before on Maui, I'm sorry."

The courier angled his clipboard at her. Under cause of death the form read: drowning. Doreena took the pen the man proffered and signed, but her fingers stiffened around it and her signature came out sharp and angled, unlike her usual arching loops.

She took the box into her childhood home. Grandfather who had never been sick a day in his life, never missed a day at his job cleaning the halls of the elementary school, would not be returning. Doreena sunk onto the living room sofa. At some point, Mrs. Dammerung left a plate of cookies on the table. They sat side-by-side with the brown box stamped with the maroon-winged AeroFlux logo. Mrs. Dammerung's pfeffernusse were a proud family recipe passed down from her German grandmother. Doreena bit into one, tasteless dry crumbles, and the powdered sugar flaked onto her black slacks. Grandfather was gone and he'd left without answering any of her questions, ever. He hadn't answered her when she'd hinted or when she'd confronted him and now he could never tell about her parents. He'd left her for Maui, left her alone, and left her heritage a mystery.

When she looked up again, Mrs. Dammerung was gone, the carpet held a spray of powdered sugar, and cookies dotted the floor. Doreena clasped her hands to her chest. Had she done that; thrown those and yelled at her neighbor? She hadn't meant to, now she'd have to find some way to apologize.

She reached for the box. Inside was a copper canister the courier had said now contained her grandfather. When she lifted it out, it was surprisingly light.

At the bottom of the box was an envelope. She touched the letters across the front. They were nearly smooth except for the press of plain ink into the pulped wood. There was a little of her grandfather in the letters, Doreena thought, as she touched her own name written in his hand — the enormous D devolving into a scrawl. Beneath her name was the bump and lift of something enclosed. Whatever the object was in the envelope, she hoped it contained answers.

~ 30 ~

MIRROR ISLAND: MOVING

New people, new places and new ideas; Doreena dislodges

Doreena did not get a chance to open the envelope right away. The other piece of mail she received along with her grandfather's ashes was a final eviction notice. She had to move out of her childhood home to make way for the White Spires condominium project, immediately. Apparently, the city's acquisition of the neighborhood had been going on for some time. Her grandfather had mentioned it, but it still blindsided her. She'd never expected moving to be her sole responsibility, or that she'd be going anywhere without him. But not even *The Mirror's* top salesman could persuade C-Town's city planners at this late date that it was a bad idea to replace the historic homes on Maple Street with condos. The homes were too near the lucrative downtown core, and C-town, with its tight borders, needed density to grow. It was a losing battle, especially since the developer was Mark Traynter, Rock's older brother.

Doreena thrust her hands down on the counter of the C-town Planning Office and squared off with the urban growth director in a classic gesture of power. The urban growth guy held his arms out and his palms up and Doreena easily read his body language. He respected her position at *The Mirror*, and he'd like to pacify her, but, honestly, there was nothing he could do.

"At least include some low-income housing," Doreena said, thinking of Mrs. Dammerung. "Some of my neighbors have lived in those houses for years. They can't afford a new condo. Maybe on the top floor."

"The top floor is for the penthouses," the planner said.

"Well, maybe the floor beneath that."

Doreena packed her possessions while the chainsaws buzzed. The trees shading the block fell. A black Traynter bulldozer plowed into the first home on the block as she stacked boxes in the back seat of her car.

"You're glad you didn't have to see this," she said to her grandfather as she placed him, in his copper urn, beside her on the passenger seat. She placed the envelope on her lap as she drove away tracing her name with her finger again. In her rearview mirror, the bulldozer reached the middle of the block and rolled over grandfather's hibiscus. Each spring, he'd filled vases with bouquets of the blooms and placed them on her bedroom dresser so that she saw them first thing when she awoke. He told her that although the fragrance of hibiscus was renowned, in fact, only the white one had scent and the plant had once been nearly extinct until the Hawaiian people had created a special preserve to save their native flower. In her memory, her childhood on Maui was all fertile beach and lush jungle, the only aspects of the past her grandfather mentioned freely.

She kept hearing Mrs. Dammerung's parting words, "Poor child, left alone." The words made her feel exactly that: poor and alone. Fighting sluggishness, Doreena stepped on the gas, before the bulldozer could scrape through the soft fir floor of the house, which held her childhood in its grooves and stains. She left the downtown core, with its sparkling high-rise condos, of which White Spires was soon to be the latest, and centennial homes outfitted with third bedrooms, and took Burrows overpass to the low rent district. As soon as she entered the unfamiliar territory near the outskirts of C-town, she began to tremble. Her hands gripped the steering wheel, but inside, they shook. Across from the Aeroflux Industrial Complex, stood a pre-Revolution era brick building, The Narborough Apartments, her new home.

On her way into the building, staggering from queasiness as well as the weight of her largest box filled with photographs, Doreena stopped and stared at Hawaii. A tear ran through the top of the poster and red, block letters stretched across the bottom quarter of the page — HAWAII. Between those two spaces lay paradise. A pearly white shell cupped a swath of blue in a shade lacking a good Pantone match. On the right a palm tree leaned in, its fringed fronds falling green over blue. The box began to slide down the front of her flannel shirt, but she didn't look away. When the door in front of her clanked and swung open, Doreena stumbled back still staring at the poster.

"I'm closed," a woman said. "Moving in? You want that glass door, there, up to the apartments."

The box slipped. It landed on its side with a clatter of frames and a cascade of photos, which began immediately to melt into the wet pavement. The woman reached for them with wrinkled hands ringed with large stones.

"No, I've got it," Doreena said. Hands flat, she swept the photos back into the box, but when she hefted it up to the shelf of her hip the bottom sagged.

"Just a moment. I've got what you need," the woman said.

"Never mind." Doreena turned to go, but the envelope with grandfather's letter, which had been on the top of the pile was gone. The glass door the woman passed through was locked. It clanked when Doreena pulled on the brass handle. She peered after the woman into a dark, cluttered space. A light appeared in the back and a body moved into it. The woman, probably as tall as Rock

Traynter, walked with a strange spread-legged gait. She returned with a crisp cardboard box imprinted with the AeroFlux logo.

"My letter?" Doreena said.

The woman patted the front of her sweatshirt pocket. A fringe of silver hair peaked out from under her hood.

"Let's get these things into a firm box. I don't blame you for getting distracted by Hawaii. She used to be one of my favorites, every bit as lovely and close, too. But you've been." She picked up one of the photos. "Did you grow up there? Off-continent?"

Doreena could see the rest of the question, "Where are you from?" crinkled in the corners of the woman's eyes. The picture the woman was holding was one of Doreena's favorites. It was taken of her on a Maui beach. She was a toddler grinning in the sand and holding her chin in cupped hands. Her legs and feet were hidden somewhere behind her in the surf. Her curly hair, which now even the stiffest gels and hairsprays could not wrangle into a professional look to meet Marilyn's approval, framed her child's face adorably and her matte brown hair shone with glints of copper in the island sun. But as much as she loved this picture, Doreena had been disappointed to find it tucked into the back of an end table while cleaning out the house. She'd mistaken this moment on Maui for an actual memory, but all she'd remembered was a photograph. It explained why she'd seen herself with the eye of an amateur photographer looking out and perfectly placed in the center of things. All she knew of her life before C-town was what her grandfather had given her, a flat, incomplete picture with MAUI running along the bottom in red letters.

Doreena grabbed the picture. She did not like this woman's acquisitive touch. "We moved to C-town when I was three. That photo is all I know of it."

"Well, keep it close. You'll want warm dreams. It gets very cold in an old building like this."

"Of course, it does," Doreena said bitterly. "Seems like I get cold in October and stay that way through March."

"Makes sense if you grew up on Maui. The body sets its internal thermometer early. You always carry the weather of your childhood with you," the woman said lifting handfuls of Doreena's things and moving them quickly from one box to another in the rain. The woman nodded across the street at the AeroFlux complex. "There've been more people moving out than moving in with all the layoffs. You an engineer?"

"Oh, no, I work at *The Mirror."* Doreena said. Just mentioning *The Mirror* made her feel more solid and certain. Her grandfather's death wouldn't change anything about her job; there would still be ads to sell.

The woman dropped a handful of photos into the box. "Don't be asking questions here. This is a haven. None of them engineers can afford Hawaii, but they can dream. A lot of them wish they could leave." Underneath her sweatshirt hood, the slits of her eyes were a shadowed blue.

"Don't you dare quote me."

"I'm not a reporter. I'm on your side. I'm in sales."

Speaking of sales, she was behind on hers. Her manager, Marilyn, would be after her soon. She could hear the pep talk; "You've got to produce if you want to stay number one." She nodded toward the Hawaii poster in the store window. "You know, you put something like that in *The Mirror* and you'd get a whole new clientele. They'd drive out here. It would only have to run six months and they'd never forget you." As soon as she said it, Doreena could see the poster scaled in full color on an inside page in the entertainment section.

"I'll stop by on my way out tomorrow. What is it you sell here?"

But she was alone on the street. The envelope was back on top of her box, and the silver-haired woman with the odd way of walking was gone.

Marimbas greeted Doreena when she entered The Narborough apartments. Maracas and steel drums sounded up the stairway. On the third-floor landing, an easy guitar and mellow male vocalist joined in the music muffled behind one in the row of black doors. A sepia haze of smoke held the scent of burnt salt. Doreena strained to keep her arm pressed around the AeroFlux box. She knelt on the stairway, afraid if she set the box down now she wouldn't be able to heft it again. Her arms were limp from unaccustomed use. Puddles on the landing and a skiff of black sand led down the hallway fading into the trail of brown carpet. The music and the mess, she guessed, came from behind the same door. She continued up to her apartment. The tarnished plate read C-4. She went up and down the stairwell freighting her things, until she'd stacked boxes so high in the entryway, she couldn't see into the living room. She didn't remember what it looked like back there. Her only impression of the place had been, "small," but she'd signed the lease in a hurry. There weren't many decent places to live in the industrial part of town. This one, cramped and cold, was all she could afford.

After moving all her stuff, Doreena managed to hang her work clothes before sprawling spent on her bed hugging her grandfather in his urn and the letter to her chest. The warmth of moving dissipated as she lay in the mildewed room beneath the tinged blue ceiling. She placed the copper urn beside her on the floor, down by the tremor of marimbas, and read grandfather's letter. His rolling script matched the voice she heard in her head. The letter was typically terse and directive but lacked his usual logic. In absence, he'd become vague:

Dear Doreena,

Hold me. Do not bury me. Do not release me unless your life begins to shift. Keep me with you until you feel transient. Then release me. Please not in C-Town. Never there. And carry some of me with you at all times.

Love,

Grandfather

It was baffling. What did he mean, "transient"? Why "not in C-town"? Where else? And where, where was mention of her parents? He knew that what she wanted most from him, any information about who she was and where she came from, but he'd left her no clues. He'd carried all her hope away with him. Accompanying this short missive was a long list of his usual directives and one bizarre request. She was ashamed to note she had not been doing most of the instructions including the one at the top of the list: Eat regular meals.

The bizarre request concerned the necklace coiled in the bottom of the envelope. She swung the glass vial capped with a swirling silver plug on its knotted chain. Grandfather disapproved of "flashy" things: "Draws too much attention of the wrong kinds." This would be her first piece of jewelry and it was beautiful, but as she read what he wanted her to do with it, she didn't want it anymore. His instructions said to fill it with some of his ashes. She imagined wearing grandfather's ashes around her neck his death resting always on her chest. She already felt the weight of his loss. She didn't want to do it. Worse, she didn't want to figure out how to do it, how to get some of the ashes from the urn into the slim-lipped vial. Even opening the urn terrified her. She'd never seen cremated human remains. The urn was small, but somehow, she kept picturing organs. As a child, her grandfather had read to her from illustrated anatomy books. "And this is where your heart is for pumping blood," he would say touching the picture and then her chest. "And your kidneys, and your liver and your pancreas."

She'd thought he'd wanted her to become a doctor, but he'd stopped when she was older. And he had a phobia of hospitals: "Stay out of them, Doreena. You'll be better off. Those are places where people go to be sick and then die. Just be a happy, healthy girl and you'll always be well." As a child, she had crawled into his lap after a long day of teasing at school to hear him croon and pet her, "Healthy girl." As a teenager, she'd no longer been comforted. They had argued. Everyone was deciding what to do with their lives and he wasn't helping her make choices. He never pushed her toward anything.

"You are fine where you are," he said. "Don't let them get to you."

"I can't just be *happy*," she said. "I have to do *something*. That's the way it works."

He could have expected more of her. Then what would her life have been like? Mrs. Dammerung was right. Grandfather had left her hopelessly handicapped, poor, and alone and unsure of her place in the world without him, and now he'd left her with the task of taking his ashes and fulfilling his wishes. In the morning she knew, somehow, she'd manage to do what he asked. Afraid her thoughts of ash and organs would bring on the nightmare that she'd been having again, Doreena resisted sleep, finally getting up and taking two blue sleeping pills so that she wouldn't be useless tomorrow at work. In the nightmare, her hands were missing. She was sure she could find them within *The Mirror's* pages, but there was no way to turn the silicon sheets with her blunt wrists.

On Monday morning, the cold woke Doreena. The apartment was still, the pulsing marimbas gone. She hunched naked in the shower shivering while she figured out how to adjust the faucet. Finally, the pipes groaned and she angled her stiff, aching shoulders into the slim stream of heat. She used up all the hot water and then carried grandfather to the bathroom and twisted the urn's cool lid.

Her hands slipped around it. She imagined the lid flying loose and grandfather spilling onto the tile and mixing with the previous occupant's debris. But on her next try the lid came off cleanly in her hand. Inside, grandfather was sealed in clear plastic. His powder was chalky brown with a hint of pink like a pasty cheek. There were chunks, but they didn't look like bone. She pressed a finger into the baggie and a cakey clump gave way. She snipped off a corner of the bag and looked for some small implement. She eventually used the end of a make-up brush to guide traces of grandfather into the necklace vial. Grandfather disapproved of make-up, a showy way to draw attention to oneself, but she'd started wearing it when she began work at *The Mirror.* Marilyn said it was part of a professional sales appearance and grandfather couldn't argue with that. She's made her first trip to Denrigger's make-up counter and come away with an expensive collection of color-filled tubes she could easily afford at the time.

Once filled, Doreena capped the vial and hung it around her neck. The necklace felt lighter on her chest than it looked. Grandfather's ashes were nearly the same as pink-brown shade as her skin. Now that she had it on, it seemed somehow less grotesque, so long as she kept it hidden and no one ever asked what was inside. One she grew accustomed to the oddity, it actually felt comforting. For the first time since grandfather had left, Doreena thought about breakfast. But transferring the ashes had taken time and now she was late for work. As she raced downstairs, she bumped to a halt on the third-floor landing and her face slapped up against cold, wet rubber.

The man she ran into on the stairs of the Narborough was wearing a wet suit and carrying a surfboard nearly as long and wide as the hall. "Hey sorry. I didn't mean to snag your *da kine.*"

Whatever that was it sounded lewd. Cold water dripped off the end of his board and soaked through the shoulder of her rust-colored sweater. He smelled dank, fishy, and seasoned like one of the seafood restaurants downtown, Watertown or The Dungeness.

He swung the board around to the side holding it under one arm. "Oh, hey. Well, I can see the sharks circling. We can meet and greet another time."

His wet suit ended at the knees exposing his taut brown calves. Muck colored sand dusted the backs of them.

"Your music is too loud," she said.

"The Steelheads," he called back. "Everybody loves them. Give it time."

The street outside the Narborough was dark. There were no phosphors here along the street or across the highway at the AeroFlux industrial complex. It was even blankly dark across the awning where the business name should have glowed. Doreena hadn't gotten the impression from the woman that it was a new business. New business owners were quick to identify themselves. But if she didn't have any phosphors yet, she must be new. Really new. Fantastic, that meant big sales, Doreena would get this place lit up in no time. The woman would need print ads and radio, dots and phosphors, to work her way into the hearts and minds of C-town. This find was pure luck and great timing; just what Doreena needed to lift herself out of a downer month.

The door to the business opened with a chime. There was a decidedly un-C-town spice to the shop's mustiness. Variants of the Hawaii poster in the window covered most of the brick walls. The posters showed random sets of sky, water, sand, and foliage in shades of blue, white, and green cocked at various angles. They could all have been the same place except for the names stretched beneath them in block red: Tahiti, Jamaica, Sri Lanka, Trinidad, Tobago, Belize. The store was a jumbled collection of bric-a-brac, too cluttered for browsing. The owner appeared to have no retail sense. Many of the objects were vaguely familiar in shape but made out of strange materials. There were dolls and sculptures, tapestries and baskets, hats and brooms, and stones, seeds, powders, coins, and grasses. Whatever kind of business this was, it definitely needed *Mirror* advertising. Doreena would suggest a huge discount sale to get rid of inventory.

The woman came down a hall from the back toting two industrial-sized thermoses from which the spicy scent wafted. She was wearing that same gray hooded sweatshirt, and some kind of sarong tied around her waist over leggings. Her silver hair was slicked wet to her forehead. She didn't exactly look ready to greet customers.

"You," the woman said.

Doreena patted her bag. "I've brought my things for you, the rate sheet and contracts. I'm sorry I was distracted yesterday. I could have got you set up right away. I didn't realize this was a new business. I'm sure you're anxious to start."

She looked for a counter, but seeing none set her bag on top of a table that lurched to the side as she did so. She removed a sheaf of papers. "I bet we can get you running in print tomorrow and the radio up this week. We're quick like that."

The woman dropped the thermoses and the table rocked. "Not interested. Get out."

"I'm sorry," Doreena pressed her palm down on top of the sliding papers. "I didn't mean to rush you. I'm just trying to help. When did you open?"

"I've been here awhile," the woman said.

"But I've never heard of you."

"Just leave, please. I don't need any."

Doreena noted the woman's crossed arms, a defensive gesture indicating resistance. She extended her hand; a move designed to break through the woman's psychologically erected barrier. "Let me start over. I'm Doreena Moriena."

The woman didn't budge.

"Listen, you can't run a business in C-town and not be in *The Mirror*. No one will know you are here. You need some nice phosphors."

"The people who need to know; they know. Besides I live here. These are just my things."

"But this is a retail space. You can't have a residence here. That's against city ordinance. And you can't run a business in the dark. That's illegal."

"There isn't really any business. It's a museum. You know, a place to keep old things." The woman smirked, as she did so her lips and eyes nearly disappeared in deep folds of skin.

"I know what a museum is." Doreena said, thinking of grandfather again.

On weekends as a child, grandfather had often taken her often to the C-town museum. He had read to her off the placards beneath aerial photographs of what had been farmland before the construction of C-town's condos, offices and Traynter Tower. He'd showed her the old farm and logging equipment with jutting metal teeth. They'd walked down the hall with the photographs of the Traynter's ancestors and mannequins dressed like Rock's great-grandmother in long dresses with buttons down the front and high-necked collars carrying babes in trailing white lace. Every time they went, Doreena asked her grandfather about her own ancestors, but he always evaded: "We're here to learn about the Traynters. They built this town." Even so, she'd persisted. She'd been sure one day he must tell her about her own parents. She didn't even know what they looked like. She had pictures of hibiscus shrubs, coconut palms and pineapple plants, but none of them.

This place didn't look anything like C-town's official museum. It was too small and disorganized to contain a history. The photos were in color and the many little objects lacked weight and permanence. "What kind of a museum is this? These things don't look very old."

"No, just out of date. You can't get them anymore so that makes them history. My what an unusual necklace," the woman said pointing at Doreena's chest.

Doreena had taken the necklace out and absent-mindedly begun to stroke it while thinking about her grandfather. She tucked it quickly back under her cowl-necked sweater. "Just something my grandfather left for me."

The woman stepped forward and enfolded Doreena's hands in hers. Her hands, like the rest of her, were very long and she wore rings of polished stones. Doreena wondered if her grandmother's hands had looked anything like these.

"I'm sorry. Listen, I'm Hobart. It's always nice to meet the neighbors, but I'm not having anything to do with your *Mirror.* We're not hurting anything here. It's OK for people to dream."

"Dream about what?"

"Leaving C-town," the woman said. "Yes, yes, these are all things from off continent back before the borders closed. People come here to think of other places. It's natural. When times are stressful, people want to go look for a place where the food's plentiful. That's the drive that pulled us across continents."

"Who?"

"I mean people in the broad sense. Eons ago. Humankind. Kind as we can be. That's all it is an evolutionary drive. You can't stamp it down. Me and mine never tried to. Somebody starts getting antsy it's best to let him go search for higher ground. That's all it is. No harm."

"Except that it's irresponsible." Doreena said. "You leave people alone with bills to pay."

"So, you know something about that? Listen, it's better to be left in the lurch than kept company by someone who's staying around just to share their misery. Going through the motions doesn't do anyone any good. So, I doubt Rock Traynter would be happy having The Travel Museum in his paper anyway."

He wouldn't be very happy knowing that you weren't in it either."

"Well, maybe he's not a very happy person and there's nothing you or I can do about it. I'd appreciate it if you'd let us be. We're out of the way and not trying to attract undue attention. Now, I've got to take the boys their tea." Hobart hoisted the thermoses and swung them towards the street. "Get out of my shop."

"So, it is a shop." Doreena said. She couldn't remember the last time she'd failed to make a sale in person. As she left the museum, Doreena cast a backward glance at the posters: St. Martin, Dominique, Costa Rica, New Zealand, Aruba, Galapagos. She could still see them as six months of ads: full-page, full-color. She could see the awning lit up in tropical phosphors - pink, turquoise, yellow - lettered in avant-garde Tiki-Tiki font: The Travel Museum.

"Those posters would look great as a section in the C-town style pages."

"Honey, I hope that's not your car."

The driver's side window of her car was busted. Glass littered the sidewalk. There were scratch marks around the face of the radio where the thieves had tried to dislodge it, probably before deciding it was too much trouble for such a cheap system. They should have known from looking at the car that there wasn't anything good in it. Like all the cars in C-town it was an old model, but not old enough to be classic. The punks must have been lured by the pile of CDs on the passenger seat, and then disappointed by the selection.

Hobart put a hand on her shoulder. "I'm sorry. This is a bad neighborhood for petty crime. You never want it to look like you have things worth taking."

"Apparently, I don't." Doreena said.

"Could be worse." Hobart tilted her chin at the AeroFlux engineers gathering on the sidewalk in green union sweatshirts. "You've still got your job."

"Not for much longer if I don't make any sales."

Doreena lifted the lock on her door. Getting a replacement window for her car was going to be trouble but Hobart was right, she'd rather that than spending the day circling a burn barrel. The chill wind whipped Doreena's curls into her eyes as she headed for the overpass to downtown. She blasted the heat but only managed to singe her fingers where they curled around the steering wheel.

Channels of fog lay beneath the freeway blanketing the swamps around Lake Traynter. Downtown, the fog lifted. Pink sun lit the cityscape and the smell of fried dough from the city's bakeries sweetened the freeway exhaust.

Doreena fished around in her CDs, inserted *Stellar Sales*, and skipped to track 2 "Redefining Your Place in the World" and repeated with the narrator, "The secret to the irresistible pitch: stay positive. Your sales destiny depends on commitment."

A paycheck was never a certainty in sales. The top seller today could be on the street tomorrow. It all depended on effort. She was already wondering if she would be able to make rent and whether she ought to report the illegal business she had discovered to Marilyn this morning or wait a little longer and see if she could bully Hobart into a sale.

~ 31 ~

MIRROR ISLAND: MANGO

Mirror Island arrives

Arriving at the reflective, black Traynter tower, Doreena cast a longing look back across the street at The Lofts, the condos overlooking Broad Street where the Traynters lived. Once a year, Rock and Marilyn invited the entire *Mirror* staff up to watch the C-Town Founder's Day parade from the balcony. Everyone looked forward to the yearly procession of floats and city services, police cars and fire trucks. The reporters, pressmen and sales force competed to predict which of the floats in honor of the Traynters' ancestors would earn the Grand Prize. The reporters usually won. Rock gave a speech reminding them how an independent C-town had persevered despite the collapse of the United Government. They all left bloated with pride and blackberry punch. Doreena wished she could afford to live in The Lofts. How easy it would be to cross the street and come to work each morning. She tallied how many full-page, full-color ads she'd need to land each month to live there. The entire entertainment section wouldn't cover the rent.

She grabbed a paper off a stack of slicks on her way into *The Mirror* and skimmed the front page on her way up. It was a mass of dueling headlines partitioned into an acceptable layout of boxes and sidebars. The reporters had made a busy night of it. The biggest headlines read: Rees Named New AeroFlux CEO, AeroFlux Fires 300 Union Workers, and Who Needs Maui? City Fathers Question Flight Risks.

The sales office smelled like the fish fertilizer her grandfather sprayed around his hibiscus. They'd cleaned the carpets over the weekend again. Across the room, Tom was already pounding the phones. He had the best phone sales of any of the force and many of the lucrative categories: automotive, banks, real estate. But Doreena bested him on volume with retail and restaurants. No one was a better closer than her on the streets and while Tom left at 5 to get home to his family Doreena worked late. She hadn't taken any time off to mourn her grandfather, but it still felt too long since she'd been in the office at her routine and focused on sales. Tom waved her over as she passed by his cubicle. He had his arm around a petite woman whose head barely reached his shoulder.

"Meet Diane," he said. "She's new; just got back from her first ride around with Marilyn."

The woman looked up at Doreena with tiny, black eyes. Above them she'd painted seven lines of metallic eyeshadow in shades from pale green to gray. Everything else about the woman was acceptably professional. She wore a tailored suit and crème scarf. Her hair was a wild, feathered red, but so lacquered in place it barely moved.

"It's hard at first," Doreena said. "But if you stick with it, Marilyn's strategy works every time."

"Don't worry," Tom said. "She'll cut you loose as soon as she's broken you in."

"She said my make-up was unprofessional," Diane said. "I like my make-up."

"Marilyn's on a tear," Tom said. "She's got a special assignment for us, Doreena. Top priority."

Doreena tensed. Special assignments took time away from commissioned sales.

"Heads up. Put on a happy face," Tom said, looking past her.

Marilyn rounded the corner and stood between them, monochromatic as always. The color of the day was red: lips, nails, shoes. It was a real patriotic red too, like the C-town fire trucks, and could not be mistaken for the deeper AeroFlux maroon.

"Stop sniveling, Diane," Marilyn said. "You're part of our winning team. I want you to feel like a winner, look like a winner, act like a winner, sell like a winner."

Diane slunk off to her cubicle, her desk still bare and unadorned.

"So, what's the target?" Tom asked.

"The publisher wants AeroFlux," Marilyn said. She always called Rock, "the publisher" at the office. "And this absolutely has to happen. Whatever it takes. Top priority. It's now or never. We could lose them."

"Lose them?" Tom asked.

"Yes. You don't read your own paper? This morning's headlines. The City Fathers are talking about revoking AeroFlux's permit to operate. That means no more imports. No more flights to Maui. We'll be completely isolated from the outside world. I want you to reel them in, put them in the pages of *The Mirror*."

Doreena exchanged a glance with Tom. Neither of them could afford imports or vacations to Maui. So, if C-town evicted AeroFlux it wouldn't make a huge difference to them. However, the idea of an isolated C-town clearly panicked Marilyn, and it was big news that C-town wanted to bring AeroFlux into its connections of dots and phosphors — and potentially a huge commission, even if they split it. Before the plane crash, AeroFlux had been off limits to the force. Rock hadn't wanted to give the company too much access to his town. This was an important sale. An enormous get for *The Mirror.*

"We're on it," Tom said.

"If you can't get an appointment today, let me know," Marilyn said. "I promised the publisher we'd get this done, ASAP." Marilyn turned to go and then trained her eye on Doreena. "Stop fidgeting. What's that? A little gaudy, isn't it?"

Doreena shuffled nervously. As Marilyn hustled back to her office, she tucked the vial of grandfather's ashes back under her sweater. She had to stop playing with it before it became habit. Wearing human remains probably wasn't even legal.

"Relax." Tom said. "We'll get it done. Hey, you see my latest?" From a desk filled with family photos, he picked up a picture of his wife and kids, this one in a hand-painted frame, and held it out to her. In this photo, too, the family was all pink-cheeked smiles. "We were out at Lake Traynter this weekend. There's actually a nice patch of green there, if you can believe it. The lake reeks, but the kids had fun and Bonnie packs a mean picnic. We had a great time. Saw some guy actually trying to surf on it."

"Surf?" Doreena recalled the smack of the wetsuit against her face this morning. "Um, pathetic. I mean, are there even any waves?"

"It was weird, yeah, but he sorta got upright a few times. Gotta admire that."

"Admire what?"

"Someone who knows what he needs to be happy and goes for it. That's talent."

Doreena frowned. Here it goes. Tom had that look: the married person's default concern for singles. Even though she hadn't told him about her grandfather's death, he pitied her just like Mrs. Dammerung. He should worry more about his own sales.

"So, you're thinking of taking up surfing?"

"No, I've got my family." Tom said. "I'm just saying it's important to have something in your life that makes you feel that way."

"Yeah, like a big commission," she said, tired of the lecture. "You better call AeroFlux and see if they'll even see us after we sicced The Stew on them and slammed them in the headlines."

"Don't worry, if they want to keep doing business, they'll see us," Tom said.

If she hadn't been loyal to *The Mirror* and in need of a big sale, Doreena would have wished AeroFlux would refuse them and give the City Fathers another reason to send them packing. Without AeroFlux, her grandfather couldn't have left her.

By late afternoon, Doreena and Tom were headed out to AeroFlux in the drizzle. Red brake lights — circles, triangles, squares — burned through the fog still thick beneath the overpass. Cold air rushed in through Doreena's open window. Tom, pressed up against the passenger door, caught her glance.

"It's not you. I'm just trying to preserve my hair."

"Sorry. It got busted out last night."

"Expensive. It's hard to get replacement glass. I had a customer once said it ran him a couple weeks pay."

Doreena imagined a long winter ahead of driving around with an open window.

"So, where'd the new girl come from," she asked. "She looked a little fragile."

"Ah, that's interesting," Tom said. "She was a flight attendant on Rock's flight. One of the people he helped save. He hired her, I think, to make a point to AeroFlux. They may be C-town's biggest employer, but *The Mirror's* the best steady work in town. Not likely to kill you in a crash anyway. I'm curious to meet this new guy, Dalton Rees." Tom lowered his voice. "Even Rock hasn't met him." He picked up a stray CD at his feet and smirked turning it over. "This looks like Marilyn's handiwork." He peered around at the backseat. "A lot of it. Do you really listen to this stuff?"

Tom pushed the CD into the player and a man's voice began to lecture, "to get people on your side a highly motivated seller creates connection."

"That one's not the best," Doreena said.

At the next light, she turned and pawed through the collection of cases behind her until she found *Stellar Sales.* She fumbled with the CD case in her lap as they exited the freeway. When they stopped at the turn lane into the AeroFlux plant, Doreena leaned forward to switch out the CD.

"Oh man, we have to cross the picket line," Tom said.

Hundreds of striking workers lined the street in front of the AeroFlux plant. In their matching green union sweatshirts they looked like a row of arborvitae hastily planted to meet some C-town building code requirement. Just like this morning, the same huddle of 10 or so circled the burn barrels in front of the AeroFlux landmark sign, with its maroon-winged logo.

"They won't be happy," Tom warned.

When the light changed, Doreena directed the car around the corner. *Stellar Sales* piped up, a woman's voice, "Say no? They won't want to."

"Nope, not happy. They're glaring." Tom said. "Tell you what, if I was out of work I'd be at home with my kids for a few days while I looked for another job. I wouldn't spend my time standing around. You?"

Doreena looked from the AeroFlux protesters to the low rectangular plant in front of her to Tom sitting beside her and imagined what she would do with a few uninterrupted days off. She sat on the sofa staring at the remains of her grandfather in the copper urn on the coffee table in the empty, still house until the bulldozers tore in or, updating her vision, sitting in her cold, dark and cramped apartment, silent except for the occasional marimba vibrating beneath her feet. Tom seemed to be baiting her again, trying to get her talk about, well, she didn't even know what his point was anymore. She didn't appear happy enough for him. What difference did that make? What business did he have making her feel inadequate? She was *The Mirror's* number one salesman.

"Not everybody wants to have a family, Tom," she said as a blue haze spread across her vision. It was as if an advertising designer had leveled out all the magenta and black and placed a cyan filter on the world. Doreena blinked hard and clutched the steering wheel. She saw her hands in a blue haze around it, but also felt her palms fold into fists. Her fingernails dug into her palms. The draft from her open window disappeared and the canned heat blasting her fingertips dispersed.

Real warmth permeated her skin. It created an instant thaw as if she'd burst through time to August instead of beginning to warm in March and slowly adapting to the onset of spring. Blue sky, white sand, and blue sea spread out in front of her. The planes of color met in sharp lines. It looked as though she'd stepped directly into the surface of the HAWAII poster except the colors moved. Prisms of sunlight glinted along the crystalline sand and the sea shimmered. Doreena squinted and held her hands before her eyes. She twisted around and a wave of green leaves rolled ahead of her. Green skeins brushed her hands and face. She lifted her buttocks searching for solid ground to stop the undulating sensation. Her hips shifted against sand. She placed her hands on her bare thighs to steady herself. The world rocked and her clothes were gone. Ahead of her a spicy froth of decomposing and blooming vegetation wafted from the verdant shadows. From behind her the scent of salt-soaked flora and fauna rose. The air thrummed a sound like hummingbird wings. A flash of white drew her eyes into the jungle. A hibiscus blossom stretched five-petaled fingers to her. Thin crimson veins ran into its center. She recalled its name: *kokio keokeo*. It was the only hibiscus flower that held scent her grandfather had told her. And with that rising scent, she felt his presence.

"Grandfather?" she said.

A woman's voice, layered like a muted choir, answered. "Pretty girl," it said or, maybe, "Big kitty."

A tumble of red and green churned down through the branches and landed in her lap. Its smooth skin nested against her thigh. She reached for it with both hands and heard a squeal like a wild pig — no — tires.

"Doreena!" Tom shouted.

She remembered she had been driving and rammed her foot forward. Her shoeless heel ground into sand. She was naked on a beach and then the headrest slammed the back of her neck. The cowl of her sweater scratched. Her hands curled around the steering wheel as she wrenched it around. The car spun toward the AeroFlux sign and the union workers in a blur of green and red. Metal crashed, and the car thudded to a halt. Maroon-wings splayed over the splintered windshield. The car had smashed to a stop in the AeroFlux sign. Doreena exhaled; head bowed. In her lap lay an oval fruit, a mango, with its red and green skin intact and a sheen of soft blue on its surface. It tumbled between her knees, leaving a trail of powdery glitter like the dust from a moth's wings across her lap, and plopped into the purse at her feet as the door beside her opened. A man leaned in and touched her shoulder.

"Are you OK? Are you OK?"

He kept shouting and she realized he expected her to answer. She didn't know how. There was tightness all around her. The rocking had stopped, and she was being held, stiff, in her own dry, cracked skin. It ached. It hurt. She tried to nod.

"Don't move. Just sit still."

She couldn't at first, move at all, and then her body began to shake, head, chest, and limbs. She was colder than she'd ever been, and her skin felt scraped and sore.

"Anyone have..." the man said, and then turned so that she didn't hear the rest of it. The reddish ring of his hair was shorn around a balding patch. In the sun, she imagined, the core of each hair would shine like the ripe inside of the mango in her purse.

The man took off his jacket and tucked the tweed around her. The fabric held workshop smells — must, oil, cleansers. The hibiscus scent was far away now, and the name of the flower escaped her.

"K, K, Ko, Ko," she said trying to remember.

"She's in shock," the man said.

Sirens blared outside. Ambulances sped toward her in a line like a Founder's Day parade. The passenger door opened, and she looked to the side and saw Tom slumped in his seat, blood on his face, a medic leaning in beside him. She stopped shivering and unbuckled her seat belt. A police officer stopped her.

"Help him," she said. "He has a family."

"We will. Tell me what happened. That man says you were rounding the turn and then started veering. He swerved, grazed the side of your car and then you jerked the car straight into the sign almost like on purpose. You on some kind of medication?"

She shook her head. "My vision. Something went wrong. Everything went blue."

"Black?"

"Blue."

The cop looked at her like he thought she didn't know her colors.

They put Tom onto a stretcher, hoisting it to their shoulders and moving towards the ambulance. The medics made the lift look easy, the way Tom probably, on weekends, swung his kids onto his shoulders, effortlessly. Then the medics came for her, easing her into their arms. She stared at the mangled intersection of her green car and the red AeroFlux sign. The man who had given her his jacket stood aways off clutching his bare arms. A barricade of union workers hovered behind him hissing, "Scab."

"This is not the time for that!" a cop yelled.

They lifted her into the ambulance. The man came forward with her purse and placed it in front of her. What was the word she'd been trying to remember? "Kio, Kio?"

"Did she just say cuckoo?" a policeman asked.

The medics shrugged and slammed the ambulance door.

"Wait!" she yelled, remembering. "I can't go. Don't take me."

The sirens began again, this time with her inside them. She was going to the hospital afraid because her grandfather had told her never to go there, and afraid because for the first time in her life she did feel out of sorts, even sick, stiff, and palsied. Doreena stared into her purse at the undeniable mango with its shimmer blue rind. She wanted very much to take it out and hold it and press its soothing skin to hers, but she did not know what the paramedics would make of that and thought it somehow safer to keep the fruit secret.

~ 32 ~

MIRROR ISLAND: RETINA

Under the island influence, Doreena cannot see clearly

In the commotion of the emergency room, Doreena lost track of Tom wheeled away behind one of the sets of swinging double-doors. She hoped his family would come for him quickly. As her grandfather had warned, once inside the hospital Doreena sickened. "They'll imagine that there's something wrong with you, and the next thing you know there will be," grandfather had said, and he was right. As the doctors, nurses and interns guessed what could be wrong with her, their speculations flowed alternately over her body. Doreena's blood surged red into the test tubes as expected. They tested for epileptic seizures, diabetic shock and multiple sclerosis and Doreena felt faint, lightheaded, and stiff.

The description of MS seemed most apt: the slow way the stiffness settled into the joints. The brief interlude of ocean had showed her how bright and painless the world could be and how her limbs could loosen. She felt dull and tight here by comparison. But if she admitted this, and let the hospital diagnose her with one lifelong disease, what was to stop them from giving her another?

"You'll get sick and eventually you'll die there in one of their hospital beds," grandfather had said.

"Don't worry," one of the nurses said patting her hand. "Adult onset for these illnesses is uncommon. You are probably fine. We are just being cautious."

Most people outside the hospital in C-town were fine. It was only when they entered the hospital, and admitted some weakness or susceptibility, that they became sick. Doreena wanted to get back to her work at *The Mirror* where everyone was well.

"I'm perfectly healthy. I've never been sick," she said. Doreena would no more disobey the doctors' authority than she would argue with Marilyn at *The Mirror*, but she could try to sell them on her health. The medical team was annoyed that she had no records, did not know if she had any allergies, and had never been to a doctor before. "It was my eyes. I saw things," she said, trying again to distract them from their mission of fitting an illness to her.

Finally, they brought her to the ophthalmic surgeon and placed her in front of a machine that shone harsh beams like blue sunlight into each of her eyes blinding her temporarily. They guided her to a small room and left her alone waiting for the doctor and her vision to return.

"Dr. O will be with you shortly," the nurse said.

After a while, a man in a lab coat with small, black eyes entered.

"Luckily, there was an opening in the OR tonight. We should be able to save your vision," said Dr. O.

"But I can see," Doreena said.

"Not for much longer if we don't operate."

He tapped at a console and two images appeared on a screen behind him. They were nebulous midnight blue globes shot with dark, wavy, and off-center yellow blotches like errant rivers and yolks. Waves of blue like sheer drapes hung down the globe on the right.

"You have very healthy veins," Dr. O said. "Those spots are your optic nerves, part of your brain. Your retina detached there in your left eye. You can see the outlines of it slipping off. That's what's causing those yellow bubbles you're seeing. The floaters."

The blue waves did remind her of the haze she had seen just before the beach appeared. But those yellow splotches, was that all it had been: the beach, the water, the sun, the sky, the jungle and the hibiscus? Floaters? The diagnosis was inarguable. Her name was printed in the bottom right corner of each image in ultra-bold, condensed. It reminded Doreena of the way she drew up large sales contracts in advance penning in the business owner's name so that it seemed inevitable. All they had to do was sign. She should do that for AeroFlux.

"The retina is delicate like wet tissue paper. We'll reattach it with a laser," Dr. O said, pointing at the diaphanous blue waves flowing through the left image.

"I can't miss work," Doreena said, she wondered if Tom would be back to work tomorrow and whether they'd be able to get another appointment with the AeroFlux CEO. "I have to make a big sale."

"Don't worry," Dr. O said. "It's a short procedure. We'll send you home tonight."

They propped her eyelid open in a steel clamp in front of a buzzing laser. Her eyelid strained. Her eye teared and then the laser seared it dry. Wisps of smoke rose in her peripheral vision. She tasted charcoal and disinfectant in the back of her throat. Once this was over, if it ever ended, there would be medical bills and car repairs. She would return to *The Mirror* without interruption or accidental arrivals of beach.

"Will I still be able to see color?" Doreena asked.

"Oh yes," Dr. O said. "This doesn't touch the rods and cones. That's more a function of the optic nerve. This isn't brain surgery exactly. It just comes close. Were you worried we were turning you into Rock Traynter? It takes more than a simple operation like this my dear to become head chief of C-town. Yes, it takes a special vision; indeed, the man is more than merely colorblind. But you, you'll still see all the colors you want: AeroFlux red and New West green."

Doreena stayed quiet for the rest of the operation. She hadn't meant to begin a political discussion.

The man could have his opinions but as a *Mirror* employee she had no interest in hearing any criticism of her publisher. Not everyone appreciated the way Rock and the City Fathers had preserved C-town's way of life, but her family, she and her grandfather, had always been staunch supporters.

"This is the best place for us. We wouldn't leave if we could," grandfather had repeatedly said. "And we've got Rock Traynter to thank for it." He'd been so happy, at first, when she'd told him she'd taken a job at *The Mirror*. It was only in the past few years that he'd become strange about it and they'd started to argue over dinner.

"Enough about that place, Doreena. I've had it," he would say.

"But I'm *The Mirror's* number one now."

"Yes, yes, you are. I know. But what else? What else is there?" He sounded like Tom when he talked like this. She could feel him pressuring her to be unhappy, to be restless, and it frustrated her. If he'd wanted her to do something different with her life, he could have told her, he could have taught her. He had always been all she had. She'd always done what he wanted. He could have shaped her into anything, but it was too late for him to change his mind now. She had her job at *The Mirror*, and she loved it every day. She was part of the operation that kept C-town stable and solid. She was content and secure, and he couldn't convince her to feel otherwise.

"Well, we could talk about my family. Why don't we talk about that?" she said, and that always ended the discussion. It used to make him apologetic.

"I'm sorry, Dori," he'd say. "Tell me again about how you upsold The Watertown."

More recently, he'd grown silent and pushed his plate away. She'd begun working later to avoid him. But they always ended up having dinner together whenever she got home.

After the surgery, Doreena was in a cab outside of the Narborough building with a bandage over her left eye trying to locate her wallet in the recesses of her purse. Beneath the bandage her numb eye bulged and throbbed. She didn't remember getting into the cab, but she remembered them asking if there was anyone she could call for a ride home. There wasn't. Tom was in the hospital, too, and she wasn't ready to face Marilyn's disappointment over AeroFlux. She'd suggested the cab and was glad they'd let her go. She feared staying overnight in the hospital and finding out she required more surgeries. Now, if only she had enough cash to pay the driver. Impatient, he reached back and flipped on the overhead light. Inside her purse, Doreena's fingers slid over silkiness, the fruit. It was still there. Somehow, she'd expected it to disappear along with the hanging drape in her eye, but the fleshy oval thing remained.

The driver stared at her in the rearview mirror. She pushed the fruit aside and found some bills behind it, enough to pay for two curries at Raja's. She stumbled out of the cab, head down. For the next few weeks, she had to keep her head down so that her eye would heal correctly. "The gas we use now absorbs back into the eye much faster," Dr. O had said. "But you have to keep your head down to hold the shape of the retina."

On her way up to her apartment, Doreena clutched the smooth stair rail. Grey-brown sand dusted the second-floor landing, but the surfer's marimbas were silent. On the worn wood floor of her apartment, just under the door lay a sheet of sherbert paper. Next to a hand-drawn picture of a palm tree, someone had gotten carried away with tiki font. Tomorrow night, The Surfers, — Was that a club, a support group, a band? The flyer neglected to explain. — were meeting 7:30 p.m. at the Labor Temple. She tucked the flyer into her purse beside the smooth mango.

Before bed, Doreena emptied the baggy the hospital had given her. There was a tube of ointment, a vial of eye drops, a bottle of codeine, and a doughnut-shaped plastic air pillow. She took two pills and sprawled across her bed face down in the blow-up ring inhaling plastic fumes. She hoped Tom was OK. She imagined his wife and children sleeping beside him in the hospital chairs.

As she fell asleep, a wash of blue swept over her. Her right eye opened wide to a blue haze. She jerked awake into a crush of inflated plastic. She was afraid to see floaters and that her retina was detaching in her other eye now. She'd be blind. She flailed, her arms swimming through the bedspread, remembering the car crash, and afraid she was about to strike something ahead of her. But the bed stayed firm beneath her belly. She stretched her arms ahead of her and saw her body below her in a glassy blue shell. She rode the tingling haze into a sunlit land.

This time, when she arrived on the beach, she lay like a seal on the sand. The water lapped her toes. She propped her head up on her elbows and rested her chin in her hands. The bandage over her eye had disappeared along with her pajamas. Her back grew warm in the sun. She could see clearly with both eyes in vivid color. She looked up the white beach to the wall of jungle green. In the shady vines, she could see a flutter of white, the hibiscus petals. Doreena brushed her curls out of her eyes. She lay as she had as a toddler on the Maui beach. When she'd found the photo, her grandfather had told her a little of that time. Grandfather loved photos and she could always get him to talk about them.

"I like the way they capture a moment. They make it something solid that you can hold in your hand, but it isn't really caught. The people in the photographs they go on. They stay fluid."

They had lived together in a hut by the roadside selling coconut palm weavings to tourists.

"Everyone thought we were native," he said. "We looked like we were. Especially you."

They'd eaten pineapple and coconut. He'd bought a camera and decorated the entire hut with photos of her. They'd spent their days walking the beach, sleeping under palms, Doreena had climbed trees and he'd taught her to count using seashells and stones.

"It sounds so wonderful," she said. "Why did we leave?"

He laughed once. "You were too hard for me to keep track of in that wild place all by myself. You were climbing trees like a monkey and scuttling along the sand like a crab and always wanting to go in the water like a fish. It was too much, too much."

Another time he'd been serious. "It wasn't safe," he said. She'd thought he'd meant politically, but later, when she'd caught him in a reflective mood after a dinner in which he hardly eaten anything, he'd elaborated, "The water, the sand everything constantly shifting. It wasn't safe for you. We needed to go inland, somewhere much more solid." She'd known that he wasn't talking about politics or the United Government, but about them, something unique and dangerous about herself that she didn't understand and which he refused to explain.

She remembered her grandfather telling her about the little lemon-yellow fishes she'd played with as a child. She stood and turned toward the ocean. It was clear blue all the way out to the skyline. Palms waved at either end of the bay. She waded into the water. In the shallows the fishes were there, tiny flashes like darts of sunlight above the wavy sand. Tiny mouths puckered over her toes, tasting. Up the beach, a forked red mouth of a trail cut into the jungle green. Beyond it, coconut palms waved and pineapple plants bristled. She bent and touched the purple flowering pohuehue vine winding through the sand and reached for a mango resting in its coils. She peeled away some of its red-green skin with her teeth. Juice sprayed her cheeks as she bit in, dipped her tongue into the hole and gnawed toward the seed.

She heard the woman's voice again, "Look up."

Doreena threw her head back. The sun scorched her eyes through a blind of palm fronds. She panicked, suddenly remembering the doctor's words, "Keep your head down or you'll damage your eyes."

She was looking up into puffy white clouds, and then she was face down in the inflated plastic pillow, feeling the flannel of her PJs and her bare toes brushing the cotton bedspread. She lay in a lingering palsy and sweat as though awakening from a nightmare, but a ripe, green fruit peel scent competed with the plastic surrounding her nose and mouth. Whether it was real or not, the disorienting motion of her travel to the beach lingered.

In the bathroom, the bandage covered her left eye again, but the throbbing had stopped. She wanted to look and see if it was healed. Nothing in ALL CAPS on the sheets of aftercare instructions said she couldn't. She unwound the bandage and lifted the patch of gauze. Beneath it her eyelid swelled around her scraped eyeball. Red speckled the white. Her brown iris bled like an unfertilized egg. Her vision through the eye was cloudy with translucent edges. It looked painful and as she looked it did begin to throb. She put in the eyedrops as directed and the stinging released blood-spattered tears. The beach seemed more distant now, more dreamlike.

Her feet grew numb on the icy tile, and she noticed a sparkle of sand between her toes. She bent to examine it rolling a few grains around in her palm under a finger. The grains were delicate white, not the course gray-brown skiff on the stairwell. When she went to brush her teeth, she plucked a sinewy strand of orange, a bit of mango, from between the gap in her two front teeth. She was afraid to think what this all meant. She felt debauched and hungover, as if she'd done something sinful, and she thought she'd better get to work.

It took her a long time to get there. She ended up head down waiting for the C-town center bus. In the relative light of dawn, she'd managed to spot her car, the mangled hood collapsed into the guts of the engine, where the AeroFlux workers had pushed it across the street. It looked irreparable. As she waited for the bus, the slow wend of passing cars made her self-conscious of standing alone on the street like a hooker or a transient outsider living on the abandoned Freeway outside of C-Town. She imagined a long winter of standing in the dark like this unless she could sell enough to afford repairs. She relaxed when she saw the leg of wetsuit come up beside her and recognized her surfer neighbor.

"You're not taking your surfboard onto the bus?" she asked.

"I'm heading out to Lake Traynter."

"Isn't it early?"

"Always do the best thing first thing. Then the rest of your day is golden," he said. He bent down to peer up at her with one green eye. The other was covered by a matte of dirty-gray curls. "What happened to you?"

"Eye surgery," she said. "And I totaled my car."

"So, you're going to work?"

Until he said it, it hadn't occurred to Doreena that she could have called in sick and spent the day lying in bed with her head down in plastic worrying about her declining commissions while the union workers across the street began another day of protest. Her scorn was guilt fueled. The beach dream had left her with lingering shame, even though she was now rightfully in her stiff scratchy suit headed to work and this guy was in a rubbery wetsuit about to waste the day on a waste-filled lake.

"Yeah dude," she said. "I guess I could try to surf on a man-made lake. Are there even any waves?"

"Not really," he said. "But you gotta get stoked about something."

His head disappeared from her view of the pavement as the bus wheezed to a stop in front of them. On the bus, he placed his board across the aisle from her. It was covered with stickers, SEXWAX, STOKED and REEF, and decals of tiny islands sprouting palms and clusters of Hawaiian blossoms. Instead of taking the direct route into town across Burrows overpass, the bus wound along the industrial strip and then through the marshlands.

"Nice mango," the surfer said.

"Mango?" she asked.

"Yeah, there."

She looked down at the fruit — the mango, with its glazed sugar sheen, which was still in her purse. She put it on the other side of her, away from him, to hide it.

"Where'd you get that?"

"It's a long story. I was listening to a motivational tape. I had a car accident. It appeared. I work at *The Mirror*."

"Ah, that makes sense. Mangoes, motivation. Sounds like transference, a psychological thing."

"I'm not crazy. That's a real mango."

"Yeah, I saw, a real motivation manifest."

"But how did it get here?" Doreena muttered. It was hard to take the surfer seriously, hard to care what she said to him, or what he thought. He was wearing a wetsuit on a bus in C-town and he seemed to take the mango in stride. "It's not like I carry fruit around with me."

"You don't?"

"Not usually. I mean, tropical fruit, where would I get that?"

"Good question. And even then, why carry it around? Fruit's for eating."

"I've eaten some."

"So, there's more where that came from? I'd be interested to meet your source, Betty."

"Not Betty. Doreena," she said.

He bent down again so she got a flash of green eye, muck-colored curl and a bit of tooth. "I'm Alonso."

The bus stopped. The surfer disappeared from her view and lifted his board.

"You can explain your fruit fetish tonight," he reached across her legs and pointed at the sherbet paper about The Surfers in her purse beside the mango. She shoved the flyer deeper into her purse and snapped it shut.

"You gave this to me?" she asked.

"Nope."

"Who then?"

He gave an easy shrug and hopped off the bus. It left him standing on the gravel roadside piercing the gray sky with his board. His curly hair flopped across his forehead in a tangle a lot like her own lay naturally, but it looked right on him.

Once the surfer was gone, Doreena thought of an explanation for the mango. Maybe The Traynters had brought them back from Maui for each of *The Mirror* employees. By the time the bus pulled up a few blocks from Traynter Tower, Doreena expected to see mangoes on each of the salesman's desks. If she was going to sell AeroFlux today, they could all do with some mango motivation. Satisfied with the explanation, Doreena couldn't wait to get to work and leave her woozy, guilt-trippy hallucinations behind. She was *The Mirror's* steady number one not some surfing derelict. At work, Marilyn immediately called Doreena into her office.

"I've been looking for you all morning," she said. She did not sound pleased.

~ 33 ~

MIRROR ISLAND: MARILYN

A sense of stiffening

Doreena's eye surged rhythmically beneath its bandage as she peered up at Marilyn with her one good eye. Marilyn's color of the day was scarlet: lips, nails, suit, and shoes. Doreena sat in her inferior position in the low cushy chair forced to peer up at Marilyn, prominent on the edge of her desk framed by the display of gold embossed awards behind her.

"Tom's out, broken clavicle," Marilyn said. "You and I will be going to AeroFlux this morning. It's critical we get them on board. Are you ready to corral Dalton Rees?"

Doreena nodded and suppressed a wince, which she hoped Marilyn would attribute to her injured eye. It had been a long time since she'd gone out on a call with her boss. Ride-a-longs with Marilyn had been frequent Doreena's first year at *The Mirror* and the intense scrutiny had been exhausting. Under Marilyn's tutelage, Doreena had changed aspects of herself she had thought were ingrained.

"You're blinking too much," Marilyn had observed after one of those early sales calls. "Liars blink a lot. You need to slow it down."

"But it's a reflex. I can't control it?" Doreena said.

Marilyn had waved her protest aside. "Of course, you can. It's easy. There's nothing about yourself you can't control. Someone like our publisher doesn't even stop there. He controls the world beyond himself, even his own environment. Listen, reflexes are only useful for people who aren't paying attention. Maybe they'll save you in a pinch if you just want to breath and keep your eyes wet. I'm teaching you to have heightened awareness, to operate at a very high level. I want you to use everything other people take for granted to your advantage."

There were ways Marilyn liked sales done and those were the ways Doreena had learned to do them.

"Our publisher tells people that the paper is called *The Mirror* because it reflects everything that's happening in C-town," Marilyn said. "But *The Mirror* means something else to The Force. Mirroring is our most powerful sales technique. Closely observe the body language of your prospect. Reflect their gestures back to them. Subconsciously, they will begin to see you as like them, and that's when you've got them. Mirror neurons in the brain fire in response to these gestures. You can impose your will on someone from the outside effecting them at an internal level. You know they won't refuse to advertise in *The Mirror,* but I want you to dig deeper. Create that lasting connection. Upsell."

After that first year, Doreena became a honed sales professional, a sharp instrument of *The Mirror* sales team Marilyn called The Force. The mirroring technique came, although she'd never express it like this to Marilyn, almost reflexively. Doreena outsold everyone on the force mirroring the position of clients' hands and guiding those hands to sign bigger and bigger contracts: full-color, full-page, placement in the Entertainment pullout section.

Now she laid her hands on her knees, awkwardly, palms up. She'd become an expert at the mirroring technique, but she was afraid to use it with Marilyn who would know what she was doing. She never knew what to do with her hands when Marilyn was watching her closely. She worked to keep her postures open and receptive. The mirroring was so ingrained, she fought to keep her fingers splayed and not mimic Marilyn's hammer fist.

"Let's go over this play by play," Marilyn said. "I'll start off with positioning and branding. You make the sale. I'll finish with pricing and placement. You get them to sign."

After the lecture, they headed out. Marilyn drove them across the overpass in Rock's infamous Ford, a stunningly restored vintage car with a pea soup paint job that only a colorblind man could have overlooked. The car had been a classic even before the revolution, but it smelled new. As they drove past the picket line onto the AeroFlux complex, Doreena slumped to avoid the glaring men in green. Crumbled bits of the landmark sign poked through the lawn.

"No worries. Tinted windows," Marilyn said. "You really did a number on that sign."

From the parking lot to the building, they walked under metal curved liked the hull of plane. Marilyn appraised Doreena. "I don't suppose there's anything you can do about the bandage. It's clean anyway. Try to look up during the presentation at least."

The AeroFlux lobby was a silo with black screened walls. In the center was the base of a red sculpture that Doreena knew without looking up was a giant pair of wings. Inlaid in the marble floor was a map of the old United Government. Arching stripes of crisscrossing gold indicated AeroFlux's old flight patterns joining the raised bronze cities. C-town lay on the edge of the Northwest, a bronze island, with one thin strand of gold crossing the Pacific Ocean to Maui.

"Please have a seat and watch our film," the receptionist said. "Mr. Rees will be with you shortly."

Doreena and Marilyn sat on the low bench that ringed the room and the black walls flashed blue as the film began. The United Government promo encircled them. The movie family, three beaming generations, set out from The Capitol, a flag adorned temple. They piled into a small electric car, a modern kind not available in C-town, and embarked on a road trip to visit long lost relatives spread across the once united land. They headed southwest across the continent and visited with homogeneously friendly folk in the bayous, grain fields and deserts. This was the supposed expanse of the UG. So far, Doreena could not find any specific fault with the film's portrayal of the UG. Aside from the suspiciously well-chosen lighting and the steady cheeriness of the traveling family she could not pinpoint any factual errors.

Then the fictional family drove up the West Coast. They passed through redwood forests and along the lighthouse dotted beaches. They sped down an empty evergreen-lined freeway into mountainous, forested Cascadia and sallied along to the flat sea-level meadows of Island County. This part of the film was blatant falsehood. In real life, on their way north, the family would be driving over scores of squatters encamped on the Freeway. And the island areas of Pacifica, depicted in shining blue, were already largely underwater as the Rust Red Seas with their poisonous and choking algae-packed waters were rising. Only those with no other place to go attempted to live there on the remaining peaks. It was no place for a holiday and any relatives who'd once lived there were likely dead. Still, the UG family continued their fantastical jaunt entering what the film referred to, in pre-Revolutionary terms, as the Great Pacific Northwest and its capital New West.

Marilyn groaned. She turned to Doreena. "They were showing this propaganda when the plane crashed. Rock was furious. It's one thing when they use this kind of thing overseas to keep up the façade, but to use it on our own people. You see how they set New West up as the capitol with no mention of C-town at all. We're completely off the UG's radar and AeroFlux is in bed with them. We've got our work cut out for us."

Doreena's eye throbbed. She searched her purse for her pain pills, but all she had in there was that weird mango. The rest of the film was basically an AeroFlux commercial. The little blond boy and his spry grandfather toured the plant with awestruck faces and ended up staring at the enormous metal wings in the lobby repeating the company's motto, "Traveling all ways into the future." The film ended when the well-traveled family returned to the UG capitol for a hug beneath the old flag. It fluttered through the final frames.

As the screens faded to black, a man approached them. Everything about him had an off-continent look. There were foreign angles to the cut of his hair and suit and even an odd tilt to his facial features. Doreena rose to greet the CEO.

"I'm Dalton Rees," he confirmed extending his hand.

Doreena left his hand extended, untouched, deferring to Marilyn's lead. His hand remained empty an uncomfortably long time until she looked down and saw Marilyn sitting with her head in her hands and hunched shoulders trembling. She was crying. Seemingly, overwrought with emotion. Doreena completed the handshake with the executive.

"I'm Doreena Moriena with *The Mirror,*" she said. "And this is Marilyn Traynter."

At last, Marilyn stood her eyes wet with tears. If the emotional display was a sales strategy, Doreena wished Marilyn had given her a heads up.

"Could it be there is a little patriotism left even in C-town's most stalwart supporters?" Rees said. "It is nothing to be ashamed of Mrs. Traynter. The film, as it was designed to do, affects many."

Marilyn flushed.

"This room. It reminded me of the plane, before the crash. They say the lack of control, the womb-like environment on a plane makes people more emotional," Marilyn said. "The UG and its partners are excellent at manipulation."

"Mrs. Traynter," Rees said. "I am so sorry for the unfortunate incident on our jetliner."

Rees led them into a small conference room decorated at intervals with black and white photographs and left them while he collected his associate. Once they were alone Marilyn, still weeping, pulled her aside.

"The presentation. You''ll have to handle it, Doreena. I can't. That film. It reminded me of my grandmother. She lives in the southeast and I haven't seen her in years," Marilyn said. "Please, let me collect myself."

In fact, Doreena felt perfectly capable of giving the presentation on her own. If anything, it made her less nervous to have Marilyn watching her than to have to stand beside her jumping in at random moments and knowing that Marilyn was judging her every word and nuance. The best would have been to give the presentation on her own. But she also felt guilty, Marilyn was so broken up by the fact that she hadn't seen her grandmother in years that she was unable to speak, but Doreena was able to carry on even though she'd lost her grandfather days ago.

"That's fine," Doreena said. "I've got it."

Rees returned with the man who had given Doreena his tweed jacket at the accident. He was wearing another jacket identical to it.

"This is one of our engineers, Earnest Wilde," he said.

To remove awkwardness about her eye patch, Doreena quickly explained about her recent eye surgery before beginning. Then she started in on her pitch. She watched both men's analytical and authoritative posturing and instead of glossing over the technical part of the presentation she gave them a more detailed description.

"The City Fathers strive to keep everything available to the citizens of C-town just as it was. We drive the same cars, communicate the same ways, and eat the same foods as we did before the economic collapse. Our quality of life has not diminished. We've been insulated from the effects of the economic collapse of the United Government. However, in recent years there is one great innovation we have come to depend upon. Advancements in quantum information theory allow citizens of C-town to share greater unified thought. Quantum dots, bits of information and ideas, are embedded into the silicon sheets of *The Mirror*. The information is then not only read in the normal fashion by newspaper readers, a circulation of more than 100,000, but also absorbed into their mindset and into the collective group of C-town. This process is enhanced by the polarized photons that transmit quantum information in radio waves to the phosphorescent lights that shine throughout C-town. Every business that uses *The Mirror's* day and night system, print and radio, dot and phosphors, becomes part of the fabric of C-town on a quantum level an indissoluble part of the collective working for our fair city. Truly, information is physical, and *The Mirror* is C-town's daily source."

Repeating the tagline left Doreena flush with excitement, as did the men's engaged and interested reactions. They were both leaning forward, now, and nodding slightly. They'd begun the presentation, both of them, with hands clasped and fingers interwoven and pointed up in displays of confidence. But her words had toppled those steeples and their fingers now pointed towards her. That was important because confident leaders were less receptive to new ideas. Now, she'd gotten their attention. They were ready for her pitch. Marilyn had started off the presentation leaning back in her chair with her arms crossed, closed into herself, trying to regain her control, but even she was leaning forward now. Her arms were folded on the table in front of her, she was looking up and watching Rees.

"Your company's aim has always been flight, traveling. Traveling all ways into our future. You look at any means to connect people geographically. *The Mirror's* mission has always been information. We look for any means to connect people by information sharing and by thought. Advertising in *The Mirror* is not just a way to strengthen your brand or to advertise your message. Being in *The Mirror* means becoming a part of the fabric of C-town and entering the hearts and minds of its citizens."

Doreena could see Marilyn nodding now. She knew she liked the way she'd worked the AeroFlux mission into her pitch. Her eye was throbbing, but she thought she had them. She explained the terms and conditions. She laid the rate sheets, the mock-up and contracts in front of them. She could see Rees signing the bottom of a yearlong full-page, full-color contract. At the end of her presentation, she paused and then asked Rees to sign.

"No," he said. "For the same reason we never have. AeroFlux is a monopoly. We have an established brand and we operate outside of C-town."

Surprised, Doreena looked at Marilyn. Her fists betrayed her anger. She gave Doreena a curt nod. Doreena felt the stiffness of Rees refusal, but she had to go on with the next assault. She hated this part, attempting to batter through another's will. His hands were splayed fingers wide on top of the table, in forceful refusal. She mirrored the position and cleared her throat.

Marilyn jumped in.

"Mr. Rees, you're new, from off-continent. You aren't familiar with how C-town does business. So, may I remind you that you've never refused to advertise in *The Mirror*? We've never invited you. But things aren't looking good for AeroFlux now. It looks like your faulty maintenance is to blame for that crash and now you've gone and laid off 300 workers. You need an image campaign."

"We wouldn't need an image campaign if we were allowed to import the goods we needed to properly maintain our fleet. We wouldn't be laying off workers if we were allowed to look for new revenue streams and export goods. We can't employ people to build planes when there's nowhere to fly," Rees retorted.

Doreena glanced at the engineer in the tweed jacket. He was leaning back with his arms crossed now. He gave her an apologetic little smile. Now that their bosses were fighting there was no chance of a sale. Uncomfortably standing in the center of the room, Doreena drifted to the side and began to look at the photographs. Most were aerial shots. There were sweeping views of inland Island County taken before the perfect circle of Lake Traynter had been dredged inside the C-town city limits. Vineyards surrounded hourglass-shaped Silver Lake; the county's only natural body of water. Farmlands spread around the small, flat speck of C-town before the AeroFlux industrial complex had sprawled to the forest and Traynter Tower rose to dwarf even the old growth firs.

She heard Marilyn's voice go from shrill to dulcet pleading behind her.

"Don't do this. You know what Rock's planning to do? Cancel that last flight out to Maui. He says we won't need it anymore."

"What?" Rees said.

Then another photo caught Doreena's eye. It was a photo of men assembled in baggy metallic flight suits. They had UG badges affixed to their shoulders. In the center of them, a man who looked just like her grandfather held his helmet under one arm and saluted with the other. Even in the shadow of his salute, she recognized the three furrowed lines across his brow and the dark mole on his cheekbone beneath his left eye. At the bottom ran the caption, Captain Leonid "The Chief" Moriena and the crew of the AF-896 bound for SPIREMine (Soviet-Prussian Interstellar Resource Excavation Misson).

Earnest, the man in tweed, approached her. "What is it?"

"My grandfather, that's him."

"Hardly," he laughed. "That's a historical photo. It'd have to be your great, great, grandfather maybe. That's one of the crews heading out to mine the energy source, back when we thought we had discovered an unlimited supply of power — before the destruction of that planet resulted in the collapse."

Then, he asked, "But which one did you think?"

"The one in the center, "the chief". His name was Leonid Moriena. He died last week. But he was just a school janitor."

"A family name perhaps," Earnest said.

"I don't know much about my family history, and I've always been curious," Doreena said. "He never mentioned a connection to AeroFlux."

They turned and saw that Marilyn and Dalton were standing, shaking hands. They'd seemed to reach some kind of agreement although the contract was still unsigned. Doreena caught the end of their conversation.

"I'm serious, he means to do it, turn this place into a real island. He'll freeze the flights out to Maui. He says if C-town has a real vacation spot we won't need to travel. We just need some kind of a getaway."

Dalton laughed. "In C-Town? What's he going to do build a resort on Traynter Lake?"

His eyes lingered a bit too long on Marilyn's scarlet chest.

Marilyn raised her eyebrows. "Good guess."

"No, really," he said, incredulous. "Well, if anyone can do it."

Before they left Earnest asked Doreena for her phone number.

"I'd like to get my jacket back," he said. "And I'll see if I can find out more about this Leonid Moriena for you."

Back at *The Mirror*, Marilyn brought Doreena into her office and closed the door behind them. Closed-door meetings signaled failure to the entire Force. Doreena was on edge the moment it snipped shut. She stood holding her hands behind her back as Marilyn started in on her about the lost sale.

"You were doing well until he said no and then you just dropped it. I had to jump in. The problem is you lack follow through. You don't commit. Rejection ought to energize you, not demoralize you. You just don't get the thrill of the hunt. I understand it with Tom. He's good, but he'll never be great. For him it's all about his family. He's just doing what it takes to support them. But you, Doreena, you could go all the way. You are sales. You could really be the best, but you lack passion."

Doreena wanted to protest. She was the best, usually. Her sales had only recently slipped, and she was still on Tom's tail even if he did have the more lucrative categories. But Marilyn was right. Demoralized. The word stuck with her. It rang true. It wasn't the first time she'd heard that other criticism either: lack of passion. Wasn't that what Tom was always going on about? Her grandfather had accused her of it during one of their last big arguments. At least it seemed now that's what he'd been getting at. She'd been cooking large ethnic dinners, too much food for the two of them especially when they were upset and barely picking at the meals. It was her way of hinting, trying to get him to open up about her family history.

"Do you like this dish?" She would say. "Maybe it's part of our tradition."

On Founder's Day she'd made dishes of mashed root vegetables: red, orange, and yellow. The sodden steaming mounds filled the house with an earthy scent. Her grandfather sucked sullenly at the tines of his fork while she talked about *The Mirror.* He'd interrupted by flinging his fork across the room.

"That's enough!" he said. The fork had stuck into the wall, breaking the illusion of solidity. The handle had vibrated as he yelled. "Enough about Founder's Day. I'm done paying homage to Rock Traynter and his perfectly preserved town. Would a little change be so bad?"

"You've always thought so!" she said. "I'm sorry. I didn't mean to go on. It's just been a great week with all the Founder's Day specials and then the party watching the parade."

"It's the same every year. Don't you ever get tired of it?"

"The loft has a fantastic view," she said.

"No, not the party. The whole thing, *The Mirror.* That hard place."

"Well, it's my job. It's not so hard." Doreena got up to serve him some of the mashed potatoes. "I thought maybe this was something mom would have made. I was imagining it, anyway."

Grandfather lowered his head. "Never mind. I'm a hypocrite. I'm as bad as Rock Traynter. I've done the same thing to you."

"Done what?" As she said it, she felt her entire body stiffen. It was as if her clothes were wrapping more securely around her; the zipper on her pants wrenching closed, the buttons on her blouse a notch tighter, the apron tie cinching and even the elastic around her underwear and bra squeezing closed. She felt heavy and overstuffed, as though it were the end of the meal. She clutched the bowl of potatoes to her chest.

Her grandfather looked up at her and shook his head sorrowfully. This relieved the pressure, and she began to move again.

"She didn't cook," he said.

She stopped with the spoon over his plate, this time of her own volition, waiting for more. He knew she savored every tidbit about her origins, especially her mother, but he just spooned the dish into his mouth and chewed silently.

"Your grandmother would have liked this. She had her own garden. She liked to garden." He got up from the table and lifted the rolltop desk. He handed her the red notice. "I'm sorry. I'm not in the mood to celebrate the Traynters. This is the last Founder's Day we'll have in this house."

She took the red eviction notice. The city had sold all of Maple Street to Traynter Construction to develop condos.

"Oh, grandfather I'm sorry," Doreena said. "But we can move, all right. Maybe even buy one of the new condos."

"I don't have the energy to move." He looked out the window, his gaze lingering on the hibiscus. "It's been so long since I've seen any hummingbirds."

"It's just the wrong time of the year," she said.

She could see he was sad that he wouldn't see it bloom again and that's when he'd said it. "Doreena are you happy? Isn't there something you've always wanted to do?"

And now his words had the opposite effect on her. She swooned with a sudden lightness. The zipper, the buttons, the tie and the elastic bindings around her loosened. She touched the window-pane to steady herself afraid that she might topple through, smashing on top of the hibiscus shrub. "Like what?"

"Do you ever imagine things are different?" he asked. "I just want you to live, be passionate, be happy."

Her hand was light on the thin glass window. It wavered beneath her touch. Light shimmered in the pane. She thought for a moment, her hand might pass through. This tremulous nature of her body disturbed her much more than the onset of stiff, heavy, awkwardness. That felt safer and more familiar.

"Grandfather," she pleaded. "I don't know."

"Look, never mind. It's just me just getting old. You're fine, Doreena, you're fine just the way you are. I don't mean to be critical."

Now both of the odd feelings were passing and she was returning to her usual state-of-being. The way she felt most of the timc at home and at *The Mirror*. But Doreena wasn't ready to forget the strange sensations. They were part of something she needed to know.

"There is something I've always wanted. That would make me happy," she said. "To know about my mother."

She waited. But he said nothing. And she felt no different now than she had always felt, like anyone who'd lived in C-town all their life. They returned to the table and finished their meal in silence. Afterward, he'd come to the kitchen.

"I won't always be here," he'd said, and left her alone to wash the dishes, so startled she'd forgotten to serve her homemade pies. Months later he'd told her he would retire and travel to Maui. When she'd asked when they would leave (she'd have to give *The Mirror* notice) he'd said, "No, just me. You can't leave C-town, but I have to go."

Never mind he'd said. Her grandfather had told her never mind about being happy and then he'd told her nothing.

Doreena looked at Marilyn standing behind her desk. There was a new photo perched on the edge, a personal one. It showed Marilyn on a Maui beach in a broad brimmed hat. Her face was covered in shadow. The photo had been printed in black and white, the way Rock Traynter would see it. The bright sun destroyed any delicacies of shading so that the sand, sea, and sky melded into a gray sheen. She could see why Rock preferred C-town. The overcast days would be easier on his light-sensitive eyes and the textures of its buildings more visually appealing than the flat sand and sea.

Doreena did not know what these people meant: Marilyn, Tom, her grandfather. She thought she was performing up to expectations. What more did they want from her?

"I'm committed. I'm passionate. I'm happy," she said.

"I almost believe you," Marilyn replied.

"You're the one who was crying. I've never cried," Doreena said. She knew better than to draw attention to her lack of tears. It was an oddity about her, an unfair advantage, like how she'd never been sick. But she was angry, and letting it get the better of her, or she wouldn't have tried to argue with Marilyn at all. "Not so much that I couldn't make a sale. What about your happiness? Worry about that."

Marilyn's response frightened her. She'd been holding her hands with her thumb on top of her clenched fists in her usual hammer fist lecturing style. But now her fists dropped. Her hands opened, palms up in a receptive posture, onto her desk. Some of the meaner pressmen took pellet guns to the flocks of pigeons that dripped white onto *The Mirror's* reflective black surfaces. Marilyn's hands looked felled and limp like those downed, pellet-stung birds. She moved to the door and opened it.

"Maybe I will," she said as Doreena walked through.

That night it was silent on Doreena's way up the stairs to the Narborough. She felt heavy and stiff, but empty. She looked in the cupboard, but she wasn't hungry for anything in there, any quick thing she could eat alone on her couch. No, not even that, she wasn't hungry at all. She hadn't been since grandfather had left. She knew she should eat regular meals, but she was tired of taking orders especially from someone who was no longer with her.

She thought of Tom in the hospital and felt guilty because she hadn't gone with the rest of the Force to visit him. But she wouldn't go back to that place. She called him instead. She told him about the AeroFlux failure and apologized for the accident.

"It's OK. We'll bring them around," he said. "And it's nothing serious. I'm healing. I'll be back in soon."

His words were innocuous enough. He hadn't accused her, but the phone call left her feeling angrier. It wasn't serious for him. She was the one alone, with Marilyn mad about the AeroFlux failure, and the wrecked car and the sinking sales. Anger thickened and stiffened her like a shell. If it settled in, she'd soon be immobile beneath its weight.

~ 34 ~

MIRROR ISLAND: ALONSO

Mirror Island returns

In the morning, those stiff, angry feelings weighed even more heavily across Doreena and her eye still throbbed as she boarded the bus to work. Her need to escape those feelings would soon cause her to make an unusual choice, a deviation. Doreena was going to follow the surfer off the bus, although at the moment she worried about her sales and her bills, the usual motivations. With her good eye, Doreena watched the sun spilling pink over C-town's marshlands. The bus' slow detour around town gave her plenty of time to plan her sales strategy for the day. Sell more; that was her strategy. She needed new clients, quickly, before her year-end review. She couldn't afford another zero day. *The Mirror* didn't float zeros and she needed commission for car repairs and rent. Doreena stared at her knees inches in front of her eyes. Her head still ached with the pressure of sleep, but even with the smelling salt offensiveness of bus, she could barely lift it.

"You OK?" Alonso, the surfer from her apartment building, swayed over her. Again, she envied his mussed curls.

"Just cold," she said. She pictured Alonso later in the day. He'd be standing on this same bus, dripping wet, going back to the Narborough. Then he'd flop down on his bed in his smoky sandalwood and clanging marimba apartment. He'd stare at the ceiling and daydream.

"So, what do you do the rest of the day?"

He shrugged. "This is the part that matters."

The bus slowed and he hefted his board. The assault of colors — yellow, turquoise, pink — pained her one eye. "See for yourself. It's something you have to experience."

Doreena knew that was wrong. Bad experiences were just bad. Everyone did not have to have them individually. Her grandfather had taught her that. "There's no sense following folly," he'd said. It was possible to benefit from the experience of others. This was why she'd had so few bad experiences: she'd escaped the random traumas — accidents and illness — that occasionally befell her co-workers.

But Grandfather was gone, and with him his insulating, protecting influence. Since then, she'd experienced both. But she now wondered as she never had before, hadn't he kept her away from some good experiences, too? Her co-workers celebrated engagements, marriages, and births. She hadn't even dated. Maybe it was time to experiment with her life.

"You think I'm the kind of person that blows off work?" Doreena said.

"You're more than your job," he said. "It's just a job."

"Just?" she said. "You know I work at *The Mirror*, right?"

As the bus stopped, Doreena surprised herself by rising from her seat and following Alonso down the aisle. Their brief exchange had left her feeling a bit more fluid. It was a relief to feel the easy movement of her limbs as she descended the short set of stairs. Alonso looked weird enough on his own, a surfer in a swamp, but she added to the oddity squat beside him in her scratchy suit. Even the bus driver, who must have seen everything, smirked as he pulled away. The dawn lit the frizz of her bangs framing her face and pinked Alonso's curls. As the cold air filled her lungs, Doreena's head cleared. She felt more awake, and alarmed. This was not what she was supposed to be doing.

"Excellent," Alonso said.

"The other salesmen do this all the time. I'm sure," Doreena said.

"I've never seen any surfing salesmen."

'This kind of thing: slacking. It was going to be a zero day anyway."

She justified avoiding work. Only a new sale could save her figures and what hope was there of landing a new client in C-town, where there was, by design, never anything new? She was part of the system that kept it that way.

Doreena's gray pumps crunched into the gravel and Alonso flip flopped beside her until they reached the dirt path down to the park. It cut through a blind of chirruping cattails hiding a marsh full of birds and amphibians. Even with the heels of her pumps sinking into the mud, Doreena could keep pace with Alonso's easy stroll to the water.

She'd been to Traynter Lake twice. Once with her grandfather when she was in elementary school. She remembered the long bus ride, lobbing hard bits of bread at hissing geese and the reflective black surface of the lake. Grandfather had squeezed her hand hard, crippling her fingers, when she'd reached for the water. He hadn't let her touch it. When she'd asked to go again, Grandfather had said, "No, it's too cold and those birds are mean." He preferred to keep her in town. Her high school graduation picnic had been there, but Doreena had been too anxious that day to enjoy it. People kept asking her what she was going to do next and she didn't have a plan. Besides, graduation hadn't seemed like much to celebrate. They'd all only done what they'd been told to do, she more than most. As it turned out, it wasn't a big deal. Afterward she'd gone to work for *The Mirror* and continued to live at home with her grandfather. Change was optional.

As they approached the brown sludge of Lake Traynter rimmed with gray sand, Doreena heard her grandfather's disapproval "People are always doing silly things. That doesn't mean you have to. My sensible girl." Doreena was already beginning to blame Alonso for her plummeting numbers and her unpaid bills. The geese, still holding sentry on the lawn, hissed at him as he stopped in front of a sign posted by the C-town Planning Department: Construction Scheduled.

"Rock's really going to do it," Doreena said. "He's going to turn this into a resort. Imagine hotels and restaurants, here."

"Damn. They're taking this too. We have got to go."

"Go where?"

"Away. Anywhere we can get to."

Alonso jumped down the rocky bank. The smooth sludge surface of the lake steamed with the digestive stench of cannibalistic algae and angry goose innards. It promised an icy entry. Swimming in there was the last thing Doreena would want to do, especially first thing in the morning.

"You get cold?"

In response, Alonso plucked at his wet suit.

"Even so."

"When I get out there, I'm in my zone."

He splashed in up to his waist holding the board high before he slid vertically into the water and crawled on top of it. He paddled out to almost the middle of the lake where gray-green water fell from a ringed metal spillway. Doreena sat on the lone bench near the water. She pulled the sides of her suit around her and crossed her arms. She could hear Marilyn critiquing, "Open postures, open postures. Closed body language is bad for sales."

"I'm just cold," she said, aloud to no one, except the geese.

Out on the lake, Alonso managed to stand up and surf the effluent a few feet before crashing. The water had a greasy sheen to it like the stretch of a lower order salesman's pants. On his way home, Alonso would drip red algae onto the bus, grimy lake water into the Narborough and trail brown sand up the stairs and into his bed. The gunk he picked up in the lake would mat in his hair and reek. The thick clouds of incense he burned would barely masque the stench. Maybe he'd shower first, strip out of his rubbery skin, before he could begin the rest of his long do-nothing day.

In the middle of this sudden, imagined stretch of Alonso's bared torso, a blue haze washed over Doreena's vision turning the pink sky violet. A tug across her skin accompanied the haze. She associated the feeling with swerving toward the union protesters, the vulnerable men, and the impact of the car into the AeroFlux landmark sign and shied away from the pinching sensation, the lift and pucker of her skin. For a moment, she hovered over the translucent watery outline of herself sitting on the bench, long enough to see that there was no harm in disappearing here. She was reluctant to leave her cares in C-town completely behind, but she could already feel herself irresistibly warming. She stilled in the grip of the haze. The pinch softened to suction. Warmth embraced her. Waves rose and fell in front of her.

She was sitting on the sand, hugging her bare knees, feeling the sun on her rounded spine and watching the ocean rise and fall. It occurred to her that she should have been scared, or at the very least startled to be pulled out of her expected reality into this one. But everything about this place soothed her. Even her nudity was a comfort. It had been easier to come here than it had been to step off the bus. The place seemed to ask and expect nothing of her and she didn't feel a twinge of guilt about anything she had left behind. Her only concern was that she might not be here long enough to get all the way warm. She stayed still as long as possible so as not to break the spell. When she felt absolutely warm, as though the sun's rays pinioned her, and her legs cramped, she finally rose. She looked from one end of the beach to the other. Palms swayed at either end of the bay. Behind her lay a wall of green. Flowered pohuehue vines grew through the sand below them. A sweet scent drew her toward the jungle. She pressed her face into a cluster of five-petaled hibiscus and inhaled. The bandage over her eye was gone again, along with her wool suit. She squinted with one eye and then the other watching the red tipped stamen of the flower jump side to side. It was dusted with beady pollen that reminded her of the newspaper's quantum dots. The colors of Alonso's surfboard were here, but set in motion: the yellow sun shimmered, the turquoise sea rippled and the hibiscus blossoms, large enough cup her breasts, fluttered in the breeze. The liquid intensity of the colors filled both Doreena's eyes. She looked up.

Through the leaves, velvety yellow triangles or waxy emerald rounds, a path cut up a hill. She took a few steps onto the exposed red soil as it curved into the jungle. Fruits grew here in a clearing: hanging green guava and mango overhead and pineapples sprouting at her feet. She picked up a fallen smooth-skinned mango. Ahead, the path continued up a short steep hill and disappeared. The leaves rustled. A woman's voice trilled from far away. "Calm sea meat," it said or sounded. Leaves whispered across Doreena's face. She clutched her necklace in one hand, the mango in the other, and turned to run back to the beach. She tripped on a vine and fell forward, falling face down, into the dirt.

The vermilion path turned black. Rubbery arms clamped around her and pressed her into a cool, wet torso. Alonso dripped onto her wool suit. The stench of the man-made lake on him was unmistakable. She'd left the magic beach behind. Gray sky framed Alonso's muck-colored curls. The creases around his eyes and mouth glowed with the dawn. He looked older this close up, even her own age. His hands were on her shoulders.

"Where are you running to?"

"Did you see? Did you see me go?"

He shook his head. "You were sitting there." He pointed round at the bench. "And then you were running up the path."

She'd brought back another fruit. She palmed the mango and hid it behind her back. It tingled in her hands. "I've got to go."

He pointed. “There's your bus."

She squeezed the mango. Her fingernails slid through the soft, trembling rind, under the thin, smooth skin and into the slippery, wet fruit.

"Wait." He grabbed her shoulders. He reached down and pulled at a white flap between the buttons of her blouse. A piece of petal, with a soft blue sheen, tore off in his hands. A faint sweetness went up with it. The rest of the blossom slid down Doreena's shirt and lodged at the waistband of her scratchy skirt.

"What's this?" He slid the petal between his fingers. Did he feel the slight vibration of its powdery surface? "What else are you hiding in there?"

All the fear that had eluded Doreena on the beach, caught up with her now. The place, the island, that had seemed so serene before now felt dangerous. It had come and gone, captured her, in ways she could not control. It was because she hadn't gone to work. If she kept to her routine the island couldn't come. It couldn't take her unwillingly. She'd given it an opening. The bus wheezed as it accelerated toward the park. Doreena turned. She dropped the new mango into her purse beside the first one and began to run up the hill. Her skirt bunched around her thighs catching on her thick stockings. Her pumps slipped. Stepping sideways onto the grasses for traction, she sank in mud up to her ankles and lost her shoes in it. She yanked her heels out of the mud and they came up with a sucking sound. Ahead, the bus had stopped. She hurried toward it in muddy stocking feet, with a goose-like waddle, sweating through the frizz of curls on her forehead. Clumps of mud fell from her shoes.

A group of surfers got off the bus: among them were two blond twins, younger, stockier versions of Alonso; the older woman, Hobart, from The Travel Museum; and a dark-haired seal-faced man who was nearly as tall as Hobart. They stared down Doreena.

"She's cool," Alonso said. "Come see the damage. They're building a resort."

Doreena climbed on board the bus and sat on the edge of the disabled passengers' seat. She wiped her brow and brushed her eye bandage. Through the window she saw the surfers standing statuesque around the C-town planning department sign. On the way into work, the cold seeped back into Doreena's skin along with the accompanying stiffness. Just before she reached her stop, she reached into her purse for one of the mangoes. It vibrated in her hands. She squinted into the gloss of its faint blue rind and saw a reminder of the glint of island sun across the ocean. She lifted it carefully to her lips and touched the outer layer with the tip of her tongue. It was light and tingly with the faint taste of saltwater taffy. With the taste of it on her tongue the stiffness vanished, but the island consumed her thoughts.

In *The Mirror's* office, the island receded. Her being seemed to settle into place, neither too stiff nor too fluid, but exactly as she needed to be. The idea that she could suddenly shift into some warm, foreign realm was ludicrous here. She took the back way up to the sales office detouring through the pressroom which stank of beryllium and silicon as the sheets for that day's run curled onto the cement floor. Today's headlines were: "Who needs Maui? One last flight" and "Resort planned for Traynter Lake." Doreena stopped off in the basement bathroom to bathe her stocking feet in the sink and wash off her pumps. She squished them back onto her feet, toweled flecks of mud off her suit and dabbed at a brown smear across her bandage until only a yellowish splotch remained. Her eye throbbed beneath it. She was relieved to be back at work, but aware she would not make a great sales impression.

On her way up the stairs, she heard Rock yelling at The Stew outside the newsroom. "Keep the pressure on. Keep digging. I want those headlines."

"I'm on the outside of this 'cause that's where *The Mirror* is," The Stew said.

"Then get in. That's an easy fix. Everyone knows I'm temperamental."

It made her glad that in sales they only had to answer directly to Marilyn, not the even more intimidating publisher who was stern and tumultuous as an avalanche. Lacking a car, Doreena's sales ability was severely handicapped. She zeroed out on cold calls, while listening to Tom, back at his post, nailing call after call. In desperation, she left in the afternoon to see what was in walking distance of *The Mirror*. The owner of The Watertown held up his hands, "You've got all I can do. What happened to your eye?" Doreena left quickly. She usually softened up the restaurant owners by having lunch, but she couldn't afford it and besides she hadn't been hungry in weeks. Doreena kept waiting for her skirts to loosen, but they were binding around her waist as usual.

She walked the rest of the block in a daze when she passed the words "Coming Soon," scrawled across butcher paper in a front window. A vacant shop? What was coming? A new business of the right kind meant opportunity — if it was in her category. Doreena tried to see in around the edges of the paper. What had been here before? A vacuum repair business, an auto shop? There had been some kind of a fire, she remembered. She tried the door. A red and blue animatronic bird squawked as she entered. Ukulele and accordion music played somewhere behind a collage of wicker tables and chairs. The bird's head jerked to train one plastic eye on her.

There wasn't a trace of smoke left inside. The only smell was new carpet. The tables and chairs gave her hope. A new restaurant? A man stepped out from behind them in checked pants wiping his hands on an apron. He twitched with the unmistakable energy of a new business owner, but there was something else familiar about him in the way he stood, the way he moved.

"My first customer. C'mon back."

She followed him past a back counter stacked with fishbowls through a swinging door.

"Yeah, I've got a lot to do on the décor. But it's the food I love," he said.

The kitchen smelled of baked salt. He reached over a tray lined with white blobs and scooped one onto a cracker. "So, it's lacking presentation. You gonna tell me it doesn't taste good?"

Doreena bit in. Cod. Her hope ebbed. "Seafood?"

The man frowned. "Yeah. We open in a couple of weeks. I expect to see you back. But you don't look very excited."

"No, it's good. A new restaurant. I'm just the person you want to see." She'd start him off with a quarter page, two colors. He'd need a big splash. Restaurants were tough. He'd be lucky to last a few months. She'd have to maximize her commission meantime.

He smiled. "I thought you were. Listen, it'll be better than you think. I've got a connection. We'll serve Silver Lake wines."

Again, there was something familiar. This time in the confident curve of his lip. But Doreena felt sorry for the guy. All the restaurants had Silver Lake wines and all the owners thought they'd finagled something special. C-town didn't allow imports, but the winemaker, just outside of town, was an unofficial exception. Doreena reached into her briefcase for her broadsheets to begin her pitch.

"So, when will I hear from the city about the liquor permit?"

Doreena held out *The Mirror*. "I'm not with the city."

The man's lips tightened, and his fists clenched. The only other time *The Mirror* had gotten that reaction was that woman, Hobart, at The Travel Museum. But if Hobart disliked the paper, this guy loathed it. He looked ready to pull it out of her hands and tear it into shreds. He looked ready to tear into her, too. Normally, her association with *The Mirror* was a source of pride. It was her job, her place. Recently, though selling for *The Mirror* had begun to feel unpleasant and possibly even dangerous. What was it with these new businesses? Didn't they believe in advertising?

"I thought you were with public health," he said.

Doreena backed into one of the tall refrigerators. As the cold seeped through the lining of her wool jacket, it clicked. This location had been the plasma center before the fire. All this stainless steel had been used to store blood. He must have gotten this space cheap.

His eyes narrowed. "Yeah, yeah. I'll buy an ad. Fuck him. You got a contract on you. I'll sign it now."

She wanted to leave, but she needed the sale. And no matter what this guy thought, she owed everything to *The Mirror*, everything she was for the past nine years. A new business had to be in *The Mirror* and it was her job to make it happen. Doreena reached into her briefcase and extracted a contract and rate sheet. The guy glowered, grabbed and slammed both documents down on the counter. The edges dipped into fishy waters. "I'll take a half page to announce the grand opening, full color and then I'll sign a six month, no, make it a year, for a quarter. Tell him I'm going to stick around. And I want radio, too. I want this place lit up, phosphors everywhere, the brightest spot on the street. Gimme a pen."

Doreena reached into her purse, where her hand brushed the cool-skinned mangoes, and handed him her gold closer pen. Too quickly, the guy scrawled his name at the bottom of the contract. Doreena could already hear Marilyn, "You only get commission on qualified buyers." A too good to be true contract smacked of desperation. It usually meant the business would go under before they could collect. But what was she going to do, argue? At least she didn't have to go back to the office empty-handed. Doreena thought of the mangoes and suddenly wished she didn't have to go back to the office at all. A little blue haze, a little suction and she wouldn't have to worry about *The Mirror*.

"And tell him, I don't want any deals. I'll pay it," he said.

He? Doreena read the signature Gavin Traynter and, suddenly, she got it, the swagger in his step, the curve of his lip — this was Rock's little brother. They were marked with the same pallor capped by dark hair, Rock's shorn close and Gavin's swept across his forehead. Gavin's eyes were a pale gray. Everyone wondered what color Rock's eyes were under his redundant shades. Could they be this dove color, too? This was the ingrate son who hadn't wanted anything to do with either family business: Traynter Construction or *The Mirror*. He'd wanted to make his own way. No wonder it irked him, trying to do his own thing and still beholden, as they all were, to *The Mirror.* Doreena stuffed the contract in her briefcase. He'd advertise alright, but Doreena wouldn't get to keep commission on any contract signed Traynter. Today was another big zero. No commission. No rent. No other way to spin it for the boss.

How had the island come earlier? Had she been doing anything special? No, it had just happened. She couldn't will the island to come, but she tried.

"You don't think I can make a go of it do you?" Gavin said, misreading her look of concentration.

"No, it's just, well, seafood." Doreena said, then she sighed. There was no use trying to bluster a Traynter. "No, I don't. You won't last three months."

"You know I'm a bartender, right?"

"Everyone does."

"Well, I can cook too. People like seafood."

"Yeah, but there's The Watertown, The Dungeness and Surf n' Turf. It's all seafood. You need a hook. Something more exotic."

"In C-town, exotic, right. What would you recommend?"

Doreena had her hands in her purse, stroking the mangoes, as though that would bring the island near. "How about an island theme? Do this place up in Tiki font."

"A Tiki Lounge? That's a nice schtick. But I'd still be serving the C-town usuals and that means fish."

Without thought, Doreena held up the mangoes one in each hand. "What about these?"

Gavin turned the fruits red over green in his hand. Then he held them up to his nose and inhaled. The shimmery blue flowed into his nostrils. His nose twitched. He pulled it away and stared at the red and green skins with the soft blue glow.

"What is this some kind of fruit-based phosphorescence?"

Doreena shrugged, reminding herself as she did so, of Alonso.

"And it's edible? Is it safe?" He pressed two fingers into the stuff, tasted it and smiled.

When he finally held the swinging door open for her, his apron was splattered orange. They were both smiling like kids building sandcastles on the beach.

"Where did you get this? Does Rock know about this? No, never mind. I'm a Traynter. I can keep secrets. Just, can you get more? This is exactly what I need."

"I'll let you know," she said. "And I'll tell you where you can get some authentic décor too. And what's with the fishbowls?"

"Those, you'll see. You know I'm a bartender, right?"

"Everyone does."

On her way out, she touched her tongue to the lingering sweet at the edge of her lip. It was 5 p.m. on a Friday, the perfect time to get fired. But back at the office, no one noticed her or her deficient sales. Instead, the hammer had fallen on The Stew. He was gone. Rock had canned him.

"You should have heard them shouting," Tom said.

"I'm next, I know it," said Diane. She'd yet to log even one sale.

Even Marilyn looked shaken and her odd color of the day, a casual rosebud pink, most unprofessional really, made her appear unusually fragile.

~ 35 ~

MIRROR ISLAND: SALES MEETING

Doreena entangled, exists on Mirror Island and in C-town

On a Monday morning, Marilyn called Doreena into her office and announced that she was going on maternity leave. As *The Mirror's* number one salesman Doreena was now in charge of the sales floor. Doreena had known she was in for a bad day as soon as she arrived at work after another arduous bus trip so long it felt like an actual journey. It surprised her when she arrived at Traynter Tower instead of somewhere different. "See me!" had been scrawled in red beside her desk.

In Marilyn's office, the color of the day was pink again like the inside of an island fruit. Pink flowed at the cuffs of Marilyn's billowing blouse and rippled down her front. It made the double-strand of pearls at Marilyn's neck blush. It shone on her cheeks and lips and even in the highlights of her black hair. Around her, the glass furniture and shelves of sales awards met the pastel rays with an icy glare. The florescent light overhead dulled the cake-frosting color to cooked-salmon at the tops of Marilyn's shoulders. Marilyn, in pink, no longer looked like she belonged although she told Doreena what to do with her usual primary color directness.

"You'll manage in my absence," she said.

When she was done, she struggled to rise from her chair, the wheels slipping forward under her pregnant center, and Doreena had to position herself beside it so Marilyn could use her as a hoist.

"Just a wave of nausea," Marilyn said. When she had collected her breath, she made a giggly dressing room sound. "I forgot; I made an appointment to check out the birthing suite. There's so much I need to do to get ready."

Her tone was conspiratorial, and although the meaning of it was lost on Doreena, she was drawn into a conversation about room service and whirlpool tubs as if Marilyn were planning some kind of exotic getaway rather than the grueling procedure of giving birth. Marilyn carried on as though Doreena were one of her sisters (she was rumored to have a large family somewhere outside the UG). It was as though Marilyn were suddenly having a conversation with someone completely different.

She began talking faster with a trace of some off-continent accent. Her hands punctuated her gestures and Doreena could not have mirrored the movements subtly, or kept up with them, if she'd tried.

Doreena wondered who she was now, or who she was supposed to be, in Marilyn's mind. It was disorienting, but she liked the conversation they were having. The fluid energy of it put them on equal footing. They could even have had a friendly argument. She wanted it to continue and expand to other subjects. She could talk to Marilyn about how she lived at home, and never dated, about how strict her grandfather had always been and how he left her for Maui and returned as ashes. She wanted to share everything. This is what it would be like to have a sister. She especially wanted to tell Marilyn how it felt not to know her family or her people. This seemed like something Marilyn would especially understand. She might even be able to help her, somehow.

Then Marilyn stopped abruptly. She seemed to remember herself and who and what and where they really were.

"Well, you're in charge," she said, speaking the way she usually did at *The Mirror.*

Doreena looked at pink Marilyn who was leaving work early to run some personal errand. Her face stiffened into a familiar scornful expression, a borrowed expression, one Marilyn usually directed at her. Doreena recognized it from the inside out. It was the look Marilyn used on her when she lost a client or wore the wrong thing to work. The look meant, "How unprofessional!" Doreena expected Marilyn to react to the look in a shrinking way, as she did. But nothing about Marilyn appeared to diminish. She seemed oblivious to the How Unprofessional look. Doreena thought that was a weakness. As sales manager, Marilyn, did not have to share her figures. Now Doreena wondered what they were. Her own sensitivity to nuance had propelled her to number one. It was her greatest asset and the reason she excelled at face-to-face sales.

As acting sales manager, Doreena's first task was the weekly motivational sales meeting. She did not have a successful attitude about it. Everyone dreaded the Monday morning meetings in the conference room so cold they called it The Meat Locker. The Force hated how they took time away from sales and openly griped, but Marilyn considered them an essential part of her management strategy.

"I'm motivating you, like it or not," she always said.

Doreena waited with her hand on the icy door handle watching the salesmen make their way towards her through the glass corridors. She anxiously looked around before pushing her way in.

"Our publisher is really concerned about sales. So, he'll be at the meeting," Marilyn had said, last thing before she left. "Listen, put on a good show. Don't let Rock bully you."

Rock was waiting for her inside. In minutes, the rest of the Force filed in stopping short when they saw Rock and shoring the edges of their cups from the rise of coffee tsunamis with their hands. They exchanged grim looks behind the publisher's back. Last in, Tom, and the new girl, Diane, went back out in search of chairs. No matter how many people were expected at a meeting, there were never enough chairs. Doreena avoided looking into the mirrored shades covering the publisher's eyes instead watching her wisps of breath rise.

"That's why we call this The Meat Locker. You'll learn," Tom said to Diane who was shivering in a sheer floral blouse.

Doreena tucked her chin into her turtleneck. Through the tinted glass of the conference table, she could just make out the hatch marks on her watch: 9:56 a.m.

When Rock began to speak, his voice boomed steely gray. "Don't worry I won't take up much of your time. I can't. Sales are down. We're the only newspaper in town and our numbers aren't good."

To a man, The Force mirrored Rock's posture leaning forward with their hands clasped on the glass surface in front of them. The exception was Diane. The new girl was holding her arms. The closed off posture communicated inattention, but she was probably just cold. Under the table though, the salesmen's feet began to relax. They held wide stances, their legs twitching and feet shuffling. This movement suggested an ease and impatience, which agreed with what Doreena had observed herself after Rock had been speaking awhile. They'd heard this before. Rock was giving them a variation on, "The Higher-Calling Speech." Marilyn began most meetings with this speech where she reminded them that they weren't just selling ads; they were selling thoughts at a quantum level. These thoughts shaped the reality of C-town and were what kept the town intact, preserved its economic stability, and made it a tranquil predictable place to live. The alternative was the chaos and deprivation outside. There was no governance, social order or commerce in most of the rest of the UG. It wasn't even possible to get basic commodities. Rock's Higher-Calling Speech was nearly identical to Marilyn's. She'd probably gotten the gist of it from him, but there were slight differences. Where Marilyn used "security" and "stability" Rock went on about "loyalty" and "tradition".

The speech was supposed to make them all feel part of something bigger. It usually worked on Doreena. This calling tied her to *The Mirror* and strengthened her commitment. The speech made her feel a certain way. In thrall of it, her spine straightened, and her mind fastened on *The Mirror* as she planned her sales attack for the day. But today was different. She was distracted thinking about how she was going to handle being sales manager and what she would say when it was her turn to motivate. The jumpiness of the Force below the table indicated they were thinking about their own commissions and just wanted to get back to sales. Was this the way it always was? Was she the only one the speech affected?

"So, if you haven't been fearful for the state of your city, it's time to begin," Rock continued. His words clanged. He stopped and reached for his shades, a sure sign that no one would like what he was about to say next. The salesmen glanced to the side trying to look away, but the room held no distractions. Unlike the AeroFlux conference room with its historical photographs, the walls here were bare. Each man ended up staring down into the table, where they could see Rock reflected. He removed a layer of shades and revealed the second shinier pair underneath. These smaller circles still hid the outer corners of his eyes and the tiny array of muscles that Doreena always looked to distinguish a real smile from a false one: crinkled meant genuine smoothness meant false. Rock's shades disguised the difference. The Force had a running pool as to the color of the publisher's eyes. So far, no one had been able to claim it. The list of possible colors had become increasingly creative as the obvious choices were taken. Diane had added cerulean to the blue category that included lapis lazuli, azure, turquoise and aquamarine. Having seen his brother's eyes Doreena guessed one of the grays would fit: flint, steel, or granite. Her early choice, if she remembered, back when the pool was new had been a simple combo: gray-green like the surface of Lake Traynter.

"We're not tolerating dissidents anymore," Rock continued. "The fabric of this city is stretched thin. It's been difficult keeping this town together and operating insulated from all the chaos outside and we can't afford to be lenient. People who don't have C-town's interests in mind won't be a part of this organization."

Above the table, the salesmen looked the same, hands pressed together on the tabletop, but, below the table, legs were crossing. It was a classic defensive reaction. They were literally protecting their genitals as though they were about to be kicked. Diane's arms still clenched her upper body, but her feet crossed at the ankles indicated it wasn't just the cold twisting her body into knots. They all knew Rock was talking about how he'd fired The Stew, once his favorite reporter, and telling them they could be next.

"Businesses who don't have C-town's interest in mind will be marginalized." He meant AeroFlux and the cessation of the Maui flights, but what Rock said next was new. "Some businesses we've been selling to have been trying to use *The Mirror* to dissent from within C-town. We'll continue to sell to those businesses because we'd rather have them in our pages than out, the City Fathers will work to bring them into the fold, but meanwhile if I catch anyone on my staff patronizing any rogue businesses, if I hear of any involvement, I'll fire you on the spot."

Doreena immediately thought of The Travel Museum and Gavin Traynter's new restaurant, but a wave of puzzled glances passed among the salesmen. This was apparently news to most of them. Rock turned his head her way. She could feel his gaze on her beneath those opaque shades and saw herself reflected in them as a metallic shadow. Where would she be without *The Mirror*? Everyone she knew was here. All she had without it was a small, apartment in a dark part of town.

Then, he unclasped his hands and leaned back in his chair. "Marilyn is on maternity leave. Doreena Moriena who has been our number one is taking over in her absence and it's time I turned this over to her, our motivational speaker."

Doreena caught Rock's use of the past tense. Already, he knew her sales were slipping. How far had she fallen? She stood. The chill of the leather seat clung to her skin through her wool skirt. She positioned herself at the front of the room, an elongated closet, and looked down the table at the sales staff wedged around it.

Around the room, the Force turned their attention to her and, in the transition, when they stopped mirroring Rock and waited for her to begin their gestures revealed their emotions. Some leaned back. They touched their mouths and faces. They propped their chins in their hands. Diane made swirling circles with purple pen on her notepad. Didn't she know *The Mirror* hated doodlers? They were impatient, bored, and leaderless. She saw this all in a flash and knew that once she began this individual dissension would dissolve into a unified image. When she started to move, they would move with her. She would be the mirror and they the reflection. The prospect terrified and exhilarated her.

"Maybe Doreena needs a round of applause to get started," Rock said.

Leaden clapping followed. The Force wanted to get this over with. The best she could do would be to keep it short. Doreena ran her hands down the sides of her wool skirt wishing for pockets. By the time she readjusted the bandage over her left eye, the room was silent again. The Force hung waiting in front of her like slabs of frozen beef. She clasped her hands in front of her and watched them do the same up and down the table in rows of white knuckles and wedding rings. It was almost the gesture Rock had used but his fingers had extended confidently out towards the center of the table, whereas hers were closed, holding something in, hiding an intention. She was the sales manager, a stiff, solid role, but a fluid feeling of leadership also rushed over her. They were under her direction. Would they follow? Where did she want to go?

Doreena launched into a few safe lines from Stellar Sales, but the words sounded flat and strangely uninspiring in her own voice. "What should we, as sales professionals, say? What motivates the buyer to come to the point of purchase?"

Mangoes, Doreena thought, and as soon as she did, she knew it was dangerous, but once she started, she could not stop thinking island thoughts. Motivation mangoes, mango motivation like the surfer, Alonso, had said on the bus. This time, when the blue haze began to wash over Doreena's vision, she recognized it. The island was coming. Even in an undercurrent of relief and desire to leave the cold conference room and the cold stare of the salesmen and flow to the warm place, she fought it. It was wrong to disappear and a terrible precedent. If the island could take her from here, from the certainty of *The Mirror* office and the routine of the Monday morning meeting then it might lift her from anywhere at any time. She would never be entirely sure where she was or where she belonged. As the soft suction pulled at her skin, Doreena flung her arms wide grasping handles of air. The blue rushed her like a wave. As she flowed back with it, she looked through a translucent backless version of herself into the still bored faces of the sales force. She watched them mirror her gesture. They unclasped their hands on the table. Their palms opened up into that most encouraging sales sign, a gesture that meant they were receptive to experience. Doreena thought if she could just clench her hands into fists, she could prevent the rush away to the island, but she could already feel a little of the warmth rising, soothing her skin and lessening her resolve to stay. In the peripheries, her fingers stretched. She heard herself say, "I'm motivating you like it or not." The Force laughed. Then, they were gone.

So much for her leadership skills. No one came with her to the beach. She arrived on the island alone. She stopped struggling and listened to the waves. The haze squeezed her and released. The clench of heat and spiced saline reminded her of stepping into C-Town Dry Cleaners at first. Then a fresh wind blew off the ocean. She faced turquoise waves and wiggled her bare toes in pink sand. The bandage over her eye was gone again. She stood in a surround of bright light and walked into the surf. Sand scrunched underfoot. She squatted and shuffled forward. Her tailbone dipped into the warm water, and she pushed her fingers into the smooth wet sand. She squinted into the translucent blue at sparkling white shells and darting lemon-yellow fishes.

In the back of her mind, she remembered vaguely that she'd been afraid come here. The island's sudden arrival or her sudden departure, she wasn't sure which, was wrong. It wasn't supposed to be possible, but that didn't seem important now. She was happy to have the place to herself and glad the sales force wasn't around to spoil it. All her personal concerns: moving, falling sales, car accidents, her eye, money trouble with rent, car repair and medical bills melted away. Even the bigger anxieties placed on her by *The Mirror:* responsibility to manage The Force, rogue businesses, AeroFlux, The Travel Museum, Gavin Traynter's restaurant, plummeting sales threatening the stability of C-town eased. She relaxed into a perfect, comfortable, tranquil release. It seemed impolite to worry about work here. She remembered grandfather tiring of her talk about *The Mirror.* It was like that. She could almost hear him as if her were sitting across from her at the dinner table, "Just be quiet a moment. Eat, eat."

Doreena looked back over her shoulder at the waving jungle greens hiding mangoes and other fruit behind them. She was almost hungry now, or at least the sensation of sweet, juicy pulps would feel good on her lips and down her throat. She heard the voice call and understood it this time, not "calm sea meat," but "Come see me." But she didn't want to leave the beach. This one place seemed perfectly safe and pleasurable. So why go? Not that the island wasn't safe, but all safe places had boundaries. Within the UG, there were enclaves: Maui, D.C., and Cascadia. Island County, Cascadia was safe within the borders of C-town or New West and unsafe without, all around Silver Lake and down the long stretch of Freeway. Even C-town was only safe in those certain neighborhoods Mapleton, Denrigger Hill, and Rosemont brightly lit by phosphors. Dangerous unknowns lay on certain streets, in the industrial part of town across Burrows overpass, in Lakeside and Marsh Creek and out by the border along the forest. On the island, the line between the white sand and the green jungle seemed a likely barrier, as impassable as the one between the sea and the sky. Besides there was something, she thought, she wanted to do here, now.

Grandfather's ashes dangled from the chain on her neck over the low waves. They sparkled pink like Marilyn today or a blush wine and the glass vial glinted in the sun. She looked past the ashes at her bare knees, and then up and down the beach. It was a long curve with palms at the ends of the arch and empty. There were no sails in the water, no ships in the bay. Along with all her other worries, her anger about grandfather's death and the loss of her family mostly faded. A sadness lingered. Her wistful feelings in harmony with the island's nature grew. It wasn't just that she'd lost grandfather. There was more she was missing. A desire to move, to do, built and became a physical pressure that expanded her skin. Doreena stood suddenly and raised her arms to the island sun. Her torso stretched. She arched her back and the sun's rays warmed the length of her body in a long slow glide. "Come see me," the voice sang again from somewhere in the jungle behind the hibiscus.

Then she heard the sound of popping hungry fish mouths — no — applause. Hearty, lively applause like waves slapping a board filled the air. She caught a glimpse of her translucent blue form in front of her before she snapped back into it like a shell. She stood before the sales force. Her arms dropped to her sides. The Force smiled and applauded. Afraid she was naked she hunched forward clasping her hands in front of her and twisting like a jungle vine. But the bandage over her eye was back along with her wool suit. The Meat Locker cold began to seep in through her clothes. The light was so dim she could hardly see. She made her way back to her seat feeling along the tops of the chairs. The salesmen began to rise and make for the door. Doreena turned to Tom and Diane.

"I'm sorry," she said. The words came out in a whisper. Her throat was dry. "What happened?"

"No, don't worry about it. You did great," Tom said. "And I'm not upset Marilyn tapped you to manage instead of me. It was a good choice. Besides I don't envy the time it'll take away from your commissions." Tom dropped his voice and looked up at Rock talking to a couple of the Force by the door. "Hey, did you get that bit about rogue businesses?"

Doreena nodded. She was searching Tom and Diane's faces for clues, but they were acting like nothing unusual had happened. "His brother Gavin's opening a restaurant. He signed a contract the other day, but he's no fan of *The Mirror*."

"Hmm. Well, where is it? So I can stay the hell away," Tom said.

"Just around the corner, seafood."

"Oh, no worries. No one's going to risk their job for a seafood joint," Diane laughed and her rainbow of eyeshadows shimmered like the sides of a fish.

"I ran into another one, too. A business that wouldn't buy in. Near my apartment."

"Well, get them in, Doreena," Tom said. "Rock sounded serious. He fired The Stew. No one's safe."

They stood. Doreena turned back to Diane.

"I did great?" Doreena asked.

"Yeah, I think you even motivated a couple of us," Diane smiled. "Me for sure. I'm ready to give it a try again."

As they passed by Rock, even without seeing his eyes, Doreena could tell his attention was on her. He turned toward her, but all he said was, "You surprised me. I didn't know you had it in you. Marilyn's doing a very good job with you."

Then he turned his ominous attention to Diane, "See me in my office."

Tom and Doreena exchanged a look. Neither of them had ever been in Rock's office.

Back at her desk Doreena opened her bottom drawer and looked for a mango in her purse. She was thirsty deep down and felt dry inside like a stale crust. Her search was fruitless. She'd given both mangoes to Gavin Traynter. While she was rummaging, a few salesmen stopped by to tell her what a great speech she'd given. She wondered what she had said. No one had noticed her disappearance. Doreena reached for her coat. It was time to get out and sell, even if she had to walk around the same oversold blocks, she didn't think she could handle hearing anymore how good she'd been in her role as sales manager, how surprisingly so. When she looked up, Dianc was bcside her, her face streaked with the cascading green and yellow shimmer of her eyeshadow.

"He fired me," she said. "I'm leaving now."

"Oh, Diane," Doreena said. "I'm sorry. I'll go down with you."

"I'm OK with it. I guess I can try that new restaurant now," Diane said. As they walked toward the elevator, she flung her long red hair back over her shoulders. "Have you ever noticed there are no windows?"

"What?"

Diane spun pointing around the office. "No windows. Not by our cubes or in the conference room or even in Marilyn's office."

Doreena shook her head. When they arrived on street level. Diane pointed up. "Look at the outside, see how the building looks from the street."

The outside of Traynter Tower was a pillar of black reflection. It was all windows. "I see what you mean. But that's usual for office buildings, isn't it?"

"You ever been in Rock's office?" Diane asked.

Doreena shook her head. Like all of the Force, she hoped never to be asked in there. Rumor had it the only person who'd ever enjoyed their time alone in Rock's office was Marilyn.

"That's where they are," Diane said. "The windows. His office goes all the way around the outside of this entire floor. He can walk all the way around the city. He can see everything."

Doreena imagined Rock looking down and seeing C-town around him in shades of gray. "Did you see his eyes?"

Diane shivered. "No. You can have my guess in the pool if you want: cerulean."

"Well, good luck. You'll be looking for a new job?"

"Yeah," Diane said. "I'm thinking something with windows."

Doreena watched Diane walk towards the parking garage as she headed the other way aimlessly. She felt sad that Diane was leaving. She'd thought, from their brief conversation, that they could have been friends. That would have been something new, a friend at work. Marilyn and Diane were both free of *The Mirror*. How could she escape? There were ways: sick days, maternity leave, and windows. But the easiest way was the island. It just came for her and *The Mirror* went on as always.

As she walked the downtown district, she began looking for the blue haze, waiting for the suction pull and thinking about when she would go back. Once she allowed herself to think about it, she could not stop thinking about when the island would come. The very effective, motivating ocean view remained ahead of her as she walked the streets. She remembered the feeling of wanting to rise up on her toes and reach her arms up into the worshipful gesture on the island. Her sun stretch was a posture she couldn't even catalog. She did not know what it meant because it was not something people did in C-town. But her desire to do it, the way she'd wanted it, struck a chord. Was that the feeling that Marilyn and Tom and her grandfather had been talking about all along in all those many conversations where they'd asked her: What drives you? What are you passionate about? Isn't there something you want to do? Doreena wanted to raise her arms and stand under the island sun. She wanted it, a way out. Now if she could only figure out how to get back and how to control it.

It occurred to Doreena that it wasn't just locations that were safe or unsafe. Thoughts had borders, too. That was what *The Mirror* was all about, gathering the right thoughts together and using them to protect C-town. *The Mirror* advertisers, the full-page, full-color spreads taken out by the City Fathers were the safe thoughts, those outside of *The Mirror* like AeroFlux and The Travel Museum were not. Now Gavin Traynter with his rogue business was trying to blur the lines. Within her own thoughts, concentrating on her sales and her income was safe. Island thinking was dangerous and unknown. But she could not stop thinking of it; how she wanted to go back, and how, after all, there was no reason not to if she could find a way. She'd apparently been better in absence, than she'd ever been trying. She could spend her time motivating the sales force by remote while living on the island if she could only control getting there again.

~ 36 ~

MIRROR ISLAND: SURFERS

A growing island addiction

Doreena wandered the blocks around Traynter Tower going through the motions of work while waiting for the island as she always did now. Although she'd never gone further into it than the grove of fruit, she was sure it was an island. There were no traces of other people on the land or water so it must be out of the way and it had that insular feel that reminded her C-town, actually, a place that existed on its own where everything that happened boiled up from the inside. Doreena found that she went to the island about once a day, every day, always in short bursts, never at the same time, either morning, noon, or night. The timing of the island departures each held its own tortures. Longing for the island came with a particular kind of dryness, a stale, toasted feeling deep within. It was strongest when she returned from the island, faded as she tried to go about her routine and then ached like a phantom limb as the island subsumed all her other thoughts. Her need for it was like thirst. Never had she been so conscious of her insides before: she didn't get sick to her stomach and her menstrual cycles were mild. It was easier to tell when Marilyn's menses began, marked by increased pressure at work, than to take note of her own period which always began quietly a few days later. But for some reason, the island focused her attention on her gut, and a series of unseen internal events.

If Doreena went to the island just as she was waking, she arrived at work warm and content. The feeling faded by midday leaving her restless and distracted. She was in agonies by evening fairly crackling inside with the dry feeling and "island, island, island" her every thought. Returning to her apartment after work, she went immediately to bed, to bring the island sooner. When she went midday, at her desk or while talking to a client, it divided the day into two equally trying sections: waiting to go and longing to return. If the island eluded her until nighttime, she would wait for it the entire day and sit up far into the night and could not sleep unless it came. Of all the unpleasant patterns, Doreena had decided that going to the island in the morning was least agonizing and it was worst when it waited until night because she worried that it would elude her all together and a long islandless day would pass. She'd start to think she had only imagined it and worry it would never come again. The island occupied her thoughts especially when she was at work, at *The Mirror* office, trying hard not to concentrate on her sales. She looked for the blue haze and felt for the soft suck around her skin. The island retreat never took her when she most wanted it, which was most of the time. It always appeared to surprise her.

Today was shaping up to be the worst kind of day when there was no island until night. Doreena walked around Traynter Tower passing the same storefronts pretending to herself that she was still trying to make sales. She needed her island. Even in her wool overcoat and scarf, the cold numbed her. Still, she didn't go. Steam fogged the windows at Raja's. She wished she could afford a five-star curry to warm her from the inside, even if she wasn't hungry. Her hand crooked to open the door. Her fingers were so stiff, from the outside in with cold, and from the inside out with the crisp island desire. Inside, the restaurant was hot and moist as boiled potato. A strong marsala tinged the steam yellow. As much as Doreena wanted to join the few diners inside, she waived the menu away and asked to speak to Mr. Elitamby instead. The owner came right out wringing his hands on his yellowed apron.

"I didn't want to neglect my favorite client," she said.

"I'm glad you've come. We've missed you, Dori. And I've been putting off a call. I wanted to tell you in person. You've been so good to us," he said. "We have to close. It's no good without the Maui flight. We can't get anything. We're into our last stores, all the spices we squirreled away during the collapse."

"Oh, Mr. Elitamby."

In her mind, Doreena struck a line through Raja's on her dwindling sales sheet.

This would be her fourth cancellation this month. That was bad, but almost as bad was the thought of no more curries, the only heat that cut through her cold.

"My dear, it's a tough spot." Mr. Elitamby hung his head. "The City Fathers, they used to make sure we businessmen could get everything we needed to keep things running as they were, one way or another. But things have changed with that new AeroFlux CEO. They don't like him, so they'll turn us into New West where we can only get local goods. What I wouldn't give for cardamom."

Mr. Elitamby held Doreena's fingers as he spoke, an extended handshake, as was his custom. Doreena thought of the mango in her purse. She bet there were spices on her island if she knew where to look. But there was no guarantee she'd see it again.

Around the block, Doreena looked back over her shoulder while passing in front of Gavin Traynter's restaurant. He'd named it the Tiki-Tiki Lounge, but inside and on the menu, it was just a smaller version of every other seafood joint in town. The restaurant looked empty, unsurprisingly, since Rock had refused to run his brother's ads after all and threatened to fire any *Mirror* staff he caught inside. Doreena had overheard some of the lower ranked salesman wasting valuable time gossiping about the new rules.

"Can he do that?" one of them had asked.

"Hell, yeah, he can. If you're that stupid, maybe Rock should just fire you now," another had responded. "This is at will employment. Means he can fire you at will."

Doreena ducked down the next alley and knocked on one of the gray metal doors. After a while, an aproned Gavin Traynter opened. He waved her into the Tiki-Tiki Lounge kitchen. Doreena reached into her purse and handed Gavin a couple of mangoes. "I know it's not enough to make a difference."

Gavin smiled at her and took the fruit. "Thanks, though, I appreciate the thought," he said. Reaching for a small paring knife, he began to slice through the red and green skin. "And these are delicious. I've been dreaming up recipes: Mango Salsa, Mango Martinis, Mango Spritzers, Mahi-Mahi with Mango Butter Sauce."

He held out a bit of the melty orange fruit to her on the end of the knife. Doreena took the slice of mango and rolled the wet slip of it around in her mouth. The liquid comforted her and a soft, fluid feeling washed over her when Gavin looked at her.

"You know, it's not like I'm Rock's enemy," he said. "I'm a Traynter, too. I love C-town as much as anyone. I've never wanted to go anywhere else. I'm perfectly happy here. I just wasn't interested in the family businesses: construction or *The Mirror.* They're all about controlling the town. Seems to me like too much work."

Doreena stiffened and responded instinctively. "It is a lot of work," she said, the Higher-Calling speech leaping to mind. "C-town couldn't be what it is without Rock and *The Mirror*. It would have fallen apart with everything else."

"Well, we could relax the control a little bit. Some free trade. Some imports," he said.

"It's a slippery slope," Doreena said, glancing at the slices of mango sliding off the side of the cutting board and beginning to feel ashamed. "I have to go."

"Yeah, right," Gavin turned away. "Well, if you find a way to get more imports. Let me know."

Doreena left the kitchen with sweetness on her lips but returned to the office guilty about her lackluster sales and traitorous visit. She worked late leaving phone message after phone message and missed the early bus. She sat at the stop as the phosphors for the boutiques flickered out at 6:30 p.m. and the ones for the bars flared to life. A layer of grime covered the street. Soggy scraps of silicon newspaper lay in the gutters like pink algae. Her body was stiff with cold, her muscles tight with a feeling she was beginning to associate with C-town. It trapped her. She wanted her beach, to walk the length of its salt-washed, pure, unspoiled sand. On the bus ride home, she imagined circling her island. The ride was so slow, she could have walked all the way around it she supposed if not for its palm-edged ends. Instead, she trudged up the stairs to her apartment.

Inside she took a mango off the top of the pyramid of tropical fruit accumulating from her morning island visits. She pressed its smooth skin to her cheek. She imagined she could feel island warmth pulsating inside it. Instead, she went to the window. She stood still in her wool coat and scarf massaging the mango. For a moment, she felt the island coming. She held her breath and wrapped her arms tight around herself to keep from gasping and reaching and wanting the beach to come too much and breaking the spell. She willed the suction to grip her and pull her free of her wool trappings and finally released the day's tension and discomfort. What she wouldn't do for just a moment, it was usually just a moment, warm and naked, on the beach. The sun would be high overhead as always. No matter when went she went it was always, always into the bright light of noon. The weather was the same, hot and balmy. Hibiscus and pikake, Hawaiian jasmine, infused the air. The fruit was so sweet, and mostly water; it didn't require an appetite. She would peel back the green skin of a fresh guava with her teeth and dug into it up to her gums lolling her tongue into its pink flesh. The juice would drip from her chin soaking the sand.

The mercurial island didn't come. In the industrial section of C-town below, she could make out the tar-covered rooftops and the brick edges of the buildings. Then there was the open darkness of the swamp and the lake beyond. Far away, downtown, phosphors glowed violet. A long night of longing stretched out in front of her alone. She squinted and imagined the glow as the blue haze. Rock Traynter would stand like this in his windowed *Mirror* office looking out at his gray city. The difference was that he controlled what he saw. If she could, would she want to see her island like that stretched out below in front of her? The idea frightened her. As it was it was, the island stayed hidden up in the jungle behind her. But she did want to control it, to be able to make it appear when she needed it. The pressure of not being sure of something as essential as her location was stacking up inside of her like her pyramid of mangoes. An idea came to her, and Doreena rummaged in the bottom of her purse. She came out pinching a soaked and mealy scrap of flyer between fingers coated in a brownish-orange rotten mango mush. The surfers were meeting tonight. They had traveled. Maybe they would know about the island and give her a clue about how to control it. Doreena filled her purse with mangoes and headed out into the night.

In the rain, without phosphors to guide her and unused to dark streets, Doreena searched for the Labor Temple. Her hair dripped in wet curls by the time she found the square, brick building with pale orange illuminating "bor Tem" over the locked double doors. A man approached, a moving piece of night, except for the beige bag slung across his back. She recognized Alonso when he whispered, "This way, you here for the meeting, right? Round back."

She followed the algae-musk that clung to him behind the building and down a stairwell into the temple's winding corridors. Dim fluorescent bulbs flickered across Alonso's wetsuit. Mold blackened the chips in the walls. Icy water dripped onto her coat through cracks in the ceiling. The carpet released a fetid odor as it sank beneath her feet. They entered an unmarked room where men sat in a circle of folding chairs with wet suits peeled down to their waists and drums poised between their knees. The building's pipes creaked and groaned, and warm air hissed down on them from the Reznor box overhead.

A pile of canvas bags lay in one corner. The men, the blond surfer twins and the seal-faced man from the lake among them, looked up at her as she entered.

"What's with the *malihini*?" one said.

"She's alright," Alonso said. "I invited her. Let's get started."

He shut the door behind them, sat down and swung the bag between his legs. He unzipped it revealing the taut hide tops of a pair of Congo drums. One by one, the men reached for their bags. They flicked the tops of their drums with their fingers. In the drumming, Doreena began to be able to tell the blond surfer twins apart. Both of their hands moved fluidly across the drums, but one of them had a lighter touch and the other a thin scar on his right hand. A rhythm emerged and intensified, widening the room with its echoing waves.

After a while, Alonso rose and gestured to Doreena to sit in front of his drum.

"I don't know how," she said.

"Just tap it," he said. "When it feels right."

Doreena joined the rhythm with hesitant touches of the drumhead. After a while it was like she'd been doing this forever and could go on doing it forever. The drum sound reverberated through the small room as if it were trying to escape. A bead of sweat slipped through the fringe of her drying hair. She soaked it up with the rust-colored cowl of her sweater. The drums dropped into a low steady tapping. The men began to chant strings of strange words interspersed with a few she did know: Easter, Cat, Destruction, Fire. A fluid feeling rippled through Doreena until the chanting trailed off into a low hum, the drumming stopped, and she realized she hadn't longed for island since she'd seen Alonso. Now the stiffness of wanting it returned. She wrung her hands over the drum.

"Welcome to the surfers. Those are the names of the islands we love," Alonso said.

He pointed around the circle of men and began rattling off foreign words. He'd gotten halfway around when she realized he was introducing her to the surfers. She was usually good with names, her sales training had armed her with mnemonic devices to remember introductions, but she couldn't keep track of these ones: Ehukai, Hapitit, and Barritz. The men, alike in their wetsuits, didn't offer much in the way of distinguishing guideposts. The twins were easy though: A-Bay of the light touch and J-Bay, with the scar.

"Those are our names, also some of our favorite surf spots," Alonso said.

Doreena was sure these surfers who held drum circles in the basement of the Labor Temple and called each other by made-up names, were the kind of people her grandfather had been keeping her away from her whole life. "The odd ones," he'd forbidden her to befriend. The first girl she'd met when she'd started school had been one. "Stay away from her, she's an odd one," her grandfather had said. Since he worked at her school, he always knew who the "odd ones" were. The other kids, the not odd, never approached Doreena. She'd gotten used to being mostly alone, but she'd never learned to identify the odd ones for herself or understood what grandfather really meant. Now she thought she understood the difference between them and most of the people she interacted with in C-town. It wasn't something she knew but something she felt, not only emotionally, but as an actual physical reaction. The surfers, came with that unsettling, but rather pleasant fluid-feeling that reminded her of the island.

"I'm Doreena Flora Moriena, nice to meet you," she said, in the stilted, distant tone she'd use with any of her clients, but then a wave of feeling swept over her and the next words rushed out. Her voice stayed low, but there was a new vibrato quality to it. "Did you say islands? Do you know how to go?"

He shook his head. "We got holed up here coming out of a surf meet in Westport on the coast. We were heading south when everything went to hell and the freeway clogged. We've been saving up for a Maui run, but so long as we're here we're trying to loosen things up adding our ideas to the mix. Eventually, we'll hit the road again, but it's gnarly out there. Meantime, we'll hunker down."

"What do you mean loosen things up?"

Before he could answer, the door swung open and a surfer giantess taller than all the men entered. Her silver cap of hair took on a blue tint in the dim light near the ceiling. It was Hobart from The Travel Museum. The woman's odd name must be a beach somewhere.

"What's the hold up?" Hobart spotted Doreena, trained eyes on her, grabbed her elbow and torqued her around. "You know she's with *The Mirror*, right?"

"She's cool. I'll vouch," Alonso said.

"Not good enough." Hobart's grip tightened. "Rock sent her to spy on us."

"No," Doreena said. She tugged her arm free and dumped her purse, so the mangoes rolled over the concrete floor. "I'm here on my own."

The surfers stared down until Hobart picked one of the fruits up, then the rest of them followed suit.

They faced Doreena in a ring, mangoes in hand.

"Where did you get these?" Hobart said.

"I have a connection," she said.

"Who are you working with? Who's your importer?"

"It's just me, now."

"You? You can get in and out?"

Doreena shrugged. "Sometimes, it's kind of unreliable."

"I bet. I don't believe it." Hobart said, but she was staring at the fruit in her hand. "We may be able to help."

"Help?" Doreena said. "Help me what?"

"Move product," Hobart said. "For AeroFlux."

"Mangoes, motivation. Motivation, mangoes," Alonso said. He'd bit into one of the fruits and a drop of juice gleamed in the corner of his mouth.

"Don't look so surprised. I know what you're doing. You're not the only one. A lot of people aren't happy with the way things are. We're working to change all that. See there," Hobart pointed up to a large vent near the ceiling above pyramid shaped structures that jutted into the room. "Those are for acoustics. *The Mirror* works on a quantum level embedding dots in the fabric of the paper, spreading the ideas throughout C-town and infiltrating people's consciousness. It's the same way any communication works except *The Mirror* purposefully creates particles of thoughts with a specific intention, keep C-town insulated and uniform. Our drumming works the same way, but we put the message in the music. We want to counteract *The Mirror* with free form openness and flowing thought."

"Flowing," Doreena said. "Loosening things up."

"Yeah, Rock's got us all constipated," A-Bay, the light-touch twin said.

"Like a kidney stone. Let's show her the new product," J-Bay added.

A group of the surfers stayed behind and resumed drumming while Hobart, Alonso, and the twins, led her down the hall through swinging double doors into a large room with a concrete floor. The phosphor lit room was moist and hot and the walls lined with banks of computers and audio recording equipment. Faders glowed. Spools of blank pink silicon were stacked in one corner and a river of broadsheet flowed across a press covered with a fresh array of pale blue dots. Fleshy blobs of silicon bubbled in vats beside tubs of phosphorescence. It was an eighth the size of the equipment in *The Mirror,* but there was no mistaking the setup of the press or the smell. She'd stopped noticing the chemical burn in *The Mirror* office, but now the warm silicon reminded her distinctly of her childhood. Her bedroom had been on side of the house that caught the afternoon sun along with grandfather's hibiscus. Her windowsills were lined with invisible women, anatomy dolls, the only kind grandfather allowed.

"These dolls show what real human bodies are like inside. Those others are just plastic. They don't look like real people. There's nothing inside them. They're hollow. You look like a real person," he'd said.

She'd thought maybe he wanted her to be a doctor, but he'd discouraged this. "Don't be around sick people. Be healthy," he'd said.

She had seven dolls in various stages of exposure: skinless, lacking major organs and utterly skeletal.

In the heat of summer, they melted a little and the hot plastic smelled a lot like this.

A man stepped out from behind the vats wearing a lab coat, a welder's mask, and swim fins. The footwear actually seemed a smart choice on the puddle-covered concrete. He flopped toward them with a curling piece of silicon slung over his arms. "The front page."

Hobart skimmed it, nodded, and passed it to Doreena. The silicon broadsheet was still warm and tacky to the touch. The numerous minute indentations of the embedded quantum dots tingled in her hands. The masthead read *C-Town Traveler*. The headline, Citizens Held Captive: Last Maui Flight Set, ran below followed by: AeroFlux Exports Electric Cars to New West: Still Banned in C-Town.

The scientist lifted his mask. He wasn't a scientist at all. He was a journalist.

The Stew was a traitor. He was running an underground newspaper to compete with *The Mirror*.

"This is why Rock fired you."

"No, Rock doesn't know about this. If he knew he'd shut it down and banish us all." He stepped forward and held out his hand. "I go by Madagascar here."

"C-town's a one paper town," she said.

"Not anymore," Hobart said. "It'll take time. Lots of editions to change this town, but we've started. We're providing an alternate vision."

"That's dangerous," Doreena said.

"It's an adventure," Hobart said.

"That's what you call travel when it gets dangerous," Alonso said.

J-Bay and A-Bay looked at her with mango wedge smiles.

"I think we can help you," Hobart said. "If you can help us."

"Me?" Doreena said. "How?"

Hobart walked over to a stack of folded fresh papers. It was a slim edition with just four pages. One of which was a full-page, full-color ad for The Travel Museum. It was a scaled down version of the HAWAII poster, just like Doreena had envisioned.

"We need more advertisers," Hobart said. "If you know anyone."

Doreena immediately thought of Gavin Traynter and Raja's and began to think of a number of other clients who had turned her down over the years. She wouldn't have thought so before, but she could see now how maybe these businesses didn't like *The Mirror*. Would they be interested in this new vision of C-town?

"I might. I'd have to think about it," Doreena said. If she did, they'd be traitorous thoughts.

She walked back to The Narborough between Hobart and Alonso. The rain had eased, and a layer of fog settled in to the marshy lowlands. The surfers walked in companionable silence, with Doreena awkward among them, but too absorbed in a flurry of thoughts to make conversation herself. The evening hadn't been at all what she expected. The surfers hadn't helped answer any of her questions about the manifestation of the island and they'd raised all kinds of new ones about C-town. Did AeroFlux have a secret importing business that Rock didn't know about? She felt confused and torn between the security and familiarity of *The Mirror* and the strange possibility of joining with the surfers in their underground paper, a possibility that made her feel entirely different inside.

"There's nothing inside them. They're hollow," her grandfather had said about ordinary dolls. He'd wanted her to have anatomy dolls with their insides showing instead. An odd thought, occurred to her, had he'd been afraid that there would be nothing inside her? Maybe she did feel kind of hollow at *The Mirror* office, certainly she had felt still and silent and innocuous inside. Now, she was stirred.

Hobart left them at The Travel Museum and Doreena walked up the stairs to her apartment with Alonso. Everything about his posture said casual complacency. It agitated her. She was fairly seasick from being around him and the surfers. She imagined her insides roiling like hot silicon. She was building up some kind of internal momentum. And where was it taking her?

"Alonso, so, is that some kind of a surf spot too?" she asked.

"No, that's my real name. But I go by lots of things," he said, and gave his easy, liquid shrug. "Right now, my handle is C-town. They say I'm so grounded they gotta call me where I am. My place, my name, is always the one I'm in."

He left her on the stairwell wondering where her place was: with *The Mirror* or the surfers. And that's when the blue haze, like a blur of crowded quantum dots, dropped over her vision again, and sucked her into the island. That wild, nameless place, that she'd managed to forget for just a few hours, overwhelmed her again.

~ 37 ~

MIRROR ISLAND: BABY SHOWER

A new visitor to Mirror Island

Doreena struggled to get her bearings. She'd been flitting in and out of the island frequently and it was becoming harder to keep track of where and when she was. Even when she wasn't on the island, an island-ish feeling lingered so that she did not feel truly present in C-town where no one seemed to notice either her absence or her disorientation. As far as she could tell, the person she was supposed to be in C-town continued to exist and do what people expected. That person, that Doreena, seemed less and less like her actual self, who was really on island time. At the moment, Doreena wasn't sure where she was; everything around her was light-filled and shiny as if she were looking out to sea. Everywhere bright colors dangled like flowering vines, but the overpowering scents weren't of the island. They were forced, stale smelling assaults of musk, rose, and orange instead of drifts of jasmine and lily. Doreena snapped fully into her C-town self when she recognized the reflective glass counters and the hanging displays of necklaces and scarves: Denrigger's Department Store. In her hand, she held the silken straps of a shopping bag. Inside was a puzzling beribboned box gift-wrapped in yellow paper. She could not remember buying anything.

"Have a great time," a voice trilled. Diane was behind the counter rolling a collection of lipsticks under her palm on the glass top. A great time, where? How long had Diane been working at Denrigger's? Doreena searched her face for clues, but it was an illusory sheen of rainbow-colors.

"I'm actually a little sorry I'm going to miss it," Diane said.

"Do you miss *The Mirror*?" Doreena asked.

"I like it here. Rock only gave me a job because he felt sorry for me after the crash," Diane rolled one of the lipsticks at her. "Here, take this, a free sample. The color'll be just right on you."

Doreena dropped the lipstick in her purse. On the street outside the department store, a sliver of sun shone through the clouds. There were quite a few people around, most of them in jeans. It was probably a Saturday afternoon. She pressed her back against the brick wall of the store and waited. Either she'd remember where she was going to go, or the blue haze would pull her away again and it wouldn't matter.

The pull didn't come and the distant winter sun never penetrated her wool coat. Beneath the coat, her legs were bare and her feet chilled in open-toed sandals. The impractical footwear looked like something new she was wearing to please someone else and that reminded her: Marilyn's baby shower. She began to walk the blocks toward Traynter Tower and the loft. She would have taken the bus, but her purse was empty except for the lipstick and a couple of mangoes. Although she walked slowly, she made it to the loft before the island ever came.

It was strange to be going to the loft on a day other than Founder's Day. Even with the sun burrowing its way out of the clouds, there was a cold, gray cast to everything. The street looked dingy. If a parade of C-town's firetrucks, police, and dignitaries were to roll down the street now, it wouldn't fool anyone; there'd be a dearth of civic pride.

In the mirrored elevator on the way up, she applied the lipstick. Marilyn liked her to have color. It was a weird shade called Scarlet Tangier. It made her lips look like wedges of something slightly rotten and emphasized the gray tones of her skin. With all the time she'd been on the island shouldn't she have a little tan? Doreena looked closer. Pulling back the flesh of her cheek below the bandage she was still wearing on her eye in C-town, she examined her winter skin. There was no hint of tan, but there was a strange bluish cast beneath it and a kind of sheen, almost as if one of Diane's metallic makeups had been applied just beneath her skin. When the elevator door opened, Doreena stepped quickly off anxious to escape her reflection.

Her hand poised to knock on the Traynter's door, Doreena worried she'd run into Rock although she didn't think it likely he'd be at the baby shower. If she did see him, for once she'd be glad of his glasses. She wouldn't be able to look him in the eye. He might see treachery. She'd sold ads in the *C-town Traveler* to both Gavin Traynter's Tiki-Tiki lounge and Raja's. Traitor that she was, it seemed wrong to show up at Rock's home, but Marilyn, whose mood of late had been sprightly, had invited her to the shower and she couldn't imagine turning Marilyn down for anything. Marilyn greeted Doreena at the door patting her shoulders in lieu of a hug across her broad belly.

"You made it after all. I was beginning to wonder," she said.

The color of the day was spring yellow. She wore a billowing yellow crepe blouse, there was a glow of yellow across her cheeks, eyes, and lips and a sunny tint to her nails. A blonde woman beside Marilyn offered to take Doreena's present and coat. Doreena was surprised when she removed the coat to find herself in a pastel floral-patterned dress she didn't remember owning in a light, clingy fabric she couldn't imagine selecting.

Marilyn introduced her to a circle of women already gathered on the crème couch. "These are my friends from the club. And this is Dori, she works for us at *The Mirror.*" Marilyn rattled off their names: Victoria Fort, Bea Mitchell, Alexis Sand, and Deidre Denrigger. Unlike when she'd been introduced to the surfers, Doreena knew she'd have no trouble remembering names, even if the women were similarly attired in spring dresses. They were iconic: Fort Family Auto, Mitchell's Medical Supplies, Sand Valley Farms and Denrigger's Outfitters and Accessories. These were *The Mirror's* premium customers, the full-page full-color regulars and the businesses that kept C-town operating independently. Fort Family Auto repaired and resold C-town's vehicles. Ed Mitchell was CEO of C-town General Hospital as well as its medical supplier. Sand Valley Farms provided most of the city's food and the Sands were rumored to own the one overlooked illegal import as well, Silver Lake Winery. Denrigger's manufactured clothing and cosmetics and, of course, ran the department store. These were the wives of the C-town City Fathers.

It was strange company for Doreena and discomfiting to be around this new softer version of Marilyn, her professional veneer cracked by the swelling baby. The women settled in on the couch to watch Marilyn open her gifts. Doreena stared out the window to Traynter Tower and wished the island would come soon. Marilyn bent over her belly and picked up a gift from the pile at her feet. She unwrapped a blue button up sleeper and held it up.

For a moment, a familiar, critically appraising look crossed Marilyn's face the one she directed at ad placements and sales figures and Doreena herself. Then she returned to her complacent abeyance and gave a lenient maternal smile. On cue, the women cooed in unison and then one by one as they passed the sleeper around. The blonde woman, Deidre Denrigger, nudged Doreena and thrust the sleeper into her hands. It was impossibly soft like the island sand, or hibiscus petals, or clouds. She smiled in imitation of the other women, but she could feel how it didn't reach her eyes and hoped Marilyn wasn't looking. Her smile caught in the dry cracks around her mouth. Her skin felt dry as sand.

She wanted the island. She ached for it. Worse still was knowing she didn't have to do this. If she went to the island, the women wouldn't even notice. If anything, she'd do this better once she left here and focused on the island. The shell she left behind would do what they wanted and expected and be perfectly behaved. She'd lost all interest in living this C-town life. She didn't care if she controlled the C-town Doreena, if she could remember where she'd been or what she bought, but she desperately wanted to control the island. She wanted to go there now. The worst part about being in C-town was not knowing how long she'd have to endure it. She would have cried, but the terrible dryness made it impossible. She balled her hands into the sleeper, her nails clacking on the teeny-tiny buttons, and noticed Deidre staring. She patted the garment smooth and passed it on.

"I know that look," Deidre said.

"I'm sorry. Just a hard day, " Doreena said. "I'll be OK."

"Honey, it just gets worse. How old are you?"

"35."

She nodded. "Yep, that's about the time it really hits. You start feeling there isn't any time. Well, if you have trouble, Marilyn knows a great fertility doctor. How long have you been trying?"

Doreena understood the woman had mistaken her longing for the island for a ticking clock, longing for a child. Doreena could see the similarity, but if only it were that easy. It seemed easier to get pregnant and have a child than to control her mysterious island. Still, it was nice to have someone to talk to about the horrible feeling. And Deidre's wide expression, her broad face, her leaning forward posture made her easy to talk to. Doreena looked at Marilyn's swollen belly.

"Six months," she said, for that was how long her grandfather had been absent and the island had been growing in her life.

"That's not long sweetie," Deirdre smiled. "Keep trying. Does your husband want children too?"

Doreena frowned. Husband? She hadn't even been on a date. Before the island, her life had been all about *The Mirror*. It struck her now what a strange abbreviated life she'd been living. She'd never even thought about having a family of her own or children. Deidre had turned away sensing she'd asked a sensitive question and returned her attention to Marilyn. Marilyn held Doreena's gift. Doreena wondered what was inside. She worried for a moment that she'd done something odd and wrapped up a mango or a seashell. But her gift turned out to be a plush, yellow, pink, and blue patchwork bag covered with pouches and pockets.

"This is perfect," Marilyn pronounced, swinging the bag over her shoulder. "For all his things."

The women cooed agreement.

There were too many gifts. They paused for refreshments. Doreena clutched her little paper plate with its slice of yellow cake. She'd been eating only island food, fruit and coconut water. She hadn't been hungry for anything else. Still, her new dress was snug across her belly, hips, and thighs. She didn't appear to have lost weight. Out of politeness, she dipped thc tines of her fork into the frosting and tasted it. It was lemony in a bottled-up way, like sweetened detergent.

She turned to a shaken Marilyn who was gripping her shoulder for support and tottering. "Excuse me. Just a big kick. Do you want to feel?"

Doreena didn't. There had always been a professional barrier between herself and her boss, and she didn't like the familiar way this new Marilyn kept breaching it. Touching her distended belly seemed disconcertingly intimate, but Marilyn pressed her hand to it anyway. She could feel everything through the thin blouse, the warm swell, the flesh stretched taut over the cushion of water and the undulating life within. The blue haze dropped over her vision, the yellow blouse turning a pale green. The suction surrounded Doreena, but it stretched by extension around Marilyn. She pulled harder to get away, but Marilyn held fast.

"No, it's my place. You'll spoil it," Doreena said, but there was no doubt that the island was embracing Marilyn, too.

As they left, Doreena could see her transparent shell still standing cake in hand, but there's was nothing left of Marilyn in C-town. Her billowing yellow blouse, skirt and matching undergarments dropped to the floor. She simply vanished.

They arrived on the beach together. The colors of the day were peach, dusk rose, and tawny brown. Marilyn was naked except for the double strand of pearls around her neck and the baby bag still slung over her shoulder. Her hair was loose. Whatever clasp had secured it at her neck had been left behind with her clothing. Her belly marbled with blue veins and stretch marks soared out in front of her.

Doreena expected Marilyn to be hysterical and order her about in a panic as she often did at *The Mirror*. But Marilyn did not look in the least alarmed. Her face went through a series of expressions Doreena thought were probably quite similar to her own her first time on the island. Marilyn looked delighted holding her arms wide and her palms up to the island sun. A bit of wonderment touched her smile as she gazed at the tranquil sea. Her fingertips curled as though she wanted to grab the edges of the scenery and pull it around her like a blanket. Then a wary expression crossed her face. Doreena looked to the jungle. She listened for the chilling voice, but there was only the sound of waves. She noticed Marilyn's hands on her belly and saw she'd misread the source of her concern.

"No, there's the kick. He's all right. It hasn't hurt him in the slightest," Marilyn said.

She turned to Doreena and stared into her eyes, but it didn't bother Doreena. Her hands hung comfortably at her sides. She didn't worry about how to hold them. Their nudity didn't bother her either. The island had removed the walls between them, and she was at ease with their intimacy.

"It's some kind of fairy tale place, like my grandmother used to read to me. I should be afraid, but I'm not," Marilyn said. "What is this? You've been here before, haven't you?"

"It's the island."

Marilyn looked up and down the bay and then nodded as if this were explanation enough. "What's back there? Through the leaves?"

"There's fruit, really delicious." She took Marilyn's hand in hers, which felt like the most natural thing in the world to do as if they were childhood friends, as if they were children, and led her up the sand to the grove of fruit. As they entered the grove, Doreena spotted a cluster of five-petaled crème-colored flowers among dark green leaves she didn't recognize, but Marilyn did.

"Frangipani," she said. "Like my grandmother used to grow."

The grove was larger now and there were large-leafed banana trees among the pineapples, coconuts, and mangoes. They gorged on fruit and their chins were dripping with juice when the concerned look crossed Marilyn's face again and her hands returned to her belly. "Is this food safe for the baby?"

"I've been eating a lot of it," Doreena said, but it occurred to her as she did it that the fruit could be responsible for her queasiness.

But Marilyn's concern quickly faded. "I can't imagine anything here would hurt him."

She began gathering the fruit and filling the pockets of her baby's tote bag. "In case we need it for the trip out," she said, looking up the red jungle trail. "Is that how we get back?"

Doreena shuddered. "No, we don't go there. I just go. Just like we came."

"You just go. When?"

"There's a little warning. Things get fuzzy."

"Mmm," Marilyn said. "Well, stay close."

"Come on, let's go back to the beach."

They sat hand in hand staring at the waves.

"I still feel like I should be afraid, but I can't be. I'd be perfectly content to sit here forever. There's *waiwai* here. That's Hawaiian for prosperity. *Wai* alone means water. *Waiwai* prosperity. It's the feeling you get from waves, the sound of abundance." Marilyn mopped her brow. "Mmm. I'm getting really hot. How long will we be here? I just start to wonder."

"I can't say. This is longest I've ever stayed. It's usually just quick trips, flashes really. Why don't we go into the water?"

"Is it safe? There aren't sharks or anything?"

"I never thought so. I've just seen little yellow fishes."

They waded in up to their waists. The water magnified Marilyn's pregnancy, the bottom of it billowed out like a pale pink fish, while the top of it broke through the water sitting on the surface a little island of its own.

"I'm still wearing my pearls," Marilyn said, fingering the strand around her neck. "I guess I really never go anywhere without them. What's your necklace?"

Doreena touched the vial between her breasts. "My grandfather."

"Gave it to you?"

"Yes, but it also is him. His ashes." Keeping secrets seemed pointless now.

Marilyn wasn't disturbed. She laughed. "Was he a pixie? Human remains aren't sparkly blue."

"Blue?" Doreena held the vial around her neck up to the sky. It was the same brilliant tourmaline. "It used to be pinker. More like the sand."

Marilyn examined Doreena's necklace. "Ashes are a chalky beige. I have my grandmothers, in an urn. I looked inside once just to see." As she held it, the blue began to bubble. It twisted in the light changing color: blue to green to yellow and silver. The chain slipped into Marilyn's hand, fell through her fingers, and slid through the waves.

Doreena was quickly after it. She dove under the water but lost track of it in her own turbulence. She waited for the water to settle and then swam down scanning the ocean floor. She finally spotted the necklace pressed into the side of a piece of coral and half covered with sand. Only the blue tint on the whiter sand gave it away. It looked so fluid and translucent at first, she thought the glass had broken and grandfather had floated into the sea.

When she surfaced, Marilyn looked afraid. Again, Doreena looked toward the jungle. It was the only part of the island she feared, but the green wall was still and silent.

"Is the baby, OK?" she asked.

"You were gone so long. You didn't come up for air. I thought you'd drowned. I wanted to come after you, but couldn't," she said, putting her hand to her belly.

Doreena inhaled slowly. She put her hand to her chest. She hadn't felt out of breath.

"I found it," she said. "The last link is missing, and the chain's all tangled."

"You can reconnect it to the next one."

They left the water and sat back down on the beach. Doreena held the chain in the air and tried to untangle the tiny knots. She was no longer at ease with Marilyn beside her and couldn't enjoy either the heat or the color. She could feel the other woman waiting like sitting beside someone at a bus stop.

"I guess this is what it must have been like for Rock when we went to Maui. Now that I'm thinking about getting back. I can't enjoy it. He never really liked Maui though. It's no loss for him to cancel the AeroFlux flights."

"I guess the scenery loses a lot in grayscale," Doreena said.

"I imagine. If something happened to you, could I get back? Would I go by myself?"

"I don't know," Doreena said, still struggling with the necklace. She wasn't even sure what would happen now. She thought she should touch Marilyn when she felt the pull back, but the return trip was faster. It offered less warning, and she wasn't sure how it would work with the two of them.

"Give it here," Marilyn said, holding out her hand. "There's a trick to it."

Doreena handed the knotted tangle of silver necklace over; she'd been making it worse. Marilyn put the necklace down on the sand and slid her finger back and forth over the chain several times. Space slowly opened up between the knots. "It wants to untangle, but you have to remove the resistance. It's gravity that keeps the knots bound. When you put it down, they loosen easily."

When the chain was one loose circle again she picked it up and refastened it around Doreena's neck.

As she did so, the blue haze dropped. Doreena touched Marilyn's arm. "It's happening."

Marilyn hugged her, anxious to get back.

Doreena saw her C-town shell in front of her standing in front of an open door with Deidre and the other women. Deidre was shouting and her words began to register between each crash of the waves, "Where...she...don't...disappeared!" With each word the points of her hair fell back and forth sweeping the line of her jaw like a razor. As Doreena clicked into place. The woman's lemony breath hit her face, "Where's Marilyn?"

Doreena realized with embarrassment that they were standing in Marilyn and Rock's bedroom.

Marilyn was nowhere in sight. Had she left Marilyn behind? Could she go back and get her?

Then a woman screamed. "Call an ambulance!"

The women dashed as one to the living room. Doreena behind them. Marilyn stood there completely naked beside the cake table, exactly on top of her discarded clothes. There was a pleasant look of surprise on her face, but the woman behind her; it was Bea Mitchell whose husband, Ed, directed the hospital, looked terrified. "Call an ambulance," she repeated.

"I'm fine. I'm fine," Marilyn said. "I went to lie down for a spell. You know how tiring it gets."

"I saw you disappear," Bea said.

"And your clothes!" Deirde exclaimed.

Marilyn looked down pointedly stepping off her pile of clothes. Doreena scooped them up for her. The indignant women, who knew when they were being lied to, were blocking the hallway to the bedroom so Marilyn slipped into the bath. Her nakedness did seem unnerving to Doreena now, so she waited outside listening to the women whispering. She clutched her necklace afraid it might have slipped off again in the transition. Her queasiness was at a pitch. Her body felt slack on the outside and watery within. She lurched toward the door and pounded on it. Marilyn opened the door as Doreena's mouth began to fill with water. She staggered forward sloshing. She dropped to her knees in front of the toilet and for the first time in her life vomited. Clear fluid streamed into the toilet and left an iridescent sheen on the surface of the water. Doreena's necklace hung over the toilet and inside it was turquoise so bright, even she could not imagine the ashes bore any resemblance to human remains. Behind her Marilyn, clothed again in billowing yellow, was holding back her hair. Her hands were cold on the back of her neck. Doreena felt better now and pushed to her feet. They stared down into the bowl and looked the sparkling, blue fluid. Marilyn tapped the metal lever and the blue swirled away. Watching it go, Doreena felt the loss of it and almost wished she could drink it up again.

"I want to go home," she said, meaning the island.

"Yes, you'd better. You look strange. I'll call a cab," Marilyn said.

"Marilyn," a woman called. "Are you sick? Is the baby, OK?"

In the entryway, the women were standing looking curiously past Marilyn now at Doreena.

"Good news, actually. She's got morning sickness," Marilyn said.

The women looked skeptical, but then another called, "Marilyn, what's this?"

Alexis Sand of Sand Valley Farms had found the baby tote bag filled with illicit island fruit. She had mangoes, guavas, and passion fruit in a ring around her and was holding up a pineapple. "Where'd this come from?"

"I'll explain," Marilyn said.

"Damn right you will," Bea said.

Behind her Deirde was holding a paring knife, there was an orange opening exposed in the mango she was holding and a small smile crossed her face. She began to cut off slices for the other women.

Doreena made for the door, but before she left Marilyn grabbed her arm. Her voice dropped to a whisper. "Come get me. Next time. I want to go again."

In the mirrored elevator on the way down, Doreena peered at her skin again. The bluish tint was even more pronounced. Her dark eye sparkled, a midnight blue. Doreena looked beneath her bandage. Her eye was healed if there had ever really been anything wrong with it. Grandfather had been right hospitals, were just places people saw sickness. She'd stay away from C-town General. She doubted they had a cure for her. Her body was filled with glittering fluid and the inside of her mouth tasted of saltwater taffy.

~ 38 ~

MIRROR ISLAND: TIKI-TIKI

C-town gets island-ized

When Doreena concentrated on her work at *The Mirror*, the strange island-ish feeling inside her, the blue, slish-slosh receded until she felt, for the most part, as solid as she'd ever been. Every time she returned from the island, it got harder to orient herself to C-town or feel as if what happened to her here mattered, so she'd been making an extra effort. Doreena spent more hours at work, even while she was betraying the enterprise secretly selling ads to the underground paper.

Doreena wondered about her grandfather's ashes and began to reconsider all his admonitions and the strange way she'd been raised. Her exposure to other people had been monitored. They'd lived in controlled isolation. C-town had been perfect for them. But why? What had he known? Grandfather had told her not to date, but in his absence, she was finally testing boundaries. They were hers now.

She'd invited that tweedy man from AeroFlux out to lunch, ostensibly to sell an ad. Whether a legitimate one to *The Mirror* or a covert ad to the *C-town Traveler* she hadn't decided yet. Then he'd suggested dinner instead and now she was spending more time than unusual in front of the bathroom mirror styling her hair with a new product from Denrigger's.

An open canister labeled Moonbeam Waves balanced on the edge of her bathroom sink. She left two finger-dip impressions in its glistening surface and smoothed her hair with the gel. A collection of new make-ups gave her features shiny angles. She didn't remember buying these cosmetics or these clothes: a blouse with fluttering silk sleeves and a pleated skirt that flapped at her thighs. She imagined Marilyn's critique, "Women of a certain age weren't meant to wear short skirts." At any rate, the fabrics were too light for the weather. Feeling foolish, she was searching in the closet for a sweater when the knock came.

Earnest stood on the threshold holding a cluster of white carnations pinked by the light filtering into the hall. "For you," he said handing her the flowers.

She had no vases.

"Are you still up for this?" He looked at her uncertainly and she stiffened in an off-kilter, disjointed way that increased her awkwardness. There were expectations here, but she didn't know the dating requirements.

This was why she didn't date: the lack of direction. It wasn't just that her grandfather forbade it. "You don't want to be alone with a young man," he'd said. "They get all kinds of odd ideas about women at this age. Be an independent young person." She'd taken that advice to extremes. Her island trips happened so independently; she couldn't depend upon them herself. Besides, Earnest wasn't exactly a young man. He wouldn't have odd ideas about women. Doreena slipped the carnations into the sink and then stepped into the hall closing the door behind her. She was always doing that kind of thing, she realized, sneaking to avoid attention, the way her grandfather had taught her, instead of just admitting she didn't have a vase.

As they left the building, it was silent: no marimbas. On the street, the sunset dimmed to a clear blue twilight. Earnest held the car door open for her. Inside, it was immaculate and pine scented. When he started the engine, a solemn voice intoned, "Photons are packets of energy. The building blocks of light."

Earnest switched the player off. "Let's try and do this without physics."

"I listen to a lot of audio books, too," Doreena said. "Mostly sales stuff for work. The one I'm listening to now is all about how you have to plan to succeed." It put her at ease to talk about work. She was beginning to identify the stiffness it created inside her, but at least it was familiar. "No, the book says it's not enough to just try. You have to do. You have to execute your strategy for success."

"Execute. Which book is that?"

"It's called Motivational Toolkit."

Earnest laughed. "Doesn't sound very motivating."

"But it is," she said.

"You know, you could be listening to the wrong books. Personally, I say why not plan for failure? You learn more from failure. Besides, then you can be audacious. When we take on something big sometimes all we can do is try. If you aren't willing to fail, you'll never push your boundaries."

Doreena thought of the surfers with their little underground press and a couple of ads trying to influence Rock Traynter's C-town or of herself trying to get to the island. She tried now thinking of the blue haze, willing the island to appear. Nothing came.

"Trying doesn't get you anywhere. It's not enough," she said.

As they crossed the overpass, Doreena shielded her eyes. Downtown glowed. The car passed into a blue haze that reminded her of being pulled to her island, but this haziness persisted. All the light here came from the bottom up, radiating just to the tops of the buildings and leaving the night sky shrouded. On the island, the sun-struck colors were crisp and bright. Here, the buildings were just visible through the aura of phosphors. The city looked coated in a numinous gel giving it a sleek wavy look, like her hair. It bore no relation to the smog-stained despair of buildings she passed through every day on her bus ride home. They passed beneath Traynter Tower in the city center. A deep purple veiled its windowed face. Its black light cast a halo of glowing white storefronts around it.

"It's a one newspaper town. I like working at *The Mirror*. C-town is the only place in the United Government that has any stability. I think we'd be crazy to give that up," Doreena said, continuing the argument she'd been having with herself while Earnest parked.

"Look, on the left," Earnest said. "Are you sure you want to go to The Watertown?"

The Tiki-Tiki Room was the brightest spot on Beaumont Avenue. The war for C-town's ideology was being fought in phosphorescence and this was the front of Gavin Traynter and the surfers' resistance. The Tiki-Tiki tangle of phosphors hid any businesses beside it and outshone even Bette's Boutique, Night and Day Chocolate and Coffee, and Sand's Corner Drugstore. Jungle vines glowed around the golden luau font letters: Tiki-Tiki. White flowers spun along the sides. A red and blue flashing parrot pointed at the entrance with its beak. Cars lined Beaumont. Earnest circled and found a free parking space down an alley a few blocks away. The butcher paper cover over the front window was gone and the name was lettered across the glass in slim luau font. Diners milled beyond Tiki-Tiki.

"I can't go in there," Doreena said.

"How can you not?" Earnest said. "Look at them."

The place was packed with people wearing palm frond and flower blossom patterned shirts and shifts. Many cradled fishbowls and sucked red, white, or blue beverages out of them through wide straws. All were laughing.

"I could seriously lose my job just for stepping inside," Doreena said.

"Ridiculous," Earnest said, and held the door open for her. "You can't be fired for eating out."

As she stepped inside, Petey, the animatronic parrot, squawked and trained his cold eye on her. A muggy heat embraced them with layered scents of baked salt and floral spice. A greeter in a plastic grass skirt placed plastic leis over their heads and led them to a table by the window. She handed them menus shaped like tiki idols. The wicker chairs crackled as they sat.

Earnest removed his tweed jacket. Underneath, he wore a short-sleeved work shirt. "Are you going to be too warm?"

Doreena's silk sleeves fluttered below the heater. She was comfortably dressed as if she planned to come here. "Just right, actually."

The place seemed to be trying hard to engage C-town's dormant senses. Gavin Traynter had taken her advice and acquired a lot of relics from The Travel Museum to add to his décor. But for all its brightness, the place was a pale imitation of her island.

"This place reminds me of Imagination Land," Earnest said. "The treehouse with all the singing birds? Come on, I'm not that much older than you. Before the border closed, your parents never took you down the 'Way?"

"My grandfather raised me," she said releasing a sugary scent as she poked at the wax candle adorning their table.

"Well, he took you then. No? Never?"

"We were pretty serious people." She looked up at the painted ceramic birds dangling over each table. "One person's paradise is another's nightmare, he always said."

The menu was boring. It was the same fancied up fish and chips fare that was served at The Watertown. But Gavin, a bartender by trade, had tried to make up for it with the drink menu renaming old standards to fit the Tiki-tiki theme. There was a long list of specialty drinks from Kill the Pig to Voodoo Cannibal.

The waiter interrupted. "Start with drinks?"

Earnest looked at her expectantly. Her grandfather had forbidden drinking too. "Lowers the inhibitions. Makes people do stupid things," he'd said. But it seemed to be something adults did on dates. She was keeping the waiter waiting. When she finally looked up, it took her a few seconds to recognize Alonso in a shirt patterned with orange surfboards hanging down over black slacks. She was used to his wetsuit.

He winked at her. "Hey, lookin' especially *wahine*."

"You too," she said. "You look good in clothes."

Earnest coughed. "Maybe a bottle of wine?"

"Nah, not here," Alonso said. "You want The Great White." He pointed mid-menu and winked again.

"OK, two Great Whites," Earnest said.

"No, one," Alonso said, making a note of it. "Share. You need more, we'll move you up to The Flaming Great White." He winked again. "Don't worry, you can handle one great white. Tiger sharks are the real killers."

When he left them, Ernest bent low over the table. "I meant to tell you; you do look beautiful tonight. I mean, especially."

"It's not me, really," Doreena said.

Alonso returned and placed a huge fishbowl between them. A toy surfer floated on its frothy blue surface.

"Is this what we ordered?" Earnest asked. "The great white? It's blue."

"Yeh, Curaçao," Alonso said. "Now, look in there, and give me a moment."

They bumped heads over the bowl as they lifted up out of their chairs to look in. The tiny surfer even had hibiscus patterned board shorts.

"Sharks. In the ice cubes," Doreena said.

"Make room," Alonso said. He poured shots into the drink from on high, brandished two thick straws and stirred. The shark-shaped ice clinked as the white syrup swirled through the blue. The little surfer boy rocked.

"Hang ten, lil' dude." Alonso said and left them.

Doreena grabbed her straw and sucked. "Coconut liqueur."

"Strong," Earnest said.

They ordered the codfish special, and the food arrived on large blue plates in bamboo holders. It was covered in a chunky red and orange sauce with a golden sheen to it.

"So, your grandfather raised you?"

Doreena clutched her necklace and sipped on the drink. Earnest moved bits of fish from one side of his plate to the other. "I work at AeroFlux. I'm an engineer. It's an interesting place." He paused.

When she didn't respond, he said. "So, I know you're in sales and not much else."

"Well, there's not much else."

"No?"

"No," she said.

He would have made a terrible salesman. His body language was exactly opposite of the confident sales posture Marilyn had taught her. His shoulders were slumped, his eyes were downcast, and his hands were hidden under the table fumbling, she imagined, with his palm frond patterned napkin. He was persistent though; give him that.

"So, speaking of hopes and dreams...what are your passions, uh, um, do you have any hobbies? I mean what do you like to do?"

Doreena sucked down the last of the Great White. The surfer boy tipped against the side. "Pretty much this."

She wondered what kind of conversation they would have been having if she were on the island. What kinds of things would she have said? This would be so much easier if she weren't here. Earnest stopped trying to get her to talk instead launching into a long explanation of physics. The drink had been good. She wanted another. She could feel herself growing warmer from the inside out.

"So, it looks like we're ready to move up to The Flaming Great White?" Alonso said the next time he checked on them.

It turned out to be an event drink. Alonso pulled them over to the bar counter. The buoyant accordions ceased, replaced by ominously slinking cellos.

"We didn't want to make a fuss," Earnest protested.

"Too late," Alonso said.

Gavin Traynter came out of the kitchen in his orange and red smeared apron. "Ah, my favorite saleswoman," he said. "I forgive you your employer." He tossed a towel embossed with a parrot over his shoulder. "Everyone gather round," he bellowed.

All around, diners abandoned their plates and circled the bar. Gavin lined up shots in layered colors like a sunrise in front of Doreena. "Suck them down as fast as possible before I light the last one," he instructed waving a tiki-torch shaped lighter down the row of shots. Her eyes followed the flame. The crowd chanted, "Shark, shark." Earnest gripped her elbow. She sucked and swallowed in a boozy rush and then Gavin lit the final float of cherry brandy on top. It flared up and out and then he dropped another little surfer boy on top of it, into the drink. He landed on the turbulent froth of baked waves, ice cube sharks clinking beneath him.

Doreena rocked. The people around her grew hazy. Her skin felt sucked loose like the approach of the island. She already felt warm and far away. She looked for the oncoming waves but saw only the reflection of the bottles and the glasses hanging against the mirrored bar. The bar-goers began to sing. The waves of the song rushed over her. She swayed. They swayed. A swish of grass skirts. Feathers floated down from the ceiling. The parrots, macaws, and mourning doves on their perches over the diners cawed and cooed. This was the best she'd ever felt off island. It was as if she had brought it here with her.

Petey squawked. The swaying stopped. Silence. Space opened up around her, except for Earnest at her back. She carried the song on out into the void, "Your own special hopes, your own special dreams, loom on the hillside, and shine near the streams."

Rock Traynter, the silencing force, the crowd scatterer, looked down on her. He removed one pair of sunglasses. Underneath he wore another, and another, and another and another, as if he had no eyes.

"That's my boss," she said to Earnest. She stared up at the now silent ceramic birds. He'd chased the island away.

"Hey, my brother finally comes to check it out," Gavin said. "A drink, man? No? How about dessert?"

Rock turned from her. Just above his collar, the hair on the back of his neck was trimmed in a neat dark line. "I'm not here to stuff my face."

"Well, it's a restaurant, Rock. That's my business: feed the people. So, how's about it, everyone? In honor of this visit from C-town's illustrious publisher, the one and only, oh, well, not the only game in town anymore. Dessert on the house. Alonso, bring out my new cake. There's plenty to share. How's life in a two-paper town?"

There was a tremulous flapping of nervous applause. Rock stared down the last of the diners until it stopped.

Doreena plucked the surfer boy from the bottom of the glass and licked the last of the burned boozy foam off of his surfboard.

"Do they make these in *wahines*?" she said leaning into Earnest.

Rock barreled toward her. In a black suit, he looked tall as Traynter Tower. He walked past rocking her into Earnest. "Marilyn!"

The crowd parted and towards the back by the kitchen Doreena saw Marilyn in a flaming red dress. A man helped her up from her chair. The dress' plunging neckline drew attention from her distended belly.

"That's my other boss and that's..." Doreena recognized the AeroFlux executive. "That's yours." She said to Earnest. Then she giggled. "Hey, it's like a double date at work."

"Shhh," Earnest said.

Alonso passed out small plates. Slices of her island's contraband mango were splayed over creamy cheesecake tops.

Rock steered Marilyn by. His hand just under the cap of her sleeve made a red band where he gripped her. He pulled her to the bar. "Nice place, Gav. Mom and Dad would be proud. No wait. They wouldn't. And here's our number one salesman."

"She's here on her own time, Rock." Marilyn said.

"Own time? The job's 24-7, keeping this place together," He raised his voice. "Maybe you don't get it. Maybe you're a little too content if you want to risk it all to play at exotics. When's the last time you were out on the 'Way? If C-town isn't good enough, maybe you've forgotten. None of us have our own time or it all unravels."

Rock's face was red around his shades. Doreena peered up at him. What color were his eyes? Steel gray? She touched the lei around her neck and felt the skin soft petals of frangipani. The five petals opened toward her like a hand. She removed it and held it up to Rock on tiptoes. "Any night, any day. In your heart you will hear it. Come away. Come away. Here am I your own special island come to me. Come to me."

"You're drunk," he said shrugging the lei off his shoulder, so the flowers slipped to the floor.

"I want to see your eyes," she said. "Are they purple? Green? I'm so sorry, you can't see all the beautiful colors. You're colorblind."

"And you're worthless. Don't come in Monday. You're fired," Rock said. He stomped on the flowers as he pulled Marilyn to the door. An island perfume rose. Rock yelled at Marilyn on the street in front of his pea green car.

"I finally get it," Doreena said. "C-town's like an island."

"Let's go," Earnest said.

Doreena reached into her purse as Earnest pulled her to the door. She held up the last mango. "Who wants mango cheese-cake?"

She lobbed the forbidden fruit toward the bar. Gavin caught it in one hand.

Earnest supported her on the way to the car. By the time they reached it, she was feeling cold and steady inside again. The drink and the island feeling were fading.

"Do we have to go? I want to go back." The tear she wiped from the end of her nose sparkled. They pulled up in front of the Nar-borough. "No. I don't want be alone. Take me to your place."

"I'm sorry," Earnest said. He walked her to her door.

"Come in," she begged.

"No," he said. "That wouldn't be gentlemanly. Here. Alonso said you should have this."

He handed her a birdcage covered in a buttoned up Hawaiian shirt patterned with orange boards. When Earnest left she peered underneath. Inside, the parrot slept. Petey's feathers were sleek, shiny, and very real.

~ 39 ~

MIRROR ISLAND: SURFING

Wallowing in the island and taking a lover

On the first day of unemployment, Doreena got up and dressed as usual. She craved *The Mirror* and her routine. Nothing could be more frightening than spending day after day aimlessly in C-town without her position or people: Rock, Marilyn, Tom, the Force. It sickened her to think of it, but there was no sparkling blue fluidity to her illness now. Her mouth was dry. Her stomach tight. It was as if there were sand caught in her chest and throat. She felt strange inside, shifting, as though she could crumble from the inside out.

Meanwhile, Petey preened. The stiff robotic thing had been transformed. Instead of carrying her away last night, a bit of the island had crept over and remade Petey as people imagined him to be — alive. His orange beak clacked against the bars of his cage as he bit at it. She pushed a few slices of mango into his cage remembering how last night the Tiki-Tiki lounge had changed. At first, she'd just felt woozy with the effects of the monster drink. Fishbowls! Only Gavin Traynter would serve alcohol in fishbowls. Then it had felt like the island was approaching, but instead of pulling her away the suction had settled over everything around her. Momentarily, there had been real flowers and birds and probably a grove of fruit back behind the kitchen doors and even the air quality had changed from a stale heat to a fresh circulating warmth.

Rock's entry had swept the island out, but Petey was proof that it was more than a mirage or a hallucination or a drunken moment. And if the parrot was real, then that sloshing feeling inside herself might be, too. Whatever it was, it wasn't comfortable. There was something ominous hidden inside her that she didn't want to explore too deeply, like whatever was behind the wall of jungle green on the island.

"Leave C-town alone, Petey," she said to the bird. "I want to go away, not bring my island here."

She went downstairs and waited for the bus. The uniformity of the street made it easy to pretend it was just another day, until Alonso arrived and stood beside her in his wetsuit. It was always jolting seeing him there dressed like that. When the bus lurched forward, she surfaced, startled, from her thoughts.

"I broke *The Mirror.* I'm broke."

"Don't talk like a regular," Alonso said.

"Where am I going?"

"Surfing, I figure. You brought your board." He swung a dingy yellow board out from behind his blue one and leaned it against her. "My old one."

She leaned her head against it. The peeling corners of the Sex Wax sticker tickled her cheek. The bus was lit by florescent blue overhead. The marshlands outside the windows were dark. The surface of the muck-covered lake, she imagined, was just starting to gleam like a greasy curry as the sun rose. "Surfing, you figure?"

"What else."

"I'll freeze."

He dropped a suit across her lap. She recoiled from its flailing neoprene appendages.

"No, you'll just look like an elephant. What? All baggy-skinned. What? It'll be too long for you."

At the park, Doreena stripped off her wool work clothes and pulled on the clinging wetsuit. Its faded rippled skin stretched over her own. It hugged her, holding her upright. She felt straighter, although it sagged a bit about her waist and neck. With effort, straining against thick, sticky material, she pushed up the sleeves and cuffed the legs. Her feet were bare on the pebbled beach as she waded into the sinking sludge at the shore.

"It's cold. It's gross."

"No, it's a kind of beautiful. Like you in that suit."

"Thanks, I feel like a toad."

It was odd the way, as she entered the lake, the wetsuit kept the water away from her skin, but she could still feel the waves moving around her. She was there, but not there, in, but not submerged, cool, but not cold, insulated from everything. It hid her porous skin. Only her feet and her hands treaded through the chemical-laced lake. She learned to keep her mouth closed so the putrefied algae never touched her tongue. It tasted digested like it smelled.

She never managed to stand up on the board. Alonso didn't give her much in the way of instruction. He was into his own thing, after his own stoke. She could barely see the dull ripples that kept him spired above his board. Left alone Doreena lay on her belly, and, with nothing better to do and no distraction, could not help but contemplate her insides. She began thinking about her grandfather and her parents, whomever they might be, and then about The Force and work, her surrogate family. Who would she be without *The Mirror*? Yet, her thoughts cycled round and round to her own belly distended beneath her and what was inside it: the thing that sometimes felt hard like a stone, grainy as sand or fluid like ocean. Only the thin board lay between her and the gray water. Feeling heavy now, she imagined sinking down into it, the board, and then, the lake.

Alonso came back to her, buoyant with stoke, whatever that was. To him, it was nothing that she'd lost that job, a bad piece of work anyway. So, for a while with him she was untroubled because that's what he saw and expected. Although what she noticed about being with him now was that for the most part, he didn't think about her at all very much or have really any expectations. This left her free to drift — or it left her adrift. She was musing on whether this was good or not. She was used to her grandfather and *The Mirror*. She was used to being held in place.

When she returned to her apartment that afternoon, her clothes were piled in the hallway outside along with her box of photographs and the caged parrot. A red post-it stuck to the door of C-4 said, "Eviction notice." This was Rock's revenge. She'd always known he had that power to take away her livelihood and her home. Alone, with her head in a fog after grandfather's death, it had taken forever to move all the boxes. Her stuff didn't look like much now: wool suits and sweaters, tattered photos under broken glass and the addition of the mangy parrot. He looked like he was in rapid decline for lack of some tropical nutrient. His feathers were faded and loose around his eyes, so his dimpled skin showed as he blinked at her. She picked up the photos and the cage and went downstairs.

Alonso opened his door in a swirl of blue sandalwood smoke. She'd caught him in his black pants and Tiki-Tiki shirt on his way to work.

"I saw all your stuff," he said and waved her in. "No problem. I have plenty of room so long as I make rent."

Actually, his apartment was smaller: a studio with one large window facing the promise of C-town sun. It was cluttered with jade, soapstone, and wood figurines, leering painted masks and fibrous painted mats on the floor and walls. It looked a lot like The Travel Museum, un-C-town, off continent, and vaguely illegal. The mattress rested on the floor covered by yellow and brown batik. Doreena sat and examined the split ends of her curls.

"I can't keep it together."

"The bird can stay, but the cage has to go," he said.

She heard the latch spring and flapping. A couple of red feathers floated in front of her. Petey'd shit all over, but, whatever, it wasn't her place.

"And I don't care."

"I hear that," Alonso said. "Tiki-Tiki is booming. Happy customers. You need something to get by, I can ask Gavin for you."

"About a job?"

"Yeah, work. I don't recommend it. You can totally squat here, but I'm not staying. I'm on the last flight out."

"Maui," she scoffed. "It doesn't matter. All I want is the island. It's all I think about. Never mind."

"Tell," he said. "I like islands."

"It's out of control, really short trips, like dreams, but full-color, full-feeling, texture, breezes." She stopped.

"Maui?"

She shook her head. "Somewhere else, and I bring things back with me: sand, fruit, flowers."

"Mangoes?"

"Yes, the mangoes."

"Good surf?"

"Blue. Waves taller than Lake Traynter."

"Sold. Let's go." He grabbed the two boards, blue and yellow, leaning against the wall.

"You don't get it. I can't control it. I just go."

"Take me." He dropped the board on the bed and sat behind her with his legs around her. "Try now."

"You aren't going to work?"

"I've time."

"You believe me?"

"'Course, there's the mangoes, this parrot, and you. You seem like you've got some secret. Besides, this is just the kind of thing I believe. I've got to. You say you're going to whisk me away to paradise, I say, yeah."

Alonso breathed on her neck, and it made her skin hum. If she stayed here, it would be on the batik in his bed. It didn't matter whether he liked her, especially. He'd take whatever wave came in to ride and here she was, the next set. It was like he'd made his life easier by deciding in advance: Be with willing people, believe good things.

In a weird way, this reminded her a lot of how her grandfather lived. He'd made a lot of their decisions, a lot of *her* decisions, ahead of time so that there was no need to evaluate anything on a case-by-case basis. Grandfather's rules were just different: Avoid everyone. Don't believe anything. One of his rules had been to avoid situations like these. He'd been frank about sex, curt and clear. He'd described the physiology of the act in all its anatomical correctness. "But that's not the part that concerns me, the normal, healthy human body functioning of a young woman. That's fine. The part that concerns me is what no one ever mentions. It's the part that happens to your brain, the neurochemical reaction. Sex changes your chemistry. It changes you inside. It bonds you to another person. In a way you may not, you won't, be able to control and that will happen no matter who it is, no matter how wrong for you. No one will tell you that it changes you forever. It changes people's chemistry. It bonds you to people before you have a chance to make up your mind about them. You can't be yourself and have sex, before you know it you'll be someone else."

Grandfather's intensity on this point had frightened her, as had her schooling with its graphic and intentionally scary depictions of birth, so that she'd never even been in a situation like she was now. Alonso had his hand on her neck, but it felt like he was stroking her inside, reaching into her as though she were a puppet, making her insides buzz and hum. The incense smoke in the apartment grew opaque and shiny. The blue haze settled in and the suction throbbed. Alonso's arms tightened around her even before she said, "Hold on. We're going."

The sun touched her face and shoulders in warm welcome. The ocean cast its breath across the shore. The waves sucked in and sighed through the sand. Alonso's chest rose and fell against her back. Her eyes squeezed tight; orange glowed through her lids. Would he still be there when she opened her eyes? He was. His eyes, blue-green with golden flecks, watched the sea. The boards were behind him. They'd arrived. She'd never seen his face so smooth with all the creases filled in. In C-town his skin had a gray cast to it like everyone's. Here, he looked golden. Watching him was even better than staring at the surf or sun. He reflected joy. The breeze flowed through every golden strand of hair on his arms, chest, and thighs. She'd brought him bare-skinned.

She quivered inside warm, ripe, and juicy as island fruit. She wanted him to want her as much as he wanted those waves. She stretched her arms out to him and put her hands on his thighs. "Change me inside," she said.

He didn't even look to wonder at that. He was even more overcome by the island than Marilyn had been on her first time. He was too enchanted by the island to be afraid or question anything. This worked to Doreena's advantage, since she'd decided to have him. Her insides were messed up anyway. Sex with Alonso could only make them better. She wanted what he had: that easy happiness and some sense of internal peace. If nothing else, it'd be a chemistry experiment. He held her shoulders for balance. He stroked her sides and his hands, like hibiscus blossoms, covered her breasts. Then he pushed her down onto the sand soft as fine sugar and pink. He moved her up and down against it. She felt like she was being polished like the stones on the ocean floor. When he came, trembling, staring at the waves, she rolled over and sat astride him. Then she watched the waves and rocked them both until their smooth backs and thighs blushed with sand and the raw skin underneath clung to it like a new covering. Now Doreena felt she would stay on the island forever.

"If we brought the boards, couldn't we have brought clothes?" she asked.

"Didn't think of it," he said. "I'm not too attached to mine."

The waves were cresting higher. Alonso reached for his boards. "I've got to get out there."

He handed one to her, but she was in no hurry. He waded into the water. She watched him stroke out to sea and catch some waves, riding high. She sat and the sun, always high in the sky when she arrived, now moved through the sky. When Alonso returned to land, it was late afternoon. He stretched his lean torso. She took his hand and led him back to the jungle trail and showed him the grove of fruit. The voice was silent. They ate banana and pineapple.

"We're still here," she said.

"So where? An island?"

"I've never been further from the beach than this."

He held up a mango, a different kind than she'd seen before, a lighter color. "This is a Bombay. You can only get these on Jamaica, which this isn't. This is some magic place."

"It's not real?"

He shrugged. "Real as paradise. Real enough for me and plenty to eat. Come on. It's time for your lesson. You've never actually caught waves. There wasn't much stoke to be had on the lake. Not really."

"You went there every day."

"I've traveled the world looking for the best waves. I didn't stop in C-town because I found them, I just got caught. Stuck. But stoke is stoke. You do what you have to do to be good wherever you are. Don't be miserable, that's the plan."

Carrying both surfboards, he led her into the water. "Lay on your stomach. Imagine you are moving buckets through the water with your hands."

Doreena paddled mid-inlet on her board and then lay with her cheek on it, feet dangling in the water, rocking on the waves the sun stroking her back. She peered through her fingers, squinting past the sun at Alonso bobbing beside her. He sat up, the board between his legs, looking out to sea and the setting sun. If she saw the island at night, Doreena was sure she'd stay forever. The sun struck only the far side of each two-tone wave. One side captured the shimmering light. The other looked dark and elusive with unknown depths.

"Could there be sharks?" she asked.

Alonso shrugged. "Well, it's the kind of water they like. Warm. Could be anything in a place like this. I think this place is a tulpa. Something I learned about in the Himalayas, in the mountains, BC, before C-town."

"I can't see you in the mountains," she said.

"I didn't like it much. It was cold, heavy. It didn't matter how many layers of gear you had on. The place had a cold heart, no escaping it. I stank too. That was the worst," he said. "Out here, the sun bakes you clean and the sea salt is pure. There, man, I was trapped in a bulky coat with my own bacteria. I could smell them eating off me, getting nice and full."

"Why go?"

"A pilgrimage. My friend said the mountains would be like waves, but taller. The lack of oxygen would be like being underwater but face up. They say there's kind of a euphoria that comes with drowning. It's all about the stoke."

"I don't get that. I don't even know what you mean."

"Sure, you do," he said, still looking at the sea. "What's to get? It's when you are in exactly the right place and time. That's all."

"The Himalayas don't sound right."

"This one night made it. We reached camp on a plateau. We pitched our tent and lit a fire in this charred rock ring. It was a place on the locals' route. We made this tea the locals had given us and spiked it with grog, a local brew, the kind that tastes toxic at first, but then you keep on and there's nothing better. That's what I miss, tasting places: curried pineapple in South Africa, Blue Mountain coffee in Jamaica, mochi in Kyushu. Every shore has its flavor. You can't import it. That was it. That night, just sitting around that campfire. Jeanne called it our trip to Shangri-La. Man, she was a cool girl."

"A girlfriend?" Doreena said. The jealous edge to her voice was unmistakable. So, the sex had done something different to her, just like grandfather had warned. But Alonso didn't seem to notice. He was lost in the Himalayas.

"Yeah. I was the one who'd always said, 'Don't mistake a woman for the stoke. She can be in it, but she never is it.' Then I followed Jeanne into the hills. I lost all cred with my mates, but she was a mad wave rider. All the surfer girls are wild, but she was fearless and then she'd crash down afterwards on the sand, like a sea cat, wouldn't move for anything. Whatever she was doing, she was all in."

"What happened?" Doreena asked.

"We were sitting by the fire. The moon rose with a blue aura around it and these sherpa stepped out of the fog. They were little men, but in these huge yak hides. They joined us by the fire. We shared grog. They were probably our age, but they looked older, wiser with weathered skin, you know. One of the guys had a gap in the front row of his teeth, like he'd lost one to a yak hoof or something. They started telling stories, in English. They must have been guides. They sounded all prophetic the way people do when they choose their words carefully. So, Gap Man says, 'You heard of the village, Vitskaya. They make thought monsters there, like yetis.

They are always thinking there, to keep warm. The tulpas like fog to hide in.' It was so weird. I remember it, exactly."

"I mean, what happened with Jeanne."

Alonso shrugged. "We split at the village. She wanted to stay. I went back to Thailand. My wave bros were merciless, said I'd missed some of the best Thai sets they'd ever seen. So. But my point is, this place feels like a tulpa. Maybe the surfers made it, you know, drummed it into being. We've all been dreaming of a place like this."

Even Doreena noticed the approaching swell, the one that made him swing to his belly on the board. He pivoted and she was looking at the soles of his feet. The wrinkled arcs would fit perfectly in the palms of her hands. She paddled after him pressing buckets through the water and making progress.

"The surfers," Doreena scoffed. She didn't like what he'd said about her island being a manifestation of the surfers' dreams. With Marilyn and Alonso's visits, there were fruits and flowers on the island she had never seen before and it looked much less like her few memories of Maui than it had, but it was still her island.

"Maybe your girlfriend was the tulpa."

She rose as he did when the wave was nearly on them. She clutched the sides of the board lifting up with the wave and then standing. It rose faster and higher with her on top. Up over the sea, her steady haunches held her in place while her torso soared. A sound like a gull's cry escaped her. She sped behind the waves' white emissaries over the rippling expanse of blue gliding toward her island and its pink sand shore. She looked down, in love with the sea that carried her forward, and wobbled. The board dropped away in a moment. She smacked the water. Her neck bent. The emissaries beat her down. Her shoulders scraped hard. Her cheeks bulged with sea. She thrashed and opened her eyes spinning in the wave, twisting toward the light. Pain braced her right arm when she reached for it. She struck out with her left through dark bubbles, then light-filled ones, until she breached, spat seawater and sucked air. Her back stung. The island had turned on her.

Opaque water flowed around her. The horizon held remnants of sun. This was the darkest the island had ever been. A few escaping rays touched the tops of the palms in the distance. Around her the sea lay like black glass, as though she were swimming in the mirrored reflection of the boardroom table in The Meat Locker or in the glass surface of Traynter Tower. She went cold inside. Where it didn't burn, her skin cooled beneath the water. Her face radiated heat. She draped her arm over the surfboard floating by, then jerked back. Not her board. Sharp leather hide sliced her forearm. Purple clouds billowed in the water around her. A torpedo-shape sped toward her and the pointed snout of a shark slid by. Its body followed — a bolt of lavender with black racing stripes. The creature's dot of an eye passed over her as it swayed. Doreena blew out all her breath and sank. The shark snapped around. Then she was clamped onto her and dragged her through the sea. She struck its nose. It released her and she surfaced. The breeze flowed over her cheeks. It clenched her waist and pushed her thigh. He pushed. She looked into Alonso's eyes. They'd turned an anxious green.

"Get up on the board," he said.

They were still in the water with the shark.

"Get up on it. We'll ride out."

She slunk onto the board. He crawled on behind her, half on top of her, his heaving breaths pressing her back. He swam, his limbs in the sea with the swaying shark. The lighter moving patches of water with hidden teeth flowed around them. Doreena clung to the board and willed the shore closer. The blue haze buzzed. "It's ok. It's happening. We're going back."

She reached back for Alonso's hand, but he twisted out of her grip. He slipped off the board, shooting her forward. "Nah, I'll take my chances. Been waiting for this a long time."

The waves behind her were black-tipped fins. Ahead of her were peaks of brown and yellow batik. Then, she was alone on the bed. At some point, she'd have to look and see how much of her was missing. She tried to steady herself to see tangles of torn flesh. She'd heard the warning once: "Shock can kill you."

When she looked, there were just the usual rolls of pale stomach and sprawled legs, intact. Her right arm, more or less the correct shape, was swollen into a disproportionate lump of fierce reds and blues. It would have looked natural on the ocean floor with urchins. But she was not broken or mauled. She was naked, soaking wet with her lips still salty. It had been that close. The cuts on her back where the coral had scraped it raw bled onto the batik.

She stayed in bed all day, and the next, waiting for the island return and thinking about Alonso. The light cycled through shades of lavender: lavender-twilight, lavender-yellow, lavender-orange, lavender-dusk to black orchid night slowly, frequently she was sure, but the blue haze, the fuzzy sheen, it never came. She lay limply, neither hungry nor tired, breathing shallow breaths. She thought of the rolls of her stomach fleshy from sales calls and office sitting. It had been weeks since she'd eaten much and days now since she'd eaten anything, but her body stayed the same. It didn't change.

She lay and waited for the island to return. The waiting hurt. She couldn't make the island come. She couldn't get back to Alonso. She couldn't control it. At one point she heard shuffling at the door and against it. Then she heard voices outside, Alonso's surfer friends. She didn't get up to open the door. She just sprawled. Maybe the sex had changed her inside and she'd never see the island again. Maybe he'd stolen it from her, and she'd lost her grandfather, *The Mirror*, and the island.

Later, a steady pounding awoke her from a nightmare of being shaken in the shark's maw. It wrangled her out of her prone position. She wrapped the bloodstained batik around her. When she got up to answer the door, her legs and arms were stiff as planks.

Hobart stood at the door; her hand red from knocking. "We haven't seen you in a while. I didn't know you were here. C-town in there?"

"Alonso's gone." Doreena said. "He's not coming back."

"He wouldn't head down the 'Way by himself. Oh, had enough cash for that last flight to Maui, did he?"

Doreena shrugged.

"That woman's been looking for you." Hobart pointed at a red notice stuck to the door. "You see this? You know you can't stay here."

Doreena bent her head in her hands. Her curls felt stiff too. "I'm not leaving." The island would have to come and get her.

"The wrecking ball comes through that window Monday morning either way," Hobart said, pushing the door in."

"Gads, vile smell. What's that?"

Doreena turned toward the stench of decay behind her. Petey lay on the floor, one sunken eye looking up at her from his featherless head. She had neglected to feed him.

"Grab your wetsuit," Hobart said. "I'm getting you out of here."

~ 40 ~

MIRROR ISLAND: DROWNING

Finding a way to control the island and populating it with men

With Hobart's solid influence, Doreena at last left Alonso's apartment. She met the surfers on the shores of Lake Traynter. Their company gave her a fluid feeling. They greeted her casually, and then paid little mind to her. The surfers stayed together, but each occupied his own space and was there for his own reasons. They were all doing the same thing but had arrived at the decision to do so independently. She hadn't thought she would ever miss Marilyn's scrutiny and firm direction, but she did. Mostly, she missed the structure and discipline of *The Mirror*, the way the work gave her a purpose and held her in place. The surfers had no expectations of her. They were companionable, but distant. They didn't mind that she was there and wouldn't notice if she left, but at least coming to the lake with them gave her a place to be and something to do.

"We're here every morning," Hobart said. "A lot of us hold odd jobs or own our own businesses, but we make them work around this. This is where we have to be and then the rest of the day goes fine."

"How about the *Traveler*?" Doreena said.

"It's not making much of an impact. C-town seems the same as it ever was. But we have to make the effort. They've got to keep drumming. It's part of us living our lives the best we can while we're stuck here."

Doreena didn't want to go into the water. The lake never looked appealing, and she was still afraid of sharks. There couldn't be any in that cold, gray water, but it was so dark below the surface that she wouldn't be sure what lay beneath. She wanted her clear island ocean. This dingy, rancid water did not compare. Why should she enter this when the island might come at any moment? It was still fresh in her mind and her longing for it occupied her thoughts. There had to be a way, something she could do to make it come, to get back there.

She sat on the bench beside the lake and watched the surfers, encased in black, solemnly laying their boards across the best waves C-town had to offer. The outfits looked ridiculously alien on the streets of C-town or on the bus, but they had a regal quality like a kind of armor here. She had been sitting here watching them in the mornings for a few days when J-Bay, one of the youngest surfers, came out of the water and sat beside her. He looked like a younger more compact version of Alonso. He had the same dingy blond hair and lithe build, but a shorter torso. His face was smooth and lacked the creases Alonso had at the corners of his eyes. It made J-Bay hard to read.

All the surfers were difficult that way. They had languid hands. They didn't gesture with them when they talked. Their hands rested on their kneecaps or hung by their sides unless they were surfing or drumming. J-Bay's hands were on his knees now. There was a coat of bronze hair across the backs except where the scar cut across his right hand. He leaned on the bench, and it held him propped with his legs stretched out across the sparse grass.

"I don't blame C-town for leaving," J-Bay said.

It took Doreena a moment to remember that he meant Alonso. Alonso's name was wherever he was. She wondered what it would be on her island.

"He's not C-town anymore," she said.

"I thought we were all going to go together. I mean, it happens all the time. Somebody just gets it in their head and goes to whatever surf spot they've heard of and they might tell someone or just go because they get called to a break. It was like that for me once at the cape. I just left and went to Durban. I didn't even tell A-Bay and he's my twin. It was like I had to. A-Bay got choked on that, but he caught me up later and he understood. It happens. But this here, has been different. We've all been stuck since Westport and that bad luck. I thought all for one, one for all, you know. For now, while we're all here, surfing this trash lake. That's what the underground was for, making cash for the Maui flight, for all of us. Then, Rock goes and cancels that way out, too. So, I guess we've all lost, except Alonso."

J-Bay's hands were as loose as ever over his knees, but his voice betrayed tension. Doreena felt a pull across her chest and recognized it as a strain from her new connection with Alonso. She'd been jealous of Alonso's old girlfriend and now she wanted to protect Alonso from J-Bay's bitterness.

"It's not his fault. He didn't go to Maui."

"No? Well, where is he?"

Doreena shrugged and now she heard her own bitterness. She wondered if Alonso, on his end, had spared a thought for her at all. "I don't know the name of the place. My grandfather never took me out of C-town."

"Sorry for you. Sometimes, I hate this place."

He said it with passion, but Doreena marveled at how still his body remained. His hands had moved from the meditative posture over his knees to the bench beside him, but there was no tension in them. They lay like the rest of his body. How did the surfers do it? Doreena was sure she never looked that relaxed except maybe on the island. When she imagined herself, she was always standing at attention beside Marilyn's desk with her hands clenched behind her back to keep them from aimless fluttering. She wasn't laid back like the surfers, except when she'd been with Alonso. Doreena put her hand on top of J-Bay's. It was different than touching Alonso, but similar. Her body eased as her focus moved to the place where their hands touched. Alonso had wanted to see the island. He'd touched her and they'd gone. Could she make it happen again with J-Bay?

"You really want to get out of here, don't you?" she asked.

She leaned into him and pressed against him wetsuit to wetsuit feeling the give of their neoprene skins. She touched her lips to his. They were thinner and cooler than Alonso's. He pulled back and looked around. She wasn't sure how he'd react to her advance and there weren't any clues in his face, or hands or eyes but there wasn't any doubt about the changes in her own body. The neoprene stretched to accommodate the sudden swelling of her hips and breasts.

"Come on," J-Bay said. He led her to a sheltered part of the shore beside the cattails. Their sex there was gritty, uncomfortable, and awkward amid peeling neoprene and sour lake smells. But J-Bay's touch reassured her. The places where they met skin to skin quickly heated up and created the islandish sensations. Doreena thought it was working and they'd make the island come. It took ages, but finally she forgot about the grit beneath her and dissolved in J-Bay's embrace. When the blue haze came, she sighed with relief and pleasure. "My island."

It came with a waft of cool salt and floral scented air.

"What? Are we tripping?" J-Bay said.

He was lying on top of her with his wetsuit peeled down to his knees looking up towards the jungle. He stank a little of lake, but she was naked and her skin felt fresh. She stretched her arms over her head and wiggled her toes in the sand. J-Bay rolled off her, spun around and staggered toward the sea. The surface held only white capped waves and a glaze of sun.

"That's where I left Alonso alone with the shark," she said. She'd been so concerned with getting back to the island; it was the first time she'd thought about whether Alonso might be hurt. "I don't know if he made it."

"Where are we?" J-Bay said.

"On my island." An emptiness gnawed at her, a resurgent hunger and thirst. "Come on, I need to eat."

The broad leaves brushed her body as she led J-Bay into the jungle to the grove. In the clearing, Alonso sat in the middle of a pile of fruit his teeth close to the green skin of a guava. His long body was unblemished. He sucked in breath when he saw her, and Doreena felt his eyes on her. She knew he noticed her body was different now. Although she hadn't been eating, it was plumper. Her hips and breasts felt stretched and viscous. It pulled. It was J-Bay. He was noticing her now and her body was ripening with his attention.

"J-Bay." Alonso said and nodded.

"You made it," she said. "The shark."

"Tiger shark. The board took the damage," he gestured behind him. Her board was missing a hunk in the middlc. "A couple of bites and he pretty much lost interest."

"When it came for me, I froze," Doreena said. "But it was like it could sense me."

"They can. In seawater we all produce electric fields and that's how sharks find us. They have these organs, electro receptors, ampullae of Lorenzini, that sense movement in the water. Fascinating creatures."

"Scary. I don't know how it got there." She looked around at the rinds of fruit. There were a few tiny green flies hovering over the rinds. She brushed them away from her face. "Has it been long?"

He shrugged. "Days? It's hard to keep track of time. Listen, you looked great. Just before, I mean, when you were surfing. You have good instincts. When you were up there, it was like your life."

"I did for a minute, didn't I?" She stretched her arms out. "I was flying, riding above everything."

"That's it," Alonso said.

"Yeah, I get it. Then wham!" She clapped her hands. "Fish food!"

She tumbled forward and knelt beside him, a mango between her knees. She reached for him. "Forget about the sharks. I missed you. Hold me."

He touched a curl beside her face and then pulled back. "I can't risk it. It's too good here."

"Hey," J-Bay said. "Man, where are we?"

"When you get out to the waves, you won't care," Alonso lobbed a mango at J-Bay who caught it with an easy stretch of his hand. "Paradise. Bali Hai. Wherever."

He stood and grabbed his board. "Let's go."

"What about sharks?" Doreena said.

He shrugged. "I'll risk it. It's worth it."

He'd risk sharks, but not touching her. As they were walking down the beach the suction came at Doreena pulling her back. She stumbled forward in the sand and reached for Alonso. He pulled away from her and caught J-Bay's arm. "If you want to stay here, you can't touch her. Don't make the same mistake I did, no woman before the stoke. You can't have both."

She returned to the lake alone. Alonso stayed in paradise. When the surfers asked where J-Bay was, she told them about the island.

"I don't know how it started, but I go to an island. There's a perfect beach and waves and all the fruit you can eat: mangoes, coconut and pineapple. I couldn't control it before, when I went by myself, it just happened. I got into an accident the first time because I was driving and then it came, but now I know how to get there on purpose. I can take people with me. I've done it a few times."

"Alonso and J-Bay," one of the surfers said.

"Yeah, that's where they are."

"Where is where they are?" a surfer asked.

She shrugged. It was an easy gesture that she had stolen from Alonso. Now that she was doing it, seeing it from the inside, she could feel what it really meant, not so much, 'I don't know.' as, 'It doesn't matter'. "Alonso called it paradise."

"Kiss you and go to paradise," a surfer said. "Now that's an offer."

"I've heard that one before," said another.

"Hey, it works sometimes, bro."

"I'll show you," Doreena said.

She reached for A-Bay, J-Bay's twin, because he seemed familiar, but he pulled away from her. "Nah, someone else. I don't like to do it...my brother and I don't share girls. It's caused us trouble in the past."

"The Cape Town girl," one of the surfers said. "Legendary."

"Hey, I believe you," another said, the seal-faced surfer. She didn't know him, but she knew his gestures. His hands were limp at his sides and his shoulders low fixed in a permanent shrug. She went to him, put her arms around his neoprene torso and lifted her lips to his. She kissed him with all the surfers watching. She thought of her island and her mouth felt warm and pliable as though she tasted the sun-ripened fruits. A thrill went through her when the suction pulled, the surfer's arms tightened around her. The haze dropped and she brought him over. He was dazzled and unafraid as Alonso and J-Bay had both been. The new surfer went by Barritz. She stayed for a while with the three of them this time surfing and lying on the sand and eating fruit before she came back to the C-town lakeshore where the rest of the surfers were still waiting.

"Where'd he go?" they asked.

"The island. I told you I took him," she said. "What did you see?"

"He disappeared. He vanished."

"And me?" she asked.

"You were still there."

"I saw her for a moment kissing air."

"No, she was just standing."

"She didn't do anything."

"What's the trick?"

"There's no trick," she said. "We just get together and the island comes for us. If there's something really important to you, like your surfboard, you can bring it with you if you're touching it."

They were skeptical, but they kissed her. She took them on top of the gritty sand until it became island soft beneath them. It was different every time. Sometimes the island would come instantly, other times it took a while touching and kissing and making love on top of the surfer's board until the island flowed around them and pulled them into its embrace. Each surfer was the same. He reacted with delight and once there, he refused to touch her. No one would risk it. No one wanted to leave. Doreena wanted Alonso to be jealous that she was making love to all his mates, but he only looked happy to see his surf bros.

"It's fine for you," she said. "But I'm the one who keeps going back."

For a while, so long as there were surfers, she could go to the island whenever she liked, taking the next one in her arms, but the more she populated the island with her men, the more she wanted to remain there to watch them skimming the waves.

When the suction came, she ran at them, she held her hands out to them, pleading with them to try and hold on to her or to take hold and come back with her.

"Come back with me. I'll bring you back," she said. But none of them would come near her outstretched hands and as they saw her desperation grow, they began to keep their distance.

Then only A-Bay was left in C-town as sure transport to her island. He was the youngest of the surfers, by two hours after his twin. She wanted to take him, but she resisted the impulse to do so right away because he was the last. Then she'd be left waiting alone. He didn't have any reservations now. He begged her. "Please. It's my turn. I want to see that my brother's OK."

"He's fine," she said. "Once you get there, you won't touch me either."

"I will. I promise."

"No. You won't. You'll want to stay like all the others, and you won't take the chance. Alonso'd take Tiger sharks over me. Nobody wants to come back here. Nobody wants to get stranded on the wrong side."

It was hard not to touch him when she wanted to and wanted the island. She was in the habit of touching easily now whomever she wanted, and it was hard to resist reaching for him. He had moved into Alonso's apartment with her, and she'd give in soon. Then all the surfers would be on the island, and she'd be in C-town with nothing to do and no sure way to get out. She'd put A-Bay off as long as she could.

"Leave me alone," she said. "Or I won't take you, ever." He knew by now though how desperate she was for the island and how much she needed him to get there.

"I'll wait here," he said.

She went to the lake and found the one surfer she'd forgotten, Hobart. The older woman had kept her distance since Doreena began talking about the island. She'd never trusted Doreena, *The Mirror* salesman.

Now the woman waved her over. "Come on, you're always here, but you're never out here," Hobart pointed to the middle of the lake. "Let me show you how to get a rise out of this."

The surfing lesson was cold and useless. They went close to the enormous, coiled aluminum tubes that spilled ripples of gray-green water. Doreena could not stand up on her board in the little drifts and it stank of amalgamated fish, algae, and chemicals that each, alone, might have been bearable. Hobart tired of her sullen student and left Doreena clinging to her board. Moments later, Doreena looked up and the surfer giantess bore down on her, a dark spire against the light gray sky, looking as if she were pulling the skim of the lake behind her. She crouched in one swift movement and stopped in front of Doreena slipping off the board into the water. A gleam shone in her eye, a touch of enchantment, as though she'd glimpsed the island in the distance as she stood over the lake. That look made Doreena want to climb up the trellis of skin in the corner of Hobart's eye and sit inside that shiny mote of bliss. She didn't understand what it was about this experience on the cold, dank, lake that the surfers loved. But she saw the effects with certainty in Hobart. She wanted to see Hobart on her island, what she would look like gliding on the waves in that idyllic place. She leaned toward her.

"Let me show you the island."

"Don't get ideas," Hobart said.

"But they've all gone. You have to believe me. Don't you want to see it?"

"What, you want to kiss me? You want to make love to an old woman, after all those surfer boys? No, listen, it's not that I'd find it so terrible. Don't look so hurt. It's just that I've been around a while. I like to think I've learned a little. These aren't little pleasures to go into lightly. When you make connections with people, you get tied up in all their shit. That's something to think about. It seems to me like you've got some pretty serious shit to wrangle.

I don't know I want to take all that on. Just touch you. But there isn't any just. Not that I've ever seen. It's never just anything."

"You will, though. You'll just go to a beautiful place and then you won't have to even pay attention to me anymore," Doreena protested.

"Oh, I doubt that. Before this stop in C-town, I traveled the world and it seems to be a rule that once you've been somewhere your odds of going back skyrocket and once you've made a connection with someone, even fleeting, chances are you'll see them again. You can hide for a while. Staying in a small town and keeping to a routine creates a kind of buffer, but eventually, when you move on, it'll open the floodgates and suddenly all those people and places you thought you left behind start pouring out. No, I don't want to get whisked away no matter how pretty. I've seen paradises before. Been to lots of pretty places, and I always wanted to move on after a while no matter how beautiful. I've been running away from my shit all my life. Now, I've started something here in this town and I want to finish it. I started that Travel Museum and I'm attached to it. I like being a business owner. Who woulda' thought."

In the back of Doreena's mind, she recognized Hobart's tone, it was the riff she'd heard from Gavin Traynter, Mr. Elitamby, and even Rock and Marilyn. Entrepreneurs got passionate about their businesses as if they were life-changing experiences. She knew that, but as Hobart talked all she could really think about deep down inside herself was the rejection. It hurt. Hobart didn't even want to try to go to the island with her. It bothered her that she couldn't see Hobart's hands, they were hidden under the lake and under the board. The creases in the corners of the Hobart's eyes looked prominently like laughter.

"You don't want to touch me either," Doreena said.

"What, are you mad about it?" Hobart said. "Seriously?"

Abject, Doreena swam for the center of the lake. She lurched stiffly through the cold water. She felt desperate, awkward, and ridiculous because of it, but that didn't make the pain of feeling out of place, out of time, and out of control any less overwhelming. Something was happening inside herself. She was on the verge of some discovery and she didn't think she could handle it alone in C-town. She stopped when she reached the lake's center and stilled the paddling movements that were keeping her afloat. Her body sank a little into the gray water. She paddled again, softly, and bobbed to the surface. Then she stilled, sank, and went under water. It covered her face and then the top of her head. She hid beneath the water and opened her mouth to let the air escape. The bubbles wobbled out. She sank further into the gray-green darkness until her toes touched the silt. This was exactly what she'd done when the shark had come for her: frozen and sank. She wasn't trying to drown, only submerge her growing panic. She wished there were sharks here now. It would be better if there were a real threat from the outside, better than this hidden, gnawing attack from the inside.

Underwater her mind drifted to a calm, cold place. Maybe the blue haze would appear on the other side, or maybe she'd find a way to stop wanting it. Her arms floated up over head as if detached. She opened her mouth again and the wastewater flowed in. There was nothing she could do to escape. She'd held the trap inside herself all along and now it sprung. She sank into the murky water gaining weight on her way down, daring the haze to rescue her, but the island had abandoned her leaving her marooned on the wrong side of her life. Her toes stirred up a cloud of dark particles when they touched the lakebed. In time, her body leaned over sinking at an angle to lay among the debris. She'd drown or the island would save her, either way, if Alonso was right, there'd be euphoria.

Then her arm was yanked into a vertical position again, her body followed. A hand grabbed hers and pulled. Doreena struggled to stay down, but her kicking lifted her up instead. Her suddenly buoyant body rode up through the water and surfaced. A neoprene arm circled her waist. Doreena gasped for air and stared into Hobart's blue eyes.

"What are you doing, girl?" Hobart said.

As Doreena shook her head, the blue haze dropped. Hobart's eyes became vivid blue and the blue in the world, in the peripheries, around them deepened so that even the gray slick of the lake shone with a cyan coating. The suction wrapped around them and in moments Doreena lay on the beach gasping in the warm sun with Hobart beside her. Hobart's big hands adorned with rings were visible now beside her on the sand. The seal-like wrinkles in her older skin seemed to soften in the island sun.

"So, you brought me anyway," Hobart said. "You gave me no choice. Now our lives are entwined."

Doreena stumbled to the waves and rinsed her mouth of the lake water with its chemical residue. She spat seawater and it left a sweet aftertaste. Doreena looked across the sea. The waves were small and the surface empty.

"Come on, I know where they are," she said. "I'll take you to the surfers."

She led Hobart toward the jungle. As they walked up the beach she noticed how, on the island, Hobart's strange gait finally looked right. It was a spread-legged straddle that kept the thighs apart and came naturally in the heat.

As they approached the trail, Doreena noticed that the beach ahead looked different. It had been bare sand laced with purple flowering pohuehue. Now there were low growing shrubs with fleshy yellow-green leaves bearing white five-lobed flowers among the vines. She knelt to examine it as they passed by.

"Sea lettuce," Hobart said.

Doreena lifted her head and turned back toward the jungle. A heady mix of spice, jasmine and frangipani streamed out of it. The island air had always exuded a light floral scent, but it was perfumed now like the inside of Denriggers. Doreena stepped on the red trail cutting into the jungle. The island continued to evolve. Foliage proliferated. Multi-colored green striations ran vertically from the blue sky to the red trail showing numerous variations on a jungle theme like Pantone swatches. There were plants and flowers she'd never seen before, and the jungle was alive. Restless cawing, clicking, buzzing, and rustling betrayed the creatures hiding in its green depths. Hobart stopped in the middle of the jungle.

"It doesn't make sense," she said, looking around. "Frangipani from Central America, South African protea, Hawaiian hibiscus and this," she pulled a branch with green way leaves and white blossoms toward her and put her face into it. "This is gardenia from Tahiti, Tiare. All these scents are mingling now, but if you could smell this one on its own you wouldn't forget it. The Tahitians' got an international patent on the scent."

She looked up at the trees. "That's traveler's palm from Madagascar. There's a double coconut you only find on the Seychelles, and South American jacaranda. These shouldn't all be growing together. They all require different soils and temperatures and rainfall. This is either a fey place or there's an incredible cultivator somewhere." She pointed up the trail. "Up there?"

This idea bewildered Doreena the way it had when Marilyn had asked about sharks in the ocean. She'd never considered what might be in the depths of the jungle or further up the red trail. She'd heard the voice calling down but had assumed it did not belong to a person.

"I've never been much further than the beach, just a little way in for fruit."

Hobart grabbed Doreena's arm, "I said I didn't want to come, but this island. You're right. This is something different."

The surfers lounged in the grove feasting on fruit. Before it had been a simple stand of coconuts, with a cluster of pineapples growing at the base of the trees and a surround of glossy dense mango shrubs with pink unfolding leaves and flowers. Now trees, shrubs, and clusters of dark green shiny leaves at all heights in the size of fingertips, palms, or entire arms pressed around the clearing. Ovoid green, yellow and gold fruits dangled into the space and lay scattered across the fibrous floor. A cry of "Hobart!" went round, then the surfers returned to languid eating and napping. Hobart handled the fruits and named them. Some she picked up from the jungle floor and tossed in the air, reassured by the weight of them as she caught them in her hands.

"Lime, papaya, papaw, guava, rambutan, durian, passion fruit, jackfruit, breadfruit, Tahitian lime," she said.

"I think it's got everything from anywhere we've ever been," Alonso said. He'd risen from where he'd lain beside a tree gnawing coconut and stood beside them. He stood on the far side of Doreena with Hobart between them. The surfers were wary of Doreena now, her unpredictable leave-taking, and kept her at a distance. In frustration, she'd lunged at a couple of them once or twice when she felt she was about to go. Alonso stepped back from her now. He wasn't even near her and still backed away. He'd felt it before she had. The suction began and stiffened her body.

She reached for Hobart, "Don't leave me."

But Hobart had followed Alonso out of arm's reach.

"I mean to go back. But not just yet. They need me. You need to bury those," Hobart said, turning to Alonso and pointing to a pile of decaying rinds and peels.

Doreena's last glimpse of the island was a haze of brown buzzing flies and then she was in Alonso's apartment at the Narborough. Her hands were a flurry of motion in front of her. She held a suit jacket folded in half over a suitcase. A-Bay sat on the edge of the stripped bed. The bloodstained batik lay crumpled on the floor with a pile of clothing. There was a roar behind her, a thud that made the room vibrate and then the shatter of breaking glass.

"What's that?" she said.

"They're tearing the building down," A-Bay said.

"Why aren't we at the lake?"

"It's closed to the public. They've started construction on Rock Traynter's new resort."

"What am I doing?"

"Packing," he said. "They want us out of here yesterday." He pulled his shirt off, threw it on top of the laundry and grabbed her arm. "Doreena. Please. Just get us out of here."

Doreena shoved the suitcase off the bed and pulled him on top of her. They writhed together on the bed to the roar and crash of the wrecking crew until the haze dropped and the sound became the roar and crash of island waves. Doreena looked at A-Bay his skin gone island gold and his curls backlit by the brightest blue. His face lit up with delight and triumph and tears formed in her eyes. She'd done it, brought the last of them. But before her tear had time to fall, the suction pulled her back. It was her shortest island visit yet and then; she was back on the bed in the Narborough alone. A thud landed against the wall nearby and then a shower of glass crossed the room. Doreena only had time to grab Alonso's tip jar. She left everything she owned and rushed down the dust-choked stairway out onto the street.

Doreena pulled her wetsuit up and zipped it staring as the Narborough fell. Its ordered bricks lay in jumbled piles at the bottom of chalky clouds of dust. She looked through the empty windows of The Travel Museum beside it until the construction workers chased her off the site. Where had all the things gone? She watched them destroy the building from across the street until it began to get dark. Then she rode the bus downtown clutching the tip jar between her neoprene-covered thighs. The bus was filled with islandless strangers who avoided her gaze. There was only one person left in C-town who had shared the island, only one person who gone with her and come back. She went to the Traynter's loft.

"Why are they always tearing down my places?" she said when Marilyn answered the door.

The color of the day was black. Marilyn held her black and white patterned scarf across her nose and mouth. Doreena touched her curls. They were sticky and stiff, matted with blood, salt, and her scalp's own accumulating oils. She was unwashed and layered with scents of stale sex and lake water. She must look frightful and smell worse. But it would vanish once she reached the island; her skin would be clean and pure.

"It's about time. Where have you been?" Marilyn asked.

"Busy."

"You can't stay here. You're lucky Rock's out."

"I won't," Doreena said. She reached for Marilyn's belly. She did not know for certain what it was about these other people that brought the island, but she thought it was something like the pulse of life. The life inside Marilyn, sex with the stoked surfers, and Hobart saving her life. It was that emotion Tom and Marilyn and her grandfather had been hinting that she'd been lacking — passion. She devoted her life to *The Mirror*, all her energy and effort, but some spark within her had held back. She hadn't even noticed its absence, but it had been obvious to others.

"Wait." Marilyn said. "I've been thinking a lot about this."

Doreena sunk into the crème-colored couch. Her wetsuit was stretched and torn in places. She plucked at it while she waited and listened to Marilyn talk on the phone in the other room. After a while, they went down to the street where a silver AeroFlux truck was parked. Marilyn lifted the back of it, inside were crates stamped with maroon wings. She hoisted herself up into it and Doreena followed.

"Most of them are empty," Marilyn said. "Now we're ready to go to the island. Here's what we're going to do.

She grabbed Doreena's hand and placed it on her belly. She put her other hand on the crate. The baby flipped. The blue haze dropped. The suction pulled them onto the island. She landed beside Marilyn and a pile of crates. She was salt washed clean again and floral scented. Her mind, dull and stiff on the streets of C-town, felt lively again.

"What's all this for?" Doreena said, staring at the crates. Around the jumbled stack of gray squares, the island scenery appeared too bright, and it vibrated slowly around the edges of the stack. For the first time, the island itself, the whole scene, looked not quite real, not quite solid.

Marilyn was about to answer when the surfers began to come in from the ocean to see the latest arrival, the unlikely looking stack of crates on the sand.

Marilyn turned to Doreena. "You've been busy."

"What's all this?" Hobart said when a circle of surfers had gathered around.

"Well, good this might help," Marilyn said. "I think it's time we began a major exporting business. I want to start bringing this place back to C-town. The fruit definitely, maybe even the sand."

A murmur went round the surfers as they began to protest, but Hobart stilled them holding up one big hand. Her polished stone rings shone in the island sun. "Wait, this could be what we've been looking for. The next iteration of *The C-town Traveler*. Think about it. This would really change things. This could be a way to open up C-town."

While they talked, Doreena looked for Alonso. He was the last to leave the sea, but eventually he began to stroll toward them. He was one of the few of them that had come to the island unclothed. Most of the surfers had transported their wetsuits with them. Still wet, Alonso's body glistened. She wanted to touch him while he was still cool from the sea.

"Hey bros," he said as he passed them, and kept walking toward the grove.

"I've got a proposal," Marilyn said. With the surfers gathered around her, it looked like a sales meeting on the sand.

Doreena left Marilyn with her new force scheming about an export business with AeroFlux and the surfer's help. She didn't care. She followed Alonso into the jungle to eat fruit. She slipped mango between her lips and let it slide around in her mouth to savor the juice. Alonso gnawed on a pineapple core. He held his muscular torso in his hands with pale pink fingernails. "I eat all the time, but I swear I can feel my ribs."

She heard voices up the trail in the jungle, Marilyn directing the surfers. The palms rustled as they passed.

"What are they up to?" Alonso asked.

"I think they're starting up a business. Try the coconut," Doreena held a chunk out to Alonso. "I never eat, but I'm fat as ever." she patted her hips and swiveled them in front of him. "Feel."

"Is that what's with all the crates?"

"I guess, they're going to bring the island back to C-town bit by bit. I don't care. I don't want to go back there. I don't work for her anymore."

"You sure about that? I mean, you will go back, right?"

"I can't stop it," she said.

"You and C-town are still tangled up."

She reached for his hand, then sighed when he pulled away. "Fine. I'll see what's up." Doreena followed a line of broken leaves, exposed stalks, and bent stems up the narrow red trail through the jungle. She listened for the voice but heard only doves cooing in the trees. A red macaw, like Petey, arched in the sky its wingspan stretching across the path as she reached a clearing where a waterfall fell into a pool beside a yawning cave. It was the farthest she'd ever been up the trail, into the jungle, and off the beach. A line of crates stretched out of the entrance. Inside, Marilyn and the surfers stood around them.

Doreena crept forward and lifted the cover of the nearest one. It was filled to the top with green-skinned mangoes. She thought she heard the voice beckoning within the rush of the waterfall, spun around and froze. Someone grabbed her from behind. She elbowed back punching into hardness before she knew what she was fighting and then going limp when she spied Marilyn's pregnant belly. She didn't want to hurt the baby. Marilyn wrapped an arm tightly around her and pulled her back towards the crates.

Doreena cried out when she saw Alonso coming down the trail. The waterfall muted her, but he turned towards the cave and stepped into the clearing. She reached for him, but he held back watching at a distance. He couldn't help. He still wouldn't touch her.

"What's this?" Alonso asked the surfers. "What do you think you're doing?"

"Saving C-town," Hobart said, barely audible in the roar of the waterfall — no — it was the engine of the truck.

Doreena struggled as the suction surrounded her wicking the moist air from her skin. She forgot about Marilyn and the baby and pulled hard against the suction digging her heels in. She was lurching toward the beach. It had been just feet away. If wasn't fair that she hadn't had any time there. One minute she was struggling in Marilyn's arms and the suction, and the next she was free. She stepped back and her heel scraped a crate and then slid down a metal ramp. She lost her footing and her legs shot out from under her. She tumbled down the ramp and her tailbone struck pavement. Pelting cold rain replaced the mist of the waterfall. She was in C-town again sitting on Beaumont Street staring up the extended ramp leading into the AeroFlux truck.

She looked for Marilyn where she had last been standing inside the truck. But it was empty. She looked back at the stack of crates behind her. The driver in his coveralls appeared looking down at her and over at the crates. He was standing in front of a loading zone sign and Doreena realized what had happened. He had pulled the truck forward, just a few feet, but Marilyn would have reappeared exactly where she'd left C-town for the island. Since the truck wasn't there anymore, that meant in the air over the street.

"Idiot, you moved it," Doreena said.

"What, you wanted to pay for the ticket? Parking ordinances are strict downtown."

Doreena ran around the crates afraid of what she'd find. A cluster of people had gathered and in the distance sirens wailed. The fall would only have been from a few feet up, but even a drop from that height, that and Doreena's fighting, could have hurt the baby. Marilyn sat beside the crates. Strangers held her hands.

"Don't worry the ambulance is on its way," a man said.

The street was wet and dark. Doreena couldn't tell if the spreading sheen over the gravel was a rising coat of oil or slowly pooling blood. Marilyn's face, peering out of her dark overcoat, looked small and pale. The color of the day was black and white.

When the EMT's arrived, Doreena got pushed aside, but before they left one of them yelled at her to ride along. "She could use a friend."

"I'm not," Doreena said, but stopped short. She wasn't sure it was true anymore that Marilyn was just her boss. They had waded into the ocean together perfectly at ease. Maybe they were friends now, on the island anyway. Even so she had to refuse, she would not go to the hospital again. Her eye had finally healed, and she didn't want anyone to see anything else was wrong with her. They could make her sick or worse, somehow cure her of the island. Besides, if Marilyn lost the baby what could Doreena possibly do to comfort her. Marilyn might even be angry. She might blame

Doreena or the island for putting the child at risk. As the ambulance sped down Beaumont, she watched the driver load the crates of stolen fruit into the truck. It wasn't long before her thoughts returned to the island. All she wanted was it, again, soon.

~ 41 ~

MIRROR ISLAND: INSIDE AEROFLUX

Mirror Island evolves and enslaves Doreena

The next time Doreena returned to the island, it enchanted her again and displaced her fear. Her shoulder blades slunk down her back. Sweat trickled between her thighs and she stepped her legs wide so air would flow between them. Her heels were heavy in the sand and her arms rested at her sides. With her eyes closed, the saline breeze seemed blossom filled. Layers of floral sweetness crested and fell around her. The Hawaiian hibiscus and pikake scent that reminded her of grandfather and home floated somewhere within the flowing breeze, no longer distinct, but still there under the layers of scent.

The inlet around her beach was filled with surfers. They gathered like dark spears and charged toward her to the shore as if they'd scented her arrival. They could hardly have seen her in the glare of the sun appearing on the shore, as she imagined, a blush of honeyed brown blooming on the pink sand.

Doreena turned toward the jungle noticing again its new density and diversity. There were stairways of palms with fringed leaves stretching in the blue sky, crossing over each other and fingering each other's trunks. The vegetation was a Pantone booklet of blue-green, red-green, and yellow-green leaves filled in with purple to black patches of shade. Some leaves were variegated with exposed bright red and white veins. Their shapes were spatulate, pointed or oblong and they folded, curved and unfurled over each other. Vines crawled everywhere, twining and wrapping around rough trunks. Red and white flowers shone like headlights and brake lights blooming through the jungle traffic. The iron red trail leading up into the jungle seemed wider. It cut a path into the foliage like a leering tongue. The jungle looked impassible anywhere else.

The surfers were behind her now, a half-circle of men baked in neoprene and salt. They, and their stifling scent, were too close to her, as if they were all seated behind her on the C-town bus.

"Where's Traynter?" they asked.

For a moment, she thought they meant Rock and froze trying to remember if she'd brought him and afraid of what changes he would bring to this shifting place. But it seemed impossible for Rock to come here. She would never get close to him and there was nothing island-like about him. Of course, they meant Marilyn.

"In the hospital," Doreena said. "She's on bed rest to save the baby. She nearly lost it."

She shaded her eyes and tried to see beyond them to the empty beach, but they stood shoulder to shoulder in front of her. Stripes of pink sand showed between their wetsuit clad hips and legs but there was no room for her to pass through. The men stood in a quiet arc between her and her beach.

"She'd want us to continue," Hobart said, stepping forward. Her cap of hair shone silver above them. Most of the men's wetsuits adhered to their plank-like torsos, but Hobart, lean as she was, had a small round of belly. Her wetsuit pressed out in just one place like a trapped roll of a wave. Doreena wanted to get away from the woman, but she didn't want to get any closer to the jungle. Instead, she dug her toes into the sand.

"Come see what we've been working on." Hobart said. "It's just up the trail."

"Alonso?" Doreena asked.

"He's exploring," a surfer said. It was seal-faced Barritz, the first one she'd brought over. He nodded toward the jungle. "Come on. Don't you want to take a look?"

"I want to stay on the beach," Doreena said. She'd dug her feet into the sand so it covered them. She wiggled them now and the sand cracked. They were all close around her. The only open space was behind. The tongue of the red trail licked her back. "I'm not here all the time like you."

J-Bay pushed her first.

"There's no time. She could go soon. When she brought my brother, she was only here for a few seconds. We don't know when she'll return so we have to move. We can't be shy about it."

Doreena stumbled back and Hobart walked toward her. The surfers jabbed at her until she stumbled off the last patch of pink. Her feet slid into the warm mud of the trail. It oozed red between her toes. The next shove sent her sprawling forward toward a plant with one enormous blossom mounted at its center. She reached for it to catch her fall, but the tender stem pulled free and she fell with the blossom cradled in her arms. It was the size of a baby's head with feathery fringes instead of petals up its sides. It was one of the foreign plants from far out of C-town Hobart had pointed out when she arrived. She remembered the name, protea. Doreena crashed onto the mud trail and put the sticky protea blossom head aside. She pressed her hands into the mud to raise herself up. It coated her palms and spread up onto the backs of her hands. She shook it off and red flecks landed on the leaves. She wiped the excess on her thighs. It had an eggy mineral smell and, when she touched her tongue to a fleck of it on her lips, a burnt caramel taste.

She walked steadily up the trail with the surfers packed behind her, but the menstrual scent of spoiling fruit made her stop at the entrance to the grove. To one side a swath of melon rinds, lime peels, rambutan husks and coconut shells, stretched beneath of a flurry of tiny brown flies. They moved like Brownian motion.

"Brownian?" she said aloud. "What's that?"

They shoved Doreena on toward the cave. Along the outside of the pool, water lilies stretched over a jade green slurry, but back by the cave a waterfall churned the center of it into peaks of green and white. A stack of crates blocked the entrance to the cave, with the maroon-winged logo plastered up the sides. Beside the crates was cargo: loaves of breadfruit, stacks of strawberry guavas and pyramids of passionfruit and papaya. A-Bay pointed.

"Just touch the crates," he shouted, and she didn't know if he was as angry as he sounded or just trying to be heard over the waterfall.

"I don't want to," she yelled back.

It would have been easy for any of them to grab her and lift her to the crates. But none of them wanted to touch her for long, so they pushed her one-by-one, making her stumble toward the crates. When she was up against them, the surfers stopped. They continued shouting.

"Now what?" J-Bay said. "Are we going to stand here? I saw some great sets on the way."

"Find some way to restrain her," Hobart said.

They bound her wrists and ankles with vines and creepers and tied her to the crates.

"We have to do this. He's got everyone trapped in C-town. This is our chance," Hobart said.

"But you're here," Doreena said. "I brought you. We can enjoy it."

"It's not for us," Hobart said. "There are surfers everywhere."

They left her with her breasts, belly, and thighs pressed up against the rough splintery wood. The waterfall splatter occasionally struck her exposed back. Insects with long legs and translucent glittery wings walked over and pressed proboscis to her skin mistaking her for the open blossoms of the nymphae lilies that they loved. Drops splashed in her mouth and eyes where it fell from the crooks of the jade green rocks perpetually enlivened by the cascade of water pouring down. White veins glistened through wet stones, while the dry cliff beside it stood stolidly matte gray with tufts of course moss growing in its cracks.

When she could no longer hear the surfers, Doreena squirmed against the vines. Immediately, some of them loosened. She was sure she could get free, in time. Maybe she could find another beach, some sheltered cove on the island, the others didn't know about. She would crawl through the jungle and find it. Maybe Alonso would be there. Some of the vines crushed as she struggled. The sinewy strands opened, and their juice slid over her skin. The woodier creepers scratched. The sinewy cords stretched and snapped. Dangling cords swung around her body as she struggled.

"Come see me," the voice called from trail.

She freed her arms and began to tear the vines apart with her hands. All she wanted was to get away from the crates and the voice and be back on the beach. She was almost free when the suction pulled. The vines crawling across her skin began to hiss. She flailed wildly against a blur of green and then gray as she landed writhing on a C-town street. A truck braked beside the stack of crates and released a hissing exhalation.

After that, Doreena spent all her time on the island strapped to the crates. The surfers pushed her into the jungle as soon as she arrived. Her back and arms were covered with rounds of fingerprint-shaped bruises like the spots of some exotic animal. She fought back, but the harder she struggled the harder the surfers pushed and the tighter they pulled when they bound her to the crates. They had ropes now. Her C-town-self had betrayed her, and she had brought them.

At the mouth of the cave, Doreena shivered. Each time became colder and drier: her rough tongue swelled in her mouth. The skin of her hands cracked. Her skin looked pale, shot through with pronounced aquamarine veins. It had been a long time since she'd had any island fruit, but instead of the lightness of hunger, her body felt heavy like freight. Her time in C-town consisted of hazy, half-remembered events. She thought she was coming to the island more often. She couldn't remember what she'd been doing in C-town anymore. The island was all she thought of. She stood with her cheek pressed to the crates and her eyes closed to the drops of water. When she smelled the green nectar of her favorite fruit, her body surged like liquid. Her breasts and hips swelled, and she knew the youngest surfers were behind her.

"Look what we brought," J-Bay said.

He held a mango up and tore through the green skin with his teeth revealing the wet orange flesh. She salivated at the ripeness of it. The rope burned her twisting wrists.

"Let me go," she said.

"I'll feed you," J-Bay said. He slipped a wedge between her lips. The juice slid down her throat. "We need some things from C-town. Bring us women we can touch."

"And beer," A-Bay added from somewhere behind her.

J-Bay moved closer. His arm brushed her breast on its way to her lips with another mango sliver. She stretched her neck up for it, snapped and caught the tip of his finger in her teeth. There was a surge of salty liquid when she clamped down. The suction began. When J-Bay pulled away his flesh ripped between her teeth. Then, he was gone.

Words came into focus in front of her: Quantum. Hawking. Brownian. She was staring at a bookshelf shaking. She spit the fingertip into her palm and closed her fist around it.

"Is that a yes?"

She turned. Earnest knelt on the floor behind her. She recognized him, but not this white-walled place that smelled of orange cleanser.

"I meant to wait until we got to the restaurant." He reached into his pocket and held up a ring.

Where was she? Had it been so long since she'd been lucid in C-town? She tried to bring herself into the moment, but she could still feel the roughness of the crates at her back, the splinters in her thighs, the ropes tight around her midsection and the cold spray of the waterfall across her back. Her chest tightened with longing for the lull of the warm, pink beach and she wished she could take just one deep breath without thinking about it. The pupil-sized round stone on the ring in front of her held a flare of yellow like captured sunshine. The sun: she missed the sun and her grandfather even more. It seemed wrong to love a single person more than the sun, which everyone depended on, but she did. She'd give up the sun to see him.

"Oh damn," Earnest said. "You don't like the ring."

"Earnest." The sound was difficult. Her tongue was dry and light and curled like peeling bark. That was his name, wasn't it? "It's beautiful."

His narrow shoulders in a thin white office shirt shrugged. "Ah, good. There's that. Diane helped me pick it out. She said she was sure you would like it. I should have waited to ask you though. Let's go," he said picking up his tweed jacket and heading for the door. "Forget this. I'll do it properly in the restaurant."

She followed him out and threw J-Bay's fingertip into a juniper outside when he wasn't looking. Earnest held the door to his car open for her. She remembered seeing it sitting on the side of the road beside the landmark sign where she'd crashed the first time she'd gone to her island mid-day. The car was bare inside with the same industrial orange smell. Inside, she ran her pink fingertips over the matching silk of her dress. The wet streets shone with reflected moonlight. The phosphors on Beaumont cut into the dark casting a pale pink skyward over the city.

They parked across from the Tiki-Tiki Lounge, and Earnest held open the door for her again. The silk dress swung round her hips, and she teetered forward on strappy gold sandals. Earnest held up an arm to help steady her. She shivered on the street but in the restaurant the warmth floated quickly up under her dress. The place was packed with people dressed in similar outfits of raw silk and linen in light yellow, pink, or blue. They wore leis of fresh frangipani and jasmine. Live birds, Petey's cousins, perched beside each table preening. White feathers floated down to settle on the bamboo floor. A live band played by the bar. The place had been completely islandized.

"The Steelheads," she said.

The waiter sat them by the window and handed them menus of woven grass. A peach slip of paper clipped to the front advertised the prix fixe menu.

Coconut Satay braised coconut chunks with a side of Tahitian lime sauce.

Savory Tropical Truffle Pie seared plantains and chunks of taro root mixed with shredded coconut covered in a light puff pastry. Comes with a side of braised breadfruit served with mango chutney.

Guava Duff a light fluffy cake stuffed with hot guava compote and served with custard and topped with fresh slices of strawberry guava.

All around them diners were eating and drinking pieces of her island: cooked, braised, sautéed, and pureed. This was where all the goods from the crates were going — or at least many of them. They lifted it to their lips on forks and spoons and devoured it.

"You've barely touched your drink," Earnest said.

There was an orange drink in front of her in a tall flute glass. She took a sip. It was mango and anise and coolly sweet. When she put the glass down, Earnest reached for her hands across the table. She pulled away. His chin dropped with rejection and his shoulders caved.

"I'm sorry," she said and placed her hands in his. It was the least she could do. She wasn't mean like the surfers to deny him a comforting touch.

"I thought about having them make the Great White for us like we had our first time here together. I was going to have them put the ring around one of those little surfers. Listen, I didn't mean to rush the proposal. You know, we've just been so happy these past months. I'm just excited for us to make it official. Especially now."

Months? Had he said months?

"Are you OK? Are you feeling all right?"

"No. I don't know how to explain. If I say it's not you, nothing to do with you, you won't believe me."

The waiter set an enormous golden puff pie between them. It smelled like the end of an island day with the baked scent of taro, plantain, and coconut rising off the sand. She poked through the top of the crust with her fork and it came to her. She knew how to explain what was happening to her to Earnest. She saw the word emblazoned red across the golden puff crust just as it was on the yellow jacket of one of the books on Earnest's shelf.

"At least, wear the ring while you think about it," he said. He leaned in and stroked her ring finger.

The blue haze dropped. She yanked her hand from his.

"Teleport," she said. "I teleport. And you're not going with me."

She left him staring through the rising steam of the pie with a wounded expression. The surfers tied her to the crates again and abandoned her. The dank ropes clung to her skin. A black mold grew on them and the rotten scent attracted iridescent-backed beetles. Her beautiful beach was only 200 feet or so away. Why couldn't she teleport to it from here? The voice called louder from up the trail. It had begun to ask for her by name. On the beach, it only whispered. She drooped against the ropes and closed her eyes. She kept them squeezed shut even when the sound of shifting leaves signaled someone's approach. The ropes slipped off her chest.

"Doreena, it's me," Alonso said. "What are you doing here?"

She shrugged and coils of rope dropped to the wet green stones at her feet covered by a skiff of coarse brown sand by the crates. Instead of the ocean, she saw Alonso.

"Where have you been?"

"Around. This really is an island."

"Is there another beach? A hidden one?"

He shook his head. "Not really. Not that we can get to. It's at the bottom of a cliff. No way down."

He finished untying her and she reached for him, but he still refused to touch her.

"Even now?" she said. "Come with me. I'll bring us back to that beach you saw."

"You can't control it."

"I'll try. Don't you trust me?"

"I trust you. But my time here, it's too precious."

The surfers came quickly. They must have been just below in the grove eating fruit. J-Bay, the first up the trail, called back, "It's Alonso."

"What've you been doing?" Alonso asked.

"Saving C-town," J-Bay said.

Alonso pointed at the crates. "Like this?"

"We've got a little export business going."

Hobart arrived leading the rest of the surfers. "It's not just us. Other people are stuck."

"Yeah, and what if we want to go back? What if we get bored?" J-Bay said.

Doreena looked for a way to get past them to the beach, but the only clear way was up the path where the voice called. Maybe though, if they were distracted by Alonso, she could duck into the jungle a little and get past them. It wasn't very far to the beach. She just wanted to feel the pink sand under her feet and get a little warm before she left. She had decided to try it when her skin tingled and the suction began. She sighed.

"Get her to the crates," J-Bay said. "She's got that look."

The surfers turned to her. J-Bay pushed her but as he did she grabbed his wrist and climbed this arm. She threw herself onto him, wrapping her arms and legs around him and digging her nails into his shoulder blades. J-Bay rocked off balance and stumbled toward the pool. The surfers crouched around shouting but no one, not even Alonso, made a move to help either of them. As the suction gripped them, A-Bay finally lunged and grabbed his brother's shoulders, but he slipped on the rocks and tipped the three of them into the pool. J-Bay pushed away from her chest and neck, pressing against her throat and submerging her even before the cold water rose over them. The chain of her necklace became an icy collar. It loosened and slid down her neck. She forgot the twins and grabbed for it, clutching at her watery collarbone, ribs and hips, but it sank toward the dark rock bottom of the pool.

She was sucked away from it, sinking toward a sheet of white. When the suction released her, she smacked up against ceramic tile. It chilled her cheek as she lay on it with the pink silk of her dress slid up around her hips. She was in the bathroom of the Tiki-Tiki lounge, but, for a moment, with The Steelheads pulsing through the floor, it felt as if she were back in her apartment at the Narborough. Doreena got up and stumbled to the sinks. She squeezed coconut lotion onto her hands and wrung them together while she got her bearings. In the mirror, she stared first at her bare neckline, then at the emptiness of the bathroom behind her. The Narborough, that's where A-Bay would be. She'd taken J-Bay to the island from the shore of Lake Traynter, but she'd been in the Narborough with A-Bay. But where was her necklace?

Two women entered the bathroom one in silver sandals and the other in bejeweled thongs. "Did you lose something?" they asked.

"My necklace," Doreena said. She scanned the shiny white floor expecting the necklace to emerge from a reflection or in the lines of grout.

The sandals and thongs walked back and forth across the floor with her for a while.

"I don't think it's here. Sorry," sandals said.

Thongs stood beside a small grate in the floor. "It could have slipped down there."

"No," Doreena said. "It was too big."

Sandals pivoted toward the door. "Then it's definitely not anywhere in here."

Doreena followed the women out past the band and the bar and the bamboo partitions. Earnest sat at a table by the window. Across from him was a half-eaten slice of pink cake and an empty chair. She sank into it, but her chest, bare without the necklace, felt as if it were floating.

"You were saying an island? Which one?" Earnest asked. "Where?"

Doreena looked around trying to recall where they were in this conversation.

"I never understood where all this could come from," Earnest said. "In the old days, there would have been someone asking questions, but now all we've got is *The Mirror* and no one's doing any investigative reporting. But this can't all come from the same place."

"It does," she said.

"When does this happen?"

"It just did," she said.

"You were here eating cake," Earnest said.

"I leave some part of myself behind. Like a shell. It does things while I'm gone."

"Like eat cake?" Earnest said.

Doreena touched her hand to her chest. "I've lost my necklace."

Earnest looked at her then ducked his head under the table. When he popped back up, he raised an eyebrow, at her and said, "I remember it. You always wear that one. It's very unusual. Can you show me where you went?"

"No." she said avoiding his eyes and watching the band instead. The Steelheads' lilting rhythm rose above the metal drums. It seemed disconnected from the objects, emanating directly from the players' fluttering fingertips. "You wouldn't want to come back. And I always do. I always come back. I know you can't believe this."

Earnest tapped his fingers on the table. "Well, in theory, it's plausible if not probable. What you're saying reminds me of quantum entanglement. You and this other place could be connected like entangled particles. Einstein called it 'spooky action at a distance'. But when did you first teleport?"

"After my grandfather died. After I moved into the Narborough," she said. "I think that was the first time. No, I am sure it was."

"The Narborough across from AeroFlux," he said. Then his voice dropped, and he muttered. "There could be side effects."

"What?"

"Let's get out of here. Stay with me," he said. "I want to show you something."

Earnest drove them to the industrial part of town. Across from AeroFlux a gap rose in the night sky where the Narborough had been. She looked at the patch of sky that had been Alonso's third floor apartment. There was rubble below. Would A-Bay have appeared there in the sky? Would he have fallen? Couldn't the island have placed him somewhere safely on earth? It had dropped Marilyn, but only a few feet. Chain link circled a collection of cranes and bulldozers. She could imagine A-Bay sprawled with his limbs twisted over the crushed rocks, but she didn't tell Earnest to stop as they passed the site. She couldn't believe the island would do that to him and what was she supposed to do, explain to Earnest how she'd had teleportation sex with all the surfers?

Miles passed. They entered the forest at the edge of town and the pavement ended. They turned onto a dirt road. The forest was even darker than the city without phosphors. She could barely see the road behind them.

"Where are we going?"

"We're almost there."

They parked in a clearing. The moon shone just over the tops of the evergreens, casting a silvery light on the long grasses so it looked as if they were flowing over the small hill. Earnest leaned out the car door. He stuck his hand into the hillside and she caught a gleam of electronics. The hillside began to hum and the side of it opened. A road dipped into it. Inside, it opened like an airplane hangar. Its sides were lined with cars.

"We're in AeroFlux," Earnest said. "Those are the electric cars they've been selling to New West and the UG."

"Cars? AeroFlux? The future of flight is cars?"

"With all the flights grounded, what were they supposed to do? But yes, one of the possible futures anyway."

They drove past miles of the small, green cars packed alongside the tunnel like jungle leaves. After a while their rounded hulls, grew slimmer and pointed. They looked like nothing she had seen before, a completely new design.

"The latest models," Earnest said. "The flying cars. But this isn't what I want to show you."

They parked beside concrete steps where the road ended. Earnest led her up them and down a dark hall. He grabbed her hand, and it reminded her of trailing her grandfather at his job. He'd worked as the night janitor at her school and the halls had had this same chemical smell. Earnest unlocked a door that opened into darkness. The air moved freely over Doreena's head and opened up far out front of her where distant surfaces glimmered. The room vibrated.

"We're in one of the sub-level mechanic bays," Earnest said. "Let's wait for our eyes to adjust."

As her eyes began to distinguish color in the darkness, Earnest strode toward an enormous teal tube. It looked like one of her old sleeping pills, giant-sized, and ringed with metal clasps. She hadn't bothered to try to force herself to sleep in some time. Earnest tapped the tube with his fingers and she half-expected it to chime. Instead, there has only a dull thud against the thick metal.

"This is it," he said. "We used the inside of an autoclave— an enormous heater used to bake composite materials, the heat changes the chemical structure so that they become an entirely new material stronger or lighter."

He hovered over a screen filled with spinning numbers. "AeroFlux is visionary. That's the secret to its longevity. That's why it's been around so long. The concept from the beginning was flight, not just hunks of flying metal. Not airplanes, not jets, but flight. This is where all the experimental projects are done. Not just flying cars, but ways to fly. This is one of them. In a way, teleportation is flight, the most efficient form. This could be the source of your island right here. They've been testing it a lot. There could have been unforeseen side effects."

The teal capsule thrummed as Earnest waved his hands about explaining.

"I think I meant to marry you," Doreena said.

He stopped; his hands drifting to the side.

"I got all dressed up," she said. "But I can't. Whatever this machine has to do with it, I think, I'm definitely that, what you said earlier, that tangled up effect."

"You really don't remember us, do you?" Earnest said.

"I've been gone. On the island. And I haven't told you the really spooky part. I haven't told anyone. It's calling me from the top of the island louder and louder and I don't know how much longer I can ignore it. I'm afraid. I hear a voice."

"Shhh. Me too." Earnest grabbed her hand and pulled her into the tube. They huddled at the back of it and heard the door open.

"We're moving," she whispered.

"It's vibration, like super-sized Brownian motion," Earnest pulled her close and took her hands in his.

He whispered. "Doreena, we have to get married. You wanted to." He squeezed her hands so tight her fingers ached. It was like shaking hands with Rock Traynter. "Maybe you don't remember us, but you have to remember the baby."

Earnest pressed his hand to her belly, and she felt it suction up to his touch.

She stared down at the little swell. "Baby?"

Then footsteps echoed through the chamber and the opening to the capsule clanged. Large eyes peered down the tube into the darkness at them.

“Thanks kids, I never would have found this without you," The Stew said.

~ 42 ~

MIRROR ISLAND: AEROFLUX PRESSER

The demonstration of teleportation fails, Doreena loses the island

The next day, The Stew's handy work was all over the front page of *The Mirror*, "AeroFlux in export scam, City Fathers to meet." AeroFlux executive Dalton Rees called Doreena at Earnest's apartment.

"It's pushing our timeline, but we have to show them teleportation. They need to see that the opening of C-town's borders is inevitable. I'm calling a press conference. We'll give a demonstration of the new technology," Rees said.

"What does this have to do with me?" Doreena asked.

"I want you to tell them about the island."

"You know about it?"

"Earnest and Marilyn told me everything. Listen Doreena, you work for AeroFlux now."

Everything was happening so fast. Doreena couldn't keep track of it. All her life, C-town had been one stable, steady place. It was devoted to recreating and preserving the comforts of the past. The

City Fathers discouraged innovation as part of the city's Growth Management Act.

"That's a losing strategy," Earnest explained. "You can't defy entropy. It's impossible to stay in stasis. If you're not moving forward, you're falling apart. You always have to be looking ahead."

"That's just a Western way of thinking," Doreena said. It was something her grandfather had often said as he read the C-town CounterPoints, the space where Rock aired dissenting voices on the editorial page of *The Mirror*, so that he could rebut them. Doreena didn't know what her grandfather meant by that, except that he wanted things to stay the same. But where was Eastern? On the other coast of the UG? Somewhere off-continent? And if grandfather liked this different way of thinking, why hadn't her shared it with her?

Now AeroFlux was breaking ranks, creating new flying cars and exporting them and researching other modes of transportation such as teleportation. Somehow, she'd gotten herself tangled up in that too; AeroFlux wanted to annex her island as though it were just another business line. Doreena couldn't believe she'd gotten involved with AeroFlux, until she checked her bank account. It was loaded. She no longer had to worry about buying lunch or paying rent. But she had found herself worrying less and less about these things anyway, since the island made it unnecessary.

In the same way, these new events, this heightening tension between *The Mirror* and AeroFlux troubled her little, even though she seemed to be right in the middle of the two companies and the two executives. These were the troubles one read about on the front page of the paper, not the ones that normally impacted her life, and she thought the island would absolve her of any complicity in the mens' schemes. It would come for her in time. She depended on it.

Earnest dropped her at Denrigger's on his way to work. Doreena met Diane. "Look at my bank statement. Can this be right?"

"Only if you're involved in something illegal," Diane said.

"Exactly." Doreena said. "I need to do some shopping. I have to look like the kind of person who belongs on an island."

"Follow me," Diane said. "Island clothing coming up. We need the fourth floor, and you can afford it."

They switchbacked up the escalators. The goods displayed on each floor grew brighter as they rose. Wealthy people weren't afraid to attract attention. On the fourth floor, they'd left behind any traces of basic black, beige, or brown shoes, handbags, or undergarments. A flurry of silk in macaw-like colors draped the racks. Doreena looked through the glass sides of the escalator to the last of the business suits below. Eggshell, lavender and sea-green were in for spring. The blue, black and gray suits were on sale. Diane fluttered ahead of her through the designer dresses. "I know just the thing. I've been eyeing this all month."

"The thing" was a mannequin wrapped in yellow. Doreena couldn't look away from the pheasant feathers curled over the top of the mannequin's head.

"We have a saying here at Denrigger's, Diane *non est disputandem*," Diane said. "It means: Diane is always right about clothes."

The dress cost more than a month of sales at *The Mirror* even before the accessories Diane threw in: the matching boots and cape-like shoulder wrap. But if there was one thing Marilyn and *Stellar Sales* had taught Doreena, it was the importance of looking the part. Since her island experiences had begun, Doreena had noticed how other people's thoughts had a physical effect on her whether she felt stiff or fluid. She could feel what they thought and feel herself becoming what they expected. Now she wanted them to see her as someone who belonged on an island.

The Denrigger's clerk emptied her bank account and handed her a striped crème bag. It swung at her side, feather-light, holding her return in trade for all the time she'd spent tied to those crates. There are royalties to come, Dalton had assured her, "What they wouldn't do for a little tropical fruit." The surfers had been delivering the island fruits to C-town, but AeroFlux had plans to export her island goods to the rest of the UG.

"I'm wearing it," Doreena said. She put the dress on in the fourth-floor lounge, adjusting the swath of fabric across her hips until it clung to her frame, folding into the places she put it. Outside, she paused beside the mannequin. The dress hung loose on its stiff figure.

"It's good," Diane insisted. "You look like I've always imagined you. From the first time I saw you, I think I saw something islandish inside you."

"Really?" Doreena said. It was strange the way people saw things sometimes, and strange to think they noticed her at all. She was always busy watching others, she never thought of herself as the kind of person who was seen. "I'm surprised you thought of me at all. And how could you know about the island?"

"Well, maybe not the island, but you were kind of far away and thoughtful and you seem exotic," she said. "Didn't you think about me?"

"We thought you wore too much eyeshadow and weren't very good at sales," Doreena said.

"Both true."

"And you seem very birdlike, exotic, too."

On the way in to AeroFlux, Doreena stopped by the black and white photo and picked her grandfather's face out from the team of astronauts standing among the proud crew of mechanics that had worked on the AF-897 spaceship. They wore flight suits with the old AeroFlux logo; the same wings but in a cubic style with blunt, shorn-looking feathers. The modern logo was streamlined, its wingtips like blades.

She'd researched the flight since she'd first seen the photo and knew how heroic the men had been. The astronauts were going to stabilize the world's economy; they were seeking a new energy source on a distant planet. It had worked for a while too, until the mining operation had caused the new planet to implode. How had grandfather survived and come to raise her? He must have been so much older than he looked. She clutched at her necklace, but her hands cupped air. She thought of how she would look to him. Exotic, Diane had said. Ridiculous, her grandfather would think.

Grandfather would not have liked it, her being here in this get up or being here at all about to get up on stage in front of everyone and take a stand against the status quo in C-town. She was going to attract attention, exactly what he'd always wanted her to avoid. Ever since grandfather had died, it seemed, she'd been defying him, breaking rules she hadn't questioned before. It was no way to honor his memory. But he'd left her with so few memories, she thought angrily. Maybe if he'd told her about her mother...Then, what? Would she have lived a different life? She was no longer sure what she wanted. She realized she had never known. She'd had no deep desires until she'd ridden the island wave. Now it was crashing over her.

The belly of AeroFlux was already full when she arrived. Suited people sat in row after row of metal folding chairs. Workers in red AeroFlux coveralls flanked them on one side of the room and the union workers in their green shirts stood behind them on the other.

"You're here." A young woman guided Doreena up a metal platform. An AeroFlux banner swathed the teal tube behind the stage and gave wings to its jet-sized bulk. Vases of red anthurium lilies flanked the stage. AeroFlux flouted its island contraband. The City

Fathers sat sternly in the front row with Rock at their center. The Stew scribbled in his notebook beside them.

"They want to shut AeroFlux down," Doreena said.

Dalton Rees looked fresh and confident in a linen suit. "Not after this they won't. The island changes everything."

The chairs buckled and squelched against the concrete floor as the crowd shifted, waiting for them to begin.

"After you," Dalton said. The top of Doreena's boots flexed around her thigh as she ascended the platform. She could feel Rock glaring at her through his double-glasses. She'd still never seen his eyes. Were they gray like the concrete floor, or teal like the teleportation tube? She had not expected to make it this far without feeling the pull of the blue haze. She had not thought that the island would abandon her to this. She adjusted the useless yellow capelet around her shoulders. It was still cold.

Dalton commandeered the microphone. "Welcome to AeroFlux," he began. "The inner bowels so to speak. This is where the real work of our company gets done. As you know, AeroFlux has always been about flight: from the days when our jets sailed the open skies of the United Government, until our fleet shrank to flights out of C-town airport, until a few years ago when all flights out were cancelled except those regular trips to Hawaii and then last week when our very last flight to Maui left and the City Fathers eliminated the rest. Today, C-town is an island, isolated, no longer a peninsula even with a single line of contact to the outside world. We've all been grounded. AeroFlux has been criticized for defying that destiny. Yes, we've been selling cars to our neighbors to the south, New West. But while I am grateful to the City Fathers for what they have done to protect the way of life in C-town, and I appreciate the insulation they created from the chaotic world out there, I don't apologize for fighting their isolationism or for trying to keep your jobs open. As you know, AeroFlux is not about jets or airplanes. We've never been about mere machinery; we're propelled by an idea: flight."

Dalton paused and looked from one side of the room to the other across the sea of red and green. The standing workers were leaning forward now, swaying on their feet. Like a conductor, Dalton pointed from one side of the room to the other. The floor rumbled as the AeroFlux employees began to stamp. "The future is flight," he said. The workers cheered. "That's right. And we'll do whatever it takes. Whether it's jets or flying cars, we *will* fly into the future. Today, we are here to demonstrate a new technology which will change the direction of C-town and the UG for all of us."

Dalton turned to Doreena, "They're ready."

She swayed uncertainly in her boots. She couldn't believe she was still here. She'd stayed through the speech. The City Fathers and Rock glared up at her, their hands stiff in their laps. There was not the slightest tinge of blue in the yellow-gray, fluorescent light of the room. The cool, dry air flowed around her. Where was the haze and the suction? When would the island rescue her?

"Let's skip my part," she whispered. "Go to the demonstration."

But Dalton stepped away and gestured to the microphone, "They're ready for you."

Doreena's breath reverberated through the hangar in time with the whir undulating from the jet-shaped machine behind the platform. Earnest, among the red coveralls, caught her eye. He nodded. For once she heard the words repeating inside her head in her own low voice, not Marilyn's or Stellar Sales', "Believe in your product. Be persistent. Speak as if to one person you care about." When had she become her own employer?

"I." The microphone squawked as she began to speak. "I want to live on an island. We all do. But not the kind the C-town fathers have created," she looked down at Rock in the front row, "the bleak fantasy of a colorblind man." He stared up at her from behind his two pairs of glasses and even though she could see no trace of his eyes or feeling she didn't like to look at him. All he'd ever done was give her a job and ask her to work hard for *The Mirror*. The trade had never seemed anything but acceptable, and now here she was cutting down his dream. The security and longevity of C-town that Rock had sustained would evaporate. "I've been to a place with sun and light and tropical breezes. I've been to this place. I've teleported. The future of flight is teleportation."

That said, she was a traitor, just like The Stew.

Rock sat unmoving with his fists clenched on his knees.

"Yes, I think, a demonstration," Dalton said.

The workers behind them shuffled. The machine thrummed. While it came to life, Earnest took the microphone and explained the science. Doreena recalled some of what he was saying from their conversation over dinner, "light waves travel 300,000 kilometers per second...oxygen molecules travel 480 meters per second...there are 26 trillion particles for every 70 kilos of body mass."

Doreena raised her arms, reaching for the island sun, eager to shed her awkward shell. The machine popped. The sky flashed blue; an effect which Earnest had explained was caused by the charged Fermi sea of electrons and polarized photons. There was a chemical smell of lithium niobate crystals used to steer the photons down the optical fibers hooked around the room. Doreena looked for the waves but saw only an ocean of black suits shifting on their metal chairs.

A worker joined Dalton on the stage. They turned toward the teal tube, their backs to the crowd. Doreena looked at Rock as he sat leaning back on the metal, his hands steepled in confidence. The doors at the back of the room swung open and the surfers, in wetsuits, cut a black swath through the divide of AeroFlux red, and union green, workers. Doreena looked up at them in wonder. How had her surfers, her islanders, as she now thought of them, returned without her? All those times they'd let her go, never knowing when she'd return. She'd left them stranded on the island, but they'd never minded. They'd never been afraid. They looked afraid now, and angry, the island had released them when they wanted to be contained.

"She's there," J-Bay shouted as the surfers ran down the aisle of chairs in their squeaking neoprene shoes. AeroFlux security blocked them at the stage. There was a grayish cast to all their faces and their wrinkled wetsuits hung. They were all back, every one of them, and they looked like starved seals. It was clear that the island fruits had not been truly feeding their bodies. And yet, all she had been eating was island fruit, too, and she was as fat as ever. Her body was sleek and swollen from it, while their bodies had wasted away. Only A-Bay was missing.

"I didn't have anything to do with it," Doreena said, before Dalton took the microphone from her. "It's this machine."

"Obviously, we had to rush this demonstration in light of today's headlines. Apparently, we don't have the power to move this much mass. But, if we can isolate it within the tube, we can continue the demonstration with a few volunteers," Dalton said. "Go. Let's keep it moving."

They descended the stage, and he pushed her toward the machine. The Stew hustled forward with his notebook and security waved him inside while holding back the reaching and shouting surfers, "We'll go. Doreena!"

"I'm sorry. There isn't room for everyone, perhaps one of the City Fathers?" Dalton asked.

Rock stepped up. "I'll stand in your machine."

Doreena wanted to back away from his gray bulk, rather than crowd with him into the tiny tube, afraid that any contact with him would be razor sharp. She also feared his effect on the island.

"Perfect," Dalton said. "Maybe one more. Doreena?"

Doreena turned from the desperate faces of the surfers. She could see how they blamed her for their reappearance in C-town. But what had she ever done? She'd delivered them to paradise and borne back the fruits of their labors. She pointed to Earnest. He'd wanted to marry her. He'd given her a ring. And he was the one who'd explained how all this technology worked. She felt guilty to betray her own tribe, but Earnest quickly stepped inside, and the decision was made.

"I'll come back for you," Doreena said to Alonso and Hobart and the rest of the islanders as she stood in the dark, pressed closed against Earnest and The Stew and the two executives. The tube reeked with the competing scents of their colognes: chemical earth versus chemical sky.

The arrival of these men on the island would be a kind of pollution, she thought, now that they were close around her and preparing to embark. First, Marilyn and then the surfers had come to the island, and they'd changed it. Marilyn's fears were responsible for the sharks. The surfers had made the island bigger and diversified the variety of plants and animals. These powerful men would shape it too. She could have tried to stop the demonstration, but Doreena desperately wanted it to work.

It had been too long since she'd seen the island. She felt brittle and afraid. She put her own desire ahead of the island's preservation. What good was it, if she wasn't there? She was already planning to escape to the far side of it, to find a way to another beach either the inaccessible one Alonso had seen or one he had missed. She would even climb up into the jungle if that were the only way. The workers closed the metal lid with a clanging staccato and sealed them inside.

"Now, we teleport," Dalton said.

The machine thrummed. Earnest took hold of her hand. The blue current flowed around them. Shapes circled in the dark around the scratching of The Stew's stylus. There were many sensations similar to the onset of her island. There was the hazy blue light of the Fermi sea. The claustrophobic press of bodies in the dark suctioned around her.

Earnest had told her a few different theories about how teleportation worked. The most likely, and most demonstrable, being that it was not a transfer of matter or particles at all, but a transfer of the information carried on them. He had described things that were very small, and she found hard to visualize. She did not have a scientific background, but what he said meshed with her own island experience. It was likely that she had not been transported to a new location at all, but simply copied, which explained how she continued to live her life on C-town. The information that made her had been replicated.

Then, Earnest had gone into a long and complicated philosophical discussion about the soul. Scientists, he said, had discovered a lot about matter and mind, but there was a level of understanding, between the microcosm and macrocosm, they could not grasp. Earnest called this, “the mysterious gap”. Neuroscientists, in their studies of the brain, didn't know what caused consciousness. Quantum physicists, in their studies of matter, didn't understand the behavior of specks of it at the smallest levels. Earnest made it sound as if these two remaining mysteries were connected and about to be revealed.

In short, he could not say what had happened to her soul. Most likely, it did not replicate. "That's the no cloning theorem," he'd said. "Quantum particles can't be duplicated." But it might remain in two places at once entangled in C-town and on the island. The danger was decoherence, that the connection was fragile and if they tried to pin it down it might disappear altogether, he said.

Earnest explained about entangled particles, how bits could remain together acting in tandem even when separated. He used the term nonlocality; which meant that time and space did not matter. Doreena, who had always been discouraged from thinking about anything mysterious or theoretical, found these musings perplexing; except that it all fit within the realm of her recent experience. But she remained concerned about her soul. She had often felt like her soul had been split between the two places: C-town and the island. Often in C-town, she had felt soulless. A terrible thought occurred to her: What if she and the island had always been entangled, long before she'd ever actually experienced it? What if much of her soul had been living on the island unknown to her? This felt true. The idea resonated. There had been so many times that her grandfather and Tom and Marilyn had accused her of lacking something, some intangible quality, some passion, some happiness without which all her stalwart devotion fell short of some ineffable standard. They'd said the same thing over and over again bewildering and confusing her, now their words carried a clear meaning: they'd been calling her soulless.

In the AeroFlux teleportation tube, after a series of pulses, there was a single bang and then a painful pop passed between her ears. The lid clanged open. Dim light shone through the porthole. Doreena peered around Rock's shoulders wishing she had the strength to shove his bulk aside in her haste for the island, but something was wrong. The island was nowhere in sight or feeling. Cold air flowed in at them off the AeroFlux factory floor. Doreena thought she could collapse from weariness and the weight of her disappointment, but her body was so stiff it upheld her. The surfers, gray-faced, stood shivering. Their hands usually so languid at their sides, twitched with sadness. They looked cold and exposed even in their suits. Even Alonso and Hobart looked drained and fidgety.

The islanders were the flaw in Earnest's theory. While entanglement described her experience perfectly, it did not explain what happened to the islanders or Marilyn. They did not appear to live two lives while on the island. They disappeared from C-town returning to it exactly where they had left. Earnest had had other theories of teleportation. It was possible, for example, that it worked more like reincarnation. In order to teleport, a particle had to be destroyed and rebuilt. Maybe only the soul could teleport. Maybe that's what had happened to hers and where it had been all along. There were other ways it could work, but Earnest's science could not explain why she was different. Doreena thought she knew: It had to do with how she was tangled up in the island. It was her place, and they were only tourists. Their souls could visit, but not inhabit it. The failure of the demonstration proved it. It was her island, and it was gone.

She was the last to leave the tube leaning stiffly into Earnest, letting him help hold her upright. Rock took the stage. He applauded and the City Fathers joined him. "A marvelous demonstration. Truly. It reminds me what's at stake. We're not experimenting. We're preserving our way of life. That's something no outsider can appreciate. Although all you'd have to do to understand is step out onto the chaos of the 'Way, Mr. Rees here makes it seem like C-town is a prison, yet nothing prevents him from leaving. Certainly, we encourage him to go."

"We," he gestured at the silent teal tube, "cannot be affected by this machine. We cannot rely on technological solutions to innovate for us again and again and pull us back from the brink of disaster. That is not the answer. We all remember how that works. It may prevent us from plunging into the abyss, but we remain poised on the brink and eventually, inevitably, we fall. The spaceship, the new power source, the mining of another planet; you remember. All that saved us for a while. But eventually it imploded, and we plunged into economic ruin anyway. Even if this teleporter worked and brought us goods from the outside, it wouldn't do what you wanted it to do for long and it would create further dilemmas. The only thing that can prevent chaos, and make our society safe and sane and whole, is political will and personal responsibility. We draw a line in the sand, and we step back from the edge. We step back from the edge. We don't wait for a crutch, or a savior, or a mechanism to wrench us away. Citizens of C-town, the answers are within our grasp. All we have to do and continue to do is make choices. It is within our power to move: in our minds, our bodies, our hands."

His voice made the microphone redundant in the hollow hangar and as he spread his arms wide his hands, long and spatulate, the ends of them looked as if they could pull the room together. Beside him, Dalton looked reedy; with delicate hands suited to fine-tuning. In a tug-of-war, Rock Traynter would win.

Earnest squeezed Doreena's arm. "I was wrong."

"It was supposed to be possible," she said.

But Earnest's science seemed a flimsy thing now, just as Alonso's tulpa theory had seemed when she'd been in the very real jaws of the shark. Earnest's scientific reality was too fanciful, and Alonso's fancy was too real. Doreena didn't know what the answer was, but she didn't like feeling trapped in C-town when all she wanted was the island. It actually felt worse now that the surfers were with her, the opposite of what she'd been thinking and would have expected. It had been better when she could imagine others enjoying her beautiful place, better than imagining it emptied. The new plants and flowers that the surfer's thoughts had fertilized would be drained of life and left wilting and then rotting in the island sun.

"For the longest time," Rock continued. "We've struggled to keep our standard of living at accustomed levels. We've sacrificed. In a few months, we will be rewarded. Traynter Resort will open — all the luxury of the world in your backyard. The next time we meet, you won't be disappointed. Traynter Construction and Traynter Hospitality Services are hiring now. Turn in your applications today. Thank you very much for joining me here to see this very powerful demonstration. Nothing happens without *The Mirror*. We all see where we are truly going now."

The security guards let the surfers pass into the blue machine. They laid hands on Doreena at once and they kissed her, but nothing happened. Hobart and Alonso bent over the control panel, but the machine stayed silent.

Earnest held her. "So, there's no island."

"There is," Doreena said. "I've been."

"Are you sure?" Earnest said.

"Of course, she's sure," Alonso said. "We were there, too."

"All of you?" Earnest said. "You brought them all? Then how are you here?"

"Last night, we all landed in Traynter Lake not long after J-Bay left."

"You guys come back to where you left from," she said. "But I am always somewhere else."

She was still trying to get her mind around how the island affected her differently, what it could mean, and whether that was the key to getting it back. All she knew for sure was that neither science nor myth would transport her.

She remembered her argument with her grandfather when he'd abruptly left her for Maui. She'd felt betrayed that he planned to go without her. "But you always said, home is where I am." she'd said. "Where will home be when you are gone?" Where was grandfather now? When people died, they disappeared, he said. That was all. It hadn't bothered her at the time. But it did now. She clutched again at the empty space at her breast where her grandfather's ashes should have been. An idea came to her and then went when J-Bay interrupted it.

"Doreena," he said, and it was difficult to look at him because his face was so drawn with famine and the gray of C-town. "Where's my brother?"

"A-Bay and I left from the apartment," she said. "But the apartment isn't there anymore. It's been torn down. The third floor, all of it."

Doreena and the surfers walked across the street. They cupped their hands against the window of The Travel Museum. Everything was gone. The walls were bare brick, stripped of every poster.

"I can't believe I let it happen," Hobart said. "I should have been here. I said I'd come back. What did they do with it all?"

Next door, the construction workers were erecting the Lakeside Hotel, part of Traynter Resort, in the footprint of the Narborough. Doreena pointed to the empty sky where she'd held A-Bay close in the apartment. "There."

They stepped onto the site and wouldn't leave when the construction workers confronted them. "You can't be here without a hard hat. It's not for tourists."

The manager stalked toward them in a bright orange vest. When he looked up from under the shadow of his hard hat, he stared at J-Bay with a haunted look.

"I'm looking for my brother," J-Bay said.

The construction worker was stiff and silent for a long while with his hands hidden behind his back. "Your twin, must be," he finally said. "I'm sorry. We didn't know who to call. We found him this morning." He pointed at rubble beside a pile of steel girders. "We didn't know who he was." His voice dropped and he looked away from J-Bay. "They took the body to the morgue."

She looked at the surfers, cold and haggard and saddened by the loss of one of their own. It wouldn't be long now, she thought, until they would leave her. After, the island they wouldn't be able to make do with the cold waters of the lake. Doreena looked up at the drifting clouds. The island had placed A-Bay, its supplicant, in the empty sky and dropped him. This was what it was capable of: abandoning him and her and all of them, disregarding their safety and their fates. Still, no matter how uncertain she was of the island in principle, she still wanted it.

~ 43 ~

MIRROR ISLAND: ROCK TRAYNTER'S RESORT

Withdrawal, the island abandons Doreena and her islanders

Doreena and her islanders came together again in the Labor Temple, in its dripping rooms permeated with silicon stench. They waited for the island to return. The drum circle went silent as soon as Earnest entered. The AeroFlux employee didn't belong here.

"It's OK," Alonso said to the islanders, as Doreena rose and followed Earnest into the hall. "She'll be back."

In the pressroom, Doreena leaned against the wall while Earnest talked. The presses were still and silent now. The *C-town Traveler* had been neglected and then abandoned. The islanders had given up.

"Nothing's going to change this place," J-Bay had said and not even Alonso or Hobart argued. But they still loved drumming; it was all they had left now that the lake was off-limits. The plaster shook as they resumed their beats.

"Come back to the apartment with me," Earnest said.

"I told you I'm waiting for the island. You don't believe me."

"I love you," he said. "Let's work this out. You said you were pregnant."

"Then I lied. And if I were, you might not be the father. Those guys in the next room, they've all been to the island all except you. How do you think they got there? We went together kissing and making love, our bodies connected, creating a magical island energy which you've never experienced. You couldn't with your cold steel tubes, your factory, and your machines. You broke it. My connection to the island was fragile you said. Now, it's gone."

"You're, this is, crazy. You're blaming me? I'm sorry, but I can't take this anymore. I've tried to help you for the baby's sake," Earnest said.

"Look at me, what baby?"

"Fine. I'm leaving. I won't ask you again." In the dripping hallway, his retreating figure grew shadowy as he walked upstairs to the street. "You said you heard voices." he called back, casting echoes. "Maybe you should see someone."

Alonso joined her in the hallway and wrapped his arms around her.

"If the island's a delusion, I still want to have it," she said. "I'm sorry I made you miss the last flight to Maui and now you're stuck here with me."

"It was my choice," he said.

The islanders that went out to work reported that C-town looked more C-town than ever. The Tiki-Tiki Lounge closed. They began to talk about leaving.

It was worse here without The Travel Museum and the lake to surf on, and still no sign of the island. "We were going to steal one of those flying cars," J-Bay said. "But they're gone too. The tunnel's empty. Still nothing?"

"Whatever it was, is gone," Hobart said.

"We can't stay here. I think we should take our chances out on the 'Way, just walk 'til we get somewhere. Anywhere's better," J-Bay said.

Hobart nodded. "If I thought I could, I'd go."

They looked to Alonso. He nodded. "We'll go, but let's get some things together first. I want us to have a chance at making it somewhere. Soon."

When Doreena left the Labor Temple, no one tried to stop her. The islanders, or maybe they were just surfers again, weren't like that. They were used to each other coming and going and finding their own way. They let each other make their own mistakes: like when Alonso had left the Thai set to follow the chick Jeanne to Tibet or J-Bay and A-Bay had tried to share the same girl in Cape Town or Lonnie had surfed the Tank Roll on a day when no one else would touch it and he went under forever. Everyone had known those decisions would bring pain, but that was life, and death was life, too. Loners came back to the tribe a little wiser, with scars to heal. Or, as in Lonnie's case, if they did not come back, the surfers all went out to the sea together to sit upright on their boards and link legs and tell the stories of a man's stoke quest through the night until the sun rose.

Doreena walked across town to see the condominium rise where grandfather's house had been. Staring at the crisp, beige squares of building over her childhood home and the absence of hibiscus, she felt empty and faint. She was neither hungry, nor thirsty, nor sleepy. There was nothing to take her mind off this either. She wished she could go to work. There, a feeling like this wouldn't even register. She returned to Traynter Tower. It was overcast and in the reflective surface of *The Mirror* building she stood: a yellow blur like a remote sun in the slick gray surface. She sank to the street, and huddled.

In the morning, the pressmen in their gray coveralls and then the sales force in their suits entered the building. No one looked her way or spoke to her. Rock's pea green car rolled up, its chrome fenders shining through the timid morning light, into its reserved space along the street. At night, a waft of silicon from the presses followed the men out. Doreena stuffed papers into her boots, now a grimy shade of yellow. She tucked her boot legs under her, pulled her capelet around her shoulders and insulated herself with silicon sheets. The headlines read "Traynter Resort: C-town's Paradise in Progress." She stared up into the pink glow of the phosphors and the dark line where the top of Traynter Tower intruded. The long, still night passed. When the sky began to gray, she rubbed her back. The ridges of the brick wall were etched along her spine.

That day, not long after he'd arrived, Rock Traynter left *The Mirror* building. The editor, Vic, followed him out.

"So sorry for your loss," he said.

"My son, my son," Rock said, pushing Vic away. He lurched toward his car; his feet twisted over each other, and his broad shoulders sloped to the street. A noise like a gull's cry rose from his throat as he hung on the open door of his car.

It was hard to see Rock like this, his stalwart form and voice eroding in waves of grief. Doreena watched the editor turn away. She knew at once what had happened, the only thing that could have affected Rock Traynter like this. Marilyn had miscarried. The bed rest had not saved his son.

Rock tore his shades from his eyes, both pairs in one fluid motion, and pressed his hands into them. There was a flash of light color: his eyes mounted in the winter sky. But, which: gray, violet, amber, green?

He sank into the car, head bowed. His black-suited leg stuck out of it trembling. "My son."

Then he looked up. It was as if he held the island in his piercing blue eyes. The color looked powerful enough to transport her and she wanted to go to him and find a way into his eyes, bright with sorrow. But her body was heavy and slack on the street. The car door slammed, and Doreena shrugged off her soggy translucent pink broadsheets. She bent her legs and, like an animal mired in mud, struggled to rise off the street. The muck-colored heels of her boots caught in a crack of the pavement, and she lunged forward. She lurched for the car as it pulled away, "Marilyn." She sat on her heels and brushed a skiff of dust away. It came from her side, moldy brown with a sheen of gold like the bottom of a dry creek bed. She picked at her clothes and a chunk of brown crumbled in her hand. She rose quickly and nearly fell. A ring of mud circled the place up against the building where she'd been sitting. Clouds of black gold dust drifted from her shoulders. It fell around her as she walked across town to C-town General. The doors opened automatically. She stepped into the sick place, crumbling.

"Marilyn Traynter," she said at the front desk, her voice raspy. "Marilyn Traynter's room."

The receptionist didn't acknowledge her but reached back for her sweater. "Hey Joe," she said. A security guard who'd been staring into a fish tank turned around. "You wanna' step out for a smoke?"

With the receptionist gone, Doreena used the computer herself to find Marilyn's room. She left smudges of golden-black glitter across at keyboard.

The room was on the third floor. She made her way up unnoticed. Marilyn sat in bed staring out the window. The color of the day was gone. Everything was white, as if all the color had congealed in Marilyn's black eyes. Even her hair, frizzed up against the pillow, had a dull cast to it. Doreena approached uncertainly, but Marilyn turned and regarded her at once. Doreena instantly felt more solid.

"Why didn't you come sooner?" Marilyn said. "They say that I have had a miscarriage, but they haven't been to the island, and they couldn't possibly know. What's happened to my boy is beyond the reach of medicine."

Doreena stared at the grime-filled lines in her hands and pushed her thumb across the powder. The muscle in her palm arched. The bones splayed across the back of her hand showing through her gray skin. "I'm so sorry. It's my fault."

"He's on the island. I left him there," Marilyn said, she reached her arms out. "Take me to him."

Doreena knew she meant the baby. Marilyn didn't know the island had left them without consolation. They had only each other. In sympathy, she bent close to Marilyn to let her arms enfold her. At first, it seemed Marilyn's arms might pass through her muddy clothes, but they finally caught her around and gripped her waist. But when the hospital room remained, Marilyn released her.

"It's gone," Doreena said. "Whatever it was, AeroFlux's experiments or the islanders' tulpas. We'll have to go on without it. There is no island now."

"No, my son is there," Marilyn said. "He is. Other things people want are there. Things not possible in C-town."

"Yes, but those are only small things: fruit."

"But he is small, so small, and like a kind of fruit."

Doreena was silent. She found herself wondering whether it was possible. There were still so many things about the island she did not know. Maybe they would open up one of the fruits on the island, a durian or a coconut, and find Marilyn’s son inside it nestled like a seed. How could she argue with Marilyn? Why say it was impossible?

"I left him. How could I have done that?" Marilyn said, staring into her hands. "It was because I didn't want him trapped here. No one likes a cage. With even a little open door to Maui, we coped. We adapted. People do. But he shut us in completely. Stupid. You have to leave people a way out to make them feel safe and accept their containment. If you trap them, people will start looking for a way out and they'll find one, like rats. Try to close all the gaps and a new one opens. Leave an opening and the majority will stay in, they won't even notice." She looked up and her black eyes darkened. "That was your mistake, Rock. Shutting down those flights to Maui. Hardly anyone could afford them anyway. You should have left them hope. Then I never would have gone to the island, and my son would still be here in my arms."

Doreena turned and saw the man behind her barricading the doorway. She clutched her hands to her chest. She wished for the ghost-like quality she'd had before, so that he couldn't see her, but her hands were cleaner now, her usual honey-brown tone coated with an ordinary layer of dirt. She was any laid off worker. And even though Rock's eyes were hidden again behind his double-glasses she could feel the vise of his attention. His fists were clenched. "Why are you here? Get out."

"Wait," Marilyn grabbed her wrist. "It's bullshit about AeroFlux and the Islanders. I've been there with you. You can get it back."

She scrutinized Doreena. Her gaze felt like girding. It made Doreena hold the posture of *The Mirror's* top salesman. "Where's that necklace? Your grandfather, you said. Blue. You vomited blue."

Doreena grasped at the air between her breasts again. "It's gone." She balled her hand into a fist. "Oh. Gone."

It had been in one of the twin's hands as they passed into the blue haze. Inside J-Bay's scarred fist. And then, A-Bay and J-Bay had fallen away from her. She'd dropped to the tiles in the Tiki-Tiki Lounge bathroom. A-Bay had fallen through the sky and J-Bay into the lake with all the other islanders after him once she had lost the necklace and their connection to the island.

"That's it," Marilyn said, whispering quickly. "You remember where you saw it last. Listen, my mother told me it's difficult for women to manage other women. We resist each other, the way we resist our mothers; because we see in each other what we dislike in ourselves. You see in me the cold reserve and the need for security that binds you. I see in you someone too adaptable and weak-willed to act independently. But we must accept ourselves now. We have to accept authority, but only so that we can learn to outgrow it. Do so now. It's not our fault we live in C-town and have had to operate within its perimeters. Don't punish the child for it. Go. Get the necklace. Bring back the island to me. My son is there, alone, and too small to forage, too young to eat fruit. Please."

"Get out," Rock said from behind them. He grabbed Doreena's arm and spun her toward the door. He looked startled when he laid hands on her. "I've seen you around. Stay away from *The Mirror* and my wife."

"But Rock, she can get us back to our baby. There's an island and I'm still pregnant there. I know I am. He's there. The doctors said there wasn't anything of him to bury. Nothing came out."

"Stop raving," he said. "You lost the baby, Marilyn. It's gone. It's over."

"No," Marilyn said. "He's there. I'm pregnant still. I am."

"She's more pregnant than you," Rock said.

Marilyn ignored him and pleaded with Doreena. "Promise me, you'll go back. Promise me you'll find him."

Doreena remembered how they had walked on the island beach, not holding hands exactly for it was too hot, but side by side with their fingertips occasionally touching.

"Of course, I will," she said, feeling the burden of the promise in her belly.

With that, Rock turned to her furiously. If Doreena had not seen his naked glistening pain-stricken eyes earlier, she would have thought him monstrous. "Find your own child. Ours is lost. Lost. Leave us."

He pushed her through the door, and she fell to her knees in the hallway. That morning, in her fragile state, such a push and a fall to the floor would have crumbled her, she had been close to becoming another layer of grime on the C-town street. Now she caught herself. The flesh of her hands and knees pressed against the mopped Formica. Talking to Marilyn had restored her solidness, although there would be a black-gold glittery cast to the bruises forming on her knees and a pit weighing in her center as if she had swallowed a stone.

The islanders hadn't left the Labor Temple. They'd stacked their backpacks in a corner of the room. When she told them about the necklace, Alonso and Hobart agreed to help her search the lake before they went. J-Bay threw up his hands. "I'm done."

"One last try," Hobart said. "There's something to it."

At night, they walked the three miles along the road and climbed the chain link fence to get to the shore. The marshes and cattails were gone, replaced by sands that glowed in the moonlight. Alonso massaged a handful of the coarse grains in pale green, pink and yellow. "A synthetic."

They entered the sanitized lake in wetsuits. The cool water held no smell. It thinly splashed her bare hands and face. They strapped lights to their foreheads like pilot fish and swam ahead into the beams. The phosphors in the grains of the synth sand, newly thick and three feet down, glowed as they combed through it.

"It will be further out," Doreena said. They couldn't see anything in the glow anyway.

"We landed far out," Alonso said.

The synth sand covered the bottom of the lake for 20 feet, but the same old muck lay at the lake's center. Its bottom was green-black gunk, a mixture of decomposed fish, algae, and C-town effluent. They dug through it raising particle-clouds into the murky water. The brownish silt looked like a dull version of the slough of her body on the street. They found a bicycle tire, rusty cans, glass bottles, fish bones, and folded remnants of *The Mirror* that swayed like kelp.

"When I get to the bottom, I've got just enough breath left in me to stir up the sediment," Hobart said when she surfaced. "Could be anywhere in there, buried. Or," she looked to shore, "Back there in that fake stuff."

"But we know it's here somewhere," Doreena said, casting an arc of moonlit waves as she turned round. "Somewhere in this circle."

"Unless it slipped through the filters," Hobart said. "The ones they're using to clean this. I'm sorry, but it was small enough. Are you even sure it was J-Bay grabbed it? Could be buried under that new hotel."

"I'm pretty sure I remember seeing the scar on his wrist," she said.

That first night of searching the three of them dove until the first gray tinge of daylight. On subsequent nights, they swam straight to the middle. Hobart tired after ten or so dives and waited for them on the shore. After a week, she stopped going with them.

"I still think it went through the filters," she said. "You're still trying? It's raining tonight. So, you really think it will bring back the island?"

"Either way, it's my grandfather. I should find it." Doreena said. She clutched the hollow of her chest. "I know it's there. I can see it, you know."

Alonso walked with her through the rain. She snagged her wetsuit on the chain link. The surface of the lake rose in onyx peaks but underneath the water her view of the cloudy bottom was no more obscure than usual. It was even a tinge warmer below the lake than above in the pelting rain. But they didn't find it that night. On Friday it was clear and Alonso dove with her again. She surfaced and found him floating on his back staring up. "Just resting. Beautiful moon. You should take a break, too."

"I can't stop looking when I know it's there," she said.

"I think you'll have to. This isn't good for you," he said.

Even without mirrors at the Labor Temple, she knew what he meant. She'd noticed the blue-gray cast to her arms and legs and how the dry cracks in her hands had swollen and filled in with overlapping lines. They hung at her sides like damp gloves. She'd become accustomed to the cold water; she never slept. She barely needed the headlamp anymore. She could see better in the dark and she'd begun, faintly, to glow like synth sand.

At the end of the next week, J-Bay said he was leaving. "Who's coming?"

"Wait," Alonso said. He threw a copy of *The Mirror* down on the floor in front of the islanders' drum circle. "Traynter Resort Opens July 20," the headline proclaimed in the biggest point type since the AeroFlux crash.

"One last try. In daylight." Alonso said.

"Fine. One," J-Bay said.

"That's all we've got. The public can come to the opening, then members only," Alonso said. "They'll keep us out."

On July 20, the islanders wore half-wetsuits leaving their arms and legs bare. They were ready to try the wave machines, only Alonso talked about searching the lake. Crowds covered the beach along the resort even early that morning. The new hotel fronts gleamed beyond. Vendors sold shaved ice, caramel apples, and chilled pears along the walkway. Nearby The Steelheads were setting up their marimbas. Boats zipped across the lake's surface close to the hotel. Parasails with rainbow chutes rose behind them. The place was pleasant, but uninspiring. The islanders ran over the multicolored faux sand with their boards overhead, slipped into the water and headed for the waves. Alonso and Doreena swam past them to the center of the lake. The water had been filtered to a clearish green like colored glass. Sunlight shone through the clouds of stirred silt as they searched. After several dives, they came up empty-handed.

Alonso came up for air and inhaled: a long anxious ah. "I still can't stay down long enough. We may not find it."

Doreena remembered looking for the necklace in the island's ocean when it had slipped through Marilyn's fingers. The water had been clear and lit. She remembered gliding back and forth over the rippled sand. When she'd returned with it, the giddy island flush was gone from Marilyn cheeks.

"You were gone so long," she'd said.

Doreena didn't remember that "ah" of inhalation or being out of breath when she'd come up from the island's ocean.

She dove again, this time without taking the many small breaths to permeate her blood with oxygen as Alonso had taught her. She imagined the fine links of the necklace's silver chain. She combed a large square of the lakebed muck with her fingers. Then, pressure wrenched her chest. She shot up to the surface and sucked air.

Alonso swam to her. "You, OK? I was worried. You were down so long."

"Don't," she said. "Let me look alone."

"What's wrong? Listen, we may have to accept it's just lost."

Doreena held up her hands. The sun shone through the gray, clammy edges of her skin. "Look. I can do this. I need you not to worry. I want to find it. Let me do this."

She went under before he could reply. His legs churned the water above. The pressure circled her chest. She fought to stay down: Just don't think about it. Find the necklace. He wants me to find it. The wetsuit weighed on her. It held her limbs close. She unzipped the suit and peeled it off. The water flowed over her bare skin. The disembodied wetsuit floated above her, its limbs dangling. She opened her mouth. A puff of sparkling blue billowed into the green lake. Yellow fishes appeared in the specks and grew as they swam. Her body, heavy and fluid, began to sink. She followed the fishes down to the murky lakebed.

She reached for the first glint of silver, expecting it to flash away from her hand. It stayed. She tugged at a buried loop and a bright chain uncoiled from the drenched loam. A vial floated on the end of it. She rose with the necklace in hand and broke the surface in silence. Alonso swam to her, and she could not read the expression on his sunlit face. His hands were cool on the back of her neck as he fastened the necklace for her. They swam together past the boats with water-skiers and parasailers toward the celebration on the shore. The islanders glided off the wave machine induced crests to follow them when Alonso beckoned.

On shore, the islanders crowded around her to hide her nudity. Loudspeakers screeched and spread a distortion of voices over the crowd as the ceremony began. There were familiar faces in the throng, members of the salesforce, barely recognizable, out of uniform, in linens and Hawaiian shirts. They raised flutes of sparkling wine. Marilyn stood beside Rock and the City Fathers, in dark suits, and their wives, in floral dresses, on a platform in the center of a swimming pool. The color of the day was gray. A plane flew overhead trailing a Traynter Resort banner and leaving a wake of colored smoke across the cool blue sky.

On the beach, Doreena opened the vial and dumped the contents of the necklace into her hand. The ashes were gray as the lake bottom. She took a pinch between her finger and thumb. She would not risk being parted from her grandfather, or the island, again. Like charcoal, the first pinch caught in her throat. The next was flakier and saline. Pinch by pinch, she ate the ashes. The last few were pink and sweet like saltwater taffy. Finally, she licked the traces of sweet blue that stained her hand. She looked up past the blue tip of her tongue at Earnest.

"I thought I'd find you here. I've missed you," he said.

A faint blue haze ebbed into the edges of her vision.

"It's coming," she said. "The island. Get me to Marilyn. I promised I'd bring her."

Alonso pressed her back, Earnest held onto her arm and the islanders surged forward through the crowd. She could hear Rock ahead of them his voice reverberating through the microphone giving the kind of speech one would expect, filled with the same pride-filled language of Founder's Day, all about C-town: unity and strength, loyalty, and tradition. As they neared the front of the crowd, Doreena could make out Marilyn standing on a stage erected on a platform across a swimming pool. But there was some of kind of commotion ahead of them in addition to the fanfare of the resort's opening day.

Suddenly there was a swath of green around her, as though she had stepped into the jungle and was running through it. A group of people near the front of the crowd had unzipped their coats and shrugged them off to reveal their green union sweatshirts. Their shouts rose over Rock's voice, tinny through the microphone. At first, she thought, they were yelling, "Fight, fight, fight!" and Doreena was afraid that if fists flew, she and the islanders might never make it to Marilyn. But as the voices coalesced. They gained strength and resonance. They were saying, "Flight." Not, “Fight." "Flight, flight, flight, flight," they chanted. “The future is flight!”

They raised white-backed posterboard signs, blocking Doreena's view of the stage. "Marilyn," Doreena shouted and the islanders echoed her. They continued to push her through the waves of bodies with white placard crests. They broke through the crowd and waded into the pool towing her along past people standing in the water, drinks in hand: Dalton Rees, Rock, and the City Fathers. Marilyn reached for her, bending down from the stage. Rock was behind her with his arm around her waist, pulling her back. "Stay back. She's crazy."

Sparkling wine splashed from Marilyn's cup down to Doreena's outstretched hand and bubbled through the raised hairs on her arm. They stretched fingers toward each other. Doreena felt a hand on her thigh, Alonso's, lifting her up and Hobart pushing at her side. With a pang in her abdomen, Doreena stood in the center of the mass of reaching people as the blue haze dropped and the tentacles of the island grabbed hold and yanked.

The suction squeezed her tight. It juiced her making every drop of her island. Through the blue haze she could see the jumble of them; the salesforce, the union protesters, and the islanders; the City Father and their wives; Tom, Diane, and Marilyn; Rock and Dalton; and Earnest and Alonso. She could see the front of the protest signs: "Maui forever!" "Jobs now!" and "The future is flight!" They were all touching someone who was touching her. Those desperate to be caught up in the chaos and those desperate to avoid it all tumbled toward the island. Some of the islanders had grabbed green bottles of sparkling wine as the haze dropped. They lifted them to her, grinning.

~ 44 ~

MIRROR ISLAND: THE CAVE

A surrogate mother, Doreena gives birth

They arrived on the beach in the middle of a hurricane. The wind, keening, whipped around Doreena. Her hair flew across her face. She held a handful of it aside and peered out at the crashing waves beyond the gritty, streaks of air. The ocean churned rank with the contents of its upturned depths, seaweed, and decaying fish. Up the beach, palm leaves slashed from the ends of bowed trunks. Sand shot into her eyes. She shoved her fists into them until tears came. A hand grabbed her shoulder.

"Is this it? Your island?" Earnest said.

Her hair whipped forward to curtain their faces. They shouted to hear each other over the pained wail of the wind.

"The others. The others are here," she said.

He pointed up the beach and she began to crawl. Through the pelting rain, a cluster of people huddled in knots across the sand with their heads ducked to protect their faces. Most were naked, their backs gray and the bones of their spines arcing up to meet the whips of sand. Others, an opaque hunch of shoulders, still wore their suits. The City Fathers and Rock began to rise. The sleeves of their suits hung with the weight of the rain. The naked ones lifted pale faces. The Stew unwrapped his body from around a camera. A harsh light swept over them. Doreena shielded her eyes.

Rock squinted. His eyes were naked crystal blue. "What is this?"

"It's not usually like this," Doreena said.

"We need to get out of this storm," Earnest said.

Doreena pointed to where she knew the trail began. A field of slick vegetation thrashed around the opening, hiding it. "Follow me."

Marilyn's shoulder brushed Doreena's. The color of the day was white. One hand fingered her pearls and the other lay across her flat belly marbled with stretch marks from where it had expanded more rapidly than her flesh could follow. Marilyn had hoped to be pregnant again on the island. She was not.

"My son is lost," she said.

"It's my place," Doreena said. "I am the one who is entangled in two worlds at once. I am the only one who can carry it inside of me."

Suddenly, Doreena's belly swelled. It felt like unfurling. Her belly blossomed, then it gained weight. It hung low and stretched until it looked ready to burst. Doreena pressed her hands to it. When she did, she could feel the entire island inside her, but when Marilyn looked at her the island kicked, and she was a surrogate mother about to give birth to Marilyn's child. Thc first contraction rolled Doreena like a wave. She fell forward, legs splayed in a lurching step. Sparkling fluid gushed between her thighs. It splashed a blue lined pattern across the sand and pooled. Doreena grabbed Marilyn's arm and pulled her to the trail. "Shelter."

She took a last look back at the beach before they ducked under the thrashing branches. By the sea, the surfers, with their black arms raised, were dancing. In the center of them, Alonso leapt. His whoop rose over the wind. His arms and legs scrawled across the sky. The wind caught him, and he hovered before he dropped to earth to leap again.

Up the trail, the lagoon beside the cave bubbled with sand. Eggy steam rose off its surface and the keening wind gained words, "Come see me. Come see me." Doreena pulled Marilyn into the cave. The warmth of it stifled like *The Mirror* office. With each step, the ceiling of the cave lowered, and the heat and sulfur grew. They went deep into its low angle where a black, damp moss coated the stone walls. Doreena sank to the cave floor with her back against stone so hot it burned when she shifted. She could barely see her arms and legs in the darkness, only the rise of her belly and its pale glow.

Rock had followed Marilyn up the trail, with the City Fathers huddling after him, too frightened to be left alone on the beach and depending on Rock, as always, to lead them to safety and shelter. But the men stopped when another round of contractions sent Doreena's cries echoing off the cave walls. They stood in the entrance to the cave blocking the light and leaving the women inside to their mysterious business.

Marilyn touched fingertips to Doreena's forehead. "You're going to have my baby. Just breathe."

Doreena clenched her fists. She did not have to breathe, or eat or sleep, but this task required the anatomy she had played with and pretended to have as a child. This was not the time to relinquish that. She puffed; she panted; she tilted her chin to the roof of the cave where the dark fuzz of rock above her shifted. Two glinting ovals appeared, and the rock grew features and became familiar. She knew that face, those three long lines across the forehead and that sun-darkened spot beside the cheekbone where she had liked to kiss and inhale the traces of hibiscus pollen.

Between her legs, Marilyn's fingers brushed her opening. "I see him. That's right. He's coming now. Push."

Grandfather's head and shoulders pushed through the ceiling of the cave. His hands slipped free of the rock and reached for her. His arms were angled and black, then round and blue and finally his familiar shape and flesh color. The rock singed Doreena's back. Her ankles were in a vise. Marilyn screamed and backed into a crook of the cave. Doreena caught grandfather's hands, warm and soft, in hers and pulled herself closer to him again.

"I've missed you. Is this where you've been? I thought you were gone."

"I was supposed to grow old and die," he said. "People do. I tried to follow the rules and managed to make myself age in the normal way. It wasn't hard to be what people expected. When they saw an old man, they didn't pay me much attention. But I didn't know how to make myself die. What we are does not have a lifecycle with such an obvious beginning and end. I didn't want you to have to care for me through some long illness that would have been a lie. I just wanted to disappear so that I wouldn't worry you. But I never have had the strength to let you alone. And I could not completely leave you."

"Tell me who I am," she said.

“We are inorganic helical structures made of plasma with a collective consciousness. We had never experienced an individual identity until Leonid Moriena joined us. He and his family died a long time ago, but his desire to know you was so strong that our empathic systems responded to his pain and preserved his identity. To fulfill his desire, we created the first individual among us: Doreena Flora Moriena. We learned "I". But it felt wrong, to be one person in a unified world. I saw us as a kind of pollution, hardening the place. But I did not want to give you up, so I brought you here to C-town to hold you in place and protect the rest of them. I wanted to keep you, but it was selfish, and I am sorry."

"You could have told me," Doreena said.

"If I had, it would have changed you."

"What about my mother?"

"Don't you see? She doesn't exist."

He pulled his hands from hers and the flesh color pulled away with them. His hands were gray and black underneath a hard sparkling shell beneath a thin flesh tone.

"Wait," she said, and her words held him steady above her. "Stay for the birth of your great grandchild."

"There's no child," he said. "You shouldn't be doing this."

Doreena pointed at Marilyn who, overcoming her fear, had begun to move closer. "But I am."

While they had talked, Hobart had joined them crawling back into the cave beside her. She took Marilyn's place between Doreena's legs. "I've got it. We're in new territory here."

When the baby finally exited her body, it came out in an easy gush, Hobart held it up. There was no umbilical cord. Strands of deep blue crisscrossed its tiny body.

Marilyn grabbed for it. "My boy. My baby boy."

Hobart pushed her aside and laid the baby on Doreena's belly. It huddled there, its skin a translucent pale blue tingling silently.

"Is he OK?" Marilyn asked.

Hobart leaned close to Doreena. "She's not breathing."

"Yes, she is," Doreena touched the child's back and its lungs lifted under her hand. Grandfather's hair had begun to fall. It drifted down in blue sparkles.

"Tell me the truth," she said.

"You don't want to know."

"I do," she said.

"Then I must tell you she was an ugly thing. We became her, but she grew stiff and hard among us, she clung so fiercely to her shape. She wanted everything to be like it had before on her own planet. I smashed your father and then I smashed her too. I destroyed them, but I coveted you. I took you from her arms. I held on to you when I should have let you go returning to the fluid blue, the electrically charged plasma sea. When I took you to C-town and you grew up and began work *at The Mirror* I could see you becoming like your mother. I thought I wanted you to be solid and permanent, but when I saw the dark reflection of your mother in your face, I felt only regret. I wondered what you could have been, if I hadn't been so afraid of losing you."

The keening voice rose commanding Doreena to come deeper into the jungle.

"Isn't that her?" Doreena said.

"No. Now, listen, you've recreated Doreena. What will you do to her this time? Who will she please?"

The wind blew against grandfather. It carried away his flesh-toned surface, revealing t the dull gray, then navy and amethyst, jade, and light blue agate, and finally the palest blue particles swirled away in the wind. Shimmering blue showered her and the baby. Doreena, he'd called the child, too.

"Then who?" Doreena asked. "Who is up there, above us?"

"We must soften. We all go together." His face crumbled down to his lips, the powder of them caked and the words fell with them, "soft, soft."

With grandfather gone, Marilyn grew bold and approached. She lifted the baby off Doreena's chest and powder fell. Doreena unclenched her hands and two handfuls of pink powder dropped with a shifting sigh.

"Put it back." Hobart said. "It needs to nurse."

Marilyn placed the baby at Doreena's breast, leaving her hand on its back. Doreena sat up to see it. It was a boy now: warm, pink, and mewling. He suckled at her breast. He might grow up and ask, "Who is my father?" Would she tell him Alonso, Earnest, one of the surfers, Rock? How would she explain? He would be uncomfortable and awkward in his humanity as she had been. She would evade his question fearing to distort him with the truth. Answers would never give him a solid sense of sureness. Like rain on sugar, information would dissolve him. She understood now why grandfather had never explained her identity. He barely understood it himself. They were alien to each other and, also, made of the same stuff.

A rumbling erupted from deep within the cave. A belch of sulfur filled the air with a scalding steam.

Hobart pulled Doreena to her feet. "Get away from the cave," she yelled to the others.

Outside, the voice said, "Come, come. Don't make me wait any longer. I am his heart."

Doreena wanted to run to this voice. Nothing would stop her from reaching her mother.

~ 45 ~

MIRROR ISLAND: CLIMBING

Doreena discovers an island of skin

The women were all outside when the shaking earth collapsed the cave. Its wet rock maw crashed closed. The wind whipped by them, and the voice cut through it crying, "Come see me." The lagoon roiled. Marilyn, focused only on the newborn's face, held the child up to Rock. "Our boy. It's him."

"Their skin. I see. All the colors, in there." Rock turned away as if blinded.

The child's skin changed colors as they examined it. The child had yet to make a sound, but the shifting colors wailed at Doreena. When Marilyn spoke, it looked apricot pink. When the City Fathers looked on, it faded to shades of ashen gray. The child had been Marilyn's idea, but now Doreena reached for it.

"Give it to its mother," Hobart said.

"Please," Rock said. "You can see that is not our child."

Marilyn's features stiffened into her sales manager mask. Her lips all but disappeared as she handed the baby to Hobart, who passed it to Doreena. "You have to nurse him," Marilyn commanded, but she looked lost with her arms still outstretched. "He's cold without a blanket."

Doreena remembered all the blankets Marilyn had unwrapped and held up at her baby shower in light yellows, pinks, and blues. There were none here. There had been no preparation for this birth. As she brought the baby to her breast, Earnest peeled off his jacket exposing his thin shoulders to the wind. It pressed into his white shirt and the whorls of his chest hair showed through the thin cotton. He swaddled the baby in the suit jacket. It still held oil and cleanser smells as it had when he'd pressed it around her after her car accident outside AeroFlux. He'd thought she was stuttering from shock, and it had felt nice to be cared for then. With him standing close, she almost thought she could parent this child that clung to her breast. Then sated, the child released. Her breast dripped a sparkling blue liquid that shared only the density of milk. The child's mouth shone with it. The voice screamed again, and Doreena began walking up the trail. She could not mother this child in ignorance. She had to know her history, how everything fit together. Wet leaves brushed her body as she began to push through them.

A thunderous sound shook the jungle, but the report came from a precise point on the trail behind her instead of filling the sky. Doreena turned back toward it and Alonso and Earnest followed. The color of the day was dusk gray. Marilyn wore an abrasion of stress across her taut face. The revolver waving in Rock's hand shone silver and surprising as the inside of an oyster shell. The things people brought to the island. They clung to the objects that made them feel secure. She'd arrived naked and empty-handed but for grandfather's ashes. Marilyn had brought her pearls, Diane still wore seven-shades of eye shadow, the surfers brought boards and wetsuits, the union workers had their signs and sweatshirts, the City Fathers had their suits and Earnest his tweed jacket. She'd expected Rock to have his glasses, the double-layers protecting his sensitive color-blind eyes from the light, but his eyes were unguarded. Instead, he had this weapon in hand.

"Here?" Doreena asked.

"Some kind of devil," Rock said.

A body lay face down across the trail. A red wound peeked between the plucked pink nubs in its back. Blood trickled from the hole into the rust red of the trail. Hobart turned the wounded man over. Dalton's slack eyes looked up at them. The AeroFlux executive had arrived on the island with vestigial wings.

"Take him down to the beach." Doreena said. The islanders hoisted him. The earth rumbled and Doreena turned back up the trail. She had to get to mother and get answers before the place fell apart.

"Where's she going?" Rock said behind her. "We should all go back to the beach and try to signal a ship."

"There's no ships in a place like this. Surely you can feel that? It's her," The Stew said. "You have to touch her to get back."

Doreena hurried up the trail. Rock was coming now, after her, the revolver in hand. She fell up and then slid down the path, mud coating her legs up past her knees. Alonso caught her arm and pulled her up in one swift motion, she went lightly to her feet momentarily weightless. She stepped into the greenery along the side of the trail and a mash of vegetation and mud formed a crust around her feet until at the top of the trail her feet slapped stone. She climbed a series of ledges until her thighs ached. Drying strands of blue afterbirth clung to them. They looked like external veins on top of her translucent skin.

She was turning into one of her childhood dolls, her seven invisible women. She saw now grandfather's reasoning: he'd wanted her to learn anatomy so that she would grow correctly on the inside. She wasn't sure now if she had. She'd never been sick, and yet, she'd given birth. She cradled the pale blue, shallow-breathed baby inside the suit jacket. Hot as stone, the child radiated heat. Through the jacket, her fingers burned, but she hugged the babe closer. It reminded her of the heater blasting her fingers around the steering wheel. The baby was so hot she could hardly bear it, but if she let go, she was afraid she'd lose direction.

The City Fathers grunted, tearing through the foliage as they came behind her. At the top of the trail, the jungle opened and dark sky showed through the slats in the broad leaves. Alonso reached from behind and parted them. Wind blew in. Diane, Alonso, and Earnest stepped into the clearing after her. They were drenched and smeared with mud. Moss and bark crowned Alonso's matted curls. Doreena brushed fuzzy wisps of tangled green out of her eyes. A clearing of lawn ran right down to a bluff. The manicured swath looked like grandfather's front lawn, but the sea crashed below, and the air smelled singed and salty.

Alonso brushed her shoulder and pointed left at a tower of land inclined into the sky. Clumps of green wound around its base but thinned towards the top to sparse tufts in rock clusters. A plate of stone angled down from the top. A bolt of faint blue struck the pinnacle, illuminating two spires. The voice called down.

"I hear it too," Alonso said. "Up there."

"Mother," Doreena said.

"Get back here. Get us out of here," Rock said. He stood with the City Fathers in the clearing and smeared red across his thighs as he wiped his muddy hands on his slacks. Doreena began to climb the hill stepping on the patches of grass between the stones. She held the baby in one arm and used the other to steady herself as she ducked low to the rocks, so the wind rushed over her back. She would reach her mother.

"Enough," Rock said, turning to The Stew. "Bring her down."

"I don't work for you here," The Stew said.

As Doreena climbed, the incline narrowed and grew rockier. In the dim light, it was difficult to tell which rocks were solid handholds and which stones would crumble when she reached for them. Doreena clung to the tower of land, Alonso beside her. Earnest and Rock followed below.

Where the tower became more sky than stone, Earnest stopped ascending. "I can't," he said.

Rock searched for handholds. "I can't see where to put my hands."

On the lawn, The City Fathers held Marilyn back. She strained between them leaning into the wind.

Doreena climbed dangling the baby. With each hoist, the ground dropped away, and the wind rushed in. Alonso climbed beside her. "We can make it."

A shot fired behind them. This time, Doreena knew the lonely sound came from Rock's revolver. It was there in his hand. He had stopped climbing to fire it. A hole gaped in her thigh and red trickled out like it had from the wound between Dalton's pubescent wings. She moved the leg and pain flared through it. The block of flesh hung. It wouldn't bear weight. She wouldn't be able to go higher. She would never know who she was or where she came from. She would have to go down now, as Rock wanted, to take them all back to C-town where everything would be the same as when they had left it, nothing changed. She would feel the same way as she had before: awkward, trapped and stifled but now she would be aware of it and there would not be even one escape.

"Do you want me to take her?" Alonso said.

Doreena held the baby in one arm swaddled in the suit jacket. "No."

"You have beautiful tears," he said. "You could bottle them."

The tears evaporated as the wind burned across her cheeks. Glittery traces flew through the air in front of her. Doreena bent her head to the baby and whispered. "I won't let it hurt you."

She looked down at her thigh and watched the red deepen to purple. It shimmered out of the wound. There was so much she'd found she hadn't needed: hunger, thirst, sleep, breath. Of all those irrelevancies, pain was the hardest to release. She'd always been uncomfortable encased in her skin, uncertain how to stand or where to put her hands every time she'd been in Marilyn's office. She'd strained to make the movements that seemed so natural to others, to go out to lunch, to talk. This pain seemed an extension of that. Discomfort was the way she moved through the world. It clamped her into place as she walked the streets of C-town. But what scared her most was how much she'd grown to need it, even as she grew numb to it. Without pain, she wouldn’t need release and the island wouldn't matter. She wouldn't want it so much anymore.

Still, she let the pain go because she wanted to see what would happen if she allowed herself to be different. It faded. The wound with its deep blue core remained. She reached for a higher rock and pressed her foot into a step above. Her leg renewed, braced her. Alonso stared at her the way he watched an approaching wave, more awed than afraid. It was just the expression she must have had the first time she'd gone to the island and found herself standing on the sudden stretch of sand, wanting to take all the sun inside of her.

She had arrived effortlessly, immediately, and naturally. She had allowed that feeling to wash over her again and again: This is who I've been all along. But it hadn't lasted. The island hadn't been something she could control, and she had never been alone in her desire for it. They were all looking for an untamed place like this: the surfers, the City Fathers, the sales force, the AeroFlux executive, Rock and Marilyn. They were all refugees and they'd stirred the island up.

"I never, ever, ever wanted to leave the beach," she said. "All I wanted was to stay there. I would have stayed and stayed."

"I know," Alonso said. "I get that."

Her legs lifted her up to the top of the island. More gunshots and shouting chased her through the air, but the bullets missed her, and she climbed steadily up. Alonso followed. The wind met them at the top of the plateau with a push. The slab of rock, shining wet with rain, capped the jungle mount. Violet lines ran through the gray stone, the same dark color as the billowing clouds above. Thunder shook the hillside and far off clouds flashed white underbellies. Most of the island, surrounded by dark sea, was visible. Jungle green cut down its side. The cave lay far below under a distant overhang and a deeper emerald patch marked the location of the lagoon. The beach, however, was hidden. She imagined it calm and empty but remembered her islanders had taken Dalton there. His body lay somewhere on it bleeding. Still, the beach was the safest place on the island. Maybe the only safe place anywhere.

The City Fathers huddled at the base of the pillar. Rock, once he had emptied the gun, had climbed back down to them. He stood like a column with his arms crossed over Marilyn. Earnest clung to the stone, white, where she had left him. The plateau she and Alonso stood on stretched wider than the island below, a teetering black plate. An onyx path led to crumbled stone ruins where the two pillars stood. Doreena and Alonso followed the path and stood beneath them. They were two statues, seated on rock thrones, with familiar features etched on their chiseled faces. Doreena knew them from her grandfather's description.

"My parents," she said.

She listened for their voices, but even the wind silenced. Doreena took Alonso's hand, and they walked around the statues. There, a woman, with powder blue skin, sat. A pale blue hibiscus blossom held waves of hair behind her ear.

"Grandmother," Doreena said.

"Come sit, child." Grandmother patted the grass. "Put Doreena down."

Doreena knelt and set the baby down on the lawn. She crawled toward the woman, kittenish.

"Your grandfather brought you to Maui because it was so soft, on island time, with everything in motion. You were thriving but growing more and more autonomous and independent, foreign, and hard for us to understand. You wanted to touch everything, and we were forever pulling you back and reforming your fingers and afraid of losing you. We teach our own to tune — *zza, zza, zza* — to the vibration of togetherness. But for you, he carried a pocketful of stones and shells and when you got too excited sat you down and made you count them to keep you focused on each separate object and make you solid in yourself. But that place was too loose and flowing. Time and space and individuality were subdued. So, he took you away to a place where it would be easier to contain you in rules and schedules and borders. He suffered there; except he loved you. When he was lonely, he'd watch the hazy motion of the hummingbird wings that reminded him of home. And we stayed here on this island of our own and waited."

"What happened to my parents?" Doreena said.

"Your mother's dying thought was water, your father's too. We don't know anything as certain as death only hard and soft the way water can be. They are not those statutes, but the sea that surrounds us. Leonid thought he killed them, but he only destroyed his own idea of them: the part of them that only cared for self-preservation. It grew hard and stiffened everything it touched. Your grandfather wanted to save the softness in us, but he wanted you too. We could feel you starting to solidify in C-town, becoming uncomfortably stiff and slow. We brought you here to help you and now feel."

The woman touched Doreena's chest and she felt the slosh, slosh of waves in her breast. "We missed you. We are always with you. We came to find ourselves again, explorer."

Grandmother looked at Alonso. "Some are soft inside. Some are stiff."

"Like my mother and father?" Doreena said.

"Like fear. Your grandfather was afraid to see you as you could have become on Maui. Like this," Grandmother swept her pale blue hand across the lawn.

A mound of blue powder lay on the grass where the baby had been. Doreena could see the movement in its dust, the constant flow beneath the surface of a calm sea. She reached for the child and black sparks shot across the loose surface.

Grandmother's hands clenched the grass. "Mustn't fear."

Doreena reached for the baby and stroked the soft pile until its back reappeared. Its tiny limbs reformed. Then she picked it up and held it. She thought this baby pink and human again. She held it to her breast. "Is this what happened to me?"

"Yes. Your grandfather held you. He wanted to know you," the grandmother said, weaving vines with trumpet-shaped blossoms through the grass. "But you were never really born, we made you out of us, a kind of cultural misunderstanding. We did not understand individuality, really. You were always unhappy alone. We're going home now. Will you come be with us?"

Doreena plucked at the grass: smooth and slick and spiked. Amber light outlined the rolling clouds above. Alonso held her hand.

"I'm too stiff now," she said. "Too human."

Grandmother reached for Doreena's right hand. She held it in hers. "Relax." She shook Doreena's hand and stroked her palm. As she did so, Doreena's skin paled and stretched smooth and pools of cobalt blue appeared in the center around a remnant of flesh with the faint trace of her heart line across it. Alonso anchored her left hand. It tingled in his tight grip.

Grandmother dipped her fingertip into the pool in Doreena's palm. Waves flowed in over the island of skin. "We are together. Explore more but stay soft." Grandmother gazed up at the pillars, which flashed gold and then darkened to burnished black. "The stiffness must go."

As Grandmother dissipated in a blue haze, Doreena felt dust falling on her face and hands. The thrones were crumbling, toppling to dust. The sky boomed. Doreena and Alonso began to run down the incline. It slid with them becoming less steep with each step. They rejoined the citizens of C-town who stood now at the edge of the bluff. Behind them oncoming rolling dunes of black gold dust enveloped the mountain, the stones, the trees, and the jungle.

"Get us out of here," Marilyn said. Her voice felt hard like stone.

"Doreena?" Alonso asked, and his voice ran over her like water.

"I'm not going back," Doreena said.

"You have to," Marilyn said, she reached for the baby. "We have to go. We can't stay here."

Doreena looked over the side of the cliff. Far below was another beach, a half circle of white around a bay filled with white water cresting over the pink sand at the bottom of the red and white striated cliff. It was the last calm untouched spot; the place she had wanted to get to when she was bound to the crates freighting cargo from the island to C-town. Now that she could see it, it seemed difficult to get to, though not impossible. Could she fly down to it or sail around to it from the side? There would be flowers below and another grove of fruit and she and Doreena could live there peacefully if no one would ever bother them. But a human child couldn't grow there in such a soft place. That was the reason her grandfather had taken her away from Maui. The baby would dissolve into pink sand and blue water, and she would go with it.

Or she could take this child back to C-town, where it would relive her own life. She could never raise this child to understand itself differently. She saw how it would grow up into the same solid uncertainty as she herself had. She could see the baby standing here at the edge of some other precipice or maybe the exact same precipice and also trying to decide. It was not unique. It was part of herself. She could give it to Marilyn to raise, but she knew in a way she had already done that, given herself over to *The Mirror*. They would mummify the child to hold it in place. She looked around at the islanders, Hobart and Alonso, they could care for her, but they would not know how to raise a child in C-town. This new Doreena would get no further in understanding than she had, if she could not help it begin its life at some further point of discovery.

"We don't need her to get back," Marilyn said to Rock. "Touch the baby."

It was true that they needed a way back and she was the only one who could provide it. Doreena leaned far over cliff, she held up the child, a baby girl again now as when she had been born, parted her arms and let her drop between them. Immediately, Marilyn began to scream. Doreena's mind went with the baby as it fell and she felt herself in two places at once: falling from the cliff and standing upon it. As the baby fell, its shape grew nebulous, and she felt the passing rush of wind and the fearlessness of her fall through the sky towards the sea, which looked both hard and soft from a distance. The red and white striped cliff running down to the sea passed like scenery. After the first few tense, disorienting moments, she began to enjoy the glide.

Then Marilyn leapt off the cliff after it, and Rock teetered on the edge. "Damn it, woman."

He spun and jumped, flailing. Marilyn's fingers stretched toward the child, but midway through the sky the blue blur of it stopped as if it had hit a wall. A swath of blue blanketed the dark sky, calm washed over Doreena, and then it was gone. That part of herself she had cast away, burst into a portal over the sea holding a door open to C-town. Another boom shook the island, but everyone stared at the infant light and the would-be parents falling toward it. Marilyn hovered in the sky above the blue nebula and Rock caught her up and held her. They swung in the sky together around the sparkling sea of air and then slipped through. The portal shuddered and contracted as they entered it. The light flashed out, then reappeared, a blurry teal glow over the sea.

"You have your way back." Doreena said to the others. "Leave me and my island alone."

The mountain behind them thundered and now the air grew thick and hot and sulfurous. Black plumes of smoke rose over the towering cliff. The Stew leapt first, followed by all the suits and the reporters and the union workers, naked and clothed. The sea below looked hard and flat, but they all took leave of her in their way and blinked through the wavering portal. Even the ones who fell short were sucked into its tide. Finally, only the islanders stood beside her on the precipice.

"Time to move on to the next waves," Alonso said.

Hobart led the way. "Come on," she said, and the islanders followed her, diving off the cliff into the portal's center. They left Doreena, Diane, Alonso, and Earnest alone on the cliff.

Earnest took Doreena's hand. He pulled her toward the cliff. "I love you. Come back with me," he said.

Doreena released him as he neared the edge. He tumbled back over it. His limbs flailed as the portal took him in.

"I'll stay with you," Alonso said with an easy shrug. The corners of his eyes and mouth were slightly raised as always. Behind him lay the crumbled ashen remains of her island.

"Let's go back down to the beach, one last time, anyway," she said.

"Is it still there?" Alonso asked.

"I want it to be," she said. "So, yes, I think so."

~ 46 ~

MIRROR ISLAND: THE ISLAND AT NIGHT

Experiencing Mirror Island at night

With the others gone, and Earnest still plummeting toward C-town, the eruption of the island stilled. Its decay blew out over the cliff on a zephyr. The spot in the sky, the infant pool, blinked out. Translucent darkness replaced the opaque smoke and billowing ash. The rumbling faded. The black-gold dust cleared into a gold-starred sky and the sea-struck air cooled. A current of jasmine cut through the sulfurous fumes. A purple nimbus around the moon glowed over the ocean. The sea lay like black silk with rumpled, pearly waves.

Doreena and Alonso turned from the cliff, hands clasped. Pawing animal noises came from behind the jungle leaves, where insects began to whir and sing. In the dark, Doreena couldn't distinguish between the red of the trail and the green of the leaves. Was this the way the jungle had looked to Rock? With each step down the trail, she stumbled as if on the edge of some dark pit. Curled fronds brushed her bare arms too tender to catch her. She no longer trusted the solidity of the land beneath her feet — the island was a transient, a traveler.

Heading down the jungle path in the dark was more frightening than falling toward the sea. The blackness flowed around her arms and legs, and it looked like the dark beneath her feet could drop away. Each step surprised her, when the island stayed firm with just the give of mud and moss beneath her feet. She and Alonso began to run plunging headlong into the dark. Ferment rose near the opening to the beach. In the fruit grove, huge luminescent eyes watched.

"Those eyes," Doreena said.

"It's a lemur. He looks a little like The Stew."

Near the opening to the beach, they examined a body-shaped indentation of sand, stained and tacky with drying blood.

"Where's Dalton?" Doreena asked.

Alonso shook his head. A stir of air made her look up into the palms with their green fringes visible mostly as fluttering movement in front of the night sky.

"Bats," he said.

"Where did all these creatures come from?"

"They came with the people, I think. People and paradise. You can't keep them separate. They always find the secret spots."

"And ruin it," Doreena said. "We bring turmoil."

Alonso shrugged. "Or calm."

"Calm sea meat. That's what I heard grandmother say at first. She meant, 'Come see me.' but I was afraid, inert. I guess I already knew that a big change was coming. Until I was ready, I wanted to stay on the beach and not do anything."

"Yeah, like that. We're calm sea meat, until we're ready. But we can't be still forever."

"No, but I didn't want someone else to tell me when I was ready for change. It might have been nice if I had listened, easier, but I wanted to feel it for myself. My time to move."

Ocean debris littered the beach. Shells decorated the sand flows. The moon, as if it had dropped down to them, was even larger here than on the cliff side. The beach shone like a strand of pearls circling the inlet of sea. It reminded her of Marilyn and how they'd waded into the water together. Marilyn had been afraid of sharks, but she'd gone in anyway seeking the coolness, naked except for her pearls, the waves magnifying her pregnancy. Marilyn had jumped back to C-town following the infant mirage. What would happen to her in that hard place?

"Do you think there are still sharks?"

"No, those were someone else's idea, your parents were just trying to scare you into action. Now there are only Spinner dolphins," He stroked the back of her hand. "You know, their skins so soft you can't wear rings, or you'll scratch them."

"I don't have any rings," Doreena said. "Earnest wanted to give me one, but I wouldn't let him."

"Just your necklace then," Alonso said, putting his hand over the glass where it lay empty on her chest.

"This is the first time I've seen the island at night. How can it be more beautiful?"

"As beautiful, anyway." He bent and retrieved a bottle from the sand. It was one of the celebratory wines snagged by an island-bound surfer meant for the opening of Traynter Resort. He swung the sparkling wine with the silver label as they approached the sea. The sand shifted and the waves rushed into the stillness. Alonso sat and offered her the open bottle. She waved it away.

"The stiffness, it's a kind of death," she said. "If we go too far from fluid consciousness, we can't get back."

"Not easily," Alonso said, sitting in his loose way. His knees were bent, and his elbows propped on them, the bottle swung between them with his wrists crossed over the opening. She imagined all the islanders sitting in a row with their languid limbs draped across the sand, Alonso the most liquid looking of them all.

"What will you do? You can't get back. To C-town, I mean," she said.

He tipped the bottle to his lips, so they gleamed wet when he answered. "Everything works out. I've never been stuck. Even in C-town I found a way to surf and found my way to an island. I'm lucky like that."

"Maybe. Marilyn said if you close up entirely, another way opens."

When he offered her the bottle again, she took it. The storm-battered label had begun to peel but the phosphors in the ink still glowed: Silver Lake Sparkling Wine. Silver Lake was a real, natural lake surrounded by vineyards outside of C-town. Marilyn said it looked just like the label. It was another trade route, Doreena realized. There were always openings, always exceptions. There were ways to get to every island if not by ships and planes there were always bridges of land hidden, waiting beneath the sea. She sipped at the wine and let the tart fizz flow over her tongue. She moved between Alonso's legs and, kneeling, placed her hands on his shoulders.

"Grandmother liked you, your gentleness."

"I really like her. I really like this place."

She straddled him letting her thighs rest over his to match his languid posture. She wrapped her arms around his neck and held the bottle against his back. He placed his hands over her breasts. The warmth of them made the rest of her skin feel cool by comparison for a moment until the feeling faded into the muggy night. His hands caressed her and her skin warmed. She tucked him inside of her. They rocked together as they had when they'd first arrived on the island, just the two of them, with Doreena's knees buried deep in the sand. Under the skin of her palms, her grandmother had showed her blue pools. She imagined Alonso, now, deep inside in the waves at her blue core.

They moved together clinging like strands of kelp in the ebb and flow offshore. Strong cycles of tide seemed to pass with the moon filling the sky above them. The island slipped away into the darkness. She was connected only to Alonso until she began to forget him too and resided only in her own body until that fell away also and her mind rose up to join the moon. Then there was only the moon, but its light touched the entire island. The wine bottle dropped from Doreena's hands and the last of the wine seeped into the sand, but she felt drunk with it, her insides filled and sparkling.

"Oh, love," she said at last.

"Those tears." Alonso caught her hands and stroked them with his thumb. The light touch made her feel the flow beneath her skin like the tides within the powder blue baby.

She stared at her hands so full of human gestures. She'd studied these movements so carefully for her job, not knowing why they meant so much to her. She'd listened to the tapes Marilyn had given her again and again with slavish persistence, somehow knowing how much she needed to learn. To fit in, she had become an expert. Foreign beings filled her insides and subconscious, so she made being human a conscious external act.

She freed her hands from Alonso's and repeated the gestures she knew. Palms up, people were open to receive. Palms down, they were ready to pull away. Fastened in a fist, a hand betrayed insecurity or anger. Fingers pointed up meant leadership or hope. Hands touching the face indicated boredom or disinterest. Hands over the mouth betrayed dishonesty or secrets. Hands could serve as clasps to fasten the arms across a body protectively.

She stood and made the movements bigger. Pressing hands to the hips made a person look larger, more threatening or in control. Hands behind the back, portrayed confidence or obedience depending on how the hidden hands were arranged: fastened or folded. Hands could dangle near the thighs or flutter and fidget through the air with nervous energy. They could touch, hold, feel, grasp or clench. They could fend off or embrace. She performed a kata of humanity across the sand and ended in front of Alonso standing with her hands clasped over the place where her heart lay still for just a little while longer.

"To create a feeling of sympathy. Put your hands in the same position as the person across from you. Subconsciously, they will see you as like themselves," she said, repeating a line from Chapter 1 of *Stellar Sales*. "Some neurons react empathetically, 'mirror neurons' they're called, when you imitate others they fire. They create a connection inside of you that extends beyond you to a person outside of you, even to a whole group of people if you are speaking to a crowd. This is possible for anyone. It isn't only me. It's just easier for me, someone of my heritage."

Doreena lifted her hands to the night. The stars shone around her fingers. Her connection to C-town lay in the thin barrier of her skin. She displayed her humanity in 10 digits. Her human experience was etched into her palms, but there were pools and islands inside of them. She stood and raised her arms to the moon stretching her fingertips up into the purplish glow.

Alonso wrapped his arms around her waist. "When did you feel it for yourself? When did you know you were ready to change?"

"When I was falling. I was in two places at once and I didn't want to be."

"Where did you want to be then?"

"Without limits, I think, everywhere. I want to experience all earth's islands."

She looked at her hands, once more, and let them go. They changed color as she released them: pink, lavender and teal. When they reached powder blue, she waved and the blue sparkles shook — *zza, zza, zza* — through the moonlight to the sand. The blunt ends of her wrists jabbed the sky. She began to spin slowly in the circle of Alonso's arms.

Her hair fell first, the curls sparkling down. Her skin swirled like the inside of an oyster shell. It looked as though she'd torn a rent in the sky and the stars were glittering down. The last thing she saw, from beneath her fringe of blue eyelashes, were the crinkles around Alonso's eyes caked with blue sparkles. She'd stuck to his tears. But still he gave her only softness. He let her dissolve without protest. As she released her container, the island, her ancestors, embraced her. They loved her not for the infant they had once coveted, but for the person she had become: *our explorer.* The peace of their mind flowed through her and she understood: They could not be separate. There were no places distant from them.

She lay at last, a blue flow pooling in the prints she and Alonso had made sharing passion in the sand. Alonso pressed his hands into her. She flowed around his fingers. His hands stirred her. There was a sensation of salt, the cut of the tiny crystals, as she mingled through his tears. So, this was what grandfather meant. He'd warned her about men, about sex, and here, at last, were the consequences. She'd been forever changed by the contact. Even now, she would not leave them. She loved the surfers and that called and carried her back to them like an island. Alonso dropped the necklace down into her and she ran over the knotted squares of its chain and into the smooth, glass vial. Then the weight of it within her was lifted. The clasp clicked closed. It fell against Alonso's chest, and she rode there, some of her, so close beside his heartbeat she vibrated. The rest of her filled the empty wine bottle. She spilled from Alonso's cupped hands, down his life and heart lines, into it and shook side to side against the glass.

Alonso sat holding her in the wine bottle while Doreena settled into her new state of being. Her sense organs were gone, but she could still sense everything. Her mind flowed between the fake containers: the glass vial of the necklace with its ornate silver top and the corked wine bottle. Now she was content, perfectly at ease in her containers, but she thought of the islanders and the citizens of C-town who were still trapped. She and Alonso were marooned on the beach through most of the night, but it was still dark when wings beat down and Dalton landed beside them. The island had healed the aerospace executive and given him the wings he had so firmly envisioned. In the necklace and in the bottle, Doreena sensed the wings above her. The billowed tents were AeroFlux red attached to Dalton's lean body. He agreed to fly them off the island and back to C-town if it were possible. In Alonso's embrace, in the necklace and in the bottle, Doreena flew up as a hazy blue powder soaring over the ocean.

And, of course, she also remained on the island.

~ 47 ~

MIRROR ISLAND: WORLD TRAVELER

Doreena Flora Moriena, world traveler

Exactly as advertised, AeroFlux flew them into the future. Dalton held Alonso's waist as he flew and Doreena, shifting like sand in the necklace on Alonso's chest and in the bottle in his hand, left the island flying over the ocean under Dalton's wings. In moments, La Merde and the other drowning islands in the rising, reddening Rust Sea appeared. Then, they flew over the scalloped coastline of Cascadia and the nearly abandoned coastal town of Westport, whose breaks had lured the Islanders into the area and then left them stranded on their way out in C-town, passed beneath them. Inland over New West, they crossed the smoky Freeway swarmed with refugees, entered the green splay of wilderness, and found the vineyards twining around the shores of Silver Lake. From this height, the scenery, even the dark 'Way, looked placid and pristine. Anything that fell from the sky would sink under the pools of color — blue, gray, or green — and be gone. The land looked as if it would not break a fall.

Then Dalton swooped toward C-town and rock cliffs spiked out of the forest. The fir tops pierced the sky and even the dirt road into town rose threateningly. The neck of Doreena's glass bottle warmed where Alonso squeezed it. They landed on the edge where pavement marked the entrance to C-town and return to solid ground.

"Are you sure this is where you want to be?" Dalton said. "I could take you anywhere."

"I'm sure," Alonso said. "There are people we need to see."

"Well, I can't go in winged. I guess I thought they'd disappear."

"No, you can't," Alonso said. "I meant me and Doreena."

"Maybe I'll fly back East. The trip from the island was easy enough."

But it wasn't any distance, Doreena thought.

"Do me a favor," Alonso said. "Wait for a while at Silver Lake. I want you to take someone with you."

There was no audible reply other than the expansion of wings. The air churned as Dalton struggled to lift from the earth again. A faint sulfur and sea scent departed with him. Doreena imagined him gliding again over the evergreens with the flat map of the world beneath him, blue rings around all the islands, her uncharted island floating not far off in a hazy nimbus. Alonso carried her the rest of the way into town on foot and in her softness, she felt the rhythm of his walk.

They met Hobart inside the reopened Travel Museum along the boardwalk at Traynter Resort. Doreena shifted inside the wine bottle as Alonso explained to Hobart what had happened to her and the plan they had concocted that last night on Mirror Island. Then Hobart showed Alonso the space. New construction smells of paint, plaster and pine floorboards masked the stale traces of mold and incense that rose off the few world-worn curios displayed.

"Doreena saved everything. We found it in one of the AeroFlux trucks. I haven't unpacked it all yet."

Hobart thumped the lids of a couple of the wooden crates. "You really want to reopen this place? I don't know how you'll find room for everything."

"I'll manage," Alonso said.

"What does Doreena think?" Hobart gazed into the bottle.

Doreena swelled and pressed the glass sides, but she stayed soft. Alonso lifted her away and the bottom circle of the bottle came to rest on the top of the crooked wood table. It rocked to the side.

"She doesn't say much these days."

Rubber band glissandos released the museum's cache of scrolled maps and posters, and they unfurled across the new floor.

"These are the places; all the best and softest places," Hobart said. "Do you think you can remember them all?"

"I love the names: Protection Island, Captiva Island, Deception Island," Alonso said. "I might forget the rest."

"Leaves more to be discovered," Hobart said.

A match struck and flame sizzled up against a stick of incense. The oily smoke rose, freeing jasmine as it dripped ash. Hazy blue wisps carried the inaugural scent through the store.

"There's nothing holding us here anymore and we all feel braver," Hobart said. "The City Fathers say they're opening this place up to trade. I think we'll go out now. Tonight, will be the islanders' last meeting."

At dusk, Alonso took Doreena to the Labor Temple. She shook against the glass up each stone step, entering the familiar drip and clank of the building. The meeting had already begun. Alonso set Doreena down in the circle of drums. Each jolt elevated her up the glass vial in the necklace and up the glass neck of the bottle. She lifted and dropped as the islanders' hands tapped the drumheads. Their voices joined and the names of earth's islands washed over her as they chanted.

Alonso dropped a bundle of maps. The dank air echoed through the paper tubes. "These are all the places we want to know; we want to share."

Each of the islanders picked up a place.

"North Island, New Zealand," J-Bay said.

"I won't make it far. Maybe Protection Island," Hobart said.

"Don't worry, me and my boys have got Kyushu and Sri Lanka. We'll get there somehow." J-Bay said. "For my brother."

"AeroFlux has reopened on the East Coast and I've heard rumors you can catch flights out of some little island up north outside the UG," The Stew said.

Doreena imagined his eyes wide and glowing like the lemur's in the dark.

When they'd all decided where they would go, the islanders gathered around her, kneeling, their knees thumping the cold concrete. Alonso uncapped her bottle. Space opened up above her releasing a breath of sour wine. The islanders' exhalations stirred her, followed by the tap and click of many lifting lids. Alonso tilted her bottle, and she precipitated down into all the differently shaped containers: ovoids, triangles, circles, ellipses, rhomboids and squares. She slid around tin, wood, glass, stone, or shell sides. Fingertips pressed into her tamping her down and she clung to the whorls. In time, she'd know each islander by his fingerprints. She stiffened a little, gaining a chalky weight, as she adjusted to her division and the myriad sensations of her separated selves, but then she stilled and softened again. *This is natural*: she heard her grandmother say.

"You'll make it," Alonso said to the Islanders. "Just remember, you'll affect her."

"Travel soft, or not at all," Hobart said.

"Go soft," the Islanders said.

And they stilled inside, she felt their thoughts soften even though they were all nervous about what awaited them outside

C-town. They all made the effort, even The Stew. She shifted side to side with each of the Islanders in the various containers. They tucked her away into pockets, bags, and backpacks. She lay in these dark nests as calm and warm as the island night. This is the allure of islands: places to let go and still be contained, she thought.

She would journey with the islanders, embodying the experiences for her ancestors. When they arrived on the islands, the islanders would pick a place and pour her out onto the sands and she would become part of those places, assisting to preserve their softness forever. She imagined it like sales calls. That was the plan she and Alonso had come up with that night on Mirror Island.

As she traveled, however, she also stayed behind in the slim vial around Alonso's neck that had once held her grandfather. She swung through the air or rested in the thrum of Alonso's particular slow heartbeat. The portion of her in the necklace, she imagined, might have once been her human heart, or the nerve endings clustered between her legs or perhaps the primitive place in her brain, the almond-shaped amygdala that loved instinctually. But she knew there was really no distinction between the part of her here, and the part that traveled. Alonso's hand embraced the vial and she clung to the warming sides of the glass.

"What about you?" J-Bay asked.

"I'm still going by C-town. I'm staying here with the museum," Alonso said. "And they've reopened the lounge. I got back on as a waiter."

"You're kidding. Here? The world awaits and you want to stay C-town?"

Alonso gave his easy shrug. As they were leaving, he pulled Hobart aside. "Head to Silver Lake." He explained to her about Dalton waiting with his maroon wings. "You might get farther than you think."

"Red wings, like a cardinal?"

"Not exactly, more like stretched skin. Bat like," he amended.

"I feel like you just said the devil take me." Hobart said and laughed. "But then I've never heard of an island underworld."

With the islanders, Doreena went out into the world and with Alonso she stayed in C-town shifting — *zza zza zza* — like sand. Her fluid form inside the many traveling vessels felt easy and companionable she wondered how she had ever survived 35 lonely years in one sole, solid body. In the mornings, Alonso poured her out into his palm, and she settled into the hooks and spirals of his fingertips and flowed down the long deep river of his lifeline and crossed the broken arch of his heart. He read aloud the headlines of *The Mirror*: C-town Opens Trade with New West, C-town Allows Refugees to Return, C-town to Begin Negotiations with the UG. Slowly, C-town was letting go, too.

At night, after a long day showing curios to passersby at The Travel Museum and evening waiting on diners at the Tiki Tiki Lounge, Alonso and Doreena surfed. At first, they just went out on the lake, where Doreena glided around Alonso's neck over the mechanized waves. But the island never felt very far away. When the weather turned warm, one Sunday in spring, Alonso walked Doreena to the street where she'd grown up. He bent down among the rounded shrubs planted in front of the condominium, its terracotta-colored siding still newly bright and clean. He scooped out a handful of the thin dry soil, lifted the silver top of Doreena's home and tilted the necklace over the shallow indent. A little of Doreena wafted down onto the soil with its infertile smells of paint and aluminum. The next morning, a hibiscus bloomed before the glass front doors.

Once believed to be extinct, the succulent petals of the white *kokio keokeo* native to Hawaii glistened faintly blue. Most hibiscus have showy, scentless blossoms, but the *kokio keokeo* is one of few with fragrance and this one's sweetness carried to the houses across the street and rose up through all the open windows reaching even as far as the 32nd floor. By the time Mrs. Dammerung, the widow who lived there, had taken the elevator down, a crowd of neighbors, the people usually only seen together at occasions such as chimney fires or ambulance calls, had gathered on the front lawn before the bush. Mrs. Dammerung wished she'd brought a plate of her grandmother's pfeffernusse cookies dusted with powdered sugar. The cookies used to be so popular at office parties and potlucks. She'd given the recipe away a thousand times.

"Have you ever smelled anything so exotic?" someone said.

As the crowd grew quiet remembering, Doreena Flora Moriena — the wanted child, the abandoned adult, the salesman, the surfer, islander and lover, ashes and dust, inorganic consciousness, world traveler and explorer, and now, the hibiscus flower — gathered all the thoughts that plumed from the neighbors enchanted by the fragrance. The globules of exotic thought, yellow tufts like pollen, stuck to her pink knobbed stamen. One day they too would blossom, flowing out into the islands of the universe and becoming so tangled up in everything that it would be impossible to be separate, impossible to stand still.

The Seasteaders: Book Three

Solarpunk Transformation Trilogy
Book Three

The Seasteaders

~ 48 ~

THE SEASTEADERS: PROLOGUE

While I am swimming, I think of what I have learned. I think of love. Love crosses distances. It expands across miles, across continents, across barriers of soul or sea. Distance does not break or dissolve love. I have loved from under oceans and come to love from beyond my body. My capacity to love is boundless and boundaryless and it is the strongest part of my aspect. Yes, I admit, I have been slow to learn love's lessons. In my first life, I was slow to love and learn. I was slow to understand our capacity for transformation. I never met Geneva Weltraum who transformed our thoughts. I was never psychic. I never knew Doreena Flora Moriena who changed our being. I never knew the liquid island of her love. Yet, those who went before me, my mothers and sisters of transformation, loved me. They were the waves of my life. Still, before I met the Mulians, I did not even think much of the capacity of love, its ancestral underwater nature. Afterwards, the stretch and reach of love became my obsession. Earlier in life, I did not think of love at all. Later, thoughts of love consumed me.

Watch me now swim to land. I reach a distant shore tired but ready to share my message at last. I begin to hum my song as I approach the land and prepare to speak.

"Love you. Appreciate you. Thank you," I say with shallow breaths when I first pull myself out of the water. "I see you and, of course, I know you."

This is how I always begin the conversation with the first person I encounter on shore--this time, a boy. I raise myself half out of the water. I am still wet with sea. While he is statuesque with shock, I say what is important before the chance slips away. I have to be direct, to assure these people of my humanity.

I was human once although I do not look it now. Sometimes the land people run away and sometimes they stay to listen; it depends upon the person.

This boy has stopped in curiosity, but my first words have scared him. He is old enough that people rarely say they love him outright anymore and too young to be thanked. He could be a young General Balor.

"I am not a monster," I tell him. "I was a child once, a person, an ordinary lander, just like you."

He points at my bare breasts, and I laugh at the absurdity that these body parts might still be the most startling thing about me.

"Oh, yes, but I was a little girl."

I wish the people could see past my appearance immediately, but it takes time. I've swum many miles through the Rust Sea. I have wrinkles and barnacles that twist across my rust red skin to horrific effect, but deep in my scars there is beauty, too--lavender, cerulean, and sea green pearlescent droplets and rivulets like an oyster shell. I hoist myself out of the water to bare it all--my twisted beauty still becoming.

If these people are willing to listen, I will have to tell the entire story so that they can understand. We are in a hurry for the waters are quickly rising, but the story can't be rushed. For decades our people have been warring on opposite isles of Pacifica over pinnacles of land. Even Sync Chrome City's psychics and Mirror Island's surfers could not stop the hatred. Perhaps Geneva should not have befriended Burrows. Perhaps Doreena should have preserved the island and not let herself become so diluted. But, motivated by loves, what choice did they have? So, the killing went on for centuries while the waves rose. We prayed for mercy, ineffectually, then stopped. It is hard to have faith in anything solid while the land slips away from under our feet.

I am here to offer a liquid solution.

I wish the landed people could just see the truth of what I am about to tell them in my eyes. In truth, though, my soul looks untrustworthy, piratical. I have the look of an Elathian Riptider. It's the way the lines have set about my eyes--a tangled combination of fear, tragedy, saltwater, wind, sun, and laughter. There's nothing reliable or settled-looking about me. I have aged into this beautiful, twisted sea wrecked shape.

I've gone where I was pulled, lived as I had to, leapt when it was demanded and left the ones I love. After I tell my story, I'll leave these people too. This is my truth may it be one of many: While others clung to the land, I departed for the sea. I went because the Mu offered peace, which I covet, having experienced none in this lifetime. There was also the offer of breath—of survival. Just that can turn the tides of fate. Just that. Just.

I follow the boy to his village where I'll place my hand upon the speaking staff, because these people have learned that lesson how to let each other speak. I wrap my webbed fingers around the smooth red Madrona wood and I tell the story I have come to tell in the public square. My real story, however, began below, as all stories will one day, in a place robbed of breath.

The villagers gather. They appear breathless. They wait for me to begin.

"I want to take you down with me under the Salish Sea," I do not say.

"I do not want to go alone or be alone ever again," I do not say.

It hurts to hold in these words. It is like drowning and at the same time I am euphoric. I sacrifice my own desires again and again to save my world, to help my people. There is no doubt that this is what I do.

The little boy who brought me before the rest of his people reminds me, too much, of General Balor. It's in the set of his lip and in his bravery.

I remember watching the old man die and how I did not move to save him.

He could have been a good man, the general, as much as any of us. The Mu have taught me that. I feel the shame of my inaction. I feel my guilt. Still, I must come before these people as a savior. They will have to save themselves, but first they must believe me. I will keep my faults and my crimes to myself. So, in this way, it is fortunate the psychics never crossed the water. It was meant to be. The world works as the waters flow.

I begin by telling these people about my first ratfin, pet. They can all relate to a child's love for a pet. The people, themselves, always remind me of ratfin -- with their squirminess, their fear, and their resistance.

Then, I tell them about my mother's bruises. These people understand that, too. They know full well the depths of war and pain.

One of the things the Mu taught us Seasteaders was a different sense of time, but even so I feel as though I am talking forever. Time rides differently on the land. I'm growing impatient. The waters are rising.

At least the story is spreading--these landers nod when I speak as though they have heard parts of this tale before. It does not strike them as entirely fantastical. It's somewhat familiar. Our plan begins to change the tides.

I, and my lovers, have been swimming and swimming and sharing our story. I hope this village tells the next one and the next one and on and on--in time this truth becomes easier to believe. The myth spreads and becomes reality.

When everyone knows and is ready to go underwater, I can be with my lovers again. Hope hurts, but I can be patient. I anticipate our reunion in salt and sea.

"The acidic water is rising," I tell the boy. "You must learn to swim in it."

I look out at the crowd.

"It could take a lifetime to rebuild the road to Mu. But please, please, consider (my love, my dear, my darling: I do not say) they'd give you more than one to do it."

The Seasteaders: Part One

LOVE

~ 49 ~

THE SEASTEADERS: LEAVING HOME

Clean, bright, washed by time, like a dirty stone plunged under a sunlit stream, the bruises on mother's cheeks and her blade-scarred forearms--the bright purple and red swatches of skin--look beautiful in my memory.

There was nothing clear or beautiful about her scars though when I standing in front of them at age seven, eye level. When I received the first coin to Mu, I was horrified.

Everything around us was a scramble.

"Hurry, Nata!" my mother called.

Her bags were lined up in the hall with everything packed. I had refused to pack my carpetbag because I didn't understand where were going. I was afraid of this change.

"I can't," I said. "I don't know what to take."

Mother said there wasn't room for everything. She pulled me into my room. My bag was open on my bed. She pulled clothes from the dresser and flung them into it.

"It doesn't matter," she said.

We had moved before, many times, inland, everyone did as the waters rose, but always before things had been important: meticulously packed and tucked into tight packages that must be carried gently and positioned into the kowal drawn cart. There was hardly room for all those things, but we had carted them carefully from the house on Salish Island when we'd left it for Orcas: when my father lost his job, after the factory flooded, and the soldiers wanted our house on the hill.

My mother had been so cautious about those things: the vase given to her by Aunt Virgie, the doilies made by cousin Tolly, the ceramic figures collected by cousin Shad. Now those same items were ignored, left high on shelves I could not reach.

Father had gone to the grocery. Mother made some excuse for why she could not go. He had had a craving for eel, so he had gone himself. I do not know why she picked that time. It was not enough time, the grocery was quite near, but it must have seemed sufficient. The wait for a lover's return is the slow ingress of a tide, but the flight from a lover is a tsunami. While we were standing there with our bags mostly packed, mother consulted her seeing shells. Somehow there was time for that?

She shook the little felt bag, reached in for one shell piece, and examined its upturned jagged edges.

"We have everything. We're ready to go," she finally said. Then, "I don't know if I can do this."

She sounded frantic. My mother had been with my father for eight years.

The rest of shells rattled in her hand. Then stopped as she closed her fist tight around them. It must have hurt. She dropped the bag and the shells scattered across the bamboo floor.

"Grab your bag," she said, staring at a piece of upturned coral.

She left the shards laying in the entryway for father to see, or more likely to step on and grind into powder. He did not believe in portents, would not be calmed by the shells, and would not agree with our departure no matter what they said.

The objects I left were dolls, ceramic figurines, and the jewelry box with the spinning dolphin inside. Things had to be left so father wouldn't suspect right away that we were gone for good, so that he wouldn't try to follow.

I cried over these things in a torrent on that day and it was really the loss of those small objects that disturbed me most. I didn't understand what loss meant, then. For a long time after that, I refused to cry over things. Looking back, that moment severed my attachment to objects. I lost my most precious things and then everything solid became unimportant. I never let myself love another material good. I tucked my capacity for love away inside. I hid it inside a thickening shell.

My mother never understood this. For her, each new item she obtained became all the more precious as it represented that which was lost.

In Mu, I learned a different way to think about objects and gained an appreciation for my mother's perspective. I understood her better after living with the Mulians. For her, all those objects had souls. They connected her to people I couldn't picture in faraway places, on islands that she would never reach again, on lands that might no longer exist above the sea.

At the time though, I saw only her foolishness, her excess, a kind of greed and focus on goods that didn't matter. I could only love ideas, the ethereal, which could not be broken or left behind, so I mistakenly thought. Mother loved her things, but if we took them, father would know we meant to leave him forever.

How to leave things wasn't a lesson my mother needed to learn in that lifetime, unfortunately. She didn't gain anything by it. Loss of beloved things was just something she suffered, another source of pain. We had to travel light.

For me, it was different: It was my time to absorb this meaning. This was the beginning of how I learned lightness.

In Mu, they believed that every object had a soul. They would no more purposefully destroy a vase than they would shatter a person's body. This made them cautious about how many objects they took into their care. They felt a responsibility for things throughout their lives and they passed on that responsibility carefully. This did not make them less reverent of Mulian life; it made them more so. Someone who cares for silent, stoic shells is even more careful with a Mulian being they can hear breathing.

In Mu, I learned that in my past life, in many lives, I hoarded objects, so in this lifetime I'm asked to learn to let go. Pacifica, in the time of the Rust Sea when everything was floating or corroding away, was a perfect place for my rebirth. I often had to remind myself that it was a blessing, truly, how thoroughly I was learning this lesson.

With the Rust Sea rising, Pacifica's islands were shrinking. Gradually, everyone had to learn to let go. For me, it was like an amputation, when my mother's flight removed me from home in one fell swoop. As a child this blessing was misery.

I took comfort in one thing: my ratfin pet, Ea.

My mother hurried me, but I wouldn't leave without Ea. I wasn't crying over this though. Instead, I put his water dish into the cage, covered it with a towel and yanked it off the shelf. Tears take over in times when there is nothing. When there remains room for action, there are no tears. When the water is rising and there is nothing to be done but drown, then it is time to cry and join the ocean in sympathy. Much later, when I left my twin soul Georgios, I jumped into the ocean and cried because there was nothing else to be done.

Then, as a child, my eyes were dry and focused. From this distance, however, many years and losses later, it was impossible not to feel sympathy for the shaken ratfin. It looked like a toy of soaked, jumbled grey fur and fin under that towel.

I picked up the cage and mother dropped my hand to fill her other hand with carpetbag handles. Mother had the most beautiful hands and I had always hoped to inherit them. Instead, in the watery way of fate, I would grow webbed fingers.

"Nata," mother said, stepping over the seeing shells to open the door to the apartment. She swung her carpetbag at the door and ushered me ahead of her. The apartment, as we left it, looked the same as it ever had except the life had gone out of the carefully arranged objects within it: vases, doilies, woodcarvings (grandmother was quite wealthy), and ceramic figurines. I held onto Ea's cage and made my mother carry everything else. She managed to take my own bag as well. I later learned that to do this she'd had to leave behind one of her own bags. It was the one with her suits in it. Later, she'd had to beg for work clothes.

Once outside, I was terrified. I was afraid of the street, the wagons and the big, hairy kowals that pulled them. I thought we would get hit standing there on the street or shat on. I worried about my father. He could have come at any time. Why had he taken so long? Had he been deterred by soldiers at the grocery? Forced conscription into General Balor's army was always a fear. Why hadn't he gotten back in time to stop us so I could be back in my pale blue bedroom? My room in the old house had been blue and they'd stained the new one in town in the apartment a light blue, too. It was a last luxury. They didn't want me to feel uprooted, so I tried not to. That was the kind of child I was, pliant as kelp.

There was a carriage waiting for us outside.

"Please, wait. We're coming," my mother said.

The driver frowned at the cage. He looked pensive and ready to leave. You could see he was sorry he'd accepted this fare, at this time of the night, and in this part of the war-torn city. We piled in and I put the cage on my lap. The kowals splashed through the soggy streets. I peered under the cloth to see Ea's whiskered little nose dripping.

"Hurry, now," he said. "It's been a soggy day."

"You know," mother said, turning to me. "It was your father's idea to get you that ratfin."

It was true. Father had a strange sense of humor, strange ideas about how to raise his only child. He didn't want me to be like anyone else. He was right, no one else I knew kept ratfin, but then I didn't know many other children. The next time I met someone who kept a ratfin for a pet I'd be an adult and the ratfin keeper would be a Riptider.

What struck me in mother's comment was her tone of disdain, a sound of separation that I'd never heard from her before. The Mulians lived long lives, many hundreds of years, and even then, they did not believe we end at death. We come and go like the tides, they said. We return with fresh lessons to cast upon the sands. There are new objects we are meant to pick up or leave: a sand dollar, a piece of kelp, a creature's body, or its calcium husk. My mother's lessons to relearn in that lifetime were: how to leave a lover and that people do not always tell the truth.

My parents didn't have many friends. They lost their first mates in the 100 Island Wars, and then kept new ones away with their private war. Maybe that's why my father wanted me to have the ratfin. They were both pacifists, who had refused to fight, which is ironic because they fought so much at home. They had relatives on other isles of Pacifica, but the war came home to us anyway.

We never lived in isolation. Even on islands, our culture came home to us. Culture surrounded us like a sea, and we were cast about in it subject to its violence or its calms. This is why I wanted so much to create a condition of peace, to find a new way.

I never considered myself to be a victim of violence because father never hit me. Mother took the blows, and they went around me. When they fought, I didn't exist. Our house was too small for me to be safe in my room, so I would slip from home with Ea in my pocket. I went to the estuary downhill from our house. In the weedy tall grasses, I sat watching the still water.

In fall, when the weather turned, my mother gave me a coat made of trumpeter feathers. It was twice the size of other kids' coats, and it could have kept Far North explorers warm. It wasn't an attractive coat, but the mottled black-green color made it perfect camouflage for hiding in the estuary at dusk. It smelled of marsh and cattails. Other kids lost their coats or whined about wearing them, but I always had mine. I took it with me when I escaped from the house, while my parents waged their private war. I imagined my mother had given the coat to me for just this purpose. She expected me to abandon her. This was where I learned to leave the ones I love in times of stress, a shameful skill I have used over and over again.

Wrapped in my coat, I would go to the water even in the winter on days when ice crisped the marsh's edges and the pampas and cattails gleamed with a coat of hoar frost. I would go even at night when I could only see the water as a glimmer, a reflection of the moon. Even in the snow, I put my coat on and went out to my safe place.

The first time that I remember my parents fought, I thought guiltily of how I had left my mother, back there, alone. I imagined her hurts. I pictured her dying. I sat on a damp stone with my feet planted on muddy earth and cried. I dripped wet tears onto Ea whose fur and scales already looked gleaming black, wet, and shiny. Ea placed his webbed paws on my chest. With repetition, though, I became accustomed to the pattern of my parents' private war. I did not imagine I had any control over these fights or could help mother in any way. It wasn't just my youth that made me passive.

I had been swept into my culture and floated with it on the outer winds of Pacifica. We were all caught up in wars and rising waters. I had not yet considered another way and it did not seem necessary to consider a course of action. My mother had bruises and tears, but she remained. My father was distant, but that was usual unless he was cheerily bringing home presents--ceramic kowal figurines for me and gold and silver bangles for my mother. Many of the necklaces and bracelets he gave her were handmade from his forge. These were his talents: battery, handcrafts, and lying. One of these I learned from him.

I learned that if I waited long enough, if I became engrossed in play, when I returned the table would be bright and filled with wet, nutrient foods--bok choy, water chestnuts, and water cabbages--and my mother would have already dabbed chamomile lotion on her bruises. This was how I became good at imagining and developed my philosophy that if you dream hard enough, you can make the world a better place--or ignore its faults, anyway. I hadn't yet learned to put my dreams into action.

In that estuary, I began my life's work again. Lifetime after lifetime, I had sought to attain what I would finally achieve in this one--so it came to me young. I knew my purpose. I saw the patterns in the world like my mother saw them in her seeing shells: ripples in the pond, flowing grasses, and fractals of leaves. I imagined arranging my world in the way my mother arranged plates and knives and napkins and dishes of rice, bean sprouts, watercress, and bamboo shoots, to realign our family. Of course, at that age, the wide world with its wars over the remaining peaks of islands was too much for me to imagine. Instead, I imagined my own small dominion. I called my invented paradise Octavia.

On that estuary, lived my imagined wee Octavian people.

They would build a colony, a tiny walled fortress while, I, an all-powerful, omniscient giantess watched over them and ordered their lives. One brave Octavian hero would be called to ride the giant ratfin back to the house for food. It would take two days at least depending on what they encountered (a fox or hawk). They'd risk everything for a dab of my mother's rice pudding, which would last the Octavian people weeks.

My imaginary land Octavia wasn't messy, disorganized, drowning, or war torn. The branches that made the city were laid neatly parallel. The people made the most of what they needed themselves. The trips to the house were merely a luxury. Octavians never fought. No one shouted or dominated. They held reasoned discussions and dissenters were cast out and, therefore, eaten by insects and vermin.

Sometimes, I would be so involved with Octavia that my mother would have to come out to the estuary to fetch me. She'd bring me in for a late dinner when the fight had passed and it was time to indulge in reunion food, a stew of vegetable gumbo.

Of course, reality, and the brutality of my home, could not always be ignored. Once I returned to the house after dark and found it empty. When my parents returned, my mother's arm was bandaged in a sling, and they avoided each other's eyes.

"I don't think he believed you," my father said holding the apothecary bottle while my mother bent over the cutting board and then laid out the thick stone plates with her one good hand.

Another time, the soldiers came across the fields riding clanging metal-draped kowals, stupidly impractical for those water-laden times. General Balor's advantage was his viciousness, not his forethought. Mother brought me inside then. I heard father yelling in the front yard. Then, I heard the thump of a man falling--and silence. Father returned bruised and dirty. Bested. I thought it served him right; until much later when I had quenched my thirst for revenge.

How dare father yell at those metal-plated men the way he yelled at mother? Later, I respected him in a way--at least he treated everyone alike. There was honesty to his impulsive violence. He could not control himself for anyone.

"General Balor says his troops need this high ground," my father said.

Not long after that, we left the house on Salish Island and moved to smaller Orcas Island and into town. I remember little of the journey, but it was not by boat. Back then there were still a few bridges.

My father told me the origin of the island's name. Of course, he was a fabulous storyteller.

"Orcas were a kind of whale, black and white, with sharp teeth. They were among the first animals killed by the corrosion leaching into the sea. They were sensitive creatures," he said. "Not like your mother."

This was a dig at mother's heritage. She was an Iron Blood and from that, proudly, she said she gained her toughness. My father turned it into an insult and punished her for it.

Fortunately for us, it was not possible to identify the Iron Bloods by appearance. Some blamed my mother's people for the rust entering the sea--as if the blood General Balor's soldiers had spilled into it were a pollutant. It was true that my mother's people--the Iron Bloods--had a tradition of bloodletting at sea as part of their burial rites. In the old days, when there were orcas, it was considered a great honor if one's body were snatched, shaken, and consumed by one of the whales.

Iron Blood was why the seas were growing red and poisonous, liars said. It was true when I licked my own blood, it tasted like the Rust Sea, but it did not sicken me. I even let Ea lick one of my wounds once, when I cut my finger on a shell, but he did not sicken, either. I did not think my blood was poison.

When we left again, the apartment this time, only my mother and I; my mother took all her jewelry. She sat in that carriage with gold bands up to her elbows and her neck weighed down by chains.

"Where to, mum?" the driver asked.

"To pawn," my mother said.

The driver drove us to the pawnbroker. It was the first time I'd been to such a shop. There were bars on the windows. Inside, it smelled of damp and muddled loss. There were few items, and most were what was left behind when homes were flooded, and people moved to higher ground.

It was at once a frightening and intriguing place. There were guns and wooden oars on the walls and tricycles on the floor: children's toys mingled with adult ones on the shelves. There were knives under the counter of all types: rusted bowies, thick hunting wedges, and long, sleek blades. There were sparkling gold rings and black, gold, and pink pearls.

We were in the pawnshop a long time, it seemed. It was a place to lose time in and a place to get lost. Was my mother hesitating? I do not know.

"It used to be all women had was jewelry, what was given, and what they could wear. I never liked all this," my mother said as she unloaded her gold onto the counter. "It's blood money. People die to mine gold and dive for pearls. It's an evil. Your father never understood how I felt, how it stung, when he gave me these things by way of apology. All this added insult, burden, and ache. It feels good to be done with it."

Mother understood instinctively, with Mulian clarity, how objects could be a burden, how they must be carried from place to place and cared for like children to survive the chaos of these times.

I watched the man behind the counter grin. He was glad to take the weight. You could see she'd spoken too much in front of him to make a good bargain.

"Happy to be of service," he said, without a trace of deference.

I didn't tell her that father had given me a jewel too, after one of their fights. It was a small pearl strung on a steel chain. Its black surface reflected purple waves in swirls of silver and green. I could not have imagined then that one day my skin would look like that. I could not imagine that one day I would be pearling.

The color was unique. I didn't think mother had one like it. Father had told me not to tell her about the gift, and I hadn't. I knew she wouldn't have liked that he had given it to me. I wasn't sure I liked receiving it myself. It felt dangerous and secret. I well knew what came with these kinds of surprises. It was the black-purple of a bruise, but it was such a pretty, small thing. I could not have refused. Now I took it out from under my shirt and released the clasp. I laid it on top of her pile of gold. It sparkled there. I wanted Mother to know I understood her lesson. She looked at me and began to cry.

"I was right to leave," she said. "I was right." As if, until that moment, there had yet been some doubt in her. Father's lies sunk deep.

There, in the pawnshop, while my mother and the clerk haggled I discovered the medallions. I looked under the case at all the gold discs. I vaguely understood the concept of pawning. The shop was filled with things stolen or lost because of poverty and fear or things abandoned as the water rose that people were glad to lose or could not take. Meaningless currency was got in return.

The medallions though, were money, given in exchange for money, and displayed as though they had greater value than the stuff kept in your pocket. It was confusing. Why? I thought they must be a kind of magic. Maybe an ill kind. I knew soldiers received them in exchange for deeds done in battle. There were special medallions given for killing Iron Bloods.

My mother, though, was not enchanted by anything in this place. It repelled her, but she lingered. Did she hope Father would find us?

She was still under father's spell--although it was seeping away.

"I never cared about those things. Just like you never cared about those toy kowals," she said.

When they'd made the deal, the man looked up startled when he saw the name on the chit and he counted the money out slowly. It made my mother nervous. She held out her hand for the coins, "What's wrong?"

She'd been tense for trouble and now she was sure this was the beginning of it. My Father was a brilliant player at card games, especially Cardinal. He was a wicked strategist--something good he gave me. He often had a trump card and now she thought this was the playing of it, some way he'd anticipated her and blocked our retreat.

"You Nata Lang?" the broker said.

My mother remained silent and glared at him, but I said, "I am." Defiantly.

Mother turned her glare on me.

"He says I'm s'posed to give you...a thing," he hesitated.

"No, we don't want anything. Just the cash," mother said. In a place like this, that should have been obvious.

"It's no mind. It's naught, but for the little 'un."

This angered me. I never thought of myself as small. In my imagination I was a giantess, the great leader of an organized society--a mighty Octavian.

He held out the coin to me, the first I received. "Take it now. No fuss. I'm s'posed to give it you." He looked at my mother. "Or I cain't give you the cash. I don't want no trouble, not of that kind, no."

My mother nudged me. "Hurry then."

I held out my hand and he dropped the coin onto it. I didn't examine it then, just noticed it was cool and light and gold. It flickered in my palm like a fish scale.

"From father?" I asked, and watched as the man spun his rings round his fingers and looked at me askance.

He scoffed, "Only if'n your a fish."

My mother got her cash and we went back to the carriage. "Take us to the dock," she said to the driver.

I put the coin in my pocket and we boarded the last night ferry to La Merde where my grandmother lived.

"It's not just me. Eventually, he would have hurt you too. I got you out just in time," mother said.

No matter that I knew it was true, I wished mother wouldn't speak truths to me so unsparingly. I didn't want to hear so plainly how father could hurt me. I see now, I've inherited her trait of blunt talk.

Mother alternated between rage and tears. She took a letter from her pocket and wept over it. Really, she wasn't thinking of me at all. Mother was still thinking about Father and so was I. We were leaving him. So I left her too, and wandered to roam the deck of the boat.

It smelled of wet metal and rust. In the moonshine, rust speckled the waves as we rode. I realized how long it had been since I'd been beside so much water. Once we'd moved to town, I'd had nowhere to run to during their fights. I'd hid in my room, but even there I was surrounded. The rooms shook and I waited for the day when my bedroom door would open, and their terror would turn on me. Now the sea spray felt so fine on my face--no matter that it tasted like rust and left my skin red and chaffed--I imagined my city of Octavia and the little people riding the waves. This was where the little people longed to be. Living on the estuary, they'd been refugees. This was the Octavian's true home, on the sea, I imagined. Some monster had made them leave it. On the ocean at night, I felt peace for the first time since our move away from the house by the estuary, my pale blue bedroom, and my marshland.

While I was standing on the deck, I took ratfin out of his cage. It seemed to me he was sluggish as I warmed him in my hands and then held him over the railing to peer down at the murk passing beneath us. I felt him shivering and pulled him close to my chest unbuttoning my jacket so he could snuggle there. Then he gasped twice and went still. There was no mistaking the departure of his soul, the sudden emptiness of his body in my hands, heavy and dead. I don't know if it was from the stress, the cold, old age or if I'd clutched him too tightly too my chest--all of these possibilities crossed my mind--either way Ea was still and stiff. My ratfin friend was dead.

Only his whiskers and fins trembled, shaking in my upheld hand. I was startled, more than anything, by my first encounter with death. It was sudden, but so much less violent than the life I was used to. I was drawn to the peacefulness in that still body. If I had known the word I would have said "transcendent". I looked at ratfin's body and wondered, "Where has he gone?" As I held him in my hands, I saw perfect stillness. Only the rumbling of the ferry disturbed him. I had the sense that he had gone somewhere. I was curious. I wanted to follow him into that space, that stillness. I wanted to explore it, as I have always wanted to explore everything. I have always been unable to leave things alone--death least of all.

The next thing I did was hold him over the railing and drop him into the sea below. The body disappeared in the night. I imagined it tumbled into the rust waves. Is this shocking and strange? Well, it startled me too what I did.

It seemed the right thing to do at the time: an Iron Blood burial at sea. It came to me naturally. In the next moment, I panicked. I thought after I did this, that I'd made a mistake: That he wasn't dead, and I had killed him. He'd wake up in the water and swim, corrode, and freeze to death, dying from exhaustion or cold. The thought has haunted me ever since. I am usually at home in the water, but when I am afraid this is why. It's not the corrosion I fear; it's the scraping fins, the wheezing whiskers, the ratfin ghosts.

I covered the cage and ran across the deck seeking the comfort of my mother's arms.

That's when the ferry broke down. It came to a grinding halt as often happened in those days. The crew began to shout and mother came rushing out onto to the deck. She grabbed me and tightened my life vest. The rusty, creaky old boat could sink. The sea and the acid billows in it were corroding the metal. I bawled on mother's shoulder, but as I had reason enough to do so, she didn't question me. She assumed my reasons were the same as hers, and she hugged me to offer comfort. I think, too, she had tired of nursing her own grief. I was a welcome distraction for once.

Eventually, they got the ferry engine going again and we landed in La Merde the next morning. I never told my mother how I'd dumped Ea into the sea. I never got around to it. She never asked after it. I just fingered the coin in my pocket and tried not to imagine my ratfin, my mother, my father, and me submerged in those rusty, murky, churning depths.

~ 50 ~

THE SEASTEADERS: LA MERDE

More than any other placed I had lived, La Merde smelled of fish and rust. The town went uphill from the ferry dock. Up was the only way to go on that mountain island. The land, when we stepped off ship, squished beneath our boots--a bad omen for the town. Even at that age, the sponginess under my feet made me anxious. In my teens, it would terrify me. Then, as an adult, it would inspire me. Later, it meant nothing, nothing. The drowning of the land meant nothing to me at all.

The sun rose as mother and I walked up the cobblestone to my grandmother's house. La Merde was bustling with townsmen, and although the town was not yet overrun with General Balor's soldiers, several men with bayonets marched along the streets. I did not then notice the pale-yellow ornamented buildings with their arches and turrets--except to note that it was a pretty town. Later, though, I would be preoccupied with La Merde's low-lying university. I did note the round dome of the Iron Blood Church. Its blue color pleasantly reminded me of my painted bedroom at home. It was shocking though to see the words Iron Blood in public. That place augured loss and sadness.

When we passed through the town and veered West up the hill, I was startled to see the red and green street placard naming the winding road ahead. It read Octavia Street--the name of my fantasy town. This seemed magical to me and poignant. The obvious, that I'd once seen the name written on letters when I was young and had co-opted it for my fantasy adventures, did not occur to me. As a babe, I had been here before.

My grandmother met us at the end of the walkway. She was thinner even than my mother and pale in a long dark dress. My mother looked surprised to see her standing there beside the tuberoses lining the walk. She'd been given to think my grandmother was bedridden. This looked not to be the case, although on our slow walk into the house, I had plenty of time of observe the overgrown gardens and the tangled roses surrounding the house.

From what I'd heard of my grandmother, this wildness was not her usual way. She was ill in some way and worse, she was lonely, and too tired to maintain her formal gardens. Later, I would find sketches of what the gardens had been when grandfather had been alive. While he'd spent time teaching and researching at the university, she'd created mazes of hedges and lined the rows with blossoms. Nearly all of it was edible. I inherited some of my bent for planning, conspiracy, and design from grandmother. She had been a meticulous, practical woman, but she, too, was learning to let things go.

The house was a mansion with two long wings. There were thorny brambles everywhere arching over the stone path and dropping half-ripe berries onto it. Vines snaked up the second story. Gnarled trees, by a trick of perspective, poked through the mossy angled roof. I had never lived in a house like this. On Salish we had lived in a mud hut with a grass roof dug into the side of a hill. It was warm and clean, though sometimes damp and wormy, but there were just a few rooms: the kitchen and bedrooms. Our apartment on Orcas was two rooms with a bamboo floor. I slept in the living area. The building was cobbled together of thatch. Grandmother's house, Tillitat Manor, was stone--and there were many, many rooms.

Inside, it smelled of anise, rosewood, and citrus. It was a mixture of the orange-scented oil grandmother used to polish her banisters and tables, the handmade rose lotion grandmother slathered on each morning, and her favorite persimmon tea from Hattie's stall in the market. The house was crammed with doilies as though the ones we'd had at home had flown here and bred. The ceramic animals had been active, too, displayed in all the nooks. The downstairs was an enormous living room and kitchen.

I don't remember much else of that first day except my mother and grandmother talking in low muffled voices. I was too tired even to eavesdrop. My mother led me upstairs to sleep. At the top of the stairs with the elegant wooden banister, I stood stock still, amazed. The long hallway stretched in either direction. There were doors and doors and rooms and rooms down the East wing and the West.

I left footprints down the dust-covered floorboards as I walked to the master bedroom. The room had been grandmother's and untouched since she'd moved downstairs. It was painted a cool blue like the roof of the Iron Blood Church. The window looked up Octavia Street where the cobblestone path steepened and narrowed. That tangle at the top was the marketplace. Mother left me. My matriarchs had plans to discuss, and I would hear their voices rising from the kitchen long into that first night. Even exhausted, it was hard to sleep in that strange new place.

The closet was filled with dark clothes permeated with a rose scent. There were mourning outfits of black boots, lace handkerchiefs, silk gloves, black crepe trousers, and dresses. Since grandfather's death and his sea-fairing funeral and her steady decline, grandmother stayed on the first floor in a smaller, warmer room behind the kitchen. She'd made that concession to infirmity. It could have been a maid's quarters, but my grandparents, even in that mansion, had never had servants.

"We are all family. You pay someone, that puts them beneath you," grandmother often said. But I had the feeling she thought someone should have helped her keep house without being asked or paid. That someone should have been mother, and perhaps myself. "We're Iron Bloods. We stick together."

There it was again the words Iron Blood spoken open as sky here in the shelter of the blue dome of their church. Grandmother did not shrink from her heritage or hide it.

Mother and I settled distractedly into the house, and it was some time before she commented on my ratfin's absence. While we were busy caring for grandmother and soothing my mother's wounded heart, many things went unnoticed--like the arrival of General Balor and the sinking of the grounds around the university. The cobbled streets by the ferry dock were growing rust red with the telltale algae--the only life that thrived in the toxic slime--moist gunk carried off the boat on the boots of the soldiers and steadily uphill. I later learned that grandmother's illness, her need for a nurse, was part of what had convinced my mother to leave father. Grandmother healed rapidly from that first feigned illness. She was no more in need of cosseting than any other elderly widow.

When mother finally did remark on ratfin's absence, I lied. "I lost him during the move," I said. "He escaped his cage."

I wanted Ea's death and his ferry sea-fairing to be my secret.

La Merde was strangely peaceful as the war was building. Balor's soldiers were recruiting from other isles and their numbers were growing, but there was no one to fight, as yet. In those early days, it was so pleasant. I wondered why we had not crossed the sea sooner. I soon found out.

"It was your father," grandmother said. "He preferred the war to the threat of my frail person."

That was true, but not the whole truth. Father had other reasons not to want us near our blood kin. In some respects, he had been right. It had been safer for me and my mother to be far away from the other Iron Bloods. On Salish Island and on Orcas, mother and I blended in. Few people on outlying isles were attuned to thinking about blood. Who cared what flowed beneath the surface of the skin? Besides, Iron Bloods kept to their own. On La Merde, surrounded by kin, we were targets. Balor's men knew where to find us.

Father never did come after us. Ferries ran infrequently between the islands and the threat of conscription likely kept him away.

That first year, he sent letters that made my mother cry.

"He says he loves you," she said.

I often heard her arguing with my grandmother after those letters came. In the aftermath, grandmother would often fall ill again. Her health seemed fragile. We'd become busy at her beck and call bringing watercress soup, tuberose poultices, and anise teas.

Later on, the letters stopped and so did the tears.

I imagined father now yelled at another woman with another little girl. He gave them pearls and his hand-carved kowals. They lined the walls of my replacement's blue room.

To make myself at home in grandmother's house, I looked for water. From the attic, a triangle of purple-red ocean was just visible perched over the thatch of neighboring rooftops between the vine-laced trees. This vantage also afforded a clear view of the steady stream of men and women leaning into the hill as they climbed toward the rising tower of smoke at the height of La Merde--the hubbub of the market where they sold smoked fish and dried herbs. For someone else, this attic might have been the perfect sanctuary, but for me it was far too confined.

I found my place when I went out to look for my next ratfin. Mother agreed I could replace my pet and grandmother often sent me out to buy her teas and the oils she needed for her lotions. Like most people, we grew the majority of our groceries, but there were a few luxuries and exotic fruits for sale in the market. I followed the line of pilgrims walking up the winding road to the cobblestone market at the end of Octavia Street. It smelled of damp algae air, mulling spices, and curry. The goods at the market center were mostly cloths and food stuffs, but I found an old woman with a pen of ratfin beside the canal. I negotiated a price with her, doing my best to bargain, but unnerved by the way she squinted at me with her red eyes as if taking an accounting of my soul. Then, when I went for my purse, I found I was shy a few coin.

"Ah sure, you are. You're wastin' my time then," she said.

I had already chosen my ratfin from among them. She was a limber beast with especially lacy, dark, torn-looking fins. I could already feel her curled at the corner of my neck where I would train her to ride. Disappointed, I turned away, but then I remembered the gold coin from the pawnbroker. I unbuttoned the small pocket by my breast.

"And this!" I said triumphantly, laying it in the palm of the woman's hand.

"Wot's this?" The woman turned the coin over in her hand and froze. Her attentive eyes, red from the market smoke, scanned the coin. The avarice in those eyes betrayed my error. I'd given her something of great value and I thought to snatch it back, but the next thing I knew she'd thrust it at me.

"This is yours, child. Keep it." Having denied temptation, she would no longer look at me, gazing instead at the ratfin. "Have a ratfin, then. Take two. This here's a nice sibling pair."

She pointed at two: a fluffy, fat one in a corner and the thin lacy one I'd had my eye on. Given permission, I didn't hesitate. I herded them into my bell-shaped wire cage and locked the clasp. They smelled of damp fur and the mullet, eel, and loche they ate. I loved the smell of the fur and fin and took it as a comfort. That was the one failing of Mu: There were no ratfin there. As I turned away, the woman stopped me. She put a fist in my shoulder and thrust me around.

"Here then," she said, when I came round to face her. On her palm lay a second gold coin. "Take it. Take it, quick. It's yours; I know it. I don't want trouble."

Startled, I snatched it up. It's a strange thing, as a small girl, to inspire fear. I see now, it was an essential, early, life-shaping experience. I felt shame. I wanted to hide. I put the coin in my breast pocket where it thumped against its mate and hung heavy in its tight nest. I thought to ask the woman where the coin had come from and would have turned back, but then I realized I'd had two ratfin from her for no price at all. I hurried off as she shooed me before she could discover I was no threat and demand payment.

Of course, I met the woman again later. La Merde was a small, close peak. She was a friend of grandmother's and an Iron Blood, too.

That day, I wasn't in a hurry to get home. I explored down another narrow street and in the middle of it I found a stone bridge across the canal trickling down to the sea. I sat on this bridge and in its lonely crevice, surrounded by high walls coated with thick, pungent yellow moss. I peered in at the ratfin. They curled at the back of the cage. The brother, the tawny fluffy one, crouched to sniff my finger. His lacy grey sister had less fur and more fin.

I took the coins out then and, on closer examination, could not imagine how I could be so stupid as to offer the dubious treasure up as money. It was thin and rather pliable, and the gold had a green cast. The decoration on the coin was worn. Later, I made a paper tracing of the pattern. There were swirls and waves on one side. On the other, wavy lines sprawled crowned by a spiked circle. The coins had an odd feel, a bit rubbery and soft. The pictures on it looked raised, as if the images were embossed, but the surface felt smooth, but convex. The sides lifted to my fingertips and if I looked too long at them shadows appeared to flow over the surface.

At home, I found a fishhook and I thought to pierce the soft coin. When I pressed the tip of the hook into the coin, I hesitated and stopped. Instead, I wound a metal wire around the outside and affixed a chain to the end of it. I made a necklace, so the chain was visible around my neck, but the coin hung low beneath my clothing against my breastbone. I hid the other coin in my back of the closet in one of grandmother's pointy black boots. From then on, I spent a great deal of my time at the stone bridge, even at night, reading pamphlets under the streetlamp.

The pamphlets were political protests in the form of comics with thinly veiled criticisms of General Balor and calls to action: Iron Blood Jo vs. General Balfour, Iron Blood Jo Stops the Flood, and my favorite, Iron Blood Jo Returns to Sea. The printing of these materials was expensive, and it was under that pretext--for the conservation of resources--that the soldiers, once they took over the town in earnest, halted their production. Also, for our benefit, as they said, they instigated curfews. In the end, the enemy ruled us. None of this martial law kept us safe.

Once school began, I read textbooks: *The History of Pacifica Isles*, *Flora and Fauna of the Greater Northwest*, and what grew to be my favorite, *Maritime Knowledge and Oceans*, written by Saul Tillitat, my grandfather. They were dry books to be sure, but I lit them with my imagination.

I learned that my grandfather had been a well-respected scholar and philanthropist. My grandparents had owned the highest point on La Merde. He'd had the foresight to buy it. As the waters encroached, they had opted to give the land to the townspeople for the farms and the market. Their own house was the next highest point and then the university. The water, the ocean around me, was rising and growing more corrosive each year. The triangle of ocean I could see from the attic window grew darker purple and red. With the corrosion, grew the anger of the people crowded on pinnacles of land and General Balor stoked the fear to raise his armies and control the remaining land and its trapped people.

I, however, was always in love with water. I loved the sound of water dripping from the rooftops, streaming down the gutters, trickling through the canal, lapping under the bridge, lapping up from the ocean and soaking the streets. I loved the plop of droplets onto the cobblestones and the tap and plash of rain on the petals and leaves in grandmother's gardens. In my baths, I loved watching the steam rise and the way it moistened my skin and then flowed in rivulets from my budding breasts. I imagined building cities of stone with canals, funnels, and fountains of water. I began to sketch them and filled page after page in my notebook with pictures of drowned cities.

One day, I was exploring in one of the dusty rooms down the West wing in grandmother's mansion. In a closet I came across sheaths of sketching. At first, I thought they were my own, that someone had stolen them from my room and rummaged through them here. But the papers were older I saw, and they were not depictions of streets. They were rows and hedges--grandmother's garden and many imagined ones.

I took them downstairs and sought nana out in her warm room beside the kitchen.

"Yes, those are mine, child."

I showed her my own drawings.

"Ah, you've inherited the habit too. Come draw beside me sometimes. It gets lonely in here."

I spent more time in grandmother's room after that drawing and listening to her stories. I thought of Octavia Street, how my imagined place had had a physical location.

"Nana, is this a real place?"

"Your grandfather thought so, but he wouldn't leave me to find out."

"What happened to grandfather?"

"Well, he left me anyway. He drown. It was an accident, on the water. It was a disease of the blood."

One day, I would see that the place we imagined, Grandmother and I, was all one city. Mu was in our blood.

~ 51 ~

THE SEASTEADERS: GRANDMOTHER'S FUNERAL

As I grew into my adolescence, I spent less time at home and more in the market. I loved to sit on the bridge with my books and sketch or read. I loved the feel of the thick mists that hung in the market--before they began to burn with acid.

The neighborhood grew more populous over the years, and it seemed that when I lowered my head into my book the streets had been empty, but when I looked up the cobblestones could scarcely be seen, they were so trodden. The streets were now filled with soldiers, a few frightened people and us--youth.

Whatever were we doing, I wonder now. Just before the war we were carrying on as if we were merely growing up and had no special role to play. I could have been frightened too; had I been paying attention.

Instead, I started spending all my time sneaking out of grandmother's house. Although I'm sure now she knew. Surely, the doors creaked. There's no one so loud as a sneak. And I went dancing at the club we all frequented.

As I began to look up more often, with rapidly growing awareness, I watched the youths dressed in black and rust heading down narrow Hector Street into some establishment. The placard over the threshold changed constantly, but the place and the crowd were always the same.

I was too young, but I got in the first time I ventured.

"You look young for your age, doll," the doorman mocked.

I was 13. In truth, I have always looked exactly my age. Even transformed as an elder, when people saw me, they could tell I had been around a while, too long, really. My purpled skin was an ageless mix of wrinkles and ocean shine, but there was a transparent, aged look to my eyes.

First, the club, our place, was called Pyrrha then Astra, then Merops, but we, the youth who went there were the same and always dressed in rust black. I was there through all the club's incantations, but I loved it best, at the end, when it was Merops.

When you came inside the club, they tied a bit of hemp around your wrist to mark you. Come to think of it, maybe grandmother noted those tattered strands about my wrist as I spooned my breakfast porridge. They tried their best to keep the place free of soldiers, but the sympathetic ones got in their rust red uniforms. We drank mugs of mulled wine and cranberry cordials. So, maybe Nana noted my bleary, dreamy, red-rimmed eyes and smelled the spice on me.

We lived at grandmother's house for several years. It would seem like no time at all in the Mulian scheme, but I do dwell on those years excessively. I remember every quiet, lonely moment of my angst-ridden youth. I still grieve for every pet.

Fluffy brother ratfin, Behn, lived a peaceful life and died a peaceful death of natural causes in his cage. I just found him still one morning, but sister ratfin, Selis, had the misfortune of managing to escape her cage. She became unpleasant in her brother's absence snarling when anyone approached the cage. I often heard her scrabbling at night and the clasp to the cage had loosened over the years. Now I suppose she might have been ill, but I thought at the time she had just become bad-tempered. One morning the cage was empty. I didn't say anything to the household, but the scent betrayed her. Selis had scuttled away into the furnace and the char man found her tiny bones.

We die like we live.

I purchased the next ratfin from the same woman, Murine, at the market. He was a smart one with a bit of a gold sheen to his black fins. He was an especially long-lived and trainable pet and Az spent most of his life wrapped around my neck--a living stole of claw, teeth, and fin. He scraped and nibbled there. My neck was often scratched and pink. Az liked to ride on my shoulders, and was a most amiable, affectionate ratfin, but he also liked to bite at clothes. The necks of my black sweaters were always frayed.

I'm sure it looked strange, but I didn't mind.

Then, around the time when I was preparing to enter university, my grandmother became truly ill. Looking back, maybe I could have remembered some odd things she said and how she started repeating the same stories of my grandfather in those days leading up to her stroke--a clot of blood in the brain. Even if I'd guessed at the trouble to come, what could I have done?

She fell in the cobblestone market but refused to let anyone carry her to the clinic. Two men brought her home lifting her between them. I knew them from Merops, I thought, and nodded.

My mother thanked them, crying.

"Ain't 'nought, she were light," they said placing her on her bed in the small room beside the kitchen, a room she rarely left after that.

I recalled how she'd said the room had been lonely when I was a child and invited me to draw with her and spent more time with her there, during her illness, I resumed drawing, but now mostly I listened to her. I see now that when I'd been a child, it was not likely she who was lonely and wanted a child to sit with her. Instead, she had seen what I was: small and in a strange place and without my familiar things. That kindness came back to her--as kindnesses will. Kindnesses nibble below the surface of events like hungry little fishes after the lichens under floating lotus leaves.

So, grandmother's kindness resurfaced to help her in her illness. I sat with her and listened.

She repeated the story of grandfather over and over again. Her brain lapped at that memory like waves in a bay. It wasn't until later when I dove under the water and entered the sea cave that I understood the significance of what she had been saying. In Mu, I understood, my grandfather had gone underwater before me.

I also took up my drawings again, and I was more skilled now with my lines and arches, perspectives, and scale. My sketches were better, but what struck me was how they were the same as the drawings of my youth. Every time I drew the imaginary city, Octavia, thinking I would undertake a completely different design, it came out the same. I knew the layout of the city and where everything should go. I knew where the large meeting dome went and the stadium and the large open lawn and grandmother's gardens and the storeroom. It did not feel right to draw it in any other way.

One day, Nana was telling her story again and she seemed far away, her eyes shimmery with tears. I did not know if I even existed for her still. Then, she turned to me.

"Nata," she said, she had not used my name in a while. "Don't you leave him. When you love, you stay."

Her voice was stern and I remembered it from her arguments with mother, the ones that coincided with father's rare letters, when, I know, her advice had been exactly the opposite.

She didn't ask me to promise. In fact, she said plainly, "Be careful, child. Be careful with promises, especially to a dying old woman and an ancestor," she said. "Though it pleases me."

But I did want to please her, I said, "I will. I'll stay."

It seemed to relax her.

Grandmother's funeral was held in the blue-domed stone Iron Blood Church. Her body was displayed on the altar during the service.

When we filed by, we showed deference to the waxen figure. This was Nana, her soul lingered nearby, until it was carried out on the waves to go in search of its next incarnation.

We said, our usual refrains, "Praise the Mountaintop." Yet, I wondered, why we worshipped that which was receding and distant instead of the life rising around us? Why not say, "Praise Water"?

It's cruel, but the person who must grieve the most, must plan the funeral. My mother, who so sunk by grief was barely capable of standing, made grandmother's arrangements. The church smelled of rose lotion. All of Nana's friends must have slathered it on for the occasion. An iron-rose tang emanated from the perspiring congregation. The air was moist, hot, and acidic. My inhalations burned.

Pastor Rotwasser's voice was a reassuring drone interrupted occasionally by sniffles, catches of breath, muffled coughs, and the raspy unfurling of handkerchiefs.

Rotwasser had evidently not been a close friend of Nana's. He did not know her or us. To him, grandmother was only the land she and grandfather had given and her death an opportunity to remind the other elders in the audience of their coming doom. He was clearly a man who feared death. All he knew how to do was proselytize to the living, and worse, he brought in politics.

We all felt the presence of soldiers nodding in approval at the back of the church. Clearly, they'd made their presence felt here in the past. The church was no safe haven, no high ground. I wondered whether the soldiers had gathered in the back of the church in their blue uniforms to pay their respects. My grandmother was beloved in town, and more so for being grandfather's life mate.

There was really nothing funny about it, but the contrast between Rotwasser's somber tone and his glib words made me want to laugh.

"It is better to bleed into the ocean at your sea-fairing than to jostle the oceans of your body into waves at the market," said Rotwasser. "For we are all going into the sea, and we must allow the waves to rise to us sooner than later. The salt of blood is better than the salt of the earth or even the salt of the sea. We raise it to our lips and drink a toast. A wise man knows his blood belongs to the ocean, while a poor man spills his blood on the shore."

It might have been a thoughtful parable to contemplate, but not at a funeral! I would have said, "The ocean surrounds me and provides me peace because I float in it. I'm lifted by the waves and the warmth of my blood and the salt. Because I bleed on the shore, I know I shall bleed well into the sea." It was the same sentiment, but a gentler expression.

Suddenly, with grandmother's death, I grew up. I became an adult. I looked at the pastor, at my broken mother, at the soldiers smirking in the doorway of the church--all these figures of authority and I saw that they were fallible and, in many ways, extremely unorganized. I looked at grandmother's friends who were feeble in all aspects, but their stalwart faces and I imagined I saw them nod. I saw among them Murine, the ratfin seller, and she did nod I am certain. Just in recognition, perhaps, but I took it as affirmation. It was my time to seize the future.

"It is better to bleed," Rotwasser repeated, and then I sputtered.

My body shook. I put my hand to my mouth, but I grinned beyond the shield of it. Undercover, I chuckled, and that sound released the floodgates. I began to giggle.

At first no one looked, but then I saw the eyes of the gray-haired ladies dart at me. Az ran around the back of my neck. Mother had been too distraught to forbid me taking him to the funeral. I'd hid him under my black felt collar where he chewed threads. I attempted to restrain my laughter with thoughts of dead Ratfin: Ea's drowned body and Selis' charred bones.

We die like we live.

To this day, I have a tendency toward spontaneous amusement in inappropriate places. I can often contain it by casting my eyes downward and imagining dead ratfin. Too much somberness or certainty strikes me as absurd. My grandmother gave me this perspective. Thinking about those small limp bodies still and black mollifies me. A ratfin's a tiny creature, but all death looms large and carries sunken, sobering weight.

At grandmother's funeral, I had not yet learned this trick, however. I began to think about my grandmother, and how I'd brought her a piece of watercress cake from her favorite market vendor. In her last days, grandmother hadn't had much of an appetite. I'd thought I'd bring her something more enticing than the tepid bowls of rice she'd been spooning down.

It hadn't been one of her good days, at first, when I brought her the slice of cake. She had forgotten me that day.

"You're bringing me poison, soldier. No, take it away," she said.

I brought the cake close to her, but she cringed and looked ready to cry. I prepared to leave it. Then, she must have smelled the frosting. Her expression changed. She looked at the slice of cake as if examining its molecular structure. These moments of lucidity were better than those in which she merely remembered my name. She looked at the world as if she had returned from inside herself with secret knowledge. She scrutinized her surroundings. I'd come with a fork and handed it to her now.

She'd detached a corner of cake holding it daintily with only a faint tremor of her hand. The frosting and cake crumbs disappeared in her mouth. She savored it. Clearly, she had never enjoyed a bite of cake this thoroughly. She looked perfectly content for a moment, just enough time for me to feel satisfaction and pride at my gift.

Then, she'd wretched. She'd spewed a trail of white down the front of her blouse and dribbled onto the cake like a macabre topping. It smelled acidic.

I was horrified, but grandmother gave out a choking laugh.

"Stand down, soldier."

I'd started to laugh at the absurdity and the hopelessness. Grandmother had not even the enjoyment of this cake left to her, and it seemed right. How could she enjoy it when she did not even know her own name? I wiped the spittle off her lips and blouse and that's when she returned in a rare moment.

She looked down. "Oh, my favorite cake. See child, I'm done for."

Then she proceeded to tell me in great, startling detail of the first time she'd ever had the cake. She remembered ridiculous information about that moment: the precise shape of the cake, the thickness of the frosting, and the exact cost of it down to the penny. She remembered the people in the market on the day she bought the cake.

"I was on a date with your grandfather. He was like your father in more ways than one. He was a fabulous swimmer," she looked sad. "Promise me, you'll set me out to sea when I'm done here."

I grew somber.

"Nana, all Iron Bloods have a proper sea-fairing."

"That's right. So...?"

I hesitated. Always be careful with promises, Nana had taught me that. It was like a test. The way she emphasized, "Promise."

"You promise, then?"

"Yes, I'll see after your sea-fairing."

She sighed. "Thank you, Nata."

She pronounced my name slowly and certainly in a mocking tone as if, of course, she knew it always. "Now, thanks to you, my last memory will be of barfing up my favorite food."

We both laughed so hard, grandmother making rasping, wheezy cackles.

My mother checked in on us. "Is everything all right?"

When had laughter become cause for concern?

"Oh yes, it's all right. It's all right. We're just dying of laughter," Nana said.

Her hacking gasps of laughter did sound like choking.

As I like to remember it, she died peacefully late that night.

I couldn't think about dying ratfin in the church at grandmother's funeral. I could only think of Nana puking all over her favorite cake and I could not stop laughing. Finally, everyone was staring at me and even the pastor stopped talking. He glared down at me as if I were a berserker laughing during battle. My mother put her hand on my arm, eventually.

I was laughing so hard I was crying. Mollified, I could not stop. I felt horrible. What if people thought my laughter meant I did not care for her? That almost sobered me, but I immediately heard grandmother saying, "I'm done for," in a childish voice. All propriety was gone. It was absurd. It was sacrilege. I could see that cake so clearly, its decadence and desirability meaningless. Sugar, a substance useless against water and death.

My mother hauled me out of the church. She pulled me down the aisle. Her fingernails poked through the skin of my forearm, but I didn't stop laughing, even in front of all those glaring faces half-shielded by black handkerchiefs, until we were out in the vestibule. Then I was silent, awaiting my mother's fury. Although she had never struck me, I expected to be slapped. Instead, mother pulled me down on the bench and slumped over me with sobs of relief.

"I'm so glad to be out of there for a moment," she said. "It's the hardest thing I've ever done. Harder even than leaving your father."

We hugged each other. I regained my equilibrium. My laughter turned to tears. Then when we turned back to enter the church there was Pastor Rotwasser behind us and a soldier decorated with badges.

"This gentleman would like to speak with you, Bettany," Rotwasser said.

The soldier took mother's arm and pulled her close. I stayed close though, so I could just hear.

"We want her blood," he said.

They would siphon the iron blood from Nana's body before they would let us take her from the church.

Mother stopped: arrested and confused. After the service, my grandmother's body was supposed to be taken to the sea in a procession. She had asked to be lowered off the dock into the rust-stained water.

So, this was the purpose of the soldiers gathered in the back of the church. They wore their blue uniforms, looked on, and waited until they could complete their duty--to drain grandmother's corpse of blood.

Had the pastor been better at his job, we would never have known. He would have just let them take her body to the back and take her blood. Likely, we wouldn't have noticed her desiccation before she was set into the water. Grandmother had become so thin, as she walked beside death. Then the water would have quickly eroded her.

This pastor, however, brought the men before my mother--as though to ask permission. There was never a question about that though. General Balor's soldiers had assumed authority long before they'd officially claimed it.

"I thought you would want to know," Pastor Rotwasser said.

"It will just take a moment," said the sergeant.

"I'm sorry for your loss," said one of the younger men. I recognized him from Merops. I'd seen him out of the uniform that marked him as one of Balor's men in a rust version that made him one of ours. Surely, he was my enemy now, but I loved him anyway as one of my youths.

The sergeant kept mother engaged. I didn't hear the whole conversation, but I heard my mother screaming. Everyone at the funeral did. Then they heard the soldiers yelling back.

In the chapel, they grabbed at the body. The old men threw up their arms and the soldiers locked their meaty hands around their elders' feeble wrists.

"Shame. Shame," the old women chanted in horror, Murine, Hattie, my Aunt Virgie and Cousin Tolly among them. They were shocked. They didn't know what to do or say. That generation was only then used to thinking of the rising, rust sea as the enemy, not each other. They hadn't yet transferred their hatred and fear to the blue uniforms.

In the end, the soldiers achieved their purpose. They took grandmother's body and drained her.

I would have fought them. I remembered my promise to Nana--a proper sea-fairing.

But my mother saved me, "Leave. Go. I won't have you here for this. It won't change anything. Go!"

She chased me away. She saved me from trouble that time, but my time was coming. The waters were rising and there was little land left to us. No one would be safe in the days ahead, especially not those of Iron Blood.

I walked up Octavia Street alone to the house, Tillitat Manor, at the top of the hill. It was springtime now and the pink and white flowers my grandmother had pressed into her lotions were in bloom as were the fruit trees in the yard. The place should have been occupied by a few of my grandmother's old friends awaiting the reception. Funerals must always be followed by food. Instead, the people who loved Nana were at the church losing a battle with soldiers gaining bruises on their thin, fragile skins.

There was a warm salad and that was fine. I went into the sunlit orangerie and filled a bowl with ripe fruits. One of my mother's friends came--Reese, a man vying to be her lover. I had scrutinized him for signs of my father, but he was shy around her and did not give her gifts, which made him seem wanting, but also harmless.

"They've taken Bettany, your mother, to jail," he said. "Virgie and Tolly, too. I'm trying to get them out. It will be all right. But can you take care of yourself tonight?"

What choice did I have? I have often found myself alone in times of trouble.

~ 52 ~

THE SEASTEADERS: MEROPS

Left alone in the big house, I went up to my room where I felt inside the dark half of my closet. I could only distinguish among the black clothes by touch: the twill jumper, the velvet pants, the silk shirt, and the lace blouse. I meant to put on my grandmother's black clothes and go out. I took off the black mourning dress and wore just the slip with a black petticoat underneath to give it flounce. I dabbed black around my eyes and red on my lips. I added black and rust striped stockings. I took the strange coin out from toe and wore my grandmother's pointed shoes. I tied the rust red kerchief around my neck.

I went to Merops. That night I met him. Fresh from my grandmother's funeral, dressed for winter in the heart of spring, I took my sketchbook to the club to dream of waterlogged cities. I met my soul mate there in the strangest of circumstances. I met my twin soul, too.

It became important to understand the difference.

A soul mate attracts in an overwhelming way with an overwhelming passion. A twin soul applies a more subtle presence. A soul mate arrives as a tsunami crashing over the land and a twin soul is the ocean washing persistently over the shore. A wise person understands the difference and knows who is in their heart.

Separation from a soul mate causes a painful rending with doubt and desperation whereas physical separation from a twin soul can be endured. It is a soft sorrow. Real separation from a twin soul is not possible. The souls stride in unison.

I met my souls on the evening of grandmother's aborted seafaring.

The next day my relatives would be released from jail (Reese, my mother's boyfriend was a lawyer--he dealt with land rights not criminal law--but what he knew was enough) and the processional was held. My grandmother's desiccated corpse, drained of her Iron Blood, was hoisted above the street by her dedicated Iron Blood friends and carried down to the Rust Sea.

My grandmother died at age 91 as had her mother and grandmother before her. My mother expected to die at age 91 also.

And I? I never expected I would live that long. Everything was on the brink in my lifetime. The corrosive waters were rising. War was overtaking every last island. The timeline of history was pronounced, and it had a palpable ridge like a raised scar. My father had been right to hide our Iron Blood. The soldiers first drained the blood from corpses for their experiments. Then, after they had some success, they wanted to drain us alive.

When they lowered grandmother's body into the sea, the waves began to churn as though dancing to the sound of the pipes played by her friends. My mother clutched Reese and wept. The soldiers were absent. They were somewhere standing ghoulishly over a vat of grandmother's cold blood, I imagined.

However, I do not want to remember that morning and what followed too quickly. I want to tell of what happened the night before when I was observing death in all my actions and embracing the darkness of music and dance. My memory clings to this origin point like kelp to a pebbled shore. I can feel every second of it like tiny stones aginst my skin.

I loved the club best when it was Merops, by then I knew the music and I recognized everyone--but not too well. The club always had a dreamy quality.

My hazed memory of Merops was colored by wine. In Mu, there was no wine. Instead, we would recreate the drunken experience by remembering Merops.

I passed the cobbled bridge and entered under the red and black "Merops" placard. Music vibrated out into the street. The alleyway smelled of cloves. I descended into the dark, toward the drums, and approached the candlelit bar. The club had always been a refuge for me, but until then I had thought of it only in terms of amusement. I hadn't made the connection yet between the growing number of soldiers on the street and the growing number of youths in the club. I knew that we were all Iron Bloods. We wore the deep rich rust color and flaunted it here, as we would not do on the street.

As a young woman, I could be excruciatingly languid in my movements, like a slow river, but Deuc was more languid still. He was singing on stage when I first laid eyes on him. His dark eyes shone in his pale face. He moved slowly and waved his hands in gestures I found unbearably attractive. From the very first time I noticed his movement; he rippled out from my heart like he belonged there. I loved his slender, ethereal quality. He moved as though his body were an apparition. He did not look like a threat of any kind. It would surprise me later--every time--how strong he was when he restrained me.

Twice, he saved my life by the strength of his own hands. Once he saved me when it is certain I would have met my everlasting death and when I no longer assumed I would live another day.

Now, to state clearly, this was exactly what happened the first time I met Deuc. I walked in the stone entryway, approached the bar, and asked for wine.

"Mulled's the special tonight. Perfect on a damp night. Have it, then?" the bartender asked.

Az, my dear ratfin, peeked over my shoulder as I assented, "Mellow."

At least this was how I imagined the conversation went. If I could go back in time, I would pay closer attention. I would try to see the waves riding into place. That's my specialty, after all.

This I know: A steam of hot cloves rose off the mulled wine as I grasped the scrolled handle of the thick mug. Though, it's true, my memory of this may not be from that particular night. A collection of nights followed thereafter when mulled wine became my drink of choice at Merops.

Now, this was important: That the bartender handed me a mug and I walked away without looking back. When I felt too confident in my perceptions, I would remember this moment. I walked away and sat in my usual corner--my usual corner!--that's how often I'd come to the bar and then walked away, heedless, beside the stage. It was no different than many other nights until Deuc came on stage.

I had never--swear fealty!—never, feared death more than the moment I saw Deuc. My heart seized. I was drained crisp, sponge dry. My lungs hurt. I clenched the mug and sucked the lip to steady myself. The steam had a sting to it and the wine sourness. When I saw Deuc, I began a romance with death. He became that to me.

I have since gained perspective and even from a weathered distance of time and war, I know that its true that the moment I saw Deuc everything changed. My feelings were true then, though not as true as they would be later. My feelings were real, that night, I was even right about the wine. It was sour under the spices and too dry, hence the special on mulled wine. In Deuc's radiance, I grew more discerning. On subsequent nights the wine would be sweeter, but never headier.

I turned toward the stage, drink in hand, and began, as we all did, to fall in love with Deuc. He stood on the stage and played the lute. He vibrated and peered out at us, his vibrations, with liquid black eyes. When I danced, I thought he stared at me, but everyone thought that.

He sang too, but I couldn't make out the words and didn't care. I danced, rocking my blossoming hips and the dark, wet lust I carried between those bones. I found the community of rust red dancers mesmerizing. In that time, everything was sinking and there seemed to be no escape from the aquatic life that chased us. The older people clung to the tops of their islands. I was of the new people: the generation that began to welcome the water. We were practicing there in Merops. I watched us dancing like waves.

Merops was a magical gathering place--a magnificent backdrop for Deuc. When I took a seat at a table and he took a break, he came and sat beside me, and we talked over steaming wine. I don't remember what we talked about. Whatever, I was rapt. I imagined he was equally captivated, but I did not yet understand how Deuc's consciousness was ruled by music, a strong current that could become an undertow. I was swept away by him headed far out past the barriers of my beliefs. That should have been a lighthouse signal, but I didn't understand the warning. Of my own free will, I would certainly crash.

When he returned to the stage, I would stand as close to him as I could from below and will him to look down at me. When he sang "Lava Hex," "Volcanoes undertow the scoria rises. Heed the river. Heed the ocean. Watch the heat." He would walk to the edge of the stage and lean back with his legs wide. The club would chant, "Heed the river. Heed the ocean." There was energy between us that I wanted to amplify. He would make eye contact with me, and I would imagine that this song was written for me. I didn't notice he looked at others too. Too preoccupied with the cays of my own griefs, I didn't understand his oceanic lyrics until later.

I went back to his room above the club many times in a besotted state. Every time, we just talked or even stared at each other. We lay on the bed. Sometimes he'd take my hand and stroke it. I wanted him to kiss me, but he wouldn't. I didn't know what he was waiting for. He made it clear he slept with everyone. I was not to fall in love with him, but it was too late. I was already in love. I fell in love with him instantly.

"It improves my music. I want to connect with everyone," he said. It was his philosophy, that we were all connected. It was a particularly painful point of view for a young lovestruck woman. I wanted him all to myself.

For months, I feared I would not see Deuc again. At times I felt I'd imagined him in a dream of clove-laden steam and had only the hemp rope of Merops on my wrist to remind me. I thought everyone must know him, had seen him in the same way I saw him. Deuc so fascinated my mind that I dwelled over him at every moment. To this day, I can hardly explain what came over me. He was standing on stage. He was singing. He was swaying side to side, and he was smoldering at me, at the crowd. He looked piercing. I was jealous of everyone, thinking they knew him and knew how to find him. I was right to be. Most people did know Deuc and had been to his room upstairs above Merops.

That night I fell in love and the next morning buried my grandmother. I'm ashamed to say that while I watched my grandmother's husk corrode into the Rust Sea, as I watched it devour her, I thought of Deuc and how I wanted his wet kisses.

~ 53 ~

THE SEASTEADERS: UNIVERSITY

After grandmother's death I enrolled in university. I spent my days there and many nights in Merops. The soldiers' presence was becoming more obvious in town. They were numerous and they often harassed Iron Blood students. There were blood checks and stops. They pricked our skins and recorded the level of "rust" therein. Students walked around with fresh wounds upon their shoulders where once we carried only books.

Merops was our haven.

At university, I began studying marine biology and was approached by professor Alexandria Belo. She sought me out. She knew I was of Iron Blood.

"I knew your grandfather," she said. "I want you to work on my new Seasteading project."

Using grandfather's technology and her theories on marine life, she wanted to build oceanic platforms that could resist the rust sea. The earth's islands were sinking, we would build our own.

I became engrossed in Seasteading and found my calling. I was going to build the place I'd always dreamed of. Later, I realized that Belo's research (and before her time, my grandfather's) was what had tipped the soldiers off and caused trouble for us Iron Bloods, but I could not blame her. Someone had to try to make a new way.

Around this same time, I became disenchanted with Deuc. At Merops, he was everyone's center, but even at the time this delusion angered me. It was ludicrous. We are all our own center.

I imagined them all grasping, gasping, and cascading after him. Every night, I drank my wine, looked for Deuc, and became more furious over my enchantment: the spell I was under, which was not, as it turned out, all his doing.

On this night, I found the music too loud, and I wrapped a scarf around my ears. It muffled Deuc's voice as though he was singing underwater. The drums and the keyboard remained just as loud and I could make out his words, but I was at a distance. I listened to the song.

The people rise up while the waters are rising,
They live on pinnacles of land;
The Riptides strip the land of trees,
They take to the waters to live.
Land so little, so much water,
Madrona, oak, pine raft on the water,
Land so little, so much water,
Madrona, oak, pine raft on the water,
The people fear the waters rising,
Living on pillars of land;
The Riptides float on the waters rising,
Just obey their commands.
The ship Kyklopes and the captains, too,
All float over the rising Rust Sea,
The Rust Sea binds, the Rust Sea binds,
Us all together, close. Us all together, close.

The song was romanticizing the Riptiders, who most people saw as selfish pirates who had stolen every islands' remaining wood which was more resistant to the corrosion than metal. Later, Deuc would explain to me his reasoning, his fascination with the pirates, but now I couldn't hear it. I felt rejected. The lyrics seemed like premonitions. I needed to get out. I needed to go away. I told myself I was done being in Deuc's thrall. I retreated to a dark place in the back of the club, one of Merops' many dark corners, to sip my wine. I was watching a different man dancing. I'd never seen anyone twist and spiral like this. He dropped to the floor and came up in a spin like a porpoise. He seemed completely in the throes of the drums, and I understood this. I enjoyed watching the experience and seeing how it looked. I had felt what he was feeling. It was like seeing inside myself. He seemed oblivious to everything but the music and the dance, but after the set he walked straight up to me in a steady line approaching my sphere of darkness. He put a coin down on the table and pushed it across to me. I was startled, but briefly pretended not to recognize it.

Finally, drunk, I said, "Another one?". "Why are people always giving these to me?" I muttered.

He picked it up and inspected it.

"But isn't this yours? It fell out on the dance floor."

It was then that I noticed the chain, the dulled silver links.

"Oh, yes," I said and snatched it up and refastened it around my neck, which took several tries. He did not offer to help.

"Who gives these to you?"

I looked into his green eyes and found myself talking. I told him about the pawnshop and about Murine, the street vendor who sold me my ratfin. He sat beside me and listened. I told him about my violent father and my escape to La Merde. I told him about Ea, the dead ratfin I had dropped overboard. These coins contained my most precious stories. I was filled with a rising tide of mulled wine and my throat opened up and my stories spilled out.

His name was Georgios. He was the bartender at Merops. I'd seen him many times, he'd given me my mugs of mulled wine, but I never really saw him until that night when he was dancing.

After I paused in my talk, he reached forward and lifted the coin off my chest. He inspected it a long time and rubbed a finger over the surface as if he were imprinting its picture into his skin. It felt like he was looking into my heart.

"Will you be here next weekend?"

"Of course."

But I wasn't. None of us were. The soldiers came to Merops that night. They darkened the doors with their blue uniforms. They made the music stop. They shut our meeting place down.

In my memory, I dwell on Merops. Someday I imagine I will swim to sunken La Merde and dive deep to find the underwater ruins of that place that I loved. Although it was the people that made it special, and they are everywhere and nowhere.

At that time, I was so obsessed with seasteading I hardly noticed the absence of Merops. Some will say this was a mistake--to let anything go without a fight, but then the fighting never seemed to advance our cause. We had nowhere to go and nothing to ask for. I poured over the blueprints, and my studies exhausted me. Looking back, I hardly understand how I could have been so tired with a perfect, painless body. I was depleted. Now I have verve for everything, the life of the sea within my soul, but, physically, I ache.

Working on the seastead project, I met Timbol, another of Professor Belo's recruits. He and I took out the rusty boats. We sloshed through the water in our bioproof-slickers, waders, and shoulder-length gloves. They offered scant protection and would corrode in a day's time. We dug into the sand beds up to our elbows.

"Hey Timbol," I vamped. "Striptease."

We laughed about the protective outfits and mocked each other's appearance, but both of us had burns on our upper arms and thighs where we'd been careless and let the tainted water splash. As the summer wore on, our faces were patchy with red from the rust ocean air. The iron was strong in our nostrils. It amazes me, looking back, that we could have been so absorbed in academics while there was a war going on. When the people you love are dying it becomes impossible for most people to think of the future, but even while the war snuffed lives, Timbol and I--and the rest of the Seasteaders--planned. We dreamt of another life, another way. It was a power that pulsed within us. It was not only our youth, although it was that, too.

Beneath the water, the older prehistoric creatures had somehow adapted to the rust water, while the younger fish died off. There were big oily barnacles with thick blackish red shells. In the water, occasionally coming close to shore when they were ill, were shark, squid, and whales. They were large hungry creatures with little to feed upon. We speculated that somewhere in the ocean there were fresh springs with more food for these creatures, or how else could they live? There was a gap in our knowledge of this new sea that kept us at a distance.

"So, Alex really thinks this is our salvation?" Timbol said looking at water where we were surveying the shore slathered in red algae. We called our professor Alex now. We had been to her house. We had met her lover, Neena, an English professor. They had served us wine and brined vegetables.

"Well, it's not like we have much choice. The land's going under," I said.

"There's Hiryana, Cos, Faroe, Corvo..." he named off some of the remaining islands. "There's still high ground and places like Noronha where the water will probably never reach."

Timbol and I repeated this argument over the value of our work often. We were reassuring ourselves. Timbol liked to spout the Peaker philosophy--that there was always higher ground out there somewhere. Some dreamed of a mythical mountain--Rainier--that rose into the sky high above where the water could ever reach.

"Praise the mountaintop. Praise top!" he'd bend his head back and point his finger into the sky. He was mocking them, but either of us would have been grateful to find the Peaker's paradise on Rainier.

"There's war, but this is our land," Timbol became serious. "Just because we can't see it, why would we abandon it? We know it's here. I know every hill and dip and shoreline and peak."

"You do, but years from now. No one else will. The time you grew up here will just be stories. They won't think of anything, but the killing sea. It's not habitable."

"They," Timbol said. "Whoever is left. We'll need a map, a cartographer, so they'll remember what's below."

"Sure," I said. "Sure." Not really caring what lay below at that time. We would leave it behind I thought.

The Seasteaders had a plan for the personnel who would be needed on the seastead: a cook, an agriculturalist, a welder, a marine biologist (Timbol claimed that role), and Timbol's cartographer. Professor Belo was working on recruiting. Of course, Professor Belo, Neena, Timbol and I would be aboard. It was a good plan, but we didn't know that Neena had no desire to go aboard and no skills that would be of use on the stead. We certainly didn’t imagine that Professor Belo would be dead by the time we launched.

"You plan for everything," Timbol said to me one day cutting off our regular argument. "I'd follow you anywhere. I don't know why I bother to argue."

I didn't deny his submission. I was getting used to the idea: People followed me. They trusted me.

"I like it when you ask questions though. It makes me think harder about the answers." I said. "To meet uncertainty, you have to be organized," I muttered to myself. It was becoming my mantra. I underestimated the level of organization required though. I thought it could just be a few others, a small island, and me.

Many people avoided the water. Most older folks (Alexandria Belo was a notable exception) clung to the land. Professor Belo's project was twofold. First, she would discover the secret formula to our Iron Blood that would enable us to counteract the corrosiveness of the sea. This was the work my grandfather had begun. Then, she had planned to build platforms on the water where we would live.

"There's one more thing," she said. "When we can get to it. Our objective will be to join the sea to leave the land behind. There's no need to talk of that yet. I just want you to know that's where I'm going."

On these new platforms, new societies could be built. Seasteads were raised platforms of metal with supports sunk into the sea, weighted and bound with floats. Many stragglers had erected them back in the day and they had once cluttered the sea. Then the waters had become corrosive, and the platforms rusted and sank. It was the time of the Ocean Settlers followed by the Rust Sea. None of the sea settlements had been very organized. They'd mostly been built by individuals--people's own houses. A few cities had planned centers and even a floating market existed at some point. When the seas had begun rising faster and people realized that the time for long-range planning was well past, organized thinking broke down, in as much as it had ever existed. First, came the mercenaries. Then, came the soldiers. War overflowed. It was easier for men to be awash, brainless, and compliant, than to think. There were many followers.

The La Merde University Seastead Project was funded by Marshall Camden, a wealthy trader who had lost his livelihood in the war but not his resources. Camden now gave freely to the university hoping to find a way to restore his business. When Professor Belo was too busy for me, I relied on Marshall, our benefactor. I often met with him in his house beside the ferry dock.

It was a stupid place to live. He had had to move his family up to the second story as the water rose, but he liked to be near his trading post. He also wanted to be ready to leave, to get to high ground, if the seastead didn't work out. The drive to tell him things was strong. He listened with intensity. In person, it felt like a magnetic pull, pulling your words, thoughts, and even a part of your soul out along with whatever news you had to share. I told him every detail of our work, but he kept a huge secret from me.

"Hurry the project along," he urged, at the end of every meeting. "The waters are rising."

But I could not feel his angst. This was such an obvious statement; the way things had been all my life.

Marshall's involvement with the Seastead was his own private rebellion. A man with his wealth and power gives the illusion of freedom, but he was tied to his business. All of his time and energy went into it. All his actions were married to it. Even friendships had become investments in maintaining revenue growth. Professor Belo must have known about the more unsavory aspects of Marshall's business and his ties with General Balor.

Left alone, for a while, the university made progress. They had developed some new materials and new designs. The university was working with La Merde to begin building out onto the water. With the land sinking from beneath us, many had looked for ways to build out onto the sea, cover the waters with steel as we had once paved the earth with concrete. There were limitations to that with the corrosive salt of our sea. Professor Belo was the first person to imagine the concept in this way: That we, freed from the land, would make our own society. This idea inspired me. I imagined it was my own. Looking back, I could see how every childhood fantasy had led me to this calling.

When Belo had identified a group of Seasteaders, she invited us to meet at a party at her place by the bay.

Professor Belo and Neena had a small hut with a thatched roof by the bay. It was one room with a kitchen, with their bed covered with a red blanket and many books and a writing station. Neena brought the food to us at a long table in the brush. We sat on cushions.

Their simple home so near the water reminded me that my grandmother's home on the hill, Tillitat Manor, was luxurious. It still had wooden banisters, a Riptider's treasure.

"Now this is our team. You've likely seen each other around or in class, but this is the first time you have met as Seasteaders," she said. It was the first time she had used the word to identify us, and I marked it. "Let's go around and have introductions."

"It's a small group," I said noting just two others at the table besides Neena, Belo, Timbol and myself.

"The twins are late, but they'll be here," she said. She looked a little concerned. "I might as well make it clear before they get here. The twins are Marshall's sons. Our benefactor doesn't want to go out with us, but he wants both of his sons involved. They'll bring skills as well, I'm sure."

Timbol sat beside me.

A girl with long, straight dark hair began the introductions, "I'm Desiree. I cook and I grow my own foods. My specialty is hydroponics and spices." She did not have an easy smile. Her hair hung straight down upon her back unmoving. There was a gracefulness to her slow movements down to the way she held her fork and passed the wooden bowls.

Merl introduced himself next. He was a gruff wiry man. "I'm studying engineering and solar power. I'm going to provide the light," he said. "We've been working on water pumps and sanitation. Waste not, want not."

Timbol explained his specialty in marine biology and agriculture. He nodded at Desiree. "I'll help with the food."

"There won't be much room in our kitchen, but I'll squeeze aside."

"I meant with the growing, but, sure, I can cook, too."

Then it was my turn. Suddenly, I wasn't sure what my role was. "Oceanography, like Timbol and, well, planning."

We heard shouting from the brush and crashing footsteps.

"I'm saying don't trust them," a low voice said.

"Ha," said the other, and the voice in that one short syllable was so familiar.

The "twins" appeared. They were tall, lean, and dark-haired. I knew them immediately from Merops. I hadn't known they were Marshall's sons, and I hadn't known they were brothers. They always kept apart: Deuc on the stage and Georgios behind the bar. I felt foolish not to have seen the resemblance.

They'd clearly been arguing, and they carried in from the woods with them a dark energy. Deuc always wore a bit of a dire furrow on his face, but the intensity changed Georgios' open face completely. His eyes drooped. His broad lips compressed. Still, they greeted Belo and Neena pleasantly and sat down beside each other. They sat across from me and I gazed at them. It was the first time I'd ever seen them side by side. Now it was obvious that they were brothers, possibly even fraternal twins. They'd never looked similar before. It was disconcerting. What else had I been missing by my inattention?

"Well, you've missed the introductions." Belo said.

"No worries, we're acquainted," Deuc said. "That's the tinker. That's the pretty cook. That's the whale-lover. And that's the dreamer--who thinks she's our leader."

He pointed in turn to Merl, Desiree, Timbol, and me.

"Whiskey, whiskey, ale, and mulled wine," Georgios said, he knew us by our drink orders and I'm sure had observed our other preferences as well in Merops.

"Well, why don't you introduce yourselves and say what you will you bring to the seastead," Belo said.

"We all know Georgios makes a mean drink," Deuc said.

"And I draw, too," Georgios said shyly.

Timbol leaned over to me and whispered, "We're not the only ones thought of it, I bet that's our cartographer."

Then we tucked into the food and drink and soon the tension dissipated. We ate well. We passed the bowls round and round. Our cups were always full. Desiree ate the whole time. She was at table nibbling little bites off of every dish.

"Pass me that one," she said. "And that one."

She savored the spices.

Merl liked the mashed root vegetables best. He dug into them, poured on the truffle gravy, and ate intently at the beginning of the meal. Later, when he was sated, he regaled the rest of us with stories while we caught up and filled our bellies.

Timbol took an even portion from the dishes that were nearest him and ate and talked in equal measure.

My plate was carefully engineered, a dab of each dish. I waited to begin to eat until I had everything arranged on the plate. I took a bite here and there and saved my favorite, water chestnut stew, for last.

Desiree and Merl bonded over their love of whiskey and began to scheme for how they could distill on the seastead.

I began to feel drunk. I loved all the Seasteaders already. I was making eyes at Georgios and Deuc and imagining what it would be like to have both of them kissing me. I would remember this shamefully, blushing the next day.

At the end of the meal, Deuc took his lute out of the case. "Let me remind you why I am here."

He began to play, and his voice was beautiful. We would need him on the sea when we tired of the sound of waves.

Then, Alex stood up and made her announcement. "I'm almost there with the formula. I tried an early version on the water, and it stopped the rust. But it's been hard to get enough to work with for all the tests and variations."

I noticed then how drawn Neena looked. She was an Iron Blood, too. Alex had been draining her for her experiments.

"I need more samples and I'm hoping you will all donate," she said.

She took us aside one by one, and we went into the house. There was a damp chill to the air. It was growing dark and cold. She drew pints of blood from us all. I remembered my grandmother's body drained of blood.

There were more nights like this. In my memory, these nights seemed infinite. We danced in the woods. Deuc sang. Belo took our blood. This was our Merops under the stars. While we partied and donated, the fervor for higher ground intensified.

The army demanded that Chancellor Freelan turn over the university land for its use. He refused and was killed. We students fought back. We didn't want our university to be used for war mongering, but we lost.

I remember screaming alongside the other students in the courtyard before the archway, "No blood for war!" I was giving up my blood, but I thought my cause peaceful.

We pelted the soldiers with oranges and precious books. We threw them down as though the symbolism alone of them being hit by tomes might make an impression. It was wasteful, but with the university overrun by soldiers there would be no higher ground to store those books. It made no difference. The books would become wet and rot and corrode in the sea like everything else left behind. Balor's army shut the university down. They chased the students out or recruited them to their ranks. Our school grounds became barracks.

I offered the Seasteaders Tillitat Manor as shelter. It was on high ground and there was plenty of room. I remember the way Deuc ogled the banisters, the hungry look in his eye I wished he'd had for me.

Then, news came of Professor Belo's death.

I remember the last lecture Alexandria Belo gave. She stood in my living room, grandmother's living room. Her dark brown hair was plaited. She wore wide skirts with pockets. She was explaining the structure of the molecules she had discovered in our Iron Blood that float over the toxic water and encase the metal in a protective shell. It was this structure that would allow us to build the platforms on the water.

She talked to us about the practical applications, many of which had yet to be discovered. To me, the real mystery was where this molecule had come from. Why had it never been seen before? Belo who was known to deliver every line and every lecture with absolute certainty, sounded uncertain about this point. It was clearly a puzzle to her how it could have arrived at such a providential time and been created to suit our need. I remember that uncertainty and I also remember how solitary and strong she looked standing before us in my grandmother's living room. Belo gave imposing, urgent lectures there. Maybe the fact that we were sunk into my grandmother's old cushions added to her stature. We felt we could not learn fast enough. The Seasteaders and a few professors and students had relocated to my grandmother's house. I offered it up for classes. I knew my grandfather would have approved. The waters were rising. We were losing land. There was no other place for students to go. The university had satellite campuses at Ertias Isle and Hierapolis--the deans left for those places--but there was no higher ground for the main institution. The Iron Bloods were left behind. Belo stayed, for Neena, I thought.

Professor Belo had survived the army's assault on the university and our faint resistance only to be struck by a pipe bomb while at the market buying her favorite cranberry and lemongrass tea at Hattie's stall. There was a part of me that wanted to take on some burden of guilt because the market was so near my house, and she might have been going to or from the university. Maybe if I had not volunteered our house, she would not have been there.

That was naught but a flash of egotism. The universe does not pay that much attention to me. It was a random act, yet the army could not have done themselves a better favor. There was no one so anathema to their cause as Professor Belo. She taught us Seasteaders that there was another way, that we did not have to obey soldiers or conventions and she gave us the tool to escape, a rust-resistant serum we could make with our Iron Blood.

~ 54 ~

THE SEASTEADERS: BELO'S SEA-FAIRING

Even at age twenty-one, I experienced the tightening of time that happens as one grows old. I now considered Belo, who died at age 40, young. Although when I first took her classes, I would not have thought so. She had left her partner, Neena, clear instructions on how to eulogize her. Her family was there as well and many children.

A sea-fairing had been assembled. Belo's body was laid out before us. We Iron Bloods filed by her corpse. When the others retreated, I stayed nearby. I leaned over her body and took one of the coins from my pocket. I reached into her mouth and placed it under her tongue. The body she'd left behind felt spongy and unreal. Then it was hoisted atop the pyre.

Neena's grief seeped out from under her veil. She recited a poem she had written for Professor Belo about the sea.

Once blue water lived,
Now red waters rust,
No one can swim within,
What lies beneath? My love.

Timbol and Georgios spoke. Deuc, Merl, and Desiree were quiet.

"Belo was fascinated with the rust whales, sharks, and squid--how they had evolved and were able to withstand the corrosion. We wanted to know why all the smaller fish, the ones people once ate and survived off the plenty of the sea, all had died."

"Do you remember that salty food she served us once at a Seastead party?" I asked. "She would never say where it had come from."

We all remembered this now.

"I thought it was something I'd imagined. It was so different. Otherworldly," Timbol said.

I thought when Neena passed me that she would hand me another coin. I was just coming out of that age when I thought everything was about me. I felt that I had dreamed this moment. Maybe I had. In reality, she gave me nothing. Belo's rickety metal sea-fairing raft, a *mokol*, was pushed out of the harbor. As it floated out, I watched the flame along with everyone else and realized that life is long, but also may be short. The flames flickered blue and then out when they touched the metal. There was no precious wood to spare for a proper sea-fairing. Unless we grotesquely coated her body in a serum made of our own blood, her body would corrode, not burn.

I wondered if Neena thought this, too, and it added to her grief.

What projects had my professor been working on? What research would now go unfinished?

Later, I thought of my own predicament. Alex Belo had been my mentor. She knew best the quality of my work and now that knowledge was lost. If it had not been clear before, with the coming of the soldiers and the rising waters, it was clear now. I had no future. What my grandparents had feared and planned for, what my parents had run from, had come to pass. It had come for me. I had no place to run.

We gathered around and sang the sea-fairing song. As I watched the pyre float out to sea, its dull blue flames flickering, I remembered the underwater quality of Deuc's last song at Merops.

Before we left, Neena took Timbol and me aside. "Don't count me among your Seasteaders anymore. Keep me out of it. But she wanted you to have these."

She gave us both scrolls (precious, rare items written on real paper made of trees) and when we compared them later saw that I had the blueprints for the Seastead and Timbol the formula for the Iron Blood serum.

Belo's death brought the Seasteaders even closer. I became resolute. In order for higher knowledge to continue in the face of war, we had to create a place apart unbound by the previous conflicts, a fresh start. We had to build the Seastead. It was imperative.

Not long after Belo's death, what my father had most feared came to pass. After the soldiers commandeered the market--and all the high ground--they came for the Iron Bloods. They jailed the elders including my mother and her boyfriend, Reese, but there were also massacres of youth in the streets. The air smelled of iron and rust-stained grooves flowed between the cobblestones.

Rumors then spread that the soldiers were being disciplined for indiscriminate killing. We took a little hope from that until they rounded up us Iron Blood students. It wasn't the killing that Balor's army disliked. It was the waste of a precious resource--our blood.

The intelligence officers did not know of Belo's serum, but her work brought attention to us. They suspected us, well, our blood, of being useful. The time for academic discussions ended.

They made a prison out of Tillitat Manor. Marshall had disappeared-- jailed or killed we could not be sure. Neena wasn't with us. Her Iron Blood was secret. Georgios and Deuc were there. The brothers roomed upstairs in the West Wing with Timbol and Merl. Desiree and I stayed together in my grandmother's room near the kitchen.

She cooked the meager fare we had, mostly rice, nothing fresh.

Why didn't we fight? We were trapped, but we Seasteaders planned our escape.

They came often and drew our blood. It was the blood they wanted, fresh, untainted, healthy young blood. I knew all of the men and women imprisoned. I didn't know them well, but many of them from Merops and from the university. We watched each other and the soldiers watched us. Outside Tillitat, nervous soldiers killed citizens of Le Merde at random. We were kept safe because of what our blood could be worth--a means to hold back the rust. Our blood saved us. Professor Belo had taught them that, but they did not know Belo had already developed such a serum and Timbol held the recipe.

Held captive in my grandmother's house, the students of La Merde University had time on our hands. Desiree, Timbol, Merl, Georgios and I played many games of Cardinal, a card game imprinted with the four directions. It was a time of great risk, but also captivity and boredom.

I knew what the others were like from their card games. I had a sense of their strategy. Merl joked through the whole game and was terrible at bluffs, but he got excited when he was winning. The more he concentrated the worse off he was. When he just played loosely, he had natural luck and would win many games. He liked to gloat even when his hand was bad.

Desiree strategized carefully but would often toss all her plans away on a risky move. She either won or lost big. Desiree bluffed and did it well.

Timbol liked to bluff but was poor at it. He played a careful game, but he liked to use power moves. He'd get excited when he was winning and when losing would play it off as if he didn't care.

"It's just a game," he'd shrug.

I, of course, loved strategy. I'd plan out long plays many moves ahead and try to predict what the other players would do. Then someone like Georgios would see what I was doing and make a play to throw me off. Georgios liked to wait and strategize. He played the most like me.

I loved the game best though when one of my long plays came to fruition and I suspected that sometimes Georgios helped me even when it was to his own detriment. He, too, liked to see a slow plan come to success.

Deuc was the only one who didn't play. He practiced his music and kept apart.

On the anniversary of my grandmother's death, the soldiers who seemed more lax and distracted than usual, relented. Desiree and I had at first begged them daily to let us go to the market. When weeks dragged on without the fulfillment of that request, we'd asked them to restock our supplies and bring us some fresh food. We needed some lentils and greens to replenish our iron. We were all looking ghastly by now.

To our surprise, the soldier said, "Just go yourself. Get back directly or I'll be done with you and your friends will starve."

Surprised by our freedom, Desiree and I walked out on to the street. There was barely a path from my grandmother's house. It was terribly overgrown, and the ground was soggy. We sloshed through rust water puddles.

There were soldiers everywhere in the market and few items for sale. The vendors looked as battered as their produce. We walked past the narrow street where Merops had been, but the sign had been removed and the soldiers pressed against us and kept us from lingering.

We purchased some rice, greens, and stringy root vegetables and placed them in the basket. We were ready to return, and I could tell Desiree wanted to get home and cook some of what we had procured.

"I want to look for Hattie, the tea vendor," I said.

"We've got to get back," Desiree said. "You heard him."

"Yes, but it was nana's favorite." That might have softened her at any other time. She knew my grandmother by reputation in life and had certainly heard enough of my stories about her, living in grandmother's bedroom, but it was a fearful time.

"No. We can't take the time."

I was steering her through the market scanning for that familiar face. "She might have some spices too, if anyone would. She might have anise, even."

That had Desiree's attention. She loved anise in her beans and greens.

When I spotted Hattie, I tugged at Desiree's sleeve, and she followed me.

"Nata, I don't have that rose orange anymore," Hattie said. "The roses won't bloom. The air and the water's too acid for 'em now. The General's chased our traders to the south away. There's no citrus to be found. We'll all get scurvy."

She did have a bit of anise and cloves secreted away and she spared them for us. Desiree smiled and relaxed. There was no one like a smiling Desiree. She was serious mostly, but I understood the desire to please her for the reward of her smile.

Then a commotion broke out in the marketplace. There was shouting. A ratfin rushed by me and I snatched it up. The scared creature clawed its way into my arms and left a couple marks.

"We're getting rid of those vermin," said a passing soldier. "Orders. They are making people sick."

"It not them, it's the rising rust and the lack of food," Hattie said.

We walked by a pile of ratfin corpses.

I hid the one I'd caught in my basket beneath the leafy greens. Fortunately, it was a smart one and its instinct was to hide.

They hauled Hattie to her feet and began to drag her across the square. She caught my eye and winked.

I wanted to help her, but Desiree grabbed my arm, "We have to get back to the Seasteaders."

Then the ground beneath us shook and a boom sounded from the harbor. En masse the market seemed to move downhill toward the sound. It began to slide. A few of the vendors began to calmly gather a few wares and move higher, Desiree pulled that way too although there was only a tiny alpine forest above us. Maybe a few people could have undisturbed huts there, but there was no farmland, no future there. The soldiers all began to run downhill. They'd been spoiling for a fight and now it sounded like there was some action. Most of the people began to move toward the water. There was one ferry. It seemed the island was sinking now or about to be overrun by another invading force. It was time to leave.

My heart quickened with fear and anticipation. Finally!

I pulled Desiree into the flow streaming downhill. There was trampling, screaming, I saw Murine, the ratfin vendor's broken body, piled at the side of the road like one of her pets. There was no helping her.

Desiree and I veered toward Tillitat. No one had been using that path. The soldiers had kept everyone away from us. Perhaps, we'd been forgotten. When we arrived, we found just one soldier waiting.

When he saw us, he pointed his musket at us. Desiree and I stopped. "Good, you're back. I've been waiting."

"We said we would come back."

I knew this soldier. I remembered him from Merops. He'd asked me to dance once. I'd said no. I hadn't been friendly to him. He was a soldier and I was concerned about my own plans.

"Good. Good." He kept repeating the word. It made me nervous. Something was wrong.

"You're no good," he spat. "Your blood is worthless. All those tests. Nothing. Just pollution. That's what brought the plague down on us."

His face grew mean, but Desiree knew what he was about.

She held up the basket. "We got some greens, a little wilted, but I'll cook 'em up nice. We'll share them with you. You look a little thin."

We all did, us Iron Bloods more than most. Even Desiree's cheeks had lost their plumpness.

"We got some spices, too. Smell." She held the anise under his nose, and he inhaled.

"You've been told to kill us," I said, finally guessing. Desiree shot me a look. She'd known and was trying to make the soldier remember we were human. He was trying to talk himself into killing us.

I saw the look in his eyes. I saw him remember my rejection.

"You should have danced with me," he said.

"I guess I should," I said.

He hesitated, grim and angry, and then shook his head. "Nah, we were both at Merops. We were free to do as we liked. Or not. Look, I'm going. If I drown, I'll do it freely. Praise the Mountaintops! But Balor won't forget you. He'll come here or he'll find you. No place you can go anyway. I'll let someone else handle the mess."

"Thanks," I said sarcastically, but Desiree saved us again. She put his hand on his arm.

"What will you do? There'll be...discipline. Stay with us?"

"No. I'd be too ashamed to desert. I'm going to go high and take my chances. There's a few places up there. Maybe eke something out. Maybe I'll see you up there. Most everything near the water is gone."

With that, he finally lowered his gun and walked resolutely up the street.

~ 55 ~

THE SEASTEADERS: SEASTEAD MEETING

Desiree and I ran up the stairs of Tillitat Manor. The house was empty, but when we yelled, "Seasteaders!" we heard a call from above. We unlocked the door to the attic and joined Timbol, Merl, Georgios and Deuc.

They had heard the boom of the landslide and after being shuffled into the attic by the soldiers had guessed what was coming next.

"That soldier was considering whether to kill us. Really talking himself up for it," Desiree said.

"Well, we would have made it difficult," Merl said. "Now what do we do? I suppose we go high and then try to launch our seastead."

Grandmother's attic smelled of rosewater, orange oil, and blood. I had imagined this meeting, this moment, when we would decide to undertake utopia, but I had thought it would be a leisurely discussion over biscuits and tea, not a hasty retreat from soldiers and chaos. I thought Professor Belo would lead us. Instead, there we were. There I was.

"I think it's already built," Deuc said.

"What?" I asked astounded.

"Belo, didn't have a chance to tell us, but I think she and your grandfather had a lot of things in motion. That blueprint you have is complete and once she had the serum...well," Deuc said.

I unscrolled the Seastead design. I stared at it to look busy, but I was intimately familiar with it: the circular rings, the platform, and the piers. Here was the kitchen. Here was the garden with the room for the raised beds, one for each passenger. Here the mechanics quarters. Up front the engine room. There were sailboats strapped to each side. These shaded patches were the solar panels. The lofted tower room would be mine, a place to get away. From the design, it did look ready and waiting for us.

"You think it's just out there?" I asked.

I didn't trust Deuc. I knew he'd act in his own interests, and I didn't know exactly what those were. He remained an enigma. It would have been simpler if Deuc were not with us. It would have been easier for me if I had not been distracted by the brothers.

"I helped her get a lot of iron out there," Deuc said.

Georgios gave him a look. "So, you've actually seen it?"

"No, but I think it's there," Deuc said.

"Well, there is a boat with a motor in my father's shed. It's a good-sized skipper already coated in the serum. So we'd have that. We could go somewhere else," Georgios said.

It didn't take a lot of time to decide. There wasn't much for us to disagree on at this point. We had to leave La Merde. Usually when we met, there was dissension. This time everyone was talking and agreeing faster than I'd ever experienced. We all wanted an excuse to set out for sea. We all wanted our seastead dream to begin to take shape. It had taken Belo years to convince the others to seastead. Then, when there was no option, of course, it took no time at all. The time for debate was over.

"We go here now," I said pointing at the scroll. "This is where the iron bloods will live."

"It will take all of us to make this work," Timbol said.

By work, he meant survive.

We would need Merl to purify the water, run the solar panels, and make repairs; Desiree and Timbol to grow the food and cook it;

Georgios to operate the platform and chart our way; Timbol to explore the depths; and all of us to bleed so we could coat the beams and keep the platform from corroding.

"We need to get seed," Desiree said.

It was decided that Georgios and Merl would raid the supplies before they left and get the boat hidden in Marshall's shed.

Timbol would get the lab materials and Desiree and I would gather up food.

"I'll get the serum," Deuc said.

None of our meetings ever went as smoothly again. That was the last time we'd be so quick and decisive.

I petted the ratfin snuggled against my neck. “You’re safe, little survivor,” I whispered to it.

"There's one more thing," I said. "I need to get my mother."

After a long silence, Deuc spoke. "Nata, the prison fell in the slide, into the sea. The soldiers said."

"They cheered," Merl said.

"My mother? Reese? My aunts?"

Georgios took my hand. "There's nothing we can do."

I let him embrace me, but then I pulled back.

"Neena, Professor Belo's widow, I can't leave without her."

Georgios gave me a look of concern, not disagreement but worry. Desiree looked surprised, but no one argued. They knew there was no point. It was clear from my voice, I was going.

"Fine, I can get the seed myself," Desiree said.

I gathered up my maps and plans and coins. We set out to do our own preparations. We'd meet at Marshall's.

I was afraid every minute I was separated from the seasteaders, from Georgios. I worried that we would not be reunited, but I was also excited. The blueprint for utopia had long been in my mind and here was an opportunity to test it.

The emigration line for the ferry off La Merde was packed. People holding packs, carpetbags, and the hands of wailing children waited in a warehouse just above the water line. The line looped back and forth. At the front, soldiers were taking tickets and searching bags and slowly, one at a time, people were boarding the last running ferry headed off the island.

It was a ferry just like the one I'd arrived on, and I wondered how far it would get before it sank. The people were headed for any available peak, the tops of another island, hoping to rejoin families long left behind. Those families would only be there if they were Peakers, people who had refused to leave. Anywhere these people were heading that was not overrun by Balor's men was not worth landing on and would likely soon be underwater.

I found Neena waiting near the end of a very long line. I hugged her.

"Dear Nata," she said. "It took me a long time, but I've decided to go. There's nothing for me here. Since I'm not an Iron Blood I can leave for another island."

Of course, I'd long since realized it was not true. Neena did have Iron Blood. It was what Professor Belo had used on her experiments, but the idea that she was not had kept her safe.

"Where will you go?"

She shrugged.

"Someplace. Where all these people are going."

"Some war-torn island, Neena? It won't be there very long."

"I have a ticket." She held up the pink stub. "And I have family on Iylla. I haven't seen them in a long time. They could be on a peak somewhere."

“Or you could come with me, with us. They are leaving the students alone now, the Iron Bloods.”

I could see the question in her eyes. I just gave her a pleading look wishing she could read my mind.

"Or you could come with me." She showed me her extra ticket, a withered slip. "They gave me Alex's. Forgot they killed her, I guess."

I remembered the journey to La Merde with my mother and how I'd thrown the dead ratfin overboard. I could escape, but to leave Georgios and Deuc. I would never do that. It was unthinkable.

"This family, they'll take you in?"

"Of course. They are family," she said, but she didn't sound excited about the possibility.

I didn't think I could convince her, so I just stood with her. I knew the Seasteaders would be getting impatient, but it was important to be with Neena for the time she had left. I just stayed beside her. While we were in that line, it was uncertain where we were going. Until a decision is made, every way is open.

I fantasized about stealing Neena's ticket so that she had no choice and had to come with us, but I didn't know what the Seasteaders' fate would be. As much as I felt it would be right for her to join us, I couldn't make that decision for her. I couldn't carry the burden of responsibility for her happiness if I were wrong.

We neared the front of the line and watched a family drama unfold. One of the children had lost a ticket. A mother and father were about to be separated. It was the father's family they were going to, so the mother would stay behind. "They'll be kinder to the children if you are there," she said.

I looked at Neena, crying for that family, and saw a way to get what I wanted.

So, I stole Neena's tickets and in slow motion I handed one to the mother.

Her eyes brightened. "Thank you." She hurried forward.

Someone saw though and there was an immediate clamor. There were not enough tickets to go around.

"They had an extra."

"Do they have another one?"

I handed the ticket back to Neena and I watched her press it into the nearest grubby hand without looking. She didn't want to make a choice either, to be responsible for anyone's fate. But she came with me.

When we got outside, I pulled her close. "We seasteaders are your family, too."

Then, I whispered the secret I hoped would make this all okay. The secret that I hoped was true.

"They built the Seastead. It exists."

"Alex's place." She stopped crying. "I hoped so. Oh, out on the water."

It was a surprise to her, not entirely, but enough that she hadn't feigned her reaction. Alex had had to keep the craft secret so the General wouldn't find it. Neena was a true lander who loved the earth and did not want to leave solid ground behind. She loved water as a poetic concept, but not as a homeland. Still, I didn't feel badly about deceiving her. I was that certain. She must have had an idea what alternative I was offering. I remembered what Professor Belo had said about where we were going, to leave it all behind. We would go to join the sea.

I took Neena's hand, and we made our way to Marshall's store. It had a warehouse connected to it just beside the water. Once, we would have called the body of water a bay. Now, the water had risen so high Marshall's was nearly in the ocean. Instead of the ocean being comfortably shaped around La Merde, La Merde was now settled uncomfortably in the ocean. The waters were rising. The soldiers, and anyone able, were fleeing the corrosive sea overflowing the island.

We found Georgios, Desiree, Merl, and Timbol staring down at a rusty metal raft like the one we'd sent Belo's corpse to sea on.

"Where's the boat?" I asked. Then, "Where's Deuc?"

Then I knew. Deuc had taken our boat.

"Why would he go without us?"

Now all of our prompt decision-making was undone. When we decided to go to the Seastead we weren't planning to fit six people on a sea-fairing *mokol*. The bottom of the raft looked hopelessly thin. The water around the house had soaked up through the concrete floor and we were lucky the *mokol* was stored upside down. The edges of it were soft and red. We didn't have any serum to coat the bottom with to shore it up. Once we were on the Seastead, we hoped, that there would be a lab where we could make more. We would each give our monthly donations of blood to create it and use it to upkeep the platform. That was the hope. Like everything else, it was really a drowning hope, but it was what we had. We had to push off into the sea.

"Where would Deuc have gone?" Desiree asked. "The only place to go is the Seastead, maybe, and why would he go without us."

"He needs us," Timbol said.

"Well, we'll shore it up with some boards," said Georgios, beginning to look around the bay for any wood. "And hope it lasts long enough."

"We've got these," Desiree said, holding up two sets of oars.

"We'll need those to row."

"That's what I meant."

"It will be slow going," Neena said. "Will we even make it before..."

Merl cut her off. "Hell, yes. Give me one of them oars."

Georgios tore his father's house apart looking for wood.

"Long ago these houses were made of wood when it was plentiful. It might be that there's a remnant under the walls, some overlooked scrap," he said. He found a piece of plywood in the bathroom beside the tub. It was somewhat soft itself, but it might buy us time.

When the *mokol* was as fortified from the corrosive sea as we could manage with such haste, we hesitated on the shore reluctant to leave the land until Merl urged us onward.

"This is no time to back down," Merl said. "Go on."

Together, we pushed out into the water over the sand. Then Georgios, Merl, Desiree, Timbol, Neena and I all climbed onto the rocking *mokol*, just skimming above the sea under our weight.

Did I mention that none of us knew how to swim? No one did in Pacifica at that time. It was an art lost when the waters grew red and blistered the skin and killed the smaller sea creatures.

The Seasteaders: Part Two

DEATH

~ 56 ~

THE SEASTEADERS: PADDLING OUT

We Seasteaders were finally leaving the land behind us. There was hardship ahead, but also a chance to change the world. An individual can make an impact, but not without sacrifice. Sometimes, the sacrifice means giving up objects and ideas that were never a boon to begin with, other times it's a loss of independence, privacy, and autonomy. I have learned that some of my most dearly held treasures were more valuable when dropped into the ocean and sunk to the bottom of the sea.

"Is change worth the sacrifice, when the loss is love and liberty?" I've asked myself. On a trajectory to change the world, there's not much choice.

The Seasteaders left shore on a rickety *mokol*. In some ways it made sense that we were using a sea-fairing craft, we also meant to make a one-way trip. There would be no coming back to the island, to La Merde, to the ruins of the university, to Octavia Street, to my grandmother's home, to the market filled with good things to eat, or to Merops. We were leaving behind all the places we knew, and we could not be sure that the Seastead existed. We knew only the plans for it, the dreams, and the ideals. How and when would the university and Professor Belo have had the opportunity to build the platform? We only hoped that the Seastead would be there. What is hope, but a hook?

"We've been working on the details," Merl said. "That says something. Filtration systems, food, water pumps. That says something was in place."

We all liked that he said this. It sounded logical and true, but I think all of us harbored doubts, except perhaps for Georgios. When I asked him later though, Georgios said he did not doubt.

"Of course, my father and Belo built it," he said. "Marshall would do anything for his sons and Alex wanted to see her vision realized."

I had some ideas, but I kept them to myself. We were scared enough. That was the moment I learned to keep my ideas to myself, at times a necessary skill.

Everyone looked at Neena, thinking she must have had some clue as Belo's intimate, but eventually we stopped pestering her with insistent glances.

"She didn't let me in on it," Neena said. "I can't believe it either. Maybe she was going to leave me. I felt we were growing distant. She spent more time at the school. She was buried in her research."

"Or she was busy building the Seastead," Merl said.

It struck me that the source of Neena's sadness, was the only hope for us. Please let Belo have been preoccupied with building the Seastead.

For now, all we could do was dip our oars into the rusty water, hope, and row toward the location indicated on the blueprint. The corrosive sea dripped off the ends of the oars and it wasn't long before the silver metal tips of the oars began to slide into the water. Dark blotches appeared on the oars' surface with jagged edges where holes were beginning to form.

Merl and Desiree started out rowing. At their best, they had both been strong: Merl from lifting pipes and digging trenches for the water flows and Desiree from lifting boxes and kneading bread. But we were all weak now from the bloodletting. Our arms were matchstick thin and the waves were thick, the sea was rough. We made slow progress. We followed the coordinates out to sea stroke by stroke as the sun dropped low in the sky.

"It's not too far, really," Timbol said.

"Oh, yeah, then take a turn," said Merl.

The *mokol* lurched over the sea and the iron spray stung our eyes. Timbol put on goggles, but we weren't all so well equipped and our eyes grew red.

The rust red water rose and dipped in the dusk. The setting sun cast a redundant rose light over the ocean waves. Amid it, we felt the sea's poisoned lifelessness. We could just see the ferry departing from La Merde heading south toward Scylla while we headed north. It threw more waves our way.

"I could be on that," Neena said. She sounded wistful and was.

"I gave you a choice," I snapped.

"Least you could have done," Neena said. "I'm not sorry now. I'm just scared."

"It's mostly soldiers, anyway," Timbol said.

The blue uniforms ringed the deck of the ferry. I wondered about the mother and daughter we'd given Neena's tickets to, had they even made it on board? Had they been permitted to go?

"Praise the mountains," Desiree said. "I'm glad you're with us, Neena, and I hope they find their way."

"Ha, praise water," Merl scoffed. "We may as well honor what's all around us."

We were now far out at sea and could no longer see La Merde, the weathervane on top of Tillitat Manor, or the distant ferry departing. I looked down at the pinkish bottom of the mokol. The rust-colored water was seeping up under the piece of soft board, turning it a pale pink. I imagined what the underneath of the *mokol* must look like: bubbling and sizzling in the Rust Sea, dark spots with jagged edges, thin beyond belief. I clutched the side of the boat only to feel the softening side, spongy, and wet beneath my hand. I wiped the pink froth of the corroding boat on my pants. My hand stung slightly from the rust touch.

"Who's scared? Let me row again," Merl said, and dug his oar in. "Row, row."

Georgios relieved Timbol and I was reassured to feel the boat surge forward. Georgios was stronger than he looked. If he'd been as strong as his will, he would have been a leviathan. We would have been to the middle of the ocean in two strokes.

As the water rose, those of us who weren't rowing watched our boots and tried to keep them out of the water, squatting high in the center of the raft, and pressing our feet up under our behinds.

Those who were rowing looked ahead and Timbol gauged our progress on the compass. For the longest time, we stared at a blank horizon filled with red. Then a blotch appeared in front of us with jagged edges marring the round red sun.

"There," Georgios said.

There looked to be metal struts rising into the beet red sun. I had never seen a structure like this so sharp and angled and created of metal. Most of the buildings and objects I was familiar with were made of curved lines of wood, which resisted the corrosive sprays, but was in short supply. The struts were the color of dried blood. It was in fact our own dried Iron Blood which coated the struts so that they could resist the sea spray. At the top rose a weathervane, just like on top of grandmother's house. Our blood was our salvation. Our blood would save us from the Rust Sea.

"She did it. Without me. Oh, Mother..." Neena said.

I didn't catch the last word. I think it was "useless."

"She did it with you," Merl said. "That's your blood, be sure of it."

As he said it, a huge spray of water rushed over the boat. At the same time, the *mokol* shook and a thunk hit the side. An arch of red water soaked us. While we hurried to wipe it off and protect our eyes, something swiped the other side of the raft.

"Merl!" Georgios called.

Merl was no longer on board. A fin rose out of the water. It was black, oily, and rust red. It was covered in a thick crust of boils raised by the corrosive sea. Merl bobbed in the waves beside the fin.

"Shark!" Timbol said.

I knew there were still some of these creatures in the water reportedly seen around islands where General Balor and his soldiers had held some of their bloodiest battles. They trailed behind Balor's ships eating waste. But what were they doing here? What was there to eat besides us?

Georgios leaned way out over the water and reached down into it with an unprotected hand.

"No!" I yelled, but then I saw him come up with the end of an oar. He swung it out to Merl. Merl grabbed the end of it and we helped haul him in. His skin was red. It would turn black and bleed.

A second strike hit the boat. There was a long-ridged plank surfacing on the other side of the boat away from the fins. I'd seen at least three fins at once rising out of the water. I wasn't counting, but I felt surrounded. There were rust sharks on one side with the *mokol* battered in between and its five scrawny Iron Blood occupants.

We clung to the sides of the boat. I felt the sponginess in my hands again. I pushed Neena into the center of the raft. The ratfin scrabbled against my neck as the *mokol* rocked.

"Hunker down," Timbol shouted.

I looked up at the platform. The distance to it was not far: a few fathoms. We could have swum there if the water had been clean and free of beasts, and if anyone in Pacifica knew how to swim. We had stopped rowing to concentrate on staying in the boat while creatures thumped against it. I imagined the bottom breaking apart. I felt the sides slipping under my hands. We waited listening to the sharks thump against the *mokol.*

Georgios was the first to pick up an oar again. "Row, row, row!"

Timbol dug in. We made it to the metal ladder that rose up to the platform. I sent Neena up first, then Desiree, clanging. Timbol, Georgios, and I hoisted Merl up. His skin burned. It was reddened, raised, and threatening to slough off. He screamed as we manhandled him, but we got him aboard. The *mokol* stayed on the water to sink with the circling sharks. The sharks would always be there. This part of the sea was their home, too.

There was also a whale, she with the big, wet, red-rimmed inky eye surrounded by fat, oily, black barnacles. We had arrived at the Seastead as promised, as hoped, but we were not alone.

~ 57 ~

THE SEASTEADERS: ARRIVING ON THE SEASTEAD

I did not expect the Seastead to be paradise. We'd lived our lives in fear of the encroaching water, with water ever on our minds, but we were not of the water. On the water was a discomfiting place.

Now, what we'd run from, the water, surrounded us. It was to be our home. It offered a fearful kind of freedom. We could do whatever we liked with no thought for anyone else's laws or hierarchies. We were free from Peaker philosophies, General Balor's orders, and soldiers' battles. We were all on equal ground here--what little of it there was.

The platform was the size of grandmother's living room. It was cold grey metal with a thick crust of applied blood on the surface. The middle of it was flat, square, and open like a courtyard or the deck of a barge. It was raised on a float and struts rose from the sides. Along each side there were rooms and glass windows. There were metal stairs up to the second deck and on the north side one more thin set of stairs to a small room at the top, a lookout. It was shaped like a square compass with a weathervane affixed to its highest point.

Merl lay on the deck, breathing heavily, panting. He stared up.

"That's for me," he said, claiming the loft on arrival with his skin burning in his weakened state.

The Seastead looked just as its blueprint. I began to search for the things I expected to see. The ground floor garden with eight two-by-four-foot raised beds was there. Green shoots were already sprouting from the soil.

We were all exhausted from rowing and it was dusk now headed towards dark, but we were excited. The Seastead was our dream and now our hard reality.

Desiree was drawn to the garden. She examined the tiny greens. “There's onions, garlic, spinach, and tomatoes already growing. And there's an herb garden in the kitchen."

"Below there will be a boiler room," I said.

The Seasteaders began to explore their piece of paradise.

"It is not paradise," I reminded myself, speaking aloud.

"But it's here," Georgios said inspecting the bloodied sides of the platform which seemed to resist the Rust Sea's corrosion.

Timbol stared over the side at the sharks. "Why are they here? What's the food source?"

"I'm sure they are drawn by all the blood paint on this thing. It's layered on, but its flaking off. We'll need to recoat it soon."

"And we're lower down than the plans call for, closer to sea level," Timbol noted.

Georgios turned from where he was inspecting the sides of the platform.

"What are we going to do for Merl?" Neena whispered to me. His skin was beginning to blacken. We did not have much in the way of medicines. Nothing to heal burns like those.

"Let's look around," I said.

Desiree was exclaiming over the kitchen, "There's refrigeration and a freezer and there are lights."

Curtains with lace frills framed the window looking out to the deck. The light shone over Merl's prostrate body. There were herbs in the cupboard, but nothing potent for healing.

Neena searched the room next door, and we heard her cry out, "There's a library and my books are in it."

The poetry anthologies she loved and copies of her own chapbooks, "The Rust Garden" and "Sea Hands," were on the shelves.

I put my arm around her, "Alexandra clearly planned this for you. She meant for you to be here one day."

"She did," Neena said. "And, but for you, I almost didn't come."

I thought of how sad I would have been to see those books without Neena and was glad I had gone after her.

Professor Belo had clearly planned this place for all of us. There were maps laid out on a table in Georgios' room and in a room upstairs on the bed there was another coin for me. This was number three. I picked it up and put it in my pocket. It felt good to claim a space, a room, with a door, and put down my few possessions.

Then I went outside and leaned over the railing at Timbol, "Nice digs?"

"Solar panels up there," Merl groaned.

"Yep, charts of the weather," Timbol said. "The gear rooms are below. Come take a look."

Timbol, Georgios, and I descended with a soft clang, the sound of movement on the Seastead, which would become so familiar.

"I found a supply room," Georgios said holding up a pair of goggles. Inside were gloves, goggles, rubber boots, hats and pants: the equipment we would need to maintain the Seastead and in case of storms.

There was a keg that had been filled with Iron Blood serum. Its sides were crusty with dried blood, but there was only sludge in the bottom.

"We'll need to replenish this soon. Timbol, can you make the serum?" I asked.

"I think so," he said.

We found no medical supplies and there was no sign that the Seastead had been occupied.

"Georgios, where's Deuc?" I asked. "I thought he'd be here."

Georgios shrugged. "I don't know. I thought so, too."

The basement was dark. Filled with a soft purple light and there was a soft, trickle of water and a bubbling sound.

"The boiler's here and the serum," Georgios said. "But what to make of this, Timbol?"

Along the far side of the room under a UV light was a hydroponic garden. The leaves growing within were a deep, nutritious green and there were ripe, bright red round hanging fruits, tomatoes, and strawberries. The water in the tank was clear and beautiful. The white roots of the plants swayed in it. A faucet above the trough let out a steady stream of clear water.

"Where's it coming from? Where's the filter?"

"I don't see anything," Timbol said. "It's trickling in from out there."

"From the Seastead deck? It's been a long day," Georgios said. "Maybe we're missing something, we're tired. Let's think about it tomorrow. We need Merl."

I wanted to go back upstairs to that quaint kitchen. We were all tired. We just wanted to feel safe, but it was clear it might be a long time before that happened, if ever.

We heard steps on the landing. Desiree descended carrying a glass of something clear.

"Guys! Check this out," she said. She held up the glass to Georgios, "Taste."

Georgios took it.

"Be careful," I said.

He drank. "Water? What makes water taste like that?"

He passed the glass around and we all exclaimed. It was so fresh and clean and sweet. I'd never had or seen water that was so clear before. We usually drank filtered water, and it was always a pale pink or yellow with traces of metal.

"It came right out of the kitchen tap," Desiree said.

"Let's take this up to Merl," I said.

We all went up except Timbol who could not leave a mechanical mystery alone, especially one that could be key to our survival. I held the glass to Merl's lips. He drank tentatively at first and then deeply. He lay back and rested.

"I've got to see the filter," he said.

"I found some lotion, too." Neena said. "A big vat of it in the closet in my room."

The women smeared it on our faces and necks. It smelled of roses. I wished I could have brought my grandmother here. Of course, she never would have left her home, but now, with nowhere better to go, and with the Seastead so clearly stocked and supplied with us in mind it felt luxurious. The lotion soothed my acid raw skin. Georgios took some for his hands.

"How does this feel?" Neena dabbed some on Merl's raw skin.

"Tingles," he said. "Nice."

His skin looked better. Neena applied it lightly gently to his face, arms, and legs. Then she carefully peeled his shredded shirt over his head and rubbed it over his torso.

We sat beside Merl listening to his ragged breaths become calmer as the scent of roses wafted toward the stars.

"I'll make us some dinner," Desiree said. "There's a store of corn flour upstairs and I'll harvest some of those tomatoes."

Just then there was a horrible clank. The Seastead shuddered and metal ground. The grinding carried on. It felt like the Seastead was ripping apart.

"The floor's moving," Desiree said.

"I found a switch," Timbol said.

"So, you touched it?" Georgios said, accusingly.

The middle of the platform was opening, a large square in the center. It was dark on the deck and what was under the metal was just as dark, but shiny. The moonlight shone down, and we saw the waves. This was the only land we had and now it was tearing apart and showing more water.

The ratfin buried into my shoulder.

"This wasn't part of the plan," Timbol said.

"Don't touch the water," I said.

The pool sparkled like a dark jewel. A fresh scent rose off of it. There was a pool at the center, and we could see stairs leading into the water and some dark shapes to the side. They looked like the heads of some sea creature. But the smell that rose from the pool was sweet and it was clearly the source of the water we'd drank in the kitchen and the water that swelled the tomatoes in Desiree's hands. The water shone. The ratfin scurried down my shoulder. It sniffed and drank in the water and then entered it gliding across the surface with its fins outstretched. Then it slipped under.

"Georgios, ratfin!" I lurched forward but hesitated to enter the water.

Georgios plunged in, he could not swim, but he lashed out and he soon had the ratfin in his hands.

I ran down the steps. The water was warm, and I reached for Georgios and then Timbol was beside me. Together we caught Georgios' hand and pulled him to the steps where the water was shallow.

"Be careful, there's a bit of a current. But thc water is fresh and warm and sweet."

I grabbed Georgios a blanket and he returned the ratfin to my neck. The ratfin nuzzled against my neck and I looked into its bright eyes.

"That's twice you've been saved. I'm going to call you In-fin."

We stared at the pool and stared. Desiree broke the spell.

"OK, I'm starving," she said, and then wandered back to the kitchen. Eventually, we all trailed after her, exhausted with our thoughts.

That night we stayed up late and gathered in the kitchen. We ate polenta with a thick tomato sauce, and we drank glasses of the water, which streamed freely from the tap.

Remembering the keg of rust-blood serum, I realized we perhaps could have saved the *mokol*. But where would we go? This Seastead was our best hope now.

"It was wasteful about the raft. We just let it sink," I said.

"I never want to be on it again," Neena said.

"We couldn't spare the blood for it anyway," said Timbol. "This whole vessel will need to be recoated soon and there's only the six of us--and we're all pretty drained."

By the time we were ready for sleep, Merl was well enough to climb up to his loft at the top of the Seastead. His lotion-coated skin was looking better, pinker and smoother.

Timbol took a room in the basement. Neena and Desiree stayed up talking. The rooms they took were on the main floor by the kitchen and library. Georgios stood with me beside the pool, and we listened to Merl clanging away in the mast, Timbol shuffling below, Desiree and Neena's chatter and the sounds of them nesting away the few items we had brought with us, tucking our few seeds and supplies into the cabinets and shelving our few books alongside the ones already supplied.

"OK, I'm to bed," Georgios said.

"I'll just be a moment," I said.

The pool in the middle of the platform mesmerized me. Why was it here? What did it mean? Moonlight shone on the surface. A faint smell of cinnamon that reminded me of grandmother's tea wafted from the surface. I saw a gleam on a ledge below and I was certain it was yet another one of the coins meant for me shining underwater. I watched at first without getting close.

I walked around the pool and stepped closer to it to get a better look. Ripples moved across the surface of the pool starting out from the center. Bubbles rose up from the center and the water began to froth. I ran down the stairs unwary of the noise. I searched for the panel.

"Close it. Close it," I said.

Timbol came out and flipped the switch to shut the lid and close the hatch to the pool. The clanging shook the platform, but I could feel the shift in movement. The metal was scrolling back, cranking into place.

He held me in his arms.

"I'm afraid of what's below," I said.

"It's OK, we're all jangly now," he said. "It'll take some time to adjust, to feel safe."

Would I ever feel safe with all this water around me?

I was slow to ascend the stairs, nervous about what I would find. The floor closed slowly. It was just a quarter of the way across. The center of the pool was still. I thought I saw a movement below a seal shape.

Desiree was standing on the deck watching it close. "What's up?"

"Just keeping the rust out of there."

"Mmm," she said. "Let's not open and close that all the time. Makes a racket."

"Sure," I assented, unsure if I ever wanted to see it open again. We could just use the water and not wonder at the source. I laughed. It was a nervous laugh. Of course, that was impossible.

Above me, Merl was looking down over the mast, staring down at the platform. From his vantage point looking down into the pool, I wondered what he had seen.

Under the roof I felt a plunk, plunk, plunk like something was knocking on the door asking to be let in. It shook the platform, but that first night, for all we knew, it might have just been the lapping of waves.

~ 58 ~

THE SEASTEADERS: MULIAN ARRIVAL

The next morning it was clear and calm for our first spring day at sea. For breakfast, Desiree made us hot corn mash with strawberries. Merl was mostly healed this morning, so it looked as though the burns were not as bad as we had thought when we brought him aboard. We ate heartily. The strawberries popped with sweetness. We were on our own at last, living the plans we had made over the past three years. Everyone but me was eager to look into the pool.

Sometimes, I wondered what would have happened if my mother had not left my father and we had stayed on Vancouver Island. I would not have condemned her to that, but still I wondered. Would the beatings have become progressively worse until he killed her? Surely that was what she had feared although it was hard to imagine such acts of violence from a family member and far easier to imagine it from the soldiers. Maybe she would have lived longer, nonetheless. What if I had never entered Merops and met Deuc and Georgios?

If I hadn't gone to university then playing at building utopias would have remained a childhood game. Much later, I would wonder what it would have been like if I had stayed longer with my companions on the Seastead. Would we have had children? Would I have died with them around me at age 91 like my grandmother? After we looked down into the pool, everything would be different, but there was no way for us to live without looking. For that, we would have had to be an entirely different kind of people, raised in a different place.

I was afraid, not just of what was in the water and where it came from, not just because I always imagined the worst, which always seemed a valid method of planning. It seemed to me the better prepared you were for defeats, the less likely they were to happen. I was more afraid because clean, pure water--an entire perfect pool of it--was a treasure, something to protect. Once we had something of worth to others, I would become afraid. Without the pool, there was no reason for anyone to try and find the Seastead. With the pool, they had reason and that meant an increased probability that they (soldiers or pirates) would find us. Soldiers, of any kind, were unlikely to be our friends.

There were so many things we could have done that first day. We had so much to do. We had to make our own food, clothing, and power. Neena could write. Merl could begin work on the boat he was already dreaming of building. Desiree could harvest seeds. I wanted to assign us tasks and begin to plan yet further ahead. I also wondered where Deuc was and wanted to take Georgios aside and ask him what he thought. However, we had arrived in our future plans at the very moment in which we foresaw no future. It was the perfect time for fate to intervene.

First, we had to drain blood and re-coat the vessel. We hoped Timbol would be able to recreate the serum. It was a question crucial to our survival which had to be answered.

At breakfast, we discussed who was able to give blood. Neena had been drained the longest of any of us so we decided to give her a rest, also Merl to give him time to heal, and Timbol to give him a better chance to think clearly. Myself, Georgios, and Desiree would give after we ate. I thought the loss of blood was adding to my irritability and nervousness, but there was no way around it.

In the light of day, the platform felt less solid than it had at night. The blood flaked off the struts and floated to the deck in the breeze. I would feel better when a fresh coat of rust protectant had been applied. We all would. I thought again that it might have been prudent to keep the small raft. Damn Deuc for leaving us without the boat. We were trapped on the water, barely afloat.

After breakfast, while everyone drank tea and looked over the railing at the ocean, spotting sharks, Merl took me aside. "Did you see something? Something that made you close the cover?"

"No," I shook my head. "Well, movement, maybe."

"Like a fish?"

"Bigger."

After tea, we drained blood so that Timbol could begin trying to resurrect the serum. He went below and began work.

Then they wanted to examine the pool. Merl went down to flip the switch and I stood next to Georgios holding his hand. There was that heavy clank. The rickety platform shifted. The grey metal floor ground aside revealing silvery waves. The water was bright, and it stretched endlessly below. Shining sliver and blue tiny fishes such as I had never seen darted through the sunlit pool. There was nothing in the center, just clear water infused with light. It looked to spiral down. Now I could see clearly, the ledge around the edge of the pool. It was four feet below around the outside and just wide enough to stand on. I saw the glint of the coin. I saw the familiar imprint of it. On the other side, were masks, strange inhuman looking masks.

We stepped into the water. It was warm and pleasant. No one felt anything strange except that we were in water, and it did not burn, it caressed our skin. Georgios stood beside me in the water. Desiree and Neena sat on the side and swung their legs in the water. Only Merl refused to go in. He was still scared from his plunge into the ocean on our way over.

"It feels soft. It might soothe your skin," Neena said.

"Nah, I've had enough of water, save for drinking," he said.

Instead, he walked over to examine the masks from the platform.

Desiree jumped into the water, onto the ledge and began to walk around. Then the current caught her, she swayed, yipped, and slipped from the ledge. Her head went under. Georgios leaned out and caught her hand.

There was a horrible moment when I thought the swirling current would pull them both under and then another horrible moment when Georgios heaved Desiree to him and onto the ledge.

I saw Georgios holding wet, shining Desiree and how quickly he'd reached out to meet her and I had a premonition. I knew then that they shared a connection. Yet, probably, nothing would happen between them so long as I was there.

Georgios stayed beside me while I reached down for the coin on the ledge. I had to fight the current to come up with it. Georgios caught my other hand to help me resist the current spiraling toward and pull me up. The coin was the same as my other coins. It was a sign. A direction.

"Let me see," Merl said, and I passed the thing to him. For the first time, I felt we Seasteaders had no secrets.

He twisted it and watched the coin flex. "OK, these creepy things are organic, a lot like these masks. They look kind of like some sort of helmet," Merl said. "They have a grey metallic sheen, but a rubbery softness."

Timbol had come up from below and he also leaned down to inspect and touch the masks.

"Rubbery. There are these hard nubs and soft tendril things. Yep, definitely organic, " he said, agreeing with Merl's assessment.

They smelled of kelp and sea salt, although this water was not salty.

While we examined them, the water began to froth and churn. We backed out of the water onto the Seastead deck.

"Should I shut it?" Timbol asked.

"Yes, shut it!" I directed.

"Let's see. Let's see," Georgios said.

We were planners, not the kind of people who reacted quickly to changing circumstance. I thought of utopias, I imagined the worst, but I wasn't prepared to fight it. None of us had a weapon stouter or more deadly than a wooden oar.

Merl picked up the oar.

It happened slowly. The bubbles rose. A crown appeared--that's what it looked like to us--lavender spikes adorned the head. Beneath that a lumpy visage. There were no facial features to fix on to. I could not discern eyes, nose, ears, or a mouth in that flakey, undulating, blue-green luminescent face. There was a short beard of tendrils and tentacles. A long silvery robe swirled around the rest of the long body, from the end of its beard for a length of at least seven feet to wherever it ended. We could not see its feet.

Perhaps it was the being's smell, foreign but spicy and sweet, of kelp and cinnamon, or maybe it was their stance and bearing, non-threatening yet confident. There was something about this being that made me regard it sympathetically as though it were myself. I wondered where it had come from and whether it had tired from its journey. Whatever it was, it was easily apparent to me that this strange creature was human, human in a way that the soldiers on the streets or even my father, when he had struck my mother, had not been. I felt at peace in their presence and then I began to feel excited. Anticipation welled up in me: What next?

The being made a low hum, a rhythmic churning came from them, and I wished we had Deuc with us, our musician. Music, not words, seemed the right way to communicate with this unusual being.

Then Neena, our poet, spoke:

"The sea, the fish, the tree, tree, tree;
Some rise, some seek, some be, be, be."

It was a simple poem, but the rhythm was right.

The emissary was pleased, I imagine. They turned to Neena and their beard and hair waved at her. He began to glide up the steps toward us. There was no up and down motion as he ascended just a gentle rocking. When he turned, we saw the twisted ropes that hung down his head and shoulders and swung heavily.

Later, I would know that the robe he wore was alive, a living shell with fluid movement, that the kingly crown was made of living shells as well, tubular shaped spikes filled with muscles. I would know that he moved on a soft muscular pod like a snail and beneath his robe his upper body was draped in cilia, and he both ate and loved with a thick trunk like appendage that came out of his side and was surrounded by eight thinner tentacles, which served as his arms, hands, and fingers. His lower body was coated in scales and rises of barnacle and that, among his kind, these creatures clung only to the best regarded Mulians. Abrador was highly respected. I would come to know Abrador intimately in all his strange nature.

It was good we did not know all that at the time--we who knew so little of the sea and who had grown up in fear of it.

Later he would tell me, "I went to greet you because I am to you, we think, the most unusual looking of Mulians, by far the most disturbing. After me, we thought, you would find the others less so, somewhat comforting. Until, that is, you went down and met the great ones."

At first glance, the emissary seemed strange, but not too strange after all we'd been through. While we feared the monotony and uncertainty of our precarious position at sea on the platform, his appearance gave us a future to focus on, a problem to solve, and questions to ask. What is life without questioning? Without mystery and puzzles?

In response to Neena, our visitor made more sound. He keened like a Rust Whale. He sang a greeting that sounded distant and muffled as if we were all underwater.

Beneath the sounds, I could feel words.

"Exiador," which meant welcome. I saw the word in my mind and felt it and recognized it from the imprint on the coins.

"They want to teach us," I said. "To swim and...I don't know, other things."

"They?" Merl asked.

"A name: Mu-lee-anns. Sea teachers. More teachers will come."

Abrador left us gifts: green algae lotion and a cinnamon and kelp-scented liquid that no one was anxious to try. These new supplies added to our stores.

He left the gifts and sank back below. Before we met another Mulian, we would have other visitors.

We would tend to the painting of the platform with our blood leaning far over the sides of the ship where the Rust Sharks swam and hanging below to get to the underbelly. It seemed to be holding up well enough.

Weeks later, Merl shouted down from the crow's nest, "A ship."

We looked out to sea and saw the galleon approaching flying a flag no one recognized.

"At least it's not Balor," I said.

"You'd rather the devil you don't know?" Timbol said.

"This time I'll take it," I said. "Shut the hatch. We don't want them to notice the water."

It closed with a clanking and the whole Seastead shook, but the motion was hidden in the ocean wind and waves. When the ship arrived, we did not get the devil we did not know. Apparently, we knew too many devils.

~ 59 ~

THE SEASTEADERS: ELATHIAN RIPTIDERS

In making our Seastead plans, everyone had been envious of the Elathian Riptiders. They were a tight clan of craftsmen who had banded together early on when the water began to rise. No one knew how the pirates had been so prescient and certain. They had hoarded wood for themselves, and they had planned to be afloat, while everyone else clung desperately to the land and fought over it. They had planned and planted and cut down trees before the soil was too wet for the hard woods to grow and the land became too soft for their roots. They had moved animals with them onto the water as well. It was rumored that they had a large and well-defended floating island to the West.

The gleaming galleon that came toward us was made of mahogany and cypress. It had planks of red and gold. It had strong, solid flanks and cannons. The flag they flew was a tree with its roots exposed. No doubt, these were the legendary Riptiders who had hoarded wood and left everyone else behind to drown.

It was alarming to see the galleon bearing down on us. It was taller than an island top and lined with guns. We had the pool, our blood, and our meager supplies to protect and no means to do so. The ship towered over us.

"We didn't make any plans for defense?" Desiree said.

"Did you?" I asked.

"Well, even if we had weapons, would you use them or expect me to use them?" Timbol said.

"No, there's no reason for anyone to end up dead sooner than we will anyway," I said.

No, we hadn't made provisions to fight. Our goal had always been to prevent suffering and there was no weapon on earth that could alleviate that. Maybe that was why the earth had to be abandoned. The galleon pulled up beside us and lowered a plank down to our Seastead. Three men descended. One of them was Deuc.

"I thought we'd have more time before we were found," Merl said.

"Deuc," Georgios said. "He brought the pirates."

Deuc was with the Riptiders. He came down after the tallest of them, a dark-haired man who looked like he'd been long at sea, who stood and walked with a swagger of authority, and his brother who had reddish hair and a thin beard and more of a swing in his step than a swagger. Beside the pair, Deuc looked trivial in stature. His delicate features and playful curly hair made him seem like a toy. If I'd had any sense of survival, I'd have turned all my attention to these stout men, but in that moment, as always, Deuc held my full attention. I told myself I was incensed by his betrayal. In truth, I was excited to see him, and I wanted his attention, too. The men were armed with worn-looking pistols and swords, which they wore like their leathers. Deuc had a sword too, but it was too long for him and looked like decoration. I went right up to him and spewed words without thinking.

"You took our boat to the Riptiders. We barely made it out here on the raft. Merl fell in. There were sharks."

"Shush," said Timbol.

The more I spoke the angrier I became. I went from cold fear to hot fury in two seconds as soon as Deuc spoke. "I'm sorry I left you, but you wouldn't listen."

"Wouldn't listen to what?"

Deuc was always remembering conversations we hadn't had. It seemed we were always arguing about arguments I couldn't remember. He came at problems from a different tack. He would hear my words differently.

"I mentioned Riptiders and you shut me down," he said.

Then I did remember, a snippet. He'd mentioned Riptiders and I'd said, "OK, but we need to focus on the Seastead." Then, he'd been sullen, and I had talked to the others. So, that was the moment he'd made his own plan. That long ago.

"You never said you knew them, and you were going to take our boat," I said. "We didn't even know if the Seastead would really be here."

He looked chagrined for a moment. He did always look apologetic, when he bothered to apologize, on the rare occasions he felt it was required.

"Oh, right. Yes, I know, and I left you just that raft. That was terrible. I'm sorry," he said. "But I knew Georgios would make it out here." Then he turned to Merl. "You should see what they have. It's larger than any floating market. There are stairs and layers. There are cities afloat. The engineering..."

"Sure, they did all that, so they make their own laws, use all the wood, and screw the rest of us," said Timbol, but Merl looked interested.

Deuc shrugged. "It's like us at Merops. It's a sanctuary."

"This is our sanctuary," I said. "You plan to plunder it."

"Do I hear welcome aboard?" asked the tall Riptider. His beard tapered below his chin and had a curl to it on the end. There was a little grey in it. It looked a little alive, like the Mulian Abrador's beard, but it blew in the breeze, and it was made of human hair not seastuff.

Until now, the Riptiders had been standing over us, looking around the deck, taking inventory. They mostly hadn't reacted to my outburst. The elder one raised a wry smile.

"There's plunder is there?" He looked around and raised an eyebrow.

Of course, he couldn't see the pool. But could we keep him from noticing the tap water?

The younger one was eyeing Desiree and looked like he might be having other ideas about plunder. To my chagrin, Desiree was meeting his gaze. We'd been away a while and although Timbol, Merl, and Georgios were all rather attracted to Desiree, no one thus far had done more than appreciate her cooking. Georgios and I were the only couple. The others were afraid to disrupt their friendship on the tiny, uncertain platform. Romance would happen in time.

"I'm sorry for our rudeness," Georgios said, stepping forward. "We were surprised to see Deuc. Can I show you around?"

"That would be most kind," he said. "I'm Randol Cox and this is my brother, Jip."

"Deuc said this ship was made of metal, but I didn't believe it," Randol said walking over to one of the struts and rubbing his fingers on it. He rubbed his fingers together and rust-colored granules stuck to them. "And this is your blood."

"You told them everything," I said to Deuc.

"Iron blood and a mixture Professor Belo invented," Deuc said, ignoring me. "It's a preservative that protects against the sea spray."

Georgios led the Riptiders to the garden and the kitchen. Sometimes he seemed to be too kind and unconcerned with his own welfare. He did not put the welfare of those he knew best before the needs or wants of those he did not know intimately. This generosity of spirit, however, never seemed to harm him.

I hadn't paid much attention to Randol. Deuc had absorbed all my attention, but as we went upstairs to view our quarters on the second floor, I studied the pirate and was surprised to see a ratfin peek out from the band of his hat. In-fin hissed his surprise and the other ratfin hid in the folds of the hat and Randol's unbound brown curly hair. In Timbol's room, we showed them the schematics for the Seastead. Randol asked questions about everything, but when Merl offered to take them up to the masthead, he wasn't interested.

"We've seen enough of the ocean," Randol said.

Jip talked mostly to Desiree. I could hear him talking about Elathe and all the goods they had there. He stopped to touch everything: the new seedlings with their tender shoots, the solar panels, the equipment in the boiler room, the sensors, and, naturally, Desiree. He had a hand on her back, shoulder, or waist at every conceivable opportunity: whenever she laughed, which was often, or to help her up or down stairs.

She raised an eyebrow at me, so I knew she was well aware of the attentions, but then she didn't seem to mind.

I made sure to lead the way downstairs and turned off the UV lights. I hoped they wouldn't peer too carefully at the hydroponic pool. They were mostly interested in the vat of Iron Blood and the formula for the serum and then Merl took them over to the pumps and boiler schematics.

Now Randol had even more questions.

"How much blood does it take to coat the ship?"

"Five pints for 1,500 square feet."

I watched him make the calculation. He'd need each of us alive. We'd designed the Seastead to be sustainable for our small group.

Down here, Jip's fingers prying into everything made me the most nervous. It was only a matter of time until he triggered the opening. But he got bored in the dark, because Desiree hadn't joined us, I suspected. She'd begged off the rest of the tour to start dinner.

"Make tea," I'd told her, and she nodded. I didn't want her serving glasses of that suspiciously fresh water.

With the tour over, the Riptiders seemed to relax. There were some curiosities on board the Seastead, but no unpleasant surprises. We had no weapons. They'd kept their pistols holstered. We sat in the kitchen and watched Desiree prepare the food. Georgios helped her chop tomatoes and kale. In-fin crawled down from around my neck and sniffed at Randol. His ratfin poked over the top of his hat and when he set it down the ratfin crawled up onto the table and squabbled with mine briefly. Then they began to play.

"Well, our ratfin are friendly," Randol said. They curled up together in the brim of his hat.

"Jip, get us some things from the ship to share with these folks," he said, the returned his attention to us. "So everyone wants to know about how we Riptiders built our island."

He began to relate the story of the Riptiders, which we all knew, but it was entertaining to hear it directly from a pirate. The Riptiders in this version were smart and resourceful, not greedy.

In the middle of the story, Jip returned with a jug of rum and some small cakes. I watched him watching Desiree and enjoying his food. His tongue loosened considerably with drink.

"Now what happened on La Merde?" he asked.

"General Balor," I said.

"Balor," Randol said. "He's a bastard. Doesn't give up either. He's troubled us more than once. We're not going to send our sons all over the seas after him though. Although we might not stop some of the younger ones from getting a mind to do just that. How many soldiers did he bring?"

He wanted information, but he had probably heard all this from Deuc and was just confirming the details.

After dinner, Merl, Desiree, Timbol, and Jip climbed into the tower. "Where's your juice?" Randol asked straight up.

But we didn't have any contraband: no drugs and our alcohol hadn't had time to ferment.

Randol sniffed at the kelp liquid Abrador had brought. "Why not?" he said and tipped the bottle back into his mouth.

I looked up and watched them watching us and wondered how much Merl was sharing with the inquisitive pirates. Deuc went out on the platform and began to play his guitar. The strumming swept over the sea.

I began to giggle. It was impossible to hide it in these close quarters from these attentive men. I used my old trick, thinking of the ratfin, but even this struck me as absurd. My body shook with laughter.

Randol turned on me. "What's so funny? Is it our hats?"

"No, ratfin," I said. "I've kept them as pets ever since I was little."

"Aye," he said. "I had them too as a lad. I used to use them for my experiments. I kept this one here, name's Darwin. He refused to die this one."

That sobered me at last. It sobered us all.

They asked us if we'd like to board their ship, Kyklopes. It looked to offer far more luxury. I was afraid that once there, however, the Riptiders would sail off with us. We'd already escaped captivity once and I wasn't ready to be imprisoned for my blood again. There was no way to escape that misfortune of birth. Still, I might have joined him. I was afraid of our rocky, unsteady Seastead with its metal clanking struts and tiny confined platform. How long would it last?

We stayed late into the night on the deck listening to Deuc's song and Randol's pirate escapades until he retired to his ship. Late into the night, I heard Desiree laughing. The next morning, I watched Jip stumble out of her room.

Later, he, Deuc, and Randol descended from the plank.

Randol strode out.

"Now show us what's under here," he said. He stomped on the deck. There was a hollow, clanging sound. "Come now. There's something," he shouted when we remained silent.

Timbol went down to the engine room and shortly after we heard the clunk and watched the surface of the platform split. I saw Deuc's surprise. He hadn't known. We could have kept it secret. But Desiree was holding her head. She'd drank and talked too much, and I looked over at Merl who looked equally hung over. Or, he had. Neena brought them out glasses of the cool water. We knew it quickly cleared a hangover.

"Might as well," she said.

Randol looked into the pool. He scanned it with his eyes.

"And you had visitors?" Randol asked.

He knew that too. Who had talked so much? I couldn't help but like Randol. He had a confident air, interesting stories, and a stout laugh. But I remembered his talk of experiments on the ratfin. There was much about him I did not know, but I knew the Riptiders did not reach out to help others as the waters rose. They had saved only their own. We Seasteaders had done the same, though. How many people were waiting in line for the ferry? Had I even looked for my own mother? What if she had somehow survived the landslide? Did it matter? We'd only ended up with a raft. How many more would have fit on the *mokol*? Not even one.

"One visitor, but yes, he said more will come," Georgios said. "Trainers. They want to teach us their ways and take us to see their place."

"What do they want from you?"

"We don't know."

"Find out," he said to Deuc. "Deuc will stay here. He wants to learn, too."

Deuc looked like he wanted to protest, but the Riptiders did not allow debate. They followed the ship captain's orders. "Of course," Deuc said.

The Riptide galleon sailed off and left a sullen Deuc behind.

"They don't consider you one of them, Deuc. You're not family so when it comes down to it you are dispensable," Georgios said.

"Yes, I know," Deuc said. "I don't need another of your lectures, Georgios. They want what they've always wanted from me, information. But they can be useful to us too. They helped build this place. They transported the metal out here. They already consider this part of their territory, but they're not going to lose life over it, unless there's something valuable. You're valuable, of course. But just as good here, out of the way, and less trouble, out of sight out of mind. The Riptiders won't fight over us out here. That source of fresh water, though..."

~ 60 ~

THE SEASTEADERS: MULIAN TRAINING

The Mulians sent three trainers to our Seastead. Abrador was not among them. The trainers vaguely resembled our first emissary. They had discernible parts: mangled-looking heads, long robes, trunks and tentacles, soft upper bodies and encrusted lower torsos, usually mounted on a soft cephalopod foot.

The one who taught us language had a long, curved head like a seahorse with a bright green sheen. The agricultural instructor had slits in the side of his robes, in shades of blue, where tentacles stuck out at crablike angles, but were covered with suckers like an octopus. The swimming instructor looked the most human, in swirling shades from peach to black, with a long slender smooth body on two webbed feet. Adi often swam unrobed in silvery loops around the pool. Adi's enormous round head stuck out of the water giving us plenty of opportunity to marvel at its spikes, barnacles, and rows of eyes sparkling like jewels.

The Mulians used the pronoun Adi, which meant simply "one of us." The swimmer never gave me any sense of gender and I thought of the swimmer as Adi even in my head.

Merl, who never picked up even a little of the language, called the trainers Green Singer, Blue Farmer, and The Purple Frog.

The first time they said their names I could not hear them. They sounded like a hum, a mewl, and a croak. I realized that the name that Abrador gave us was not his true name, but one easier for us to understand.

While the trainers worked with us, they lived in a dome-shaped globe just a little smaller than our Seastead platform about 30 feet below the surface of the pool. They came onto the platform only while working with us and on special occasions. It was a hardship for them to spend too much time in our air. The corrosion seeped too quickly into their porous skins. At night, we could see their pale, green globe lit up, phosphorescent underwater and see their shadows moving beneath its semi-translucent surface. The water carried the sound of their voices humming and singing into the night. Occasionally, I thought I heard approximations of our names and sprinkled laughter.

It must have been amusing to teach us.

We began with language lessons and everyone on the Seastead, curious, took part. It began with humming, then singing, and only later the separation of words. Their language consisted of spoken words, song, and telepathy. Much of the sense of it came mind to mind. We had to become receptive first and we practiced humming, chanting, and meditation.

Merl quickly became frustrated. He couldn't discern the speech and never heard the Mulians in his head. He pretended at first and then finally admitted, "I don't hear a thing."

He retreated to his engineering projects. He wouldn't swim either, he was too afraid of the water, so his lessons ended there. Neena also struggled with the new sounds of words, but she liked the singing and swimming. Desiree got the language quite well, Georgios and Timbol passably. Deuc picked it up quickly with his musical sensibility.

"I like it better than our own," he said.

He was best at the speech and the inflection, but I surpassed him in understanding the telepathy.

I could hear the Mulians talking in my head almost from the beginning. It reminded me of the imaginary conversations I held with the Octavians as a child, but I missed some of the nuances of the spoken Mulian because I missed the music, or I tried to translate the Mulian words into my own tongue and missed the differences.

Deuc said he could not get the telepathy, but one day I felt him singing Mulian in my head. "I had a breakthrough," he said.

The language training went slowly. Meanwhile, I tried to get a better sense of Neena and Deuc's growing friendship. One night after dinner, I instigated a game of Cardinal with them.

"Sure, I'm too tired to do anything else," Deuc said.

We were all exhausted by trying to understand and form Mulian words and having the trainers in our heads.

It was fun to have new player in Cardinal to throw off the balance of my usual planning. I was too used to the patterns of the others' play. Deuc knew the game well. He played to win, but when he got bored he began to throw hands. Neena made moves for elegance, as if she had rules all her own, playing for the rhythm of the game, without a thought for winning. She approached everything that way, making beauty and rhythms appear where there were none. They both saw the world in interesting, but completely different, ways from me. Whereas Georgios and I saw the world, as far as I could tell, exactly the same. Timbol and I were in a great deal of agreement, but there were things that interested him that I was not as interested in, details and marine life, whereas I focused often on the future and plans. Desiree and Merl were freer people less serious, more focused on their particular pleasures. Desiree loved cooking and craftwork and Merl loved tinkering and concoctions.

Neena and Deuc composed songs together. He played and she added her poetry as lyrics. They sang together. More often than not, she would grow silent.

"I love to hear my words in his voice," she said. "They sound so beautiful. It is as if I had not written them."

They were becoming good, if unlikely, friends.

Eventually the Mulians could communicate well enough with us that we could begin our swimming lessons. Already they had taken us into the water each day as part of our language lessons and we had learned to paddle across the surface. Georgios, Timbol, Deuc and I and even Neena made progress. Merl refused to have anything to do with it and Desiree managed to become buoyant, but not much more. She was beautiful in the sunlit water though with her dark hair shiny and sleek as a seal. I watched Georgios watching her.

Before we could dive, we had to apply an algae-scented lotion to our faces every morning and night for a week to prepare the skin. We entered the water in the outdoor training pool, up to our chests and they brought up a basket filled with an assortment of purple, light blue, and pale green pearlescent tentacles. They were beautiful laying still in the basket woven of sea stuffs. But they felt strange: firm and tumescent yet spongy and pliable. It stung when the trainers affixed them to our faces three on each side down our cheekbones, two along each side of the nose and three shorter ones over our top lips. These were to help with breathing, but also to cover the nose and mouth, which were culturally erotic. They tickled, but wearing them, the water felt safer. To get us used to the depths and make it easier to breathe, we had to apply the tentacles. The weird sensations disappeared when we went underwater. I caught on to it quite quickly and was praised as a good swimmer.

Once we learned to swim, our agricultural lessons began. We swam down to the kelp beds below the trainers' dome. In Mulian society everyone grows their own food.

"So, they expect us to go there? Underwater. To live?" asked Georgios.

"For as long as it takes to learn their ways," I said. "They can teach us how to save ourselves. They will show us. Besides, aren't you curious?"

"Of course, but this is enough of an adventure for me. I can't see myself underwater."

"I can," I said. "See myself underwater. Maybe I always have seen myself in hazy ripples."

He was silent. We had an inkling then of what was ahead for us.

When the lesson was over, we each detached our tentacles and placed them in small separate baskets labeled with our names. These were our tentacles now. The trainers showed us how to sprinkle our tentacles with small gold flakes, a kind of food that keeps them healthy in some way (I still found it difficult to understand our trainers' thick accents and muffled voices). I could mostly understand their ideas.

We all, except Merl who refused to take part, had deep purple sucker marks across our faces where the tentacles had been, and they gave us a glittery blue green gel to help our skin heal and to help the suckers stick better to our faces next time. I was afraid it would permanently change the quality of my skin. Maybe for the better? Softer? Now it seems a funny fear.

The lotion I applied every day to my face did begin to change the texture of my skin. It became softer and smoother, but also tougher and rubbery. One day, I realized that the tiny flakes of gold in the sparkly gel we applied to our faces was similar to the glittery "tentacle food". We were teaching them to feed off our faces.

Our skin became soft and stretchy, but after long periods of diving and being underwater in tentacles, when we pulled them off the places where the tentacles had clung began to ache and itch. Patches of skin on my face sloughed off. We had no mirrors, but I could see how it looked on the others, like a rash of pox.

They continued language and culture training, teaching us more complicated songs and rituals.

Adi told me, "Until you are able to change, you will not be able to attain your Octavia. You will always fall short of what you've envisioned."

They ought to have known. This was why the Mulians had gone underwater long ago.

They'd taken the word Octavia from me. They used it for their meaning, utopia. They'd learned the idea from me.

Toward the end of our Mulian training, the Riptiders returned.

~ 61 ~

THE SEASTEADERS: JUMPING OFF

The Riptiders made Deuc go to Mu to maintain his loyalty to them. They wanted most of us to stay above water on the Seastead to donate blood and I wondered how long the Seastead would be able to stay afloat without us.

Neena, Deuc, and I would go. Timbol, Desiree, Merl, and Georgios would stay.

I wondered at our decision to send Neena to Mu. Was her life worth less because she was an artist? But it came down to her choice, and she wanted to go to Mu. The Mulians tempted us by saying they had something down there to save us, to turn back the corrosion and purify the sea. We each had our own reasons for wanting to make the journey. Neena wanted to write poems about them and to follow the path she felt Professor Alexandra had set for her. Deuc sought to bring back secrets to the Riptiders and, also, he felt most at home adventuring amongst the fringe.

I wanted to find utopian secrets and visit the imagined city of my childhood dreams, but I didn't want to leave Georgios. My two conflicting desperate desires competed. I felt sanded by them, polished, vibrant, and ready to descend into the sea. I remembered the pain, the fear of being separated from Georgios when we were leaving La Merde and I went to find Neena. That separation was only hours. After we reunited it all seemed bearable--together--even though we were casting out onto an uncertain ocean and there was the threat of drowning, of rusting, and of being eaten by sharks.

Before we went, we drained as much blood as we could to help the Seastead, although we were already blood light. We were light-headed and dizzy. Perhaps if we'd been at full blood, the whole departure would have seemed less surreal. Maybe we would have had the sense to stay.

The Mulians arranged a special time for our departure. Our arrival in Mu would be in their season of *sivan* coinciding with their hydrophoria festival, an auspicious time. There was a full moon on the eve of our departure and Neena, Deuc, and I had tried to busy ourselves all day. Even so, we were perched on the edge of the pool too early. We had our things beside us in rubber packs. They were not many. We had few possessions to begin with on the islands, even fewer on the Seastead and our trainers had told us they would take us to get the things we would need to live when we arrived. When we'd asked them what to bring, they had said, "Nothing."

Still, Neena had to take her journals and her pens and Deuc his lute. I wanted one of everything I thought the others would have brought, I took a map from Timbol and seeds and spices from Desiree. I pondered for a while what Merl would bring and considered batteries, serum, and electrodes and finally brought a small solar panel--more as a symbol than for practical use. For Merl, preparation meant making do with what you had and using your brain to capacity. I figured he would trust to have the materials to innovate once he arrived. Georgios made me take a deck of Cardinal cards. They turned out to be a prized possession. I wanted to have a bit of each of my tribe with me for comfort. It was, I would learn, a very Mulian approach.

We waited beside the pool until the bubbling began in the center of it where the moon shone through and the spikes of Mulian crowns broke through the surface. They were lavender lengths tipped with pink pearls that glowed silver in the moonlight. I looked back at Georgios hovering on the platform behind me. He'd been making himself look busy, touching ropes and nets, or some such.

"They're below," I said. "I'm going."

He nodded. He didn't say, "You don't have to do this."

He knew I did.

"Wait," he said. "I've one more thing for you."

He slipped a coin into my hand.

"They are not the only ones that can leave you tokens."

It was a medallion he'd carved of precious wood. The picture on it was of a cypress tree. I strung it around my neck.

I gave Georgios In-fin. I unhooked the sweet creature from his place around my neck.

"Look after my ratfin," I said, handing the ratfin over. In-fin quickly crawled up Georgios' arm and curled around his neck sniffing at his ear.

"I will." Georgios said.

As I said goodbye to Georgios, I watched him watching Desiree. If I was gone long, their relationship was inevitable. I was sending them into each other's arms, but I could see no way around it. He had to work on his project here and pacify the Riptiders. I needed to go to find out about the Mulians and what lay beneath us--the key to our destiny and our opportunity to, as I had always envisioned, become one with the water. We needed to learn first and see if this was something we could accept and nurture in our world. It was foolish to think that we could sustain a love apart in those tumultuous times and at such a distance between surface and sea, but I could not turn down the opportunity to go live among the Mulians. I had to know what was below.

The moment before I jumped into the pool though, I wanted nothing but to stay on the Seastead alone with Georgios. I wanted that more than anything to be beside Georgios forever, just sitting, and holding hands.

It was almost enough for me. Almost. I remembered my promise to my grandmother, "Don't you leave him. When you love, you stay." I would break that promise because there were things I wanted more. I yearned to see the Mulian city, and I longed to create a social structure and a peaceful place. I wanted, in some way, to defeat the soldiers who destroyed my grandmother's house. It was a residual of my deep longing to step in between my father and my mother's arguments. Not to raise my fist to father, but to gaze at him and, with one look, take all the fight and anger out of him. How that rage had infected him in the first place was a mystery. I wanted to dissolve his anger so that he could float forever in love and lap at my mother's feet proffering only kisses, as she deserved.

If I had not wanted this more, then I could have stayed with Georgios. It may have been enough.

I could have given up my savior dreams, but even if I could have, I could not have been certain of Georgios and myself. There was the way he looked at Desiree. There was the way I still looked at Deuc. We did not know that our life together could be counted on, certainly not enough to risk the fate of the world, certainly not considering the world and its risks. I had no choice, being myself in that moment, but to descend. Looking back from an age, I never would have gone, but then I would not be this person I am now had I not gone to Mu. There is no way to change the decision. *Praise water!*

The Mulians pointed to the tentacles. I applied them for the last time. I would never take them off again. The places on my face where I chose to put them were where they would always be. I affixed two on the sides of my nose and one on my temple to drape down and cover my nostrils. All of these were blue. I placed a row of smaller lavender tentacles cross my upper jaw line to veil my erotic mouth and stuck two larger purple-green ones into my dimples. Neena decorated her face with light blue and turquoise tentacles and applied more than she needed. She was not afraid to become other. Either that or she wanted to be very sure to breathe. Deuc picked deep blue and black tentacles and used just a few large ones. The fact that his lips were hidden made me want to see them even more. I was beginning to find the tentacles appealing. One day I would enjoy the touch of them.

Because we were diving down so far, we wore the helmets as well. Deuc, Neena and I put on our helmets on over our heads. I felt the suckers attach themselves to my bare skin, the uncovered places on my cheeks, behind my ears, the back of my neck, my throat. The sensations were more familiar, but still odd. The shell material before my eyes tinted everything a pale green.

In my head, I was already composing letters to Georgios, and thinking of what I would say to him when I returned.

"I am sliding into the water," I said.

In my head, when I talked to Georgios, I felt like I was lying. Everything would sound adventurous, ethereal, lovely, and passionate. It was not a lie, but how could I be passionate without him? When I was with the Mulians, I felt every moment deeply. Every moment felt like my last. I held close my passion for Georgios.

Once I was tentacled, for the first 20 or so feet it was just like diving in the ocean, and then it was like diving down into the deepest, darkest ocean, but then ahead of me the water became lighter, and we entered a tunnel and it seemed to be flowing down. It grew lighter and lighter in the tunnel. It had occurred to me more than once on the platform that I did not particularly like fish or the ocean. I liked it from above, seeing it as part of the setting, but I did not like plunging into it. I did not like the three dimensionality of it, not knowing what was beneath me. I did not like the kind of polluted saltiness of it: salt that tasted of algae and tuna. I did not like the little fish that darted against my skin or the larger mammoth shapes I imagined rising beneath and beside me. The ocean sunk fear into me. Its terrors struck deep into my subconscious. Still, I went without a struggle.

Past the deep cold part of the water, it opened into a pale blue dawn. We drifted on a current past dunes and dunes of soft brown and in pockets bright white. I heard a ringing across the dunes sometimes louder, sometimes softer like ambient bells or cooing mourning doves. The further we went, the fewer and further between the white patches became and it was like an underwater desert of rolling sand. Soon, I noticed that we were traveling slowly. There was barely any current at all.

Even though I was better at telepathy than any other Seasteader, I struggled with the Mulian mind-to-mind talk. Underwater it was essential. There was no other way to communicate and the deeper we went as we traveled down, the easier it became.

I heard the Mulian voices in my head. I heard the whale song. I heard their trumpets and their bells.

I looked at Neena and Deuc. We had traveled even farther down than I had expected. After a while Adi swam to the side. We swam the rest of the way. It was warm and stagnant outside the current. Deuc swam in the strange upright way we had practiced.

"Praise mountaintop!" I thought, then corrected myself, "Praise water!" I had no difficulty breathing and the pressure of the depths did not crush me. I was safe in the Mulian currents.

I struggled to swim correctly and wondered what all my plans and ideals would come to when I didn't even know how to move. Gradually, we floated into a horizontal, upright position.

There was a current, but it flowed across what I would have thought was the ocean floor. The water was warm, but it grew colder. Sinking, I felt alone for the first time ever in my life, alone no possibility of love ahead of me, nothing left to long for. Never had Georgios felt so far away, so lost from every possibility of return. Gone. Gone. Forever. I sank with Deuc and Neena beside me and our bodies were cold, our faces foreign and tentacled. I imagined I would never again be warm.

We followed the spiked headdress ahead of us. Down. In the dark, they looked like pieces of ebony coral. Coal-colored crowns. I could barely see anything. It had been night above.

As the Mulians, Neena, Deuc and I traveled down, a pathway opened ahead, a lighter shade of blue streaking through the deeper blue beside it. The water grew warm inside the pathway. When I reached my hand outside, it was quickly chilled. Then, I could see topography below. Nothing appeared distinct, as I gazed through the moving water, but I saw round shapes, hills and valleys, roads, and a round bubble cluster surrounded by lights.

In front of me, the bubbles that moved through my hands were shiny and round. They sparkled as they accelerated towards me. Here, I lost track of my orientation, and I would not regain it. It was no longer possible to think of the direction of where I was headed as down or the place where I had come from as up. Where I had been oriented head down in a diving position, I was now moving forward as if walking. I felt pushed forward by the warm water. I could see the city. Its towers and domes were shaded, deeply etched before the backdrop of the ocean so that the whole city looked distinct and deep. It would be a long time before I saw the city from that perspective again, from the height and distance of arrival.

From above, this was how Mu looked. In the center of Mu was a golden pyramid and at the top of the pyramid was a golden sun. Extending out over the pyramid was a translucent, billowing, green membrane. The entire civilization was encased within a sack like a jellyfish. How the sun was there underwater able to be looked at directly I could not fathom. I stared and stared at it. There was warmth, but it did not burn.

Looking at Mu, I thought it was entirely possible that I would never return to the surface. How could I see this alien city and then return to my other life? That moment, when it would have been most easy, or at least possible, to go back to the Seastead, was the one moment when I was not considering it. Later, when it would have been difficult or impossible, the idea of return to Georgios and air consumed me.

Four roads in each direction extended from the pyramid. There were four towers at the ends of the roads. Each of the four sectors was a pale color: lavender, periwinkle, aqua, and green. I learned later they were colored by the foods grown upon the different soils and that the Mulians rotated the crops each year. There was a white coliseum embedded on the rise of an open, green park apart from the pyramid. Below the park, I recognized the raised beds we had learned to make to grow our food. Then the sides sloped down into darkness. Mulians lived in warren-like caves that extended beneath the surface city.

The faces of my companions were unreadable underneath their helmets. To me, in the darkness of our approach, they appeared as blobs of strange matter. But I sensed a well of emotion in Neena. She hovered above the view, swimming slowly, taking it all in. I knew she was affected. Deuc continued his movement, and I sensed his fear. This was more than we expected. He'd made a huge sacrifice to gain the political goodwill of the pirates.

We entered the city through an arch of whale bone.

"This is not our entire empire. This is the city Mu," Abrador said.

I saw masses of pink pearl crowns and wavy pillar bodies and heard a reverberating hum. The Mulians were lined up to greet us. I was elated and exhausted as soon as I saw them. How will we communicate, I worried.

I could not understand the first Mulian who approached me. It was not like language training when words were spoken often in regular and predictable patterns. Later, I learned that the Mulians were just saying standard greetings and well wishes for the hydrophoria holiday. The proper response was just to repeat the words back, but our trainers did not teach us this, so we struggled to understand and quickly became tired, frustrated, and overwhelmed.

There was a ceremony and celebration that was mostly a crowd of strange rubbery bodies, foul offerings of salty and seaweedy food and drinks, and a long reverberating hum of noise that pounded at my head and made my tentacles bounce against my face and tap at my lips and nose in an unpleasant dance. Then we were guided into a domed building.

It sparkled white and light turquoise but was overlaid by a deep blue and black pattern, a mosaic design. Beneath the dome, we were led down a dark corridor. We had entered a cave. It was dark, but shimmering reflections of water and light danced on the coral lining around us.

I felt muffled, sleepy. A Mulian trainer, I think it was The Blue Farmer, took my hand in his rubbery mitt and led me forward. How far had we traveled? How far had we come? How many times had my arms pushed aside the water, stroking into the waves? I knew that the sea beneath the Seastead was many fathoms, but I'd never dove down more than thirty myself.

The Singer led Deuc away down a corridor and The Farmer led Neena and I down another.

Neena and I would room together.

When she took off her helmet, I saw her tears and knew she had been deeply affected by our descent. Something about the air and the pressure change made us sleepy and compliant. I was led into a dark room, and I sunk down into a soft surface that surrounded me with a feeling of peace and tranquility. I could not easily sleep for the dancing reflections on the surfaces around me. On the ceiling? On the floor? I watched for a long time torn between watching the patterns and falling asleep until strangely it occurred to me that my eyes had long been closed, but I could still see the patterns, tentacles, reflections of waves and light undulating across the ceiling, distinctly moving behind my eyelids. I became annoyed tossing in the bedding, which felt like it was made of the softest sand, but still loose and gritty. I wanted only the silence, calm, and peace inside my own head. I wanted only to sleep. Suddenly, the light and movement stopped. At last, I slept.

I awoke in a small room with slick wet walls and soft blue gleam under a blue light. It was like a dream of death. I felt glued to the bed I was in--a shell shape, half buried in its sandy covering and moved by waves. I had vague hallucinations and felt a tickling along my chin. I put my hands to my mouth and whiskered tendrils suctioned against my fingertips. I pulled them aside in horror and fascination. These were my tentacles. On my face. I slept again. When I woke up the soft tendrils were still there. My lips and mouth, once thin and wrinkled, felt full and wrinkled instead.

A smooth headed Mulian appeared in the doorway and then at my bedside. Adi (again the Mulian pronoun seemed most appropriate) had small tendrils around their mouth. It looked like a soft pink mustache. One day, I would kiss a tentacled mouth like this and discover a new sensation.

Adi poured a hot liquid into a small, ornate silver cup. Its rim was etched with Mulian swimmers. The drink was salty and spicy. I recognized it as the kelp-green liquid Abrador had given us on the Seastead. The liquid was intoxicating. *Mélange*, the Mulians called it.

Neena rose from another shell bed in the room and we both felt rejuvenated after drinking the mélange. It removed the pressure and fuzz from our minds.

When the Mulian left us, we began to explore. We walked out of the dark sleeping room and followed the light down the open hall. We did not dare open any doors, but at the end of our compartment was a cave with pool in its center lined by smooth green stones. There was a porthole in the wall of the cave looking out to the ocean. The water within the pool bubbled and frothed and a sweet scent rose from it.

Neena and I slipped off our clothes and into the water. I let it bubble up around my face. The water I was sitting in did not appear to have a floor just a seat and stones, but in the middle, there was just a darkening of the blue and it may have gone down further, how far I did not know.

"What did you think when you saw the city?" I asked Neena.

"It made me want to write," Neena said. "Alexandra was right. If she led me here, she was right to do so. I only wish she could have seen it."

As we sat in the tub, a small grey eye appeared at the porthole. The eye was surrounded by a deep grey. A humpbacked whale peered in at us. She frequented these depths. I was reminded again of how far underwater I had come as if an enormous creature had swallowed me.

The Seasteaders: Part Three

MU

~ 62 ~

THE SEASTEADERS: IN MU

In the morning, our language trainer Green Singer arrived. I was glad to see her, but she would not say more than a few words in our language. We were to speak only Mulian now. She brought us our first Mulian robes. They were long rubbery capes that fell below our feet and trailed behind us. They would protect us from the cold sea and cover our strange looking bodies. Cloaked in the rubbery draping we looked almost Mulian. Neena wore pink. My robe was deep purple. Deuc's was nearly black.

For many of the Mulians, the capes hid their soft mollusk feet. When I'd first seen the crowd of robed Mulians, I'd thought the robes were identical, but up close I could see the difference between them, Neena's robe had swirling patterns, mine looked like waves, and Deuc's looked like the night sky. Neena immediately put her robe on over her nakedness, and I don't think she wore any other clothes again for the rest of the time we were there.

"It's so *vahoma*[1]," she said, remembering the Mulian word for soft, a combination of breath--va--and water--homa.

The robe was soft and pliable but held its form. It felt like the same texture as the coins I had received, but thinner. It was, like all objects in Mu, a living thing with its own will.

Neena and I, testing the language with a small vocabulary and some discomfort, always spoke in short, simple sentences now. It had the effect of making us sound earnest and sage.

Long, winding complicated sentences like General Balor's speeches only had the effect of making him sound disconnected. I tried to remember this lesson, but I also found I soon began to miss being able to use unusual words and have long conversations. I missed the ease of understanding.

Soft was not quite the right word for the robes. Now we used the nearest word, one with the essence of the meaning we wanted. These simplifications made us sound quaint.

The robes were sleek against the skin. The underside of the robe was a little wet and malleable so that it was like wearing a coating of lotion. Our skin grew soft. Georgios, how I wanted to touch you with my newly soft skin. I did not want to return, however; I wanted to bring you to me. I could have asked for it. Maybe it could have been done, but it seemed the decision had been made. I had to explore Mu and you had to map the ocean.

I was not comfortable unclothed, and I always wore a short shift underneath my Mulian robe. Deuc hated the robes and would only wear them for formal Mulian gatherings, but usually he was shirtless with jeans on in a makeshift half robe he invented and wore like a kilt. The Mulians found his display of his under body scandalous. Because of this, some of the younger ones began to adopt Deuc's style. I wondered if the Mulians ever regretted our intrusion.

"It's hell to work in these things," Deuc said, although we were given separate gardening robes, which were shorter and rougher on the outside and of a paler color that matched the kelp-green crops. These robes were specially made after the harvest celebration and blessed to sow bountiful crops. Deuc only reliably wore his robe in the cooler months.

Once we were dressed, the trainer took us to get the things we needed to live in Mu and to show us to our gardens, which were told to plant immediately. Every Mulian grew their own food, and we would not be accepted into this community if we could not.

The quantity of things the Mulians deemed we needed astounded me. In addition to our gardening tools and supplies, they included a bronze tea service on a platter, an incense burner, a collection of vases, a broom, and various sizes of ornately decorated bottles filled with spices and salts. I had never had so many objects in my life and could not discern for the life of me why all of these were needed for a short stay in Mu. I grew suspicious and wary. My trainer went to one of the large dark caves and retrieved these collections for us. I imagined they came from a large storeroom. I was right about this. However, there were no manufacturers. Instead, the workers in the storerooms looked after the objects, cleaning, polishing, and mending any object that had lost their previous caretakers and finding the best new homes for them. In fact, these items had been made long ago, and we were receiving sets that had been used by ancestors who had moved on. The sets Neena and I received were similar but different. Hers was pink and blue. Mine was red and bronze.

Objects and caring for objects was a large part of Mulian culture. It was part of their purpose to care for what they had. The objects were treated like living beings with souls. We were expected to spend time each day polishing the items, to keep them in their proper places, and to use them with reverence and respect. There were punishments for losing or harming things.

Our cache of objects included our gardening tools: bronze trowels, a bucket, and a shovel with a bronze handle. These implements were retrieved from a storeroom, but then kept in the greenhouse. We were assigned chests there in which to keep our work robes and gardening tools.

"Later, I will take you to retrieve your seeds," The Blue Farmer said, in a reverent tone. "First, you must be received by the community. Return now to your home and I will come for you at sundown."

Neena and I looked at each other. Of course, we had not been paying attention and could not tell exactly where we were. After some time, it became easy to find our way. The city was arranged in quadrants. By observing the light and color, you could find your way. Although, the colors shifted quadrants with the seasons. When we arrived, our cave was located in the south end of the blue quadrant.

Neena and I often sat and talked in the bubbling pool within our cave to process new events and prepare ourselves for the next encounter. Once we had our objects, our next initiation into Mu was to meet the Mulian council.

We put on our robes. The hardest part was arranging our hair. The Mulians, of course, did not have hair. There were no brushes or gels to contain locks and wisps, but they did have clasps for the robes and to restrain their tendrils; so, we used those. Not long after we arrived, Neena found the tools to shave her head. Her hair, after that, grew in slowly, fine and pale green. We decided it was a result of living in the *homa* of Mu--the light, breathable liquid that the Mu lived in--faintly sweet and not salty. The homa also had a soft scent to it that changed with the seasons. At hydrophoria, in the summer, it was permeated by a damp lavender scent.

I was reluctant to give up my hair and taking note of what happened to Neena's head made me more so, although her shaven look did, along with her robes, give her an elegant and youthful appearance. Instead, I kept my hair and let it grow and tangle within my tentacles. By the end of my time in Mu, I had long dreadlocks that began to look like sleek tentacles and then chains of barnacles as those attached to us, a sign of respect and our Mulian integration. By then, many aspects of my appearance had changed.

Green Singer came to lead us to the council. We stopped and got Deuc from the lavender sector. I was relieved to see he was wearing his robe and had his long hair pinned back with a shell.

We walked past the living stones underground and up a ramp to the lawn around the coliseum. It had low walls and a sunken center. There were bells chiming and a large group of Mulians--in all their sizes, blue, green, and lavender shades, and sea-creature shapes--assembled on the open lawn before the coliseum. This was our first Mulian concert. Green Singer took us out among the Mu. They surrounded us on their pale blue-green field, standing on a hillock with their concert encircling us.

From my early days in Mu, what I remember most is music. My hearing was impaired when I first got there. My ears felt constantly plugged and the pressure would not relieve. It wasn't until I'd been there six months that I noticed one day while harvesting kelp that I could hear with crispness that I'd been lacking, and I cried with joy and relief. The Mulians farming nearby wondered at this strangeness. They, who did not cry, came and tasted my tears with their tentacles, which made me cry harder at my alienation, at being surrounded by odd creatures, at being separated from my loved ones. I think the event earned me some respect though among the Mu. I, with my ability to create sea-tears, became in their minds more of a sea creature after that. It was one of many times I was overwhelmed by my experience in Mu.

However, when they first brought me to the park to hear their strange instruments, sound still had that flat, muffled quality that reminded me of having earplugs in and of being underwater. It felt remote. They sang us welcome.

I looked at Deuc in his long, strange robe and thought of him shirtless on stage at Merops with his deep underwater voice layered beneath the electronics.

"I wanted to be taken seriously," he told me later, explaining why he had dressed in the Mulian style at that time and rarely after. "Now, I don't care. Clothes are tools, not art. They either keep us at the right temperature, protect us, or help us tell a story."

In Mu, there was no stage with a band of performers around it, however. Everyone performed. We were all part of the music. There was no celebrity. We worshipped each other. The concert took place in an open space with more light reflected from the water above the dome, casting waves of light down upon us. Mulians sang and, I later noticed, added sounds with tiny instruments of clacking shells, beads upon their garments and metal clasps. I did not notice these details at my first Mulian concert. I stared up at the dome and looked at the strange beings around me uncertainly. A heavenly music emanated without a clear source. It was beautiful and disorienting and it went on and on. As it did so my anxiety grew. The music was no longer beautiful, but a menace. I did not know when it would stop. I did not know when I would have a chance, to eat, to drink, to rest, to be alone as I so often needed to be in my early days in Mu. Later, when I acclimated, I could stay for hours at these concerts and participate. The first time, however, I was lost without time or perception of the culture. It was torturous in a way that now I cannot fathom. I do not even understand myself how I could have hated it so much then and loved it so much later. How we can change in ways unfathomable to ourselves. Praise water!

Light emanated from the music. There was light when the Mulians spoke. When they whispered in the dark, they betrayed themselves with light. We topsiders (as the Mulians called those who lived above the ocean) were the only ones who could hide in the dark. The Mulians were a community. We were outside of it, but only because of our lack of understanding.

Beside me, Deuc and Neena were also uncomfortable. When the Mulians finally finished with their welcome song, we topsiders were exhausted. Abrador lead us onto a hill to meet the Mulian Council.

The Council of Thirty-Three stood in a circle, covered in barnacles and tentacles, their faces indistinguishable to us that first time. They spoke, as one, in unison. We felt them speak.

"We know your people are on the brink. The waters have turned against them, and they have turned against each other. We know what this is like, to face extinction and to be afraid. We think we can help by offering a learning."

"Yes, that's why we are here," I said.

"It will take time," Abrador said.

"How long?" Deuc asked.

"Two years," said Abrador.

"No," I said.

"No," Deuc said. "You never told us our visit would be so long."

"But you knew this," Abrador said to me, and I realized that I had known in a way. I had said goodbye as if I'd known and if I hadn't imagined it Georgios had known our separation would last years, too.

"There are only 200 Mulians remaining," the council spoke into us again. "We have only the minimum to repopulate the world, a small number easily hidden, but ready to repopulate the world should humankind fail. But we would rather not take to the surface again. We are content here. We would rather you succeed, and we stay beneath the ocean."

"It will take time," Abrador repeated.

I knew in my heart that I had understood this all along, but I thought anxiously: They've taken me prisoner. Until I can speak their language, it is not safe for me to be free. I can never leave until I pass this test. I don't know if I can ever learn the language. They speak mind to mind. What if I cannot learn? They speak in bubbles, pockets of air. They speak in sounds like waves, so long underwater; all the tones are hushed, except for the deep, grunting breaths of air. I can hardly hear. How can I understand them?

They wanted us to learn their ways. They wanted to help our species, but we had to know them to do so.

I watched Deuc watching everything, calculating what we could take back to the Riptiders once the time--two years--had passed. Would it be worthwhile?

"The flutes," Abrador said, he meant the column of freshwater we'd swum down from the surface to the deep dark sea and finally the homa domes of Mu . "They don't last forever. We can't make them at a whim. We must work now. The flute will go and then, in two years' time or so, it will return."

"You are going to send us back?" I asked. I wanted to extract a promise, but Abrador turned from me.

For the first time, it occurred to me that I could die down here in this foreign land of Mu.

"Can I send word back?" I asked. "To Georgios."

"There is no way to send words, but we can send song," Abrador said.

I would learn, as soon as possible how to sing in Mulian. I would send back songs so Georgios would know I would be longer than we had thought, but that I would return.

When we had agreed to stay, I took Deuc aside.

"If I die here, Deuc," I said. "You make sure they send my body home. Promise. I want to know I will return to the air and land."

I told it to Neena too, but she seemed unconcerned. She was comfortable here. For this, I trusted Deuc. He understood my attachment to the Earth above.

While I remained in Mu there were many things I missed: foods, smells, textures, tastes. It wasn't only Georgios. But when I look back at my time in Mu, it seems I thought only of Georgios and that everything I did was so that I could return to him.

~ 63 ~

THE SEASTEADERS: MULIAN LOVE

I could not rest until I learned Mulian song, sang it to the messenger, and knew that my thoughts had been carried to Georgios.

Fortunately, the messenger was close by. She was Varuna the Whale whose eye had greeted us that first day and who frequently lingered outside our quarters. I knew Varuna from the Seastead as well. She had surfaced there in the flute of clear water out of reach of the rust sea and the rust sharks. When I grew skilled enough, I could sing directly to Varuna mind to mind, but in those early days in Mu I was anxious. I needed to be sure of some tie to Georgios, some way to communicate with him.

We were told not to leave Mu proper, but I have never been obedient. I have always had my secret getaways: the marsh, my room, the market, Merops. I must have space to get away where my mind can roam free with its plans. Mu had many crevices, but none had that forbidden feel which drives me. The Mulians told me I could not go outside and so that was where I wanted to go. I had many havens in Mu. I loved to spend time in the wet gardens. I loved the temple and the lawn outside the coliseum. Perhaps, I wanted to swim in the sea outside the safety of the Mulian *homa*, because I spent so much time looking up into the lavender rimmed inky eye of Varuna the Whale. There looked to be wisdom in the deep blue ridges of her face.

When I felt sure and Green Singer agreed, that my song could be sung well enough for Varuna to translate, I put on the helmet again and slipped down through the water pool portal in my room out of the sweet homa and into the salty sea of the deepest ocean. My body felt free my limbs flowing behind me like the tentacles of a jellyfish. Varuna, who loomed so large outside of my translucent roof, was now further away than I had expected. She swam in the depths outside, encircling the core of Mu and I had to swim through the open translucent space. I pressed my hands against the field and slowly entered the murk. I was deep below, and I felt the pressure around me, as I had not before in Mu. It was not unbearable, but the salt of the sea felt rough after the softness of the homa. I was becoming more Mulian already than I realized. I swam to the whale and lashed tails and fins brushed my bare skin in the dark. Still, I felt relaxed and at ease, as always when I went away on my own. I went out to the whale, and I touched her ridges. She was large but welcoming. A fin spun the wrong way in my direction could end me, but I felt safe beside her bulk.

I called to Varuna. I felt we understood each other, both of us at peace in the deep sea. I did not have to struggle to communicate, to grow food, or worry I would offend her. I went close to her, and I sang to her of my longing. I hoped Georgios would understand enough Mulian to know that I would be away for longer than I had expected but that I loved him more than ever and would return. Would he understand that from the thrumming of a strange whale appearing alongside the Seastead? It seemed unlikely, but Varuna's clear eye reassured me.

I continued to go outside into the sea and sing my messages directly to Varuna. The more I went outside though the more aware I became of the dangers. It seemed worth the risk to get away. I knew of the electric eels, the sharp teeth in the dark, the lashes of leathery, ridged flails with poisonous darts. There were also currents that could change and make it difficult to return through the barrier. I knew of these dangers, and I came back sometimes with poisons in my system, bites, or electric scars. Usually, Varuna protected me.

Abrador warned me of other dangers.

"You should not venture out," he said.

I was not aware he had known of my travels. He could tell I was not dissuaded.

"At least do not go without a companion from Mu," he said. "There are other tribes of peoples, other Mulian enclaves. They will drain your iron blood and use it as medicine. They do not care about you."

Of course, this caught my attention and made me wary and fearful, but it did not stop me. I could not take another Mulian with me always; this would defeat my need for isolation. The longer I stayed in Mu, the more cautious I became and the less frequently I ventured out. As it grew colder below and the lavender and sun scent faded, I could commune with Varuna directly while sitting in the pool in my room and staring out at her big eye. I no longer needed to go out and I would not risk it.

Munan. It was in those first months that I learned the Mulian word for lover. *Munan.*

The Mulians intrigued me, but I did not see them as partners. My thoughts were too much with the surface, with all the plans for how we might survive the rising Rust Sea. It was entirely possible, I often felt, for me to overcome the differences between our bodies. There was always something sensual about them. They were made up of so many textures and unusual ridges and lumps. However, I could not bridge the gaps between our minds. I thought I needed that connection to the sky, the wind, the trees, and the flowers: surface world things. I sang songs to Georgios every day and sent them to him via Varuna the humpback whale, but at night I began to talk to Deuc.

"I'm learning about the music," he said.

He talked endlessly about the new rhythms and harmonies he was learning and what they meant. We wore the long robes with nothing underneath. I thought about Deuc's "nothing underneath" more than I wanted to. Often.

We grew close. I didn't notice that he never talked about himself: his family or friends. He never asked about me. I noticed this but didn't much care. In Mu, all my plans seemed far away and on hold.

Our encounters began in a chaste fashion, stroking hands and exchanging soft kisses. I did not imagine this tenderness had been his style at Merops. I did not think of Georgios or feel guilty about in these moments. I was lonely and I felt this touch was necessary to my peace of mind, my sanity. I envied Deuc's easy way among the Mulians and how he kept to his own habits and made new ones. Whereas I felt the Mulians were dragging myself underwater, forever. I was subsumed by their ways. At times, working in the garden, learning their crafts, I gave in and let go. At other times, when I could not find Varuna the Whale to send my songs to Georgios, I resisted. With Deuc, singing music from the surface and doing things of which the Mulians would have disapproved, I rebelled. In my heart, I knew, I could not be as I once was. I clung to Deuc as if he were shore. He was essential to my transition.

We were so different, Deuc and I. He was more moved by the arts and had a carefree attitude whereas I was interested in structure and wanted to plan each move. He was fiercely independent, quiet in an insular way I sought to penetrate, but could not. He was more often silent. I wanted to speak about everything. I missed Georgios, who loved to talk through ideas, too. Yet, I was adaptable in Mu. It was necessary. We each saw our way as an asset and the other's way as weakness. However, when Deuc and I were together, I began to have fantasies that I could become more like him, that I could be a partner to him and adopt his ways and be well. We would have fun together.

I have always been like this. I want to live out many lives. I see the threads of each of them. I am ready to join any one at any point. I saw this one life held out to me and, of course, I wanted to pick it up. In many ways, I wish I were a ratfin. Their lives are short so they may rapidly move on to the next life and see what awaits. I missed In-fin, who I had left with Georgios. I'd be satisfied in any life; so, I have often thought. For these few months, I saw my life with Deuc unfolding before me and I wanted to fashion it into a fine garment and wrap it around me.

Hear me on the shores of the issue. *Munan.* Deuc and I were lovers. To let someone come so close to you, to bond their life with yours, and create a connection between bodies — it is an obvious thing, and a dangerous one. Obvious, because we are all connected to everyone in this way. Dangerous, because most of the time we do not imagine it, but sex breaks that spell. Suddenly the thread is visible. Through my life, I have learned to follow my intuition and to devise which feelings indicate a path to tread and which ones to avoid. Seeing Deuc, I felt guilty. I was stealing a life path that was not mine. Neena knew when I spent the nights away from our cave or snuck in late.

"I don't think much of Deuc," she said, and in her Neena way made this sound as directed, but non-critical as possible. "I don't trust his intentions."

I struggled not to be defensive. A bad sign, I knew. "It was a brave thing for anyone to come down here."

"Sure, that, but it's a bit of an escape, regardless. Don't forget he sold us out to the pirates."

One night though, I came back and awoke to find Neena and all of her things gone.

When we met in the garden, I asked her where she'd gone.

"I've moved in with Haya and Tubal in the green quadrant," Neena said. "You should stop by and see the place."

Tubal worked in the object room restoring and caring for the metal pieces. The Mulians did not manufacture anything but cared for what they had. Haya worked on the friezes and murals that decorated the Mulian caverns. They had larger quarters, finely decorated, in the green quarter.

This time Neena was the one who looked sheepish and sounded defensive. She'd taken two Mulians as partners, joined their household, become part of a *munanhoma*. Tubal and Haya were respected artisans. Maybe in La Merde, if there had not been war, I would have found it odd in that society. On the Seastead, no one would have thought much of it. Here in Mu, we were all outside of the usual tenets of society. It made sense. Why should Neena be alone?

I was hurt that she'd left me, but relieved too. Our garden was becoming lush, our Mulian kelp was growing thick and high. We were melding into Mulian society. It was good to see Neena happy and it kept her from saying more about me and Deuc.

~ 64 ~

THE SEASTEADERS: EGGS AND SKIN

The Mulians have many celebration nights, and Deuc and I were together on one of these in the darkest, coldest time of year, when it felt too cold to venture out into the sea, and there was a crispness and a frosted tang even to the warm *homa.* We were drinking an intoxicating Mulian mélange, their word for tea, and Deuc began to tell me his father's history. Balor's soldiers took the island Marshall was on, Corvo, and he was made to join them. He killed, but he was smart, and he saw a way to stop killing.

"I gave Balor the idea," Deuc confessed. "I said we should watch the Iron Bloods. He just wanted to get to La Merde. He thought he had relatives there. Some of the soldiers were friendly to me in town because of this. They gave me the contact with the Riptiders and I told them about the Seastead."

"You gave them the coordinates."

He nodded. I took a drink and digested this. I envisioned the Seastead overrun with Balor's men: Merl, Timbol, Georgios, and Desiree would all be killed or enslaved.

"So everyone we love up there is dead."

He shook his head. "I don't think so. I told him there was nothing worth taking out there, just a rusting hulk that wouldn't last. That you had some kind of serum, but it was faulty."

"Faulty."

"See, I told him the truth."

"You don't think Balor will have to see for himself?" Of course, he would.

"There are better places. There are legends that attract his curiosity: there's Noronha, the island of ascension, and Hiranya, the island of the sun. There are rumors of islands made of gold and of vast stretches of clear seas. Those will capture his imagination more than a pile of rust and some people he already let go. He'll seek those first."

"You don't think much of our Seastead."

"It isn't much. I know you have these hopes for it and ideas. But really, it's rusting metal, soon to sink like everything else. If we make it back up, we'll have to join the Riptiders on Elathe, if they'll have us."

"You're wrong," I said, speaking boldly in a way I hadn't to Deuc before. I sounded like the woman who had planned the Seastead again, not a Mulian farmer. "We have plans for a society and that's much harder than most people think. It isn't gold or mahogany or glory. It is a lot of dull meetings trying to get people to agree and communicate, but it's what can come of all that planning and meeting and organization and lists, see. It's like prayers. They seem like meaningless ritual, until they are answered. It just doesn't happen fast. You have to be patient."

I was talking to myself. When I looked up, Deuc was speaking also to himself. He was talking about his time on Elathe about the wooden planks, towers, and turrets. Our conversation had become a forked river.

"I told him a lot of things, not all the truth. On Corvo, he killed my sister. I don't wish him well. You would have thought he would remember that."

I caught the tail end of his diatribe.

"I'm sorry about your sister. Praise water. People only remember what they want to."

"Praise water," Deuc said, and he rarely did offer praise.

I understood what Deuc had done, his further betrayal, and what he had said. We spent the night together, but it was our last. In the morning, my mind clear, I knew I was done with him, repulsed by my weakness and for needing him to help me adjust to the strangeness of this Mu. Whatever intoxicating pheromones I breathed off Deuc's body had worn off. The sheen of him was scraped off my fantasy. I remembered that Deuc was here reporting for the Riptiders.

I gave Varuna the Whale a song for Georgios to warn him of Deuc's betrayal--a sad and warring song. There are no wind instruments, drums, or trumpets to convey the march forth of General Balor and send Georgios a proper warning. In whale song, war only sounds arrhythmic and desperate. I hoped Georgios understood.

I received a soothing reply. It was the first and last time I heard from Georgios in Mu. Varuna sang me the notes I have told her mean Georgios, my surface love. I knew it was a response to my song because I heard my notes repeated in it. I was comforted, but I had to be. There was nothing I could do except demand that the Mulians find a way to return me earlier. We were waiting for the return of the freshwater flute that could carry us to the surface. Perhaps, there was another way if I insisted. But what would that accomplish? I had to discover all I could about the Mulians. I could not go back to Georgios unchanged. I had to learn enough to be worthy of him so that we could never be parted again.

I imagined what I would do if I were on the surface and heard that General Balor could be approaching. I realized I would not be so alarmed. Balor had always been a possibility. Deuc's betrayal might hasten it, or not. Deuc was right. What does Balor want with a hunk of rusted metal? He wanted land. The Seastead would be a last resort for him. It was only the fellowships and actions of Neena, Georgios, Merl, Timbol, Desiree, and I that made the Seastead desirable.

At first, I missed Deuc's kisses and mourned them and his company, but my interest in him or any distraction waned. Deuc, Neena, and I grew fatter and sleeker like seals on the fruits of our own harvest and in the clean kelp-scented environment. Deuc and Neena made peace and began to compose music together. Deuc played the lute and Mulian instruments. Neena wrote the lyrics. For the first six months, we all looked fabulous. Soon, I felt gorgeous, plump, and soft. I wished Georgios could see me. After six months, I had acclimated to Mu.

I understood Mulian and felt comfortable. What a difference words made. Deuc and Neena took to playing at Mulian concerts and with a small band of musician artisans. I visited Neena sometimes in the green land in her new cave with Tubal and Haya. Their cave had many more objects and a more settled feel than mine. It was truly Mulian. We surfacers spent less time together than we had the first six months. Not knowing what Deuc was doing made me somewhat nervous. Was he seeing things I was missing? But I was glad to be free of him.

I was with the Mu for about nine months before I was allowed to see the room where the new Mu waited. The homa was beginning to become warm again and there was the faintest hint of lavender in the liquid around us. The rookery where the new Mu slept was deep underground by a hot spring rising from within the earth. It had a nutritious mineral smell like rising bread. It was a warm incubator where the Mu lay their young. I thought of the young as eggs, but this was not quite right. The Mulians called them Mua, which meant simply new Mu. I wished Timbol was with me to better help me understand the physiology. The rookery had a sleek gold coating and barnacles that rose from the floor like stalagmites with translucent pearl-shaped dome tops. Inside I could see moving gelatinous green, blue, and lavender threads. As they grew, they congealed and shrank, and they became gold coins embossed with tentacles stacked on the sides of the room.

"The Mua await the day when humanity fails and they can repopulate," Abrador said. "Some say it would be in our best interest to watch you fail. Some even say that we should hasten it. But I could not doom another civilization to our fate. It is cruel to be few and alone."

"You would rather help us," I said.

"So, it seems," he said. "We are ready to repopulate the earth, but it is not our desire to take over the world or to return to the surface. We have been hidden so long and have experienced peace. To return to the surface would be to accept responsibility, to intermingle and to admit, that this time, there is nothing in reserve. We 200 are all who are left. It is to mix and be changed and to possibly subject Mulians to war and passions again. It is to admit the end of our utopia in a new beginning."

In the eggs, I saw the Mulians' secret selves. I saw how fragile they were with those threadlike tentacles encased in gelatinous discs and how near to extinction. Still, it was not likely to happen, if ever, for hundreds of years, but the Mulians know, they can easily imagine, they can empathize with a species on the brink of survival.

"It is not your time, Abrador," I said.

He was easy to convince, as he did not want it to be time for the Mulians, yet.

"Then, if it not our time, you must *hovana*," he said.

I did not really understand the word, possibly some combination of transcendence and transformation, but it frightened me.

"I like myself as I am," I said.

"I like you, too. You misunderstand. *Hovana* does not mean to lose."

But his words, his careful words, did not calm me.

No long after this, I began to eat true Mulian mélange, which was thicker and savory and more than tea.

We had all avoided the slick food ever since we'd realized what it was made of: the skin the Mulians shed, cured and spiced. We'd had it on the first night but had not known what it was although it reminded me of the food Professor Belo had served us when she first brought the Seasteaders together at her party. If I had known what it was--peeled skin and the cells of immortality--I could not have imbibed it. According to legend, those who eat the skin become immortal. Yet, the Mulians held funerals.

"Those are the ones who choose to end," Abrador said. "The skin sheds as the spirit overtakes it and grows. The younger ones eat it. It is filled with a kind of oil that allows for immortality, secretions that cause longevity. It becomes thinner and thinner--the body, the skin, the corporeal self, until it dissipates.

One night the Mulian Council invited us to a special banquet. It was the hydrophoria feast almost a year to the day we had arrived.

"It's time for you to eat our food," Abrador said.

Of course, I ate their food, although I grew my own. He meant their skin.

Only Deuc refused. "I grow enough food," he said. He would stick to his own crops. He was not afraid of offending the Mu. He never was.

They invited me to feast, and it felt normal to eat the soup and it tasted so good, thick, oily, and spiced like a kelp curry. By now, I was used to the rubbery texture. The stewed mélange was the fattiest substance the Mulians ate. It was crisp and delicious. As a soup or tea, it left a thick oily smudge at the bottom of a cup or bowl and in a ring around the inside of the gold bowls and cups which then had to be carefully polished. Neena ate of it too, of course, but for her, I think, although she did not say, it was less of a change. I noticed that Abrador did not make a point of asking her to eat. There was a glow about her now and a lavender cast to her skin. I think she had been eating her Mulian partners' mélange for some time.

I was in the garden one afternoon, when I first became disturbed by the effect. I bent down and saw a splotch upon my skin, blight, like rust. After a while, I noticed changes to my skin, splotches of red rust color and hardness to the coating. My hair grew together and clumped. It was rusty and wiry. Neena looked different too, more traditionally Mulian, but also mottled with red. We, with our Iron Blood, began to rust.

"Did you know this would happen?" I asked Abrador.

"It's something different about your blood. We didn't know. Not exactly."

I began to cry, and my tears had a rust tint. They were light pink pearls of water. The tears always moved the Mulians to take pity on us surfacers.

"Come with me to the rookery. There's the first sign," he said.

We walked to the warm Mua cave, that hot sulphuric, yeasty room, where the eggs waited. His tentacles pointed towards the domed roof. I stared for the longest time uncomprehending. Abrador only waited for me to make the connection on my own. I heard the sound first a gentle plink, plink, plink. In the top, there was a pinprick of blue light, and it was dripping fresh water.

It was the beginning of our flute home.

"It's returning," he said. "And so will you in time."

We had about another year in Mu, but from this day, our return would be less than half the time we had already been away. I still remembered Georgios and loved him. From this day, my thoughts turned to home. Never, in my entire time in Mu did I think about staying. How different would my life had been if I had lived in that moment and settled among the people around me as Neena had? But I, I was always thinking of what I had left, and then of my return. In this regard, I was no help to the Mulians at all. I was not present.

At that time, as I began to change my skin, Abrador, was no help to me. I was horrified to see my way home now, horrified to see my rusting Mulian shedding, webbing hands. Now when I felt most monstrous, I began to face my return. How could I go home to Georgios like this?

~ 65 ~

THE SEASTEADERS: THE RUINS

Now that I had seen that pinprick of light that promised my way home, I was obsessed with thoughts of return. Yet, there were many months until the flute would be large enough to transport us upward. We could not go in the bitterest cold either. We had to wait for the flute to form and the seas to warm.

We surfacers had gained comfort within our Mulian routines. We lived as the Mu lived growing our food, caring for our objects, and participating in music and ceremonies. The time would pass slowly now, too slowly, I thought.

Neena and I began to plan a trip out of Mu--not to the surface but to see more of Mulian society and the other Mulian enclaves. I had been out only on occasion to commune with Varuna but had stopped once I could rely on telepathy. Neena, however, had never been outside the confines of Mu into the sea. We wanted to see the ruins of the old civilization. The Mulians often spoke about Mount Meru.

Tubal and Haya had told Neena there was a festival when the enclaves gathered and made a processional to the ruins at Meru.

"They said they would take me then," she said.

"But doesn't that happen only once a decade?" I asked. The Mulians had a complicated calendar of festivals and rituals that I barely understood. "We'll be long gone by then."

"So, let's go now, just you and me." She wanted an adventure with me like when we had first arrived and met Varuna. I wanted that too.

Now that I could envision my homecoming, I was reluctant to leave and endure danger once again. I knew that it was dangerous in the sea among the predators outside of the Mulian dome. Still, there was a long time to wait until the water flute would be ready for our return and I wanted the time to pass quickly. I could not spend all my days waiting and thinking of Georgios. I found myself going to bed earlier and earlier, hurrying the days on.

The journey with Neena would provide a distraction. We intended to be gone many days. We'd swim through the ocean and go to the next Mulian enclave.

"Don't make the trip," Abrador said. "It's ill-advised."

In typical Mulian fashion, however, he was not convincing, and we knew we could do as we liked, make our own mistakes. We would not be dissuaded. Neena wanted some adventure, and we would never be in Mu again. This was our chance.

Neena came to stay with me as she had done those first weeks. We sat in the whirling, bubbling bathing pool together. We added some scented salts to it so that a lavender steam grew thick in the cave and watched the eye of Varuna the Whale through the dome. Then we put on our helmets, let the suckers attach to our faces, neck, and shoulders and dove down and swam out into the sea.

It was still quite cold and the *homa* was crisp and sweet reminding me of the inside of an apple. It made me tear up thinking of that surface fruit. The ocean was colder. I hated the chill and the openness and regretted being outside immediately, but I could hear Neena beside me. Our telepathic communication was strong.

Happy to be out with you. Adventuring!

She was joyous. She seemed much younger and freer than when we had first met. Her grief, although always with her, was less heavy upon her these days. She could remember Belo and smile. She could forget Belo at times as she enjoyed life without the consequence of guilt.

Varuna accompanied us through the ocean part of the way, but she did not like to stray from her grounds between Mu and the Seastead. We ventured West toward the other enclaves and the ruins at Mount Meru.

We managed to avoid sea predators. The other Mulian enclaves treated us kindly, but suspiciously. Mulians were not travelers, and they did not appreciate the concept. Travelers could not grow their own food or care properly for their objects. We had nothing with us.

Emptiness, the Mulians said. That's how our concept of traveling translated. Neena explained that her partners were caring for her objects while she was away. I had asked Deuc to take care of mine, but I could not imagine that he would place a high priority on polishing my tea set while I was gone. He never adopted or understood the Mulian view that those objects had souls.

The Mulians in the other enclaves treated us kindlier when we proved we could sing their songs, but they were difficult to understand and I realized what an effort the Mulians in our enclave made to slow their speech so that we could understand them even now after we had lived with them more than a year.

We made our way to the gold and silver pillared enclave closest to the dome, where we interrupted a festival of warming and fertility. The Mulians there were the most welcoming of any we had encountered. They were all drunk on a kind of mélange and soon got us intoxicated as well. They offered us strips of their mélange and sang louder when we accepted them. They were crisper, sweeter, and oilier than any other mélange we'd had. The strips dripped a viscous honey-like liquid.

Everyone was playing an instrument of some sort: bells, lyres, small drums or seashell castanets. The Mulian singers made slow liquid caroling sounds. They were singing of the past and the future, a beautiful, marvelous mix of images that became indistinguishable to us. The Mulians at this event moved in unusual ways, a kind of dancing. They shed their robes and displayed the barnacles and shells embedded in their skins. Tentacles and fins, thin and fine, thick and lumped, were all outstretched.

It was a fertility rite, one of the few times the Mulians copulated without an intent to produce eggs. I wondered if something similar was being celebrated back at our home and how Deuc would handle it. Well. He would handle it well, I imagined. Would Neena be sad she had not been there with her partners? She did not look sad now.

I wound up in a nook with a Mulian covered mostly with soft blue feathery tentacles and a dart-shaped tail. I observed how much my appearance had changed, but then I stopped observing for once and just enjoyed touch and telepathic communication. When the mélange wore off in the morning, I wound myself into those feathery tentacles again, just to prove to myself that it had not been a mistake.

The blue Mulian stayed with me.

"I can show you to the ruins," they said.

I found Neena. She only nodded at our feathery blue guide. I did not observe how she had spent the night. The last I knew was of everyone dancing with tentacles intertwined. Neena was never inclined to be judgmental and even less so now. We headed outside the enclave down a pebbled path, a carefully constructed shining path made by the Mulians for ceremonial purposes. When we could see the ruins ahead of us, pillars stuck into the side of a craggy underwater mountain flecked with gold. My blue tailed Mulian lover left us there.

"We Mu only go to the ruins at Meru, only for the ceremony," they said. "It is better not to disturb the *illisants*."

"Illisants?" I asked Neena.

"Ghosts," she said. "My partners explained to me. The gold mountain, Meru, is where the ghosts live. It's where souls, who are not Mulian, wait to be reborn in the new Mu. The illisants wait in the objects that the Mulians tend."

We found Professor Belo's ghost, there. I remembered placing the Mulian coin, the Mua in her mouth. We did not see her, but she spoke to us. It nearly broke Neena's heart again.

"I made the water flute for you, in the Seastead, with that coin," she said.

I listened for my grandmother among the voices of the ghosts.

"Her blood was drained before her sea-fairing. She could not arrive here," Belo said.

It was another reason to abhor Balor. It stoked my hatred that he had taken grandmother from me again.

It drained Neena and I to meet with these ghosts and hear their tales of the afterlife.

"I see why the Mulians undertake this only with support, when they all go together," I said. "I see why Abrador warned us away from here. I don't like to feel so much hate and anger for my father, for the soldiers, for the Riptiders, and even Deuc. What will I do with it? It's so hard to tamp it down once rage rises within."

"That's war," Neena said. "Let it go."

It was easy to say.

We climbed to the pinnacle and looked down over Mulian society. There were twelve domes and glittering paths between them. Where we came from was the furthest East. There were many domes we had not entered. Looking up, real or imagined, we could almost see sunlight above coming from the surface.

We still had our necks craned back staring into the ocean when Neena said, "I'm not going back. I'm staying."

I laughed at first, not realizing she was serious, imaging she meant the ruins and then it dawned on me, she meant she would stay in Mu.

"Is it because of Belo?" I asked.

"No," she said. "I made my decision earlier. I want to live with Tubal and Haya. You can take the knowledge back. I'll stay here."

"But we'll need you." I meant on the Seastead where we all had our roles.

"It will be different," she said. "Besides, you never needed me. I was always extra, an aside to Alexandra's plan. I want to stay here with Alexandra and my new partners."

"You still miss her?"

"I miss her more. Every day there is something I could have shared with her. My sadness grows, but my grief lessens. I can handle it better, even as the tragedy becomes greater, because I see all the times together we have lost," Neena said.

"That makes sense."

"So, you agree? You won't fight me this time?" she asked, and I understood why she had wanted to make this journey with me. She still remembered how I made her leave the ferry dock at La Merde. She worried I would somehow be able to convince her to return.

"No, of course not, if the Mulians will let you, you can stay and with my acceptance. I won't try to sway you."

"The Mulians have already agreed," she said. "Look at me, Nata."

I looked at her carefully and noted her pliable lavender skin and clinging barnacles. She looked Mulian.

"I see. You've changed. Yes, stay. I won't try to convince you otherwise," I said.

"Good," she said. "Because you can be very convincing."

"I still have to go back," I said, imagining how I must look, Mulian and oceanic but also rusting and sloughing because of my Iron Blood.

"Nata," Neena said. "I believe you will. Listen. I've never been sorry I came with you to the Seastead."

Thank you. Love you. Appreciate you. She said telepathically. It struck me that those were the most important words, always the ones I had needed to hear. The ones I needed to say before I left everyone behind. Thank you. Love you. Appreciate you.

Neena and I returned to Mu through the dark cold waters. We watched the predators carefully and fended off any that came too near. Varuna greeted us when we arrived far enough East.

As soon as we returned, I went to the rookery to see the flute. It had opened wider and was the size of a fist.

I began to count the days and I went often to watch the progress of the water flute. Sometimes it seemed big enough I could slip my hips through, and other times shrunken so that it would pinch my waist, but still it grew. I calculated that it would be done earlier than they had told us. I pressed Abrador to tell me it was ready.

Finally, he said, "It will be ready soon...your flute home."

"Deuc and I can go now."

"If you want," he said. "Let us have a farewell ceremony. We have begun the preparations."

"Of course," I said. "We will miss you."

At the time, I wasn't sure I would. My thoughts were all for the surface and centered on Georgios. I longed for him now just as I had on the day I left, although I realized that much of what I had left of him and of my love was only memory.

~ 66 ~

THE SEASTEADERS: FAREWELL

I imagine if I had not eaten the mélange or if my blood had been different, I would have remained beautiful and young in Mu. I could have changed my life for Deuc. I could have been a different person. It cannot be, of course, but I do love to imagine how Deuc and I would have stayed together in Mu. I would have taken up an instrument too, a Mulian flute, and we would have played together in the green, purple, and blue anemone covered Mulian fields. Imagine this life of contentment and love so different from the life I actually lived. This was a stream I did not follow.

Or imagine, Deuc and I, we could have gone to the surface together and then presented our finding about the Mulians to the Riptiders. Would they have taken us in as heroes or merely more useful slaves? Would we have known the difference? Could we have convinced ourselves otherwise, adapted to servitude so completely that we did not know differently? We would have been captives certainly and, in some way, I could have lived with that, rested with the Riptiders, without any responsibility and lived a simple life on someone else's craft that someone else was steering. It even seemed noble to me to do so rather than to always struggle selfishly after my own idea of perfection. Who was I to say what was best? But I did not let this tide pull me along either, and this outcome could not have been, because my blood would not let it be.

I ate the mélange and it changed me. It turned my skin to rust and wrinkles. With my monstrous visage, life with Deuc no longer seemed an option. I had chosen to eat the skin and be more of the Mu, and he had not. Deuc had not changed. Although he seemed more comfortable among the Mu than I, and he had made friends among the musicians, there was no question of him staying underwater.

When my skin changed, Deuc didn't treat me much differently, but he was spending more time with the Mulians. He was most often on the field trying out new rhythms and instruments with the younger Mu. Then, when I began to think more about going home, when it preoccupied my thoughts, I spent more time with Deuc. This time, there was nothing romantic. We were returning to the surface, and we were the only ones who shared this experience and that desire.

"Sometimes, I think, I wouldn't be sad to stay here, but then I remember," Deuc would say, "Sky, birds, wind, apples..." and he would go on and on like that listing all the things he missed from home until I joined him and added to his list.

"Berries, wood, velvet, ratfin...I miss In-fin." I told him about my life in the marshes of Salish Island. I told him about the feasts my mother prepared for us.

Neena joined us too, but not so often and she was silent.

"Would you ever stay?" I asked Deuc.

"Praise the mountaintop, no. Never. I know where I belong. This place, Mu, it doesn't make sense to me. It's so far underwater. It's too small and confined. Besides they don't want me."

It was true, the Mulians would not let him stay unless he ate mélange, and he would not. They did not want him to be alone. They did not want him to try to mate with their young Mu. Only, I think, because it would not work, and they needed the eggs. It was practical, not prejudicial.

"Would you?"

I was honest. "No, I got what I came for: understanding. I wanted to do this, but I'm for the surface."

"You want to be with Georgios."

"If he'll have me."

Deuc doesn't say anything, but in Mulian I hear him. *Of course.*

There are no doubts for him. I wish I had such confidence, but one's own life must always seem uncertain. That's the drive to live. If we saw our own lives with the matter-of-factness that allows other people to see them, we would too easily be able to solve our own troubles.

And *become bored* by them, Deuc thought.

I did not agree. I was not bored by planning and slow progress. Building community, making relationships that would last, and seeing our work together wash over the years fascinated me endlessly.

With the decision made, and as time went on, I thought more of Georgios. When I'd arrived, I had thought of him every hour, I was composing letters to him in my thoughts that I was unable to send. I learned to compose songs instead. Then, as time went on, my hourly preoccupation with him, Georgios hovering ever in the back of my thoughts, began to fade. Instead, I thought of him daily or only when some new occurrence brought him to mind. Now, though, in preparation for the return, I thought of him on the hour again. I felt his presence as strongly as when I had left. I worried, however. Was it truly him I recalled? Or had I reinvented him in my imagination while I lived in Mu? Who was it I wished to return to? Was that person real?

Then, as the preparations for our sendoff became evident throughout Mu and going home became a certainty, I grew nervous about his reception of me. What was I going back to? Aged, crusted, and rusted as I was, I could not imagine a romance with Georgios. How would he see me now? I couldn't imagine how we would live together in the rust world. In the two years I had been below, we had been ages apart.

We had not been able to exchange words. We had exchanged only songs. I listened to the one song he had sent me over and over again and I read into it what I wanted until I was sure I knew him and his state of mind. Then not. I second-guessed myself and was uncertain all over again. Recently, there had been no songs at all.

The last song I sent him was titled "Homecoming." The words I meant for it were these: "My love, I miss you, I have missed you. My love, won't you welcome me home. My love, I am different than when I left you. You may never like to touch me again, but I love to touch you. In my mind, my skin becomes silken. I rust. I rust. Why have I suffered so without you? I know so much, but I am lost. Only let us be together again and maybe the future will become clear. Or won't matter. My love. My love. Mu send me home."

I wrote the words but knew he would hear only the notes from Varuna the Whale. I imagined he would know my meaning, but I hardly understood myself anymore. This song, more than any of the others I had sent, sounded the most like keening whale song. Maybe he would not even recognize me. Surely, I'd become too strange for him. I felt too strange for myself! But I wanted him. I'd spent too much time wanting him not to want him anymore. I was always one to stick to a plan.

On the day before our departure, the Mulians held a special ceremony for us. I went to it on my own. How well I knew my way around by then. I had no fear of the place, then great fear of it, and no fear again within the boundaries I knew. I looked around my cave-like room one last time with its walls, pearlescent as the inside of a shell, pearlescent as my changed skin. Inside Mu, as I have gone to rust, I have felt like an oyster, gelatinous, limbless, tough, liquid, and malleable. All of these. I ran my hand over the smooth, polished stones that ringed the pool where I often bathed and where I once dove into the portal to the sea. It's been a long time since I've been in the sea. It's safer inside, among the Mu, where I speak the language. I lifted the stones and peered into compartments filled with spices, foods, and objects. I take only my coral flute with me. I want to take the silver tea service, but it will be too impractical to swim with it and it would be wrong. The Mulians need these things. They love them. They do not have the capacity or desire to make more. These objects must be left to be cared for by a new Mulian.

I was sad to leave my water garden, which I had so carefully tended, and which fed me. I gave Neena the last of Desiree's tomato seeds. The nightshade grew well in the homa and larger and juicier in Mu than the vines ever would have in the rust air on the Seastead. If Neena harvested the seeds carefully, she could enjoy them for years to come. The Mulians, especially Neena's partners Tubal and Haya, were developing a taste for these surface fruits, too.

I wondered, would I miss the smell of kelp and cinnamon? I anticipated that I would miss the sound of the humming of the whirlpool and Varuna's cries. I would miss the Mulian music and the chorus of lyres and voices, all the sounds the community made when we celebrated and sang. I gazed up through the translucent ceiling and watched the shape of great Varuna the Whale glide overhead. She was so ominous at first. Then we became friends. I walked down the dark corridors of the living walls woven of kelp and covered with purple barnacles like jewels. The corridors were dark and intricate, but I knew them. I saw the phosphorescent markings directing the Mulians through the passageway. I remembered when I could not see them, and the hallways were like a maze.

The corridor emerged into the huge lawn, a mossy bed if looked at it closely, soft, and tumescent, a rolling lawn with small hills. The anemones were in bloom, and they covered the lawn in bright purple, green, and blue. They gave off a heady lavender scent. Already the music--harps, flutes, and chanting--had begun, I saw the council elders standing on a knoll before the coliseum and the 200 Mulians from all of the enclaves gathered round. I looked at their faces, their tentacles. This time of the year, there was a golden cast to their skin. I saw them. I felt them. I heard their minds. I knew nearly all of them by name. I looked up at their sky, which was not sky, but a translucent dome into the outside world. It had become sky to me. How much had changed in two years, I felt safe with them and loved them and this place.

The Mulians sang the songs of farewell and Neena and I ate the dish of mélange that contains some of everyone's skin. Even Deuc ate the dish this time. He would take some of them with him. It would make him live longer, perhaps forever. It was oily, thick, and delicious.

The homa around us felt light and sweet. I often shivered in Mu unused to the cold and the crispness, but on the last day of my leaving I felt comfortable.

"It is springtime above," Neena said.

The Mulians made presents of new robes for Deuc and I. They were long and sleek and sky-colored, a surface sky blue. We wore them and danced in the community circle so that everyone could see. The younger Mu teased Deuc. He showed them his naked torso underneath his robe. I was wearing a shift under my robe in preparation for the surface. The Mu gave me a packet of kelp and mélange tea. I wondered how long it would last me on the surface. They gave Neena gifts, too. For her it is not a farewell, but a welcoming celebration. A homecoming. She received more objects and instruments to care for, a sign of her acceptance. The Mu have not welcomed a permanent newcomer in ages. I saw Deuc watching her and imagined I detected jealousy in the look. Deuc always wanted to be loved most, the way the Mu loved Neena.

When we arrived, the Mulians had not welcomed a surfacer for decades. I knew that we would be legendary among the Mu and long remembered. If I were to return, even after hundreds of years, the Mu would call out, "Nata!" If any other surfacer were to arrive in Mu, the first question they would be asked, "Do you know Nata?"

I did not expect ever to return to Mu. Still, I could not believe I would be able to leave.

I enjoyed the celebration, but my thoughts were already surfacing.

I thought, just let me live long enough to leave this place. Just let me see home and the surface and the sun once again. Let Georgios hold me. I would have promised something, but I had nothing left to give. I had given up everything down to my skin, so I thought. I thought I had already made my great sacrifice for the world. I did not know that my two years in Mu were only the beginning of what the world would ask of me. What did I have left to sacrifice for the future I envisioned? Whatever it was, I would be asked to give it. And I would. I could not refuse that unknown future all of the gifts it required.

~ 67 ~

THE SEASTEADERS: SURFACING

At that last celebration, I found my voice. I sang my desire to the Mulians. I sang of the surface. They stood and were briefly silent. Then they led Deuc and I in a procession down the lawn to the rookery. The elders left us at the entryway, for Mulians rarely enter the nursery unless it is time to procreate, an act unique from sexual intimacy (which occurs frequently and indiscriminately everywhere). Deuc and I descended the stone steps with Abrador as our guide again.

We entered the dark corridors and passed through the portico into the warm circular room filled with living orbs. I had not been so warm for some time except in the steeping pools. If Deuc and I had been Mulian lovers we would now kneel beside the eggs of pale lavender, blue, and green and sing until they broke open spilling a kelp plume into the viscous liquid of the room. Slender tentacles would rise out of the orbs and attach themselves to the front of our bodies and entangle us. The new Mu would be born out of our union and the souls of the Mu waiting in polished objects or from the souls of surfacers called from the ruins. They would be reborn. Neena would wait here hoping one day to be reunited with Professor Belo. Deuc and I could have lived another lifetime together in this way.

Instead, we looked up at the flute of water, a turquoise waterway back to the surface, and prepared for the journey home. Deuc put on a helmet again, but when I reached for one Abrador shook his head. Had it been that long since I'd looked in a mirror? I knew my face had become lumpy, but could I also now breathe water and withstand pressure differently?

By ingesting the mélange, I had become a sea creature. I did not need a helmet to breathe or to protect me from the pressure of the dank sea. This change embarrassed me. I did not want Deuc to know how complete my transformation had been. So, I took the helmet anyway and wore it although I did not need it. It was of no use to me, but I wanted it as a souvenir.

Deuc and I held hands when we stepped into the stream. It was instinctual, I think we both were frightened of what our return to the surface would mean for us. I could barely feel his fingers in the rusted webbing that had become my hand, but I was grateful he did not shrink from it, and I felt close to him. I could hear him telepathically.

Let us go.

We had come to rely on each other. I thought how I would never return to Mu and how I was grateful to leave. I was out of my element here, but I felt comfortable sometimes, too. I remembered descending to Mu in the water flute, how days passed coming down, and how we had the current with us.

To return, we must fight the flow of the flute to ascend.

It was light at first from the glowing dome of Mu surrounding its warm homa. When we passed through the deepest depths of ocean, it grew dark. We rose past the blackest depths of the ocean where the creatures shine with phosphorescent lights and bare sharp, glowing white teeth. We rose through the navy depths and closer to the aquamarine. We slept through some of the journey. We shut our eyes to pass the time. When the world around us had become teal blue with a sense of sunlight, Deuc, close by, got my attention. He held out his hand.

In his palm were two golden coins, spirits of the new Mu. They were not a gift.

Look what I stole, I heard him say.

The coins could be planted to create water flutes and purify the water. We could build more platforms and plant the seeds in the center. We could plant them off the shores of La Merde and live on the island's highest point with a fresh water source. That's what Georgios would want to do. He'd always loved the land. His attraction and need for it was not so strong that he would cling to it uselessly, to the point of death like his elders. However, land was a source of security for him. He would keep to the land, if he could. Those ways were not Deuc's. He preferred adventure to security. His purpose for the coins would be different--a bargaining tool. He would give them to the Riptiders. Deuc's theft saddened me, but it also held possibilities for us all I could not help but see.

Finally, we rose to where the light penetrated, and I could see the dried blood color of the rust ocean around us outside the cone of the flute. Rust sharks circled to snare the few stray fish that swam inside the flute and sometimes slipped free of the shelter of the freshwater cone. Deuc and I were careful to stay to the center of the flute as far from the toxic rust ocean and its mottled red sea creatures as possible.

The flute grew narrower as we rose, and Deuc and I kept further and further apart within it. We were remembering that we were at odds on the surface and perhaps even enemies. I felt his thoughts turning to the Riptiders, while I thought of the Seastead.

We were approaching the surface, and our battle of wills was beginning.

Riptiders, Deuc insisted.

Seasteaders, I responded.

An impulse.

A plan.

Freedom.

Collective action.

We heard each other plotting.

I hated that he had stolen the newborns. The Riptiders could not have them. I was making plans. I was already plotting against him.

Before I could surface, Deuc grabbed my foot. *No. Let's go back to Mu. Let's be together.*

We knew I had imagined we could break open eggs like Mulians together, he had likely heard my thoughts, but I could not believe he meant it.

The Mulians don't want you. People like you. Thieves. I was harsh and blunt.

He returned the favor. *You're too ugly for the surface, Nata. Georgios will gag when he sees you.*

We told each other hard, ugly, hurtful truths and approached the surface wounded.

Then, he grabbed my shoulders and pulled me down. He meant to drown us both. I struggled against him, but he was stronger. Finally, he pulled off my helmet. I surrendered, I feigned a struggle, but then grew still. I could still breathe, but Deuc did not know it. He did not know me very well after all. He had not really seen all I was capable of. But I knew.

Then Deuc threw off his helmet. He had no care for objects. He had not adopted the Mulian ways.

We will be reborn. It will be different.

He meant for us to die together. He preferred that end to being a traitor, at least. But I had already been transformed and I had my dream for the Seastead, for our utopia. I would not accept nothingness for either of us. When Deuc passed out from lack of oxygen, I pulled him to the surface. The sunlight was blinding, the air, moving about us felt wild, free, harsh, and frightening. It whipped and burned the surface of my skin and I gasped at the slice of it down my throat when I breathed the air again. My lungs pricked as if they were numb and waking. My chest captured all my attention as I struggled to breathe.

The surface was loud and moving frenetically: the waves, the wind. It roared. It blared. It frenzied.

The flute was in the middle of the ocean. It was a clear, clean pool surrounded by the darkest rust red sea I had ever seen. The corrosion had worsened. Rust sharks were swimming around the outside of the flute waiting to catch a fresh morsel.

I pulled Deuc to the surface and I tried to revive him, breathing for him, mouth to mouth, but I no longer had a mouth like that. I draped my face, my tentacles, over his and when I pulled back, I saw he was breathing again. My tentacles had saved him. When my eyes adjusted, I watched Deuc see me for the first time in the stark sunlight of the surface. I saw his horrified expression and then a more exaggerated version of the same meant for my benefit. I knew for certain now I was monstrous. I had changed more than I guessed. At the same time, I marveled at Deuc's beauty. His time in Mu had given his delicate features depth and polish. When his skin dried in the air, it shone like a stone plunged underwater.

I wanted him to live. Even if he was to be my enemy and would go to the Riptiders. What choice did I have? I reached for the packet of mélange and slipped some skin under his tongue, treading water with him in my arms, until he was able to speak.

"I was a spy," he said, the first words I had heard spoken in air for two years. The words leapt loudly out of his mouth and smacked against the surface of the sea. "One of Balor's men. I deserve my death."

Perhaps he did, as we all do, but I could not give it to him. I cradled Deuc, bobbing in ocean while I scouted our bearings. It was difficult to see at sea level, but I swam in circles within the shelter of the flute until I caught a shadow in the fading light. I saw a rust-colored strut rising. I edged closer to gauge the distance. The Seastead platform was about 500 yards away. I'd have to swim through the corrosion to get there.

After all the glittering, smooth, shine and curves of Mu, the sharp, dull Seastead struts looked ugly and unnatural. Deuc saw the Seastead too and he started for it. He pulled away from me and soon I saw the prehistoric shark fin lunging toward him. I swam out and grabbed his arm to pull him back, but I didn't see the other shark. The rust shark hit me, circled back, and tore along my arm and side with its rough hide.

Below, I saw Varuna the Whale's big eye. She had followed me to the surface and braved the corrosion again. I realized every time I had sent a message to Georgios, I had asked her plunge into the red rust. She sacrificed so I could sing to Georgios and be comforted. I swam through the corrosion and made for the whale. I expected the waters to burn, but I felt only fear. The sea was not even cold. Deuc's soft skin quickly became raw from the rust sea. He could not stay here. I gave him to Varuna.

Take him back, I sang.

I returned him to the sea as I had dropped my ratfin's corpse from the ferry, but I knew Deuc was alive.

His face tentacles attached to Varuna's side and she dove down with him. I sent Deuc back to Mu. I did not know what the Mulians would do with him. Varuna would tell them of his crimes. They didn't want him to stay forever as a member of their community, but I hoped now they would have no choice though they might well punish him for the theft and the betrayal. There were few transgressors in Mulian society. I did not know what form that punishment might take, but he would likely never see the sky again. Perhaps, that would be enough.

I thought of all the times Deuc and I had sat together in Mu and dreamed of the surface. I thought of what he had missed: the sky, the air, the quality of the sound, the apples and tomatoes. He was barely able to take a breath. He looked once at the sky before I sent him back. I betrayed him for utopia. My lover. My friend. My enemy.

I did not return the two new Mulians, he'd stolen, but kept them for myself. I did that.

I was alone. I swam to the Seastead and climbed up the metal ladder. I heard my clanging steps. Everything sounded louder on the surface. The wind felt sharp. The sun glared over the waves, beginning to set. It reddened the seas even more. The air moved and dried my skin. I had forgotten this and the strong smell of iron, the rust sea, the rust air, salt, and rotting fish. The salt stung my tongue and tentacles. The wind ran a harsh brush over my rusted appendages, and I saw the little red rust flakes flying around me, tiny pieces of my shedding skin, rust-tainted, airborne mélange. The platform looked like a husk.

The pool in the center of the Seastead was open and filled with thick, viscous rust sea. The Mulian flute had changed location. There was no source of fresh water for the Seastead now. No one was here.

"The Riptiders have taken them," I thought.

The Seastead looked old and empty. After life in the polished, swirling, purple-blue-green layers of Mu, the Seastead's metal struts looked faded, but there was a fresh layer of the brown dried-blood serum on it. If it hadn't been tended, it would have dissolved into the sea long ago.

I was shy at the thought of seeing Georgios, and I put on my long, formal robe--a gift from the Mulians. It covered most of my body from neck to toe. It was luxuriously soft. It protected me from the wind. I was a pillar of silver blue swirls. If I put my helmet on now, I would look entirely Mulian. Even without it, I was afraid I would be unrecognizable. All that remained of me were my very human clumps of hair. I wanted to make myself presentable, if not beautiful, for Georgios.

As the sun set, the floodlights came on. Then three people emerged from the kitchen. I could not hide in the shadows. They saw me fresh from Mu, after a long journey and a struggle, bedeviled with barnacles, disheveled from travel and fear.

I thought, *I love you Georgios. I do. I did anyway and I remember I love you.*

Then I let my mind become silent in fear and anticipation. My plans dissolved. There was nothing past the moment when Georgios emerged.

My love, my dear, my darling.

I remembered what it was like when I first saw the Mulians. I knew on sight that they were human, wise, and worthy of love although they looked so strange. I looked worse than they did. I was of Iron Blood, shriveled and red.

Later, when I saw myself in a mirror for the first time in years. It would be both better and worse than I thought. If I didn't think of myself as human, if didn't remember young Nata, it was better. My face was a collection of new lumps and textures, but my eyes were still my own, startled, and the whole effect was softer than I feared. Encrusted was not the right word after all. My face had been built up, but it was pliable and smooth in spots. Still, I could be terrifying at first glance. Imagine spinning around in air and coming face to face with a fish. It might be a beautiful fish, but unexpected. And I was not a beautiful specimen. Monstrous. Ugly. As Deuc had said.

When I first saw Georgios, I was stunned. I could not reassure him. I could not speak. I hummed. I sung my homecoming.

Georgios told me later, however, that he knew me immediately.

"You were humming that last song you sent me," he said. "Of course, I knew you."

I cried when he said that. Later, if I wanted to cry, I had only to remember, "Of course, I knew you."

Of course, he did.

We embraced and my rough, barnacled, finned arms scraped him. He pulled away and was gentler afterward when he lightly touched my arm. I was amazed that he wanted to touch me. Later, he told me he wanted nothing else. He loved me. He loved me still. It was a miracle. Once, I had wanted to save the world from the rust sea. Now all I wanted was Georgios.

Timbol and Desiree were also there. They were more cautious of me. Much had happened while I was away.

"Merl is with the Riptiders. We have a lot to tell you," Georgios said. "In-fin is here." He held out his arm and my now elderly ratfin walked down his arm to me, hid in my locks of hair, and curled around my rubbery neck as if he'd never left me. My dear lovely friend.

I watched Georgios and Desiree carefully. I remembered the song he had sent: wistful, romantic, and full of longing. Somehow, it had reminded me of Desiree's cooking and sensuality. I knew they had been together. I watched them still.

That night we played the game Cardinal as if no time had passed. It took me a while to remember it. The cards looked unfamiliar. Then I slid right back into the time when we had played every night. It was as if I had never left, except I fumbled a bit with the cards in my changed hands and I could feel the strangeness in my face when I smiled. Georgios looked as if he loved me still. Could it be by some miracle that he did? I stole sidelong glances at him from behind the cards. I drank the Mulian tea. I did not yet share it with the others.

"Where is Deuc?" Timbol asked.

"He stayed in Mu. I don't think he'll ever come back," I said. I had no idea how the Mulians would treat him. "Neena stayed too. She lives with a Mulian couple now."

I tried to tell them some of what Mu was like, but the words caught in my throat, and I became overwhelmed with remembering. I repeated the same words over and over: lavender, dome, stones, farming, singing, tentacles, barnacles, silver, ruins, tea, kelp, cinnamon. I felt they could not possibly understand. Yet, they were nodding.

After the game, Georgios and I went back to my room, which was left waiting for me untouched. I looked at my forgotten things. There were maps and fabrics that I had not seen for two years. I felt my youth return to me.

Georgios came close.

"You didn't look happy to see me."

"I am afraid."

"Why?"

I looked directly at him.

"You sent me all those songs and I sent one to you. Didn't you hear me?" he asked.

"I heard you," I said. "But I am different now."

He cradled my face in his hand. I was a child. I was a ratfin. I was his.

"I am so glad you are home," he said.

It was more than I had hoped for.

We were awkwardly together. It was not like the easy passion we used to have. I was uncomfortable and uncertain. But there was love, lust, and hope. We could be together again, even like this.

"There is so much I have to tell you," I said.

I knew I would never be able to tell it all at once. It would be years before I could explain what had happened, what it was like. The most difficult part of my journey had come. I was home, but I had to do everything I had delayed by my absence. I had to create the society in which we could live. There were so many rules to the surface life, and they all must be followed.

The first rule was war.

The islands war had continued in my absence and in the morning, with Georgios beside me--praise water, may he never be parted from me again--we heard the clunk of the ladder. There was no doubt who owned the ship alongside the platform. It was not a pirate galleon. It was not the Riptiders' Kyklopes. It was a vessel of war. The rust soldiers came aboard. I hid in the kitchen and listened. Who knew what they'd do to someone who looked like me. Timbol, Georgios, and Desiree greeted them. We anticipated takeover and madness. But it was not that.

The soldier who stepped forward was middle-aged. He had short sandy brown hair. Something in his carriage reminded me of my father.

"The old man. He just wants to come aboard. This is the last place he hasn't conquered."

"Then you leave," Georgios said.

"Then, we leave," he said.

I wanted to show myself, but I was afraid of these men who had been fighting too long, and would not see me for what I am, a peacemaker. So I stayed hidden.

General Balor came across the plank and boarded my Seastead.

He was an old man now and his breath came in thick, rasping heaves through wide open blue lips. He was sucking for air like a fish on land. He was dying.

I watched him all night and when the soldiers went to sleep, I sneaked out to sit beside him on the Seastead deck where he stayed in the open night air, the better to breathe. He had gone inside himself and my crooked visage meant nothing to him, but he could feel my peaceful presence. I held his hand in mine. I had the mélange with me, but I did not share it. I did not want him to live forever. I wanted him to feel peace and to be reborn with it. When the moon lowered, he took his last breath. I sung him to sleep, to death.

I could have saved him, with the tea perhaps, but it was not what the Mulians would have wanted. It was not what I wanted for this man who killed family and took my homeland. I felt better with him gone, relieved. On the Seastead, General Balor was given the sea burial denied my grandmother. His soul would dwell in the ruins of Mu as hers would not. Perhaps, his soul would return to us one day. I hoped he would have some memory of peace then.

Afterwards the soldiers lingered and made us doubt that they would leave as promised. Then they stripped the Seastead of any useable metal and stole the last of our Iron Blood serum. War was the first rule. The fight for land would continue until we were all gone and underwater.

I knew then what I had to do. I knew the rightness of the decision even while the weight of it settled into my stomach. It had the excited hum of a right choice instead of the heavy dread of a wrong one. I had learned to recognize this difference in Mu, and I would put it to use now. I could move forward confidently, even though it was the last thing I wanted to do.

I love you. I appreciate you. Thank you. May we never be separated again in this life or any other. I see you and, of course, I know you.

~ 68 ~

THE SEASTEADERS: IRON BLOOD

That morning, the honor-bound soldiers left, but there was no doubt that they would come back with a new general. It was only a matter of time before the Riptiders came to find us and claim our blood for their serum and their safety from the sea. They would enslave the Iron Bloods. I didn't know what they would make of me.

I wanted to stay with my family--Georgios, Desiree, and Timbol--on the Seastead. I wished we could live in the peace I had planned for. I wish we had had more time, but I had to adapt to the new adventure and act on what I had learned.

After the soldiers left, I called my friends, my family, together. I showed them the new Mulians, the souls Deuc stole, the purifying coins we could use to stay together and have another life.

"That is what I want to do then," Georgios said, as I had expected.

Then there was a long silence as the others considered. It was as if were were at Cardinal again, everyone examining the cards in their hands and seeing the possible plays forward.

“There's another way,” Timbol said at last. “Not just for us four, but for everyone who is left.” He had seen it. The look on his face was grim and resolute.

"We can live in the sea," Desiree said, staring at my face and truly seeing me. “We can change like Nata has and become more

Mulian. We've been running from the rust sea, but we can make it ours."

I sighed with sadness but drew a breath in with relief. They saw the possibility, too. I was no longer alone.

"But the land," said Georgios.

"We can help purify the ocean again," I said.

"Once we are inside it," Desiree said.

Georgios looked from one of us to the other. He reached for our hands. "Yes," he said.

We talked long that night and for several weeks. It was not a hasty decision; true ones never are. While we thought, we played Cardinal, and I made love to Georgios and every time was ecstatic and likely one of the last. We did not drain blood to make more serum. The Seastead creaked and rocked, and we let it rust.

Finally, it was agreed. Georgios, Timbol, and Desiree began to drink the mélange every day and I taught them. When they had learned and their bodies had changed enough to welcome the sea and to be protected against it, we chose a day. It was the morning after a windstorm that shook the Seastead so the metal shrieked. We woke and saw bits of it had fallen off into the sea. There was a froth of rust corrosion around the platform.

It was falling apart. It was time to go. We said goodbye, and we sang each other songs, and finally we each dove into the sea and swam in a different direction. My family had become rusty, tentacled, and webbed like me. I went North, Georgios West, Desiree swam South, and Timbol headed to the East. I was not as sad as the last time I left Georgios. This time we were united in purpose. It was difficult to tell them I loved them when I was so afraid of death. Everything sounded ominous, like the last fearful goodbye.

But I had gone away and been reunited once. I knew that all these barriers between us; they do not exist. I knew that there was a strong chance that I would see Georgios again although it could be far away. I believed that when I saw him next, that time for certain there would be no reason for us to ever part again. I looked long into his eyes, the green pools, before we parted ways. No matter how he changed, I would recognize him: "I see you, of course, I know you."

Our plan, the Seasteaders' plan, was what it had always been, to survive in a beautiful, planned, considerate way. This time we would take to the water to find the many creative ways that people had managed to live outside of the water. We would offer those people our blood and the Mulian mélange, the skin of the Mulians and show them a way to live in the water and to swim forever. We would evolve back into the ocean of our ancestors.

Setting out across the sea in search of a settlement, I felt strong, as though I could swim forever, and had been, swimming forever. I undulated through the water fishlike and fast. My Mulian robe billowed around me. It looked like a cooling wrap over the burning red sea. I went alone, but also with the Seasteaders' plans and the Mulians' hope.

I swam for days before I reached a small peak. Long wood docks stretched out over the water. As I hauled myself out of the water, I noticed the scar where the Rust shark had brushed me in my conflict with Deuc. It had scraped away some of my rust hide. There was a slice across my side of beautiful, luminescent pale green, lavender, and blue pearlescent skin.

I saw hope that one day I'd shed the rust from my skin. When every islander left had learned to swim, I would be beautiful. Then, we could plant and spread the freshwater flutes.

We could never lower the water. We had lost the land forever, but the water could be clean again and fresh and we could learn to live within it.

While I swam in the rust sea, I felt the rhythm of one of Neena's poems. I sang one of Deuc's songs in my head. I heard the calls of whales. I remembered the Mulians. Although overwhelmed with my own survival, I would never forget them. One day, I would find a way to help them, too.

I considered the Mulians and how, while I was with them, Abrador and the elders had seemed so wise. However, Abrador was like me: different, focused on the future, and made odd and separate among the Mulians because he took an interest in the surface world (as I had taken interest in living on the sea).

The Mulians understood we were dying, but they were not wise deities above us. They were merely compassionate. They saw our days were limited as were theirs. They had compassion for our species, were benevolent, and desired to help. They placed a few Mulian coins in the way of a young girl. There was so much more they could have done, but they were afraid to act on their compassionate impulses. They were concerned with their own survival, and they were disorganized. They could not agree and plan and they needed to keep themselves secret for fear of being hurt. They didn't trust us. Most of us, I believe, would have been trustworthy. We could have helped more people faster if they had come forward. Professor Belo, myself, my grandmother, the people of La Merde, even those at Merops and the Riptiders would have helped, I think. Only General Balor and the men he poisoned would not...but maybe even they could have been convinced. If the Mulians had had the will and the courage. Maybe. It is difficult to tell, always, how goodwill, may be received. I could be wrong, maybe if the Mulians had taken more risk it would have been disastrous. I don't know for sure what will happen next. I have only our hopes. I do know what I am doing now in this moment. I am swimming. We are all swimming.

We swam toward the islands where some people escaped the sea on the peaks. In a land of islands, many preferred isolation, what they were used to, and what they told themselves they wanted. The peakers wanted to stand apart. For them, we swam to each enclave and offered to share the gift of immortality and the ability to live in the sea. We would also share the music. We sang to them.

We must do this. We must act on our best impulses, this is what Georgios, Timbol, Desiree and I decided. Maybe we all had different motivations in a way. Timbol loved to explore. Georgios wanted to do what was right. Desiree sought to become something more and obtain a transformation. I was in love, and I felt if we succeeded, if we endured this one more fated task of separation, Georgios and I would be a certainty. I would have earned it. There was also, we all felt it, compassion for the world, the sea, and its people.

When I finally reached a landed place, the first people I met were afraid of me. I am a monstrous legend to them, a frightening myth. I swam on. The next place I stopped, there were a few people who joined me in the waters, and we received a visitor: a Mulian I did not know. He brought sad news. I saw him and immediately feared: What had happened to Georgios or Deuc? The first words I understood from the stranger: "He is dead."

But who? Which one of mine? They were at a loss to describe him. They described the similarities. Never had the brothers seemed so alike. It had never occurred to me how much they were alike, one and the same--not the physicality. The Mulian friend described their auras. These were nearly identical. For the first time, my tribe made sense to me. At that point in our lives, we were all shades of purple and white.

The light one. The light one. The one filled with light.

Finally, I knew who was meant. I began to cry, the salt tears that always endeared me to the Mulians.

I understood, Abrador had died.

He wanted me to know. He wanted to say thank you.

Thank you. I appreciate you. I love you. I see you and, of course, I know you for who you are.

That is all the stranger came so far to say. I remembered Abrador's reply when I said I thought the Mulians were helping us, "So it seems."

Were we not helping them in return? I had hoped Abrador would return. Would the Mulians come to claim their heritage on the surface of the sea? Were we not just preparing the way for them?

The Mulian messenger also left me a packet of mélange. It was a special brew that Abrador wanted me to have. It was made of his own skin. I shared it with the people on the island so that they would come to live with me forever in the sea. It tasted like sweet *homa* and tomatoes.

~ 69 ~

THE SEASTEADERS: EPILOGUE

Here we return to the beginning. I begin my speech to this crowd of islanders as they look at my strange, red pearled skin.

When I returned from Mu the idea of being separated from Georgios and the Seasteaders again was unbearable, but I bore it. Now I'm bringing my experience and wisdom back from Mu and sharing it with all humanity.

The paths to Mu must remain hidden from the generals, soldiers, warriors, and Riptiders who would plunder them. The rule of peace must prevail.

After my speech, I swim on to the next enclave and the next. I no longer fear that my blood will lead me to an early demise.

I celebrate my 91st birthday. The older I become, the more Mulian I look and behave. I am silent except when I hum. My skin is leathery. It sheds in strips which I make into mélange. I am aging. I am evolving. I feed my mélange to In-fin.

In-fin, my long-lived ratfin friend, is my one concession to myself. I would not be alone and without a companion again. I taught him to swim beside me. I fed him my skin.

The next time, I crawl up out of the sea I am luminescent and beautiful, shiny, and clean, and I know I have an alluring strangeness. Now my task is made much easier.

The people will come to me faster lured by my hum and my song and enchanted by my luminous skin. They watch In-fin shake off his lacy wings and see his whiskers twitch. How will Georgios and the others be, younger than I, with their thick rust skins and oily coats? Will people recognize them for what they are? Salvation.

Someday, soon I hope to see Georgios again.

When next we go to Mu, when next we jump ship, we will go together.

Shel Graves is a reader, writer, and utopian thinker who lives by the Salish Sea. She is a solarpunk author published in the anthologies *Glass and Gardens: Solarpunk Summers* and *Glass and Gardens: Solarpunk Winters* from World Weaver Press edited by Sarena Ulibarri. Shel earned her MFA at Goddard College, Port Townsend, a utopia which no longer exists. Shel is an ordained animal chaplain with the Compassion Consortium and as Shel Graves Animal Consulting, www.shelgravesanimal.com, aims to create a culture of compassion and pay attention to animals.

May we all be confident, at ease, playful, and safe.

www.ingramcontent.com/pod-product-compliance
Lightning Source LLC
Chambersburg PA
CBHW021239020826
48980CB00024B/343

* 9 7 9 8 9 9 8 5 4 8 6 3 5 *